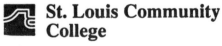

THE MUSICAL IMAGE

A Theory of Content

Recent Titles in
Contributions to the Study of Music and Dance

20th-Century Microtonal Notation
Gardner Read

Movement to Music: Musicians in the Dance Studio
Katherine Teck

The Coming of Age of American Art Music: New England's Classical
Romanticists
Nicholas E. Tawa

Theological Music: Introduction to Theomusicology
Jon Michael Spencer

Philosophy and the Analysis of Music: Bridges to Musical Sound,
Form, and Reference
Lawrence Ferrara

Alfred Einstein on Music: Selected Music Criticisms
Catherine Dower

Salsiology: Afro-Cuban Music and the Evolution of Salsa in New York City
Vernon W. Boggs

Dancing Till Dawn: A Century of Exhibition Ballroom Dance
Julie Malnig

Mainstream Music of Early Twentieth Century America: The Composers,
Their Times, and Their Works
Nicholas E. Tawa

Televising the Performing Arts: Interviews with Merrill Brockway,
Kirk Browning, and Roger Englander
Brian Rose

Johann Sebastian: A Tercentenary Celebration
Seymour L. Benstock, editor

An Outward Show: Music for Shakespeare on the London Stage, 1660–1830
Randy L. Neighbarger

The

MUSICAL

IMAGE

A Theory of Content

Laurence Berman

Contributions to the Study of Music and Dance,
Number 30

GREENWOOD PRESS
Westport, Connecticut • London

Library of Congress Cataloging-in-Publication Data

Berman, Laurence D.
  The musical image : a theory of content / Laurence D. Berman.
    p.   cm. — (Contributions to the study of music and dance,
  ISSN 0193–9041 ; no. 30)
  Includes bibliographical references and indexes.
  ISBN 0–313–28434–2
  1. Music—Philosophy and aesthetics.   I. Title.   II. Series.
ML3845.B377   1993
781.1′7—dc20   92–32210

British Library Cataloguing in Publication Data is available.

Library of Congress Catalog Card Number: 92–32210
ISBN: 0–313-28434–2
ISSN: 0193–9041

First published in 1993

Greenwood Press, 88 Post Road West, Westport, CT 06881
An imprint of Greenwood Publishing Group, Inc.

Printed in the United States of America

The paper used in this book complies with the
Permanent Paper Standard issued by the National
Information Standards Organization (Z39.48–1984).

10 9 8 7 6 5 4 3 2 1

Copyright Acknowledgments

The author and publisher gratefully acknowledge permission to quote beyond the fair use limit from the books listed below:

Auerbach, Erich, *Mimesis*, trans. Willard P. Trask. Copyright © 1953 by Princeton University Press. Reprinted by permission of Princeton University Press.

Einstein, Alfred, *The Italian Madrigal*, trans. Alexander H. Krappe, Roger H. Sessions, and Oliver Strunk. 3 vols. Copyright © 1949 by Princeton University Press. Reprinted by permission of Princeton University Press.

Fassett, Agatha, *The Naked Face of Genius*. Copyright © 1958 by Agatha Fassett. Reprinted by permission of Houghton Mifflin Co. All rights reserved.

Kaufmann, Walter, *Tragedy and Philosophy*. Copyright © 1968 by Princeton University Press. Reprinted by permission of Princeton University Press.

Stevens, John, *Words and Music in the Middle Ages: Song, Narrative, Dance and Drama, 1050–1350*. Copyright © 1986 by Cambridge University Press. Reprinted by permission of Cambridge University Press.

W.W. Norton & Company requests that the following wording be used:
Reprinted from *Source Readings in Music History*. Compiled and edited by Oliver Strunk, by permission of W.W. Norton & Company, Inc. Copyright 1950 by W.W. Norton & Company, Inc. Copyright renewed 1978 by Oliver Strunk.

Winn, James Anderson, *Unsuspected Eloquence*. Copyright © 1983 by Yale University Press. Reprinted by permission of Yale University Press.

Copyright acknowledgments for the musical examples are placed under each example in the book; however, European-American Music has made a special wish to be acknowledged on this page for having permitted use of Examples 8.3c and 8.6.

To my mother and father,
Ina R. and Manuel K. Berman

Acknowledgments

This being my first book, I have in mind the idea—perhaps it is only an illusion—that there must be a certain style appropriate to acknowledgment pages. And so recently I have been perusing the front matter of some publications with an eye to finding a few conventional turns of phrase. What I have found is not so much a certain style as a certain tone: to read these authors' remarks is to believe that the entire composition and production of their works took place in a state of permanent beatitude. Were these writers never faced with even a momentary setback? Did they not once meet up with the common indignities of the trade—unnecessary delays in the evaluation process, indifferent editors, hostile evaluators, multiple rejections of one's manuscript? Well, courteous Reader, I will not conceal from you that I have suffered all these, and still others that it would be undiplomatic of me to put a name to. Not that I care to dwell on such things, but to my mind the rubric "Acknowledgments" connotes something of a balanced, if not total account; it means acknowledging the negative as well as the positive, the not-so-great along with the great, the bitter along with the sweet—in the hope, of course, that the sweet will seem all the sweeter in the end.

That said, I now feel free to admit that even in the dimmest days (both chronologically and psychologically) of this experience, there were the definite bright spots. Two in particular come to mind. The first was the extremely gracious and enthusiastic reception I had from Doris Kretschmer, humanities editor at the University of California Press. She was so committed to publishing my material that she kept the evaluation process going against heavy odds, probably longer than reasonable hopes would warrant. She went many extra miles for me, and I will never forget her for them. The other person, in the early period of the manuscript's life, to whom I am very grateful is Anthony Newcomb, Professor of Music at the University of California, Berkeley. After making a favorable review of my ms. for a press that eventually rejected it, he believed enough in my work to persuade another press to take it under consideration. No reflection on him that the ms. failed there as well.

Over the course of several revisions, the book, in whole or in part, has been read by and/or discussed with a number of close friends and colleagues: John and Dorothy Crawford, Robert Gartside, Midori Hayashi, Leon Kirchner, Steven Matthysse, Kathryn Reichard, Lin Haire-Sergeant, Rebecca Saunders, and Erik Sundquist. All their interest, encouragement, and good advice mean more than I could say. Of these I must single out Steven Matthysse, who not only read two complete versions but also made contact on my behalf with a distinguished press. He could hardly foresee—no more than myself—that this would be the nadir of my encounters with publishers.

Happily, my fortunes turned around in the summer of 1991, when the book was accepted by the Greenwood Publishing Group. The two Greenwood representatives who materially aided in that process were Mary Blair, at that time acquisitions editor, and Marilyn Brownstein, senior editor of the humanities department. My sincere thanks to them both. I also wish to thank Maureen Melino, copyright permissions editor, for all her help in securing the permissions, and Mark Kane, production editor, for his advice with respect to numerous mechanical details.

"Production" on this book actually began many years ago, when long-hand scrawl first had to be converted into word-processor print. Three people were involved in successive stages of that operation: Francis Doughty for the first chapters of the earliest version, Bea Bradley for the rest of this version as well as for several intermediate rewritings, and Ellen Troutman for the version presented to Greenwood. They have my gratitude for the excellent results, and my special admiration for their successful grapplings with minute script and heavily crossed-out passages.

The final stage of production—the so-called camera-ready preparation—has been in the capable hands of Karl Berry and Kathryn Hargreaves since the summer of 1991. They have been responsible for every aspect of the physical layout of the book, including musical examples and title pages, and they have gone about their business with such care and sense of personal commitment that by now the book seems to have become theirs as much as mine. Working with them has been an undiluted pleasure and I am very much in their debt. Only the dust jacket has been an independent project, consigned to the elegant and imaginative eye of the graphic designer, Edward Plotkin. My thanks to him for the handsome result.

I would be singularly remiss if I didn't pay special tribute to two people who have become more and more influential in my life as the years have passed. They are Nicholas Tawa, Professor of Music at the University of Massachusetts/ Boston, and Luise Vosgerchian, Walter W. Naumburg Professor Emerita of Harvard University. Not only did each of them play an important part in bringing about the successful outcome at Greenwood Press, but they have helped immeasurably in the development of my career as a whole—indeed, have helped on so many fronts that it would be difficult to enumerate the ways and means. I think of them as my guardian angels, and words don't begin to express what I feel for them.

Finally, I come to my parents, who frankly had nothing to do with the realization of this book, except to sit by rather helplessly while I ground out the bulk of the following pages over many summers in a second-floor room of their house. I remember not a few late nights when, on their way to bed, they would pass that room, casting pitying glances at their one and only locked in mortal embrace with yet another stubborn phrase. It is altogether natural that the book should be dedicated to them—small and inadequate token of the blessing it has been to be theirs.

And so, gentle Reader—you see that I, too—opening remarks to the contrary—have experienced beatitudes of my own in the course of this venture. If you are embarking or are in any way involved in something similar, I wish you well, which is to say that I wish you fewer hazards than I have had to deal with. Just remember to live long enough to overcome them.

Contents

PART I: INTRODUCTION AND THEORY

1   Archetypal Criticism, or an Alternate Poetics of Music   ·   2
2   The Archetypal Model   ·   19

PART II: MUSIC IN RITUAL AND EDUCATION: ETHOS

3   Dialectic between Ethos and Pathos in Ancient Greek Thought   ·   62
4   Ethos of the Christian Liturgy   ·   76
5   Ethos of Courtly Love   ·   91

PART III: CLASSICAL HUMANISM: PATHOS

6   Reawakening of Pathos   ·   110
7   Emotional Music, or the Rhetorical Variety of Pathos   ·   130
8   The Pastoral Mode, I   ·   157
9   The Pastoral Mode, II   ·   179
10   The Epic/Heroic Mode   ·   197
11   The Satiric Mode   ·   226
12   The Many Faces of Classicism   ·   257

PART IV: TRANSCENDENTAL HUMANISM ... AND BEYOND: LOGOS

13   Romanticism and Melodrama   ·   278
14   Innigkeit, the Romantic Alternative   ·   295
15   Age of Irony: Modernist Music   ·   312
16   Formalist Alterations of the Archetypes   ·   344

Contents

EPILOGUE
17   Analysis and Culture   ·   364

Bibliography   ·   374
Subject Index   ·   383
Music Index   ·   389

PART I

Introduction and Theory

1 Archetypal Criticism, or an Alternate Poetics of Music

The Musical Image has as its primary task to identify and classify the kinds of content in music that are traditionally thought to lie beyond pure musical syntax and structure. These contents are none other than what has long existed in the popular mind as the basic matter for musical expression—human emotions, human behavior, natural environments and occurrences. But according to the central premise set forth here, the same contents ultimately, if not directly, correspond to the fundamental ideas or patterns of thought running through and unifying Western culture. Such patterns or archetypes permeate musical imagery quite as much as they do the imagery of the other arts; the contention is, contrary to formalist ideologies which have ruled musical scholarship until very recently, that music is as capable of participating in the expression of the archetypal contents as any other symbolizing activity. And the contents *are* archetypal, both because they deal with elemental human concerns and because, within the framework of the culture, they get dispersed and projected into all realms of experience. It is, in fact, just by virtue of inhabiting every corner of experience—of being continually with us—that certain concerns do gain for themselves a kind of universality; and thus it is that the "universals" could just as readily be called (and perhaps less grandly) the problems of everyday life. Viewed as such, the content of art is simply the content of life delivered in an intense form. And conversely, the content of life is in overwhelming part the imagery of art filtered down into the diffuse and random remarks of everyday discourse. Scott Buchanan beautifully summarizes this latter point in calling attention to the fact that the conversation of 5th-century Athenians was riddled with quotations from the *Iliad* and the *Odyssey*: "As Homer speaks for all men, so all men speak like Homer."[1]

Several problems threaten to arise when treating popular materials, and they should be considered before proceeding further. Above all, there is the danger that the contents in question being stereotypes, the stigma of the stereotypical will cling to the treatment itself; because it is dealing continually with familiar ideas and information, this book could give the impression of merely rehashing what everybody already knows. I count, of course, on careful readers to be able to distinguish between the "truistic" nature of the subject matter and the efforts I am making on behalf of that subject matter. In essence, those efforts consist, first of all, in ordering a number of archetypal themes into a hierarchically based conceptual model, and then in showing how Western music developed over time a repertoire of expressive modes and for what artistic and cultural reasons. In short, the orientation of this book (but for the presentation of the model itself in Chapter 2) is historical. What emerges, however, is not a traditional history of Western music, but rather a history of certain root-themes of the culture as expressed through musical images. The book bears some comparison to the traditional survey; for instance, the conventional period-designations of musicology are preserved—as is, to some extent, chronological order. But the qualifier "to some extent" is important, for if archetypal thinking is basically thematic in character, then the basis of the organization of this text should also be thematic. Thus, the history of medieval music is presented in Chapters 4 and 5 as a history of two themes— the decorum of the Christian liturgy and the code of courtly love—while in the chapters devoted to Classical humanism the focus is steadily on the complex interaction between outward human behavior and the inner life. This latter focus is particularly evident in Chapters 8–11, where human character is broken down into a number of conventional types (the warrior, the shepherd, the authority figure, a host of human types from the world conventionally defined as satiric). At the same time, within the bounds of any one of these chapters, the treatment is chronological.

To the extent, then, that this study outlines a theory of content and then applies it to the entire span of Western classical music, it is trying for a certain comprehensiveness. Of course, to be comprehensive about such a subject within the scope of a single volume is to be schematic about it at best. But this is not necessarily a drawback: the possibility of a reader supplying illustrations and even entire historical steps that the author failed to include could be viewed as a strength, a sign of flexibility. This presupposes, of course, that a given conceptual framework is so designed as to allow for such a possibility: the author must be reasonably sure that illustrations and historical steps missing from his account can nevertheless find a proper and comfortable place within the framework. The relative success or failure of the model introduced in Chapter 2 thus rests on that sole condition. Or to put it somewhat differently: if the condition is met, comprehensiveness will have been served.

Today, models are being called into question by a growing number of critics on the grounds that they are mechanistic in nature and easy crutches for the lazy-minded. If that is true, the model presented in Chapter 2 is a multiple offender, reducing as it does the fundamental ideas of Western culture to a finite group of twelve terms. The present love in criticism for the problematic, the ambiguous, the fragmentary, the self-contradictory is very much in back of the growing suspicion about models, especially if the model is of the old closed-system type. On the other hand, absence of a model can also be viewed with suspicion: the kind of criticism that prefers leaving questions unresolved to stabilizing and settling them could be faulted, for instance, for fostering laziness in the form of self-indulgence; for if there is no *a priori* frame of reference, there is nothing to answer to, no accountability. I raise this case only in order to bring out the futility of pointing the finger at any one theory or another, given the fact that a theory is ultimately an intellectual projection of one's temperament, the rational means of confirming one's deepest intuitions about the world. A model is only as good as the uses to which it is put. Musical semiotics, for instance, has a reputation for having lingered unduly in the precincts of abstraction and hypothesis, but there is no reason that cogent and concrete analyses will not be produced in its name. Nor should we imagine that deconstructionist strategies, given as they are to seeking out the unstable and open-ended, can never serve in the interests of bringing problematic questions to stable conclusions. Nor must we believe that something "inherent" in reductionist, closed-system models precludes their use in the *ars subtilior* of interpretation. At any rate, interpretation is a matter for another day; theory is the matter at hand (albeit a theory whose fixed principles mean to be measured against an evolving historical process).

As to my aim in devising a theory in the first place, I realize that it is motivated in no small part by what Leonard Meyer has recently described as "our need to stabilize the world."[2] A few sentences after making this remark, Meyer adds: "The need to envisage leads us to search for orderly predictable patterns … This is the goal of all our theorizing."[3] Although I subscribe thoroughly to this idea, I would have to assert it with less confidence than Meyer, if only because of deconstructionist claims to doing a different kind of theorizing. But whether directed toward the stable or the unstable, theorizing is undeniably the result of a need, one so deep-seated that it provides its own justification. I could, nevertheless, spend a moment justifying my own brand of theorizing by observing that a conceptual framework serves only as a jumping-off point for interpreting phenomena: a tool for the interpreter, it is in no way constituted to reflect the diversity of the phenomena themselves. The phenomena in the present case being an indeterminate number of "world views," they have played some part in the formation of the archetypal model, but only a part, and only indirectly. Other factors, such as the purely practical consideration of keeping the model within manageable proportions or the business of seeking out only "orderly predictable patterns" have had a larger part. Several other factors will be discussed at the end of this chapter and the beginning of the next. For the moment it is enough to say that given the choice between two clearly differentiated systems—on the one hand, an open conception forecasting infinite possibilities of meaning, on the other hand, a reductionist approach offering only a portion of the total meaning—I will unhesitatingly choose the second, in the conviction that it will yield something I can hold on to and in the hope that something can eventually be brought to interact with other aspects of meaning, i.e., with meanings governed by other closed systems. By "other closed systems" I have in mind the techniques of syntactic analysis that constitute the basis of music theory such as we understand it today, plus some long-abandoned notions of musical rhetoric which are now coming to be reevaluated and recast for contemporary consumption. There is no question that the meaning of an artwork—its "total form"—is far more than the archetypal content dealt with here. But this book must restrict itself to an examination of that content, a sufficient enterprise in itself.

Image and Content

Before proceeding to the archetypal model of Chapter 2, we must turn for the remainder of this chapter to the four key concepts underlying the model—image, content, archetype, and convention. Because these terms mean different things to different readers, it becomes all the more important to explain their particular usages here. We begin by noting that the terms fall into two distinct pairs, though the pairings are by no means symmetrical in all respects. Image and content, for instance, qualify each other so completely that the one is virtually incomprehensible without the other; yet, for the purposes of this study, content is in a privileged position with respect to image, insofar as the archetypes of Western culture constitute the sole content of the image, whereas not all archetypes need be—or perhaps even can be—expressed in image form. Similarly, archetype and convention are in a hierarchical relation, the conventions being the local and variant forms of the archetypal thought patterns. But the archetype is *restricted* to the role of thought pattern—of content—whereas the convention is at one and the same time both content and image; it functions as the code joining content to image. We see that the four concepts are not so much laid out in a row as that they form a conceptual ring, in which the abstractness of the two middle terms is complemented by—or, more precisely, made manifest in—the concreteness of the two outer terms.

Several pages back, reference was made to popular notions about the kinds of content deemed susceptible of musical expression. These notions are not confined to the modern Western world, if we are to believe Friedrich Blume, who once wrote that "all peoples … from the antique high cultures of Asia and Europe onward through a history of several thousand years" carry the conviction that music "is not only sound and form as such but signifies something beyond."[4] By "all peoples," Blume would presumably include all but those who have subscribed to the formalist views dominating musical thinking (at least, academic musical thinking) for the better part of our own century. In formalist analysis today, it is customary to treat a piece of music as a self-contained organism—to establish its "structure" and then examine the interrelation of its parts in order to see how they work together to form the unified whole. This syntactic approach is assumed to explain the piece, to reveal its form and thus its "meaning." But already in listening to the opening line, say, of the *Appassionata* sonata of

Beethoven, I have a distinct sense of a meaning emerging—a meaning which, because it differs from the kind dictated by rational thought, we customarily call "mood" or "character." Syntactic analysis, which deals only with entire pieces, has nothing to say—indeed, deliberately avoids saying anything—about such meaning, charging that "character" is a matter of reflex response and therefore has no bearing on objective inquiry.

Yet, character in music is an old and persistent idea, going back at least to Plato and Aristotle. They call it *ethos*, because, as Aristotle writes, "Music has the power of producing a certain effect on the ethical disposition of the soul."[5] From repeated evidence of this power, he concludes that pieces of music "actually contain in themselves imitations of character."[6] Given its ethical action, Plato maintains that music is a "more potent instrument than any other" for training the young mind.[7] But precisely for this reason the music proper for education must be selected with extreme care. Plato would have disapproved of the *Appassionata* outright, as not being the kind of music conducive to the shaping of character; its storminess and violence would have only set a bad example for youths in whom teachers were trying to instill a love for temperateness and sober courage, in preparation for the ultimate goal of education, namely, philosophy. Plato was suspicious of the arts in general because he believed they fed the passions. Artists over the ages have persistently disagreed with Plato, claiming that art examines—and must examine—all aspects of human character and behavior, the bad as well as the good, in order not merely to dramatize such things but to be edifying about them. Already Aristotle gives strong support to this claim through his famous distinction between universals and particulars.[8] Universals, Aristotle says, are those things that happen to all human beings sooner or later, and are therefore of fundamental human concern. Poetry deals with universals, though it will normally present them in the form of a particular set of circumstances. In the tragedy of *Oedipus Rex*, the acts of killing his father and marrying his mother are unique to Oedipus, but the grief he suffers in discovering those acts is something with which we all identify, because grief eventually comes to every one of us in some shape or form. If Oedipus' circumstances were exactly coincident with our own, we would in a certain sense be too close to them to take their proper measure. (This runs parallel to the situation we often observe today among survivors of the Nazi concentration camps, who find it too painful to contemplate re-creations of events connected with the Holocaust.) Theoretically, it is when the action represented *could be* ours but *is not* ours that we stand the best chance of grasping its significance, of discovering the universal element in it. So goes, in effect, the poet's answer to Plato. Art does not feed the passions; on the contrary, it takes the passions out of the world of subjective experience and lifts them into the realm of the universal. In this new form—in the form of art—storminess and violence become edifying.

Music being an art, it is assumed here to behave no differently in essence from the other arts. While each branch of knowledge presumably involves a kind of content distinct from that of every other branch, the arts, philosophy, and religion seem closely allied in the ultimate objects of their interest, namely the primordial concerns just identified as the "universals." They concentrate on the human being as a whole—or perhaps more precisely, on the human condition as a whole, which Alexander Pope in his *Essay on Man* broke down into three basic relationships: (1) man with himself, (2) man with society, and (3) man with the cosmos.[9] The universals themselves can be characterized in terms of a number of oppositions: (1) life-death, (2) harmony-conflict, (3) change-eternity, (4) body-spirit, (5) unity-duality, (6) fear-desire, (7) joy-sorrow, (8) love-hate, (9) reason-will, (10) order-chaos. This is not meant to be an exhaustive list, and is in any case only a suggestion of the categorization that will be worked out in Chapter 2.

In spite of their common interests, religion, philosophy, and the arts express these interests in different ways: religion in the form of myth and ritual, philosophy through rational discourse, art through images. In addition, there are the distinctions to be made in terms of the materials with which the various arts create their imagery: words for literature, line, mass, and color for the visual arts, tone and rhythm for music. These material differences lead us to consider the very different capacities of the arts for specifying subject matter. Literature tells stories, dramatizes actions and even explains, often in great detail, the motivations behind those actions. Painting has trouble with motivation, although it has proven effective enough in representing landscapes, interiors, animals, the human face and body, bowls of fruit, vases of flowers, angels, devils, gods, fairies, monsters, ghosts, elves, sprites, in short, all manner of objects and creatures, factual and imaginary. Music can neither depict nor represent; incapable of generating subject matter, it seems to be about nothing at all.

In the course of these last statements, we have slowly drifted away from the question of *what* the arts express to *how* they express; we have been moving from the area of content *per se* toward a definition of the image. In particular, we are concerned to know something about the specific mechanisms of *musical* expression, for if depiction and representation are—or appear to be—beyond music's capacities, then what means are available to it for presenting its contents? What are we to understand an image to be in the strictly musical sense? To begin to answer that question, we must first acknowledge the initial barrier certain readers will have to cross in widening their hitherto exclusively visual idea of a concept to include the world of sound. *Image* ordinarily connotes something impinging on the eye. And—with specific reference to music—there is a hallowed Romantic tradition (still alive, moreover) which holds that music, having transcended the realm of words and pictures, is thus the "nonimagistic art" *par excellence*. Nevertheless, application of the term "image" to sound experience does have precedents—Ferdinand de Saussure's original designation of the *signifier* as "sound image," for one,[10] Susanne Langer's persistent use of the term in *Philosophy in a New Key*, for another. Langer labors valiantly in her book to raise image-making to the status of a "nondiscursive symbol" and to represent music as fully participating in this form of symbolizing.[11] Granting for the sake of argument, then, that all the arts work by images, but music, unlike litera-ture and the visual arts, cannot describe or represent a subject matter, the only conclusion to be drawn from these propositions is that subject matter and con-tent would not be synonymous terms. We may, of course—and do, in fact—say that the tragedy of Oedipus is "about" a man who killed his father and married his mother, but that is not the primary content of the piece; the story itself is only a means of giving form to a content—of coming to grips with the universal problem of suffering in the world and with the source of that suffering we call "evil." Subject matters as such—stories of heroes in literature or Madonnas in painting—are images, not contents. And if that is so, then we may now reaffirm what was already stated above for the musical image, namely that it is a shape made out of tones and rhythms, just as a visual image like the Madonna is made out of line, color, and mass, and a literary image like the story of Oedipus is made out of words.

Such a definition, however, would appear at first glance to make musical images *identical* with the entities familiar to anyone acquainted with the funda-mentals of musical syntax—motives, phrases, periods, sections, and the like. And in fact, just like syntactic units, images come indifferently in small and large sizes; even an entire piece or a process such as fugue can be properly called an image. But images are *not* identical to the units of musical syntax. When we think of a musical shape as being a motive or a phrase, we take the perspective of structural analysis and become interested solely in a description of the interior actions of a piece—how the motives and phrases relate to each other and how they combine to build up an entire syntactic design. When the same musical shape takes on the status of an image, we think of it as being "possessed of" or expressing a content. What has changed here is not the musical shape itself but our conception of it; if it seems to us to resonate with heightened significance—to carry an element of the world beyond the pure form—we feel that it has become more than a motive or a phrase and we give it the name *image*.

Archetype

Assuming for the moment that the above argument is well taken, it still falls short of suggesting a mechanism by which the musical image could indicate its content. People all over the world and since time immemorial may well believe that the human emotions comprise the basic content of musical imagery; they may say that they *know* the emotions are in the music because they *feel* them so strongly. But if music, unlike literature and painting, is incapable of designating—of explicitly pointing to—its content, how is it possible—indeed, *is* it possible—to demonstrate in a genuinely rational way the existence of something that is merely (however strongly) felt? The conception of the archetype as developed by the literary critic Northrop Frye, in his *Anatomy of Criticism*, holds the key, I believe, to getting past this inexorable question of musical aesthetics. Frye's method, which is worked out for literature, will have to be considerably reinterpreted in order to be useful to our purposes here, but the basic conceptual framework of his book is so broad as to have significant application to all the arts. The great appeal of archetypal thinking is in its ability to show how individual images, beyond the borders of a single artwork, relate to each other: a host of images from different artworks are seen to fall together into a class. "I mean by an archetype," writes Frye, "a symbol which connects one poem with another and thereby helps to unify and integrate our literary experience."[12] Frye's intention is to provide a historical connotation not found in the more famous conceptions of Plato and Jung. With Plato, the archetypes correspond to those original Ideas, those Ideal Forms, of which the world of physical appearances gives us at best the dimmest apprehension, and true knowledge of which can be obtained only by way of philosophy. What Plato predicates as totally exterior to ourselves Jung views as totally inward—a product of the "collective unconscious," an element inherent in the mind process of the human race as a whole. But whether taken in the Platonic or Jungian sense, the archetype has something of the primordial and universal about it, something that either is situated "before time" or belongs to "all time." Frye does not negate these notions but his ingenuity rests in the flexibility with which he takes the archetypal idea and places it "in the course of time."

Frye designates myths as the archetypes of literature. A myth is a story concerned with things of exceptional significance—a society's religious beliefs, its origins, destinies, and so on. It is not too much to say that myths are conceptions around which a society defines itself—without which, in fact, it could hardly keep going. But myths are also *stories* and as such, they contain the fundamental themes of literature. "Poets," Frye says, "can hardly find a literary theme that does not coincide with a myth."[13] (Or conversely stated, behind virtually every literary image lurks a mythological archetype.) Frye sees literary images, therefore, as the "displacements" of myths, the variants that have come about as part of the normal evolutionary process of literature. Frye's view of archetype suggests a hierarchy, one in which the original archetype—myth—stands at the head of historical time, while structures of thought crystallizing in given periods and localities are not discounted from archetypal status. By this conception, archetype takes on a highly communal character, being that component in the image which translates the thoughts and values of a given society; it is the *conventional* aspect of the image, that part of it which governs its communicability and causes the reader, listener, or spectator to recognize in any *particular* image a *typical* content or pattern of thought.

The references above to society and history lead us to grasp an important additional distinction between Plato's and Frye's concepts. Since myths deal with matters of ultimate significance, they are unquestionably about the concerns listed earlier as the "universals." However, the archetypes are not to be confused with the universals themselves, which are those things that happen to everybody and are thus common to the human race as a whole, above divisions of society and history. The archetype is a way of conceiving a universal—a way of solving a problem posed by the universal—and, no matter how "universally" applicable it appears to be, it must have originated in, or contributed to the formation of, some social context. To illustrate this fact, we may take the example of the experience described by Ernst Cassirer as the "momentary god." Cassirer writes:[14]

Every impression that man receives, every wish that stirs in him, every danger that threatens him can affect him religiously. Just let spontaneous feeling invest the object before him, or his own personal condition or some display of power that surprised him, with an air of holiness, and the momentary god has been experienced and created.

The vision of the momentary god is clearly a powerful experience, but it is also an ephemeral one. Members of archaic communities who have such visions are called shamans; but in order for shamans to be recognized as such, they must have been able to give form to their visions, to endow them with some kind of permanence and communicability, in short, to create symbols out of them. When a shaman finds the way of clothing his vision in imagery so powerful that it proves irresistible to the other members of the community, they embrace it as their own. The vision becomes, so to speak, common property, and it is then held in place by the symbols (images, rituals, doctrines) that the shaman originally conceived, or at least got under way. The significance of his very original and personal experience has crystallized into a communal content, a shared point of view.

History teaches us that points of view diverge widely from community to community. Therefore, however broadly disseminated archetypal contents get to be, they are far from ever gaining literal universal status; they will always bear "the imprintings of our parish," to use Joseph Campbell's expressive phrase.[15] Campbell says: "It is clear that the actual images and emphases of any mythological or dream system must be derived from local experience."[16] And, in another place he speaks of "socially authorized mythologies" whose[17]

effectiveness was such that they determined the form and content of the most profound personal experiences. No one has yet reported of a Buddhist arhat surprised by a vision of Christ, or a Christian nun by the Buddha. The image of the vehicle of grace, arriving in vision from untold depths, puts on the guise of the local mythic symbol of the spirit, and as long as such symbols work there can be no quarrel with their retention.

A given community can have a geopolitical, chronological, ethnic, or economic base, or any combination of these, the biggest communities being those designated as "primitive," "oriental," and "occidental." Indeed, it is only the notion of the archetype itself that enables us to think of these largest communities as having any reality at all—that makes it possible for us to imagine an entity as comprehensive, for instance, as "Western civilization." We realize that if there is anything to link us to our past—to the "roots of Western culture"—it must be certain fundamental patterns of thought by which great minds early in our history endeavored to make sense out of the world and which are still alive in our thinking today. We can therefore speak of archetypes as having "universal" significance, insofar as they are common to the culture as a whole, in other words, are found contained in the products of those communities, modern as well as ancient, which fall within the framework of the culture. Of course, certain artifacts, by reason of their age and fame, or because of the explicitness with which they reveal their contents, occupy a privileged place in the archetypal hierarchy. Such is the case for Greek myth-stories and the Bible, where literary critics customarily look for their archetypes. But the same archetypal content—if it really is a fundamental pattern of thought—can run through any and every manifestation of the culture, be that manifestation ancient or modern, a masterpiece or a mediocrity, whether it comes in visual, verbal, or musical form, or in the shape of an image, concept, ritual, or doctrine. This leads us to realize that we never encounter the archetype directly but only the symbols that are its manifestations. With specific reference to the arts, then, a given archetype would be a fundamental content common to a host of images which in other respects (chronology, nationality, social purpose, artistic idiom) appear quite disparate and unrelated.

Convention and Style

In itself, the archetype is a static and abstract notion, and it becomes truly understood only when it is articulated in its variant forms. The experience of the modern West has been such that the opportunity for studying "variant forms" is far from minimal: for reasons best left to the cultural historian to explain, evolution rather than preservation has been the rule. As a result, earlier forms of archetypes often accumulate meanings they did not start out with, or find themselves divested of original meanings. The Greek gods, for instance, have lost any aura of divine holiness they might once have possessed; at the same time, they continue to function vigorously in the interests of our archetypal visions of glory, beauty, and power. Divine significance for the Western world has been embodied in the figure of Christ for the better part of 2,000 years, but a quick review of religious paintings since the Middle Ages will show that even divinity, at least in the West, has been subjected to continual revision and reinterpretation.

What we are observing here is the phenomenon of "localization," or what cultural historians like to refer to as the *Zeitgeist*—a point of view which prevails over any single belief in this or that, a configuration of beliefs that dominate in a given place for a given period of time. It is on this local level that archetypal contents take on certain "conventional" characteristics, assuming a more specific orientation and emphasis in keeping with the dominant values of the epoch or community in question. Thus, the theme of the hero assumes quite a different aspect, depending on which society is describing the hero's attributes. With chivalry, the emphasis is on loyalty—to one's liege, one's lady, and one's God. Galanterie stresses elegance, grace, and wit; with Florentine humanism it is genius and breadth of interest; in Neoclassic France absolute authority embodied in the person of the king. To take a related example: the medieval conception of chivalry and courtly love, the pastoral tradition in Renaissance Italy, and the *style galant* of mid-18th-century Europe are all united by virtue of an archetype which we may identify as: refinement of manners or the cultivation of social virtue. The same general content can be traced back in ancient times to Plato's discussions in the *Republic* about the improvement of judgment and taste and even more remotely to handbooks of etiquette in ancient Egypt. Yet, when we line up a galant piano piece from c. 1750, a pastoral madrigal of the 1580s, and a courtly love song from 12th-century Provence, we notice striking divergences in the respective images. What we commonly say is that there are striking differences in *style*.

With the notion of style we come to the core of the present theory, which is that style provides the concrete and objective means by which to identify archetypal content. If the contents of a given community are the patterns of thought—the conventions, values, ideals, and basic assumptions—*typical* of the community as a whole, then artistic style, which is the *typical* element in the imagery of a given art form, will be a clear indicator of those patterns of thought. Thus, with respect to the musical examples just mentioned, it is the position of the present theory to say that the changes of style from piece to piece reflect the general differences in values and perspectives of the communities to which the pieces belong, and that the differences in values affect, in their turn, the archetypal content tying each piece to the next. If all this is true, then it is the responsibility of archetypal criticism to show what the changes in values are and if possible to explain how and why they came about. The archetypal critic thus becomes something of a cultural historian.

The principle of the *Zeitgeist* is, of course, not unknown to the music historian; he is thoroughly aware of the principle in theory, though in practice he tends to disregard it. The typical strategy of the history survey is to present a cultural background at the openings of those chapters in which a new style period is introduced. The author, thus satisfied that he has made an adequate rundown of the fundamental perspectives of the age, then proceeds to discuss musical style as if those perspectives did not exist. What I am proposing is a far more intimate connection between style and local content, a treatment that gives more than token acknowledgment to the idea that style is the formal complement to perspective and perspective the metaphysical complement to style. In all fairness, it must be admitted that in public criticism, generally, and among some scholars, there exists the tacit assumption that images do fall together into classes, at least on the level of an individual composer's style: that is, a figure or gesture from a given piece of a composer will be compared with one from another of his works and something of the same "meaning" imputed to both. Few would disagree that the drum-roll motif at the openings of Symphonies No. 34 and 41 of Mozart have the same essential character. This kind of thinking is also common in connection with composers who are contemporaries or compatriots, and whose imagery has strong stylistic affinities; or with composers from different generations, many of whose images bear such a striking resemblance to each other that the younger composer's style is considered derivative. This is certainly true of the relation of the early Scriabin to Chopin, and the conclusion usually drawn from this case (correctly, it seems to me) is that the stylistic relation proves a "deep, spiritual sympathy."

Music criticism has noticeably shied away from such comparison, however, when the images in question fall into two distinct style periods. In this respect, musical scholarship has been much less bold than the corresponding movements in literature and art. But perhaps with good cause. The most obvious reason is that without the explicit indications of subject matter that depiction and representation provide, it is difficult to recognize a recurrent pattern of thought in an image conceived in a different style. A secondary reason has to do with the relatively restricted history of music when compared with that of her sister arts, and the influence that has had on a cyclical interpretation of events. Whereas the living history of ancient literature and art has provided the possibility of a number of conscious "Neoclassic" resurgences over the entire course of modern history, Neoclassicism in music did not find expression until the "Back to Bach" movement in 19th-century Germany. Be that as it may, the idea of juxtaposing Verdi and Monteverdi still strikes us as material for a parlor game rather than a topic of serious inquiry. Yet, we recognize the "tragic" quality of expression in the music of both composers, despite the divergences of style. And just as readily, we recognize heroic statement in composers as chronologically and culturally removed from each other as Brahms and Lully.

Our ability to find the same basic pattern in sharply divergent images has already been discussed in terms of an earlier example. And so, the main thrust of archetypal thinking should be clear: to provide an objective framework for the principle that content articulates itself into patterns of thought which, by virtue of their "typical" and recurring character, become dominant at certain given moments and in certain given locales. This reflects a cyclical view of the evolution of ideas. But the cyclical view is qualified by a linear conception, which recognizes the change of form in the recurring pattern. For contents are embodied in images, and modern Western artists have been continually manipulating images and putting their individual stamp on them. Thus, the original pattern is both recognizable and never quite the same. Between the original pattern and the individual image falls an intermediate stage—a hierarchy of archetypal states, the crystallization of content into conventional modes and *styles*.

Toward the Building of the Model

As was already stated, the history presented in Parts II, III, and IV of this book is one that interprets familiar musical events in terms of a group of fundamental ideas. Because these ideas cut across the traditional barriers of period and style, they serve to unite our total experience of Western culture: history takes on the look of a set of variations on a number of recurrent themes. The task of archetypal theory is to create a framework by which to examine correspondences between the fundamental ideas and their manifestations in a given art form. In devising this framework, however, we would do well to be aware of certain methodological problems. Myth, Frye asserts, is the structure that provides the necessary link in literature between content and image. But how are myth archetypes to be applied to music? Not directly, it would seem, for myths are made out of words, while music is wordless. As the good critic he is, with his sights fixed steadily on the formal aspects of literature, Frye is eager to point out that it is not the content the artist deals with directly, but the *image*; it is from the body of imagery available in his particular art form that he will fashion the materials of his own work. "Poetry," Frye explains, "organizes the content of the world as it passes before the poet, but the forms in which that content is organized come out of the structure of poetry itself."[18]

Frye can afford to make this statement for poetry because there is a general agreement among literary critics as to what "the content of the world" is. The same statement applied to music, however, causes us to think of "structure" as pure syntax and to interpret content in the spirit of pure formalism. Alternatively, it leads us to think of the image itself as the basic structure by which to get to the problem of content. But the image proves to be a false route; for even if we were to succeed in fashioning a sizeable number of image classes, how would we characterize them ("drum-roll" image? French overture image? hunting motif?) and how many would we have to amass before we had assured ourselves that we had provided an adequate coverage? For the purposes at hand, the image approach is as unsystematic as it is cumbersome. But most importantly, it fails in the primary aim of conceiving the experience of Western music as a unity, for if an image class derives its identity from a single style period (as it most characteristically does), it cannot transcend the barriers that divide one style-period from another.[19]

The conclusion to be drawn from all this is that the "structures of content" we are looking for are indeed the archetypes themselves, provided we understand the meaning of *archetype* here not to extend to "image class" or "convention" but to be confined to "fundamental idea," or "original pattern of thought." In order to erect our framework we must confront the archetypes directly; we must first consider how the universals have been articulated in terms of Western culture as a whole, and for this purpose it is right to turn to religion and philosophy, as well as art, for our evidence. Frye's emphasis of the structural value of myth suggests that he will explain all literary phenomena in terms of myth, but in actual practice he does not adhere to this principle. He is as willing to use propositional thought and theological doctrine to bolster his arguments as the myth images themselves, and references abound in his writings to Plato and Aristotle, Augustine and Aquinas.

It should be clear that a terminology resulting from an archetypal approach will be very different from the kind by which earlier ages conceptualized musical expression: those discrete states of mind—joy, sorrow, rage, tenderness, and the like—collectively known in the 17th and 18th centuries as the "affections." This does not mean that the so-called Doctrine of the Affections will be ignored in the new critical scheme; on the contrary, it should be encompassed by the new scheme in such a way as to demonstrate that the sorts of contents music has traditionally and popularly been thought to express are truly there. The question as to whether the contents are "truly there" has, of course, been the chief stumbling block of musical aesthetics in this century. The formalists do not accept the reality of such contents. They prefer instead to acknowledge the age-old practice of assigning conventional meanings to musical imagery, and then reject the significance of conventions altogether. Here is Stravinsky on the subject:[20]

Expression has never been an inherent property of music. That is by no means the purpose of its existence. If, as is nearly always the case, music appears to express something, this is only an illusion and not a reality. It is simply an additional attribute which by tacit and inveterate agreement, we have lent it, thrust upon it, a label, a convention—in short, an aspect unconsciously or by force of habit, we have come to confuse with its essential being.

Stravinsky's position, in effect, is that if only we could prune away the unnecessary conventions of meaning from a piece of music, we would see it for what it really is—a beautiful design of interacting tones and rhythms. For somewhat different reasons, there is a branch of the new criticism which downplays the conventions as being "dubious truisms." The tendency in this criticism to call into question all past wisdom would seem to leave the straightforwardly conventional stripped of its former reality. But if the new revisionist interpretations like to view experience as made up of essentially odd twists and hidden surprises, how does oddness find its own identity? Does oddness not eventually have to be measured against a conception of normalcy? At any rate, this study proceeds on the principle that to discover what is individual in an artwork means first to know what is conventional about it—to know what it has in common with other works. Indeed, totally aside from whether artistic conventions are negligible, the more crucial question would seem to be whether they are avoidable; for conventions come about through processes so deep-rooted in our consciousness that one wonders how they could be prevented from taking shape even if a conscious effort toward this end were made. In spite of the existence of more systematic kinds of learning, the indisputable fact remains that most of our information is assimilated through association, in the largely random context of exemplary action and dialogue. This process of association applies to musical experience as it does to all intelligible acts. Whatever measure of agreement there might be among us as to the meaning of a given musical image, that element of agreement presumably comes not only from the capacity of images to travel, so to speak, from piece to piece, so that we get to know them in numbers of musical contexts and configurations, but also from the fact that in the context of an age or cultural unit of some kind they come into contact with extramusical experiences.

The more radical of the new critics do not deny the existence of the associative process; rather, they deny its essential relevance for the progress of current intellectual thought. They evaluate such thought on the basis of a construct whose extreme poles are defined by "old-fashioned shibboleths" and "innovative ideas," and they inevitably veer toward the latter pole. This is understandable in light of what cultural historians have told us about the gradual erosion of shared meaning over the last two hundred years and what that signifies in a concomitant erosion of communal feeling. Unquestionably, conventional meanings—assumptions, values, ideals—are "real" only because a great many people believe and agree that they are real. Begin to doubt the mythic power of these meanings and that is all that is needed to turn them into dubious truisms. For the radical new critics, shared meaning as a way of thinking about cultural phenomena is outmoded and dull; fluidity of meaning comes to stand for all that is bold, new, and exciting. But once again we must ask, as we did in the case of oddness vs. normalcy, whether "new" has a chance of making any sense without a notion of "old." And let us not be misled into thinking that the new critics, in celebrating meaning as fluid, open, nonhierarchical, in constant flux, etc., are operating from anything but a distinct point of view. Meyer has recently written that it is impossible for anyone to escape an ideology (a point with which it would seem impossible for anyone to disagree).[21] In the case of many of the new critics, the general position they are working from is an ideology of modernism, on the basis of which they form their own communities, power bases, and modes of action for carrying out specific modernist agendas.

As for the ideology guiding the present study, the central place accorded to shared meaning is for all practical purposes fixed and unchanging. Archetypal thinking may work more readily for the art products of earlier centuries, where conventions were, as a rule, more straightforwardly applied than they have been in recent times. But in the view of archetypal criticism, the clarifying force of the archetypes extends (though not necessarily in equal measure) to all artifacts of the culture, without exception and irrespective of time period. Even the most radical solutions (or experiments, if you will) in the musical language of our own century must in part be described and evaluated in terms of what they broke away from. But when all is said and done, it is not so much in relation to musical scholarship as in relation to everyday musical experience that shared meaning makes its most important stand. We spoke above of cultural phenomena drawing their reality from the very faith in that reality that numbers of people invest in them. No stronger case could be made for this effect than in the area of the beliefs surrounding the popular reception of music. For the majority of listeners in the Western world, human emotions are what music has been "about" for several centuries and continues to be about today; such listeners equate nothing other than happiness and sadness with music's expressive *raison d'être*.

In *The Corded Shell*, Peter Kivy makes a great deal of the divide separating the frames of reference of the ordinary music lover from those in which 20th-century musicology has made its chief advances. (Indeed, the situation is so divided that the selfsame theorist who treats a musical work in the classroom as a pure design of interacting tones and rhythms may well turn out in the privacy of his or her living room to be the listener for whom music conjures up all manner of extramusical worlds and feelings.) Kivy wants to search for a language with which it would be possible to "emote over music (without losing your respectability)."[22] For critics who share Kivy's aim, the central topic of discussion cannot be merely "music" in some general or abstract sense; it must be music as we *immediately* experience it—compose it, perform it, listen to it. This needs to be said, I think, because so much of the recent criticism seems pointed toward interests which, though construed to be related to musical expression, do not participate in it in any truly material way. Particularly because of the level of intellectualism in this criticism and its tendency to borrow terminology from extramusical sources, the discussions slip almost ineluctably in the direction of those sources, with the result that one is left with the impression of having read not music criticism, but literary criticism, philosophy, cultural history. I will be the first to admit that in the pages to follow I am not totally innocent of that charge, though I hope it will be apparent to the reader that the time spent in the domain of extramusical content is ultimately for the sake of examining how that content enters the musical image and, as it were, takes up permanent lodgings there.

There is something almost painfully paradoxical about the basic stance of the critic—the fact that despite the preoccupation with a world of images, the critic interprets those images in terms of a world of concepts: he pushes the content of art up (or down, depending on one's viewpoint) to the level of propositional thought. While this is the rightful role of criticism, the responsible critic will be acutely aware of the pitfalls involved in making something explicit and literal out of imagistic significance. Careful not to destroy the fabric of the original aesthetic experience, the critic has to learn to explain artistic content in terms proper to art. A critical theory which holds that art is connected to life must pay attention to life in order to be clear about the nature of that connection. Yet, in acknowledging the open door between art and life, we must also notice the threshold to be crossed. Content in the world of everyday experience is unsystematic and diffuse; in the environment of an artwork it becomes focused and unified. If art is to any degree a systematic way of getting to the meaning of things, then criticism will always need a systematic vocabulary to describe artistic experience.

And yet, the primordial element in music should make us wary of being too systematic. Milton's now ancient claim that poetry is "more simple, sensuous, and passionate than philosophy"[23] seems as true as ever—and perhaps most true of music, with its primitive, visceral ways of transmitting the culture's fundamental thoughts. But these fundamental thoughts, when lodged in musical imagery, have effectively already taken the form of cultural stereotypes. And it is in *this* form that composers, performers, and listeners alike, in the direct experiencing of a work of music, hold the archetypal contents in their minds; it is the stereotypes that they finally hear in the work's inner reaches, not the piling up of intriguing and disparate meanings. Critics should remember, after having donned their professional hats, that part of their musical being remains composer, performer, or listener. Keeping one's sights fixed on the actual experiencing of music while being actively engaged in talking about it: that would seem to be the critic's main task; that (to slightly transpose Meyer) would be the goal of all our verbalizing.

Notes

1. Scott Buchanan, ed., *The Portable Plato*, p. 9.
2. Leonard B. Meyer, *Style and Music: Theory, History and Ideology*, p. 88.
3. *Ibid.*, p. 89.
4. Friedrich Blume, *Renaissance and Baroque Music*, p. 111.
5. Quoted in Oliver Strunk, ed., *Source Readings in Music History*, p. 19.
6. *Ibid.*, p. 19.
7. Buchanan, p. 389.
8. S.H. Butcher, trans. and ed., *Aristotle's Theory of Poetry and Fine Art*, p. 35.
9. The poem (with modern spelling) is found in Alexander Pope, *Collected Poems*, pp. 181–185. Pope divides *Essay on Man* into four "epistles," of which the first three are entitled: (1) Of the nature and state of man with respect to the universe; (2) Of the nature and state of man with repect to himself as an individual; (3) Of the nature and state of man with respect to society. The fourth epistle—Of the nature and state of man with respect to happiness—reflects the predominating Enlightenment perspective of his own time.
10. See Jean-Jacques Nattiez, *Music and Discourse: Toward a Semiology of Music*, p. 4. For a succinct introduction to Saussure's original theory of semiotics, see Ferdinand de Saussure, "Course in General Linguistics" in *The Structuralists from Marx to Lévi-Strauss*, Richard and Fernande De George, eds., pp. 58–79.
11. Susanne K. Langer, *Philosophy in a New Key*. See especially p. 93 and pp. 144ff.
12. Northrop Frye, *Anatomy of Criticism*, p. 99.
13. On this point, see in particular Northrop Frye, *Fables of Identity*, pp. 30–38 and 55–58.
14. Ernst Cassirer, *Language and Myth*, p. 18.
15. Joseph Campbell, *Creative Mythology*, Vol. IV of *The Masks of God*, p. 89.
16. *Ibid.*, p. 654.
17. *Ibid.*, p. 85.
18. See Frye, *Anatomy*, p. 97, pp. 106–107; also Frye, *Fables*, p. 53, pp. 141–142.
19. Having said this, I am reminded of Leonard Ratner's and Wye Jamison Allanbrook's independent and very successful efforts in assembling groups of "topics" for later 18th-century music. In one aspect of the present study—in that aspect which attempts to track the development of a repertoire of expressive modes—the point of view is not unlike theirs. But for the reasons just given, I see it necessary to approach the problem from a different angle.
20. Igor Stravinsky, *An Autobiography*, pp. 53–54.
21. Meyer, *Style and Music*, p. 160.
22. Peter Kivy, *The Corded Shell*, p. 132.
23. Quoted in Frye, *Fables*, p. 57.

2 *The Archetypal Model*

Pastoral, melodrama, comedy, tragedy, satire, and epic are terms familiar to literary theory, most of them since ancient times. They also represent distinct and fundamental ways of viewing the world, and are therefore genuine archetypes. Because they look like literary categories pure and simple, part of our task is to show how they apply every bit as much to music; consequently, they are used extensively in Parts II, III, and IV of this book. In the present chapter, however, they figure less importantly, giving place to structures which are even more elemental in character (and of which, it will be argued, the categories of pastoral, melodrama, and the like are complexes). On the basis of criteria outlined in the previous chapter, the model to be presented is constructed in the form of five dichotomies:[1]

(1) *comic/tragic* (apprehension of the world, subjectively as pleasure and pain, objectively as good and evil);

(2) *romantic/ironic* (sympathy and antipathy—our impulse to be drawn toward an object or to draw away from it);

(3) *mythic/humanistic* (the need for absolutes—the need to question);

(4) *hieratic/demotic* (cultivation of the extraordinary—significance in the ordinary);

(5) *Apollonian/Dionysian* (this dichotomy embraces a number of interrelated perceptions, ranging from the more ontological—finite-infinite, form-feeling—to the more personal and temperamental—sober-intoxicated, control-abandon).

Once more, it should be noted that this collection of dichotomies, as elemental as they might seem at first glance—as much as they might appear to correspond to the most basic impulses of human nature—are already alive with cultural resonances. Impulses may be individually felt, but they are culturally comprehended: once an individual has moved from the stage of merely experiencing an impulse to that of acting or reflecting upon it, he or she has entered the realm of archetypal mediation. In short, the five dichotomies in question have been selected with a particular eye for their significance as products of Western history. It is not that non-Western cultures are innocent of any notion, say, of the comic and the tragic; it is simply that the comic and tragic connotations presented here have been shaped by the specific experiences of Western societies, and are thus understood and interpreted on the level of communal belief and attitude, not on the level of individual response. Finally, it should be added that the archetypes in question, modes of thought that they are first and foremost, can easily be construed to function as modes of expression—a fact that makes them particularly well disposed to serving in the interests of explaining artistic experience.

Comic/Tragic

Walter Kaufmann, in his book, *Tragedy and Philosophy*, reminds us that "Tragedy is primarily a form of literature developed in Athens in the 5th century B.C., and all other uses of the words 'tragedy' and 'tragic' derive from this. (The notion that events of some sort are tragic and that literary works deserve the name of 'tragedy' only by derivation is the opposite of the truth.)"[2] In other words, the "tragic sense of life" or "tragic world view," as Kaufmann calls it, will best be revealed through the great tragedies themselves. Considering the whole panoply of tragedies in Western literature and faced with their enormous variety, Kaufmann asks what the indispensable ingredient common to them all is; for, if that ingredient can be identified, it must be at the core of the tragic vision. He concludes that it is human suffering:[3]

Sophocles' *Electra* ... does not even "end badly"; nor is a *deus ex machina* required to prevent a tragic ending: heroism prevails, the good triumph over the wicked, and freedom is won. What makes the play a tragedy in spite of all of this is that, like *all* Aeschylus' and Sophocles' surviving tragedies, it presents on the stage an immense amount of suffering—so intense and so profound that no joyous but serious conclusion can expunge it from our minds. Even as Cassandra's agony is not forgotten, Electra's anguish stays with us to remind us of the dark side of existence.

Kaufmann's reference to the "dark side of existence" implies that the comic belongs to the "bright side." It also implies that the sensuous experiences of darkness and light are conceptually linked (for reasons that will be given a few pages hence) to the emotional experiences—the *pathe*—of suffering, or pain, on the one hand, and of happiness, or pleasure, on the other. In the first instance, therefore, the tragic/comic dichotomy presupposes the human capacity to differentiate between pain and pleasure: in order for something to be painful, it must be *felt* as painful. What is commonly called "evil" would then be simply the objectification of something subjectively experienced as pain. In short, pain and pleasure imply the existence of human sentience. Until such time as an objectively verifiable construct of human sentience presents itself, each of us is free to devise our own constructs. For the present purposes what we need is something that provides a common ground for the archetypal contents under examination, without causing us to get mired down in arguments about human sentience in its own right. I therefore propose a sixth dichotomy, a kind of "super-opposition" from which the five dichotomies to be defined in the following pages can all be shown to derive. In spite of the fact that the names assigned to this opposition—Eros/Thanatos— suggest Western origins, it is important to assume its primal character, that is, its identity as a universal experience beyond the reach of any given culture (while belonging in a very real sense to them all).

■ *Eros/Thanatos*   Like the Apollonian/Dionysian duality to be discussed later in this chapter, the terms Eros and Thanatos have ancient Greek roots and a modern interpretation. In this case the credit for the latter is usually given to Freud for his reference to the terms in *The Pleasure Principle*. Freud defines Eros as the life force and contrasts it with Thanatos, the death instinct, which is not a wish for literal death, but the will to reach what James Hillman has described as the "state below and after the actions of life and ... deeper than they—that is, what is symbolically attributed to death."[4] As another author writes:[5]

Classical Indian philosophy has always followed the Thanatos principle and rejected the principle of Eros: the ideal state, the goal, is the reintegration of the self into the perfect whole, the "release" of the individual life force from the debasing influence of the senses so that it may be reabsorbed into the undifferentiated godhead. This is the "blowing out of the flame" (*nirvana*).

Applied to everyday experience, Thanatos, like Eros, is *desire*, but a kind of desire pointed toward the ontological and archetypal, toward meaning free of personal and sensory implication. Thanatos signifies a desire to "know," and is thus directed to what the Greeks called *logos*; Eros is a desire to be, and leads to *pathos*, because it is inextricably tied up with natural life and the distinguishing features of that life, namely the senses and the individual self.

Viewed in this context, the tragic/comic dichotomy aligns itself with Eros, pain and pleasure being the products of desire generated on behalf of the individual self: pain is Eros frustrated, pleasure is Eros fulfilled, and any symbolism embodying the one or the other experience expresses respectively the tragic or comic vision. Since Eros is natural desire and experiences motivated by Eros are secular in character, the world religions have typically worked to redirect the course of nature and temper its power. If the "higher" religions are in any way deserving of the name, it must be in their common impulse to break free of nature and move on to a higher plane of being. The Christian pattern of life, death, and resurrection outlines a basic movement from the tragic to the comic, the comic now attainable only beyond the limits of the natural world. The *contemptus mundi* of Christianity—the view of the here and now as essentially tragic—is striking, especially when we remember the fervor with which the glories and pleasures of nature are celebrated in ancient literature and again in Western art since the late Middle Ages. Yet, this transformation in significance is not always apparent in terms of the artistic imagery itself. For instance, the most prestigious elaborations in Western art of the movement from the tragic to the comic mentioned above are, in fact, Christian-based examples: Dante's *Divine Comedy*, the *Paradise* poems of Milton, and Handel's *Messiah*; but in spite of obvious changes in meaning, the same design characterizes a number of types of modern secular experience, including the medieval quest stories, the Puritan work ethic, political revolution—any situation in which the factors of struggle and breakthrough and the ideal of individual self-fulfillment are evident.

▪ *"The Wheel of Nature"*   The same design applies to both sacred and secular artworks because in either case the source of that design is nature itself. The practice of associating our own progress on earth with that of the physical world goes back to earliest recorded times, human life being coordinated in the old myth stories with the seasonal cycle of the year and the solar cycle of the day. Human birth is symbolically equated with dawn (birth of day) and spring (birth of year), the climax of human life with summer and the rising of the sun to its zenith, and so on as worked out in the diagram called here the "wheel of Nature." Shakespeare's *Passionate Pilgrim* contains a very straightforward statement: "Youth like summer morne, Age like winter weather/Youth like summer brave, Age like winter bare." Dickens writes at the opening of *A Tale of Two Cities*: "It was the best of times, it was the worst of times … it was the season of light, it was the season of darkness, it was the spring of hope, it was the winter of despair." The figures of literature spill over into everyday experience, as when Haydn remarked to a friend, just after finishing the winter portion of his last completed work, *The Seasons*: "This part is myself."[6]

To accept the notion of the archetype is to believe strongly in the stability of meanings. And yet, such stability has its practical limits. Although tragic and comic contents are most clearly conveyed through images that make the most of the dark-bright (night-day) duality, darkness and brightness are not restricted to carrying tragic and comic connotations. In terms of the cyclical diagram just presented, night appears exclusively as a tragic image. But in the second act of *Tristan and Isolde* the lovers spend a great deal of time telling each other how the day brings anguish and the night bliss. This ostensible reversal of meaning seems to be a typical problem of lovers; we hear the same sentiments expressed in Act III, Sc. ii of *Romeo and Juliet*.

Figure 2.1: The "Wheel of Nature" or the Comic/Tragic Cycle

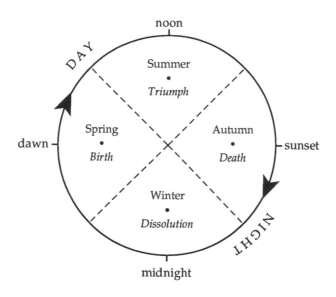

Juliet: Come gentle night; come, loving black-browed night,
           Give me my Romeo; and when he shall die,
           Take him and cut him out in little stars,
           And he will make the face of heaven so fine
           That all the world will be in love with night,
           And pay no worship to the garish sun.

All this is understandable from a practical point of view, since day will separate the lovers and night bring them back together. Nevertheless, it is not their practical circumstances that interest us so much as their positive feelings toward the night—the fact that, for them, night's terrifying aspects have given way to something alluring and seductive. Darkness as a tragic image has effectively been supplanted by darkness as a romantic image. This distinction should become clearer once the romantic/ironic dichotomy has been explained. The point to be understood now is that each dichotomy is itself a frame of reference which can alternatively surface and recede. This simply reflects the capacity of the human consciousness to carry a number of frames of reference simultaneously, to wander freely among them, mix them up in any combination and intensity, and come out with a "primary context."

To take an example from painting: the prevailing darkness of Rembrandt's mature style may have tragic weight in some instances but not necessarily in all; it may, given a certain image, signify mystery and obscurity, in which case the imagery would correspond less to the tragic and more to what has yet to be identified as the Dionysian archetype. Deciding whether the tragic or the Dionysian factor predominates in a particular case eventually entails examining aspects of Rembrandt's imagery beyond the familiar *chiaroscuro*. In a related vein, the charming *Girl with a Watering Can* by Renoir—from the National Gallery in Washington, DC—is an unambiguous symbol of the comic vision, not merely because of the overall brightness but because every image element in the piece signals the comic feeling—the youthful subject herself, the garden, the rose bushes in full bloom (the fullness of summer), the rich and tender grass. The relative brightness or darkness of an image, in short, needs the reinforcement of other elements to set a well-defined context. No more than with the archetypal connection between darkness and tragic content, brightness is not sufficient unto itself to ensure a comic interpretation, as will be borne out by the work of Vincent Van Gogh, whose incandescent yellows and limpid sea-greens overrun one troubling canvas after another. We need not consider here the dichotomy that would best explain the significance of brightness for Van Gogh's style, but it is clear that such brightness is much more problematic in respect to the conventional meanings than is Renoir's.

In music, the distinction between major and minor has enjoyed archetypal status since at least the middle of the 16th century. It will of course be objected that the major/minor dichotomy has no consistency of meaning, since the common conception of major as bright and happy and minor as dark and sad is contradicted by hundreds of "sad" pieces in major and quite as many spirited ones in minor. The problem with such an objection is that it fails to accept the force of a convention, to recognize what the chief function of a convention is—which is to foster, not understanding directly, but the communicative basis on which understanding can be built. In other words, a convention should have general application, but it is not required to serve with the same force in each case. That the Gavotte from the third English Suite of Bach can be simultaneously spirited and in the minor mode must be for much the same reasons that brightness does not function as a comic archetype in a number of Van Gogh paintings. In the case of the Gavotte, the force of minor as a tragic archetype is not much felt, presumably for reasons close to those Nicola Vicentino already recognized in his treatise on "modern practice" of 1555:[7]

When the composer wishes to write something sad, slow movement and the minor consonances will serve; when he wishes to write something gay, the major consonances and swift movement will be most suitable; and although the minor consonances are sad, swift movement will make them seem almost gay, for the ear will not grasp their sadness and infirmity because of the swiftness of the movement.

Modifying what Alfred Einstein once referred to as "the primitive and childish character of these observations,"[8] we might acknowledge something in the prescriptive aspect of Vicentino's presentation as being childish, but not the observations themselves. On the contrary, Vicentino proves himself right on target in noting that the major-minor opposition cannot stand alone in determining a tragic or a comic context. Leonard Meyer has defined the shaping forces of such contexts as "those elements of the musical organization which tend to be constant, e.g., tempo, general range, dynamic level, instrumentation, and texture."[9] Extending this list to include meter and mode, and applying it to the sarabande of the same English suite mentioned above, we can identify three factors in particular—slow tempo, minor mode, and heavy texture—as forming the conventionally tragic feeling of this piece (Example 2.1a).

Example 2.1a: Bach, Sarabande

Example 2.1b: Dowland, Lacrimae Antiquae Pavan

To what extent a kind of unconscious faith persisted between 1550 and 1750 in the usefulness of such conventions for effective expression and communication may be brought out in the juxtaposition of Bach's Sarabande with the *Lacrimae Antiquae Pavan* of Dowland, written at least 120 years earlier (Example 2.1b). For still another reason it is right that Dowland's piece should be placed alongside Bach's, for the pavan as a type carries the same sense of stateliness and dignity for the Renaissance as does the sarabande for the high Baroque. But in mentioning stateliness and dignity, we are made aware of the presence of another archetypal content. We could just as readily characterize the Bach Sarabande (or the Dowland Pavan) as "solemn" instead of tragic, and there might well be a gain in doing so. In the characterization "solemn" there is, to be sure, the tragic element, but there is the additional factor of *behavior*, which is missed in the world of purely subjective emotion governed by the tragic vision. "Solemnity" connotes bearing (stateliness and dignity) as much as it does inner feeling (grief), perhaps even more so; and if that is true, then the sarabande under discussion may be less primarily attached to the tragic vision than to what will eventually be defined as the hieratic archetype.

To summarize the main points of this discussion: the tragic/comic dichotomy involves negative and positive emotions which presuppose a condition of natural desire; as desire is either frustrated or fulfilled we experience the affects of sorrow and joy. This runs counter to traditional religious teaching, where the natural world and the desire that springs from it are represented as root causes of evil and thus inevitable symbols of the tragic vision. If the comic vision has a place in this world, it is largely due to the development of man's worldly nature—a development particularly encouraged in the West since the late Middle Ages through the ideology of self-fulfillment. Up to now the comic vision has been characterized in terms of the tragic vision—embodied mainly in the movement earlier described as the pulling away from the tragic realm of necessity toward the comic realm of freedom. We should recognize, however, that the comic vision has a significance in its own right, which is the human capacity for play. Often in everyday life the consequences of tragic events cannot be permanently overcome, but that does not preclude the presence of the comic. It is in fact in some of our darker moments that humor is put to its best uses—in dispelling fear and finding relief, and thus generating renewed energy.

This last observation serves to point up a basic opposition within the dichotomy itself, one that distinguishes between more active and passive phases of the tragic and comic visions. Up to now we have been dealing essentially with the passive phase, with what is commonly called the "human condition" and whose basic thrust may be summarized in the question, "What is the world doing for (or against) me?" With the "human capacity for play" referred to above, we are in the presence of the active phase of the comic vision, since the tendency to play remains independent of the nature of a given situation. As already suggested, a painful situation, far from negating the capacity for play, may indeed stimulate it. This active phase of the tragic/comic dichotomy is perhaps best epitomized in the question, "What am I doing for myself?" Contrasting the comic and tragic visions on the basis of their active phases, we may say that a human being, faced with a difficult situation and at the same time under the influence of the comic vision of play, will do everything possible to get around the situation and minimize its difficulties, whereas the same human being, driven by the tragic vision of necessity, will see the difficulties as unavoidable and meet them head-on.

Romantic/Ironic

Complementing the tragic/comic dichotomy in its connection to Eros is the romantic/ironic dichotomy. Natural desire signifies not only the instinct to act on behalf of oneself but also the capacity to differentiate between loving and hating and the need to find objects to which to attach those feelings. At the root of the romantic and ironic archetypes, then, is sympathy and antipathy—our inclination to be drawn toward an object or to draw away from it. Something or someone does or does not appeal. Since both the tragic/comic and romantic/ironic dichotomies involve the concept of "positive and negative emotion," it is important before going further to emphasize a distinction on that point.

The comic and tragic are the positive and negative poles of a perspective that proceeds directly out of a preoccupation with self, with *what is happening to me*. In the romantic/ironic conception, the emotion is directed away from the self, toward an object which becomes interesting by virtue of its own attributes and not in relation to one's personal desires, to one's aspirations to power. With the tragic/comic, the experience of the outer world is perceived as impinging with its full weight on the sentient subject, while with the romantic/ironic, it is a matter of looking at something apart from oneself and liking or not liking what one sees. The word "perspective," which has been mentioned immediately above, does seem to be appropriate to the action of looking outward, but if we are going to use the word here, a qualification is necessary. For this "perspective" is not identical to the kind described in Chapter 1, which was rather a product or amalgam of social beliefs and insights, a point of view shaped through a process of acculturation. Here, the connotation is much simpler, and more personal: the romantic/ironic dichotomy works from a perspective "of the heart."

The heart is hardly a seat of psychic life in the literal sense, but poetry has so persistently depended on this metaphor that criticism can use it as well. In any event, we understand immediately what it is to embrace something "with all one's heart," to "give one's heart" to something, or to "hold one's heart back." The instinct for disapproval built into the ironic impulse, contrasted against the typically approving atmosphere of romance, suggests that irony is a more "serious" kind of consciousness than romance. More "sober," no doubt, and more complex, for reasons that will be discussed below. But no more "serious" than romance, insofar as "seriousness" can be equated with avoidance of excess; for the possibility of falling into excess applies equally to both impulses. To one of an ironic cast of mind, the romantic outlook will always look excessively romantic; and, of course, the reverse must also be true. The fact is that the two archetypes form such a complementary relationship that the effect of the one presupposes the presence of the other. And so, while within the framework of the dichotomy itself, romance represents the positive pole of emotion, and irony the negative pole, they are both subject to positive and negative value judgments, to the extent that their effects are felt to be within or in excess of certain limits. Romance can be considered positively as the preservation of hopes and ideals, the willingness to find the value in things, the confidence that human beings can act nobly and generously. Negatively interpreted, romance is a voluntary "blindness," an immaturity, an inability to confront harsher realities, a form of escapism or forgetfulness. Viewed positively, irony is the voice of awareness, the wise voice which warns to proceed with caution and keep an eye open for folly and injustice. Viewed negatively, irony is the loss of all idealism, the dry croak of cynicism and disillusion. It should be recognized how one archetype serves as a corrective to the other.

■ *Romance and Its Artistic Expressions*   In his definition of the "mode" of romance, Frye identifies several genres as falling directly under its umbrella: legends, folk-tales, fairy tales, and the medieval prose stories of chivalry and adventure known as *romans* in old French, and called *romances* in English.[10] At a later place in his first essay, Frye refers to *pastoral*, calling it the chief vehicle of "romantic comedy," in which is favored a type of expression "best described as idyllic."[11] We will concentrate on the pastoral here for several reasons, first because it has the longest lineage of any of the genres belonging to the romantic mode; second, because its development in the history of music is enormous; and third, because it brings out strikingly the qualities of sentiment we have just been discussing in relation to the romantic impulse.

Paul Alpers tells us that Virgil's *Eclogues* were written "in imitation of— and in some cases closely modeled on—the pastoral poems of Theocritus, one of several brilliant poets who wrote under the patronage of Ptolemy II in Alexandria, in the middle decades of the 3rd century B.C. Theocritus' *Idylls*, as they have been called since Roman times, are a collection of thirty poems (some thought to be spurious) of which ten are pastorals. Scholars have made many efforts to find antecedents in ritual and poetry, but it seems that Theocritus genuinely invented this form of poetry."[12] Thus, if we are to believe Alpers, the story of pastoral begins with Theocritus; his *Idylls*, together with Virgil's *Eclogues*, are generally considered to constitute the high watermark of pastoral poetry in the ancient world. That Theocritus was a member of a sophisticated group of court artists and that he was writing more than a hundred years after the great moment of Athenian tragedy had come to an end are both important facts. Country life is the setting of pastoral poetry, but one can be quite sure that if this life is being described from the courtly point of view, a "faithful representation" is not the central aim—this in spite of the fact that many particulars of a shepherd's daily routine such as shearing, milking, and cheese making figure continually throughout the poems. What does seem to be the central aim of pastoral is to provide an answer to the epic and tragic traditions—to break away from the great world of gods, kings, and warriors which is the necessary locale of those traditions and to move into quieter zones. It has long been held that the need to evoke a simple, comparatively untroubled existence is typical of the escapist urge of courtiers who would be free of the cares and intrigues of the court. While that consideration should certainly not be ignored, it would be unfortunate to restrict interpretation of a symbol to one impulse, and a negative one at that.

When we begin to read Theocritus, we see other meanings emerging. Above all is a sense of human community, immediately expressed in the opening lines of Idyll 1:[13]

> *Thyrsis:* Something sweet is the whisper of the pine that makes her music by yonder springs, and sweet no less, master Goatherd, the melody of your pipe. Pan only shall take place and prize afore you; and if they give him a horny he-goat, then a she shall be yours; and if a she be for him, why you shall have her kid ... I pray you, master Goatherd, come now and sit ye down here by this

shelving bank and these brush tamarisks and play me a tune.

Goatherd: No, no, man; there's no piping for me at high noon. I go in too great dread of Pan for that ... But for singing, you, Thyrsis, used to sing *The Affliction of Daphnis* as well as any man; you are no 'prentice in the art of country-music. So let's come and sit yonder beneath the elm ... And if you but sing as you sang that day in the match with Chromis of Libya, I'll not only grant you three milkings of a twinner goat that for all her two young yields two pailfuls, but I'll give you a fine great mazer, to boot.

There are few passages in Theocritus quite as "idyllic" as this one. Indeed, even fights are possible, as in Idyll 5, where two shepherds have a pretty sharp exchange of words (though not of blows). But in the end, the tone is harmlessly bickering rather than menacing, and one has the impression that after the dust has settled, friendship will be restored. What is very characteristic of these pastorals (as well as of Virgil's *Eclogues*) is the assiduousness with which the poet imposes limitations on the range of expression. Those limitations seem embodied in the atmosphere itself. Pastoral themes and motifs can run a certain gamut: they may go from the loftier images of mythology (Daphnis in Idyll 1) to figures of quasi-farce (Idyll 5), but the focal point of pastoral imagery remains the countryside, and this locale has an influence on whatever happens within its boundaries.

It is as if through the countryside the poet has found the means to produce a less ambitious, scaled-down, essentially quiet art, one which consciously goes about avoiding the storm-tossed feelings of epic and tragedy. The expressive range is consequently circumscribed, not necessarily for the sake of providing escape from the "harsh realities of life," but to emphasize certain ways of being in the world which can be cherished as decided virtues in their own right: peace and friendship, and—on a different symbolic level—the cultivation of poetry and music. The Idylls, then, are of a particular romantic purity, because they exist primarily to express the ideal of sympathy between men. Friendship and song are the key concepts in Theocritus—friendship because it is the ideal proper, song because it is the indispensable means by which the bond is made and the ideal realized, by which one communicates "from the heart to the heart." The magical and therapeutic value of music is continually celebrated throughout these verses. Human song is often compared—and favorably—to natural music, as in the opening of Idyll 1, and it is treasured above most other human experiences:[14]

Of songs be my house the house alone,
For neither sleep, nor a sudden spring day
Nor flowers to the bees, are as sweet as they.

Finally, it also serves as consolation (Idyll 11):[15]

Thus did Polyphemus tend his love-sickness
With music, and got more comfort thereout
Than he could have had for gold.

A world resounding with music and including only the gentlest aspects of nature is clearly not a representation of this world nor even of the factual countryside. It is rather a spiritual landscape, an image by which we come to realize that gentleness, sweetness, and harmoniousness are the very properties of human sympathy.

Theocritus delivers a message which is not escapist but idealistic. He intends his poetry to be "touching" and "affecting," which is to say that he risks making it sentimental—a risk he can well afford to take, given the freshness and zest with which he tells a story and paints a scene. Virgil has been called a more "sentimental" poet than Theocritus, not in the sense just used, but in the sense Schiller conceived the word for the purposes of literary criticism and distinguished it from "naïve." What Schiller seems to have meant is that the "sentimental" poet is more reflective or self-conscious about his own impressions than the "naïve" poet, with the result that his own "voice" (i.e., his sentiment) seems to resonate through his words in a way that the naïve poet's voice does not. It is impossible to show in any detail here to what extent this characteristic might apply to Virgil, but the last five lines of the first Eclogue, which Alpers acknowledges have "become, for many readers, the hallmark of Virgilian pastorals,"[16] may give an indication of the effect.[17]

> Tityrus: Still, you could take your rest with me tonight,
>   Couched on green leaves: there will be apples ripe,
>   Soft roasted chestnuts, plenty of pressed cheese.
>   Already rooftops in the distance smoke,
>   And lofty hills let fall their lengthening shade.

To feel the impact of these lines, it is necessary to know that the eclogue concerns a dialogue between two farmers, one of whom, Meliboeus, has been dispossessed of his farm by invading troops, and will be forced to "leave for thirsty lands— Africa, Scythia, or Oxus' chalky waves, or Britain wholly cut off from the world."[18] Tityrus' farm, on the other hand, has been spared through the intervention of the commander. Tragedy thus enters the idyllic setting, and the dialogue alternates between Meliboeus' distress and Tityrus' evasiveness, until in the final lines quoted above, Tityrus makes the heartrending gesture of inviting Meliboeus for one night. And the gesture is heartrending, not only because of Tityrus' need to console his friend and his inability to do so beyond the duration of one night, but mainly because of the understated dissonance set up between human (inner) suffering and natural (outer) beauty. In the last line of the eclogue, which is justly famous in the annals of pastoral poetry, one imagines hearing Virgil's "sentimental" voice—the voice of solemn and sustained sympathy—sounding through the images.

Almost as famous as Virgil's last line is the characterization it elicited from Erwin Panofsky: "that vespertinal mixture of sadness and tranquility which is Virgil's most personal contribution to poetry. With only slight exaggeration one might say that he 'discovered' the evening."[19] Panofsky's conception is so evocative that it is still the conception that is most generally associated with Virgil. But another insight of Panofsky's made in the same essay is even more important for present purposes, for it leads beyond Virgil to a consideration of what happens in poetry when the tragic and romantic visions intersect:[20]

Virgil does not exclude frustrated love and death; but he deprives them, as it were, of their factuality. He projects tragedy either into the future or, preferably, into the past, and he thereby transforms mythical truth into elegiac sentiment.

Whether Panofsky is right in regard to Virgil himself is of no concern here.[21] What is important is that he has identified a type of expression which seems to be a direct counterpart of the idyllic feeling discussed earlier—and for much the same reasons. Once again pastoral imagery forms an expressive region whose limits must be respected; in this case, the beauty of the pastoral world—"the superhumanly perfect surroundings of Virgil's ideal Arcady,"[22] as Panofsky has put it—softens the effects of tragedy, takes away its sting.

And so, what remains is elegy, or the expression of solemn sympathy, which is another name for subdued pity. Aristotle, as we know, speaks of the capacity of tragedy to arouse both pity and fear. What elegy seems to arouse is pity without fear. That this coincides with the conception of the romantic impulse established many pages earlier can now be shown. Tragedy involves a mixture of the romantic and the ironic, since there are some elements in tragedy to which we will be drawn and others from which we will draw back. Elegy, containing no element of irony (Frye writes: "The elegiac presents a heroism unspoiled by irony"[23]), seeks to draw us toward an object only and thus elicit only our pity. From these statements we can infer a structural picture as follows: sympathy and antipathy are the root conditions of the romantic and ironic tendencies, respectively. When sympathy is colored by the tragic vision, it turns to pity; when influenced by the comic vision, it becomes tenderness. Similarly, antipathy becomes fear on the tragic side and ridicule on the comic side. Idyllic expression dominates the comic side, elegiac expression the tragic side, of the romantic archetype. The corresponding expressive structures for the ironic archetype will be discussed in due course.

It should be clear from this discussion that the romantic archetype is the origin of that quality in Western art which we call "touching," or when it comes in somewhat stronger form, "moving." What we mean by these terms refers to the power of the work of art in question to suggest that its imagery embodies feelings of tenderness or pity. In the excerpt below from the *Iliad* concerning Agamemnon and Iphidamas, we have the texture of genuine tragedy, since the elements of both fear and pity are present.[24]

Then wideruling Agamemnon seized the spear in his hand and drew it toward him furiously like a lion, and pulled it from the hand of Iphidamas, and smote him on the neck with his sword and loosed his limbs. So there he fell, and slept a sleep of bronze, unhappy youth, far from his wedded wife, bearing aid to his townfolk—far from the bride of whom he had no joy, yet much had he given for her.

But in the line, "So there he fell, and slept a sleep of bronze, unhappy youth," and especially with the repetition "far from ... far from," there is a strong premonition of that "sentimental" voice we have associated with Virgil—something that we call "warmth of expression" and that betokens the movement of the human heart.

In the reconstitution of Arcadia that takes hold in 16th-century Europe, the names, personages, and devices of the ancient form are perpetuated; the entire vehicle is kept quite remarkably intact. One will, of course, detect slight modifications in orientation; pastoral comes to be somewhat more closely linked with gentility than gentleness, with entertainment than edification. But all in all, cultivation of physical beauty is not a frivolous enterprise. And the motifs of pastoral art are particularly well suited to developing a canon of beauty that places a high value on such attributes as proportion, grace, delicacy of ornament, elegance of line, and a certain sweet harmoniousness of the whole—a canon, moreover, that will hold good for the "civilized" West until the dawning of our own century. The implications of this agenda will be examined at length in Chapters 8 and 9 and elsewhere. For the moment it is enough to say that during the better part of the 16th century, poetry and music were joined in what remains to this day the most intense and single-minded illustration of the pastoral idea (the Italian madrigal being arguably the purest tribute ever paid to elegiac expression). Also, it is worth noting that contrary to the experience of ancient Greece, where pastoral poetry grew out of a need to counteract the forces of epic and tragedy, the history of music in modern Europe shows the shepherd-musician-lover to have emerged earlier than the warrior-leader. The pervasiveness of the love theme in 16th-century secular music leads us to recognize the tenacity with which certain aspects of the courtly love idea (now done up in pastoral dress) held on long beyond the Middle Ages, while, reciprocally, the gently impassioned complaints of the courtly troubadours would seem to justify characterizing their love songs as "proto-elegiac."

▪ *Irony: General Remarks*   Polyphemus, the monster of Handel's *Acis and Galatea*, is essentially a comic figure because he is made to express himself in an exaggerated manner. What precisely is being exaggerated is the *recitativo accompagnato* style normally assigned to serious operatic heroes and heroines in the throes of intense passion. The incongruity of a monster singing *recitativo accompagnato* is already a type of exaggeration, or distortion, and this distortion produces a comic effect (Example 2.2). It is important to realize that the word "comic" here has a more complex connotation than in its usage with respect to the comic vision, where the only implications are enjoyment, pleasure, and play. The use of "comic" in the present case is related, to be sure, to the category called comedy, which has a strong element of the "comic vision" but contains a perhaps even stronger dose of *humor*. Humor is not always pleasant, as the terms "black humor" and "savage humor" should make clear, and the reason is that

Example 2.2: Handel, Recitativo accompagnato from *Acis and Galatea*

humor relies for its success more often than not on the presence of something to belittle, to bring down to size. This predatory or attack quality would mark humor as a form of cruelty were it not for the fact that the object under attack is usually represented as deserving of it, and also somewhat immune. In the Greek satyr plays it is the gods and great heroes themselves who are ridiculed, and the fun of the action is due not only to the fact that gods and heroes are known not always to behave admirably, but also to the fact that they are big enough to survive the onslaught. The main strategy in mocking a god or a hero is to assign him a style—a manner of speaking and moving—which is as far from his habitual style as possible, in other words, to divest him of all outward signs of dignity. Handel's treatment of Polyphemus works in the reverse direction, the heroic style being assigned to someone who is unacquainted with it and therefore cannot use it properly. This second strategy, which perhaps best corresponds to Dryden's term "mock-heroic," may well be funnier than the first, because it lampoons the style and the temporary bearer of it simultaneously. Humor, more than any other type of expression, relies on convention, since if there is no recognition of the convention being broken, the humor has no point.

Breaking a convention is a form of inappropriateness (at least in the eyes of those who take the convention seriously), and "inappropriateness" refers to something which is "not right." But to detect what is not right requires that fault-finding faculty which has already been defined as the ironic impulse. Irony, then, is at the bottom of humor, since humor must always show some measure of disapproval of its target. The "satiric" is that element in comedy in which humor is given a particularly disapproving edge, and perhaps the classic modern examples are the comedies of Molière. In works such as *Tartuffe, L'avare,* and *Le malade imaginaire,* the chief protagonists are so sharply etched that they come close to being archetypes in their own right for the vices they embody. That vices such as corruption and hypocrisy are major interests of the satiric outlook attests to its strongly didactic nature: vice is not presented gratuitously, but for the sake of discovering it, holding it up to derision, and ridding society of the disease. At the heart of satire, then, is a basic idealism, a view to making the world better than it is. But instead of presenting its idealism directly, in the spirit of the romantic mode—in images of beauty and loveliness—it works indirectly and negatively, showing us what is grotesque and absurd. If satire is not our most complex form of expression, it is certainly far more sophisticated than any of the types that belong to the mode of romance. Ironic expression, in general, cannot be straightforward, because irony, by definition, is built on a discrepancy, the discrepancy between what the world is and what one would like it to be. More precisely, this discrepancy, while recognized by all but the most naïve, becomes for the ironist the most significant truth he knows, the guiding force in how he acts. There is in the ironic character always a tension between feelings of dissatisfaction and a latent idealism, and this tension is reflected in qualities typical of ironic expression—evasion, circumlocution, deprecation, sarcasm. The Greek word "eiron" means "dissembler in speech," someone who says the opposite, or very nearly the opposite, of what he means. Dissembling is not necessarily synonymous with covering up the truth. An *eiron* expects and wants to be understood: his inability to speak straightforwardly is simply consistent with the way he sees the world—as a field of strange contradictions and uncomfortable discrepancies. Not surprisingly, the complexity of the ironic mentality leads to a wide variety of artistic forms, which it would be of little use to enumerate in advance of an investigation on an individual basis.

If the archetype of satire, which represents the comic side of irony, is particularly rich in ambiguities and shades of meaning, and for that reason difficult to categorize, the tragic side of irony, which may be labeled "nihilistic," presents difficulties of another kind; for it is logical for artists to have shied away from giving an exclusively nihilistic message, from presenting, in other words, a world of absolute fear and despair. The latent idealism in satiric expression disappears with extreme tragic irony, since the kind of introversion the mind can perform on ridiculous objects is not much possible with truly fearsome ones, which demand being taken seriously and at face value. Few pieces, therefore, devote themselves totally to tragic irony, but literature is not poor in vivid pictures of hell on earth. Whenever we come across a parched desert, a dungeon, a bleak and lonely moor, or even a palace infested with human ruthlessness, we have the makings of a world of tragic irony. The horrors of human degradation have rarely been treated with such ferocious intensity as in *The White Devil* or *The Duchess of Malfi*, but greed, lechery, and incomprehensible malevolence make up only a fraction of the themes in this category. Physical squalor, painful death, carnage, betrayal, madness—all these aspects of harsh reality have been translated time and again into artistic images of fear, almost in imitation of those ancient rites which exorcise evil by conjuring it up. But the reality represented does not even have to be so harsh; it can be the dull, flat grayness of spirit that creeps into occasional verses of Lucretius and covers whole pages of *Madame Bovary*.

One can almost believe that this muted, gray, unlovely world is the true home of tragic irony, that the worlds inhabited by the monsters of Elizabethan tragedy are too colorful and grand. With monsters there is always the danger that horror will turn into fascination: Edmund, Mephistopheles, and Jezebel are cases in point. The human faculty for switching mercurially between the romantic and ironic "perspectives of the heart" has already been acknowledged: what at one moment repels us can often in the next moment appear quite dangerously exhilarating. Fascination with the horrible seems to be due to the power of the romantic instinct to perform a psychological operation on an object that would normally belong to the realm of tragic irony. Panofsky has shown how under the softening influence of pastoral, tragic feeling is replaced by elegy. Frye extends this principle to the entire romantic mode:[25]

Romance ... is characterized by the acceptance of pity and fear, which in ordinary life relate to pain, as forms of pleasure. It turns fear at a distance, or terror, into the adventurous; fear at contact, or horror, into the marvellous; and fear without object, or dread (*Angst*) into a pensive melancholy.

What one comes to realize is the extraordinary complication and enrichment of feeling that can proceed from this principle. Especially where 19th-century Romanticism is concerned, the ramifications are almost endless. We also come to realize that the romantic archetype, on the tragic side, effects a reversal of thought which parallels that of the ironic archetype on the comic side: in these two areas of expression there takes place a uniting of opposites such that the positive force of romance combines with the negative force of the tragic vision in the first case, while the negative element of irony fuses with the positive force of the comic vision in the second. The inherent tension in these combinations may explain why they have enjoyed a far wider dissemination than the others. Certain it is that the double negative of tragic irony and the double positive of idyllic senti-ment pose their problems: unless delicately controlled, each risks falling into an aesthetically undesirable pattern, the first into a forbidding sadism, the second into a saccharine prettiness. It has already been mentioned that the problematic character of the ironic view makes it resistant to classification and generaliza-tion. Nevertheless, from the above discussion the basis of a method has at least been indicated: the contrasts hard/soft, bitter/sweet, contentious/harmonious become sensuous signs of the ironic and romantic impulses respectively, and it follows directly from this that such contrasts can serve significantly in identifying ironic and romantic contents in musical imagery.

Mythic/Humanistic

If the two dichotomies just discussed are linked to Eros, with the dichotomy now to be addressed the governing force is Thanatos, the desire to know, the desire to make sense out of the world. The impulse of the present dichotomy is therefore to *logos*. But that having been said, we must also recognize a certain asymmetry in the relation of the two terms, mythic and humanistic, to the source-impulse, for the mythic mentality is undeniably the earlier—and the more necessary—means of expressing Thanatos. In the early days of human history, the need to have answers for the condition of the world—to provide explanations for its origins, its workings, its ultimate fate—was overwhelming, and myth filled that need. In the last 4,000 years or so, each of us has come into a world already fitted out with a mythic structure, that is to say, a "culture." Under such conditions it becomes a matter of accepting the structure in its entirety or calling into question some of its constituent parts—institutions, rituals, even beliefs that for whatever reasons seem no longer to serve the functions for which they were originally designed. When the second of these alternatives is invoked, the humanistic impulse is at work.

Since myth envisions a world order that is divinely authorized, any antithet-ical function could be said to represent the secular viewpoint. The sacred-secular opposition may in fact serve as a starting place for a definition of this dichotomy, but as we proceed, the definition will be seen to include connotations ranging beyond the sacred-secular. For instance, the humanistic outlook, while pointed toward *logos* by virtue of the dichotomy itself, also encourages *pathos* by virtue of an inherent anthropocentricity; in Western art since the late Middle Ages, man's interest in himself has grown with each passing generation, the workings of his emotional life being examined in ever-increasing and painstaking detail. In any event, the terms mythic and humanistic must be recognized to have acquired over the course of time multiple and even conflicting meanings—meanings which will require some immediate looking into if confusion is to be avoided.

With "myth" we are confronted with two connotations of the word that are diametrically opposed: to the mythographers it means a story which contains the absolute, literal truths upon which a society is founded and sustained; in common usage it means a gross misconception, if not an outright lie. In recognition of this antimony, Mircea Eliade opens his book *Myth and Reality* with the following statement:[26]

For the past fifty years at least, Western scholars have approached the study of myth from a viewpoint markedly different from, let us say, that of the nineteenth century. Unlike their predecessors, who treated myth in the usual meaning of the word, that is, as "fable," "invention," "fiction," they have accepted it as it was understood in the archaic societies, where, on the contrary, "myth" means a "true story" and beyond that, a story that is a most precious possession because it is sacred, exemplary, significant. This new semantic value given the term "myth" makes its use in contemporary parlance somewhat equivocal. Today, that is, the word is employed both in the sense of "fiction" or "illusion" and in that familiar especially to ethnologists, sociologists, and historians of religions, the sense of "sacred tradition, primordial revelation, exemplary model."

The change in point of view about myth can be fairly easily understood if we consider that the word was attached to a corpus of stories that underwent a thorough desacralizing process in modern Europe. (Christian stories, by contrast, were called "gospel," and for good reason.) But, as Eliade shows, desacralization of Greek myth did not have to wait for modern times: the process was well under way in ancient Greece. Already in the eyes of the philosophers, mythmaking was an inferior kind of thought. "Contrasted both with *logos* and later, with *historia, mythos* came in the end to denote what cannot really exist."[27] Still another way of understanding the debasement of the concept of myth (if not the word itself) is to recognize that what stands as the truth for one community must be a lie for a community with a different system of beliefs. In our capacity as critics it is easier to allow for this fact than in our capacity as believers. For the present purposes, however, it will be necessary to begin with the acceptance of the concept in its original intentions, that is, as something which concerns itself with a reality beyond the human, or even more particularly, with events responsible for the coming into existence of this world. The most important myths, therefore, are cosmogonies—explanations of origins, stories concerning ultimate existential realities. In archaic societies power in this world is directly tied up with the cosmogonic myths, since every human action is considered an imitation of a divine model, an action that was accomplished in primordial time. A decision as to the rightness of an action cannot be taken until the story of the corresponding divine action has been revealed. As Eliade relates, "A rite cannot be performed unless its 'origin' is known, that is, the myth that tells how it was performed for the first time."[28] And in another place he writes, "the cosmogony is the exemplary model for every creative situation: whatever man does is in some way a repetition for the pre-eminent 'deed', the archetypal gesture of the Creator God, the Creation of the World."[29]

■ *Greek Impiety: The Break with the Mythic*   Deity for such societies is the literal truth, the ultimate reality, and the vital information regarding deity is stored in the myths. Against this conception, the composite picture of the Olympian gods is bewildering, if not entirely incomprehensible. In many places of the *Iliad* and the *Odyssey* the gods are not drawn even as objects of esteem, let alone awe. And these representations are bothersome to not a few ancient Greeks. Xenophanes, a philosopher of the 6th century B.C., would reject the immortality of the Olympian gods on the grounds that they "do all manner of things which men would consider disgraceful: adultery, stealing, deceiving each other."[30] Plato advocates another solution, namely excising the passages in Homer in which the gods are cast in a bad light, thus enabling them to regain something of their essence as deity.[31] For deity, as opposed to humanity, is at the heart of the matter: Zeus and his troupe look and act too often like nothing more nor less than human beings. The gods as described in the Homeric epics come off as clear, sharply etched, beautiful superhumans, which is to say that they seem not different in kind from humans, only different in degree. Richmond Lattimore calls them "immortal men and women, incomparably more powerful than mortals, but like mortals susceptible to all human emotions and appetites, therefore capable of being teased, flattered, enraged, seduced, chastised."[32]

By contrast, Jehovah, the Hebrew god, though quick to anger and to mete out punishment, is not subject to anything we could call "frailty" or "appetite." His anger is like that of the gods of all archaic religions, justifiably aroused: a human offense has been committed, and if it is not immediately evident to the offenders, it must be hunted out and discovered. In Greek tragedy of the 5th century, the gods have become hostile for no apparent reason:[33]

> The gods have ceased to care for us.
> The only grace they want from us is our destruction.
> Why stop to fawn upon our cruel doom?

or:[34]

> Linger not, maidens, stay not by the house.
> Come to behold great and new deaths,
> many agonies, never yet suffered;
> and none of this is not Zeus.

This outlook strongly suggests an assumption followed by a disappointment, the assumption being that the gods have a responsibility to help those who are weaker than they, the disappointment being that the gods have failed in their responsibility: since human pleas have gone unanswered, the gods must be hostile. Perhaps the most disturbing picture of a god to be found in Greek literature is drawn by Euripides in *The Bacchae*. Here, Dionysus takes his revenge on Pentheus, the king of Thebes, for being a nonbeliever. Pentheus' punishment is to be torn to pieces by the maenads, the frenzied worshippers of Dionysus, with no other leading the pack than Pentheus' mother, Agave. The final tragedy is Agave's when, coming out of her frenzy, she realizes the victim to be her own son. While in true Euripidean fashion the author never discloses his own feelings, the questions raised by the play are unavoidable. More than just indicting maenadism (which may still have been practiced in places not far from 5th-century Athens) and the god who sanctioned such worship, the play seems to ask whether all religion is not loss of reason and therefore the road to horror and destruction.[35]

Greek "impiety," however, is perhaps best expressed in the satyr plays of the Dionysian festivals; here, gods are lampooned and sent up at will, and even Zeus is fair game. Of course, the satyr plays are not to be taken seriously, but neither, it seems, are the gods. Furthermore, ridiculing the gods is not confined to the satyr plays, since a good deal of it is done in the comedies of Aristophanes as well. At any rate, the fact that Dionysus, the sinister power of *The Bacchae*, can turn up a year later as the perfect idiot of *The Frogs* is inconceivable in Judeo-Christian terms, not because it implies an ambivalence (which is understandable by Judeo-Christian standards), but because it expresses the ambivalence in such a blatantly irreverent way.

The discrepancies between such displays of irreverence and the fact that religious observance continued to be a part of everyday life seem difficult to reconcile, especially when the documentation is scanty both on the literary and ritualistic side. Yet, such a disunified situation may not be so very different from our own. The difference is, of course, that in our own time, we have sufficient information to understand how the heterogeneous parts relate to each other; in the Greek picture the relationships are largely missing. But the heterogeneity itself is of tremendous significance, for it points to the uniqueness of the Greek experience by comparison with those of all the other peoples in the Asia Minor region. At some point earlier than Homer, the mythic structure of archaic society must have begun to show the first signs of disintegration. At that point the idea must have occurred to someone that perhaps the gods should not have total say as to the way men live. In the archaic conception of things, men adjusted their lives completely according to the dictates of divine law; men, of course, made day-to-day decisions but only after consulting with the shamans, priests, and oracles—the representatives of divine authority. The decisions taken in primitive societies, in other words, were not so much concerned with *what* to do as to when and how to carry out something that was already divinely ordained. The revolutionary aspect of the Greek conception is in its movement away from myth and toward humanism; indeed, the history of Greek culture for centuries on end seems centered on the tension and the interplay between these two outlooks.

Lattimore has put the point very nicely when he says, "These gods have, in relation to men, absolute power ... But one thing the gods-as-persons of Homer do not do, they do not change human nature. They manipulate Achilles, Aieneias, Paris but they do not make them what they are. The choices are human; and in the end, despite all divine interferences, the *Iliad* is a story of people."[36]

■ *Mythic vs. Humanistic in Ancient Literature*   Since ancient Greek literature and the Old and New Testaments furnish virtually all the source material for later Western thought, we cannot leave the subject of these sources without briefly considering their relatively mythic or humanistic orientation. The humanistic bias of the Homeric epics manifests itself in two distinct ways—in a sustained interest in the diverse aspects of everyday life and in the exploration of human action and motivation. The first is especially true of the *Odyssey*, in which activities such as cooking and sailing or places such as the orchard where Odysseus finds his father are described in minute detail. The second is brought out forcefully in Homer's habit of adopting direct discourse for his protagonists—of letting them speak for themselves (a strategy already acknowledged in ancient times, most significantly by Plato).[37] Direct discourse enables us to perceive the inwardness, the very dynamics of human feeling; but a clever use of narrative construction can do much the same thing. In the *Odyssey* the hero's return is drawn out over the last three of the twenty-four books, with a concomitant buildup (and eventual release) of the psychological tension. By comparison, terseness and stasis mark the recognition scene of Joseph and his brothers in Genesis 45, greatly moving as it is and even though the passage is quite lengthy by Old Testament standards and Joseph has a chance to express personal feelings.

Homer's continuity is the opposite of static; it is swift and flexible by virtue of his ability to change the point of view. This capacity to see the same situation from a different angle and thereby create a multidimensional emotional effect is perhaps the core of the humanistic genius; this is already the "modern" way of viewing things. Moreover, the suppleness of perspective seems directly related to a concern for things human—an intense interest in the volatility of the human condition as opposed to the relative fixity of the divine order. Kaufmann has recognized the presence of this concern in the *Iliad*, which he describes as a "profound *humanity* that experiences suffering as suffering and death as death, even if they strike the enemy."[38] To see yourself in the enemy is, indeed, the most humane of sentiments, and to what extent Homer possesses this sentiment will be acknowledged by any reader who has felt the predicament of Hector as keenly as that of Achilles. Sympathy for one's enemies is not readily found in the Old and New Testaments, in spite of admonitions to "love thy neighbor" and turn the other cheek. The reason is simple enough: an enemy is someone who does not believe like yourself and is therefore on the wrong side. In the *Iliad*, the enemy is on the *other* side; and he has ended up there because of circumstances—because of an offense which everybody realizes is trivial and not worth fighting over, but which must be avenged if only to reaffirm one's value as a human being.

Because the humanistic tradition is very strong with us in the West, we find the presentations of inner and outer conflict in Homer and the Greek tragedies extremely satisfying and meaningful. For the greater part of the world, however, such stories can be more bewildering than satisfying, leaving open too many ethical choices. No single lesson can be learned from them, no irrevocable truth that one can take away as a guide for right living. What both Auerbach and Kaufmann have said about the sufferings of the Old Testament figures and the changes registered in their personalities is quite true, but the final fact is that the collective existence of these figures is tied to Jehovah's will. There is no action recorded in either the Old or New Testament that does not have a mythic meaning behind it. Saul, David, and Jonathan are vividly drawn and appear very human and "rounded" by virtue of the fact that their weaknesses as well as their strengths are shown. And David is no doubt the favorite figure of the Old Testament precisely because he appeals to our humanistic taste. But if one reads the sections on David carefully, one will discover that every action he performs is directly referrable to the judgment of a specific mythic divinity named Jehovah. The episode concerning the taking of Bathsheba would have no point if it did not include the thought: "But the thing that David had done displeased the Lord."[39]

Mythic truth aims in practical terms for the unity and solidarity of a community. Eliade has shown that for the members of archaic societies the reality of a sacred object is grounded in a static vision of its existence; it exists now because it always existed:[40]

Asked the reason for a particular detail in a ceremony, a Navaho chanter answered: "Because the Holy People did it that way in the first place." ... The same justification is alleged by the Hindu theologians and ritualists. "We must do what the gods did in the beginning" (Satapatha Brahmana, VII, 2, 1, 4). "Thus the gods did; thus men do" (Taittiriya Brahmana, 1, 5, 9, 4).

Christian *logos* and ritual adhere, at least in theory, to a condition of stasis, but given the ambitions of the Church—the geographical territory and diverse cultures it managed to bring under its influence—it would be unrealistic to infer a uniformity, in terms of artifacts and ceremonies, equal to that of the sacred objects of locally constituted societies. That Christian ritual got disseminated as widely as it did is already testimony to the Church's heroic energy. But by the very breadth of that dissemination, variety and heterogeneity were as if predestined. With particular respect to the liturgical music of the Middle Ages, what seems more surprising than the local variants in chant style is the introduction of polyphony into the liturgy sometime during the 9th century (and perhaps earlier). In view of the exalted position of chant as the music ideally suited to the worship of God because it had been given to man under divine inspiration, one wonders what to make of the advent of the distinctly different type of music that organum represents. This is a mysterious question which has not yet been (and may well never be) satisfactorily answered.[41] But whether by design or by accident, the appearance of polyphony not only signals a significant departure from strict observance, it also opens the door to an eventual proliferation of styles—a development decidedly out of keeping with the noninnovative, preservational ways of a community founded on the mythic plan.

The makeup of the Christian "community," c. A.D. 1000, militates against evaluating it on the same basis as Eliade's archaic societies. And yet, the recognized authority of the Church attests to Christianity's continuing mythic status. Unlike Greek myth, Christian myth, it should be remembered, has never been desacralized, nor has there ever been a separation between Christian myth and Christian ritual. Rather, what has happened since the resurgence of humanist tendencies in the late Middle Ages is a reduction (though hardly a breakdown) in the Church's authority—a dwindling of its spiritual influence, a cantonization of its political power. In short, mythic status persists; but the mythic unity that the early Church labored so strenuously to build up and secure has been greatly dissipated. For, despite many examples of harmonious coexistence of sacred and secular interests, the increasing hold that the notion of "free will" has exerted on the European mind (the will to a growing independence of the divine, hence a greater dependence on self) points to the elemental tension between mythic and humanistic attitudes.

Indeed, if this tension is as elemental as it seems, then it might best be described as a manifestation, in historical and specifically Western terms, of something that began life as an internal conflict between two opposing human impulses: the need for absolutes and the need to question. In the mythic view, life is felt to be a part of a greater whole, and its significance is revealed in a set of truths divinely inspired and authorized. In the humanistic view, life is felt to be wondrously diverse, and its significance is subject to human interpretation. Human insight being what it is, human interpretation has led to a great many incomplete truths, half-truths, and hypotheses. Myths have in great part been exchanged for values. Nevertheless, modern Western society has chosen to live with these, which is to say in a state of relative uncertainty. And in keeping with this preference, certain categories of humanistic art—Greek tragedy, for instance, which poses terrible questions and presents intolerable dilemmas—have enjoyed great prestige.

Hieratic/Demotic

An asymmetry enters the structural model at this point, resulting from the fact that the present dichotomy proceeds not directly from Eros/Thanatos but rather from the dichotomy just discussed. Whereas the mythic/humanistic centers upon objective significance—how do we make sense of the world, do we rely on perfect divine truth or imperfect human understanding?—the significance of the hieratic/demotic is directed back toward a human frame of reference, in particular, toward human action—how do we behave, how can we improve ourselves, how do we relate to our social and cultural environment? The nature of this significance, then, is not exactly a *logos*, that is, an objective knowledge purportedly free of the vagaries and variables of human feeling, but an *ethos*, that is, a knowledge of human character, or more precisely, a method by which to build character and shape the total personality. Insofar as we are talking in great part about cultivation of manners and social virtues, it is society itself that most often sets the ethical standards and establishes proper modes of behavior. Where social behavior is concerned, artistic images have been considered a valuable tool of instruction, capable not only of reflecting social ideals but even more actively of serving as models of harmony and grace. As to the more inward virtues of the Judeo-Christian tradition, such as obedience, compassion, brotherly love, and inner harmony, these, like the emotions, have long been viewed as susceptible of artistic expression, even though the manner in which they might be expressed is not immediately clear.

■ *Hieratic: Cultivation of the Extraordinary*   In defining the dichotomy in question more fully, we may begin by examining three statements from Aristotle's *Poetics*. In the first statement, "Tragedy is an imitation of a noble action,"[42] the traditional rendering of "noble" for "spoudaios" spawns the beginnings of a misconception, since noble has connotations of rank, while the original means something like "weighty" or "of a certain magnitude." With Aristotle's second statement, on the other hand, the question of rank really does enter: "Tragedy should represent on stage kings and other personages of high rank, in keeping with the dignity, elevation, and significance of the proceedings."[43] This and the following third statement: "Tragedy imitates men who are better, comedy imitates men who are worse than we know them today,"[44] lend themselves to two very definite inferences, the first being that the general style and bearing of kings and leaders in everyday life can elevate the tragic action, the second being that leaders are somehow "better" men not so much out of innate goodness but because they have better ways of conducting themselves than the ordinary run of mortals.

In spite of this it should be kept in mind that Aristotle's conception is based not only on the 5th-century tragedies with which he is directly dealing in the *Poetics*, but also on the epic tradition out of which the tragedies grew. Actions of great significance and scope are the subject matter, as we have seen, of Homeric epic and Greek tragedy, and the men and women represented in this literature are extraordinary, of heroic stature. Indeed, their relations with the gods would seem to be a sign of their superiority. For, whether they are in a kind of dialectical interaction with the gods as in the *Iliad* and the *Odyssey* or struggling against them, as in Sophoclean tragedy, the presence of the god confers a particular significance on all events, and the commerce that these heroic mortals have with the gods is thus the distinguishing feature that separates them from ordinary human beings. One may in fact define the heroic simply as "experience beyond the normally human." And the connection with gods and with the mythic world in general is the means by which this experience is made manifest. The images of the mythic world become in Greek literature interlaced with those of the hieratic world, and hieratic expression takes on the breadth and grandeur originally associated only with myth.

It is no surprise, then, that the language of this hieratic literature is poetry, a language proper to extraordinary individuals and experience. In fact, it may not be too facetious to say that if epic poetry intends to imitate the speech of any group of "existential" beings, that speech must be the language of the gods. But perhaps not quite; for there is another image of god-speech, already extant in Greek times, which has an altogether different character. Apollo, for instance, speaks through the Delphic oracle in short, clipped phrases, uttering pithy but often cryptic bits of wisdom such as "Know thyself" and "Moderation in all things." Such speech is called, appropriately enough, oracular, and is characterized by extreme economy of means, as if to express the impenetrability of godlike thought. I bring up oracular speech here in order to point up the enormous difference between its texture and that of epic and tragic poetry. The Olympian gods of Homer, far from being impenetrable and shadowy, are clear, colorful, full of movement, resembling in great measure nothing other than the great heroes of Greece and Troy. Thus there is every reason that gods of this sort and extraordinary human beings should speak the same language and that that language should be grandly eloquent, which is to say that it should not only connote significance, but also *show* significance.

In this conception of *showing* lies an important truth about hieratic thinking, which, in the final analysis, is a function of aristocratic mentality. The word "aristos" in Greek means "best," but it is not enough to be the best: the fact must be shown, it must be made manifest. Heroes must accomplish daring feats and risk death, athletes must win their contests, musicians must perform with skill and feeling—these things are normal by any standards. But in Greek aristocratic thought, over and above these expectations is a sense that all life, in order to be noteworthy, must look noteworthy: it must be clothed in the outward trappings of beauty and grandeur. In the light of this discussion, Aristotle's statements above take on an undeniably aristocratic tone. What was inferred earlier can now be confirmed: kings and other personages of high rank are called for in tragedy, not because they are the only "good" men, but because they are the only ones whose outward manner attains the level of dignity and elevation adequate to the tragic situation. Tragedy, in other words, requires the outward signs of dignity and elevation to be clearly present in order for significance to be felt. And, in the nature of a "hieratic" art, tragedy makes this requirement because it is indicative of hieratic mentality in general. To sum up this notion in a kind of syllogism, we might say: something, in order to be significant, must be extraordinary, and in order to be extraordinary, it must *look* extraordinary. Aristotle's third statement reinforces this notion, since, by contrasting comedy with tragedy, it effectively observes that comedy operates on a level of significance distinctly below that of tragedy. From this it follows that a style of expression must be found which is in keeping with the level of personage that inhabits the comic world. But since the comic world is more or less equivalent to our everyday world, it is right that literary comedy should imitate everyday speech and deportment in developing its diction and style of physical gesture. We might conclude from this that it is through comedy that the demotic style is born. Such a conclusion is only minimally correct, however. For while it is true that the ancient comic style might outwardly resemble a type of demotic expression which we call "realistic," the mentality governing artistic expression in general is still primarily aristocratic and thus hieratic in orientation.

In fact, a sharp separation of styles is symptomatic of an artistic climate dominated by the aristocratic mentality. And the reason should be clear: comedy adopts a low style, in opposition to tragedy's high style, because this style is proper to everyday and ordinary concerns, in other words, to concerns which, unlike those of tragedy, have *no special* significance. Erich Auerbach has stated the case very clearly with respect to a passage from Petronius:[45]

Now if Petronius marks the ultimate limit to which realism attained in antiquity, his work will accordingly serve to show what that realism could not or would not do. The Banquet is a purely comic work. The individual characters, as well as the connecting narrative, are consciously and consistently kept on the lowest level of style both in diction and treatment. And this necessarily implies that everything problematic, everything psychologically or sociologically suggestive of serious, let alone tragic, complications, must be excluded, for its excessive weight would break the style. Let us pause here for a moment and think of the nineteenth-century realists, of Balzac or Flaubert, of Tolstoi or Dostoevski. Old Grandet (in *Eugenie Grandet*) or Fedor Pavlovich Karamazov are not mere caricatures, as Trimalchio is, but terrible realities which must be taken wholly seriously; they are involved in tragic complications, and notwithstanding their grotesqueness, are themselves tragic. In modern literature the technique of imitation can evolve a serious, problematic, and tragic conception of any character regardless of type and social standing, of any occurrence regardless of whether it be legendary, broadly political, or narrowly domestic; and in most cases it actually does so. Precisely that is completely impossible in antiquity. There are, it is true, some transitional forms in bucolic and amatory poetry, but on the whole the rule of the separation of styles, touched upon in the first chapter of this study, remains inviolate. Everything commonly realistic, everything pertaining to everyday life, must not be treated on any level except the comic, which admits no problematic probing.

Auerbach's reference to modern literature in the middle of the quotation points fairly closely to what the kernel of the demotic spirit is. Indeed, one might say that Auerbach's book is an intense and protracted gaze at the emergence of the demotic in Western literature. But if Auerbach is correct, one wonders whether all comedy in the ancient world does not essentially belong to the category of comic irony. For in an environment where something of particular weight and significance must be manifested through certain outward signs (and no others) in order to be recognized as such, the demotic archetype has little chance of realizing its potential. As has already been said, such an environment is being interpreted solely from the aristocratic point of view. A value system which in effect utilizes a single principle for separating the serious from the nonserious points directly to a ruling-class influence and control.

■ *Hieratic Style in Modern Europe*   When we come to the modern era, hieratic feeling becomes an all-pervasive thing in courtly life, and much of urban life as well. Since it is characteristic of the hieratic to make itself felt, there is rarely any need to prove its presence: the outward manifestations are there for all to see. This fact alone makes it possible here to dispense with any lengthy account of the ceremony which accompanied even the most routine affairs of court life. The pomp and color of festivals, the lavishness of dress, the grandeur and ornateness of the palazzo, all make up a texture of living which is so integral a part of daily existence that it comes to appear to those in authority not only as their privilege, but even more, as their responsibility to maintain.

When outward show is sufficiently splendid and large scale, the intention of "heightened significance" is obvious. But when the aim is toward more intimate and small-scale effects, the relevance of significance is more difficult to assess. I am thinking in particular of 16th-century pastoral where the avowedly antiheroic ethic militates against size and pretension. We have said that pastoral is situated in the romantic archetype, and this is as true of Arcadian pastoral of the 16th century as it is of any other type. Yet, in Arcadian pastoral there is also a strong hieratic influence, and if that is so, then the pastoral imagery must express, through its very sensuousness, the feeling for the out-of-the-ordinary which is at the heart of hieratic thought.

Perhaps we can approach the problem through the idea of beauty. The word "beauty" has figured quite continually in our discussion of the archetype of romance, and it seems to be naturally connected to that archetype. In its romantic connotations beauty signifies a quality inherent in objects to which we are naturally drawn. There is in this meaning of beautiful a sense of spontaneous reaction, a strong initial movement of the heart. Such a meaning persists in Arcadian pastoral, but there it is overladen with hieratic connotations and enforced by an aesthetic which guides virtually all Renaissance art. This aesthetic has already been called "imitation of nature"; but the term needs qualification; for someone of a demotic frame of mind would certainly understand by this a "faithful representation of everyday reality." That everyday reality is to be closely *observed*, according to Renaissance thinking, there is no doubt, as is exemplified by Leonardo's anatomy studies, to take only the most famous case. But that nature should be observed for its own sake is not a sufficient artistic enterprise; one learns from nature not by copying it, but by reassembling it—by taking its best parts and discovering the secret of its beauty. This ideal of improving on nature is a persistent one in Renaissance art theory, perhaps no more clearly expressed than in the following passage:[46]

And of all the parts (the painter should) not only render a true likeness but also add beauty
to them; for in painting, loveliness is not so much pleasing as it is required. Demetrius,
the ancient painter, failed to gain the highest praise because he strove to make things
similar to nature rather than lovely. For this it will help to take from all beautiful bodies
each praiseworthy part, and one must always exert himself with study and skill to learn
great loveliness; this may well be difficult, for perfect beauty is not in one body alone, but
(beautiful parts) are dispersed and rare in many bodies, yet one must give all his labor to
investigate and learn it. It will happen that one who is accustomed to aim and undertake
great things will be easily capable of lesser things. And nothing is so difficult that it cannot
be mastered by study and application.

The conception voiced in this passage can find expression in images and objects
that run the gamut from the delightfully superficial to the more impressively
sustained. But behind all of them persists the notion, clearly neo-Platonic in
inspiration, that man has imposed his own form on nature, as if imitating the
original creation of nature out of formless matter. In art, nature is raised to a
new level of interest; it becomes, so to speak, an "upper nature," one on a plane
distinctly above ordinary nature, the world of everyday reality. Thus, the hieratic
ideal realizes itself in the Renaissance by creating *art*, or perhaps more precisely,
by making everything into art.

Elizabethan literary theory and practice provide very fertile ground for examining the relations between nature and artifice. In her study, *Elizabethan and
Metaphysical Imagery*, Rosemond Tuve argues valiantly against the critics whose
approach to Elizabethan poetry is principally to see it as a rhetorically figured
language, and for the position that responsible theorists and poets of the age are
always seeking a just relation between ornament and subject, a way of "fitting
the sound to the sense."[47] She is right, of course: there will always be the type
of poet who engages in a profusion of ornament because of a lack of discipline,
or more probably, for want of an integrating idea; but with the best poets there
is a sincere attempt to convey "the essential vitality of which the external detail
is a manifestation."[48] When Ben Jonson writes in his preface to *Sejanus* that the
proper obligations of a tragic writer are to "truth of argument, dignity of persons,
gravity, and height of elocution,"[49] we not only re-hear the voice of Aristotle, but
we also imagine that Jonson means to integrate the tragic elements by means of
a unified conception. "Figures" have certain properties and not others: some
are fit for magnifying, some for lending grace and harmony, and they should be
used accordingly. Drayton says of the improper use of a seven-line stanza that it
"softened the verse more than the Majestie of the subject would permit."[50]

Elizabethan criticism of the type just mentioned could be multiplied at will.
Yet, there remains the inescapable fact of the figures themselves: in both the
theory and the poetry, figure and ornament are present to a degree that makes
it clear that they are a constant—and conscious—preoccupation. Whether it is a
love sonnet or a tragic soliloquy, figurative speech is a given, a consistent feature

of the diction in a way that is not true of poetry in the last two hundred years. Elizabethan theorists will refer to style as a "garment," to "the flowers" of rhetoric, or to an effort to "dress up meaning." All this attests to the status of ornament as a general condition; and it is so, not only (as Tuve says) because ornament serves to convey the significance of the subject in question, but more forcefully—and more to the point of hieratic thought—because ornament, in and of itself, conveys a feeling of heightened significance. The following passage from Puttenham's *Arte of English Poesie* brings out the point very clearly:[51]

Even so cannot our vulgar Poesie shew itself either gallant or gorgeous if any limb be left naked or bare and not clad in his kindly clothes and coulors, such as may convey them somewhat out of sight, that is from the common course of ordinary speech and capacity of the vulgar judgment, and yet being artificially handled must needs yield it much more beauty and commendation. This ornament we speak of is given to it by figures and figurative speeches, which be the flowers as it were and coulors that a Poet setteth upon his language of art.

The use of the word "beauty" here is particularly apposite to our argument, for not only is the beauty of poetry enhanced by a certain artificial handling, but it is enhanced just to the extent that it is divorced from ordinary, everyday speech. A more pointed example of how the hieratic moves to "methodize nature"[52] would be difficult to find.

▪ *Demotic: Significance in the Ordinary*   The crystallization of a genuine demotic mentality in Western art is a story too complicated to relate here. Auerbach gives us a fascinating picture of it, and some aspects of his account will be of use in Chapter 4. All we can do here is to outline the basic principles which separate the demotic and the hieratic archetypes, and to offer a few isolated examples as illustration. Two types of art with distinctly demotic tendencies—genre painting and rustic pastoral poetry—will serve as the sources of our examples. In genre painting we have an art that depicts scenes of everyday life. As the Praeger encyclopedia points out, "It does not deal with any particular stratum; there are genre pictures showing life amongst the aristocracy, the middle class and the peasantry."[53] This seems to be true if we compare the interiors and personages of Terborch's paintings, which look distinctly upper-class, with those of de Hooch's, which are working-class or burgherlike. Steen's and Brouwer's scenes of debauch and merriment are almost always in the satirical vein, and belong unequivocally to the category of comic irony. But when we turn to de Hooch's glimpses of women sweeping a courtyard or scrubbing tiles, or of a mother casting an adoring glance at her child who has just come in the door, we experience an altogether different feeling. What seems most remarkable about these pieces is their soundlessness, an effect achieved pictorially through a space greatly relieved of detail and ordered into neat compartments of verticals and horizontals (picture frames, window frames, door frames). Here we must adjust our historical eye for a moment, and imagine how plain, primitive, and lacking in verve a painting in this style would have looked to a contemporary Italian. To us, it is as if a deeply moving significance has been found in a place where the hieratic mind forgot to look. Similarly, in the Le Nain brothers' pictures of peasant life we find a serious dignity—a dignity without pose, without stateliness, without ornament, without any of those accoutrements of dignified behavior by which hieratic art would render the feeling. And that is just the point: demotic thought means to show us that dignity is not *behavior*, not something we see, but something we feel out from an object. Demotic art believes in eloquence, but a kind of eloquence which must to a large degree bypass ornament and be judged by other standards.

Just what these standards are is difficult to say. The effects of hieratic imagery are very much on the surface, in keeping with the hieratic ethic of outward show. But since the contents which are significant to demotic thought are not manifested in clear, unequivocal outward signs, how are we to recognize their presence in demotic imagery? To some degree, demotic images will appear as a reaction to hieratic ones: the former will look plain, modest, even homely by comparison with the latter. In essence, this means that the demotic style can borrow much of its imagery from the ironic archetype—images which have a certain harshness and rudeness of quality, a certain "rusticity"; but the demotic, in keeping with *its* ethic, will soften these images, or at least transform them into something more redemptive, more positive.

■ *"Rusticity" and Simple Eloquence*   A decisive step in the demotic direction is taken by English poetry at the opening of the 18th century: rustic pastoral art emerges as an explicit reaction to the Arcadian type described in the romantic/ironic section above. In the preface to his *Shepherd's Week* of 1714, John Gay outlines the aspirations of the new pastoral:[54]

Great Marvell hath it been (and that not unworthily) to diverse worthy wits, that in this our Island of Britain ... no Poet ... hath hit on the right simple Eclogue after the true ancient guise of Theocritus, before this mine Attempt. Other Poet traveling in this plain High-way of Pastoral know I none. Yet, certes, such it behoveth a Pastoral to be, as Nature in the Country affordeth; and the Manners also meetly copied from rustical Folk therein. In this also my love to my native Country Britain much pricketh me forward, to describe aright the manners of our own honest and laborious Ploughmen, in no wise sure more unworthy a British Poet's invitation, than those of Sicily or Arcadie.

This passage bears the distinct suggestion that Britain, great realm that it is, is made all the greater by the labor of the "rustical Folk" and that their contribution merits being celebrated and dignified in verse. But the true measure of dignifying these folk consists not simply in describing them but in *adopting their tone*. In a confession of extraordinary awareness, Gay tells us just how far he is willing to go in this endeavor.[55]

That principally, courteous Reader, whereof I would have thee to be advertised (seeing I depart from the vulgar Usage), is touching the Language of my Shepherds; which is, soothly to say, such as is neither spoken by the country Maiden nor the courtly Dame, it having too much of the Country to be fit for the Court, too much of the Court to be fit for the Country.

Gay's plight epitomizes the problem of court art in its interaction with folk culture: how to capture the spirit of the original, without abandoning the fundamentals of one's traditional mode of artistic expression. For Gay is finally writing a poem, not a compendium of colorful samples of the "vulgar Usage." His poem is an imitation, not a documentary, of country life. Yet, there is the inclination to be true in some degree to the everyday experience, in the hope that something of the flavor of that experience will seep into the artwork. The court artist is attracted to peasant vigor, presumably because he recognizes something alive in it that can enliven his own style. But when Gay refers to the "plain High-way of Pastoral," vigor does not seem to be the essential quality he has in mind. At the end of his preface, he writes: "It may so hap, in meet time that some lover of *Simplicity* shall have the Hardiness to render these mine Eclogues into such more modern Dialect as shall be then understood."[56] Simplicity—plain speech—may indeed be a kind of vigor, but one detects a new point of view in Gay's appreciation of it. What the simplicity of rustic speech connotes here is not "simpleness" but a capacity to express sentiment directly and without affectation. If up to this time the motivation behind "rusticity" has been comic relief, whereby the rustic tone serves to guard against too much loftiness and dignity, Gay's intention is to point out the distinct possibility that rusticity has a dignity of its own.

Less than forty years after *The Shepherd's Week*, Thomas Gray will add significantly to demotic imagery with his *Elegy Written in a Country Churchyard* (1750). This 128-line poem, so famous that it was known by heart by countless schoolchildren not too many years ago, gives definitive shape to rustic pastoral's counterpart of the Arcadian shepherd—the honest laborer. Gray sums up the dignity of this unsung class of human being in an epitaph that occupies the last twelve lines of the poem. In the opening lines, day is drawing to a close, leaving the poet alone with his thoughts:[57]

> The curfew tolls the knell of parting day,
> The lowing herd wind slowly o'er the lea,
> The plowman homeward plods his weary way,
> And leaves the world to darkness and to me.

If, as Panofsky says, Virgil invented the evening, Gray has memorably re-created it for the English-speaking world. Gray's countryside is one he could actually have visited, full of the rude images of peasant life—"moldering heap," "straw-built shed," "blazing hearth," "lowly bed," "sturdy stroke"—and he dwells on these lovingly. Later in the poem the great world is evoked—to its great detriment, so it turns out, since Gray compares it unfavorably to the virtues and "solemn stillness" of country life. In the ninth stanza beginning, "The boast of heraldry, the pomp of power," Gray shows the emptiness of worldly ambition and grandeur— their ultimate worthlessness, since "The paths of glory lead but to the grave."

In great part, the *Elegy* is a social poem, reflecting a class consciousness from a distinctly demotic vantage point. For, as stated earlier, the demotic's reaction to the hieratic on one important level of meaning is a social one, the vision of a depressed class being given a voice, or, in a yet wider sense, the struggle of the individual spirit against authority. In Gray's poem the individual spirit is typified as a sober and steady strength, and the poet means to find imagery that corresponds to those qualities. It is hard to believe that Gray is using the same rhymed couplet as Alexander Pope, so different is his rhythm from that of the poet of *Pastorals* and the *Rape of the Lock*. As the lowing herd wind slowly o'er the lea, so Gray's lines amble on in a gait so regular and dumpy that their grace, if such it is, must be judged by other standards. The gentle four-square rhythms, the clear horizontals and verticals of linear and periodic symmetries, and the "moderato cantabile" tempo are worlds apart from Pope's "vivace" arabesques. But in the end the rhetoric has its own eloquence, a new and different kind of seriousness.

The egalitarian mood that takes hold in the latter part of the 18th century marks a turning point for demotic art. The main literary genres of the last two centuries, the novel and the drama, are surfeited with stories of ordinary people struggling with authority, aiming higher, and making triumphant breakthroughs. To what extent music can embody this pattern will be explored on several occasions in later chapters. But the central theme of demotic thinking—the idea of significant things appearing in unlikely places—is of much older vintage, considering that it received a great thrust forward, if not its actual start, from Christianity itself. With the story of the Christ child born in lowly circumstances we have the case of an image which gives all others of the class—small farmhouses, white clapboard churches, gospel singing, scenes of cozy domesticity such as are found at the end of Dickens's *Christmas Carol* and Copland's *Appalachian Spring*—an immediate and familiar resonance.

Apollonian/Dionysian

The definitive treatment of the Apollonian/Dionysian duality (and doubtless the source of the majority of the popular references to the subject in contemporary criticism) was made in modern times by Nietzsche in *The Birth of Tragedy* (1872). Inspired by Schopenhauer's conception of music as an imitation of the "will,"[58] Nietzsche separates music, which he calls the "nonimagistic" Dionysian art, from the Apollonian arts of sculpture and architecture.[59] The Apollonian impulse, he says, corresponds to the energy given to man to dream and create images; under the influence of the Dionysian impulse man sinks into an ecstasy and enters into contact with the will, which Schopenhauer had defined as "the inmost nature of the world and our own self,"[60] thus outside the boundaries of space and time. According to Nietzsche the birth of tragedy in ancient Greece represents an exceptional synthesis of the Apollonian and Dionysian tendencies:

"By a metaphysical miracle of the Hellenic 'will', they appear coupled with each other, and through their coupling ultimately generate an equally Dionysian and Apollonian form of art—Attic tragedy."[61] In spite of this extraordinary event, the two tendencies, says Nietzsche, remain essentially opposed.

It is hardly surprising, given his specific interests, that Nietzsche should have found in the Greek experience itself the source of his two terms. Of course, the credit goes to him for having abstracted a simple philosophical construct out of a welter of religious and artistic developments, but it must also be recognized that the collection of attributes contained in this construct had already been assimilated by the Greeks themselves into a number of myth stories about the two gods from whom Nietzsche's duality takes its name. As critical tools, Apollonian and Dionysian are most commonly used in connection with artistic temperament and performance: the coolly controlled Apollonian approach of one performer will be contrasted with the hotly impassioned Dionysian manner of another. The qualities "cool" and "hot" agree in the main very well with the attributes normally associated with the two gods in question. Not all of Apollo's stories present a god thoroughly calm and self-possessed (he could at times be quite spiteful and cruel), but his gentler and more harmonious traits have persisted in the popular mind. He is remembered for his incomparable mastery of the lyre (the "civilized" instrument, as opposed to the "barbaric" aulos) and is thus universally acknowledged as the god of music. His limpid beauty and supernal composure are celebrated in a succession of 5th- and 4th-century Greek sculptures which must have had no little influence on Winckelmann's conception of Greek art as "edle Einfalt und stille Grösse" (noble simplicity and quiet grandeur).[62] Finally, he is the "soothsaying god" who, through the medium of the Delphic Oracle, preaches "moderation in all things" and "nothing in excess."[63]

The figure of Dionysus, by contrast, is surrounded from the outset by violence and madness. At birth he is taken by the Titans on Hera's orders and torn to pieces. He is later reconstructed, but Hera eventually discovers him and drives him mad. Thereon in begins an almost endless string of savage episodes: mass murders, hordes of frenzied satyrs and maenads overrunning the countryside, kings deprived of their senses and committing horrible crimes, and the indiscriminate rending of bodies, whether animal or human.[64] Always these events are tied up with the wine that Dionysus is reputed to have given the world, and hysteria and intoxication form the emotional climate in which the events take place. Also, as the gift of wine is the chief element for which he is worshipped, it is proper that his rites should be accompanied by orgy and intoxication. Clearly, the heart of the Dionysian spirit is freedom from all constraint—the *ecstasis*, total release.[65]

Ecstasis, the state that comes on through a willing surrender of the self, is a more broadly conceived notion of Dionysian behavior than violence; indeed, we will see that the historic associations of violence with the exploits of Dionysus and his followers conceals a deep-rooted prejudice. While the orgiastic character of Dionysian ritual typically brings to mind wild and tumultuous goings-on, the element of intoxication can evoke a very different picture—a virtual cessation of action, something akin to stupor and trance. It appears from this that surrender of self is an extreme measure, resulting in extreme behavior—violence at one extreme, torpor at the other. From the standpoint of Greek moral philosophy, the only acceptable behavior is temperateness, situated midway between the two extremes and achieved through the exercising of an action that stands as the diametrical opposite of surrender, namely, self-control. What Plato would particularly dislike about Dionysian surrender is its abandonment of all rationality. The rational, according to Plato, marks the true path to *logos*. The Dionysian descent to a level of consciousness where sensuality and the emotions (the *pathe*) take over and engulf the rational, moves in the exact opposite direction from *logos*, toward *pathos*. The temperateness of Apollo, though not synonymous with the rational, is nevertheless the consequence of having enlisted the rational in order to fight off the emotions and the senses. In the Platonic view (and, as a consequence of Plato, in the Western view ever since), "control" means an exertion of the "head" for the sake of resisting the onslaughts of the heart and the sensual impulses; and it is in this resistance that lies an important *ethical* value. For Plato, the effort made to withstand emotional pressures is a sign of good character; building the character—the *ethos*—of a person is an aspect of Greek education which must begin in the earliest stages of childhood and in which music is seen as playing a major role.[66] The root principle, then, on which the Apollonian/Dionysian dichotomy rests is not behavior itself (coolness vs. hotness, moderation vs. violence or torpor), but the practices that nurture certain kinds of character and their outward manifestations: resistance and control oppose themselves to surrender and abandon, and in so doing, lead in the direction of *ethos*.

The nonethical and thus unacceptable feature of Dionysianism is its willingness to give in to natural desire, to Eros. I dwell on this point because it probably illustrates better than any other single idea the gulf between Western and Eastern thinking. Of course, connections with Eros are also unacceptable to Eastern mystical philosophy because they block the way to the ultimate goal, but the very way to that goal is predicated on a vision directly antithetical to the rational vision of Socrates and Plato. The "surrender of self," far from signifying submission to Eros, means instead for the Eastern mystical mind the embracing of Thanatos, the desire for absolute truth, the will to *logos*. From the Hindu Upanishads of the 8th century B.C. to the comparatively late sutras of Zen Buddhism, the pattern persists of a discipline dedicated to the peeling off of the individual self in order to find the universal self.[67] The core of the discipline is starkly nonrational, consisting of prolonged periods of silence and meditation, the assumption of difficult physical postures, and the incanting of repetitive, trance-inducing phrases. The individual self must be thrown off because it is the obstruction to unity: as long as there exists a self separate from Self, duality prevails and the totally undifferentiated state—Nirvana, Enlightenment—has not been reached. From the standpoint of the higher Eastern religions, the individual self and the rational mind are for all intents and purposes one and the same thing: in spite of certain obvious but limited virtues, the rational turns everything into multiplicity and distinction; it is constituted as if from the outset to impede progress toward the *logos* of Eastern mysticism.

That the ancient worship of Dionysus envisioned something of the same *logos* there seems little doubt. In *The Greeks and the Irrational* E.R. Dodds draws an elaborate picture of Dionysian practices and those of contemporaneous rites that points very strongly to the will to attain a state of unity through a forgetting of the self.[68] In *The Birth of Tragedy* Nietzsche describes the phenomenon as follows:[69]

Either under the influence of the narcotic draught, of which the songs of all primitive men and peoples speak, or with the potent coming of spring that penetrates all nature with joy, these Dionysian emotions awake, and as they grow in intensity everything subjective vanishes into complete self-forgetfulness ...Under the charm of the Dionysian not only is the union between man and man reaffirmed, but nature which has become alienated, hostile, or subjugated, celebrates once more her reconciliation with her lost son, man.

The forgetting of self demands a loosening of controls, a loosening of those forces which separate one individual from another in order that the unifying power might take hold and be felt. In the Dionysian experience one gives up the individual self to become a "member of a higher community." The ultimate unification is achieved as the force of individuation and separation is obliterated and only a feeling of merging and fusion remains. In Dionysian terms the fostering of surrender leads to attainment of union. Dodds shows that Dionysian practice was sufficiently widespread and diverse to exist on a number of levels of varying seriousness; no doubt there was a strong erotic content in much of it.[70] But even if, on the highest levels, the worship of Dionysus had been conducted in the pure atmosphere of Thanatos, Socrates and Plato would have been bent on questioning its legitimacy, for Greek philosophy had proclaimed the supremacy of pure reason over all other approaches, and so the search for *logos* by a route which engaged any measure of the irrational was simply out of the question. In the eyes of the Greek moral philosopher, the irrational invariably signalled the *pathe* and the senses.

■ *The Logos of the Apollonian/Dionysian: Form vs. Feeling*   The dark connotations attached throughout most of Western history to the word "irrational" go far in confirming the triumph of Greek philosophy. Complementarily, the triumph of Greek philosophy goes a long way to explaining the suspicion with which activities tinged with mysticism—Catharism, alchemy, ecstatic Christian visions— have traditionally been regarded in the West.[71] Only Romanticism seems to have escaped the stigma of deviancy, perhaps because, as an idea centered on art, it was perceived as posing no immediate threat to the social order. What interests us in particular here is to establish how certain aims and effects of ritual practice could get translated into principles of artistic perception—how, in other words, Apollonian control and Dionysian surrender could come to be associated with the artistic notions, respectively, of form and feeling. To clarify these relationships we again enlist Nietzsche's aid, for it was he who first understood how his duality could work in an artistic context and thus become a major tool for modern criticism. In effect, what he did was to take a term from Schopenhauer's *The World as Will and Idea*—the *principium individuationis*—and to recognize in it the essence of the Apollonian "artistic energy."[72] The "principle of individuation" can alternately be called "the principle of differentiation," or that principle by which we *differentiate* the world, by which we see it as an ordering of its constituent parts. Under the influence of the *principium individuationis*, the world is perceived as something to which we have come through long-standing habit to give the name "form."

Apollonian control was described earlier as a resistance to natural human desire, to Eros; at the moment, we are discussing something that bears closer affinities to Thanatos, namely, human perception of the world. But whether construed in terms of Eros or Thanatos, "control" signifies an exertion of the rational mind; and since, as was already noted, the rational turns everything into multiplicity and distinction, it follows that the world seen from the Apollonian vantage point is a network of multiple, distinct, and interconnecting parts. In the West we have been so conditioned to seeing "worlds," "shapes," "things"— entities of any sort—as networks that we can easily overlook the possibility of another way of seeing them. Nietzsche, on the other hand, a 19th-century man particularly disposed to the aspirations of Romanticism, does not forget this possibility. Having proposed the *principium individuationis* as the Apollonian artistic energy, he proceeds to turn this proposition around and aim it at the opposite target, the Dionysian impulse, which he calls the "collapse of the *principium individuationis*."[73] Under the influence of such a collapse, we no longer wish to see the world as an ordering of parts, but as an *undifferentiated* whole, an indivisible unity.

Nietzsche's description, quoted above, of the ritual action undertaken by the Dionysian votary to attain union is now fitted out with a perceptual counterpart. This translation from the ritualistic to the perceptual enables us to see that the world taken as an undifferentiated whole is a world conceived in a totally immaterial way, that is, as "feeling." If we remember that the impulse toward union is just another expression for what Schopenhauer has called our yearning for the Will, we should begin to understand in what sense "feeling" and "form" are directly opposed. The Will, according to Schopenhauer, is the "inmost nature of the world," its totally immaterial essence, its infiniteness, existing beyond the limits of space and time, beyond form. "Feeling," the everyday word we use for inmost nature, is connected to the infinite because it is unbounded by space and time and is thus the only way we have of understanding things which, like itself, have no material reality. Apollonian perceptions proceed from experiences with materially constituted worlds, thus formal and finite by definition; the Dionysian vision deals with meanings not reached by the *principium individuationis*.

While this is not the place to go into the matter, the possibilities for application of the Apollonian/Dionysian principle to the areas of aesthetic perception and value judgment are considerable. Just as with the romantic/ironic dichotomy, the Apollonian and Dionysian perspectives qualify each other; each casts, so to speak, the negative value judgment on the other's "excesses." Viewed positively, that is, in orthodox Apollonian terms, the Apollonian adherence to form signifies order; viewed negatively, in Dionysian terms, the same impulse to form signifies repression. Viewed positively, in Dionysian terms, the Dionysian adherence to feeling signifies freedom; viewed negatively, in Apollonian terms, the same adherence to feeling signifies disorder, even dissolution. We can see how these ideas might bear not only on issues of social decorum and behavior but also on artistic issues, art being a special form of behavior. There is little contemporary art criticism, for instance, that does not raise the ideal of Classical balance and restraint to something of an absolute standard and then proceed to measure all other modes of artistic expression (notably, Romantic exuberance) against that standard. Finally, it bears repeating that the oppositions form-feeling and control-abandon show the Apollonian/Dionysian dichotomy to be founded on a two-pronged principle, one prong (form-feeling) directed toward *logos*, the other (control-abandon) toward the eternal tension between *ethos* and *pathos*. This not only suggests a certain flexibility over and above the other dichotomies for dealing with musical content but also goes far in explaining why there is hardly an archetypal theme for which the Apollonian/Dionysian dichotomy will not supply a pertinent clarification.

Summary

In defining the five dichotomies above, I have attempted to contrast them as sharply as possible so as to bring out their distinctive features. In the reality of an artwork, however, or even of a period style, they never exist singly but in mixtures and combinations. The business of reading an image is largely one of trying to discover what frames of reference are at work in the image and in what varying proportions they are being balanced off against each other. Frye's reference in *Anatomy of Criticism* to the "underlying tonality of a work of fiction" suggests a more intuitional—a more Dionysian—approach to the problem, insofar as the *whole*, in Dionysian terms, is something different from the sum of its parts.[74] The primary "tonality" of an artwork would be due, one might imagine, to the predominance of one archetypal structure over the others, the rest then gathering around as "secondary keys." Applying this principle to a single example—Bizet's *Carmen*—we may see the archetypes at work in the opera in a number of embodiments, dramatic as well as musical. The tragic vision is most evident in Don José's sufferings. The romantic mode is expressed in the theme of erotic love, in all the exotic touches of Spanish decor and Spanish custom, and in the excitement of life lived dangerously. The influence of the hieratic is felt most strongly in the spectacular and ceremonial events, especially in the sparkling pomp that accompanies the entrance into the bullring in Act IV. The Dionysian element comes through in Don José's uncontrollable passion, though perhaps even more in Carmen's seductive power, which one is made to feel (especially by a great singing actress) is not her own but the effect of an irresistible and mysterious force coursing through her. There are even touches of irony in Carmen's capricious toying with Don José, though a comparison with the dry and remorseless tone of Merimée's *nouvelle* will show how much the ironic mode has been played down for the purposes of operatic entertainment. Finally, we may say that the "primary tonality" of *Carmen* is demotic in its effort to find substance in unlikely characters and places; in this respect, Bizet has fashioned the perfect musical parallels to the *nouvelle*, drawing on the popular sources of two musical cultures and raising the material to a level of tragic significance.

The presence of modal combinations in artistic imagery enables us to make distinctions between works that fall into the same category. For instance, the *Iliad* and Sophocles' tragedies would both be classified as hieratic, despite the marked difference in general texture between Homer and Sophocles. What must account in no small part for this difference is the impact of the romantic/ironic dichotomy. The *Iliad* presents pain and horror in all their immediacy, yet a halo of glory surrounds them at the same time. Death, life, the hero, the god—all are glorious and all embody the strong romantic thrust of the *Iliad's* tragic substance. The darkness, on the other hand, which descends on *Antigone* and *Electra* betrays the relentless grip of tragic irony. Since the structures we are dealing with are archetypal in character, what in one case serves to separate can also in another case work to unite. Theocritus and Renoir are artists who lived 2,200 years apart, yet the kinship between them must have something to do with the idyllic feeling that emanates from the work of both—a feeling whose spontaneity and general freedom from reflection could easily earn these artists Schiller's epithet "naïve."

Finally, it should be realized that the conception of "primary tonality" and "secondary keys" can be used to describe any general context, from the smallest (the individual artwork) to the largest (Western culture as a whole). In between there exist two significant stages—the art epoch (Renaissance, Baroque, Classical, etc.) and the *oeuvre* of an individual composer. Given the fact that style and content have been defined in these pages as the typical and recurring in form and idea, respectively, it is understandable that the history presented in Parts II, III, and IV should take place primarily on these two intermediate levels. It is not the aim of this history, then, to analyze and explicate the *meanings* of individual images, only to find those common, recurrent elements in the image which are its conventional patterns of thought. *Concitato* is a "tonality" present in virtually all first movements of Baroque concerti grossi; in itself, it will not distinguish between the personalities of Brandenburg Concertos No. 5 and No. 6, but it very much serves to explain how and why certain musical figures and certain kinds of continuity became associated with the concerto grosso. *Concitato* is a convention of Baroque expression, just as binary form is in a Baroque dance, or the major mode is a structure of classical tonality. Every musical example that appears in the following pages is meant to represent a *type*, never to be taken on its own; if one piece or excerpt has been chosen over another, it is simply because the piece in question has been thought to be a particularly good illustration of a certain structure of content.

Such, then, are the basic propositions of this archetypal theory. Since there is just so much that can be said about a method in advance of its application, it is time to move on. It is time to see what happens when the treatment of the history of music is cyclical as well as linear.

Notes

1. Several of these terms are to be found in Frye's "Theory of Modes," the first of the four parts of *Anatomy of Criticism*. But here they are worked into a different ordering and combined with other terms, with concomitant changes in emphasis and meaning. For example, Frye bases his theory of modes on a device of narrative fiction he calls "the power of the hero." In order for this device to have any use for music criticism, it must first be shorn of its literary vestments; we must uncover the archetypal contents that lie beneath the hero's power. But, in fact, it is easy enough to see that the fictional hero is in great part a projection of our ideals and wish fulfillments, an image of what we aspire to be and how we would most like to see ourselves. Those ideals change, as was noted in Chapter 1, in keeping with the dominant attitudes of a given time and place. What we may also realize is that ideals form as much of the "vision of reality" as experience itself and that art has always been very active in the imaging of ideals. It should be added that Frye does not arrange his modes as dichotomies; and whereas his modes function in essence as literary devices, I think of the above dichotomies as the root themes of Western culture, applicable to religion and philosophy as well as to all the arts. All of this is to say that the model presented below is essentially of my own devising, and the discussions in the ensuing chapters proceed independently of Frye. But clearly, Frye's "Theory of Modes" is the great prime mover behind the present book, and my own ideas would have never taken the shape they did without the concrete inspiration of Frye's work.
2. Walter Kaufmann, *Tragedy and Philosophy*, p. 89.
3. *Ibid.*, p. 271.
4. James Hillman, *Re-Visioning Psychology*, p. 111.
5. Wendy Doniger O'Flaherty, ed., *Hindu Myths*, p. 13.
6. Quoted in H.C. Robbins Landon, *Haydn: Chronicle and Works*, Vol. V, p. 124. Haydn is referring specifically to the bass aria, No. 38, in the Winter section.
7. Quoted in Alfred Einstein, *The Italian Madrigal*, Vol. I, pp. 222–223.
8. *Ibid.*, p. 223.
9. Leonard B. Meyer, *Emotion and Meaning in Music*, p. 7.
10. Northrop Frye, *Anatomy of Criticism*, p. 33.
11. *Ibid.*, p. 43.
12. Paul Alpers, *The Singer of the Eclogues: A Study of Virgilian Pastoral*, p. 2. This volume contains a translation of the eclogues and a lengthy commentary.
13. J.M. Edmonds, trans., *The Greek Bucolic Poets* in Loeb Classical Library, p. 9.

14. *Ibid.*, p. 27. The lines are from Idyll 9.

15. *Ibid.*, p. 147.

16. Alpers, p. 67.

17. *Ibid.*, p. 15.

18. *Ibid.*, p. 15.

19. Erwin Panofsky, "Et in Arcadia Ego: Poussin and the Elegiac Tradition," in *Meaning in the Visual Arts*, p. 300.

20. *Ibid.*, p. 301.

21. See Alpers, pp. 67–68.

22. Panofsky, p. 300.

23. Frye, *Anatomy*, p. 36.

24. From Book XI of the *Iliad*.

25. Frye, *Anatomy*, p. 37.

26. Mircea Eliade, *Myth and Reality*, p. 1.

27. *Ibid.*, pp. 1–2.

28. *Ibid.*, p. 17.

29. *Ibid.*, p. 32.

30. See Kaufmann, p. 9.

31. See Scott Buchanan, ed., *The Portable Plato*, pp. 367–377.

32. Richmond Lattimore, trans. and ed., *The Iliad of Homer*, p. 54.

33. Quoted in Kaufmann, p. 249. The lines are from the *Oedipus* of Aeschylus.

34. Quoted in *ibid.*, p. 266. The lines are from Sophocles' *Elektra*.

35. See the extended discussion in Richmond Y. Hathorn, *Tragedy, Myth & Mystery*, pp. 113–142.

36. Lattimore, *Iliad*, p. 54.

37. Buchanan, pp. 375–378.

38. Kaufmann, p. 162.

39. Second Samuel, XI, 27.

40. Eliade, *Myth and Reality*, p. 7.

41. This question will be taken up at greater length in Chapter 4.

42. See S. H. Butcher, trans. and ed., *Aristotle's Theory of Poetry and Fine Art*, p. 23.

43. See *ibid.*, pp. 57, also pp. 83–87.

44. *Ibid.*, p. 11.

45. Erich Auerbach, *Mimesis*, p. 31.

46. Quoted in Erwin Panofsky, *Idea, A Concept in Art Theory*, p. 49.

47. A paraphrase of lines 364–65 of Alexander Pope, *An Essay on Criticism*. "'Tis not enough no harshness gives offence / The sound must seem an echo to the sense."

48. Rosemond Tuve, *Elizabethan and Metaphysical Imagery*, p. 52.

49. Quoted in Moody E. Prior, *The Language of Tragedy*, p. 23.

50. Quoted in Tuve, p. 91.

51. Quoted in Prior, p. 25.

52. A reference to Pope's *An Essay on Criticism*, in which the poet writes: "These rules of old discover'd, not devised / Are Nature still, but Nature methodised." (Lines 88–89).

53. Olive Cook et al., ed., *The Praeger Picture Encyclopedia of Art*, p. 58.

54. John Gay, *The Shepherd's Week in Six Pastorals*, pp. A3–[A3v].

55. *Ibid.*, p. [A4v].

56. *Ibid.*, p. [A5].

57. This poem appears in numbers of anthologies, of which one is Rewey Belle Inglis et al., ed., *Adventures in English Literature*, pp. 303–306.

58. Arthur Schopenhauer, *The World as Will and Idea*, pp. 268–269. See also Patrick Gardiner, *Schopenhauer*, pp. 229–234.

59. Friedrich Nietzsche, *The Birth of Tragedy*, p. 33.

60. Schopenhauer, p. 267.

61. Nietzsche, p. 33.

62. This memorable phrase of Winckelmann's appears in his *Reflections on the Imitation of Greek Works*. See Wolfgang Leppmann, *Winckelmann*, pp. 113–116. Winckelmann's dedication to ancient Greek sculpture and architecture is yet one more manifestation of worshipful Neoclassicism in post-medieval culture (see Chapter 12 below). He considered noble simplicity and quiet grandeur to be not only the essential qualities of 5th-century Greek art but also the ultimate standard of Western civilization.

63. Robert Graves, *The Greek Myths*, Vol. I, p. 79.

64. *Ibid.*, pp. 103–106.

65. See E.R. Dodds, *The Greeks and the Irrational*, pp. 270–280.

66. Buchanan, pp. 352–353. This point will be more fully developed in Chapter 3.

67. Edward Conze, *Buddhism, Its Essence and Development* is a particularly clear and concise introduction to Eastern religious thought. Philip Kapleau, ed., *The Three Pillars of Zen*, a compilation of lectures and teachings by Zen masters, has become something of a classic since its first appearance. A selection of key passages from the Upanishads is published in a Penguin pocket edition. For a fascinating comparative study of the Upanishads, Schopenhauer's philosophy and Nietzsche's Apollonian/Dionysian conception, see Joseph Campbell, *Creative Mythology*, Vol. IV of *The Masks of God*, pp. 333–358.

68. See n. 65 above. Also, Dodds, pp. 76–82.

69. Nietzsche, pp. 36–37.

70. Dodds, p. 76.

71. See Denis de Rougement, *Love in the Western World*, in particular Chapter 6. The book is essentially an account of mysticism in the West.

72. Nietzsche, pp. 35–36.

73. *Ibid.*, p. 36.

74. Frye, *Anatomy*, pp. 50–51.

PART II

Music in Ritual and Education: Ethos

3   Dialectic between
Ethos and Pathos
in Ancient Greek Thought

Today virtually everything Plato wrote about music is gathered together in a single chapter of a single volume in English entitled *Greek Musical Writings*.[1] This ostensible convenience conceals a danger, for it offers us the opportunity to read the material without any feeling for the larger context surrounding it. It permits us to think that Plato's theory of musical *ethos*—his advocacy of certain "modes" (harmoniai) and rejection of others on the basis of their influence in shaping human character—is some quaint relic of the past, an item worthy of a footnote in the history books but of no relevance to modern musical thinking. Indeed, from today's so-called disinterested perspective of aesthetic experience, what correlation could we conceivably hope—or want—to find between being exposed to "good music" and becoming a better person? This question could well be answered by another one, namely: how truly disinterested are our aesthetic views if ethical criteria (as already tentatively argued in the previous chapter) figure significantly in what we hold to be good music? However, that is a matter for another day. As intriguing as issues of value judgment might be, they must not deflect us from our main business here, which is to review the old Greek *ethos* theory for one purpose and one purpose only.

That purpose is to try to undo a conceptual muddle that has beset musical commentary more or less continually since the late Middle Ages. The muddle arises from a failure to have distinguished properly between two principles in terms of their proverbial relation to music: between feeling, on the one hand, and behavior, which is the business of showing or expressing feeling, on the other. The distinction is made throughout Book Three of Plato's *Republic*, though the fact that it is made only implicitly there may account in part for its having been missed later on.[2] There are other reasons as well, not the least of which is the inability on the part of modern Europeans to realize, or to accept for what it was worth, the fact that Plato's only motivation in turning to music was to establish its usefulness in improving the individual personality and thus, by extension, in contributing to the betterment of society as a whole. He is not in the least interested in encouraging the notion that music should be enjoyed and engaged in for its own sake; music is a tool of education, a means to an end, not an end in itself.

Plato has Socrates suggest in Book Three of the *Republic* that an overseer will be necessary in the ideal state to regulate the flow of music—to legislate what music is fit for public consumption, what music is not.[3] To one conditioned to believe in the arts as the ultimate embodiment of freedom, this pronouncement has the chilling ring of commissardom about it. We are relieved to find Aristotle taking a more relaxed approach: for him, all music is eventually tolerable, but certain types are appropriate for certain groups and activities, and should be selected accordingly.[4] Nevertheless, the point here is not to be offended by Plato's attitude but to learn why he so doggedly insisted on it.

Notwithstanding differences in their views on music and its place in society, Plato and Aristotle are solidly agreed on one fundamental premise (indeed, all their discussions proceed from it), namely that music has "the power of producing a certain effect on the moral character of the soul."[5] Even more specifically, a given musical configuration corresponds to a certain configuration of the soul, and will therefore activate a state of feeling governed by that aspect of the soul. Moreover, this is not a theoretical notion but one based on empirical evidence. Aristotle brings these thoughts together in the following significant passage:[6]

Pieces of music ... actually contain in themselves imitations of character; and this is manifest, for even in the nature of the mere harmonies [i.e., modes] there are differences, so that people when hearing them are affected differently and have not the same feelings in regard to each of them, but listen to some in a more mournful and restrained state, for instance the harmony called Mixolydian, and to others in a softer state of mind, for instance the relaxed harmonies [identified in Plato as Ionian and Lydian], but in a midway state and with the greatest composure to another, as the Dorian alone of harmonies seems to act, while the Phrygian makes them enthusiastic; for these things are well stated by those who have studied this form of education, as they derive the evidence for their theories from the actual facts of experience.

Given, then, music's acknowledged ethical power, coupled with the philosopher's responsibilities (self-appointed, to be sure) for showing the way toward the exercise of ethical judgment in everyday affairs, it becomes nothing less than Plato's and Aristotle's obligation to pronounce for those musical elements which will accomplish the desired aim, and against those which will not. In this respect, Plato is much more parochial than Aristotle, because he has only one aim in mind: to educate young men to recognize "forms of soberness, courage, liberality, and high-mindedness."[7] For this purpose only two musical modes are necessary, the Dorian and the Phrygian: the first to encourage bravery and endurance, the second, to foster modesty and moderation. Aristotle, thinking of music education in broader terms, advocates a three-pronged program guided by the criteria of "moderation," "possibility," and "suitability." The three criteria apply to three different classes of people: (1) privileged youth, (2) the elderly and the very young, and (3) the "vulgar class composed of mechanics and laborers."[8] The first group is the same one Plato had in mind and is thus the object of education proper. In respect to the second group, Aristotle takes into account the waning "possibilities" of older people and the still underdeveloped potential of small children and considers the "relaxed harmonies" as appropriate to their *powers*. For the members of the third group, he suggests "melodies that are intense and irregular in coloration," these being suitable to their *tastes*. Although Aristotle appears more broad-minded than Plato, it is clear that only the harmonies destined for the first group can be considered of the "ethical class," i.e., truly edifying. And in this class, Aristotle accepts only *one* harmony, namely the Dorian, criticizing Plato/Socrates for inconsistency in having included the Phrygian harmony while rejecting the aulos as an instrument: "for the Phrygian harmony has the same effect among harmonies as the aulos among instruments—both are violently exciting and emotional."[9]

Having enumerated the chief points of the old *ethos* theory, we are now in a better position to understand in what respect the theory was subsequently misinterpreted. Plato and Aristotle, as already noted, are completely agreed as to the power that music has over the soul. But exactly what do they mean by "soul," and how does their conception differ from the immortal entity envisioned in Christian teaching? Somewhat oversimplifying the matter, we can represent the Greek conception of "soul" as a bipartite affair, divided between two principles, the nonrational and the rational. To make the picture as concrete as possible, we can even imagine an entity divided into two compartments, the first inhabited by all the pleasurable and painful sensations that human beings are heir to (the *pathe*), the second in which the processes of pure logical discourse take place free of any influence of the emotions or the bodily senses.[10] The prime object of Greek education is to develop the rational principle to its highest power and reduce the nonrational to ineffectiveness: this is not only in the interests of encouraging social virtue but is also the obvious first step to be taken by the incipient philosopher. Music has no direct connection with the rational principle, its sole influence being over the nonrational; but it can, if properly applied, prepare the groundwork for rational activity by taking the sting out of the nonrational factor, that is by relieving the nonrational of its natural intemperateness. And this process cannot begin too early because, as Plato himself remarks, "the beginning is the most important part of any work, especially in the care of a young and tender thing; for that is the time at which the character is being formed, and the desired impression is more readily taken."[11] Precisely because the child is so impressionable, the best models must be put before it, and this is particularly true in the case of music, which, together with gymnastics, forms the basis of the pre-rational phase of the child's education. On this point, Plato writes as follows:[12]

'For these reasons, then, Glaucon,' I said, 'isn't training in *mousikē* of overwhelming importance, because rhythm and *harmonia* penetrate most deeply into the recesses of the soul [read here more precisely: the irrational component of the soul] and take a powerful hold on it, bringing gracefulness and making a man graceful if he is correctly trained, but the opposite if he is not? Another reason is that the man who has been properly trained in these matters would perceive most sharply things that were defective, and badly crafted or badly grown, and his displeasure would be justified. He would praise and rejoice in fine things, and would receive them into his soul and be nourished by them, becoming fine and good: but he would rightly condemn ugly things, and hate them even when he was young, before he was able to lay hold on reason. And when reason grew, the person trained in this way would embrace it with enthusiasm, recognising it as a familiar friend.'

Character forming, therefore, is a prelude to the child's later education based on reason; and this is as it should be, since the proper formation of the character will provide that ground of temperateness (one might say freedom from emotionality and sensuality) upon which reason can build. And so we return to arguments already put forth in Chapter 2: "good character" is synonymous with temperateness, and temperateness is the result of rigorous training, either in the form of programs administered from the outside, as with music and gymnastics in early childhood, or, in the case of older persons, in the form of a strict code of discipline, where the subject makes a strenuous effort to gain control over his existence and withstand the natural impulses fostered by the emotions and the senses. Failure to resist the natural onslaught of the emotions (*pathe*) produces "bad" character which, as already implied in the discussion of Chapter 2, takes on two different forms: the first, languor or lack of vigor, falling on one side of temperateness; the second, excitability, falling on the other side. Though very distinct from each other in essence and behavior, these bad kinds of character reflect the same Dionysian inclination to give in to the *pathe*, and are manifestly the result, as far as Plato and Aristotle are concerned, of improper or insufficient training.

The *ethe*, then, falling into three basic categories, are clearly separate from the *pathe*, which though not enumerated and described individually by Plato and Aristotle, are recognized by them as belonging to a different order of experience from the *ethe*, one governed by the polar coordinates of psychic pleasure and pain.[13] Moreover, we infer from their discussions the recurrent or habitual nature of character, as opposed to the momentary effects of the emotions. *Ethos* and *pathos*, in the Greek view, are thus in a functional relation with each other, where good and bad character is measured by the relative success or failure of an individual to deal effectively with his emotions. The individual must be given the means, therefore, to improve his character; and since good character is made overt and manifest through a set of behavioral habits that have been formed by the right kind of practice, the quality of the practice itself is of the essence. Little wonder, then, that music, identified by the Greeks as an indispensable element of this practice, should be subjected to the strictest standards.

It is by virtue of its educative force that music gets classified in Greek moral philosophy as an ethical, not affective, material—this in spite of the fact that

Plato and Aristotle understand perfectly well how "rhythm and harmony find their way into the inward places of the soul."[14] Corresponding to the three basic *ethe*, or kinds of behavior—the languorous, the excitable, and the temperate—the musical modes as denoted by Plato fall into three basic classes: (1) the "soft" or "relaxed" Ionian (Iastian) and Lydian; (2) the "highstrung" Lydian (otherwise known as the "Hyperlydian"); (3) the courageously restrained Dorian and the diplomatically restrained Phrygian.[15] (As mentioned earlier, only the last class is useful for educational purposes and should be kept; the other two categories being harmful in matters of forming character, Plato calls for their expulsion from the community.)

This neat classification served very well the purposes of Greek education. But it did not survive intact into the post-antique world; for modern Europe, having lost sight of the basic rationale behind Greek musical *ethos*, took to treating *ethos* and *pathos* as interchangeable principles of musical expression. We can easily understand why: modern Europeans, increasingly interested in the "passions" for their effectiveness in explaining human action and motivation, came to see music as a powerful agent for expressing human emotion. Music grew more and more to be thought of as an affective language, less and less as an ethical one. There is, of course, no error in this perception in and of itself, which reflects nothing more than a change in tastes and interests, a shift of emphasis from the social to the individual. Plato intends music to contribute palpably to the fostering of social virtue—to the making of "good citizens"—while modern Europe finds in music a primary material for exploring the inner life. Where the error intrudes is in the modern European failure to recognize that a shift in emphasis has indeed taken place. The new focus on *pathos* leads to a breakdown of the old distinction between *ethos* and *pathos*, a fact painfully evident in the musical treatises, where ethical and affective characterizations of the modes are lumped together in such a way as to obscure the simple reality that feeling and behavior—in music as in anything else—are not the same thing.

In a recent study of the subject, the author has compiled a very useful listing of descriptions of the Dorian mode, in an effort to trace an evolution in thinking about this mode from ancient times up to the beginning of the 18th century. Of the thirty entries, three from the latter part of the list are given below:[16]

[20] Johannes Lippius, *Synopsis musicae novae* (1612)
    Dorian: moderately mild, gentle, sad, serious.
[25] Johann Herbst, *Musica poetica* (1643)
    Dorian (D): splendid and also happy, joyful, merry and majestic
[28] Giovanni Bona, *De divina psalmodia* (1663).
    Dorian: modest, joyful, serious and dignified.

What is striking about this collection of definitions is not only the lack of consensus among them—a point which has long been recognized in the scholarly literature—but even more, the indiscriminate mixing of ethical (moderately mild, modest, dignified) with pathetic terms (sad, joyful, merry)—a point that seems to have occurred neither to the authors of the original sources nor to the scholar of this recent study.

We are not to conclude from this seeming disorderliness in the musical treatises that clear notions of character and emotion, and the differences between them, had ceased to exist generally in the modern European mind. Nor are we to conclude that the music was no longer able to reflect these differences, for what was largely missed in an explicit way in these early stages of musical criticism could still be transmitted powerfully, though implicitly, through the musical imagery. We should conclude instead that a very distinct functional relation between *ethos* and *pathos* continued to operate for the modern West as it had for the ancient world, though with some inevitable changes of emphasis. To put this more concretely, we would expect that because the tendency from the early Renaissance on has been to take the view that the passions contain more than a grain of creative energy—that they are not merely the destructive force Plato saw in them—the dialectic between *ethos* and *pathos* would have become correspondingly more flexible, something that would lend itself to being redefined for each successive age and each individual locale.

With this remark, we have effectively returned to the "theme of the hero" first touched upon in Chapter 1, and we realize that the "hero" is nothing other than the ultimate "ethical" man, the type we most admire, the type we most aspire to be. But we realize, too, that over time the object of our admiration continues to change: the qualities deemed most worthy by one age and one society are not necessarily given the highest value by another. We can illustrate this point with a striking musical case, that of Monteverdi's conception of *concitato* such as it was outlined by the composer in his preface to the 1638 publication of the *Combattimento di Tancredi e Clorinda*. In his guise as commentator, Monteverdi emerges as one of the few moderns to have adhered strictly to Plato's tripartite division of music in accordance with the three basic ethical categories. And yet, under the influence of the "pathetic" viewpoint of his own time, Monteverdi sees these categories not as *ethe*, but as *pathe*—or, as he calls them, "passioni od' affettioni." Here is the opening of this famous essay:[17]

I have reflected that the principal passions or affections of our mind are three, namely anger, moderation and humility or supplication; so the best philosophers declare, and the very nature of our voice indicates this in having high, low, and middle registers. The art of music also points clearly to these three in its terms "agitated," "soft," and "moderate" (*concitato, molle,* and *temperato*). In all the works of former composers I have indeed found examples of the "soft" and the "moderate," but never of the "agitated," a genus nevertheless described by Plato in the third book of his *Rhetoric* in these words: "Take that harmony that would fittingly imitate the utterances and the accents of a brave man who is engaged in warfare."

Several mistakes are comprised in this statement, the first of which is more editorial than material, namely the reference to Plato's *Republic* as *Rhetoric*. The other two mistakes, however, are material, for they find Monteverdi quoting only a part of Plato's idea, therefore misconstruing the fundamental intention behind the idea. What Plato actually writes is as follows:[18]

Of the harmonies I know nothing, but I want to have one warlike, to sound the note or accent which a brave man utters in the hour of danger and stern resolve, or when his cause is failing, and he is going to wounds or death or is overtaken by some other evil, and at every such crisis meets the blows of fortune with firm step and a determination to endure.

It is absolutely of the essence to understand that the "harmony" Plato has in mind here is the Dorian, the mode designed to foster temperateness and self-control, not angry and agitated behavior. Plato's and Monteverdi's heroes may indeed *feel* the same agitation when confronting death, but Plato's hero is clearly expected to suppress excitement at such moments and "take it like a major," to "keep a stiff upper lip." Monteverdi, on the other hand, encourages his heroes to howl and rage in the ancient epic/dramatic mode of an Achilles or a Philoctetes, both of whom come in for Plato's censure for having let their emotions get the better of them. The qualities of Monteverdi's hero tend toward the Homeric, not the Platonic; and it is something of an irony that Monteverdi himself missed that point, especially since early Baroque music drama is so obstinately patterned on ancient Greek epic and tragic models. But Monteverdi's oversight is also understandable in the light of his ethical outlook, which, like that generally of his age, was less austere than Plato's, allowing for the show of strong emotion without such a show necessarily signaling unseemly behavior or weak character. The precise terms of this ethical outlook will be discussed in a later chapter. For the moment it is enough to say that the indispensability of proper conduct, if only for the sake of maintaining stability in a social sense, was not lost on the modern European mind; indeed, behavior was so fundamental an element of European courtly life that when it came to discussing musical expression, which was generally believed to deal with the affections (the *pathe*), qualities of behavior such as modesty, solemnity, mildness and the like were, not surprisingly, classified as so many more *pathe*, instead of as the forms of character (*ethe*) that they rightfully were, and are.

We would not make such a point of these confusions were it not for the fact that a clear view of the distinction between *ethos* and *pathos* is ultimately fundamental to a rich and full interpretation of musical content: for it is one thing to believe implicitly that music expresses human emotions and quite another to identify the kind of person to whom these emotions belong. The fact that the English term for persons who inhabit plays and novels is "characters" is not insignificant; literary criticism has long recognized that these characters fall into types and has classified them accordingly. Comedy, in particular, has generated an enormous number of types—the tricky slave, the scapegoat, the miser, the coquette, the blocking parents, the braggart—and the traits of character embodied in each of these types are so familiar—so typical, so "characteristic"—that one sees at once how they might have crystallized into literary conventions and have moved easily from novel to novel and play to play.

Something of the same kind of classification, modified though it may have to be, is appropriate for music criticism, indeed more than appropriate and even necessary, if one is of the aesthetic conviction that much, if not all, music expresses the human emotions. For it makes some difference whether a "character" in a sorrowful state of mind is typed as a hero, a villain, or a fool, and, depending on which he is, whether he is likely to express that sorrow explosively, languorously, even ridiculously, or with sober restraint. In the lament from Monteverdi's *Orfeo*, the music causes the hero to sing with such impassioned vehemence that there seems no mistaking the hero's grief; whereas in Gluck's *Orfeo ed Euridice* the composer wrote an aria for an almost identical dramatic situation of such "Platonic" restraint that some have thought the music to express happiness rather than grief. Eduard Hanslick, for one, went one step further, taking this aria to be the definitive proof for the formalist position and claiming that the music expressed no emotion at all.[19]

The Problem of Pathos in Greek Musical Aesthetics

Although we have been contrasting a modern "pathetic" view of music with an ancient "ethical" view, there is good reason to believe that Plato's stern vision was atypical for his time. No ancient theory of musical *pathos* has come down to us, doubtless because it did not suit the Greek philosopher to fashion one. But the existence of a highly emotional Greek music can hardly be questioned. For one thing, there are the considerable lengths Plato went to to speak out against such a music, to the point of advocating its permanent expulsion from the state. For another, there is the implicit evidence of 5th-century Attic tragedy, of which the musical element, according to some, reached far beyond the mighty portions assigned to the chorus. Aristotle's memorable definition of catharsis, whereby the spectator's emotions of pity and fear are purged through the experiencing of a tragic drama, does not directly address the question of *pathos*, but one wonders how emotions could be purged without first being aroused. One wonders as well what part the choral music of the tragedy played in bringing about the cathartic effect. Aristotle is silent on the matter, and his silence may be significant. Granted that he is a more sympathetic witness on behalf of the arts than either Socrates or Plato (who would profess not to be?), there is nevertheless a certain Apollonian reticence that qualifies his sympathy. His ambivalence about emotional music (an ambivalence that extends to the emotions in general) is betrayed almost more by what he failed to say than what he did say.

To read Aristotle on music is to encounter a kind of thinking that will surface and resurface at various intervals in Western musical history. His is a genuine artistic sensibility, if only for the reason that he views *ethos* and *pathos* in a relationship of accommodation rather than antagonism. It is a sensibility, nevertheless,

that puts craft far in front of emotional impact. That preference, of course, may
be the opinion of the philosopher/teacher wearing his professional hat, as opposed to that of the more naïve and enthusiastic music lover Aristotle might
have proven to be in unofficial moments. But we can read between the lines
only so far. In the passage below, he is typically cautious. While recognizing
a place for emotional excitement in musical experiences, he does not accord it
a high place:[20]

It is clear that we should employ all the harmonies, yet not employ them all in the same way,
but use the most ethical ones for education, and the active and passive kinds for listening
to when others are performing (for any experience that occurs violently in some souls is
found in all, though with different degrees of intensity—for example, pity and fear, and also
religious excitement; for some persons are very liable to this form of emotion, and under
the influence of sacred music we see these people, when they use melodies that violently
arouse the soul, being thrown into a state as if they had received medicinal treatment and
taken a purge, the same experience then must come also to the compassionate and the timid
and the other emotional people generally in such degree as befalls each individual of these
classes, and all must undergo a purgation and a pleasant feeling of relief; and similarly
also the purgative melodies afford harmless delight to people.)

Walter Kaufmann has commented on Aristotle's tone of "slight contempt" in this
passage, though the tone might better be called condescension;[21] in any case,
Aristotle does not number himself among those who are given to the emotional
experiences he is describing. At the same time, he is also clearly not threatened
by such experiences, for they offer, in his opinion, pleasurable relief, "harmless"
delight. Plato before Aristotle is clearly not of this opinion, and the reason has
been cogently argued by Kaufmann:[22]

Plato had supposed that the spectators of a tragedy who see the hero give free vent to
his pain—screaming, to furnish our own example, like Philoctetes and Heracles in two of
Sophocles' plays—might become cowards. Plato had argued for the exclusion of tragedy
from his ideal city, partly because it would undermine courage and sobriety. Aristotle's
concept of catharsis suggests that a performance of *Philoctetes* or *The Women of Trachis*
will have more nearly the opposite effect on the audience: it will purge them of pent-up
emotions and sober them.

Kaufmann has used the example of tragedy instead of music to draw his comparison, but the point of the comparison is not changed. Indeed, the transposition
from music to tragedy, or vice versa, shows that Aristotle applied his theory of
catharsis to both. There is in fact some reason to believe that the idea of catharsis
first occurred to Aristotle through music, judging from what he writes in the
section on music from the *Politics*: "The term purgation [catharsis] we use for
the present without explanation, but we will return to discuss the meaning that
we give to it more explicitly in our treatise on poetry."[23] Ironically, Aristotle
mentions catharsis in his definition of tragedy at the opening of the *Poetics*, and
never returns to it again. This has led some scholars to think that an entire section
of the *Poetics* devoted to catharsis must have been lost. Whether or not this is

true, the fact remains that Aristotle's only elaboration of the idea appears in the passage, just quoted, dealing with the reactions of emotionally inclined people to melodies which have the power to excite, and thereby, to purge.

The implications of Aristotle's ideas are extremely suggestive, and we should not leave the subject before following some of them up. To begin with, we wonder how Aristotle was led to develop his concept of catharsis. Was it one of those theories derived from the "actual facts of experience" (as he claims for the theory of musical imitation of character), and did he have the opportunity to observe first hand the experiences which purportedly bring about the purgative effects he mentions? His references to "religious excitement" and to people "under the influence of sacred music" suggest irresistibly that the Dionysian ritual is in the background of his thoughts. This idea is not in the least farfetched when we remember that the governing principle of the Dionysian impulse is toward the forgetting of the self. E.R. Dodds has written:[24]

The joys of Dionysus had an extremely wide range, from the simple pleasures of the country bumpkin, dancing a jig on greased wineskins, to the *omophagos charis* of the ecstatic bacchanal. At both levels, and at all the levels between, he is Lusios, "the Liberator"—the god who by very simple means, or by other means not so simple, enables you for a short time to *stop being yourself*, and thereby sets you free.

Dodds goes on to describe the therapeutic functions of the Dionysian and related cults, the treatment of mental affliction through homeopathic cures. By the 5th century, apparently, the responsibilities for such cures had been largely turned over to the Corybantes, who "had developed a special ritual for the treatment of madness":[25]

We may note first the essential similarity of the Corybantic to the old Dionysiac cure; both claimed to operate a catharsis by means of an infectious "orgiastic" dance accompanied by the same kind of "orgiastic" music—tunes in the Phrygian mode played on the flute and the kettledrum. It seems safe to infer that the two cults appealed to similar psychological types and produced similar psychological reactions.

This information from Dodds makes it clear that the idea of the cathartic effects of music was hardly original with Aristotle (though the applications of catharsis to tragedy may well have originated with him). Whether or not he had come into direct contact with Dionysian or Corybantic practices, he had ample opportunity to know something of them through the accounts of Herodotus, Theophrastus, and curiously enough, even his teacher, Plato.[26] That Plato was aware of these activities, reported them at some length, and yet saw no reason to make an artistic principle of them, bears further witness to a strong "anti-Dionysian" streak in his nature. He has no use for violent and excited music, nor the people associated with it; they do not conform to his high-minded conceptions, to his vision of an elite brought up to appreciate a disciplined and temperate art. Or, to put it more simply, Plato takes the Corybantic treatment at face value; it is therapy, and that is all it is; it pretends to no artistic significance. From that point of view,

Aristotle's inclusion of cathartic experience as an element in a theory of art must be considered something of an innovation. As soon as we realize that fact, his concept becomes all the more intriguing, and we regret all the more his failure to have elaborated on it.

As silent as he is on the subject of catharsis in the *Poetics*, Aristotle is almost as much so about music. These two facts may be closely related. Aristotle's approach to tragedy in the *Poetics* is highly formalistic, emphasizing the plot structure as the determining factor in providing the unity of the tragic action; without this unity, the other factors, and thus the entire piece, had no hope of functioning properly. Six elements are named as the constituents of tragedy— plot, character, thought, diction, music, and spectacle—but Aristotle gives little time to any but the first two. His treatment of music is brief and exclusively technical, devoted to an enumeration of the musical sections that appear at various points along the tragic route: *parodos* ("going in," or first song of the chorus), *exodos* ("going out," or last song), *stasimon* ("stationary thing," i.e., any song between the *parodos* and *exodos* (sung by the chorus alone), *kommos* ("beating" of head in lamentation, normally a duet between the chorus and an actor on a mournful theme), and *monody* (a song by one actor alone).[27] Nothing is said about the part the chorus could play in animating or in any way affecting the dramatic ideas, and no connection is made between the chorus and catharsis. This lack of connection is consistent with Aristotle's attitude toward spectacle as well, about which he says, "It stirs the emotions, but it is less a matter of art than the others [other elements] and has least to do with poetry, for a tragedy can achieve its effect even apart from the performance and the actors."[28] From this assertion, we are forced to conclude that whatever Aristotle means by catharsis in tragedy has less to do with the experience he describes in the *Politics* than we might have at first been given to think.

The archetypal status of catharsis will necessitate our returning to the idea throughout this book. For the moment, we must pursue the problem of the chorus a little further. Indeed, if Aristotle had done so himself, he may have developed some interesting ideas. As it was, it remained for Nietzsche, 2,300 years later, to develop them. Specifically, we are concerned with the emergence of tragedy from its shadowy origins in the satyr-play, or the choral dithyramb, or both. Frye writes, "The Classical critics, Aristotle to Horace, were puzzled to understand why a disorganized ribald farce like the satyr-play should be the source of tragedy, though they were clear that it was."[29] Aristotle devotes one page to the subject in the *Poetics*, in which he says in effect that tragedy began as a form of dithyramb, passed through a "satyric" phase when it was oriented toward the dance, and its language was humorous or amusing, and became serious only later on. That the satyr-play and dithyramb had intimate connections with cult performances in honor of Dionysus, Aristotle could not have been unaware, since Herodotus refers to them very pointedly.[30] But Aristotle omits any mention of them.

It was left to Nietzsche to piece the strands together and to achieve a synthesis which, however much it may be questioned by many authorities today, still remains the only substantial and coherent theory we have of the origin of Attic tragedy. Space will not allow for anything but a bare outline of the theory here; the reader should, in any case, turn to Sections 7 and 8 of *The Birth of Tragedy*, not only to have the full account, but almost more, to experience the mounting excitement with which Nietzsche pursues an argument. Nietzsche's point of departure is the ancient tradition which "tells us quite unequivocally *that tragedy arose from the tragic chorus*, and was originally only chorus and nothing but chorus."[31] He goes on to describe this entity as a chorus of satyrs, or more precisely, as a group of votaries of Dionysus who, in the process of raising their voices in celebration of their god, become transformed into the very personalities who are Dionysus' intimates and first worshippers, namely, the satyrs. Nietzsche explains that this process of transformation—this genius for taking on another personality—is the essence of drama, of what we commonly call "acting."[32]

This process of the tragic chorus ... stands at the beginning of the origin of drama. Here we have something different from the rhapsodist who does not become fused with his images but, like a painter, sees them outside himself as objects of contemplation. Here we have a surrender of individuality and a way of entering into another character. And this phenomenon is encountered epidemically: a whole throng experiences the magic of this transformation. Such magic transformation is the presupposition of all dramatic art. In this magic transformation the Dionysian reveler sees himself as a *satyr, and as a satyr, he sees the god*, which means that in his metamorphosis he beholds another vision outside himself, as the Apollonian complement of his own state. With this new vision the drama is complete.

The "new vision" Nietzsche refers to is, of course, the dialogues and plots which make up the real drama of tragedy, the entire world of the stage. But, according to him, these elements would never have come into existence without the generating force of the chorus, the "womb" that discharged itself and gave birth to the "Apollinian world of images."[33] The heart of Attic tragedy, then, is the chorus, and at the very heart of the chorus is Dionysus. We come away from Nietzsche's exegesis with an entirely different picture of Greek tragedy than that which Aristotle has presented, one in which the performative impulse is so strong that, even apart from a performance, we would have to read tragedy imagining that catharsis proceeded, if not wholly, at the very least primarily and directly from the choral parts. One can hardly believe that Aristotle, who, after all, had the benefit, contrary to ourselves, of seeing performances which were still part of a living tradition, would not have felt first hand the cathartic effect—or the violently exciting effects leading to catharsis—of a combination of instruments, voices, and bodies incanting and stamping out the pulsating, highly charged rhythms of the proverbial dithyramb. Why, then, did he not take the step necessary to reach Nietzsche's exalted vision? He had, it appears, all the materials necessary to do so, and surely he was perceptive enough to put them together.

Two answers to this question are possible. The first is that, being close to the facts, Aristotle was in a position to know that those facts were not quite as Nietzsche supposed, and that he would have been wrong to have drawn the conclusions that Nietzsche subsequently did. A second answer seems more probable: Aristotle did not have enough of the Dionysian temperament to accept the chorus as the *heart* of the Greek tragedy. He may well have understood the chorus to be the germinating seed of the tragedy, and yet have been unwilling to impute to it the overwhelming importance Nietzsche sees in it, especially in view of the kind of tragedy Aristotle knew at the end of a 150-year evolution, with the plot and its dialogues carrying the action, and the choruses fitting into that action as best they could. To one primarily interested in structure, tragedy gave every opportunity of being interpreted in a distinctly Apollonian way. Nietzsche's concern is not with structure; it is with content—with the metaphysical. What he tells us in essence is that in spite of appearances, the germinating seed is the heart of the matter and informs everything else; every work, every gesture, every image is ultimately imbued with it. Nietzsche's is a symbolic conception, and it takes an act of faith. The distance separating Nietzsche and Aristotle is precisely the faith one has that the metaphysical is at the center of art as it is at the center of philosophy. But to a philosopher of Aristotle's persuasion there was no reason to view tragedy as a world of thought. Henry Alonzo Myers perfectly summarizes Aristotle's position:[34]

Aristotle's theory of catharsis, as it is explained in the passage in the *Politics*, admirably suits his purposes in the study of poetry. It answers Plato's extreme criticisms of poets and poetry. Poetry, Plato had charged, feeds the passions, which should be starved. Poetry, Aristotle seems to reply, provides a healthful emotional outlet, a beneficial mean between the dangerous extremes of surrender to passion and suppression of feeling. The poets, Plato had charged, are untrustworthy teachers. The poets, Aristotle seems to reply, are to be judged not as teachers, but as contributors to the emotional well-being of mankind. Indeed, the theory of catharsis is Aristotle's solution to the ancient quarrel between poetry and philosophy: the poet is granted an honored function in the realm of the feelings but the philosopher remains king in the realm of meaning.

Here, once again, is a measure of the separation between Nietzsche and Aristotle: Nietzsche does not make a distinction between feeling and meaning, and he sees art the carrier of meaning quite as much as philosophy. For Nietzsche, meaning moves on a number of levels of consciousness, and perhaps the deeper the level the deeper the meaning. In terms of the Western philosophical tradition, Schopenhauer's and Nietzsche's belief in music as capable of expressing the deepest meanings is an astonishing about-face. They are philosophers of the Dionysian persuasion, which, by Western standards, is almost a contradiction in terms. As for Aristotle, he had made his concession to the Dionysian spirit in his adaptation of catharsis as an artistic principle. He may have realized that to consider the principle further would be making more of it than it deserved; or it might even have necessitated a revision of the place of the arts in the hierarchy of human pursuits. Neither tragedy nor music seemed to warrant such a revision— certainly not the latter, whose powers were to be felt, at the very highest, in the area of human character, not human consciousness.

Notes

1. Andrew Barker, ed., *The Musician and His Art*, Vol. I of *Greek Musical Writings*, Chapter 10.

2. See in particular Scott Buchanan, ed., *The Portable Plato*, pp. 386–390.

3. Oliver Strunk, ed., *Source Readings in Music History*, p. 12.

4. *Ibid.*, p. 23.

5. *Ibid.*, p. 19.

6. *Ibid.*, p. 19.

7. *Ibid.*, p. 8.

8. *Ibid.*, p. 23.

9. *Ibid.*, p. 23.

10. Plato refers often to the "rational" and the "irrational" principles of (or in) the soul. See Buchanan, pp. 673–674.

11. *Ibid.*, p. 353.

12. Barker, pp. 135–136.

13. Plato refers to the Dorian and Phrygian harmonies as the "strain of the unfortunate and the strain of the fortunate," respectively. See Buchanan, p. 385.

14. *Ibid.*, p. 389.

15. *Ibid.*, pp. 384–385.

16. Rita Steblin, *A History of Key Characteristics in the Eighteenth and Early Nineteenth Centuries*, pp. 25–26.

17. Strunk, *Source Readings*, p. 413.

18. Buchanan, p. 385.

19. Hanslick's position will be taken up once again (and with specific reference to his discussion of Gluck's aria) in Chapter 12.

20. Strunk, *Source Readings*, p. 22.

21. Walter Kaufmann, *Tragedy and Philosophy*, p. 57.

22. *Ibid.*, p. 57.

23. Strunk, *Source Readings*, p. 22.

24. E.R. Dodds, *The Greeks and the Irrational*, p. 76.

25. *Ibid.*, p. 78.

26. See Dodds's discussion, *ibid.*, pp. 78–80.

27. This information is found in Chapter XII of the *Poetics*. See S.H. Butcher, trans. and ed., *Aristotle's Theory of Poetry and Fine Art*, pp. 43–45.

28. Quoted in Kaufmann, p. 60 (original: VI, 50b).

29. Northrop Frye, *Anatomy of Criticism*, p. 242.

30. Herodotus, *The Histories*, p. 365.

31. Friedrich Nietzsche, *The Birth of Tragedy*, p. 66.

32. *Ibid.*, p. 64.

33. *Ibid.*, p. 65.

34. Henry Alonzo Myers, *Tragedy, A View of Life*, p. 51.

4   Ethos of the Christian Liturgy

Having read at the end of Part I of this study that Parts II–IV purport to be a "history," present-day musicologists and especially historians of medieval sacred music may be surprised to find little in the following pages to remind them of their own method. Accounts of Western music in the first millennium of the Christian era normally center around the music of the Church, its antecedents and its dissemination. This is as expected, given the fact that we have little other music from the period. Traditionally, medievalists have been concerned to uncover the artifacts of chant, and to piece together from the extant information (often scanty and even inadequate when it is a question of sources written in imprecise notation) a coherent picture of the chant's development. Such a picture would include at the very least a classification of the chant by liturgical genre (introit, kyrie, gloria, alleluia, etc.) and a consideration not only of the stylistic differences among the so-called "local" traditions (Byzantine, Ambrosian, Old Roman, Mozarabic, Gallican), but also of the relationships between these traditions and the eventual "international" synthesis called Gregorian. If there is little evidence of these material considerations here, it is because the archetypal approach finds in chant a significance almost diametrically opposed to the outlook of modern historians: the historical eye sees chant in terms of variety, distinction, and evolution, whereas archetypal thinking sees a body of music unified, if not through a direct connection to the *logos* of Christianity itself, at least through the central action substantiating that *logos*, namely the liturgy. With regard to the origins of chant, for example: without belittling the historian's effort to decide how much chant borrowed from Jewish cantillation, how much from Greco-Roman practice, the archetypal critic must put the position of Christian theology in the forefront of the matter. The 10th-century theorist Regino of Prüm describes the origin of chant as follows:[1]

Natural music [Regino's alternate definition of natural music is: "music sung to the praise of God in the eight tones," i.e., *chant*] is that which is made by no instruments nor by the touch of fingers, nor by any touch or instigation of man ... it is modulated by nature alone under divine inspiration teaching the sweet modes such as there is in the motion of the sky or in the human voice.

To paraphrase Regino a little further: music made with the mediation of a musical instrument is "artificial" just to the extent that it involves something created by man, whereas the human voice is a natural thing created by God to produce natural music. Hymns sung by the human voice alone are such music and, being so, are the direct earthly imitation of the hymns heard in heaven. The archetypal critic is not required to think like Regino, but he must believe that Regino's ideas (and hardly Regino's alone, since they express the theologically sanctioned commonplaces of the time) have more to do with the content of medieval sacred music than any historical factor. The danger of the archetypal approach is either that it will get itself mired down in useless speculation about attitudes and values that are ultimately irretrievable, both because of our removal in time from the events in question and because of the spottiness of the record, or lead to restating the obvious, the obvious being the Judeo-Christian shibboleths which are part of everyday thinking in the West. These dangers are real, but they can be avoided if we fix our sights on the fact that today's religious stereotypes are reflections of a very specific set of archetypes crafted in the mythic mold. If we remember that what passes for "holiness" in the West today—those patterns of behavior and modes of worship, in other words, deemed appropriate to holiness—were established in the early Christian Church and not in any of the ancient Greek or Roman or Buddhist or Jewish rites, nor in those of the African plain or the Hindu forests (notwithstanding resemblances between some of these modes of worship and Christian practice) we gain some hope of defining the essential content of medieval chant.

Christian Ethos and Music

The *logos* of Christianity, despite the elaborateness of scriptural interpretation to which it would eventually be subjected, is, in its origins, a simple framework of ideas revolving around the figure of Christ, his teachings, and his history on earth. The final act of that history stands as both an example and a promise for all true believers that they, too, may be rewarded with eternal life. As a concept to be grasped, resurrection requires virtually nothing of the intellectual development expected of those trained in the rigors of Greek rationalism, but the ethical demands that proceed from this concept are rigorous in the extreme. The road to Christian holiness is one marked not only by self-denial and rejection of this world (traits common enough to all ascetic experience), but perhaps more significantly by feelings of guilt and self-recrimination, conflicts within the inner self that bespeak great psychic pain. The spirit of *contemptus mundi* which courses through the writings of the early Church fathers and culminates in St. Augustine owes its emotionally troubled character, one feels, not so much to mere otherworldliness as to a response to immediate historical conditions. Sensuousness became too closely allied with Roman moral corruption in the early Christian mind to have any positive value; the most casual connection with the senses inspired fear, if not loathing, and the higher forms of sensuousness—poetry, painting, music—were to be used, not enjoyed. Needless to say, the implications for the future of the fine arts would be considerable.

Even before the establishment of the first monasteries, psalmody, prayer, and readings of scripture came to form the basis of religious life. Of the three modes, prayer was the most "holy," placing the believer squarely in the role of humble supplicant, and thereby confirming divine power over the individual will. Scriptural readings, on the other hand, posed a dilemma: while in its simplest guise daily reading of scripture meant steadily calling to mind Christ's example and the basic teachings of the faith, it could also mean the more complex activity of scholarly interpretation, the unearthing of hidden and esoteric mysteries accessible only to the learned. But the Church fathers themselves saw the dangers of learnedness. In spite of the fact that throughout the Christian writings of the Middle Ages there is constant talk of the virtues of rationality and order, true Christians could not have the supreme confidence in rationality that Plato had placed in it. For Plato, the intense study of philosophy had signalled the triumph of the rational principle of the soul over the irrational. The Christian view of the soul, however, was of a single indivisible entity in eternal battle with the body. It was a question of nothing less than salvation or damnation, and the saving grace in this battle was not rationality, but faith. As Karl F. Morrison explains it:[2]

Awareness that sanctification—the introjection of the Holy Spirit—came by God's action limited the confidence that the Fathers could place in human arts, including the art of scriptural interpretation. The sense of ultimate dependence on God brought with it praise of holy simplicity and of its paradigms—the illiterate fishermen who became Apostles. Such praise sounds incongruous in the mouths of theologians and rhetoricians. But the learned were aware of the irony in their position. They recognized that, in their search for ever greater participation in God, the would-be purifiers of the arts could be overtaken by their own ingenuity: "the unlearned rise up and seize heaven by force, and, behold, we with our doctrines are entangled in flesh and blood."[3]

The several mentions of the "arts" in this statement do not refer, of course, to the arts as we classify them today but to the "liberal arts" of late antiquity which came in time to constitute the curriculum of the monasteries and medieval universities. Although the fathers saw the preservation of the liberal arts as an absolute necessity in combating the menace of barbarism and the total breakdown of "civilization" as it had come to be known in the West, they also could not believe like Plato and Cicero that the chief aim of these arts was to improve humanity;

for improvement of humanity, as conceived by the ancients, resonated too much of ideas of social well-being and of the human condition in the here and now, whereas Christianity envisioned the preparation of the soul for the life hereafter. But more than just being irrelevant to such preparation, erudition along the ancient lines could pose itself as an actual obstacle, for a Christian well versed in the liberal arts risked the danger of having achieved something for himself, with what that connoted in terms of individual prestige and loss of humility. One wonders, indeed, whether it ever occurred to the late medieval theorists of music that in continually insisting on the superiority of their own knowledge over that of the composer/singer they were not committing the sin of pride.[4] But to such as St. Augustine, the point was not lost: the difficulty an educated Christian had in dealing with his rationalism on the one hand, as opposed to the new vision of holy simplicity and denial of self on the other, was only one of many conflicts weighing heavily on the Christian conscience.

Psalmody, the chanting of simple melodies set to texts of which the overwhelming number came from the psalms of the Old Testament, was universally adopted in early Christian worship, though not without some soul-searching. The misgivings arose, understandably, from the problem of music's immemorial appeal to the senses, its dangerous "enchantments." To read St. Basil, one might think that this were not the case, since he speaks of the positive function of music in the liturgy as deriving from its inherent sweetness.[5] However, the more austere elements in the early Church argue the question on somewhat different grounds. Augustine is at times inclined to follow the example of Athanasius, "who used to oblige lectors to recite the psalm with such slight modulation of the voice that they seemed to be speaking rather than chanting."[6] But then he reconsiders this habit as perhaps being too strict and remembers how moved he was by the hymns of St. Ambrose at the time of his conversion. He goes on to say:[7]

When I realize that nowadays it is not the singing that moves me but the meaning of the words when they are sung in a clear voice to the most appropriate tune, I again acknowledge the great value of this practice. So I waver between the danger that lies in gratifying the senses, and the benefits which, as I know from experience, can accrue from singing.

This passage, justly famous for the frankness with which it reveals the Christian ascetic attitude toward music, testifies to the extraordinary restraint with which liturgical music would have to be treated in order not to overstep its bounds. And "restraint" characterizes not only the treatment but also the result: even more it is the quality that applies to the Christian liturgy as a whole and most clearly distinguishes the character of the liturgy from that of every other previously known ritual in the West, including the rite of the Jewish temple. If we take Psalm 150 at face value, where it is urged that Jehovah be glorified "with a blast of the horn, with the timbrel and dance, stringed instruments and the pipe with loud-sounding cymbals," we begin to understand what a radical change the ethics of the Christian liturgy represented for its time. Psalm 150 serves to remind us that no single factor was more responsible for the restrained hush of Christian worship than the absence of instruments and dancing—elements which had to be eliminated if no trace of the "mad Bacchanalian revel" were to remain.

Augustine, however, has more than just the contrast of noisy and quiet decorum in mind: his vision of liturgical control extends to the chant-melody itself, whose modest sliver of a single line must not in the slightest degree obscure the message carried by the words. Mindful of "some mysterious relationship" between words and music and also candidly aware of the fact that the sacred words "when they are sung ... stir my mind to greater religious fervor and kindle in me a more ardent flame of piety than they would if they were not sung,"[8] Augustine, for all that, concludes that it is the words which are the "life" of the chant-melodies, which "breathe soul" into them. It is the "holy words themselves" which constitute the true source of emotion, for the words point directly to the spiritual content, the energy of the holy idea. But the music has its own animating energy, which can serve to set aflame the words. That the music is the "servant" of the words there is no doubt, though this must not be taken to mean, as it does in the late 16th century, that the music *expresses* the words.

In viewing the chant principally in terms of its ability to set forth a message—in terms of its power to persuade—Augustine is thinking like a rhetorician. James Anderson Winn finds this rhetorical viewpoint extremely suggestive in light of the fact that Augustine would eventually devote a systematic study to the subject of rhetoric:[9]

The closest analogue to [Augustine's] acknowledgment of the practical utility of music is [his] position about rhetorical eloquence. In Book IV of the *De Doctrina*, a revision of Ciceronian principles for Christian use, Augustine says that preachers should "use the ornament of the moderate style ... not ostentatiously but prudently, not content ... that the audience be pleased, but rather using them in such a way that they assist that good we wish to convey by persuasion" (IV, 25). The emphasis on ends, instead of means, and on a moderate style, runs parallel to the admiration for the precepts of Athanasius in the passage on music.

So far the function of liturgical music has been explained on the basis of limitation and rhetorical utility, but these ascetic and practical aims in the chant, we presume, contain a more positive spiritual value. Looking further into Augustine's reasons for advocating a new rhetorical style in writing and speaking, we come to realize that he is motivated, both with regard to verbal eloquence and chant, by the same concern for that quality of holiness which we have been representing throughout this discussion as the underlying condition of Christian *ethos*. Defending scripture and the writings of the Church fathers against pagan allegations of "artlessness," Augustine argues that Christian eloquence must be judged by standards other than those of Ciceronian rhetoric. Christian rhetoric is, if anything, "anti-rhetorical" in the old sense, abandoning the high- and middle-style ornaments of antique rhetorical theory for a low style which, Augustine claims, is particularly well suited to the preacher's needs. Martin Camargo paraphrases

Augustine's ideas as follows:[10]

> Prayers rather than skill is finally the key to effective preaching; the needs and aptitudes of the audience should determine one's choice of style; and the speaker's example, his way of living, is more persuasive than his skill in speaking.

As the preacher, both in his manner of expression and everyday conduct, stands as a model for his congregation, so he has used for his own model Christ himself—the archetypal embodiment of an artless "teaching" style and of lowly surroundings. Erich Auerbach shows how the grass-roots nature of early Christianity gives Christian literature and rhetoric a bold new voice, a voice so innocent of style that it corresponds to no antique genre. While acknowledging the special role Augustine played in identifying and prescribing the new mixing of styles, Auerbach says that the development is symptomatic of Christianity as a whole:[11]

> The true heart of the Christian doctrine—Incarnation and Passion—was totally incompatible with the principle of the separation of styles. Christ had not come as a hero and king but as a human being of the lowest social station. His first disciples were fishermen and artisans; he moved in the everyday milieu of the humble folk of Palestine; he talked with publicans and fallen women, the poor and sick and children. Nevertheless, all that he did and said was of the highest and deepest dignity, more significant than anything else in the world. The style in which it was presented possessed little if any rhetorical culture in the antique sense; it was *sermo piscatorius* and yet it was extremely moving and much more impressive than the most sublime rhetorico-tragical literary work. And the most moving account of all was the Passion. That the King of Kings was treated as a low criminal, that he was mocked, spat upon, whipped, and nailed to the cross—that story no sooner comes to dominate the consciousness of the people than it completely destroys the aesthetics of the separation of styles; it engenders a new elevated style, which does not scorn everyday life and which is ready to absorb the sensorially realistic, even the ugly, the undignified, the physically base. Or—if anyone prefers to have it the other way around—a new *sermo humilis* is born, a low style, such as would properly only be applicable to comedy, but which now reaches far beyond its original domain, and encroaches upon the deepest and the highest, the sublime and the eternal.

The "sermo humilis," as already anticipated in an earlier chapter, corresponds to that aspect of demotic thought which finds the serious and significant in lowly things. Indeed, to say that demotic ways of thinking originated with Christianity would be, if not historically precise, at least archetypally justifiable, given the extent to which Christian expression and imagery have seeped down into Western consciousness. Still the question confronts us: if the "sermo humilis" forms the core of sacred Christian literature and rhetoric, is it the primary content of chant as well? Surely it must be, but rather than find direct parallels between rhetoric and music, we would prefer to argue the issue from the more basic standpoint of the Christian liturgical ideal, at the center of which is a vision of holiness in the form of humility. Humility defines an entire way of life—a coherent *ethos*—of which the liturgy and its music constitute only one manifestation. To work not for one's own glory but the glory of God, one must proceed by a route other than the epic-heroic. This is necessary not only because it is in the spirit of Christian holiness to bend to the divine will but also because humility is the rule of Heaven. What is the simple restrained rudimentary quality of Christ's existence on earth but a demonstration of the heavenly way?

The liturgy aspiring to holiness reenacts Christ's simplicity and restraint. If the liturgy is only one manifestation of the total *ethos* of humility, it is doubtless the most powerful tool Christianity had at its disposal to realize this *ethos*. As a reenactment the liturgy commands a literal bending on the part of the worshipper to a greater will than his own: repeatedly he murmurs acceptance of absolute authority over him, repeatedly he sings the praises of divine creation around him. As ritual the liturgy is a repetitive act, in itself celebrated every day, many times a day: it becomes routine, habit-forming, second nature, and thereby succeeds in fulfilling the essential ethical function of transforming "first nature" into something manifestly better and higher than it was.

From Humilitas to Sublimitas

When speaking of an improved second nature, however, we must be mindful once again of the gap that separates the Platonic and Christian ethical positions. Christianity aims at improvement of human nature not for its own sake, but for the sake of making it worthy of a glory beyond the heroic kind envisioned either by Greek philosophy or Greco-Roman epic poetry. Christian theology certainly succeeds in distinguishing worldly from otherworldly glory, but can the liturgy itself—and particularly, the music of the liturgy—express this distinction? One suspects that the Church fathers would have no hesitation in answering this question in the affirmative and in locating the expression of otherworldly glory in the humble style—the "sermo humilis"—itself. Taking the testimony of later medieval figures, we note that St. Francis of Assisi considers prayer and human respect to embody a direct connection between "humilitas" and "sublimitas";[12] for Bernard de Clairvaux, the same connection is the very definition of beauty.[13]

In light of this connection, chant may well have greater ambitions than we have heretofore ascribed to it: in its economy of means, its stepwise motion, gently arched shapes, in the sustained undramatic evenness with which a melody unfolds, chant points to the effort on the part of medieval Christendom to express a movement from the humble to the sublime. To jump forward in time for a moment and read the testimony of a 20th-century Trappist monk, we find Thomas Merton writing the following of the Gregorian Advent hymn, *Conditor Alma Siderum*: "Its structure is mighty with a perfection that despises the effects of the most grandiloquent secular music—and says more than Bach without even exhausting the whole range of one octave."[14] Surely, Bach does not compare favorably to chant in Merton's opinion; Merton is careful to distinguish Bach from secular music, but the suggestion that the music of the venerable cantor of the Thomaskirche might be grandiloquent relative to chant is too strong not to be inferred. We do not have to share Merton's bias, but his sensing of an imagery which is alien to chant is exactly on target. That element is the sound of pagan heroism blasting through the more pompous and theatrical pages of Bach's sacred music—the grandiose and monumental gestures, for instance, of the "Et resurrexit" of the B minor Mass, to take a particularly noteworthy case. This heroism, "resurrected" in its own right through the secularizing processes of Renaissance humanism, celebrates worldly glory and relies on "outward show" to maintain its significance and reality. Yet, the Baroque pomp associated with worldly heroism also came to be accepted as an appropriate expression of glory in the Christian sense. What we have, then, in the content of the "Et resurrexit" is the confrontation of two mythic traditions: on the one hand, a pantheon of golden gods and heroes who operate in a realm far above the ordinary one associated with the everyday world; on the other hand, a community of humble folk whose mundane, almost humdrum existence is suddenly discovered to be the scene of divine enactment. Compared against this archetypal mixture, chant emerges a pure and exclusive form of Christian observance because it springs from an ethical conception which, for all intents and purposes, originated with Christianity itself. Eminently understandable is not only the ascetic position represented by Thomas Merton but even more the fact that chant is established as the definitive standard against which the sacred character of liturgical music in the West must be measured. The musical artifacts of Baroque churchly pomp may be mighty in their own right, but the hushed silence of chant has stamped on the Western mind a definitive image of holiness.

A Musical Image of the Sublime

"Hushed silence" is a condition toward which chant may aspire but can never literally become. To identify the kind of chant-image that comes closest to this condition we must explore somewhat further the Christian conception of "sublimitas." For reasons that should become clearer as the discussion develops, the most likely sources of such an image are the most melismatic chants of the repertory, the graduals and alleluias, already recognized in the Middle Ages as "the jewels of the Mass." Especially with the alleluias, whose use is restricted to the joyous seasons of the year, and whose "jubilus" an be taken as a symbol, in strict allegorical terms, of joy, we get a sense of what the believer understands as "eternal radiance." In the Alleluia for Easter the clear compositional balance, the settled tonal feeling given by the seventh mode, and the purity and delicacy of the melodic outlining of G-B-D connote for us today an effect we like to char-acterize, almost by reflex, as "heavenly" or "angelic" (Example 4.1). Particularly in the melisma on *immolatus* (not shown in the example), as it floats upward and soars on to the high G, wreathing about this note as if aimlessly and endlessly, we hear more than simple Christian piety; there is the distinct impression of the otherworldly having for a brief moment *been made present*, been revealed. Merton's frequent use of the word "might" to describe a chant which has particularly moved him causes us to wonder whether these single-lined shapes—slender by our standards—could signify a grandeur for the medieval world. In one sense, the answer is certainly yes; for, given the strictly symbolic terms in which the medieval mind could see meaning in things, the grandeur of the *idea* toward which the image pointed was sufficient to produce the effect. But in another sense—the sense in which there is a certain awareness of a power in the image itself—the answer could also be yes. When we remember that the singing of the chant was, at least in the later Middle Ages, heard in a space which signified majesty of proportions by any standard, then a relationship between slenderness and mysterious grandeur begins to emerge. For the melody has an extended life, beginning as the slender and modest appeal of the human supplicant, gradually rising to take on the breadth of the space it fills, finally merging into the immateriality of literal silence. In so doing, the chant follows precisely the upward direction the Abbé Suger claimed for it about 900 years ago when he spoke of his choir at St. Denis as being a "symphony more angelic than human."[15]

Example 4.1: Alleluia for the Solemn Mass of Easter

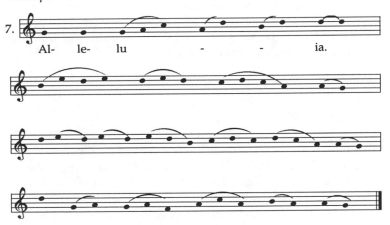

If the above account strikes our scholarly sensibilities as uncomfortably fanciful, we should pay heed to early Christian testimony itself, beginning with the remarks of Augustine regarding the *jubilus* of the alleluia.[16]

He who jubilates does not utter words; rather, it is a sort of sound of gladness without words. The voice comes from a mind diffused with gladness which is experiencing feeling to the highest degree possible [but] not understanding its meaning. A man delighting in his exultation breaks away from any words whatever, since they cannot be spoken nor understood, into a vocal sound of, as it were, exultation without words. The result is that he seems to be rejoicing indeed in his very voice but not to be able to express what rejoices him [because it is] as it were filled with too great joy.

What Augustine is trying to explain (somewhat gropingly, it might be added) is the psychological sensation of being so overcome with emotion that one cannot find one's words: verbal inarticulateness goes hand in hand with loss of rational control. The only recourse left to one in such a state is to express oneself through wordless song. In proposing this, Augustine prefigures the commonplace, made familiar to us by a century of Romantic and post-Romantic aesthetics, that music begins where words leave off. It is at any rate worth noting that the ancient connection of music to the irrational, or pre-rational, still had some currency in Christian thinking and even more that music seemed particularly appropriate where spontaneous effusion of intense states of feeling was involved.

In his recent authoritative work on the vocal forms of the high Middle Ages, John Stevens presents the familiar dichotomy between syllabic and melismatic setting of chant in a fresh and extremely insightful way:[17]

There are always two contrary principles at work in chant, which pull in opposite directions and affect our sense of the relation of melody to text. On the one hand there is the principle of psalmody, and on the other a principle which rather loosely one may call *jubilus*. The first is extremely restrained and, whilst allowing itself to be diverted from pure syllabic monotone by the needs of phrases and sentences, gives little or nothing away to individual words. The second is free, creative, and in its final forms ecstatically liberated from all the demands of a text—its characteristic genre is the alleluia of the Mass, but all melismatic chants seem to aspire to this state.

Stevens goes on to illustrate his point by presenting three different settings of the Holy Week text, "Deus, deus meus, respice in me, quere me dereliquisti?" ("O God, my God, look upon me, why hast thou forsaken me?") In the first version, a psalm recitation, the setting is (in keeping with its chant class) in unrelieved syllabic style; in the second version, a psalm verse for the Introit for Palm Sunday, the syllabic treatment is, as expected, somewhat less severe, with a number of syllables receiving two or three notes apiece. In the tract for Palm Sunday, however, the decorations are "flowingly complex and unrestrained" (to borrow Stevens's description). His interpretation of these differences runs as follows:[18]

I have deliberately chosen a highly emotional text: it is emotional in the expressive sense, inasmuch as the words express not only the grief of the psalmist but, as spoken from the cross, Christ's grief and agony, also. In the first two versions the recitation-style depersonalizes the emotion. The effect is not easy to describe: the formal monotony of the chant (almost in a literal sense) and its indifference to individual words diminishes our sense of pain, releases us from the intolerable realization, whilst at the same time enhancing through its generalizing power the importance and the significance. There is a higher level of experience than the merely personal and the chant helps us to reach it.

When Stevens comes to discussing the tract, however, his assessment is conducted according to somewhat different criteria from those applied to the psalms. We are ready to hear him say that as "the recitation-style depersonalizes the emotion," so the florid style intensifies the personal. Instead, he investigates the placement of the melismas in the melody, and, by showing how they fall randomly on strategic and nonstrategic words alike, means to persuade us that the tract shares with the psalms an "indifference to individual words." In short, he provides a structural/ rhetorical treatment of the melismas, but leaves us to wonder how they might affect a text which, by his own admission, he has deliberately chosen for its highly emotional content.

Of the responses we can make to this question, there are several plausible choices. We can, for instance, conclude that medieval liturgical music is as indifferent to the distinction between joy and grief as it is to the sense of individual words. That conclusion, besides being one of the stock answers scholars have long provided for the more general question of the medieval attitude toward the relationship of music and text, is not entirely supported by the evidence. To say, as does Stevens in the last sentence of the statement quoted above, that chant reaches for a "higher level of experience than the merely personal" is perhaps to come closer to the truth, though it confronts us with a discrepancy—the picture of a liturgy which permits its texts a range of highly differentiated emotions but demands of its music a strict impersonality. Such a discrepancy can in large part be alleviated if we do not place the Christian view of joy and grief on an altogether, or even primarily, personal plane. This is not to say that the emotion of the believer when he is recollecting such stirring events as the Crucifixion and Resurrection is not real and deeply felt, but it must also be remembered that the emotional distinction made by the Christian calendar with regard to joyful and penitential days and seasons is, in the first place, *prescriptive* (in keeping with the activities of an institution founded on the mythic plan) and secondly, *communal* in its essential conception and character. The liturgy is designed for a community of worshippers, totally aside from the personal involvement of this or that worshipper and also regardless of the apparent emotionality of certain individual texts; its sphere of operations is thus by definition removed from the realm of the personal. This is by way of saying that ritual formality will always impose its measure of emotional distance, not to mention the fact that early Christianity, by comparison with almost all other contemporaneous religions, exacted a ritual decorum of extreme restraint.

And yet, as we have already read, Stevens calls the melismas of the tract *Deus, deus meus* "unrestrained," and he characterizes melismas in general as "the breaking out of jubilant melody."[19] We have still to determine the ethical significance for chant of the melismatic style, and in particular, we are puzzled to understand why a grief-laden text such as "Deus, deus meus"—and more generally, why an entire class of penitential song, namely the tract—is allied with "jubilant" melody. This puzzlement, by the way, is not limited to modern Western thinking, for such an alliance, if it were to turn out to mean what it appears to mean, would have struck medieval Christianity, no less than the later Western world, as a misalliance. Is Augustine's conception of the *jubilus* as signifying joy too limited? Is Stevens's principle of the *jubilus* too all-embracing?

In point of fact, these ostensible discrepancies disappear once the precise character of Augustine's *joy* is clearly defined. What we most urgently need to understand is that the emotion Augustine is referring to is not the state of mind that opposes itself to *grief*, but a specifically Christian experience wherein the sentient subject—the believer—catches a glimpse of otherworldly glory. Christianity knew, of course, the traditional simple opposition between human joy and grief and developed a number of symbolisms out of it—for instance, the distinction between the Resurrection and the Crucifixion, between the alleluia and the tract. But Augustine's conception is of an intense emotion that transcends normal human joy, that transcends normal human feeling altogether; such emotion comes from the sensation of approaching divine being, from knowing, if only momentarily, the true nature of the sublime. The appropriate name for this sensation is *ecstasis*, in spite of the fact that the term evokes the frenzy and violence of the ancient Dionysian rite. That Christian *ecstasis* does not embrace frenzy hardly needs substantiation, though it is no less "Dionysian" for all that; for *ecstasis* is by definition the first principle and ultimate goal of Dionysian consciousness, dedicated to the surrender of rational control—indeed, to the surrender of self.

What distinguishes Christian *ecstasis* from the ancient version is not only behavior (Christian repugnance for vehement bodily movement, not to speak of orgy) but the very quality of the central emotion: ancient Dionysianism begins with excitement and ends in exhausted thrall; Christian *ecstasis* signifies extreme self-containment and poise of the inner life—in a word, serenity. "Serene joy," which may well be an invention of the Christian genius, unknown to earlier cultures in the West, needs little outward manifestation to suggest it; for Augustine, the wordless *jubilus* is enough. Stevens, we have seen, has characterized the *jubilus* as unrestrained, but we must measure that characterization in the general context of restrained Christian expression and against the severe restraint—the "Apollonian sobriety"—of psalm intonation. The musical distance separating psalm from tract may seem slight when compared against the contrasts of later kinds of music, but the archetypal distance is considerable—on the one hand, a rudimentary, almost matter-of-fact song-speech couched in "humilitas," on the other, a floating, weightless cantilena poised at "sublimitas."

Now that we can take Stevens's "breaking out in jubilant melody" to mean the "flowering into melody of transcendent serene joy," the apparent contradictions between text and music in the tract *Deus, deus meus* are eliminated. The element of personal suffering in the text does not disappear—it continues to make itself felt—but it is subsumed in the murmuring melismas of the melodic line, which carries the worshipper upward, so to speak, bringing him closer to divine being. In light of this purported function of the melisma, we realize that the tract as a class, despite its tragic thrust but precisely because of its melismatic style, is the proper substitute for the alleluia. During the seasons of Advent and Passiontide, an exchange of joyous (in the human sense) for penitential texts had to be made, but the Church fathers saw no reason to forego the sublime effects of wordless music. It is as if graduals, alleluias, and tracts were offered to the worshipper in recognition of the discipline he had undergone with the surrounding "humble" chants in the syllabic and semi-syllabic style. Compensated for his pains with these momentary foretastes of eternal serenity, the worshipper in the process of experiencing the melismatic chants came to know true moments of serenity on earth. If this appreciation of the liturgical situation is essentially correct, then the Christian liturgy contains an important *pathos* as well as an *ethos*. By all accounts, the greater part of the liturgy's role was ethical and instructional: through steady application, the devout believer learned submission and self-denial and studiously prepared his soul for its promised reward. But at those few moments in the succession of liturgical events when the music effectively left words behind and flew free, the *logos* for which the believer had all the time been preparing could seem immediately present before him and he could feel palpably moved.

A Footnote on Medieval Polyphony

The appropriate question to be asked here about medieval polyphony is not the historical one of how polyphony came to be, but rather the archetypal one of why it should have come to be. If chant was the perfect expression of Christian worship, why should the Church have permitted entry to a music which could only compromise the hegemony of chant—which indeed, as it turned out (though the early exponents of polyphony could not have known this), would eventually displace chant in the affections of church musicians and command all their creative resources? The general answer to that question must lie in that aspect of the hated paganism which educated Christians often found themselves powerless to resist, namely the whole universe of Greco-Roman *logos*, with all that it represented in the way of practical guidance and intellectual challenge for living in this world while waiting for the next. Had the early Christian fathers hated paganism to the extent that the *logos* of Christianity demanded and for the solitary reason that it was not Christian (which though not a reason at all, is the most foolproof way, as fundamentalist movements have shown time and again, of remaining "pure"), they would have looked at the entirety of Greco-Roman culture as business better left unfinished. As it was, they adopted what artifacts of that culture they thought could be made over in the Christian image and left the rest behind. If purity was the aim, this was not a wise choice, for it was to result in inevitable dichotomies—faith/reason, scripture/theology, uniformity/universality, insularity/cosmopolitanism—the effects of which would be permanently felt in every part and on every level of the Church structure. Eventually, this bifocal mentality of Christianity would have its repercussions in the purest aspect of Christian organization, the liturgy itself. The music of the liturgy would contain its own dichotomy—chant/polyphony—which, more than marking surface differences of form, would resonate with the fundamental differences that divided Christian and pre-Christian world views.

The final irony attached to polyphonic music of the high Middle Ages may be that, unlike the theology of the time, it left the faith/reason dichotomy as is, unable to make a synthesis of it.[20] When we confront the chief artifacts of later medieval polyphony—the organa and clausulae of Léonin and Pérotin, and the mass movements and isorhythmic motets of 14th-century France—we are struck by effects of intricacy, periodicity, weight, and solidity, qualities we are culturally disposed to associate with rationalism and the physicalness of the natural order— with, in short, the substantiality of the here and now. It remained for Renaissance church polyphony, with its arching lines (especially in the sparsely texted sections of the Mass such as the Kyrie, Sanctus, and Agnus Dei) to rediscover the floating, weightless quality of melismatic chant, and thus while embodying the natural order to suggest something beyond that order.

If these images of Renaissance church music constitute a successful synthesis of the faith/reason dichotomy, later polyphonic instances of such a synthesis are rare—rare, that is, until the advent of Romanticism, when the beyond becomes a paramount issue for musical expression. "Heavenly" Romantic music, however, embodies not so much a synthesis of faith and reason (especially since reason, according to Romantic thinking, is a state of mind directly opposed to reaching for the beyond) as it does a transformation of the proverbial solidity of polyphony into a kind of sonorous weightlessness, the effect of sounds wafting upward and away. It is hard to imagine this effect being realized without the precedent of the chant-image behind it. Nineteenth-century images such as the string tremolos at the opening of *Lohengrin*, or the angelic choir in Part I, Scene 6 of *L'enfance du Christ* or the intertwining of the lovers' voices in the final duet of *Aida* in no way replicate the floating cantilena of the Easter Alleluia, yet all work for the same mysterious, serene joy as their medieval forbear. At least as regards the melismatic branch of Gregorian chant, it may be said that medieval sacred music left an indelible imprint on Western musical imagery.

Notes

1. Quoted in Calvin Bower, "Natural and Artificial Music: The Origins and Development of an Aesthetic Concept," in *Musica Disciplina*, Vol. 25 (1971), p. 21.

2. Karl F. Morrison, "Incentives for Studying the Liberal Arts," in *The Seven Liberal Arts in the Middle Ages*, David L. Wagner, ed., p. 52.

3. The words quoted at the end of Morrison's statement are from Augustine, *Confessions*, 8.8, CSEL, 33, p. 186.

4. The origin of the distinction between *musicus* and *cantor* is credited to Boethius, though St. Augustine in his earlier *De Musica* already calls music "a science" and dwells at length on the reasons for considering art a "ratio" and not an "imitatio." From Boethius on, music theory takes on a particularly scientific cast, eventually joining arithmetic, geometry, and astronomy in the medieval quadrivium. Such was Boethius' authority throughout the Middle Ages that his bias against practitioners of music persisted even

after music theorists had turned their attention to practical matters, in other words, had begun to concern themselves with the music of their own day.

5. See Piero Weiss and Richard Taruskin, ed., *Music in the Western World: A History of Documents*, p. 25.

6. Quoted in James Anderson Winn, *Unsuspected Eloquence*, p. 48.

7. *Ibid.*, p. 48.

8. *Ibid.*, p. 47.

9. *Ibid.*, pp. 48–49.

10. Martin Camargo, "Rhetoric," in *The Seven Liberal Arts in the Middle Ages*, David L. Wagner, ed., p. 111.

11. Erich Auerbach, *Mimesis*, p. 72.

12. *Ibid.*, p. 162.

13. *Ibid.*, pp. 162–165.

14. Thomas Merton, *The Seven Storey Mountain*, p. 460.

15. Quoted in Erwin Panofsky, *Meaning in the Visual Arts*, p. 122.

16. Quoted in John Stevens, *Words and Music in the Middle Ages: Song, Narrative, Dance and Drama, 1050–1350*, p. 402.

17. *Ibid.*, p. 304.

18. *Ibid.*, p. 306.

19. *Ibid.*, p. 306.

20. In referring to the "theology of the time," I am of course thinking of St. Thomas Aquinas, the supreme exemplar of late medieval intellectualism working to eradicate the differences between monkish simplicity and intellectual complexity. The irony of *his* situation is that, monk that he was, he should carry out his task by erecting one of the most gigantic intellectual monuments known to man. Umberto Eco may well be thinking of his hero in his earliest scholarly work, *The Aesthetics of Thomas Aquinas*, when he writes in his novel, *The Name of the Rose*: "A monk should surely love his books with humility, wishing their good and not the glory of his own curiosity: but what the temptation of adultery is for laymen and the yearning for riches is for secular ecclesiastics, the seduction of knowledge is for monks."

5   Ethos of Courtly Love

The notable ethical experience of the Middle Ages, just after Christianity itself, is courtly love. Though no challenge to Christianity in intent or fact (those who espoused courtly love were no less devout Christians for that), courtly love proposed, nevertheless, a distinctly non-Christian view of the world. This needs to be said, if only because of the tendency in modern scholarship to favor formal and symbolic similarities over distinctions of doctrine. The similarities are undeniable—parallels between Christian writings and troubadour lyrics were noted by not a few medievals themselves—but they must not allow us to confuse allegory and literal belief; they must not obscure what separates the Christian view of the beyond from a vision aimed squarely at the here and now, from a code of living that begins in erotic desire and ends with enhancement of individual prestige. Once the conceptual distinctions are made, we are free to note as many analogies between Christianity and courtly love as we please, noting all the while that these analogies share little in the way of common ethical ground.

Like the chant and its relation to the liturgy, courtly music is indispensable to the courtly love ideal; the love song—the "gran chant courtois"—is nothing less than the central action by which the ideal gets carried out. By "song," however, we must understand a collaboration between word and melody of an order that goes beyond our modern conception. To the medieval mind the "poem" of a courtly love song was no more complete without its music than the melody was without its text: the first imperative of a love song was that it be sung. If this notion is somewhat belied by manuscripts which do not include music for numbers of poems—a situation which has encouraged most literary scholars to treat troubadour and trouvère lyrics essentially as artifacts to be read—it is no less real for that. John Stevens believes so strongly in the interaction—one might say, interpenetration—of words and music that he has forged out of it a whole theory of medieval song. For him, each of the two components, poem and melody, supplies its own patterns of sound—the number of syllables, pitches, accents, linear shapes, rhythmic proportions—which in combination yield a unique *armonia* of correspondences and noncorrespondences.[1] This *armonia* explains the essence of song, of what it is to be expressive in the medieval sense. Applicable to medieval song in general, this conception elaborated by Stevens means to be true of the courtly love song in particular, where the *armonia* is yielded up through an intricate network of musico-verbal patterns, a "total music" held together in such a delicate and sophisticated balance as to make the word "gran" really count for something. Though Stevens does not explicitly say so, the implication is that the "gran chant courtois" is the most ambitious of medieval song forms because it serves the highest aesthetic ideals.

In view of his position, Stevens's objections to the more or less universal claim by scholars that the music mattered less to the creators of the courtly love song than the text are not surprising. We need not review the arguments for and against this claim: suffice it to say that Stevens's position is more convincing than his opponents', not only because he pleads his own case very well but also because the best pieces of the repertoire speak for themselves. In the first place, it is illogical to imagine a lack of interest on the part of composers in their own music; but more than that, the evidence itself—the generous corpus of excellent melodies, the popularity of certain melodies as we find them appearing frequently in the manuscript anthologies, the wide-ranging practice of *contrafacta*—attests to the very opposite on the part of the society as a whole. And yet, such evidence does not force us to conclude that Stevens's theory of the courtly love song is the final word on the subject. Without in the least calling his results into question, we can add to his structural approach a treatment of the love song that examines the song for its content: by such a treatment, text and music would be presented as two faculties serving two distinct functions, rather than as equal partners in the execution of a single function. Or perhaps instead of speaking of two distinct functions, we might more precisely identify two different areas of content which text and music, each according to its respective powers, would be susceptible of handling effectively.

To get at the content in question, we must first go over the basic features that make up the code of courtly love. This is deceptively familiar territory—familiar because certain notions of romantic love which developed in the later Middle Ages have remained more or less unchanged in the West ever since, deceptively so because romantic love is only one factor in the code. Indeed, we risk misconstruing the whole significance of courtly love if we concentrate on the love element and minimize courtliness. Histories of the period repeat the familiar commonplaces about the basic theme—the devotion of a knight/poet to a lady, her proverbial unattainability, his complaints at not being properly rewarded, yet his ultimate willingness to wait and eternally hope. These are the ostensible signs of courtly love, but what is missing here is the code itself, a closed system of rules whereby a select group of individuals identifies itself through its values. In our modern culture, where the word "love" triggers an image of grand passion, it is at first difficult to understand that *amour courtois* or *fin' amor* is only incidentally about love and centrally about the society in which the love takes place. Whether the knight actually has a burning passion for a real lady is quite as immaterial as whether he is only "in love with love"; all that really matters is that he conduct himself properly according to the code. Indeed, in all these events, the object of desire, the lady herself, is of very little consequence. She is never addressed directly in the love poems; and while she is described as alternately beautiful, noble, chaste, capricious, and the cause of all the knight's distress, we never get a vivid picture of her. She seems almost as distant to us as the knight imagines her, and for the very logical reason that the situation described in the poem is seen totally through his eyes. The main subject of the poem is his sufferings and fears—and finally, not even so much these as *his expression of these*. For, although we must accept the reality of his actual feelings for the lady, it is what he tells us about those feelings that constitute the true reality of courtly love. Through the expression of his feelings he will either succeed or fail to impress us with his courtliness—his *courtoisie*, his essential *dignité*. In the last instance, the French word has been used instead of the English one because it connotes decidedly more than the outward face one presents to society, and even more than self-esteem: it signifies *worthiness*, unquestionably the central element in this courtly system of values. Both the lady and the poet show themselves worthy, though for quite different reasons. The lady is worthy in an absolute sense: she is *great*, and being so, merits the unflagging devotion of any man. The poet is worthy, first because he, among all other men, has recognized the greatness of the lady, and second, because, no matter how she ignores or even scorns him—indeed, precisely because he can never expect any reward from her—he will remain faithfully and eternally in her service.

We may now begin to understand how the love song itself occupies the very center of the courtly process. The love song is the vehicle by which the poet can hope to demonstrate most unequivocally his *dignité* in the eyes of both his lady and of those that Frederick Goldin calls his "friends," for he has expressed himself as carefully, justly, and sensitively as was in his power to do, and thus he has sought to reaffirm his qualities as a courtly man.[2] That he wants the esteem of his friends as well as of his lady is an indispensable element of courtly love, for they form the society from which the code derives its validity. "He is a courtly poet, and bound to his office among these friends: it is for them that he sings, it is by his song that they know he is one of them, it is in the circle of their recognition that he is truly situated, redeemed from exile, named, and valued."[3]

It is clear that if he is going to use his song to demonstrate his delicacy, the poet must sing in a delicate manner, he must use his "best voice." Guillaume IX, Duke of Aquitaine and the first troubadour, is very explicit on this point: at the end of his poem, *Farai chansoneta nueva*, he instructs Daurostre, presumably the *joglar* who will perform the song, to "chan e no bram": "sing this nicely, do not bray it out."[4] Goldin makes a good deal out of the meaning of this command.

He tells us, in effect, that Guillaume would not have felt it necessary to give such a warning if the practice for singing sweetly was already a habit, an established tradition. We must remember that Guillaume is the pioneer troubadour and that he is breaking new ground: the very poem which contains his instructions to Daurostre begins, "Farai chansoneta nueva": "I will make a new song." But if the new song is nothing other than the song of courtly love, then what is the old song? Apparently, it is a song which can be "brayed out"; and it can be done so, because such a rendering is appropriate to its subject matter. The subject matter, as Guillaume himself makes known in very frank language, is the *leis de con*, an expression which will be translated here (somewhat more decorously than the original) as the "law of lust." The old song-type, then, is a bawdy song; and, as it is addressed to the *companhos*, one can reasonably assume that it was intended for an all-male audience. The women portrayed in these songs are every bit as lusty as the men; they certainly bear no resemblance to the perfect, almost unearthly, creatures of the world of courtly love. In this world, everyone takes what he can get and throws propriety to the winds. Goldin writes:[5]

Under the rule of the *leis de con* all actions have the status of accidents, for this "law" allows no motive but instinctual appetite in the individual, and no other rule but chance in the world. Everyone wanders around till he or she bumps into someone else, and then lust astounds them both with its possibilities. In the world in which they wander, there is no personal dignity and no moral coherence. That is what makes it a world of fun—who wants to trudge beneath the weight of his dignity all the time? The festival spirit breathes where it will, seeking encounters without consequences. That is why these songs are merry.

The inhabitants of this world which runs by the rule of lust are the "nymphs and satyrs" of medieval fantasy (though they do not go by such names). This world corresponds to a realm of play and diversion which offers temporary escape from social and moral responsibility. Such an escape, as long as it remains temporary, has its decided benefits, but as a way of life, it leads to meaninglessness. These songs may be merry, but at their very core there is the gnawing presence of nihilism: bawdy songs are ultimately governed by the archetype of comic irony. As Goldin has written: "Nothing is real except the closest thing, and even then only the appearance is real, and only for a time. The only permanent facts are the force of desire—*am*, I love—and the embarrassment or discontent in which it ends."[6]

Guillaume IX is not unaware of the limitations of animal instinct and of the ultimate dissatisfaction it brings. We are very fortunate that of the eleven poems we have of him, about half fall into the category of the *leis de con* and the other half into the category of courtly love. As Goldin has arranged these lyrics in his anthology, we have the opportunity to watch a transformation take place in Guillaume's perceptions: from the first songs in which there is a genuine enthusiasm for the world of lust, we see Guillaume's growing disaffection with this world at the end of No. 4, an intimation of the new courtly ideals in No. 6, and the full flowering of these ideals in the "chansoneta nueva" of No. 7. Goldin's insight is in having perceived that courtly love is an answer to the *leis de con*: it supplies meaning—a system of value, a sustained reality, an *ethos*—where none existed before. But Goldin takes his thought one step further in showing that the true significance of courtly love rests ultimately in the tension it maintains with the *leis de con*: "the worshipful love it [the new song] celebrates somehow has to originate in the feelings of a carnal man."[7] In other words, only the poet's initial carnality will prove that the restraints he imposes on himself signify a real discipline, a serious *askesis*.

In this last respect—in the willingness to self-denial and to humility before the love object—we find a genuine parallel with Christian experience, quite possibly the only genuine one. Other claims for religious significance in the courtly love theme, of which the following is a prime example, seem distinctly farfetched: "The virtues acquired by the soul illuminated by divine grace are exactly those which the lover acquires when his soul is irradiated by his lady's grace: they are truly a courtly lover's virtues."[8] The civilizing effects of the courtly love ethic, though considerable, were nevertheless of a social, not religious, character. By such an ethic, the members of the society stood not only to *behave* better but also to *think* better of both themselves and their associates: the climate of the court as a whole was manifestly enhanced. More than a mere code of manners, courtly love combined elevation of the inner life with improvement of outward behavior. But we must not confuse spiritual elevation with the sensation of being visited by divine grace. Stevens refers to a love song by Bernard de Ventadorn in which the troubadour uses the word "joi" six times in the course of the first stanza ("Can l'erba frescha").[9] Lest the ecstatic incantation of the word lead us to mistake the distinctive nature of this "joi," we must make some effort to define the feeling precisely. First, the presence of erotic excitement alone rules out the kind of serene joy attached by Augustine to the *jubilus* of the alleluia. At the same time, the eroticism itself is scarcely pure carnality, for even from the outset it is tempered by the certainty of trials to be endured, and it is ennobled by the promise of the virtue to be gained through such endurance. Excitement is always anticipatory, but this anticipation is at least twofold, focused on two patently separate objects—the lady herself and the ultimate goal of personal and social worthiness.

That the courtly love song is directly responsible for conveying the complexity of feeling just described has already been suggested. The question remaining is: are text and music equal partners in the expression of this feeling or do they perform functions essentially different in kind and of varying importance? The views of earlier scholarship on this point have been at best oblique, transmitted through actions rather than through any explicit statement of purpose. It has been the somewhat unreflecting stance of most literary critics to declare the primacy of the text simply by ignoring the music altogether. Musicology has not unexpectedly tended in the other direction, though in their preoccupation with solving the rhythmic puzzles of the musical notation, the musicologists have at least had to deal at length with the prosody, if not the content, of the texts. Indeed, the great irony of the pioneering work of Aubry and Beck lies in a fundamental discrepancy between theory and practice—between initial intention and final results—for their stated working principle was ostensibly to fashion a musical rhythm based on the prosody of the text, whereas in actual fact their wholesale adoption of the polyphonic rhythmic modes succeeded in the obliteration of that prosody in far many more cases than it was preserved. In spite of the resulting distortions, not to speak of the disagreements among scholars regarding the application of the rhythmic modes to the self-same song, Aubry's and Beck's theories continued to hold sway until fairly recently in the musicological world. Not so in the sphere of literary scholarship, which has traditionally taken the opposite stand:[10]

Literary scholars, when they considered the matter at all, have tended to reject the use of triple meters in the monophonic songs of the time, whether in Latin, Provençal or French. In none of these languages does versification depend on the regular alternations of strong and weak syllables—on the use of poetic meters, in other words. The number of syllables in each line, the total number of lines, and the rhyme scheme were the only criteria for making the succeeding stanzas of a poem correspond with the first. Within these limits, constant variation of metrical patterns proves to be one of the subtlest techniques of troubadour verse. Carl Appel has shown, for example, that no two lines in the first stanza of *Non es meravelha* ... have the same distribution of accented and unaccented syllables. To devise a single metrical pattern to fit all eight lines is an obvious impossibility. This situation is typical of Bernart de Ventadorn's poems and Appel strongly proposed metrical transcriptions in which melodic and textual accents do not correspond.

In recent times, musical scholarship has largely come around to the literary position, even to the point of pronouncing the music secondary in importance to the text and of insisting on a correspondence between melodic and textual accents down to the last detail. As already noted, Stevens parts company with this view, arguing that musical and textual accents function equally and interdependently in forming a total prosody, a composite counterpoint of rhythms where accents from the two sources may both coincide and not coincide. While this theory has the appeal of flexibility and is also realistic in terms of all later traditions of solo song, it chooses not to say anything more specific about what might have guided the poets' insights in developing their musico-verbal combinations; in other words, it does not provide a working principle according to which the poets saw an upper limit beyond which the noncorrespondence of textual and musical accents could not go. Such a limit, however, must have existed and it must have come precisely when and where the noncorrespondence of accents would have begun to interfere with a proper and comfortable understanding of the words.

If this point seems hardly worth mentioning, given the universal importance of good diction, it should be recalled that what is clearly a general aim for all solo song is of the essence in the case of the courtly love song: for, taking into account the strongly discursive thrust of the text, a performance of the total song had to ensure that the succession of ideas of which the discourse was composed could be closely followed. Even a brief glance at a troubadour song on the strictly verbal plane will reveal the variety and ingenuity with which the love theme is treated. These are not the flowery dedications to *Douce dame* and *Madonna* that later ages would produce to order. On the contrary, they are meditated and quick-witted discussions the poet has with himself concerning the complexities of love relationships and the validity of his feelings. That they often run on beyond 80 lines is already indication that the poets think of their subject matter as something to be pondered, reflected upon, argued out at length.

Returning to the question of single or separate functions for music and text in the courtly love song, we cite a lengthy statement from Stevens as a point of reference. Though he is discussing one song in particular, the *D'amourous coeur* of Adam de la Halle, we understand from context that this song illustrates what he considers to be the fundamental perspective of song writing in the Middle Ages:[11]

Adam ... accepts the conventional structural "controls" of *chanson* form ... : the musical phrase coincides with the line-length; a "weak" ending in the words ... is respected in the melody; the number of notes and note-groups (in ligature) coincide precisely with the number of syllables (60 + 3) in the stanza; the overall form AAB is mirrored in the musical form. These restraints apart, the musician (in this case certainly Adam himself) was free to exercise his own fine invention. He does not have to echo the rhyme-scheme in his melody; he does not have to (and apparently never does) reproduce the sound of individual words or phrases or their stresses—which vary continuously in any case from stanza to stanza. Still less is he concerned with the meaning of the words, individually or as a totality. His sole business is to create an *armonia* which will run alongside the verse, self-sufficient, a beautiful object in its own right.

Once again, Stevens's account is both imaginative and sound, based on close observation. Only with respect to his final remark, referring to the "sole business" of the poet/musician, must a question be raised, for surely the evidence is too strong to be ignored that the poet had a serious responsibility (or if not *directly* the poet, the performer who represented him) to see to it that the music would not in the slightest degree obscure the words. We must believe that at least in the early days of courtly love, the indwelling, mythic reality of the idea spurred the poet on to examine its intricacies and enigmas in ever-renewed minuteness of detail, while at the same time the results of the examination—the poet's "findings," so to speak—were to be shared with the whole courtly community. One can easily imagine that this sharing even had a competitive edge, each poet trying to outdo the other in terms of the art and insight that he showed in prodding his own psyche. Those listening to the song in order to grasp its full substance must be able to follow the progress of the poet's mind at close range, to experience along with him the conflicts of his feelings, to hear his changes of heart through his changes of voice. Since these last were stated explicitly in the text, nothing in the musical presentation could get in the way of the textual statement: the musical rhythm was permitted a certain freedom in distorting the textual accentuation, but only in the interests of heightening the effect of the sense contained in the words. If it ventured beyond that point and contributed to verbal unintelligibility, the meaning of the song, and along with it the very rationale of the courtly love ritual, were seriously compromised, if not irretrievably lost. To this extent, then, the music must be understood as being in a supportive relationship to the text, just as Augustine had conceived the role of chant with respect to liturgical prayer. And just as with chant, so in these songs the music transcended its conceptual vassalage and became a reciprocal power, diffusing into the far corners of the poem its own enhancing virtue.

This description of music's power to animate words—to give them a greater life—is meant to restore to music some of the rhetorical value lost sight of in Stevens's more purely aesthetic conception. The two views, however, by no means cancel each other out. At the same time, there remains one matter not considered by Stevens (and most probably not considered by him because he finds no relevance or validity in it) which calls for our attention: that is the possibility that the music, independent of the text, though presumably with nowhere near the text's variety, conveyed an expressive meaning; that is, it was designed (most likely, only in an intuitive, not self-conscious sense) to capture through its own sounds and gestures something of the fundamental stance of the courtly lover. To get at this matter more concretely, we begin by looking not at the music directly, but at a typical troubadour text. Any one of a number of texts could serve, since so many display the same psychological design: (1) opening avowal of "joi"; (2) expression of doubts of one's adequacy in face of the lady's superiority; (3) perception of the lady's coldness, leading to (4) almost total reversal of the opening mood, a threat to break the bonds of servitude; (5) quelling of rebellion, the restoration of feelings of acceptance and devotion; (6) reaffirmation of the contract.

Be m'an perdut by Bernard de Ventadorn is a good example of how far phase 4, the momentary reversal, can be taken. In Stanzas III and IV, the poet praises the lady, claiming he "cannot say anything bad is in her," and promising always to "desire her honor and her good." But in Stanza V, he declares himself to have "become available to all other women, anyone who wants to can get me to come to her;" the *leis de con* has risen up without warning, posing its rude challenge to courtliness.[12] To what extent the performance was expected to deal with this about-face we can never know, but the melody's strophic structure is clearly not geared to record or reflect such a change. Of course, just as a Fischer-Dieskau or a Prey will not sing identically the five verses of Schubert's *Das Wandern,* so one imagines a performer modulating the color and dynamic level of his voice to get across the changes of feeling dictated by the text: he can sing sweetly for Stanzas III and IV and bray a little for Stanza V. Still, the fact remains that the musical imagery gives no sign of the kinds of contrast immediately apparent in the text.

From this we can conclude along with Stevens that the musician is in no

way "concerned with the meaning of the words, individually or as a totality."
And yet, it does not at all follow that these melodies are unconcerned with the
meanings attached to courtly love, for to infer such a thing is to reject *a priori* the
possibility that a melody has expressive capacities independent of the words to
which it may be wedded. Specifically, what is being proposed here is a bipartite
division of expressive responsibility, in which both text and music of the *gran
chant courtois* deal with significant aspects of the meaning of the courtly love ethic
but approach these meanings in fundamentally different ways. The text treats the
love theme as a progress in quest of the courtly ideal; alternatively, one can think
of the volatility of the feelings described in the text—the initial enthusiasms, the
subsequent hesitations, the backtrackings—as being played out against the ideal
itself, which is all the time well understood as the underpinning of the entire
experience though no less difficult to achieve for all that. The melody, on the
other hand, seems to belie the difficulty: in its uniformity of musical idea, its
single-mindedness, its evenness, it gives the impression of stating the endpoint
of the ideal from the start and of sustaining it throughout. The melody is, as it
were, the steady background against which one registers the unsteadiness of the
text. If this is so, then the sole responsibility of the music would be to capture the
general tone of behavior underlying courtliness: refinement, a certain plaintive
reserve, humility, a certain quality of seriousness that is perhaps best summed up
in the oxymoron, "restrained fervor." By this conception, the text would adhere
strongly to the principle of *pathos*, recording as it does all the vicissitudes of
the courtly man's emotional life as he strives for courtliness, whereas the music
would embody the *ethos* of courtly love directly and without complication.

Building on this hypothesis, we must now examine the melody of a courtly
love song independent of its text, in order to determine what in the anatomy
of the melody would be particularly susceptible of realizing the expressive and
ethical ends just described (Example 5.1). The contention among numbers of
modern scholars that troubadour songs and Gregorian chant are closely related
in style seems greatly exaggerated: differences in rhythmic conception and formal
proportions far outweigh similarities in range and modal usage. The symmetries
within stanzas of a typical *canso* and the structural principle of open and closed
endings are effectively absent in chant. Compositional balance is surely achieved
in chant, but mainly through melodic accretion and the strategic placement of
tonal high and low points—processes essentially empirical and intuitive. Balance
in the troubadour *canso*, on the other hand, is dualistic and *a priori*, the product of
a pair of segments designed to couple and complete each other.

But it is in regard to the segments themselves—in the shaping of an individual line—that one discovers the crucial stylistic distinction: for the chief building
block of the courtly love melody is nothing more nor less than the sustained
arching gesture we think of today as the generic *musical phrase*. Or, turning this
proposition around, we may say that our modern conception of the phrase can
trace its roots back to the courtly love song. In Gregorian chant this sustained

Example 5.1: Bernard de Ventadorn, Courtly love song

arching gesture is not the chief unit of discourse; a "phrase" as such surely figures as part of the chant's musical language, but it is built up of functionally
predominant melodic "cells" as opposed to being presented as a single, unitary
shape. What strikes one about the phrase in the courtly love song is its linear
integrity, the effect it gives of sighting the endpoint of the line from the start.
The ornaments in this phrase are not "cells" in the Gregorian sense but rhythmic
accents geared to propelling the line forward to its conclusion. This explains why
ornaments are most commonly found in league with the cadential figures, in that
phase of the line which brings the line to rest. Gregorian chant "murmurs": not
only in the extended pieces of the repertoire but in the relatively brief ones also,
the chant-line rises only gradually and somewhat waywardly, emerging from,
rather than cutting, the silence and often falling back on itself before finding its
way to the top of the melodic arch. The line of the courtly love song is, in addition
to being more clear-cut in shape, less upwardly directed toward a point of climax
and more forwardly directed toward a point of arrival.

     To reassure ourselves that we are not confusing the qualities produced by a
performance of a courtly love song with those presumed to belong to the melody
itself, we should imagine for a moment a performer delivering the text of a
song without its music. In such a case, the performer would recite the words in
controlled and unhurried fashion in order to convey the prevailing high-minded
tone, and also with a mixture of sweetness and vibrancy of voice to keep a
balance between the underlying passion and the ultimate refinement of effect:
refinement, in other words, must never become so delicate as to eradicate fervor.
Turning back to Example 5.1, we observe that the melodic lines readily lend
themselves to this kind of delivery. The gradually building arch permits each
pitch of the melody (at least, each pitch set syllabically) to be heard distinctly and
solidly, and it also encourages consistency of sound and connectedness between
successive pitches.

We have already noted the uniformity of musical idea for the courtly love song as a whole—the evenness with which the melody pursues a single mood throughout. "Evenness," however, is itself a mood; more precisely, it implies a certain character, a certain capacity to sustain feeling, to be steadfast. Now we see that this evenness of feeling may be transmitted even more intensely on the level of the phrase than on the level of the entire song, for it is in the carrying power of the phrase, in its directedness, in its unified movement toward the point of arrival (a motion, moreover, which demands being sung in one breath), that an image is invoked of a man who expresses himself clearly and straightforwardly, with a sense of purpose, without any hint of the hesitations and lapses of self-control that show through periodically in the text. One thing the phrase of the courtly love song does not do; it does not lend itself to declamatory performance, the kind of expression that seeks out specific points in the line for special emphasis and which is found in many types of later melody (in early 17th-century monody, for instance, or in 19th-century Italian opera). That kind of insistence—that more open show of passion—would subvert the basic purpose of the song; it would suggest that passion had gotten the upper hand. But if any degree of vehemence in the performance of a courtly love song is as inappropriate to the melodic contours of the song as it is to the whole conception of courtship, then what this conclusively suggests is that the behavior of a courtly love melody is thoroughly appropriate to the conception of courtly behavior in general.

Because the behavior in question is deemed virtuous in the eyes of the society that envisioned it, we can reaffirm the ethical significance of the courtly love song as being the song's ultimate *raison d'être*. In that respect, the courtly love tradition offers a parallel both to Christian thinking and to the Greco-Roman past. But more important may be its implications for the future. Singing the pangs of love has had an unbroken history in the West since the mid-11th century; also, the idea of being well regarded in the community continues to carry some weight today. Yet, these two basic ideas of the culture, once so closely intertwined in the courtly love song, no longer have any relation: with the passing of the courtly love code has disappeared any connection between singing a love song and the cultivation of social virtue. What has *not* disappeared, by contrast, is the musical image-type to which the courtly love song first gave rise—the sustained, arching melodic line which captured the steadfastness of the knight/poet and which in later ages has come to stand for emotional sincerity and firmness of conviction. Virtually every succeeding age furnishes examples of the type, as the following excerpts will at least partially show (Examples 5.2a–e). In the greater number of these images, connotations of love and courtliness play no part; the connotation of "seriousness," however, is in all of them.

By "seriousness" here, we are speaking of a kind of expression characteristic not of a situation directly, but of a person who recognizes the importance of the situation and then shows the mental force and self-possession to deal with it accordingly. Such force of character is especially admired in Western culture, though mention of it here is not intended in the least to suggest that persons

Example 5.2a: Machaut, Lai

Loy- au- té,   que point ne de-   lay,   Wuet sans de-   lay

Guillaume de Machaut: Lay "Loyauté, que point ne delay" from "The Complete Works of
Guillaume de Machaut," *Polyphonic Music of the Fourteenth Century*, volume II, ed. Leo
Schrade, Editions de l'Oiseau-Lyre, Monaco 1974, p.1. Copyright Margarita M. Hanson,
Editions de l'Oiseau-Lyre. Les Remparts, Monaco 1974.

Example 5.2b: Handel, Air from *Semele*

Where e'er   you walk   cool   gales shall fan the glade.

Example 5.2c: Bach, Fugue No. 8, *WTC* I

Example 5.2d: Brahms, Violin sonata, Op. 100

Example 5.2e: Bartok, No. 1 from *Nine Little Piano Pieces*

© Copyright 1927 by Universal Edition; Copyright renewed. Copyright and renewal
assigned to Boosey & Hawkes, Inc. Reprinted by permission.

who fail to conform to the type are unadmirable. Nor is there any intent to cast
an aesthetic value judgment in favor of musical images which embody this kind
of character and against those which do not. The two excerpts given below are
models of fine melody (Examples 5.3a and b). But in the first, Monteverdi permits
Orfeo to howl and declaim rather uncontrollably under the weight of fresh grief,
while Verdi brings his "troubadour," Manrico, to a pitch of excitement that is

clearly beyond the limits of restrained expression we have been trying to define for the better part of this chapter. It is not even that the two examples at hand are not "serious" in a broader sense: the situations presented and the responses to them are all serious; the entire proceedings of both cases are intended to be taken seriously and are willingly accepted as such by audiences. The point is that this seriousness is of a different order from the kind we have been considering. Conspicuously absent is the ingredient of Apollonian sobriety discussed at length at the end of Chapter 2. Monteverdi and Verdi surely think of their heroes as admirable and virtuous human beings, and we have no cause to think of them otherwise. But these heroes are not strictly "ethical" according to the criteria laid out here. They are not ethical in a Platonic sense, and they are no more so according to the spirit of courtly love. Their sentiments and behavior must be judged against other standards, against a different *ethos*. Though older than Plato, this *ethos* must wait for a time considerably later than the troubadours in order to be rediscovered in music.

Example 5.3a: Monteverdi, *Orfeo*, Act II

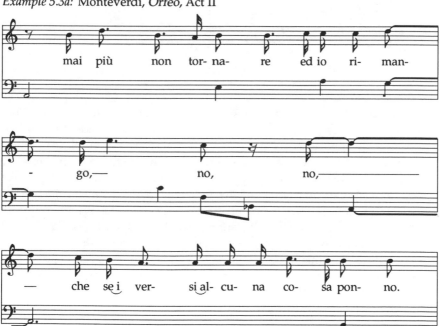

mai più non tor-na- re ed io ri- man- go,— no, no,— che se i ver- si al- cu- na co- sa pon- no.

"L'Orfeo" by Claudio Monteverdi. Copyright © 1923, J&W Chester, Ltd. (London). All rights for the U.S. & Canada controlled by G. Schirmer, Inc. (New York). International copyright secured. All rights reserved. Used by permission.

Example 5.3b: Verdi, Manrico's aria from *Il Trovatore,* Act III

Narrative Songs, Dance Songs

The present chapter should have just ended, judging from its title. But however much the courtly love song is the genre most closely identified in our minds with the troubadours and trouvères (and very probably in their minds as well), the fact remains that a sizeable amount of the troubadour and trouvère repertoire falls outside of the courtly love category. The remaining repertoire covers an enormous diversity of genres—alba, joc parti, sirventes, chanson de geste, lai, chanson de toile, pastourelle, rondeau, carole—though the diversity can be somewhat reduced by classification into either narrative or dance types. If only to put the courtly love song into clearer perspective, it is worth pondering this literature briefly. Setting aside the narrative genres, whose musical elaboration is for the most part equivalent to the recitation formulas commonly associated with the lessons and epistles of chant, we will concentrate here on the dance pieces, in part because of their relatively greater musical development, but mainly because they are, like the courtly love song, the source of an image-type which has permanent repercussions for later Western music.

Medieval dance and dance music are nothing if not essentially social phe-nomena. Whether it is a question of the self-enclosed, self-conscious society of the court or of the more open dependency of the "folk" who lived at the court's edges, the dance was a highly ordered mechanism by which a group could manifest its identity and solidarity. At the same time the essential secularity of dance was assured, indeed forced, in the Middle Ages by prohibitions against dance in the

Church. Whereas in societies before Christianity its functions had ranged over the entire realm of human experience, in the Christian mind dance was destined to be linked up with worldly pleasure and diversion. Between folk and court dancing there was doubtless some difference in outlook as well as style, the folk using dance for specific festive occasions, the court primarily interested in showing "how the privileged few wished and were able to enjoy their pastime."[13] But through all of it, the mood of joyous celebration was paramount. The poetry and prose works of the later Middle Ages are studded with descriptions of festivities and amusements, real and imaginary, in which dance plays the central role. The joy depicted in these accounts is neither the hard-won serenity that comes with Christian piety nor the anticipation of the heightened virtue promised by courtly love; it is simple, spontaneous delight, the high spirits and lightheartedness that rise to the surface when the impulse to play in human nature is given free rein. Dancing in this spirit signals the release of tension, the need to leave one's worries behind and let off steam ("music for a while, that all our cares beguile," to quote a later, more highbrow commentary on the same theme). To what extent the music of the dance song embodies these contents must be demonstrated here with one solitary example; but one example should suffice, since the basic features of the type are so persistent (Example 5.4).

Example 5.4: Anonymous, Spring song

Short phrases, equal phrase lengths, "open" and "closed" phrase-endings, and refrains are all typical, as are the frequent repetitions of whole phrases or phrase-segments. Of course, the single feature that most clearly differentiates the dance song from those we have been discussing up until now is the presence of meter, the fact that this is music governed by a beat and with fixed relations between durations of individual notes. Scholars are generally agreed that because dance songs presupposed group activity, a metrical structure is also presupposed, whether or not the song in question may have been written down in measured notation. But practical considerations aside, the internal symmetries of music and text in this piece, as in the dance song literature as a whole, make anything but a metrical interpretation virtually unthinkable.[14] And, more than any other single factor, this metrical distinction qualifies the melody of the dance song in terms of its identity as a gesture, the gesture in this case having bodily as well as vocal implications.

The tendency among modern performers to play virtually every medieval dance song at a brisk, often breakneck, speed has conditioned us to think of the entire genre as being highly vigorous, if not frenetic, in character. Were there heard, at least in the courts, if not in the villages, dances more in the stately spirit of the later pavane and sarabande or with the sinuous and flowing movements associated with minuets and Ländler? There being no dance treatises from the period and precious few choreographic hints to be gleaned from even as detailed a description of "carolling" as appears in the *Roman de la Rose*, we would be hard put to imagine the likelihood of a diversity of types equivalent to those found in dance manuals of the Renaissance and Baroque periods. Conversely, the written evidence in the medieval manuscripts does not support such a diversity; in the majority of cases the musical notation, together with the textual rhythms, conforms readily to the "skipping" pattern of rhythmic mode No. 1 (see example above). And this skipping pattern in its own turn readily lends itself to a rendering in a quick, lively tempo (though we should be careful to remember that it does not necessitate such a rendering).

But we will miss the central point of the issue if we concentrate too heavily on the historical situation and try to establish whether all medieval dance song was lusty and exuberant and in the equivalent of modern $6/8$ time. The undisputed fact is that dancing as a generic activity was connected in the medieval mind with diversion and rejoicing, whether the dance was slow or fast. To imagine how little the character of a specific dance affects the actual pleasure of the performance we have only to think of the example of a later age, where dancing the pavane was presumably as enjoyable to the participant as dancing the galliard or the volta. The crucial question to ask, then, is not what communal dancing has to do with mirth and merriment, since dancing is assumed by definition to be a pleasurable pastime, but why mirth and merriment should be connected with lively and vigorous movement as opposed to staid and restrained movement, or—to rephrase the question in more historical terms—why lively and vigorous dance music should have come to embody mirthful and merry states of mind.

Obvious as the connection may appear at first glance, the story leading up to the connection is complicated and only the briefest outline will be attempted here. There seems little doubt, however, that the story has its beginnings in the theme of *ethos* that has held center stage in the last three chapters. In a culture dominated by the notion that the "ethical" man was one who conducted himself in a dignified manner, that is, moved with deliberate and controlled bodily gestures and spoke in quiet, modest tones of voice, it was inevitable that lively and excitable behavior would be looked upon as, if not actually "unethical," at least as lacking in substance and seriousness. One is reminded of Auerbach's assessment of the high and low styles of ancient literature, in which comedy adopts a low style because its concerns, unlike the dignified and elevated proceedings of tragedy, are of no particular significance and because it treats of men who, according to Aristotle, are "worse [i.e., less "ethical"] than we know them today." The identification of quick and excited movement with play and diversion—with human experience devoid of sustained effort and development—is thus of early vintage; and it shows no sign of change in the Middle Ages, since Christian humility and courtly love, as we have already noted, share with Greek moral philosophy a common theory of self-restraint as a cardinal virtue.[15] The question is not so much of directly suppressing emotion as of controlling behavior, for, as the theory goes, all men may equally feel inner excitement, but only the "ethical man," through force of character, will inhibit outward show of his emotion; those not adequately trained in the ethical discipline will be unable to resist giving vent to the whoops and cries that signal an excited state.

To be sure, the therapeutic value of periodically loosening the controls was as much recognized during the Middle Ages as at any other time in Western history, to the extent that "surrendering to one's excitement" was an officially sanctioned act on certain designated days throughout the year—May Day, harvest time, the joyous feasts of the liturgical calendar. By and large, the Church took much the same view of the dance songs associated with spring revels and Twelfth-night celebrations as had Aristotle of the "purgative melodies" of the Dionysian rite, which, we remember, he speaks of as affording "harmless delight to people." "Harmless" is precisely the word to qualify a delight to which no lasting significance is attached. As in the stories told by Guillaume IX in his poems of the *leis de con*, the experiences in question here are unconnected, random and sporadic; they change nothing; they lead nowhere. But this is the very nature of lightheartedness; anything less transient or more reflective would rob it of its essential purpose. We may know little about how the medieval dance song was actually performed and still less about certain very basic matters such as tempo and dynamics. Yet, we are certain of its overriding function, which was to permit the dancers to work off excess tension and temporarily release them from their cares. To carry out this function in the promptest way possible, the music would have to make the dancers really move. The anonymous spring song above, *A l'entrada del temps clar*, with its fast pace and steady beat, strongly accented skipping rhythms and robust shouts of "Eya," satisfies the paradigm in all essential respects. One imagines, too, that performance of these dance songs was sufficiently regulated so as to keep the proceedings from degenerating into "mad Bacchanalian fury": the object was clearly not to lose control and risk the evil consequences that could result from wild behavior, but rather to *loosen* controls and spread the festive mood. At a later stage of musical history, Monteverdi will show us how excited music can express anger and warlike feeling, in short, take on serious and even tragic significance. But until that time, excited music would be associated with mirth and merriment, and we owe it to the Middle Ages to have provided through its dance songs at least one definitive image of the comic archetype.

Notes

1. The main points of Stevens's theory are presented in John Stevens, *Words and Music in the Middle Ages: Song, Narrative, Dance and Drama, 1050–1350,* Chapter I ("The Courtly Chanson"), pp. 13–47.
2. Frederick Goldin, ed., *Lyrics of the Troubadours and Trouvères,* pp. 108–111.
3. *Ibid.,* p. 113.
4. *Ibid.,* p. 43.
5. *Ibid.,* p. 7.
6. *Ibid.,* p. 8.
7. *Ibid.,* p. 12.
8. Quoted in James Anderson Winn, *Unsuspected Eloquence,* p. 78.
9. Stevens, p. 30.
10. Richard H. Hoppin, *Medieval Music,* p. 280.
11. Stevens, p. 38.
12. The poem is given in full in Goldin, pp. 134–137. A transcription of the melody appears as No. 18b in Archibald T. Davison and Willi Apel, ed., *Historical Anthology of Music,* p. 15.
13. Stevens, p. 164.
14. Stevens, p. 189, speaking of the music for *refrains* and *rondeaux,* writes: "to describe one is virtually to describe them all."
15. Plato's wisdom on this point is well taken: he sees the possibility of eventual and permanent alteration in our inner life—not, however, by working it out directly but by working on its outward manifestations. See especially Scott Buchanan, ed., *The Portable Plato,* p. 379 and pp. 672–673.

PART III

Classical Humanism: Pathos

6 Reawakening of Pathos

In his *Utopia* of 1516, Thomas More credits his Utopian inhabitants with the following:[1]

There is one thing in which they have excelled us for a long time: all their music, whether played on the organ or sung, imitates and expresses the natural affections, accommodates the sound to the thing according to whether the *oratio* is happy, placid, dark, lugubrious, or angry; also the sense of the subject is represented in the form of the melody, in order to affect, penetrate, inflame the souls of the listeners.

Aside from the context of the passage, which permits us to know that More is referring specifically to liturgical music, this statement is not easy to assess. Is it merely a wistful hope on the part of an avowed humanist that Europeans might follow the Utopian lead? Or does it reflect an awareness of the latest Franco-Netherlandish style? The reference to "all their music" could mean that More had already noted the presence of an affective element in the sacred music of his own day and was urging its further development. Or perhaps it is only a disguised message to English composers to emulate their continental counterparts. Whatever the case may be, the significance of More's remarks for us lies less in *his* experience with European music than in the way we have come to regard that music today. Scholars are generally agreed that a new consciousness about music—the very consciousness More is encouraging—was taking form around the year 1500 and that the best evidence of that development is to be found in the motets of Josquin. While this conventional wisdom need not be contested, there is good reason to ponder why historians have willingly accorded to Josquin's work qualities that they would deny all music written previously. When we come to read the reasons traditionally offered to explain this apparently sudden interest in musical *pathos*, we find that they are rooted, virtually all of them, in assumptions that have not undergone much recent scrutiny. Certain of these reasons, in fact—the supposedly new "expressive" relations between tone and text, the influence of humanism—raise more questions on first notice than they answer, especially when the issue involves sacred music; for as a program dedicated to re-creating the ideals and artifacts of Classical antiquity, would not humanism have come into serious conflict with Christian interests? Was not the Church, or at least the Church ritual, off limits to the secularizing influences of humanism—sanctuary against the uncertainties humanism provoked with its emphasis on pluralism and human choice? Approaching the problem from a different direction, we meet similar incongruities. We are told that the Italian humanists of the 15th century favored a soloistic vocal music sung to the accompaniment of a lyre, in the spirit of ancient Greek practice. What could such a style have in common with the craft of the *oltremontani*, who practiced polyphony and whose most impressive advances in the later 15th century had been made in the realm of music for the Mass ordinary?

If these apparent anomalies can eventually be resolved into a coherent picture, it takes some doing to bring them to that point. As a first step in the process, it is absolutely necessary to recognize that More's statement taken on its own—that is, divorced from the immediate musical realities which may have motivated it or to which it could be applied—offers nothing new either in substance or language; statements essentially identical to it turn up in medieval treatises from the 10th century on. Stevens's study, already cited, assembles enough information to leave no doubt that the notion (normally associated in our minds with post-medieval times) of a power in music to capture the sense of a text was already alive in the Middle Ages. In recent years several useful studies have emerged that try to make sense of the text/music relationship in medieval music, examining it from various points of view. Of these, Stevens's book is the most comprehensive and important, though the contributions of Leo Treitler and Don Randel are also considerable.[2] The thrust of all these authors' treatment of the subject is mainly structural, in keeping with their common conviction that grammar and number form the basis of the medieval attitude toward the setting of words to music. Stevens, however, goes beyond the structural aspects and deals with aspects of meaning as well—indeed, deals with them so authoritatively (gathering such good materials together and asking the hard questions in such a forthright and original manner) that he leaves to those coming after him little to do but to gloss his remarks and propose a conclusion with a somewhat different emphasis from his own.

Of course, much of the information found in Stevens has been available (even in English translation) for some time (for instance, Guido's "ethical" assignments with respect to the eight Church modes in Chapter XIV of the *Micrologus*).[3] But the customary manner among scholars of dealing with this information has been either to record it without comment or to pass it off as some recrudescence of Neoplatonic theory. Stevens takes a fresh look at the material and makes a serious attempt to interpret its significance. The observation he quotes from the *Musica Enchiriadis* is particularly revealing: "It is necessary that the emotional characteristics ("affectus") of the song should imitate the emotional characteristics of the things which are being sung about."[4] The shift in emphasis from *ethos* to *pathos*, suggested here by the key word "affectus," appears to be borne out by the descriptive language with which the author of the *Musica Enchiriadis* follows up his general statement: "peaceful," "glad-sounding," "mournful," "harsh" are all affective, not ethical terms. Nevertheless, as there is no effort to link these characterizations to concrete musical examples, it is impossible to know whether the author is describing actual music of his own day or prescribing a kind of music he would like to see composed—or whether in fact he is speaking of chant or a music outside the liturgy. Guido in his time and Johannes of Afflighem a generation later provide somewhat clearer applications of their ideas; we know from context that they both have chant basically in mind, and their characterizations are specific to each of the eight Church modes. But these characterizations present such a confusion of ethical and affective categories—according to Johannes, a "ceremonious" first mode, a "staid, matronly" eighth mode (ethical distinctions), a "tearful" sixth mode (affective distinction)—that we are left wondering how these might form any consistent theory of musical expression, much less bear on the practice of their own day.[5]

As stated earlier, the common musicological wisdom has been that Guido's and Johannes's remarks are too subjective to correspond to any generally accepted view of medieval liturgical music in their own time, merely reflecting a pious effort to perpetuate the form, without the substance, of some shadowy classical authority. Stevens at least makes an effort to identify that authority by locating the origin of the fundamental idea.[6]

The genesis of the idea ... appears to go back to the ancient rhetoricians. Quintilian had from the Greeks a threefold view of 'music': it consisted ... of dance, melody, and words. The threefold skills of the orator—gesture, voice-modulation and verbal arrangement—correspond to these. The orator, he goes on to argue, in order to be fully 'affective' must conform his voice to the *affectus* (emotional characteristics?) of what is being said. Lofty things will be delivered (*canere*, to sing or sound) in an elevated manner, joyful things sweetly, things indifferent in a light style.

In medieval scholarship, the inclination has been to favor Platonic *ethos* over Quintilian rhetoric as the source of Guido's and Johannes's modal characterizations; and at first glance, Guido's and Johannes's method might well seem to derive from the seminal description about imitating a noble warrior in Book III of Plato's *Republic*. But method and motives are different things: Stevens's insight in tracing the medieval taste for "affectus" back to rhetoric leads us to the further insight that the main interest of rhetoric is in *variety* of expression, whether verbal or musical, as opposed to the reductionist attitude of ethical philosophy. Plato is well aware of the range of the effects of which music is capable, but he forbids the use of all but those which will lead to temperateness and sober courage. And Augustine, though recognizing the occasional usefulness of the high and middle styles of ancient rhetoric for Christian purposes, ultimately champions the ethical viewpoint when he opts for reducing Christian expression, both in regard to preaching and to chant, to the "sermo humilis." The true rhetorician, on the other hand, embraces the whole range of effects: Johannes never for a moment suggests eliminating the sixth and seventh modes on grounds that the "tearful voice" of the former and the "spectacular leaps" of the latter might be ethically inferior to the "ceremonious peregrinations" of the first mode. Guido and Johannes accept all the modes with their diverse characters equally, because diversity being the law of taste, there ought to be a kind of music to suit each taste. This is clearly not the voice of the Greek moralist or the Church father speaking here; taste, in the ethical view, is something to be shaped, not indulged. The chief advice these theorists give for making a melody is to vary the music "according to the sense of the words" and to determine carefully "which mode is appropriate to which matter."[7] There is, in short, a sense in which appropriateness is an important criterion, but this sense is rhetorical, not ethical.

To give Johannes's and Guido's expressive views more credence than has been given in the past could well have significant consequences for the way in which we think about medieval music in general and about chant in particular. However, correlations between the theorists' ideas and actual examples from the chant literature are very difficult to assess. Of Johannes's modal characterizations Stevens writes: "The implications of these seemingly fanciful epithets are never drawn out; they do not seem to correspond to anything commonly experienced in the various modes. One is simply left guessing."[8]

In a related matter, we are not left guessing. Toward the end of his advice on how to compose a song, Johannes offers some examples from chant of what he considers to be expressions of exultation and sorrow in musical sound: "the antiphon called 'Rex autem David' not only in its words but even in its melody seems to sound forth sorrow."[9] Stevens supplies the Sarum version of this lament of David for his son Absalom and comments: "If [this antiphon] 'expresses sorrow' ... it is sorrow of an extraordinarily restrained and undemonstrative kind. The antiphon appears, in fact, to have a typical eighth-mode antiphon melody." He then gives the melody of the antiphon for the Benedictus from the Mass, also in the eighth mode, and adds the following:[10]

This joyful message for Lauds of Advent Sunday is presented in the same restrained, un-melismatic, conjunct style as David's lament and uses some of the same melodic formulae. It is hard to avoid the conclusion that Johannes Afflighemensis does what many musicians since have done—he reads into the melody of 'Rex autem David' his own emotional response to a highly emotional text ... I do not wish to seem eager to discredit the attempt of Johannes Afflighemensis to make contemporary sense of an implied relationship between words and music which he inherited in a very rudimentary shape from his predecessors. That he should want to make sense is a striking fact in itself.

Stevens concludes that this theory of Johannes's—if "theory" it should be called—is finally too rudimentary in its own turn to serve as a true conceptual framework for examining the text/music relationship in either the chant or the nonliturgical repertoire of the Middle Ages. Returning to the central thesis of his book, he says that the real medieval conception of a text/music relationship is:[11]

a matter of parallel 'harmonies,' agreements of phrase and structure, of balance and 'number', so that in song the mind and ear may be 'doubly charmed by a double melody'. Such a view does not exclude from the effects of music emotional experiences of great power … It does, however, seem to exclude—or at least, patently and consistently neglects—the close and detailed expressive relations between words and music which we find in the songs of later periods. For this reason a theory of expressive sound closely related to subject matter, a theory apparently derived from antique rhetoric, has only a limited place in 'the medieval experience of music'. It remains marginal and never finds a comfortable place in the Great Synthesis.

This is Stevens's final word on the subject, and it is probably the most thoroughly substantiated word to date. Though he does not say so explicitly, he suggests that as text expression was not of central and consistent interest to the medieval musician, there is no reason that it should be a central preoccupation of musical scholarship today: by focusing undue attention on the expressive area, the contemporary scholar runs the risk of reading meanings into medieval melodies (in the same way that Stevens presumes Johannes to have done) that were never intended by the creators themselves. Stevens's position is eminently sensible—indeed, probably the only position that can be upheld with any assurance, given the present state of our evidence. And yet, at the risk of appearing less than sensible, let us contemplate for a moment another possibility. Even granting that Johannes's observations hardly amount to a theory of expression in the modern sense and thus supply us with very little to go on, is this eventually his fault or ours? Rather than cast suspicion on his inclination to read meanings into chant melodies, it may be less presumptuous of us to credit him with the ability to detect distinctions in chant that would be impossible for us to detect, cut off as we are from the living tradition with which he was totally familiar. This reality of a "living tradition" raises the distinct possibility that Johannes's characterizations are not purely subjective, but *conventional*, shared by a number, perhaps an entire group, of individuals and linked to actual regional practices of performing chant. We should remember that his treatise had a certain vogue in its own time, and that it would have been read with respect by a considerable following.[12] And finally, the subjectivity of his observations is somewhat beside the point, for what is really at stake is the existence or nonexistence of a fundamental conception. That a notion of text expression, however vague, embryonic, or derivative it may look to us, was known to music of the later Middle Ages and was, moreover, based on affective as well as ethical criteria, seems to be the essential, and undeniable, point.

   Furthermore, a correspondence between these criteria and the musical material may have more basis in reality than has previously been claimed. Reconsidering Stevens's comparison of the two eighth-mode antiphons mentioned above, we must agree with him that the music reveals nothing of the joy or sorrow depicted in the texts; but it should also be recognized that neither joy nor sorrow, according to Johannes, is characteristic of the eighth mode. This is not to say that the music is *neutral* with respect to the texts; rather the music can be construed to complement *both* texts, the joyful as well as the sorrowful, in the same "staid and matronly" manner, to take Johannes's characterization at face value. Stevens, in fact, calls the two melodies in question (if not the mode in its totality) "restrained," which is in essential agreement with Johannes's view; and we know from everyday experience, let alone musical experience, that it is indeed not at all inconsistent to be alternately demonstrative or subdued ("restrained," "staid") about one's sorrow or joy, depending on the occasion and one's mood. In the present case, inconsistency would have resulted only if the joyful Benedictus of Advent had been set to the "tearful" sixth mode; text and music would have presented, in terms of Johannes's expressive scheme, a direct confrontation of opposing affections. As it stands, the staid eighth mode, connoting an aspect not of emotion but of behavior, is theoretically appropriate to all affective states: it does not exactly meet the content of a joyous or sorrowful text on its own terms, but it indicates a precise way in which joy or sorrow may be expressed.

In anticipation of later discussions in this book it may be well to point out at this juncture that the content of all post-medieval music, virtually without exception, will be treated as being composed of both an ethical and an affective factor and that this is considered to hold for instrumental music as well as for music joined to a text. If such a treatment seems ill-suited to the antiphons discussed above, it is only because it does violence to one of musicology's most sacred cows, namely, the vision of a placid, emotionally detached medieval Christian ritual whose chief embodiment would be the chant melody itself; the intrusion of everyday human emotion into this hushed otherworld is a difficult, nearly impossible, proposition for us to accept. But, in fact, there are instances recorded in which the element of human emotion did intrude. The decorum of Christian ritual described in Chapter 4 is an ethical ideal from which departures to a greater or lesser degree were doubtless made in everyday practice. By A.D. 1100, the chant melodies were fairly uniformly disseminated in Western Europe, but they could hardly be expected to be so uniformly sung. Ailred of Rievaulx gives a scathing report of the singing he heard (presumably in his own district), in which he compares the sounds of the choir to "horses neighing" and describes the typical singer as "imitating the agonies of the dying or of those experiencing ecstasy. All the time his whole body is in movement, with the kinds of gestures used by actors."[13] Clearly, this tendency to dramatize the chant strikes Bishop Ailred as unseemly behavior—a breach of decorum—but one wonders if there were not parishes and locales where such tendencies would have been better received. Could Guido d'Arezzo's rather enthusiastic advice to composers of chant to modulate their melodies in accordance with the affections of the text not be stimulated by practices in his own district (a section of the European world, it should be remembered, where open displays of emotion are a cultural norm of long standing)? Rather than reject this highly speculative scenario out of hand, let us carry it to its logical conclusion. Stevens, as already noted, traces the roots of these medieval ideas about affective music to ancient rhetoric, and he does so because the Greek rhetoricians had likened their own art to musical performance, as well as to dance and dramatic acting. As something of an actor, the ancient rhetorician was expected to adopt different "voices" in order to underline the changing ideas contained in his speeches. Similarly, we can imagine the medieval singer modulating his voice to fit the changing "characters" contained in Johannes's modal ascriptions: he would inflect broadly and ceremoniously for Mode 1, assume a more ingratiating, flattering air for Mode 4, take on the sounds of a staid matron for Mode 8. Improbable as this hypothesis may appear, we must recognize that much of its improbable character stems from the challenge it poses to the traditional picture of medieval Christian ritual. An emotionalistic rendering of chant strikes us, no less than it did Bishop Ailred, as "unseemly behavior" because the *ethos* of the Christian liturgy is at its core a conception of decorum, a vision of correct behavior.

Eventually, the difference between Stevens's interpretation and the one offered here comes down to a question of emphasis. In his discussion of liturgical drama, Stevens writes that in addition to the melodies themselves, "the style of singing ... conforms to the demands of liturgical propriety, not to the demands of a dramatic situation humanly conceived."[14] The choice of premises he proposes confers an inescapable tone of either-or on the conclusion: against liturgical propriety is pitted nothing less than a thoroughgoing dramatic situation. These being the alternatives, we have no choice but to infer an intrinsic opposition between affective expression and the *ethos* of the Christian liturgy. Stevens's reluctance to imagine the possibility of overcoming this opposition is more than understandable and, in the case of chant, may be well taken. Yet, by the beginning of the 16th century, the very possibility Stevens would disallow for chant has become the literal reality for sacred polyphony; the blending of the affective and the liturgically appropriate is precisely what historians accept as the norm for Church music of the high Renaissance. It would of course be unreasonable to equate medieval Church conditions with those of ducal chapels in Renaissance Italy, but it is not so unreasonable to believe that the gap between medieval and Renaissance concepts of "emotional music" may not be as wide as has been traditionally thought. In any event, in both theory and practice, medieval music produces enough evidence on its own to show that the spirit of *pathos* did not have to await the advent of Renaissance humanism for its musical reawakening.

The Impact of Humanism

Assuming for the moment that the pathetic principle must have evolved over a far more protracted period—and also more unevenly—than has been represented in the past, there is still no reason to revise our thinking about the significance of the year 1500 in the evolutionary process. We can continue to believe that this moment marks a decisive turning point in the history of Western music, provided cultural and aesthetic considerations, in addition to questions of style and technique, are factored into the account. Up until the mid-1960s, it was customary to look upon the development leading to the art of Josquin and his contemporaries as a northern phenomenon explicable purely in terms of polyphonic techniques. Since the appearance, however, of Nino Pirrotta's pathbreaking article, "Music and Cultural Tendencies in Fifteenth-Century Italy," it is impossible to ignore the implications for Franco-Netherlandish polyphony of a nonpolyphonic secular music of Italian origin with a predominantly literary bias.[15] Hindsight leads us to wonder why the Italian influence was not obvious to specialists in Renaissance music prior to Pirrotta, given the fact that Josquin and the greater number of his northern compatriots came to maturity as singers attached to one Italian chapel or another. The answer is almost equally obvious: the Italian music in question was never written down, with the result that the historians had nothing concrete to go on. Pirrotta's argument is all the more ingenious, then, for having been assembled from totally extramusical evidence. The overriding value of the argument lies in its having supplied a rationale for Josquin's achievement where none existed before. Scholars were not ignorant of the formal/rhetorical synthesis that Josquin's art represented for the polyphony of his period, but they were vague as to why the period should be ripe for such a synthesis in the first place. Pirrotta clarifies this point by drawing a direct link between the craze of mid-15th-century Italy for ancient rhetoric and the new expressiveness of the solo singing in favor at the courts—an "unwritten tradition" of music making based on hallowed ancient models.

One symptom of this link can be found in the subtly changing content of contemporary musical treatises (whose numbers alone show a dramatic rise in the late years of the century). Much of the material in these works is still heavily weighted toward the metaphysical and speculative—toward the issues, in other words, that had preoccupied Greek and medieval thinkers; the ghosts of Pythagoras and Boethius continue to loom large. But the growing rhetorical thrust of the material is unmistakable: hardly a treatise is produced which does not include some reference to the power of music over the affections. Practical advice to composers is inevitably accompanied by the observation that the chief aim of composition is to move the listeners to particular feelings.

The place rhetoric comes to occupy in the educational system of 15th-century Italy—in the everyday life of the average "citizen"—seems nothing less than all-encompassing. Not that its place in medieval education had been minimal: rhetoric was one of the seven liberal arts, and fundamental writings on the subject were known all the way through early Christian times and closely studied. The essential difference between the medieval and Renaissance situations is not so much a question of access as of attitude. With an eye constantly out for how rhetoric might serve Christian purposes, the medieval view was selective and sectarian. The Renaissance rhetorician, by contrast, embraces his art unconditionally, taking delight in all the ancient documents without prejudice and with a particular appreciation for the refinement and elegance of the classical Latin vis-à-vis the scholastic Latin of the Church and the medieval universities. More than a mere compendium of techniques and strategies, rhetoric takes on once again the virtues in shaping the whole individual it had originally been conceived to possess by Cicero and Quintilian. "True eloquence" presupposes wisdom; the "perfect citizen" is the "best orator." As an art reaching out in both private and public directions, rhetoric contributes on the one hand to the enhancement of aesthetic sensibility, on the other to feelings of self-assurance without which an individual cannot effectively navigate in public life. "No quality is of more vital concern to the state than public speaking, especially that aspect which relates to civic discussion; for the ends of the state depend upon the ability of men of affairs to persuade each other into or out of a proposed course of action."[16]

The interests of rhetoric contain in microcosm the most comprehensive and deep-seated impulses of Renaissance thought, crystallized in the program called "humanism." Kristeller writes, "Classical humanism was, if not the only, certainly the most characteristic and pervasive intellectual current of that period."[17] More than an intellectual current, humanism came to be an entire way of life, for it affected the world of action quite as profoundly as the world of ideas. The artifacts of antiquity held an endless fascination for humanist intellectuals but only partly because of their intrinsic worth; if the humanist cult of antiquity was going to have wide appeal, it must find those aspects of the past which spoke urgently to the needs of the present. Ancient philosophy, poetry, and the visual arts were subjects for contemplation and private enjoyment; ancient history, on the other hand, supplied a fund of vivid models and practical object lessons. As Lauro Martines has succinctly observed, "The humanists looked to history for what it could tell them about their own experience. Theirs was a demand for relevance."[18]

Of course, the existential realities of "history-in-the-making," in short, the varying stages of social development which different parts of Europe had reached by late medieval times, were ultimately responsible for creating this climate of relevance. It is something of a truism that the political and social makeup of the Italian peninsula c. 1400—its organization into a mosaic of compact city-states—was particularly fertile ground for the growth of the humanist agenda. The histories of Greek and Roman cities were of surpassing interest to the civic-minded Italian of the 1400s precisely because they were about cities: they had much to impart in the way of information about corporate, communal, and familial alliances, and about jockeying for power and influence in an urban setting. Study of the ancients enabled the humanists to find themselves in ancient models while encouraging in the process an ever-deepening reverence for study in its own right:[19]

Far from being trivial, the self-images projected back into antiquity were the way to bring it forward; they served to revive classical learning. Looking back to Greece, the humanists saw themselves in the company of Demosthenes, Lysius, Alexander the Great, Aristotle, Alcibiades, Plato, Lycurgus, Pericles, and so on.

Images of heady worldliness such as the humanists created for themselves and their patrons recalls the question posed at the beginning of this chapter regarding humanism and Christianity: how were these two antithetical visions to coexist? To be sure, there were repeated outcries about paganism and the "serpent of antiquity." Martines writes: "Right through the 15th century, humanists had to defend their program of study against the charge of its spreading pagan ideals and undermining Christianity."[20] Yet, humanism continued to gain ground, while at the same time the Church, though doubtless fearful of being under siege, maintained its primacy. Perhaps no single phenomenon attests more strikingly to humanist worldliness than the spirit of accommodation with which alliances were made between the Church in Rome and the various city-states of Quattrocento Italy. Scions of noble families, usually second sons, were routinely named to high offices in the Church, Cardinal Ascanio Sforza, Pope Alexander VI, his son Cardinal Cesare Borgia, and Cardinal Giovanni de' Medici (subsequently Leo X) being the most memorable examples. This picturesque practice, though often related in tones of moral indignation in the history books, nevertheless contains another reality, one so obvious that it can easily be overlooked. The stability of the Church, to be sure, stood to gain considerably each time a prince of the court and a prince of the Church were united in the same person, but that stability would have been meaningless if the message of the Church no longer continued to exert its hold over the "popular" imagination—the imagination, that is, not only of the common people but of the ruling class and the intellectuals as well. In spite of the fact that by the end of the 15th century humanism had progressed to being the new consciousness of the age, Christianity had effectively lost nothing of its mythic power.

It was in this climate of free and open interchange of sacred and secular affairs that Josquin, along with a host of northern musicians, came to maturity. This does not automatically signal a parallel interchange in the musical realm itself: one can easily picture a situation in which a musical retinue such as Galeazzo Maria Sforza's in Milan was split into two groups with distinctly separate functions and artistic interests—the indigenous, humanistically inspired *improvvisatori*, on the one hand, with their earnest and soulful imitations of the ancient rhapsodists; the foreign polyphonists, on the other hand, with their commitment to embellishing the Mass.[21] Even Serafino Aquilano's sonnet, c. 1490, in praise of "Josquino, suo compagno musico d'Ascanio" must be interpreted with some caution. The sonnet is clearly a tribute from the most illustrious of the *improvvisatori* to a very different kind of practicing musician, and one can imagine that Serafino might not have written (and sung?) it unless the sympathy extended to Josquin had been reciprocated. More difficult to imagine is how specific stylistic elements of Serafino's sung poetry (and, of course, we have no firsthand way of knowing what these elements were) might have been incorporated into Josquin's style. Probably there is no direct correspondence. What is more likely is a changing aesthetic attitude on the part of the polyphonists: they may well have discovered in the improviser's art a simpler, thus more direct, means of musical communication than they had been accustomed to. Josquin may well have felt that the polyphonic language could profit from greater rhetorical emphasis, that a measure of human *pathos* was alien neither to polyphony nor to the divine service.

In addition to the tribute of Serafino, the superiority of Josquin's music was recognized on several occasions during his lifetime, but not specifically for its expressiveness. For this latter kind of assessment, we must await the testimony of Heinrich Glarean:[22]

No one has more effectively expressed the passions of the soul in music than this symphonist, no one has more felicitously begun, no one has been able to compete in grace and facility on an equal footing with him just as there is no Latin poet superior in the epic to Maro.

Glarean greatly esteems Josquin's artistry in terms of both technical craft and expressive power. On the other hand, he is not so idolatrous of his subject that he is incapable of noting a weakness or two:[23] "In certain places in his compositions, he did not, as he should have, soberly repress the violent impulses of his unbridled temperament. Yet let this petty fault be condoned in view of the man's other incomparable gifts." From context we infer that Josquin's minor offenses have to do with lapses in modal usage, for Glarean writes that the great master would have shown better judgment in some instances had he had "an understanding of the twelve modes [the very system Glarean was establishing in his famous treatise] and of the truth of musical theory."[24] The case is reminiscent of Artusi's criticisms of Monteverdi, though unlike Artusi, Glarean does not permit these negative details to get in the way of his basic appreciation. To put a more positive construction on the matter, it may well be that Josquin had permitted himself certain boldnesses of writing (or had eschewed certain refinements) for the sake of making an expressive point. In any event, it is unfortunate that Glarean did not cite the passages in question (as he does when speaking of many of the composer's elegant and inventive handlings of modal difficulties), for we would be particularly curious to know whether these passages included the conclusion of *Absalon, fili mi*, in which the departure from the mode is so striking that virtually no modern writer passes it by without some comment (Example 6.1).

Edward Lowinsky once suggested that Josquin wrote this motet to commemorate the murder in 1497 of Pope Alexander VI's first son, the Duke of Gandia:[25]

Josquin's setting of David's dirge over the death of his son Absalom belongs to a tradition of memorializing contemporary events in a work of art by using Biblical analogies. The unusual means chosen by Josquin—the extremely low tessitura for four men's voices with the bass reaching down to contra B-flat the unprecedented key signature of B-flat and E-flat in the two upper voices, E-flat and A-flat in the tenor, and E-flat, A-flat, and D-flat in the bass, the modulatory harmony alternating restlessly between the centers of B-flat major, E-flat major, F minor, and B-flat minor; the powerful and grating dissonance patterns and appoggiaturas emphasizing the semitone in varying combinations, and finally the astonishing modulation at the end, descending by triadic motives from B-flat major to E-flat, A-flat, D-flat, and using G-flat, cadencing in B-flat minor on the words of David: "I

Example 6.1: Josquin, *Absalon, fili mi*

Reprinted by the permission of the publishers from *Werken van Josquin des Prez*, ed. M. Antonowycz & W. Elders, Volume Supplement J55. Copyright 1969 by Vereniging voor Nederlandse Muziekgeschiedenis.

shall descend into the underworld weeping"—these extraordinary means chosen by the most imaginative composer of the time were meant to give expression to the passionate mourning of a man no less emotional for his being the supreme head of the Church.

In briefer terms Leeman Perkins has described the motet as follows: "The exceptionally low range of the work, and the flats that it carries, both in the signature and as accidentals, are undoubtedly intended to reflect the extreme grief expressed by the text."[26] Referring to a moment that comes early in the same piece, Gustave Reese writes: "A suspension on a major seventh, which would obviously sound quite harsh inserted in the typical sound context of the period, helps to establish a mood of lamentation."[27] Each of these modern writers holds firmly to the belief that Josquin's music corresponds directly with the acute *pathos* conveyed by the words, and they support their belief with specific musical details. This all-too-familiar way of treating a musical problem today is singled out for special attention here only because it was totally unknown in Josquin's time. However much the humanist theorist may have believed in the musical expression of the passions, his approach to the matter was prescriptive, not descriptive: Gaffurio, the most respected theorist of the turn of the century, continues in the medieval tradition of Guido and Johannes Afflighemensis, supplying a list of ethical and affective assignments for each of the eight Church modes. The proverbial vagueness of these ascriptions is compounded here by irrelevance, for Gaffurio, as the faithful humanist he is, characterizes Mode 3 (also called "Phrygian" in medieval and Renaissance parlance) as inciting to anger and war, merely on the basis of the reputation of the ancient Greek Phrygian for arousing violent behavior.[28] He thus overlooks the fact that the actual "Phrygian" music that he knew, whether in the form of chant melodies or polyphonic works, exhibited nothing of a violent character.

Palisca's comment on this point is apt, if a little harsh:[29]

The principle that the composer should choose the mode according to the affection of the text is reasonable enough, but on what basis should the choice be made? Surely, not the affective qualities outlined in the table! [The "table" refers to the list Palisca assembles comparing the modal ascriptions from three sources—Aron, Nardo, and Gaffurio.] Who would compose a stirring martial piece in the Church Phrygian, or banish gloom with the sorrowful tritone-laden Church Lydian? Here is humanism gone awry, a sad legacy of early Renaissance musical scholarship's failure to make necessary distinctions between two totally different tonal systems, the Greek and the Western medieval.

With regard to the confusion of ancient and medieval modality, the Renaissance theorists may be forgiven for not correcting the errors of their medieval predecessors; the record on that matter was not set straight until well into our own century. It is nevertheless true that the humanist inclination to adhere to ancient authority posed a severe limitation, for it permitted ancient notions of musical *ethos* to speak for musical realities to which they had no application. But perhaps this was only the normal delay that one can reasonably expect between practice and theory. From 1525 on, the year in which Aron made his adaptation of modal theory to polyphony, the business of looking closely at musical examples from the contemporary literature became more and more the norm. Glarean (1547) is an admirable case in point, and it is not long after him that Vicentino in 1555 and Zarlino in 1558 put forth a theory of musical *pathos* free of the old modal differentiations—a theory moreover, which could only come from immediate experience with the latest polyphonic music.

Since Vicentino has been cited earlier, we will turn to Zarlino's fuller elaboration here. In effect, he divides Glarean's system of twelve modes into *two* groups, the first of which, consisting of the "fifth, sixth, seventh, eighth, eleventh and twelfth [modes] ... is very gay and lively," due to the harmonic division of the fifth "into a major and minor third which is very pleasing to the ear. Whereas in the first group the major third is often placed beneath the minor, in the second group [consisting of the first, second, third, fourth, ninth and tenth modes] the opposite is true, with a result I can only describe as sad or languid."[30] The implications of these few lines for the subject of Western tonality can hardly be exaggerated. In two bold strokes, Zarlino reduces the modal system to a *dichotomy* whose fundamental purpose is to generate a preponderance of—to use modern parlance—major or minor triads. In all fairness to the historical record, it must be added that after drawing these highly original conclusions in Part III of *Istitutioni harmoniche*, Zarlino reverts in Part IV to the tradition-bound breakdown into the Church modes, with the expected ethical and affective distinctions applied systematically. Rather than disappoint us, his tentativeness on this issue should make us realize how difficult it is to break with a deeply entrenched pattern of thought, even when the pattern of thought has proven inadequate to the facts. To have based, even tentatively, a theory of musical *pathos* on a harmonic principle instead of a modal principle was a singular achievement, and the independence of mind he showed in following empirical observations instead of ancient authority cannot go unrecognized.

We know the significance this mid-16th-century development would have for the future of Western music, but how does it relate to its own past? How far back in musical time can Zarlino's conception be appropriately extended? To judge from the commentaries on *Absalon, fili mi* already quoted, scholars today have no doubt as to the expressive impact of harmony in Josquin's work: they appear to accept it as a stylistic given. From the modern vantage point, it is virtually impossible to confront the sonorities of Example 6.1 without hearing them as harmonically motivated—the heavily laden *musica ficta*, the triadic outlining in each of the upper voices, the structural movement of fifths in the bass. In conjunction with the tragic text, the expressive intent of a harmonically dominated polyphony seems undeniable in this case. But what can we conclude from cases in which the harmonic means are less extraordinary? We can begin to answer this question by considering the following interesting insight:[31]

By making an arresting or unsettling series of harmonies coincide with a particularly painful phrase in the text, composers clearly ... were seeking to enhance the *pathos* of the text rather than its poetic or allegorical meaning. But the ability to use harmonies for such purposes came out of the experience gained in manipulating them in more obviously constructive ways ... only when a grammar of normal chord sequences had been developed could such passages as the chord series in *Absalon, fili mi* strike the ear as meaningful deviations.

That chords had to group themselves into certain conventional patterns before certain other patterns could be viewed as unconventional is a credible argument. But it suggests, perhaps unintentionally, that only the more unconventional chord series have expressive power. There is something extremely disconcerting in the notion that a work could be expressive only intermittently; we want to believe that a work is expressive throughout and that an entire grammar of normal chord sequences has the opportunity of participating in that expressive life. Josquin's *Déploration* on the death of Ockeghem and his chanson *Douleur me bat* have none of the swift changes of coloration of *Absalon, fili mi,* yet they impress us as being no less doleful in general mood. What at the very least they have in common with each other is the ingredient Vincentino and Zarlino prescribed as necessary for making a sad music—a predominance of minor harmonies. What evidence do we have for thinking that the mid-16th-century attitude with respect to major and minor harmonies was already alive, if only in incipient form, in the work of Josquin and his contemporaries? In the absence of any explicit testimony from theoretical works, we take as our guide the stylistic practices not only of Josquin's time but also of the Franco-Flemish tradition leading up to him. Scholars have long recognized the harmonic consciousness of the "Burgundian" generation, expressed in its liking for fauxbourdon and its use of block chords for underlining particular portions of text. When Martin le Franc praises Dunstable and Dufay for their "frisque concordance," this is commonly interpreted to mean that he is acknowledging more than the general delightfulness of their songs; he is paying tribute to a newly discovered "sweetness" specifically lodged in the imperfect consonances.[32] The thirds and the sixths are the work of a mentality oriented toward "triads," not only because English descant and continental fauxbourdon literally consist of three tones, but even more because the octave doublings in four- and five-voiced textures signify an ultimate reduction in the number of pitch-classes to three.

This strong triadic orientation creates a world of vertical consonance hitherto unknown. Machaut's 14th-century style provides many examples of pieces with a generally "major" sound, but their majorness is mitigated by a liberal sprinkling of dissonances. If *Rose, lis, printemps, verdure* is a more fascinating use of sonority than anything we find in the Dunstable-Dufay canon, its fascination is doubtless in the way the piece plays with color, in its ambiguous shading of the major sound with flecks of minor coloring. In the new style of the 15th century, Machaut's iridescence is given up for a purer, plainer version of major, one under whose influence a definitive, harmonically constituted convention can take form. This image-type need not have any affective connotation; in the initial stage, its status may be purely sensuous, the effect of a sonority distinct and separate unto itself. As the only other stable triad, the minor harmony will inevitably emerge as a distinct entity in its own right.[33] Polyphonic passages with predominant major or minor coloring become fixed and separated in the aural consciousness, though not necessarily in terms of symbolic association. But with this separation, the first step toward a full-blown symbolic association is taken: there develops the possibility of a sensitivity to relative differences in harmonic qualities, with the result that textures dominated by minor harmonies will take on a "darkness" relative to the "brightness" of a sound-space in which major harmony predominates.

These harmonic types are thus available as material to be applied to the affective purposes articulated by Thomas More and fellow humanists when and if those purposes should crystallize in actual practice. The effects of such a crystallizing process are precisely what scholars claim to have found in the motets of Josquin. Not that all, or even the majority, of these effects are harmonic in character: Josquin's bid to *pathos* is dramatized with a variety of means, ranging from swift changes of texture (illustrating crying or murmuring) to the use of a melodic figure such as the recurrent drooping third of *Nymphes des bois* (said to be an acknowledged and widely used convention of lamentation in Josquin's time), to a declamatory style that may well have been inspired by his experience with the Italian *improvvisatori*. If we dwell on the harmonic factor here, it is because of the unique place that the major/minor dichotomy occupies in the musical expression of the passions. No other musical material has ever had the symbolic capacity to reduce the multifarious passions to the two fundamental categories of pleasure and pain—to group the passions, in short, in terms of the comic/tragic archetype. Musical cries, sighs, and murmurs may be unequivocal signs of *pathos*, but they do not divide along comic and tragic lines: no theory of musical imitation exists by which to distinguish cries of joy from cries of horror in music, or sighs of melancholy from sighs of contentment. Given the fact that the comic/tragic dichotomy has been since Greek times the West's fundamental building block for conceptualizing human emotion, there should be little wonder about the central and persistent role the major/minor convention has played in the musical experience of modern Western culture. It is essential, therefore, to the proper reading of musical content to know just how far back this convention can be traced.[34]

Is Josquin the starting point? Has he chosen the fifth mode for his ethereally crystalline "Ave Maria … virgo serena" because he hears in its majorness the sound of "serene joy"—the mood, in short, that takes hold of the believer whenever the Virgin in all her radiant purity is felt to be close by? Similarly, has he used the second mode for the lamentation on the death of Ockeghem because he associates with its minor coloring a tragic tone? The affective dimension already seen in his music may lead us to think that his sense of harmonic expressiveness extended this far. But we must take extreme care not to impose our modern tonal bias on his pre-tonal sensibilities. In the face of the huge outpouring of Marian motets composed between 1450 and 1500 in fifth mode transposed to C, we might want to believe that Josquin was working at least intuitively with the major-minor associations in question. That this symbolism, however, was understood in the conscious way that Vicentino and Zarlino would later describe it can probably never be known for sure.

As much as we would like to have absolute clarification on this point, insofar as it would enable us to hear Josquin's works with an increased sense of their expressive intentions, there is a yet more general and important point about which no further clarification is necessary. That point concerns the roughly hundred years' progression of events that led to the initial formulation by Zarlino of the major-minor symbolism. We may not be able to pinpoint the exact moment at which a particular stage in that progression was reached, but the stages themselves, already outlined above, are not in doubt: (1) clear separation of the major and minor triadic entities; (2) intuitive grasp of the relative darkness and brightness of the minor and major sonorities; (3) definition of the applicability to music of the archetypal connections, dark/tragic, bright/comic, leading to (4) the correlations, major = happy; minor = sad.

These correlations gained relatively quick acceptance, as is evidenced in the numerous references to sad and happy music in the musical treatises and commentaries of the period subsequent to Zarlino. The same period sees the beginning of the so-called "transition" from modal to tonal thinking, an evolution that would result in the definitive exchange of the Church modes for a harmonically constituted tonal system. Historians have carefully recorded this evolution, sketching out a complicated pattern of stylistic and theoretical interactions, scrupulously noting the advances made in one locale, the regressions in another, the comparatively rapid grasp of modern tonality in Italy, the delayed reactions in Germany and France. Yet, in all these accounts, there is never a hint that this march toward the modern tonal system (notwithstanding its actual turnings and twistings) could involve anything other than questions of pure structure and technique, no indication that at the bottom of this structural development might lie a deep-seated expressive need. Composers were surely guided by their ears in a Darwinian process of sorts, one in which tonal combinations that failed to elaborate the basic progression I–IV–V–I ultimately did not survive. But just as the tonal system generated an enormous expansion in the means by which the musical language could produce effects of tension and relaxation, so too it satisfied the yearnings of the culture at large for stable and communicable images of human emotion. From the major-minor dichotomy of the basic harmonic progression emerged the pure, functional embodiment in music of the comic/tragic opposition. The significance of this symbolism for Western culture is attested not only by the seriousness with which its development was pursued over a 250-year time span (c. 1450–1700), but perhaps even more by the place it still holds today in the popular mythology about music, outweighing every other consideration of *ethos* and *pathos*.

Liturgical Decorum Redefined

We began this chapter by considering to what extent the element of human emotion might have seeped into medieval Church practice. Now, the appropriate question becomes: how, if at all, did the note of passion injected into the Josquin motet affect the root ethical purpose of liturgical music? Perkins writes that Josquin "appears to have been one of the first to draw on the lyrical and subjective poetry of the Old Testament and in particular that of the psalms for a substantial number of works."[35] By design Josquin was seeking out sacred texts that would illustrate the lessons of Christian *logos* with "something of the life around," with something of human interest.[36] In *Absalon, fili mi* a grand patriarchal figure from the pre-Christian (though sacred) past is also a man weeping inconsolably for the loss of a son. In *Planxit autem David* the same man weeps for his leader and his beloved friend. In *De profundis clamavi* the ancient psalmist gives voice to deep spiritual distress, brought on by momentary doubts and feelings of separation from God. Even when the theme is specifically Christian and devotional, as with the traditional Marian texts, one feels that Josquin is looking for a human element.

Doubtless, the new motet style had strayed from the early Christian vision: Josquin's musical gesture would have been adjudged sensual and intemperate by the Christian fathers; in their eyes it would have called too much attention to itself, it would have lost track of its liturgical place. But in the eyes of the humanists the new emotional element constituted an addition, not a replacement; it gave a richness, a supplemental intensity. It was possible on one level to be certain that the sacred work was fully performing its ritual function, on another level to look upon the same work as endowed with a beauty and expressiveness that could be all the better admired when separated from its ritual context. Supporting this new autonomous—one might say artistic—view of the sacred work was the esteem accorded the leading composers of sacred music by writers as diversified in their interests as Tinctoris, Cortese, Luther, and Glarean, with particular masses and motets often singled out for special praise.[37]

We should also recognize that in view of the extent to which the ritual was still intoned in plainchant, the time devoted to the motet was fairly limited. The liturgy provided moments—but only moments—in which the sacred objects could be mined for their human interest value and the ordinary passions of the worshipper thereby aroused. But even when examined on its own, the Josquin motet should show that its rhetoric proceeds only in part from the affective element. We have no way of knowing how *Absalon, fili mi* was sung in early 16th-century Rome or Milan—with what relative vehemence or restraint the emotional accents were delivered—but considerations of liturgical decorum must have had a tempering influence on any given performance: the individual grief-laden gestures could be given their due, but only to the extent that they would add their part to the ultimately unifying tone of measured solemnity. In terms of its ethical significance, therefore, it may be said of *Absalon, fili mi* that it represents a frank display of human emotion, though one checked by the liturgical conditions in which it took place and thus not inappropriate to those conditions. But the very inclusion of emotion meant that the conditions themselves had been altered, if only moderately. As long as we recognize that liturgical decorum had been redefined for 16th-century purposes (hence, for all future time), we can accept the notion that decorum continued to be observed, and was thus preserved.

Notes

1. Thomas More, *Utopia*, p. 127.
2. See Ritva Jonsson and Leo Treitler, "Medieval Music and Language: A Reconsideration of the Relationship," in *Music and Language*, Vol. I of *Studies in the History of Music*, pp. 1–23. Also, see Don Michael Randel, "Dufay, the Reader" in *ibid.*, pp. 38–78.

3. Claude V. Palisca, ed., *Hucbald, Guido and John on Music: Three Medieval Treatises*, p. 69.
4. Quoted in John Stevens, *Words and Music in the Middle Ages: Song, Narrative, Dance and Drama, 1050–1350*, p. 405.
5. See Palisca, *Hucbald, Guido and John*, p. 133.
6. Stevens, pp. 403–404.
7. *Ibid.*, pp. 404–405.
8. *Ibid.*, p. 404.
9. *Ibid.*, p. 406.
10. *Ibid.*, p. 408.
11. *Ibid.*, p. 409.
12. See Palisca, *Hucbald, Guido and John*, p. 3.
13. Quoted in Stevens, p. 401.
14. *Ibid.*, p. 370.
15. The article has been reprinted in Nino Pirrotta, *Music and Culture in Italy from the Middle Ages to the Baroque*, pp. 80–112.
16. A humanist statement of the period quoted in Lauro Martines, *Power and Imagination: City-States in Renaissance Italy*, p. 194.
17. Quoted in Claude V. Palisca, *Humanism in Italian Renaissance Musical Thought*, p. 6.
18. Martines, p. 195.
19. *Ibid.*, p. 196.
20. *Ibid.*, p. 205.
21. For the late 15th-century Italian view of the relative merits of "humanistic" singing and polyphony, see in particular Pirrotta, p. 89 and p. 165. Even Cortese's appreciation of Josquin seems somewhat secondhand. He thinks of Josquin as plying a craft, of Aquilano as practicing an art.
22. Quoted in Oliver Strunk, ed., *Source Readings in Music History*, p. 220.
23. *Ibid.*, p. 220.
24. *Ibid.*, p. 220.
25. Edward Lowinsky, "Secret Chromatic Art Re-examined," in *Perspectives in Musicology*, Barry S. Brook, Edward O.D. Downes, and Sherman Van Solkema, ed., pp. 110–111.
26. See entry "Motet," in *The New Grove Dictionary of Music and Musicians*, Stanley Sadie, ed., Vol. XII, p. 634.
27. Gustave Reese, *Music in the Renaissance*, p. 257.
28. See Palisca, *Humanism*, p. 345.
29. *Ibid.*, pp. 345–346.
30. Quoted in Harold S. Powers, "Mode," in *New Grove*, Vol. XII, p. 412.
31. James Anderson Winn, *Unsuspected Eloquence*, pp. 134–136.
32. See Howard M. Brown, *Music in the Renaissance*, p. 8.
33. Indications that this description conforms to a distinct reality are given by Tinctoris when he says in Book 3 of his twelve treatises that the modal system is useful for explaining single lines but that for polyphony a new theoretical language is needed, one capable of explaining harmonies.

34. It makes no difference, as has been discussed in an earlier chapter, that the equivalencies "major=happy" and "minor=sad" are not borne out in a sizeable portion of the musical literature. The major/minor dichotomy behaves neither like a physical occurrence verified by the senses nor a truth that can be logically demonstrated; it is rather a convention, a kind of thought-material that becomes truth when the culture as a whole believes in its reality. (The Latin *convenire* connotes a "coming together," a meeting of minds.) The persistence of the convention says much about the need in Western culture for a musical symbolism of the emotions.

35. "Motet," in *New Grove*, Vol. XII, p. 632.

36. See Martines, p. 250, on this point.

37. For Cortese's statements on Josquin, see references in Pirrotta, pp. 91–92. For Luther's statement, in addition to the tributes of many others, see the biographical information in the article "Josquin Desprez" in *The New Grove*, Vol. IX, p. 717.

7 *Emotional Music, or the Rhetorical Variety of Pathos*

When we come to the subject of 16th-century secular music, new questions arise regarding the *ethos/pathos* dichotomy. One could imagine, for instance, that the specific kind of tension between emotion and decorum just outlined for the sacred music of the period would not apply to a music that served no ritual function: humanist composers, on turning to secular forms, might well feel that they had *carte blanche*, that they could pursue pathetic expression free of any ethical constraint. This is indeed how composers (and theorists along with them) liked to think of the artistic situation. In actual fact, the situation was very different, if only because artists, as employees of princes and church officials, were not totally free agents. The ethical factor continued to hold strong because works of art in the 16th century (and long after) could not conceivably have come into being independent of a social context, and society has always been the chief incubator of ethical concerns. At the same time, it is important that we take, at least provisionally, the humanist emphasis of the passions at face value: we must not overlook the obvious. Just as the *ethos* of *fin' amor* had once dominated courtly culture, so in the high Renaissance the aesthetic of *pathos* caught the imagination of artist and public alike and led to numbers of artistic realizations in its name. The diverse realities of the situation—the fact that composers were making their artifacts for the tastes of specific patrons—seemed to take second place to the assumption shared by society at large that music was made to express "gli affetti umani."

Indeed, the question of first and second place is at the heart of the matter. The three chapters following this one are aimed at showing that during the period 1500–1800 (and in certain respects beyond 1800) the dialectic between *ethos* and *pathos* continued to operate at full strength. Nevertheless, a shift in the relative importance of the two principles seems to have taken place: whereas in the Middle Ages musical imagery emerged in conjunction with human types who were defined in terms of an ideal behavior, in the era of Classical humanism the human types are defined first and foremost in terms of their feelings, from which it follows that their behavior depends on how they feel. By the end of this chapter it will have been shown why this is an incomplete and thus somewhat distorted way of viewing the matter, but some of our most enduring vocal genres—the French part-song and the Italian madrigal in the 16th century, the recitative and aria in the 17th century—are born of this distortion. This being the case, it is mainly through these forms and the diverse approaches they represent that we can expect to grasp the pervasiveness of the pathetic impulse in humanistic thought. And so, even allowing for the fact that *pathos* as a principle is not our sole or ultimate object of interest, some examination of the affective intentions behind these forms is a necessary step toward taking their fuller measure later on.

Chanson

In dealing with the part-songs published by Attaignant in Paris around the year 1530, we will find it instructive as well as useful to establish separate and distinct functions for the music and the poetry (much as was done for medieval secular song in Chapter 5). This seems justified solely on the basis of the fact that the courtly love theme continued to occupy an important place in the new chanson literature. The persistence into the 16th century of a "courtly love song" (albeit now polyphonic rather than monophonic) strikes one as remarkable, provided it is kept in mind that the complexity and mythic vigor of the early troubadour lyrics had long been a thing of the past. Already by the mid-13th century, the *ethos* of courtly love—at least as transmitted through the verbal element of the song—had been shorn of its deeper spiritual content; what the poetry retained of the original conception was its force as a model for developing a beautiful manner. Courtly love poetry, in short, had long since become a network of "Douce dame" conceits ingeniously worked and reworked. *What* was said was virtually immaterial; how prettily it was said was everything.

Continuing in this vein, the poems connected to the courtly love chansons of the 16th century strive for perhaps even more restraint and self-containment than their forbears. Epigrammatic eloquence, mildness of manner, and the promise of being set to a charming tune constitute their not overextended ambitions. Charm and self-composure are precisely the attributes by which a courtly society means to pattern its social behavior; and since this behavior *is* of a strictly social kind, we are puzzled to understand where notions of *pathos* and the inner life could enter in. The puzzlement begins to vanish, however, once the poetry is connected to the music, for the music, especially in its new-found capacity to differentiate states of pleasure and pain, gives every sign of embodying straightforwardly and directly the affections reported by the text—affections, it should be added, that are indeed *only* reported, that is, treated as so many "affectations" of pleasure and pain, as pure poetic artifice and wordplay, and not intended to be taken seriously on the level of emotional truth. Or, viewed from a somewhat different angle: it is as if the words were waiting to be set to music in order to get beneath mere manner, in order to find an emotional life that they themselves have indicated but not expressed. That the music should now become the chief carrier of the affective content is a reversal of older conceptions of the text-music relationship and thus a matter of some historical consequence. If this last point has been generally missed, it may be because the chanson's demonstrative cousin, the Italian madrigal, makes the point more dramatically. In any event, the degree to which individual chansons share common melodic and rhythmic material results in a collection of highly conventional (and thus easily recognizable) affective meanings; and historians have had little trouble in breaking down the repertoire into a number of distinct types.

Of the categories identified by recent authorities, the two that deal directly with the theme of courtly love are (to borrow Lawrence Bernstein's terminology) the *chanson de complainte* and the *chanson de cour*.[1] This bi-partite division is in essence a consequence of the reductionist attitude that had overtaken the courtly love theme from late medieval times. Either the courtly love song paid the lady tribute or it wallowed in feelings of rejection and despair, but rarely did it do both at once; the psychological subtlety of the early troubadour lyrics, which came from complaint and tribute being played off against each other, had all but disappeared. This may have been a loss as long as the poetry remained in charge of the affective life of the song, but once the perception grew that the music could take over the primary affective role, a new possibility presented itself, which was that of the music developing two distinct styles, the tragic and the comic.

The effects of the new development are more immediately felt in the tragic area than in the comic, doubtless because of the more striking rhetorical resources usually brought to bear for the expression of tragic feeling. The openings of *Plaine de deuil* and *Douleur me bat* of Josquin respectively display the heavy sonorities and the "mi-fa" melodic figure and sustained minor second dissonance that quickly became conventional symbols of personal suffering. The hallmarks of the later *chanson de conplainte* are identified by Bernstein as deriving from Josquin and including the following features: broad, declamatory opening gestures, long rhythmic values, rich chordal effects, and a closing mannerism whereby one voice sustains while others repeat the closing words or the opening declamatory figure.[2] In addition, minor harmony is the pervasive coloring in the overwhelming majority of these pieces, though, speaking for the chanson style as a whole, the force of minor alone is hardly enough to determine the tragic symbolism of a musical image. The realities of the style were such that rhythm, texture, and harmony all had to work closely together in order to fix the connotations of the imagery. But in return, the images of the 1530s and 40s chansons became so pervasive and stereotypical that the connotations were unmistakable: no devotee of the genre in its heyday, turning the pages of an Attaignant print, could have misjudged the category of the chanson before him—whether *complainte*, chanson de cour, patter-chanson, or voix de ville—and would thus have failed to know what tempo to take and whether to sing the piece with smooth or choppy accents.

Though no more difficult than the other categories to recognize through its musical imagery, the *chanson de cour* (of which Claudin de Sermisy is the pre-eminent figure) is difficult to fathom from an affective standpoint. Its extreme placidity leads one to wonder whether it was not designed to provide its aristo-cratic audience with a moment or two of amiable grace—to project, in short, not an emotion but a decorum. Brown writes: "It is the very simplicity of a song like Claudin's *Tant que vivray* ... that makes its greatness so elusive ... and so difficult to explain."[3] Yet, this simplicity also contains the core of an explanation, if we think back on the 15th-century humanist ideal. Not learned polyphony, cried the humanists, but a simple line of sweet melody supported by a few chordal strum-mings on the lute; that is the direct path to the listeners' hearts, the surest way of moving them to the depths of their souls. The appeal of simple expression, then, of the Claudin chanson would be argument for the humanist position. Just the same, the argument, convincing as it may sound, does not really bring us closer to resolving our original problem, which is that of uncovering an affective source for the *chanson de cour*'s expressiveness. It is one thing to speak of aesthetic effect; it is quite another to speak of aesthetic intent and musical content—to demon-strate, in short, that the Claudin chanson, notwithstanding its elegance and quiet good manners, was meant to be more than an emblem of social accomplishment, that it was intended to carry its measure of personal feeling and that that feeling was preeminently contained in the music.

To confirm these last points, we must remind ourselves of the chanson's status as a song of courtly love. We must imagine, in other words—just as with the medieval pieces—that the author of the song is not the literal composer but a courtier who presents his song as well as composes it, and does so not only to appear beautiful and refined and virtuous in the eyes of his lady but to say what is truly in his heart.[4] Indeed, an immutable rule of the courtly love ideal is sincerity: there is no hope of attaining virtue without speaking the truth about one's feelings. At the same time, we must remember that the portion of feeling with which the *chanson de cour* is directly concerned is something less than what the troubadours first had in mind. The darker feelings—anxiety, fear, torment, and the like—having been consigned to the *chanson de complainte*, the *chanson de cour* is free to pursue its functions as pure tribute-piece, to sing the praises of the lady without interference from the world of negative emotion. This is not consistently true of the verses, where disappointment and fears of rejection intermittently intrude.[5] Yet, not a note of complaint is sounded in the music, or to put it more precisely and more literally, none of the gestures identified above as being routinely associated with the *chanson de complainte* appear in the *chanson de cour*. Claudin's chansons are particularly recognizable for the perfectly molded, smoothly arched contours of their soprano lines—graceful but not overly sinuous—and for the homophonic texture, lightly animated by counterpoint, over which the soprano is set.

It is by virtue of these hallmarks and not on the basis of the messages conveyed in the texts that the *chanson de cour* is identified and clearly distinguished from the *chanson de complainte*: the criteria for separating the categories are ultimately musical because the music is the primary carrier of *pathos*. And yet, the surface of the typical Claudin chanson is one of such supernal poise that it is easily understandable why its attributes have been routinely interpreted as signs of pure outward manner. To alter this impression, we must believe that the *chanson de cour* is an authentic expression of courtly love and see behind the song a flesh-and-blood courtier who truly feels the things he sings about. But then, what this means in terms of the affective significance of the *chanson de cour* is that its extreme musical calm can only be the direct and sincere reflection of *inner* calm—of an inner life in a state of perfect composure.

We are describing, then, a courtier whose innermost being has been totally purified of distress because selflessness has become total: any remnant of initial desire, any faint hope of reward has been distilled in the all-absorbing wish to serve. While at first glance this idealization seems merely to reiterate the goal of courtly love as originally proposed by the troubadours, in actual fact it carries the troubadour vision one step further. The troubadours saw courtly love as a progress by which the knight/poet advances by means of a stringent program of self-discipline from feelings of carnal desire to the highest state of steadfast devotion. Many of the early poems describe this progress in detail, while the melodies attached to these poems purportedly express only the end goal, the ideal. But even the melodies themselves suggest by what was earlier described as their fervor that the ideal is at least the *result* of a process: the melodies are fervent precisely because they contain the memory of the initial desire.

In the music of the Claudin chanson, no traces of desire remain; on the face of it no such carnal feelings ever existed. Devotion is projected as if it never had to be won; it is the sole quality that defines the courtier, but as it is perfect and unchanging, no other seems necessary. Such perfection in a human being does not much appeal to other, less perfect mortals, which is to say that the courtier of the *chanson de cour* might strike us as arch and stilted were it not for two other qualities ultimately revealed through the song: modesty and warmth. His eloquence (literally the eloquence of the song that represents him) comes not only from good manners and simplicity, but above all from the heart. The simplicity of the chanson is self-evident and has already been described in terms of some of the individual musical ingredients; as for the warmth, if we can locate it in any single aspect of the musical fabric, it will be in the harmony. Four-voiced, close-spaced and squarely in the middle register, the Claudin harmonies are a moderate updating of 15th-century "frisque concordance"; the fourth voice gives the Burgundian freshness an added resonance, a golden glow. Even the dissonances, sparingly used, have no value of asperity in them; rather they make the affected sonorities rounder, more substantial (Example 7.1). Not harshness but generosity is the symbolic result. The *chanson de cour*[6] is incapable of creating the slightest disturbance, which is no doubt why its mildness is usually taken for nothing more than delicate charm. In Brown's own words, "Such a chanson certainly reaches no great expressive heights."[7] That is quite true; it reaches for depth rather than "height"—for a rare kind of interiority that can be easily missed by modern ears.

Example 7.1: Claudin de Sermisy, *J'attends secours*

Reprinted by permission of the publishers from *Chanson & Madrigal, 1480–1530*, edited by James Haar, Cambridge, Mass.: Harvard University Press, Copyright © 1964 by the President and Fellows of Harvard College.

Madrigal

The idea of an Italian enthusiasm for *pathos* as opposed to a French mistrust of it is a deeply entrenched myth still routinely transmitted in the textbooks and obediently regurgitated by students in papers and exams. No doubt the myth got its start in the 16th century from the examples of the chanson and the madrigal. We should realize, however, that the myth, as stated, is heavily weighted in favor of the Italian point of view. Indeed, in the polemics that periodically break out in the 16th, 17th, and 18th centuries regarding the relative merits of French and

Italian music, French music is presented from the Italian side as cold, limp, and passionless.[8] Italian music, by contrast, is warm, full-blooded, and alive with human feeling. For their part, those representing the French side counter with their opinion of Italian music: extravagant, fatiguing, overwrought, vulgar in its emotional displays, while French music is refreshing, tender and composed, its naturalness deeply affecting.

Clearly, there is an opposition here, but not over the importance of *pathos*. The French are as dedicated as the Italians to the proposition that the passions are the rightful province of musical content. What concerns them quite as much, however, is the rightful *expression* of the passions, involving considerations not only of the outward behavior proper to each passion but also of the time and place in which a given passion can be appropriately brought out into the open. Since the Italian code of affective behavior has been traditionally less restrictive than the French, the issue here is one of opposing tastes.[9] How these differences in taste and expressive habits affected the fortunes of 16th-century secular music can be most immediately seen in the virtuosity with which composers went about finding new and striking musical imagery for the Italian madrigal throughout the century. Not that this meant the abandonment of all principles of decorum any more than the French preoccupation with decorum signalled the absence of a commitment to *pathos*. But there is no question that the Italian experience brought a new energy to the bond between music and the passions—a bond hammered into the very epicenter of our aesthetic perceptions, from which it has not yet been dislodged.

Essentially a song of courtly love, the madrigal in its first definitive incarnation (c. 1530) bears close affinities, as would be expected, with the Claudin chanson. There is no little significance in the fact that the development of this first-generation madrigal was dominated by northerners. Verdelot's *Madonna, il tuo bel viso* is for all intents and purposes an Italian *chanson de cour*, showing all the elegance and well-bred refinement of the French tribute-piece, albeit with greater textural and rhythmic variety. This last difference is already indication of an added rhetorical concern: the rhythmic flexibility with which the text is handled—the accelerating of a stream of words in one place, the prolonging of a single syllable in another—suggests a kind of emotion which must assert itself spontaneously and impulsively, in "unmeasured" fashion. The "individual" whose voice we hear declaiming this utterance is not identical in interior makeup to his French counterpart. The Claudin courtier sings a phrase in which no rhythmic or intervallic element is permitted any function other than that of contributing to the phrase's seamless unity: the evenness of line is born of the evenness "inside." The Italian courtier does not express himself with the same confidence; his phrases, though basically smooth and lyrical, show less repose, at times even revealing the effect of having been built out of exclamatory bits and pieces. This is a man who has not reached the depth of distilled emotion described for the *chanson de cour*. He still yearns, and his yearnings and uncertainties are betrayed by the vocal gestures of the madrigal sung in his name.

Such gestures, however, appear quite self-possessed when put alongside the cries of pain heard in the madrigals of the generation following Verdelot. The way in which Cipriano de' Rore seizes upon the words, "Veggio, penso, ardo, pianto" in the middle of Petrarch's sonnet *Hor ch'el ciel* and isolates them from the prevailing flow must have shocked not a few sensibilities of the period (1542) (Example 7.2). Indeed, the reverberations of Rore's bold move were felt clear into the 17th century, as we know from Monteverdi's identification of "the divine Cipriano" as the prime mover of the "seconda prattica."[10] This new-found vehemence clearly signalled an ever-increasing involvement with the passions, a need to explore all the passions without exception—sharp grief as well as mirthfulness, terror as well as mild uncertainty. What must be equally recognized is that preoccupation with the more unruly emotions effectively removed the madrigal from the sphere of courtly love, for the decorum of courtly love could not support Dionysian turbulence: cries of torment and shrieks of delight might be heard in private, but they were not matters for polite society.

A new madrigalian hero—indeed, a new hero for music in general—came into being, one less admirable than the knight/poet of courtly love, one more given to outbursts and erratic behavior. The new madrigal produced a brooding, isolated, essentially tragic figure whose weaknesses threatened to overtake his strengths; but for those very reasons, he seemed closer to the realities of everyday experience. At the same time, we must understand that the madrigalists were first and foremost dedicated to *pathos*, not to tragedy. If they concentrated on tragic experience, it was not for its own sake, but because representation of the more tumultuous and disturbing passions enabled their music to be more striking and intense. Vehement expression was the symptom of a desire to fire up the listener to a pitch of excitement undreamt of in earlier music. In the classic Aristotelian conception of *catharsis*, tragedy teaches us how to rise above suffering with "all passion spent." With intense *pathos*, on the other hand, the impulse is to arouse emotion rather than purge it, the chief object of interest being not suffering (or more precisely the overcoming of suffering), but human passior in all its intensity and variety.

As the madrigal development moved toward its climax in the 1580s and 90s, the rhetorical possibilities seemed to expand exponentially and music took on a decidedly declamatory cast: isolated gestures, excited exclamations, dramatic shifts in mood became the order of the day. Were these studies in contrast motivated by an awareness of the volatility of the human emotional system or had they actually brought the composers to such an awareness? Reference to an earlier commentary by Heinrich Glarean may shed some light on this question. It must be noted that in these observations, written in 1547, Glarean is not referring to a contemporary madrigal, but to a sacred motet composed by Josquin some 40 years before.[11]

Throughout the motet, there is preserved what befits the mourner, who is wont at first to cry out frequently, then to murmur to himself, turning little by little to sorrowful complaints,

Example 7.2: Rore, *Hor ch'el ciel*

thereupon to subside or sometimes, when passion breaks out anew, to raise his voice again, shouting out a cry.

While it is true that the issue Glarean is addressing is the *expression* of passion and not passion directly, and while it is also true that the expressive transformations he is describing revolve around the single affection of sorrow and not a collection of contrasting affections, there is nevertheless no mistaking his belief in the ebb and flow of human emotion ("when passion breaks out anew") and in the cause-effect relationship between emotion and expression. Above all, there is his faith that music has the power to record the emotional fluctuations with fidelity and precision.[12] The same faith motivates the madrigalists of the 1580s and 90s—with perhaps even more comprehensiveness, insofar as they seek to portray human passion as a perpetual dynamic, moving as if randomly and without warning from one state of mind to the next. The extreme case of this is represented in the last works of Gesualdo, where the musical imagery typically swings from a mood of deep depression to one of manic elation, with no transitional steps in between. This kind of behavior shows to what extent the older guidelines for musical expression could be consumed in the flames of *pathos*. But if the notion of *pathos* itself aroused aesthetic excitement among the Italian madrigalists, they were equally excited with the rhetorical equipment they had assembled for handling pathetic content. In examining any number of the late madrigals, one is struck not only by the delight with which the creators are manipulating their coloristic combinations, but even more by their confidence that the sensuous material is conveying emotional truth. In spite of the proliferation of rhetorical devices, or perhaps because of them, the madrigal had developed in the various Italian courts a devoted audience that responded warmly to its seductions and implicitly understood its meanings.

One rhetorical resource is often overlooked: not much is said of the presence of instruments in madrigal performance, since it is customary to think of 16th-century part-writing as *a cappella*. But instrumental coloring, when applied, could have a particularly strong influence on the general mood expressed, and we know that in intermezzi where infernal scenes were depicted, the accompanying instruments were normally consorts of trombones and/or viols. In his essay on *Psyche's Lament*, performed at the Medici wedding celebrations of 1565, Howard Brown describes the expressive implications of the piece as follows:[13]

To a 16th-century listener and, for that matter, to a 20th-century listener as well, the first clue to its expressive character would have been its instrumentation which, as we have seen, is traditional. The sound of four trombones, four bass viols and *lirone*, plus solo voice, would immediately have characterized the piece as a solemn one, quite possibly an infernal one, and, almost certainly, an unhappy one.

Thus, a low, heavy instrumental sound (which we would metaphorically call "dark") would elicit immediate associations with the tragic vision. In keeping with the heaviness, a slowness of rhythm is also prescribed. Nicola Vicentino writes: "One should not make any diminutions with lamentations or other sorrowful compositions, because such compositions would then appear happy."[14] Vicentino's observation is no doubt correct for his time, but not necessarily for a later age, which saw no discrepancy in introducing *stile concitato* into a tragic action. Vicentino would probably have been confused by *stile concitato*, but only because he equated solemnity with slowness, which is correct, and tragedy with solemnity, which is only sometimes true. For solemnity does not refer to a state of mind but to a decorum; the solemn tone was a lofty and dignified one, and was thus appropriate to tragedy, at least according to the Aristotelian definition of it. But in a newer vision of tragedy, the slow pace might not allow for arousal of the emotions to the desired pitch of excitement. The advent of *stile concitato,* then, signified the abandonment of some dignity for the increase of vehement expression.

Monteverdi wrote that he "invented" *stile concitato* for the *Combattimento di Tancredi e Clorinda* of 1624.[15] This may have been his first *conscious* use of it, but examples of it show up in many earlier places in his work. And indeed, it is an impulse which can be traced back to the madrigals of the 1580s, significantly enough to the "scenic" madrigals of Wert and Luzzaschi. In *Giunto a la tomba* of Wert, we have a "microdrama" such as composers would soon be extracting from Guarini's poetic play, *Il Pastor Fido.* These lines of Tasso from *Gerusalemme Liberata* are principally concerned with a hero's lament for a departed beloved, but the lament does not begin until the hero has first been depicted walking into the cold and gloomy tomb.[16] Thus a whole scene with a very decided atmosphere has been erected before our eyes, and it is the music's responsibility to deal with every element of it. The mood of the opening lines is properly sepulchral; the music is almost pure chant, and the source of the image seems to be Counter-Reformation liturgy, although the infernal theater scenes with trombones and viols are exerting their influence as well.[17] Suddenly, at the line "Al fin sgorgando" the human emotion gushes out in streams of musical descents, just as the tears depicted in the text stream forth (Example 7.3). Words and music fuse to create what must rank as one of the most startling effects in the madrigal literature. Part of the overwhelming impact of this moment is due to the visual illusion of gloomy space already created in the opening. Thus, when the streams of descending musical lines arrive, there is a real sense of their reverberating around the tomb, the very walls echoing with the awful wailing sounds of grief. This is where polyphony has been given a new motivation through the scenic madrigal: it has become an orchestration of dramatic relationships raised to the level of visual immediacy.

Unquestionably, the visual stimulus of Tasso's lines had helped Wert to find his extraordinary image. But what Wert had done in his treatment of "Al fin sgorgando" was more than a suitable counterpart to the textual idea; he had given to music a means of expression of immense historical importance though he could not have appreciated that fact at the time.[18] For if his tumbling musical lines signalled the beginning of *stile concitato,* then the exclusive, and thus restrictive, association that fast music had maintained over the course of centuries with gaiety and lightheartedness no longer held. Here was a fast music associated with tragedy, and whose furious energy gave every impression of belonging there. The conscious pursuit of *stile concitato* and its implications for Baroque expression will be the subject of a later discussion. For the moment it is enough to say that with this new vehemence music had not only expanded its repertoire of rhetorical devices, but far more importantly, had gained for itself truly new content.

This so-called "gain" for music is at the very heart of the matter, for what the madrigalists were ultimately searching for were equivalents in music to the

Example 7.3: Wert, *Giunto a la tomba*

various kinds of passion that had inhabited literature since time immemorial. In this effort, musicians must use literature as a trustworthy model: literature had dealt seriously with all aspects of the human condition from ancient times, while music was only now learning once again to do so. Pirrotta writes that beginning around 1560 "the madrigalists had tended to abandon merely lyrical expression (in which text and music express, or seem to express, subjective feelings) and had begun to represent sentiments attributed to fictitious characters. An opening narrative would often introduce the psychological situations they wanted to portray."[19] In making itself over in the image of drama, music was aspiring to claim for itself some of that faculty for coming to grips with human truths that had always seemed drama's birthright. Tasso, who had more to do with madrigals than merely supplying them with poetry, has this to say:[20]

Then let us put aside all that music which, in degenerating, has become soft and effeminate, and let us ask Striggio and Jaches [Wert] and Luzzasco, or any other excellent master of excellent music to lead it back to that seriousness, in deviating from which it has often drifted into regions which it is better to pass over in silence than to talk about ... I do not blame sweetness and grace; but I should like to see them combined with moderation; for I am of the opinion that music is like the other noble arts, each of which is combined with a similar flattery (of the senses), though its effects are quite different.

Tasso's commentary is two-edged; on the one hand, he seems to be saying that music is presently not at the same level of achievement as the "other noble arts" (poetry? drama?) but that it could be, if only it dedicated itself to seriousness and avoided the "soft and effeminate." Judging from their initiatives in the 1580s, the madrigalists named by Tasso did not need their mission explained to them: under the inspiration of ancient Greek tragedy and the major epic poems of their own day, they had in great part abandoned the gentler and prettier modes of human passion and were well on their way to uncovering its more disturbing dimensions.

Recitative

There is an irony in the fact that the year 1581 saw the publication of both Wert's seventh book of madrigals in five parts and Vincenzo Galilei's *Dialogo della musica antica e della moderna*. At the very moment that the final and most magnificent phase of secular part-writing in 16th-century Europe was getting under way a call was going out for the total elimination of vocal polyphony. Add to this drastic recommendation Galilei's highly polemical tone and a very selective treatment of the ancient evidence for the sake of bolstering his own argument, and one may imagine that he has not benefited much from recent assessments of his historical place.[21] Winn even goes to the point of accusing

Galilei and his humanist collaborators of favoring poetry over music and trying to obstruct music's future development:[22]

There are many ironies in the curious history of the musical humanists. Despite their desire to recover the marvelous "effects" of the ancients, the most rabid among them advocated reforms that would have deprived composers of some of their most effective means of expression ... under the cover of restoring the ancient union between music and poetry, many of the musical humanists were actually trying to assert the superiority of poetry over music, to curtail music's growing independence, to bring it under the control of texts.

This is a serious misreading of motivations behind actions, for neither Galilei nor any other member of the Bardi circle ever considered the comparative merits of poetry and music; all that concerned them was that poetry and music should be combined in such a way as to produce the most powerful kind of tool possible with which to express human passions. That Galilei may have been deluded in seeking the particular balance he did between music and poetry is of no consequence to us; our task is to see whether his ideas for reform follow logically from his opening premise, which is that the expression of the passions (gli affetti umani) is music's fundamental, if not sole, *raison d'être*.

The premise itself was hardly controversial in 1581; everyone took it to be axiomatic. The controversy begins with his assertion that while ancient music fulfilled its primary function admirably, modern vocal polyphony subverted it on two major counts: it rendered the words unintelligible and it was interested only in delighting the ear. In order to make amends, modern music had to rid itself of counterpoint and go back to the monody of the ancients. In practical terms musicians could begin by imitating the vocal gestures of the actors in the spoken theater. The idea of the singer as actor was not a particularly original one with Galilei—it had come up periodically in both pejorative and supportive contexts over centuries—but it had a special urgency in the Camerata discussions of the 1570s due in large part to Girolamo Mei's comparative theories on the prosody of Tuscan and ancient Greek poetry and also because of his researches into the various uses of music in Greek tragedy. Mei's work did much to fuel convictions among Camerata members that music imitates not so much words and the sense of words as the very manner of delivering the words; as they conceived it, the cadences of men's speech were human emotion made outward and manifest, a direct and truthful recording of inner feeling.[23]

The old story of the birth of *stilo recitativo*, which has it that the discussions of the Camerata led without detour to Peri's realizations in *Euridice*, has been largely rewritten by modern scholarship. Historians today like to invoke the declamatory tendencies of the late 16th-century madrigal and also the general strain of pseudo-monody that runs through so much Italian music of the Renaissance as evidence that the notions of the Camerata on music and declamation (one might say, "the musical aspects of declamation") are far more widespread than was made out in the past. The responsibility of an accurate accounting of these developments must be left to the historians. More pertinent to our present purposes is to discover how the outcome met initial expectations. Happily, most musicians ignored Galilei's warnings and proceeded to contribute their share to the sumptuousness and magnificence of the fin de siècle madrigal. Galilei may well have been deluded about the inexpressiveness of polyphony, but was he equally deluded in pinning all his hopes on the expressiveness of monody? To what extent, in other words, did the new recitative meet his demands and satisfy him that the "errors" of the madrigalists had been corrected?

The most obvious effect of the new style is the gain in verisimilitude, the substitution of a solo voice for multiple voices to represent the single protagonist described in the text (this verisimilitude being further enhanced when the presentation is put on the stage and made visible as well as audible). With the text now limited to one line of melody, the verbal clashes arising from a polyphonic treatment of the text immediately disappear; composers concentrate on faithfully reproducing the accentuation of the syllables as they are rendered in the spoken language. At the same time, an *exact copy* of the spoken language is not what the composers are looking for; rather, they mean to invent a music (to borrow Peri's careful distinction) "surpassing that of ordinary speech but falling so far below the melody of song as to take an intermediate form."[24] This "intermediate form" is, according to Peri, what the ancient Greeks and Romans used when singing their tragedies, the inference being that this kind of music was precisely right for the rendering of tragic emotion. Heroes of modern musical tragedy, then, will declaim in *stilo recitativo* because it captures with singular fidelity the cadences of their speech while they are in the grip of painful and intense feeling. The rhythms of recitative, besides having the energy requisite to tragedy, also have the flexibility with which to represent human inner life in all its changeableness and volatility.

But the declamatory madrigal (especially in its very late incarnation, where counterpoint has been greatly eliminated and the several voices intone the syllables simultaneously) had learned to do much the same thing. Just like the recitative, it shows the same interest in strong passion and tragic subjects and it has the same expressive ends in view, though it may accomplish these with somewhat different means. But in fact, how different are the means? If Monteverdi takes to the recitative style with such seeming ease and mastery in *L'Orfeo*, is it not partly because he has already had considerable practice at writing a disguised form of monody, as any number of passages in his first five madrigal books will show?[25] Still, the change in texture from madrigal pseudo-monody to recitative-monody is considerable. In recitative the vocal line, in no way constrained to "dance to the movement of the bass,"[26] has a rhythmic suppleness—a *parlando rubato*—beyond that of any other kind of melody except chant. Such a line has the possibility of holding back on a single tone at one place, then rushing headlong through a cluster of sounds at another, thereby conveying a sudden change of feeling from languor to excitement. But even beyond the rhythmic factor (and this is where it differs radically from plainchant in both expressive effect and intention), recitative counts on the application of subtle (and not so subtle) gradations of vocal accents, again with a mind to rendering all the infinite contrasts and "modulations" of the inner life. Finally, there is the bass line itself, which beyond its function of supporting the vocal line and allowing it maximum freedom, has its own expressive character, which Peri, when writing that the slow sustained tones of the bass are especially suited to "sad or grave" subjects, clearly understood as reaffirming the basic symbiosis between early recitative and tragic expression.[27]

The best examples of recitative leave no doubt as to the expressive powers of the language, this despite the enormous reduction of means it represents vis-à-vis 16th-century polyphony. At the same time, it is not easy to forgive Galilei his zeal in willing away the precious richness and splendor, and we are happy to think that most musicians ignored him and proceeded to contribute their share to the monument that is the fin de siècle madrigal. But if we pay very close attention to what he writes—to how he thinks—about this richness, we must conclude that he had no other choice.[28] When Winn takes Galilei to task for insisting on a solution that would rob music of some of its most expressive means, he simply fails to look at the situation from Galilei's point of view. To Galilei's way of thinking, these so-called expressive means were so many seductions for the ear; they obstructed the way to the "affetti umani." Far from being the friends of expression, they were its enemies. He writes with exceptional clarity on this point in the *Dialogo*, stating that the rules of counterpoint are[29]

excellent and necessary for the mere delight the ear takes in the variety of the harmonies, but for the expression of conceptions they are pestilent, being fit for nothing but to make the concentus varied and full, and this is not always, indeed is never, suited to express any conception of the poet or the orator.

We do not have to agree with Galilei in order to understand that the solution he proposes follows logically from a conviction that is totally sincere. And if we confront the actual recitative once again, this time ridding our minds of any thought of what it might connote in the loss of color and sensuousness (and realizing, in any case, that European music lost nothing in the bargain, but rather gained another arrow for its rhetorical quiver), we stand to appreciate the unique value of this language for dealing with human emotion; as the music which has come the closest in our culture to replicating the cadences of human speech, the recitative becomes a style without style, an expression of self from which the veneer of the outward personality seems to have been totally removed. We have a sense of being in the presence of emotion stripped down to bare essentials. The literary drama, of course, identifies a great mythical figure, like Orpheus, Pluto, Theseus, Ariadne, or Proserpina, and in performance, the timbre of voice alone will necessarily point to a recognizable "type." But the music in its stark naturalism projects a figure with no identifiable connections, no sound of rank or courtly elegance, of lofty ceremony or liturgical piety. The demotic impulse is at work here, portraying a hero who is one of us—an everyman—and who, like us, rejoices and mourns, feels defeated by circumstances, and then finds the energy to struggle past them.[30] In demotic images, there is a strong bid made for our feelings of identification and our sympathy; in this demotic monody, then, we are asked to hear the pleadings of our own voice. Galilei's vision of a music of unadorned emotion—of truth unassisted by beauty—is genuinely realized, if only for a brief time.

Aria

From quite early on in the 16th century, the label "aria" was attached to several different musical conceptions, but with the opening of the first public opera house in Venice in 1637, the course was set for affixing the label to one single genre of extended song which we still call "aria" today. The recitative, too, would be affected by these Venetian events, though less in musical appearances than in dramatic function. Pirrotta describes the recitative in Monteverdi's last opera, *L'incoronazione di Poppea* of 1642, as moving in and out of phases of "winged melody."[31] Soon after *Poppea*, the phases of recitative and winged melody would be more clearly differentiated, leading to more extended set-pieces. By the end of the century the solo set-piece had assumed its fully developed da capo form, and it dominated every area of Italian vocal music. In the opera seria of the early 18th century, it was customary at the moment that an aria was to be sung for all but one of the protagonists to retire from the stage, thus leaving the remaining protagonist to sing the aria as a soliloquy. This illusion of absolute privacy was important in persuading the listener that the feelings being expressed were totally heartfelt and sincere, totally free of the kinds of ulterior motives that could be imagined if the feelings were addressed to someone else on stage.

This device alone attests to the strong position that *pathos* continued to occupy in the aesthetic assumptions of those heavily involved in the musical culture—composer, librettist, and faithful audience alike. Nevertheless, concealed in the aria are other concerns, not so easily perceived, with which *pathos* must contend in shaping the aria's expressive character. The first of these is not so much a deviation from *pathos* itself as a departure from the view of inner life projected in the dominant musical types of the preceding era. Both the dramatic madrigal and early monody had imaged the inner life as a welter of rapidly changing and contrasting emotions; early 18th-century opera did not do away with the notion of emotional contrast but it distributed the contrasting states of mind over the entire surface of the opera, in such a way that each state of mind became a self-contained entity to be sustained for the entire duration of an aria. This "doctrine of the single affection," if it can be so called, meant that any single aria had lost the capacity to represent within its borders the inner life as a system of rapidly changing emotions, except in those cases (and they were not numerous) where the sharp division between A and B sections of a da capo form was used as the occasion for introducing a contrast of mood.

It is often said that this new way of conceiving human emotion was largely the work of one man, René Descartes. George Buelow writes that Descartes' *Les Passions de l'Âme* was perhaps the single most influential philosophical work of the 17th century in relation to musical theory and aesthetics.[32] Descartes' efforts to give a scientific, physiological rationale to the workings and effects of the "passions" resulted in his classification of six "primitive passions" together with thirty-five others, which "are composed of some of these six, or are species of them."[33] As he conceived the basic process, the passions were[34]

accompanied by some commotion taking place in the heart, and consequently also in all the blood and animal spirits, so that until this commotion has subsided, the passions remain present to our thought in the same manner as sensible objects are present to us in thought during the time they act on our sense-organs.

Clearly, this likening of the passions to "sensible objects," in addition to the business of identifying each of the six-plus-thirty-five passions by name, lent to emotional reality a concreteness such as it had never known. That subsequent theories of musical expression owe a heavy debt to Descartes there is no doubt, not only by the theorists' professed acknowledgments of the French philosopher's ideas but also by their own very "Cartesian" classifications.[35] That Descartes had the same influence over compositional developments is less certain. The later 17th-century tendency to consolidate—to establish fixed patterns, to classify all manner of experience—suggests that musical practice guided by the "doctrine of the single affection" would have happened without Descartes. One suspects that Descartes' tract had the influence it did precisely because it was conceived in terms with which its readers were already familiar; it did not so much shape as reinforce a way of thinking that had been some time in the making. Galilei already refers to the "passions," as does Monteverdi. Indeed, the Greeks also thought of their emotional matter in terms of a variety of *pathe*.

To speak of the "passions" in the plural—to think of emotion as a finite collection of separate and discrete entities—is surely to *qualify pathos*, to channel musical expression of the inner life in a particular direction. Such an approach to emotion surely seems much less "naturalistic" than the imitations of the minute inflections of human speech that we get in monody or even than the fluctuations of mood, sometimes gradual, sometimes abrupt, that make up the continuity of a single dramatic madrigal. Monody—free in rhythm, free with respect to tonal organization, free to follow the supple and unpredictable trajectory of an interior emotional action described by a text—is the paradigm of openness, of spontaneity of expression. The aria, metrically regulated and as if predestined to carry out the fixed pattern, ABA, epitomizes the impulse to closure; the aesthetic need to formalize expression is very pronounced. But to claim on the basis of this that operatic practice at the beginning of the 18th century dealt in "units of music and emotional states of characters on stage that made no pretence at psychological realism"[36] is to exaggerate the case; such a claim lends credence to a demonstrably close association between artifice and artificiality; it suggests that Baroque musicians manipulated their representations of "static depersonalized passions"[37] in an exclusively artistic manner—with a view, in other words, to arousing the aesthetic emotion of the audience without anyone particularly believing, either composer or listener, that these avowals of tenderness and torrents of anger sung on stage corresponded vitally and directly to what human beings experienced in the world of everyday reality.

Nothing could be farther from the truth. We may think from our 20th-century vantage point, replete with all its Freudian sophistication, that the Baroque way of looking at the passions was either oversimplified or overdetermined or both. That, however, in no way diminishes the power they exerted over the Baroque imagination. Nor can we believe that Baroque musicians made any distinction between the passions expressed through their musical imagery and those identified by Descartes as belonging to the existential world; the musical passions were imitations, of course, but they went by the same names as nature's "originals" and for the simple reason that they were intended (just as Galilei had argued for the power of ancient music) to "lead the mind" back to those originals. The proof of all this lies in the best examples of the *opera seria* literature. There is no denying that to move from one aria to the next in the chain of arias that makes up the opera's continuity is to make an "abrupt change from one static passion to another."[38] But within the formal confines of a single aria, the first-rate composers like Alessandro Scarlatti or Handel applied all their skill to creating a continuity which was the very opposite of static. Essentially lyrical but not without its declamatory touches (and also strongly dynamic in view of the collaboration of functional tonality), this continuity provided the protagonist with all the gradations and subtleties of voice he needed to give expression to the particular passion which presently held him in its grip. Here was the essence of the aria's psychological realism; here was emotion in all its fluid and complex ebb and flow. The method of concentrating on one passion at a time enabled the Baroque composer to give it full expression, to probe it richly and intensively. And as the composer made his way through the opera, exploring the passions each in turn, it would be hard to believe that he did not consider them his opera's central truths.

Immediately on having made this assertion, we turn to an issue which seems to belie it. After the first public opera house opened in 1637, it was clear that opera was going to have to appeal to a wider range of tastes than it had previously. People wanted to be entertained and above all, they wanted *bel canto*—beautiful singing. We may be amused by Addison's and Marcello's accounts of operagoing in the early 18th century, but in view of present-day practices, we should not be particularly surprised to learn that most of the audience came to the opera to hear the bravura arias or their favorite singer, and cared not a whit about the dramatic significance. Indeed, much of their lack of concern for plot and character was shared by the creators themselves, whose first interest was generally in pleasing the prima donna, not worrying about whether a particular aria was more in character for one protagonist or another or whether it should appear in the first or last acts. The countless cases of cutting and rearranging plots and of exchanging arias even between operas are ample testimony on behalf of that point.

Such goings-on seem to give the lie to the rather high-minded aesthetic vision of the passions laid out in the previous discussion. In actual fact, the casual attitude toward the dramatic integrity of the opera had nothing to do with the emotional content of a given aria, since the aria was by definition a self-contained unit (though judicious placement of the aria in a succession of set-pieces could certainly heighten its impact). Beautiful singing was another matter. Given the separation that Galilei had made between the passions and the senses—to the point of making antagonists out of them—there was now a serious question as to whether a music that pleased the ear could carry emotional truth. Surely, Galilei had posed something of a paradox, for prior to him the general principle of modern aesthetics had been established (and artists and art lovers alike of the humanist persuasion were quite comfortable living with it) that "delight" and "instruction" (or perhaps more precisely, in view of music's specific capacities, delight and "serious expression of the passions") were not incompatible aims. But now Galilei had said that they were, and the hedonism surrounding opera developments from the 1640s onward seemed to lend further credence to his idea.

Perhaps we can best resolve this question by approaching it from an evolutionary standpoint. Pirrotta tells us that in the early 17th-century operas it was the custom for the gods and goddesses in these pieces to sing in elaborate and song-like style, whereas human beings sang in recitative.[39] This revealing separation of responsibilities creates a natural alliance between "nonsensuous" recitative and man's earthbound and essentially tragic condition, while song is the natural language of the gods, who live on another plane of existence, immune to suffering and death. Mention has already been made of Monteverdi's mid-17th-century essays in recitative, in which the speech-like cadences periodically take off into "winged melody." Elaborating on this effect, Pirrotta writes: "The ardor of amorous passion justifies the overflowing expansion of vocal melody ... in *L'incoronazione* Monteverdi's realism lets the melody grow from the psychological 'excitement' of the heart."[40] In this example the sensuousness of song is intimately linked to the sensuality of erotic desire: the two are effectively made out of the same stuff. *L'incoronazione* tells of a universal feeling with which we can easily identify. To one under love's spell, the prosaic, everyday world comes to be a magical, romantic place, a place resounding with the magic of song. Having been exalted by love, the lover comes to feel himself relocated somewhere above the ordinary human plane, ready to break forth in "divine melody" (though divinity here should be understood to be of the order of Olympus, not of Christian Heaven).

But musicians after Monteverdi went beyond this limiting case. For them music's proverbial sweetness—its capacity to delight—no longer needed the rationale of erotic love to demonstrate its power to move. Its enchantments, so often labeled "dangerous" over the long course of history, would now be embraced for the part they played in arousing aesthetic emotion: the basic elements of music in all their visceral presence—not only melody, but rhythm, harmony, and the wonderful variety of instrumental color—were to be marshalled in the interests of serving the passions vividly and comprehensively. This is the aria's answer to the recitative. In the later Baroque period, the *divine* attributes of music are reconfirmed, this time not merely to express *human* emotion but to glorify it. The older message: "Those who live on a higher plane (the gods) must surely sing" is subtly transmuted into: "Those who choose to sing (the humans) will surely advance to a higher plane on which to live." The Baroque aria takes the old pairing of delight and instruction and raises it to a new level of synthesis.

Another kind of synthesis—that between vocal and instrumental media—was going on concurrently in Baroque music, a synthesis that not only guaranteed the virtual interchangeability of vocal and instrumental imagery but also brought the instrumental dance into the mainstream of musical thought. No genre of the period is more affected by this last development (not even the suite) than the aria, the aria category taken as a whole being a compendium adapted for vocal use of instrumental dance-types. The possibilities of the dance principle in constituting still another rhetorical resource for the expression of the passions should be clear: as recitative was conceived to be an imitation of "natural" vocal gestures, a given aria is involved in the imitation of a formal physical action, namely a particular dance-type, which in its turn corresponds to a particular state of mind. And as "state of mind" connotes precisely that tendency in later Baroque thinking to view human emotion as a collection of self-contained affective entities—of "states"—it is easy to see how the clear-cut, distinct differentiations between dance-types could in little time acquire clear-cut and specific affective associations. To what extent Baroque aesthetic theory believed in the force of these associations is brought out explicitly in Johann Mattheson's classification of dance affects in *Der Volkommene Capellmeister*, of which the following are a few examples: minuet—moderate gaiety; gavotte—jubilant joy; bourrée—contentedness and relaxation; rigaudon—flirtatious pleasantry; anglaise—obstinacy; rondeau—steadfastness and good faith.[41] The question is not whether Mattheson's affective assignments are right or wrong, or whether his verbal designations even constitute a good method for identifying affective content in music. What is significant about the method is that the content is understood to be found not in some connection to an outside text, but in the sensuous material of a musical image—an image, moreover, which is dance-based.

The scenario outlined above—of a musical culture which, with its peculiarly rationalistic view of the inner life and with a vocal music explicitly dedicated to the expression of that inner life, should fix upon the available dance material of the period as a vehicle for carrying out its expressive mission—is so logical as to seem almost inevitable. Yet, one wonders whether the musicians of the Baroque period, in quest of a treasure-trove of *pathe*, had not happened upon a storehouse of *ethe* instead. For when we think of the environment in which the aforementioned dances took on their definitive look, namely the extremely decorum-conscious and form-laden court of Louis XIV, it is difficult not to conclude that the content to be uncovered in these dances was a species not of inner life but of outward manners. We need not read far into any Renaissance or Baroque dance manual to learn that courtly dancing is an art as indispensable to a man of quality as any other aspect of his education—fencing, hunting, the arts of war. This is what Arbeau has to say on the subject:[42]

Most of the authorities hold that dancing is a kind of mute rhetoric by which the orator, without uttering a word, can make himself understood by his movements and persuade the spectators that he is gallant and worthy to be acclaimed, admired, and loved. Are you not of the opinion that this is the dancer's own language, expressed by his feet and in a convincing manner?

In view of the basic thrust of courtly dancing, it seems more likely that individual dance-types would connote outer qualities rather than inner feelings. They would suggest the outward face a person wishes to show the world, not what he is experiencing inside. The stately sarabande would reflect his dignity, the minuet his temperateness of character and delicate grace; the bourrée would show him to be amiable and quick-witted. These are all character traits by which one would like to be remembered—which are worthy, just as Arbeau says, "to be acclaimed, admired, and loved";[43] they have in short, ethical, not affective significance. But if opera arias are based on dance-types, as they are in the overwhelming number of cases, perhaps the protagonists who are singing them are expressing not so much their changing emotions as their habitual personalities. Add to this the fact that these protagonists—these "characters"—of the *opera seria* conduct themselves with a certain admirable dignity—they conform to certain strict notions of courtly decorum (whether or not they should prove ultimately to be on the side of good or evil)—and one wonders whether the Baroque practitioners of this art have not seriously mistaken *ethos* for *pathos*.

We have been slowly working our way back to the thesis initiated in Chapter 3. Indeed, the preceding chapter ended with the notion that the decorum of the Christian liturgy as conceived by the early fathers had been undergoing slight modifications in the late Middle Ages in such a way that the accommodation of the liturgy to the "emotional" motet that emerged at the end of the 15th century took place without incident. Subsequently, we saw how the rhetorical restraint of much early 16th-century secular polyphony showed it to be still fundamentally attached to the social vision of courtly love, while the later 16th-century madrigal found itself abandoning this vision whenever it entered into the private, dark world of the more violent passions. With the monody of the early Italian opera, the music (if not the literary drama) gives no hint of the social identity of the protagonists, with the result that the lasting impression here is one of having heard the voice of raw emotion unmuted by any concern for decorous behavior. This is hardly true of the aria, where the courtly factor has reasserted itself in the embodiment of the dance. It would be folly, however, to claim on this basis the abandonment of *pathos* in the Baroque aria. The dance is in the long run only one element contributing to the total image of the aria, in other words, to its total expressiveness. *Opere serie* are studded with heart-wrenching episodes and tormented protagonists, and opera seria composers were certain that their music had the energy to more than meet the emotional challenge posed by the drama; the "rage aria" and the "pathetic aria" are so named for good reason.[44]

Still, the differentiations among arias (which, we are reminded, are essentially the differentiations between dance categories) reflect not only a collection of states of mind but quite as importantly the articulation of courtly and urban society into a number of recognizable human types. In order to take the full measure of the aria's content, the listener, in addition to absorbing through the music the specific affection involved, needed to know something of the identity of the person who was feeling and expressing the affection. If historians of music have rarely thought to look for this identity in the musical images themselves, that must be because theories of art in the Baroque period never mention it; Baroque aesthetics is so preoccupied with the passions that assumptions of decorum and outward behavior, however deeply entrenched in the courtly psyche they might be, remain in that deeply unconscious state; they never, in other words, seem to rise to the surface of conscious abstraction and classification. Though unstated in theory, however, these assumptions are vigorously at work in practice, which is to say that with few exceptions, no balanced reading of a musical image is possible unless a serious effort has been made to account for the ethical as well as affective factors contained in the image.

As our discussions have proceeded, we have caused certain human types to appear from behind the musical imagery: the humble worshipper, the plaintive courtier, the merry reveller, the suffering everyman. Except for the last, these types originate in very specific and sectarian contexts of the literal world around us: the Christian ritual, the courtly love ritual, the May Day ritual. But with the increasing de-ritualizing of music in Western culture and the increasing interest of composers to connect their music to literary narrative and dramatic forms, the human types that emerge from musical imagery are increasingly fictional in nature. The "suffering everyman" is in a unique position in this picture, because he has no affiliation, no identity outside the context of his own emotion. And emotion is the universal leveller: it is, despite the diversity of our individual experiences, the one thing we all experience. We may be the authors of our circumstances, or they may have come along unbidden, but the pain and pleasure we receive from them are registered as having happened to us. This is the passive essence of passion; destined to experience our circumstances as pain or pleasure, we "suffer" them, whether we have created them or not. The "suffering everyman," therefore, is in all of us, including the "ritual" types identified above and the fictional types about to be encountered.

Nevertheless, there is an important difference in the way these two typological categories relate to their emotion. In the first category, the human type, being the product of a strong ethical position, is identified principally in terms of how he behaves, not how he feels: emotion enters in, but only secondarily. In the fictional category, on the other hand, the figures in question function first and foremost in terms of their emotion, and for the very reason that that is the way their creators have conceived them: composers working in the firm belief that music exists primarily to express the "affetti umani" make every effort to invest their protagonists with the rhetorical resources necessary to give powerful voice to their joys and sorrows. But the subtext—the tacit reality—of this enterprise is that these same protagonists have an identity beyond their emotion; in the primary sense, they are all "suffering everymen," but each is also a "kind of person" whose identity derives from his belonging to a specific world. *Ethos* may have taken second place to *pathos*, but it is still a force to be reckoned with.

Ethos being the principle by which we define human behavior and character, the "kind of person" an individual is will be understood in terms of what that individual does—how he behaves, how he acts. (By contrast, a person caught up in his emotions is someone who merely *reacts*.) In the next three chapters we will be concerned with identifying a number of human types and examining the ways in which they express themselves musically by virtue of the kinds of persons they are. It was said above that the identity of a type is also dependent on the "world" to which the type belongs. This is true to the extent that the world in question controls and shapes the kinds of actions that happen within its borders. In such a world a *decorum* is established, a mode of conduct considered appropriate to the spiritual climate—the *ethos*—of that world. The church sanctuary during the celebration of the liturgy and the ideal court which faithfully lives according to the precepts of courtly love are two cases in point.

In the next three chapters, the fictional "worlds" depicted are the pastoral, the epic/heroic, and the satiric, respectively. A fictional world contains certain recognizable features of the everyday literal world, which must ultimately be a significant source for all the fictional worlds possible; a useful analogy for a fictional world might be to imagine a detail of a photograph (a piece of the literal world) blown up to a large size and then made to stand on its own. The world of the pastoral has been described earlier as better than our own—one that combines the best parts of the real world—where peace and beauty flourish, and friendship is the basis of human interaction. Its opposite is the satiric world, a topsy-turvy place inhabited by people who behave in foolish, undignified, and generally unadmirable ways. Though opposites, the pastoral and satiric worlds share one quality in common, which is that they are both relatively small and contained. The epic/heroic, by contrast, is the great world—the theater of adventure and war—the one that tests to the limits those who live according to its rules and significantly challenges them to rise above themselves. All three worlds are ultimately "ethical," though the satiric is so by indirection, defining virtue through its absence.

During the better part of this chapter, the special nature of the musical material has enabled us to concentrate on the subject of the human emotions without much attention paid to any other factor. But on coming to the Baroque aria with its plethora of "types," we have been suddenly confronted with the realization that the "affection" or "passion" in question is not enough to account for the aria's expressiveness; we want to know who is behind the passion, who is experiencing it. This principle, extracted from the specific case of the Baroque aria, extends to all "emotional" music. In such music the expressive function is entrusted with a dual responsibility: to be true to the specific passion or passions represented in the imagery and to be true to the character of the sentient subject. The protagonist of an opera seria is certainly intended to give full vent to his emotion, but he is also constrained to sing of his emotion according to the kind of person he is; no matter how strong his passion, there is no way he can escape expressing *himself*, which is something, if not deeper than passion, at least less momentary, more characteristic. We now seek to identify a protagonist's characteristic modes of expression. Examining the major fictional worlds in which he lives should help us considerably in this process.

Notes

1. Lawrence F. Bernstein, "The 'Parisian Chanson': Problems of Style and Terminology," in *Journal of the American Musicological Society*, Vol. XXXI, No. 2 (Summer 1978), p. 212 and p. 239.

2. *Ibid.*, pp. 212–217.

3. Howard M. Brown, *Music in the Renaissance*, p. 212.

4. We must imagine this process in spite of the fact that in the case at hand the single courtier is represented by at least four singers. This double artifice is a complication of the strategy of *mimesis*, which though a fascinating subject in itself, is tangential to our central subject of musical content and, at any rate, is so rich in ramifications that it demands its own studies.

5. For instance, *J'ai fait pour vous cent mille pas* begins: "I have made for you one hundred thousand steps and many foolish undertakings" and ends: "Alas, what will become of my life? It gives me nothing but misfortune. For one pleasure, a thousand pains."

6. *Chanson de cour* translated literally into English would read "courtly chanson," which connotes something like "chanson of courtly behavior." To convey more of the inward character of the song, "chanson of courtly devotion" would come closer to the mark.

7. Brown, p. 212.

8. There are occasions in which writers of Italian nationality will take the French side, or vice versa, but that does not change the terms of the argument or the prejudices behind it.

9. Indeed, these differences in national viewpoints on the matter of expressive styles are well known through the expressive habits of both French and Italians; that they should apply to music as well as to every other aspect of living is no more than expected.

10. Oliver Strunk, ed., *Source Readings in Music History*, pp. 407–408.

11. *Ibid.*, pp. 226–227.

12. Whether Josquin would have described his piece in the same terms as Glarean is another question altogether and one which, for reasons already given in the previous chapter, is unanswerable.

13. Howard Mayer Brown, "Psyche's Lament," in *Words and Music: The Scholar's View*, Laurence Berman, ed., p. 14.

14. Quoted in the original Italian in *ibid.*, p. 16.

15. See Strunk, *Source Readings*, pp. 413–415.

16. The scene depicted here, in fact, follows on the one taken by Monteverdi for the *Combattimento*. Tancredi, thinking his beloved Clorinda to be an enemy on horseback, engages her in combat and kills her. Now, in these lines set forth by Wert, he comes to her tomb to mourn her.

17. One hears even more distant echoes of Josquin's chanson, *Plaine de deuil*, and the liturgical style he fostered in such motets as *Dominus regnavit* and *Tu pauperum refugium*.

18. It took Monteverdi, with the benefit of 40 more years' perspective, to appreciate it.

19. Nino Pirrotta, *Music and Culture in Italy from the Middle Ages to the Baroque*, p. 220.

20. Quoted in Alfred Einstein, *The Italian Madrigal*, Vol. I, p. 220.

21. Pirrotta, p. 219: "Galileo's father cuts a poor figure as a theorist and has nothing, or next to nothing, original to say ..." But see Claude V. Palisca, *Humanism in Italian Renaissance Musical Thought*, pp. 273–279.

22. James Anderson Winn, *Unsuspected Eloquence*, pp. 176–177. Though Winn doesn't identify his humanists by name here, it is clear that Galilei is included in the indictment, since in a prior statement, he writes: "The most extreme humanists, especially Galilei, wanted to eliminate every aspect of current compositional technique, to return to the naked monody that had been the Greek norm."

23. A very coherent discussion of Mei's ideas is conducted in Palisca, *Humanism*, pp. 348–355.

24. Strunk, *Source Readings*, p. 374.

25. *L'Orfeo* dates from 1607, the first five madrigal books from 1587, 1590, 1603, 1604, and 1605 respectively.

26. A remark of Peri's quoted in Strunk, *Source Readings*, p. 374.

27. In the more conversational, less intentionally emotional style of later recitative, it should be noted that the biggest change comes in the bass, where the long sustained tones of the early monody are exchanged for abrupt punctuations, which lend a certain perfunctory character to the expression and rightly earn for the style the name *secco*.

28. It was an austere choice, to be sure, but no more so than Plato's and Augustine's, and their positions are always presented as eminently reasonable. One wonders how ready we would be to accept their reasons if the beautiful music they condemned and would cast over the cliff were known to us firsthand.

29. Strunk, *Source Readings*, pp. 311–312.

30. This alternation between suffering the blows of fate and then making an effort to rise above them is the central action of all tragedy, ancient and modern.

31. Pirrotta, p. 253.

32. George J. Buelow, "Music, Rhetoric, and the Concept of Affections," in *Notes*, Vol. XXX (1973), p. 252.

33. Quoted in Piero Weiss and Richard Taruskin, ed., *Music in the Western World: A History of Documents*, p. 214.

34. *Ibid.*, p. 214.

35. Mattheson is the most illustrious of this generation, which also includes J.D. Heinichen, J.G. Walther, J.C. Gottsched, all very much affected by the Cartesian theories.

36. John Neubauer, *The Emancipation of Music from Language*, p. 50. There is a prejudice in the author's reference to "psychological realism"; his assessment of Descartes makes it clear where he thinks "psychological realism" is to be found.

37. *Ibid.*, p. 50.

38. *Ibid.*, p. 50.

39. Pirrotta, p. 249.

40. *Ibid.*, pp. 252–253.

41. Weiss/Taruskin, p. 219.

42. Quoted in *ibid.*, p. 155.

43. *Ibid.*, p. 155.

44. For a concise but telling picture of such aria conventions, see an excerpt from the memoirs of Carlo Goldoni, reprinted in *ibid.*, pp. 229–231.

8   *The Pastoral Mode, I*

In determining the kinds of music to be included in the pastoral category, we begin by referring to the criteria outlined in Chapter 2. Most fundamental among these are the qualities of gentleness, sweetness, restfulness, and the like that inhabit all pastoral imagery, though were we to stop with this consideration a full three-quarters of the literature would qualify as pastoral music. As a means of setting further limits, a division into Arcadian and rustic subclasses (already indicated in Chapter 2) works not only to underscore the social component in the pastoral archetype but even more to bring to light the key values of hieratic and demotic thinking. At the same time, this separation of rustic and Arcadian interests must not ignore the overriding interest they have in common, which is to see the everyday world reflected in the idealizing mirror of the pastoral community and thereby bring it closer to the ideal.

Taken together, these criteria serve to outline a method for identifying pastoral imagery in music. On this basis, however, medieval music would be left out of consideration altogether, Arcadian pastoral being a product of Renaissance humanism, while rustic pastoral is a later development still, in large part a reaction against Arcadian ideals. This problem can be overcome by creating a third subdivision—"proto-Pastoral"—for those medieval and early Renaissance images which conform in appearance and philosophical attitude to later pastoral patterns. The appropriate medieval music for this subdivision would presumably fall somewhere between the serious courtly love song and the dance of revelry—a kind of melody simple and regular in phrase structure, moderate in tempo, and gently undulating in linear contour. The 13th-century monophonic dance-song, *Ce fut en mai* by Moniot d'Arras, with its triple-time lilt, its perfect symmetry both in terms of phrase length and open and closed pairs, and its bright major intervals, shows all the markings of proto-pastoral expression. Essentially a *carole* (which Stevens has described as a dance having its origins in folk melody but made over in the refined image of the court),[1] this piece means to combine the proverbial fresh note of the country with the corrective of courtly cultivation.

Its preeminent spiritual successor in the polyphonic idiom of the early Renaissance is the three-part May Day or spring chanson of the Burgundian school. The opening phrase of Dufay's *Pour l'amour de ma doulce amye* is enough to reveal its pastoral-idyllic leanings: crystalline texture, softly buoyant triple-time impulse, delicately curvilinear main melody (Example 8.1). Indeed, the easy, open elegance of this music appears already to meet two essential requisites of classic Arcadian pastoral, combining exquisite workmanship with that "sparkling, folklike innocence" which court and city, in their more sentimental moments, have traditionally represented as the essence of country life. It may also be of some significance that *Ce fut en mai* and much of the Burgundian chanson literature are found in the manuscript sources written in an F-mode, suggesting that the later convention of F major as the "pastoral key" might have been already alive in an embryonic form at this early time.

Example 8.1: Dufay, *Pour l'amour de ma doulce amye*

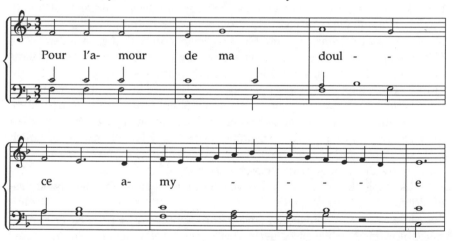

Another candidate for inclusion in the proto-pastoral category, though with some qualification, is the 14th-century Italian *caccia*. This genre presents a significant variant of the usual pastoral perspective, depicting as it does not country life directly but rather the court at its country pleasures. In *Tosto che l'alba* of Ghirardello da Firenze, the rush and excitement of the hunt, with the quick-paced ⁶⁄₈ thumping of the horses' hooves, the flourishes of the horns, and the whoops and cries of the hunters as they call after their dogs, Viola and Primera (all conveyed musically in a rare effort of the time at musical realism), is really too uproarious for classic pastoral quiet, but representation of the country as a place in the full blush of health and youthful beauty conforms precisely to the way the court likes to see its pastoral symbolism put to use. If the *caccia* teeters on the edge of pastoral, the troubadour and trouvère genres known as the *pastorela* and the *pastourelle*, respectively, fall outside its bounds for reasons that will be discussed in the chapter on the satiric mode. Of the *pastourelle* Stevens writes that it is "a genre which pretends to be popular, belonging to the people, rather than actually being so. There is a disingenuousness, a mock-simplicity, at the heart of pastoral in every age."[2] But the element of mockery goes beyond the business of putting on an easily seen-through disguise: the text very explicitly, and the music in its own way, show that they mean to poke fun at the actions they describe. That is the very antithesis of classic pastoral, which idealizes human actions by representing them as pure and innocent—as "unspoiled by irony." Since the outlook of the *pastourelle* (which is something more complex than its surface affiliations with the countryside would suggest) places it squarely in the satiric category, it will be appropriately discussed in Chapter 11.

Arcadian Pastoral

The *ethos* of courtly pastoral having been provisionally stated, we must now ask what gain there was in pastoral poets of the early 16th century resurrecting all the ancient machinery of Arcadia—how, in a literal sense, the Italian courtly culture related to this Arcadian metaphor. The fact is that ancient pastoral poetry was a storehouse of beautiful, delicately voluptuous images, images that could be taken over by modern visual and musical artists, as well as by poets, and done up with even more sensuous immediacy for the eye and the ear than was possible with words alone. Pirrotta has summarized the entire aspiration of the movement in one succinct phrase: "In a tradition of classical origin, a sophisticated society usually enjoys mirroring itself in an equally sophisticated Arcadian disguise."[3] The disguise is the perfect world of Arcadia itself. Unlike this perfect pastoral world, the everyday world of the 16th-century Italian court was not perfect, but the inhabitants of the court, by surrounding themselves with newly created artifacts embodying the pastoral realm, came into actual contact with that realm and could thereby perfect themselves. This is the ethical effect of Renaissance pastoral, an effect amounting to an action of ritual transference: the pastoral world is no longer simply a nostalgic reverie but the artistic environment in which the privileged class lives out its daily existence. Worldly beauty, long justified as a reflection of heavenly beauty, comes to be celebrated, if not entirely for its own sake, at least for the part it plays in the cultivation of worldliness and personal distinction. And so, pastoral becomes the chief vehicle by which cultivated beauty is served.

Sixteenth-century pastoral, then, is a decor extending to all the arts. Indeed, it is mainly through the stimulus of this decor that the pictorial impulses of the new music will have full opportunity to develop. As the ravishing backdrop they form, the pastoral surroundings prove to be a vast storehouse of images, containing not only the "vaghi augelletti" and "amorosi fronde" of the natural world, but also the superhuman beings of the mythological world, which, now totally emptied of their mythic content, radiate even more charm and sensuality than they did for the ancients. Tasso understands this very well when he writes: "Though I am no expert in music, I know at least what is expected of poems intended to be sung. They are smooth; they are amorous in their affection; they are colorful; and they abound in phrases (*figure*) suitable for music."[4] In *Il Pastor Fido*, Guarini would write a play with so much of the expected imagery that it would prove irresistible to musicians. Of course, the connection of pastoral with the theater was already very much a tradition by Guarini's time. From the great Medici wedding of 1539 we have an elaborate account of the pastoral intermezzi which appeared between the acts of the comedy, *Il Commodo*.[5] The particular sumptuousness of these representations is not surprising, given the family and occasion they were celebrating. But spectacle is at the very heart of the intermezzo, grand or small. The musical component of the intermezzo fulfills its function of providing the aural delight, while the visual delight is literally provided before the beholder's eyes.

In a Guarini "microdrama," such as *Tirsi morir volea*, on the other hand, the visual setting supplied by the words is meant to be captured in the music: it is not too much to say that the music in the later pastoral madrigals has a spectacular function unto itself. The word-painting in these pieces—the pictorializations—are their most obvious feature and usually the first thing discussed about them. They were already a matter of some controversy in their own day, considered indispensable to musical expression by some (Morley[6]), vilified as puerile claptrap by others (Galilei[7]). But to play down the pictorializations is to deny a unique function of these madrigals in creating a visual illusion; it is to ignore the theatrical essence of their expression. Is it possible to hear the opening of *Scendi dal paradiso, Venere* without *seeing* the superb goddess already on her way down (the illusion created quite alone by the music, since the text only anticipates her descent)?[8] Or to listen to *Scaldava il sol* without forming a picture of sun-baked silence (Example 8.2)? To be sure, it requires the text to make the scene explicit; but the music, with its capacity to imitate details which are visual in origin, does not mean to create aural analogues for their own sake, but to retranslate these into the visual sphere, so that the auditor will capture the essence of the thing in all its clarity and immediacy by ultimately "beholding" it in his mind's eye.

The pastoral madrigal is strongly depictive, then, owing to the "backdrop" of the Arcadian world. Sometimes, however, this world does not serve as the backdrop but is the entire picture. This is the case in *Scaldava il sol*, where the human elements—the shepherd and the farmer—are not true protagonists, but part of the decor. When the perfect world of the pastoral occupies the foreground, the verbal and musical expression is, or should be, as close to the purely idyllic as possible. Of all the madrigalists of the late 16th century, Marenzio is the acknowledged master of the idyllic mood. His ability to create a number of antitheses of sonority, then to modulate between them with the subtlest ease;

Example 8.2: Marenzio, *Scaldava il sol*

Publikationen Älterer Musik, ed. Alfred Einstein, 1928. Breitkopf & Härtel, Wiesbaden, used by permission.

his skill in imitating the little noises of nature, only to prove to us that they belong to the ultimate hush of rural peace, form the basis of his manner, one particularly beloved of the English. But if the idyllic were his only manner, he would not have earned the following characterization from Einstein: "Marenzio is preeminently the musician of the pastoral, of the pastoral in every sense."[9] In the Guarini texts, human suffering enters the idyllic world, and Marenzio does not hesitate to deal with it. His *Ah, dolente partita* is a particularly instructive setting, because it can be compared to two other memorable versions of the text, the first by Wert, the second by Monteverdi (Examples 8.3a, b, and c).[10] The text concerns Mirtillo's last words after being dismissed by Amarylli; and the composers deal with Mirtillo's situation in three distinct ways. Wert seems to take a middle position, his setting being the most theatrical, i.e., the most pictorial, of the three. With its shifts of sonority, its dramatic juxtapositions of high and low sound and its periodic soloistic outpourings, this madrigal evokes a picture that includes not only Mirtillo but a chorus that echoes the sentiments of the protagonist and offers sympathy. This is a device which already has its precedents in earlier "dialogue" settings (for instance, a lament for three nymphs and four shepherds by Donato from 1553), and which will live on long into the 17th century (Monteverdi's famous *Lamento della ninfa* of 1640). By contrast, Marenzio's conception is essentially nonpictorial. One could imagine, given the evenness of the expression, with its muted sighs at the opening and perfectly poised lyricism of the concluding phrases, that Mirtillo's anguish has not been portrayed; rather, the sympathizing chorus has replaced him in delivering a statement of pure elegy. The elegiac and idyllic tones are the complementary representatives of the tragic and comic visions, respectively, in the world of the pastoral. As Panofsky has observed, regarding Virgil's elegiac manner, "tragedy no longer faces us as stark reality but is seen through the soft, colored haze of sentiment either anticipatory or retrospective."[11] In music, one means of removing the expression from tragic immediacy is to imagine it assigned to the sympathetic observer rather than to the protagonist. Its solemn but accepting mood then corresponds to the one we find in literary elegy, which is a lament not for oneself, but for someone else: hero, friend, leader, mistress, or teacher. Marenzio's genius rests largely in his capacity to find in musical expression the voice of solemn and tender sympathy, thereby permitting him to capture the quintessence of the elegiac and idyllic moods. As such, he emerges the pastoral composer *par excellence*.

In Monteverdi's setting of *Ah, dolente partita*, the expression has been shifted back to the protagonist. From the prolonged and searing dissonance of the opening line—the same isolated minor second we find a century before in Josquin's *Douleur me bat*, although now raised (literally) to a new pitch of intensity—we have the impression that Mirtillo is alone with his grief: the lower lines of the madrigal are not the representation of sympathetic response, but the reverberations of his own anguished cry. In this restless setting, Monteverdi has exceeded the bounds of pastoral decorum and has pulled away into the realm of intense

Example 8.3a: Wert, *Ah, dolente partita*

Example 8.3b: Marenzio, *Ah, dolente partita*

pathos. Given the fact that Monteverdi's madrigal was published in 1603, the sharp, declamatory accents of the piece already have a considerable history behind them. As discussed in the last chapter, the tragic impulse, which became the expressive center of 17th-century monody, had already found an important outlet in the dramatic madrigal of the later 16th century. However, the rise of the unrestrained tragic tone at this time should not be regarded as signaling a waning of devotion to the Arcadian dream: pastoral and tragedy were essentially

Example 8.3c: Monteverdi, *Ah, dolente partita*

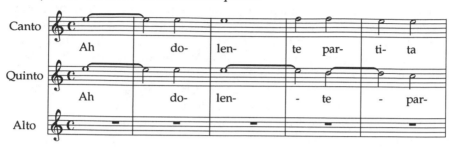

"Ah dolente partita" from *Il Quarto Libro de Madrigali di Claudio Monteverdi.* Edited by G. Francesco Malipiero. Used by kind permission of European American Music Distributors Corporation, sole U.S. and Canadian agent for Universal Edition A.G., Wien.

separate modes of expression—two different sets of tracks which for the most part ran parallel to each other, occasionally intersecting. When they did intersect, the tragic pattern, constrained to bend to the gentle will of pastoral, found it possible, as already noted, to realize only its elegiac side. This suggests that as a general rule, tragedy would be able to sing in full voice only when working outside pastoral limits.[12]

But, in fact, events coming at the very opening of the 17th century were to prove otherwise: the *favola in musica*, with which both opera and the Baroque era simultaneously got launched, turned out to be a pastoral form in which suffering had the chance to be explored in all its depth and variety. Since the *favola in musica* has been studied quite thoroughly by a number of recent authorities, only a few passing observations will be offered here. The first is that the separateness generally maintained between elegiac expression and the unrestrained tragic tone in late 16th-century madrigals must in part be due to the madrigal's relatively restricted scale. Once music was called upon to adapt to the scale (not to mention the episodic variety) of a literary drama, a "policy of inclusion" was more than likely, if not absolutely necessary. Reference has already been made to Act II of Monteverdi's *L'Orfeo,* in which a messenger breaks in on a joyous celebration to impart the news of Euridice's death. The scene is structured so as to dramatize the evil of human misfortune intruding into the idyllic world, into the Garden of Eden; this is the kind of action that could excite the madrigalists but was almost impossible for them to undertake within the scope of the madrigal genre. In *Orfeo*, the dramatic crisis of Act II offers Monteverdi, already well practiced through his own madrigals in handling the pastoral and tragic modes separately, the possibility for bringing them into a new relation: the series of idyllic dance-songs that open the act are suddenly cut short by the messenger's harrowing recitative. Here, pastoral does not transform tragedy into muted elegy, but serves as a benign foil for the terrible blow ahead.

In the years following *Orfeo*, opera gave birth to some unusual examples of expressive hybrids. Pastoral, tragic, and satiric episodes clashed and bounced off each other with unaccustomed and often fascinating abandon, and composers created the music to match. But as the century wore on, the taste grew for finding a more unified tone for each dramatic entity, eventually resulting in a theoretically strict separation of operatic genres, the *seria* and the *buffa*. This was mainly due to the rise of heroic expression in Baroque musical thought and to the ingenuity on the part of Baroque composers for finding musical ways to embody epic/heroic content. Although a full description of the heroic mode must await the next chapter, it can at least be said here that relative to the ascendancy of the heroic mode, pastoral expression, so dominant in the music of the latter part of the Renaissance, came to occupy a somewhat lesser place in the Baroque configuration of things. But we must not overstate the weakening of the pastoral influence in music during this time, or, for that matter, in the thinking of the culture in general; for the fact is that the Arcadian images maintained themselves in strength throughout the 17th century and well into the 18th, because courtly society, ever in need of a language with which to project its aspirations to high refinement and artistic superiority, had not created another dialect to supplant "Arcadian."

What we find, then, at the start of the 18th century is a kind of roving function invested in musical pastoral: the heroic and tragic styles predominate in *opera seria*, the satiric style is the mainstay of *opera buffa*, while pastoral imagery shows up abundantly in both.[13] A brief glimpse into how this works can be given by an example from Handel's *Giulio Cesare*. Caesar's opening aria strikes just the right military note for a conquering hero, while in the love duet with Cleopatra in Act II, he is permitted to be appropriately amorous; that is, he is assigned a music which encourages him to sing with a kind of soft languor. This dualism of personality is the very essence of the Baroque heroic ideal. But more than that, it is the perpetuation of the ancient division between epic and pastoral, with all the original archetypal significance of the division still intact. The hero-leader, in the Baroque view of things, is complete only when courage, commanding presence, and will to glory are matched by seasoned practice in the art of love and a continued show of love for the arts—when, in short, an equilibrium has been reached between the image of the warrior and the image of the shepherd.

This equating of the shepherd with the lover leads us to consider a phase of Arcadian pastoral not yet discussed. The *ethos* of pastoral, when compared against the *ethos* of the Christian liturgy, for instance, where a literal and specific action (holy worship) takes place in a literal and specific environment (the church sanctuary)—this *ethos* of pastoral, projected as it is as an elaborate metaphor of idyllic landscapes and gentle human actions, is not always easy to keep straight. We must continually remind ourselves that the only literal reality of these charming nymphs and shepherds, rippling brooks and murmuring streams, twittering birds and tufted groves, is their power to embody a host of qualities which the society who dreamt them up would like to possess. And then, not all, or even half, of the qualities required by this society are covered by the pastoral metaphor, for surely a Baroque aristocrat would also wish to shape himself in the image of a warrior-hero and must therefore turn to another world of actions and qualities to guide him in that pursuit. What this ultimately means in terms of literal content is that although the qualities attaching to warriors and shepherds may well be subsumed in a single person from the literal, everyday world, the epic and pastoral traditions in Western culture have conditioned us to think of warrior and shepherd as distinct and contrasting human types. The shepherd as a type, then, is limited to the extent that he does not possess the qualities of the warrior; but he is not so limited that we must think of him merely as a sweet, gentle fellow wandering a bit distractedly around the countryside tending his flock. Ancient pastoral had also marked out the shepherd as a lover and a musician-poet; and around this triad of qualities his archetypal personality has been formed ever since.

Quite independently of the classical tradition, or so it seems, the later Middle Ages had invented the perfect courtly knight who was also a true and ardent lover and sang of his love in order to prove his personal and social virtue.[14] Given the persistence of courtly love even into the 16th century, it would be surprising if some of its patterns had not been absorbed into the texture of Arcadian pastoral. Indeed, the love theme is at the very core of the 16th-century pastoral madrigal; it is the generating force of all the actions committed and all the emotions suffered by the archetypal lover-pairs, Tirsi and Clori, Mirtillo and Amarylli. But this overlapping concern of courtly love and pastoral is more apparent than real, for love is perceived in the two categories in almost diametrically opposed ways. In courtly love, erotic desire is voluntarily repressed in order to achieve a higher end; in 16th-century pastoral, erotic desire means to be fulfilled. When it is thwarted, as in the case of *Ah, dolente partita*, at the moment in *Il Pastor Fido* when Mirtillo loses Amarylli, the result is stark, unredeemed suffering, not the quiet triumph of discipline over self. Pastoral celebrates the senses, even to the point of representing sensual enjoyment as "innocent pleasure," whereas courtly love is still too steeped in the medieval tradition of self-denial to celebrate anything more than that restrained quality of emotion which is expressed through the courtly love song itself. The musical images of pastoral, by contrast, are suffused with a delicate but unmistakable sensuousness: "smooth" and "colorful," as Tasso wrote, the pastoral madrigal of the late 16th century offers in five- and six-voiced textures a sonority that has rarely been equaled for creaminess and golden warmth. In a certain sense, pastoral music of the later Baroque period may be even more inclined to celebrating the senses than the pastoral madrigal. Elegiac statement is not wholly missing from Baroque pastoral, but the preference is for a less sober tone—something more comfortable, more overtly sensuous. (We should remember that the secular cantata is made for the same audience that preferred the aria to the recitative.) Composers continued to look for this tone in the love stories of nymphs and shepherds, still the overwhelming subject of choice for pastoral music, but they concentrated on the more exciting and romantic phases of love—when it is in full bloom or still in the bud.

The conceit of the lover burnt by his or her own flame and in a state of "sweet torment" has countless variants in late medieval and Renaissance love poetry. In music, however, the fusion of elements necessary to convey this antithesis in a single image may not have arrived until the moment of the secular cantata. When it does arrive, it becomes one of the favorite "tones" of the era— certainly the central tone of Baroque pastoral; and the musical image eminently suited to rendering the tone is the *siciliana*—not insignificantly, a dance-type (Example 8.4).

Example 8.4: Alessandro Scarlatti, "Sono amante"

Reprinted by permission of the publishers from Alessandro Scarlatti, *Io son pur solo* (solo cantata). Copyright 1972 by Bärenreiter-Verlag, Kassel.

By stressing the excitement of love over its tragic possibilities, the Baroque pastoral succeeds in fully restoring the alliance between love and the physical beauty of domesticated nature (a "natural" alliance by reason of their common grounding in the senses) that Theocritus had marked out for them in his first conception of pastoral. (Marenzio, by contrast, though he surely reevokes the fresh innocence of the Theocritan countryside in his idyllic madrigals, inclines toward Virgil in the elegiac works, where we are faced with the sobering picture of the same innocent countryside becoming witness to a tragedy born of love.) The imagery of Renaissance pastoral may be of a finer texture than that of its Baroque counterpart, but for that very reason it is lacking in a quality which is effortlessly captured in the lilt of the siciliana and to which we have already given the name (in connection with the love duet in *Giulio Cesare*) "languor."

Languor corresponds to the mode of human behavior Plato designated as relaxed (Monteverdi calls it "molle" or "soft").[15] As one of Plato's three primary *ethe*, "relaxed" is the opposite of "excited" (Monteverdi's "concitato"), both being unacceptable forms of behavior relative to the "temperate" which falls between them. Plato would have disapproved of Example 8.4, with its soft siciliana rhythm reinforced by drooping melodic figures and plaintively seductive minor mode coloring, because the image represents a clear Dionysian surrender to Eros, to natural desire. Just as excited behavior is the direct result of surrender to intense emotion, so languor is the surrender to pleasure of the senses. What Plato finds "nonethical" in such conduct is its very passivity, its willingness to embrace natural desire, to give in to the easiest thing. Temperateness is the only "ethical" stance, because it signals *action*—human effort—the will to resist what was given ("first nature") and to re-create oneself. To the extent that Western culture has always recognized the ethical superiority of the active person over the passive, Plato's thought still wields enormous influence. But his prejudice against passivity in any form strikes us as excessive, supporting the notion of a personality so unrelentingly active as to suggest a serious imbalance; for surely, periods of relaxation well spent are the necessary refreshment for periods of concentrated work to follow. Artistic experience itself is the formal testimony to that truth. Even Aristotle felt Plato had gone too far in recommending the banishment of all but the most sober and temperate music from the Republic. Aristotle defended excited music on the grounds that arousing the emotions to fever pitch would inevitably lead to their being purged and thus to inner calm. Of relaxed music, however, he could only say that it "afforded harmless delight."

But harmless delight is only for the moment, whereas pastoral languor contains a genuine *ethos*, it envisages certain long-range effects. Arcadian pastoral taken as a whole seeks to foster and perpetuate an appreciation of physical beauty as well as providing the models for shaping a gentle, amiable personality. The more sensuous element in pastoral that we are now discussing succeeds at the very least in affecting aesthetic sensibility, if not human character. It teaches the eye and ear to register subtle combinations of sonority and color, small nuances and shadings. To give Plato his due, he does say that the right kind of music will "impart grace" and instill in the "rightly trained" a "delight in beautiful things."[16] But we must be careful to understand the precise locus of his sense of beauty, which is in a "sober and harmonious love of the orderly,"[17] in other words, in those qualities of rhythm, just proportion, and unified design that we particularly admire in the artifacts of ancient Greek sculpture and architecture. The aesthetic values of pastoral languor are different in kind from these classical principles, but for those of us who respond to the seductive impulse of a siciliana and its fluent melodiousness, or to a series of beautifully spaced harmonies, or a delicious dissonance, or the momentary darkening that comes from the sudden appearance of a Neapolitan sixth chord, these values are not to be despised.

The Arcadian Legacy

In the examples to follow, we meet imagery which has strong spiritual connections to Arcadia, in spite of the fact that the classical Arcadian devices may no longer be in evidence. Reference was made in an earlier chapter to the paintings of Claude Lorrain, in which the mythological beings appearing in one landscape will be alternated for factual country types in another, the landscape itself remaining all the while idyllic and smoothly Arcadian. In the slightly later paintings of Watteau, a somewhat different transposition is effected: the disguise of nymphs and shepherds has been abandoned and has given way to exquisitely gowned ladies and fancifully groomed men reposing languidly in the confines of a garden or park. These figures look like so many members of the contemporary French court, until we realize that the world in which they travel has a deliberately dreamlike look and that they have adopted—at least for the series known as the *Fêtes galantes*—another disguise, that of the *commedia dell' arte*. The psychological implications of these exchanges are too complex to study here, but we can at least define the general mood that hangs over the greater number of Watteau's works. That mood is what Milton had called in a signal piece of poetry "penseroso" or pensive melancholy.[18] Frye has described pensive melancholy as "fear without an object," or dread, being accepted as a form of pleasure.[19] This is something distinct from elegy, which is in any case an expression of pity, not fear, and where the object of pity, though removed from our midst, has been clearly identified. With *penseroso*, the object is nowhere to be found; it is a fear of who knows what.

To this ambiguity about the object may be added the ambiguity of the mood itself in its dual inclination to pain and pleasure. Possibly the single most insightful remark ever made about the languid personages of Watteau's *Fêtes galantes* was written by Verlaine in his poem *Clair de lune*: "Ils n'ont pas l'air de croire à leur bonheur" (They don't look as if they believe in their happiness). Here, everything is thrown into uncertainty: their happiness, their belief in their happiness, our perception of their belief. Watteau renders his subjects' elusiveness in a number of ways, showing them from the back, wrapping them in a quasi-veil of mist, never painting them in a primary color (not red, but dark peach, not yellow but ochre, not blue but some vague fusion of green and black that does not exist in nature). Watteau's immediate musical counterpart, both in terms of historical position and aesthetic achievement, is François Couperin, whose taste for the small-scale and for irregular rhythmic groupings and weakly defined melodic profiles betrays a national sensibility.

In the example below, the *penseroso* mood comes from a cross of the idyllic (harmonic sameness, naiveté of phrase repetition) with the elusive (*sfumato*) quality of the static drones, tendency to fragmentary, near-amorphous statement). But Couperin's real uniqueness figures in a kind of expression to which it is difficult to put a name—a muffled, murmuring tragic *pathos* that is intense precisely because it seems so suppressed. The element of pity here is not related to elegy, however, for elegiac statement is lyric and smoothly sustained, whereas the typical gestures of this music as illustrated in "L'âme en peine" ("The soul in pain") are moans of distress that would have been the vehement, declamatory outbursts of high tragedy had they not been stifled by some significant restraining force (Example 8.5). That force is precisely the small-scale, civilizing influence of pastoral: to think of the soul in "L'âme en peine" as belonging to an Arcadian shepherd enables us to see that the suffering everyman in this shepherd needs to cry out his pain, yet cannot do so beyond uttering a few barely audible sighs because of the *ethos* he represents—because of his archetypal identification with sweetness and gentle civility.

Example 8.5: François Couperin, "L'âme en peine"

For his own part, Couperin's identification with this kind of expression is so comprehensive that we can say of him (as Einstein did of Marenzio for an earlier time) that he is preeminently the musician of the Baroque pastoral. The degree to which his style is steeped in French country music bespeaks strong pastoral connections. To be sure, it must be recognized that all the small-scale dances of the French court—minuet, gavotte, bourrée, rigaudon, passepied—constitute an Arcadian reworking of a less elegant village music, which is to say that any composer using such court material would be rightly labeled a musician of the pastoral. But Couperin's pastoral leanings extend (1) to a preference for the small-scale that becomes virtually exclusive in his solo harpsichord work and (2) to an almost profligate use of folk motifs—bagpipe drones, snippets of regional melody, melodic structure imitating the tendency of folk melody to turn around on itself in repetitive little patterns—all duly transformed into an Arcadian rococo idiom acceptable to courtly style (acceptable, in other words, in terms of the stringent forms of cultivated beauty observed at the court of Versailles). "L'âme en peine" may show less evidence of these motifs than other pieces in the Couperin canon, but the folk roots of the underlying dance impulse of the piece have been carefully traced. The dance in question is the loure, and the soft lilt of its dotted rhythms points to its classification as the French equivalent of the siciliana.

Although *penseroso* was introduced by way of French examples, the Italian version may be more familiar. Not unexpectedly, the image-type is structurally clearer and more straightforward than its French counterpart: equal phrase lengths, transparent homophonic texture, steady harmonic rhythm. *Penseroso* in this Italian form gets its most memorable expressions from the non-Italian Mozart in *andante* arias and moderately slow, serenade-like instrumental movements. Nevertheless, the type is already very well defined in the *cantabile* music coming out of Neapolitan opera in the 1760s, of which the leading exponent is another non-Italian, J.C. Bach. Edward Downes, in his preface to the modern edition of *Temistocle* (Mannheim, 1772), speaks of the "aristocratic elegance, delicacy of feeling and sensuous glow" of Bach's melodic line.[20] Downes continues: "He developed a special type of aria in slow tempo characterized by a broadly flowing melody, often in the key of E-flat major, and by a dreamy yearning, nostalgic mood sometimes shadowed by a restrained pessimism, but robed in a ravishingly sensuous sound, often including soft clarinet color, mellow touches of French horn, and muted strings."[21] Downes is obviously thinking of the opening aria of *Temistocle*, "Fosca nube," in which, he points out, Christian Bach has come to the "very threshold" of Ilia's "Se il padre perdei" from *Idomeneo* and "Porgi amor" from *Figaro* (Example 8.6).

Broad flowing melody is the link between the aria-type just described and the instrumental serenade. And the relationship is not confined to the late 18th century; we can find significant antecedents in an earlier period. In the second movement of "La Primavera" from Vivaldi's *Seasons*, we have not only the same kind of musical imagery, but also a program which specifies the pastoral situation to which the imagery belongs:

> E quindi sul fiorito ameno prato
> Al caro mormorio de fronde e piante
> Dorme'l Caprar col fido can'a latto.

The scene is the idyll we have already met in *Scaldava il sol* and in slumber scenes in Baroque operas.[22] The transposition from aria to concerto or sonata is effortlessly made by virtue of the same solo function served by either high voice or high instrument, together with the measured "iterated-quaver" accompaniment common to vocal and instrumental type alike.

Example 8.6: J.C. Bach, "Fosca nube"

J.C. Bach's father has provided some examples of the instrumental "aria" in the slow movements of his violin concerto in A minor and concerto for two harpsichords, though the activity of his melodic lines removes them to some degree from the smoother, more placid line that we think of as being classic *cantabile*. Nevertheless, the relationship of melody to accompaniment makes it clear that these concerto movements are truly in the slumber/serenade tradition. In the slumber sequence from Gluck's *Orphée*, the use of the flute serves to reaffirm the close connection in the 18th-century mind between certain solo instruments and the human voice.

The serenade-type is the most common form of slow movement in Mozart's instrumental works—one more instance of his Italianate leanings. The slow movement of the wind serenade, K. 375, echoes "Fosca nube" not only in the choice of key and in the general outline of the theme, but also in the use of clarinets and horns. Perhaps the supreme examples of the type appear in the piano concertos, most notably K. 466 and K. 467. The interplay of light and shade so often applied in Mozart's later style (never more poetically and precisely than in the second movement of K. 467), together with the sustained upward thrusting of the solo line, embodies precisely what Downes has described above as "a dreamy yearning ... shadowed by a restrained pessimism." This image causes us to wonder whether Frye's definition of *penseroso* should not be somewhat recast; for pensive melancholy here seems not so much a fear turned romantically to pleasure as a reflection on the tension in human existence between pleasure and pain. The dreamy yearning is desire, not fear—a desire for the unmixed, eternal pleasure promised in the perfect world of pastoral. The restrained pessimism is the knowledge that even the pastoral world cannot keep out evil and suffering; hence, the idyllic F major stretches in the slow movement of K. 467 broken by patches of F minor pain.

The image of tragedy entering the idyllic world, evoked already a number of times in the course of this chapter, should remind us that such an image is only a projection of our own regret at the thought that tragedy must enter the real, everyday world. Mozart's *penseroso* music, in short, gives musical voice to our rather helpless and self-pitying question, "Why must there be pain?" That having been said, we might ask ourselves why we cannot—or should not—drop the pastoral disguise in interpreting the imagery of K. 467 (which, after all, being instrumental, has no explicit Arcadian references) and simply read it directly as an expression of a universal state of mind. The answer to this question is twofold, having to do with the aesthetic quality of Mozart's image as well as with its content. With reference to the first, everything in Mozart's style which speaks for surface polish and elegance and delicacy of coloring is a product of Arcadian thinking. In other words, the kind of aristocratic beauty embodied in Mozart's music in general (and by extension, in J.C. Bach's and in the tradition that nurtured them both) is reason enough for recognizing the pastoral influence. But there is also the question of content: as a quiet, gentle, soft-spoken kind of expression, *penseroso*, like elegy, belongs almost by definition to the pastoral mode, and like elegy also, it connotes a particular perception of tragedy, of human suffering. But unlike the case of elegy, where the object of pity, though at some distance from us, is known (and certainly unlike the circumstances of tragic *pathos*, where the objects of fear and pity are in our very midst), with *penseroso* there is no identifiable object, no specific event that has just taken place—only a vague and yet persistent knowledge that suffering exists, has always existed, and will continue to exist. Not only does this give *penseroso* expression a particularly reflective cast but it explains why the *penseroso* state of mind, not held fast by any specific object or event, can shift ambiguously back and forth between fragmentary feelings of dread and yearnings for perfect bliss on earth.[23] One might argue, in view of this, that *penseroso* signals a severing of the bonds with pastoral because the state of emotion in question is simply too ambiguous and complex for the traditional Arcadian shepherd to have harbored. The level of emotional sophistication here is certainly beyond Theocritus' original conception and probably beyond Virgil's Tityrus as well.[24] However, that is really beside the point: we do not have to believe in the *penseroso* feelings of an Arcadian shepherd in order to believe something far more practical and historical, namely that only pastoral among the archetypal modes was equipped to provide the imagery by means of which the content of pensive melancholy could be musically expressed.

Of the two 19th-century categories to be considered here (both French in cultural tendency) the first offers an image-type with such strong resemblances to the *penseroso* image just discussed that one is inclined to speak of a stylistic continuation. The Germanic thrust of early Romanticism explains to some extent why the German influence is largely missing here and also why this category, consisting of miniatures bearing such titles as Meditation, Consolation, and Rêverie, is usually filed under "salon music."[25] A more suitable label might be "Barbizon pastoral," in recognition of spiritual links to the school of landscape painters led by Corot. Though Romanticism is not at the heart of Barbizon pastoral, it would be difficult to find a genuine 19th-century art that did not show decided Romantic effects. But as to the main outlines of this pastoral music, they huddle closer to what comes before than to the central themes of their own time.

Most characteristic of the type is a clear-cut and persistent melody-accompaniment texture, the melody set high above the rolling accompaniment so as to yield clarity and resonance at the same time—a net effect of luminousness, not richness. Elements of spaciousness, expansiveness, and relaxation gather together to form the languorously idyllic mood. As an amplification of the Alberti principle, the accompaniment, perhaps more than any other feature, shows the inroads made by Romanticism, for its deeper sonorities evoke a picture, dear to the Romantics, of the isolated individual (the soaring solo line) communing with the natural world—lost, as it were, in the universal hum. This strongly positive sense of the individual alone in a great space, separated from the rest of society, calls to mind the earlier *penseroso* feeling, which also evokes through its yearning solo line the isolated individual, but in a spirit that reflects the socially minded 18th-century perception of isolation as loneliness. Significantly, the accompaniment of the 18th-century *penseroso* image with its repeated eighth-note chords is tense and sober by comparison with the dreamily rapturous cascades of, say, Chopin's *Andante spianato*. Yet, the daydream of Barbizon loveliness must not be confused with the full-blown dream of Romanticism, which means for Art to capture for itself the transcendental force of Nature and thereby shake the human spirit at its very core. In the end, these musical reveries, like Corot's evocations of domesticated nature (shimmering more magically than the originals in their bluish haze) are well contained within the precincts of Arcadian pastoral. Delicate and gently aristocratic, they confer on their somewhat less aristocratic public the same beneficent mixture of charm and wish fulfillment that their ancestors did in the Italian courts.

Impressionism

Placing a park scene of Watteau's alongside Monet's famous poppy field immediately brings to light the Arcadian underpinnings of both—though in the latter case any hint of *penseroso* feeling has given over to a purely idyllic mood. Similarly, the idyllic dominates in numbers of Impressionist pieces of music—the song *L'échelonnement des haies* by Debussy, the piano pieces *Jardins sous la pluie* and *Reflets dans l'eau*, the Introduction and Allegro by Ravel. Of the basic spiritual impulse of Impressionism, Werner Hofmann writes: "Impressionism is the 'voice' of the spirit of the liberal bourgeoisie which withdrew from its public duties and sought to create an earthly paradise within its private world."[26] Impressionism, according to this definition, then, is one more chapter in the continuing artistic effort to recreate Theocritan virtues of peace, intimate community, and cultivated well-being. Actually, the significance of Impressionism does not stop with the idyll of pastoral art: other phases more pertinent to modernist concerns will have to be discussed at a later time. But the original and most intuitive phase of Impressionism is hedonistic in orientation, dedicated to the innocent and uncomplicated pleasures of being alive. As the body is the distinguishing feature of being alive (the soul being, by contrast, "eternal"), Impressionism provides an answer, albeit a modest one, to Romantic transcendence: Romanticism begins with the supremacy of the spiritual and advocates grasping it through sensation, whereas Impressionism begins with the known of sensation and then proceeds to celebrate the loveliness of that simple reality.

In Impressionist painting we have what might be called a vigorous displacement of the Arcadian archetype: the chief spiritual and aesthetic values are preserved while the explicit outward signs have disappeared. Much the same could be said of Impressionist music until we realize that one of Western music's most famous works—Debussy's *Prelude to the Afternoon of a Faun*—is a genuine Arcadian throwback. We know this through the poem of Mallarmé which inspired the prelude. In reality a discourse about the act of artistic creation, the poem presents this discourse in the form of a story of pursuit and seduction. Of the three protagonists in the story, the two nymphs are directly out of the Arcadian tradition, while the faun—more than a mere substitute for the shepherd figure— is the shepherd's ancestor: he is consumed with desire for the nymphs and he is a musician, playing on his "two pipes." Indeed, the mythic significance of the faun is that all shepherds play the flute as a consequence of his original act. One trait of the shepherd, however, the faun does not possess: he is not cultivated, he is still a wild beast. He does not really love the nymphs, he only lusts after them. At this point, however, Mallarmé does some mythmaking of his own, for the ultimate promise of the poem is that if only the faun succeeds in transforming his erotic feelings into music, he will have realized himself as an artist and become truly civilized. What Mallarmé has created, then, is proto-Arcadia, the moment at which Arcadia is about to be born. As if aware of this he places the story not in the hills of ancient Greece but in Sicily on a hot summer's afternoon.

Debussy's music, on the other hand, evokes cooler climes: the instrumental sonorities, chosen with the fastidiousness of a necromancer mixing his potions, have the vernal coloring and dewiness of young and tender nature, as if the events were taking place not in the sultriness of a summer afternoon but on what Gide once called "le premier matin du monde."[27] But if the specific sensuousness of Debussy's imagery consists of qualities such as tenderness, delicacy, and civilized gentleness, then the *Prelude to the Afternoon of a Faun* comes out of the mainstream tradition of Arcadian pastoral; it does not correspond in all essentials to Mallarmé's unique and somewhat unclassical variant. Chronologically speaking, Debussy's prelude may not be the last musical word about Arcadia, but it is, of all pastoral images in music, the one to have most shaped our modern picture of a perfect place that once existed at the dawn of Western culture. For musicians and music lovers in the Western world today, Arcadia looks—and may well always look—the way the *Prelude to the Afternoon of a Faun* sounds.

Notes

1. John Stevens, *Words and Music in the Middle Ages: Song, Narrative, Dance and Drama, 1050–1350*, pp. 162–164.

2. *Ibid.*, p. 231.

3. Nino Pirrotta, *Music and Culture in Italy from the Middle Ages to the Baroque*, pp. 176–177.

4. Quoted in Alfred Einstein, *The Italian Madrigal*, Vol. I, p. 210.

5. A thorough, albeit somewhat truncated English-language version of this account is given in Henry W. Kaufmann, "Music for a Noble Florentine Wedding (1539)," in *Words and Music: The Scholar's View*, Laurence Berman, ed., pp. 161–188.

6. Thomas Morley, *A Plain and Easy Introduction to Practical Music*, pp. 290–292.

7. See Oliver Strunk, ed., *Source Readings in Music History*, pp. 315–317.

8. A transcription of this piece appears in Luca Marenzio, *Sämtliche Werke*, Vol. IV, pp. 12–15. (No. 4).

9. Einstein, *The Italian Madrigal*, Vol. II, p. 613.

10. A comparative study of settings of *Ah, dolente partita* has, in fact, been made: see Pierluigi Petrobelli, "Ah, dolente partita: Marenzio, Wert, Monteverdi," in *Congresso internazionale sul tema Claudio Monteverdi e il suo tempo*, pp. 361–376.

11. Erwin Panofsky, *Meaning in the Visual Arts*, p. 301.

12. This is what is implied in Galilei's view, and in Tasso's as well (see Chapter 7).

13. Its use in religious music, especially in connection with Christmas narratives, is also extremely important and will be discussed briefly in Chapter 9.

14. The French word *chevalier*, or "one who rides a horse," shows both the noble rank of the knight and his prime function as a warrior. But seasoned in the domestic and delicate art of courtly love, he learns to be "chivalrous." The qualities of warrior and "shepherd musician" are combined in the ideal medieval knight just as they will be in the hero of Baroque *opera seria*.

15. See Strunk, *Source Readings*, p. 5 and p. 413. "Hypo" and "hyper," the "loose" and the "high strung."

16. See *ibid.*, p. 8.

17. *Ibid.*, p. 9.

18. John Milton, *L'Allegro ed Il Penseroso*, reprinted in full in Huntington Cairns, ed., *The Limits of Art*, Vol. II, pp. 704–712.

19. See Northrop Frye, *Anatomy of Criticism*, p. 37.

20. Johann Christian Bach, *Temistocle*, p. ix.

21. *Ibid.*, p. ix. "Fosca nube" appears on pp. 33-41 of the score.

22. Slumber arias as such normally have undulating accompaniments, as opposed to the measured iterated quaver of the *penseroso* music now under discussion. The difference may be seen by comparing Galatea's aria from Part II of Handel's *Acis* to "Comfort ye" from the *Messiah*. (The *Acis* aria has a remarkably close echo in the Act II duet from *Cosi fan tutte*). There seems little doubt that the accompaniment has a great deal to do with making the slumber aria more languorous, the *penseroso* aria more soberly reflective.

23. The reflective aspect of *penseroso* thought goes a long way to explaining why slow movements of sonatas, symphonies, concertos and the like are generally thought of as having a reflective character. A further reason seems to be that the accompaniment having lost all connection with the dance, there is no suggestion of an *action*.

24. This perception, of course, does not extend to Virgil himself. It is perhaps worth recollecting in this regard that Watteau's very sophisticated *penseroso* feeling is conveyed through figures who resemble courtiers, not nymphs and shepherds. He may have thought that the Arcadian shepherd was too naïve a representation to express the *penseroso* ambiguity he had in mind.

25. Liszt's insistence on the German word "Liebestraum" doesn't make the spirit of this kind of music any more German than had this kind of piece been named a "Rêverie."

26. Werner Hofmann, *The Earthly Paradise*, p. 346.

27. "The first morning of the world" is a line from one of the opening choruses of Stravinsky's *Perséphone*, another classical Arcadian evocation.

9   *The Pastoral Mode, II*

The evolution in Arcadian imagery that we have been considering represents the updating of a *like* pattern of thought, the reaffirmation of courtly belief in the superiority of physical loveliness and artistic elegance. In the course of this development, pastoral takes a turn such as to suggest the influence of a qualitatively *different* pattern of thought—a radical change in the way educated (i.e., "cultivated") society views rural life. This new pattern—*rustic pastoral*—already presented in its broad outlines in Chapter 2, can now be explored for its musical ramifications. It is important to keep in mind, however, that the original thrust of the pastoral—its deeply antiheroic vision of a world far from the tumult of great deeds and warlike glory—remains unchanged. What Arcadian and rustic pastoral have in common is their idealization of the countryside; the gentle, essentially idyllic tone is never forsaken. Where rustic pastoral opposes itself to the Arcadian is in the idea that the idyll is not to be found in cultivated beauty and behavior, but rather in a probity of the spirit, which is an inner beauty. That Arcadian and rustic pastoral succinctly define the split between hieratic and demotic thinking has already been proposed in Chapter 2. For the hieratic mentality, rustic images are too rude and homely to carry any true significance, let alone appeal, while the demotic mind regards Arcadian images as artificial and lacking in spirituality. In the world of rustic pastoral, youth and beauty are of little account, and love is an incidental theme.

Rustic Pastoral

The notion that humble things contain a virtue unknown to those who set great store by appearances is resonant with overtones of Christian *humilitas*. It is quite possible that without the stimulus of Christianity demotic archetypes would have been much slower to take root in the modern West than they did. Never-theless, the content of rustic pastoral is secular and social in essence, grounded in *caritas*, in the impulse to feel sympathy for those less fortunate than ourselves. Just when in European history the first stirrings of this impulse were felt in lyric poetry and music is difficult to say. England in the late 16th century is a possible starting point. The wealth of variation sets on popular country tunes appearing in the Fitzwilliam Virginal Book alone suggests that folk music and polyphonic music, though clearly separate categories in the minds of Elizabethan court mu-sicians, could fruitfully interact and replenish each other. That composers of the stature of Byrd, Bull, and Gibbons elaborated folk tunes in works of no mean size or weight has a double significance. It means, first of all, that the hier-atic trappings of their own craft could do something to "elevate" the modest originals. But more significantly, it means that these composers had found in a modest, unassuming, four-square tune like *Walsingham* the makings of its own elevation, a demotic kind of eloquence which could nourish their own style.[1] In the realm of poetry: John Gay hears the first murmurings of a rustic sound in the tenderness with which "Maister Spencer" addresses the 16th-century English peasantry.[2] Gay goes on to quote a poem of "Maister Milton," in which the vener-able virtuoso of high-flown Arcadian imagery lays aside the hieratic mantle and tries for a humbler tone.[3] Likewise, in *L'allegro ed il penseroso*, Milton, though clearly painting imaginary landscapes, does it with such zest and sparkle and such affection for his pastoral types—"And the Milkmaid singeth blithe/And the Mower whets his sithe/And every Shepherd tells his tale/Under the Hawthorn in the dale"—that one is left with the impression of a rapture of a very personal kind, as if Milton had simply distilled into his verses his own delighted experi-ences with the English countryside.[4] Handel, setting this poem a century later, seems to want to meet Milton on the poet's ground, finding a style that is at once more intimate in scale than the Italianate speech of his operas and sparer in melodic design—more direct, more vernacular. But we may have strayed from our subject, for it is possible that we are talking only about a difference in national manner—between the Italian style Handel learned as a young apprentice com-poser and the English—indeed Purcellian—mannerisms he consciously adopted as early as 1713 when he wrote his birthday ode for Queen Anne. In the process of integrating the English motifs into his European style, he may have hit upon more than a popular note or two, assuming that the English court music, as has been widely claimed, is "more directly in touch with a folk culture" than its con-tinental counterparts.[5] But his motives in doing so would be only tangentially related, if at all, to what Gay had in mind when searching for a pastoral language that would fall somewhere in between the speech of the "Country Maiden" and the "Courtly Dame."[6]

The question of how far a court artist must travel down the "plain High-way of Pastoral" in order to establish the proper rustic tone is one that should probably be decided only in terms of individual cases; in the case of Handel's *L'allegro*, the problem is compounded by virtue of the fact that no specific intentions are made known. And the problem is complicated further by our own contemporary conceptions of what qualifies as "plain speech." Accustomed to later versions of rustic eloquence, we are inclined to look upon Baroque style as a whole as altogether too formal and elaborate to fit comfortably into the rustic pastoral conception. Even with Baroque settings of the Christmas story, where the themes of holiness and rusticity are closely joined, it is hard to see how the music wears the rude, plain face of simplicity, any more than in a typical manger scene by Jacopo Bassano the inclusion of a cow and a few token sheaves of hay will offset the effects of the painter's polished manner. In his Christmas Oratorio Bach successfully sets the quiet pastoral tone in the second part against the splendid pomp of the opening; but is this enough to establish "rusticity," or are the diverse pastoral effects in this portion of the piece eventually absorbed into the rich consistency that defines Bach's mature language?

While even a modest attempt at answering these questions is outside the scope of our discussion, the questions themselves at least serve to clarify a set of conditions which, taken together, form a framework for the rustic pastoral category: (1) establishment of a decorum of rusticity, as viewed from a courtly or urban perspective; (2) fashioning of an artistic style to conform to the rustic decorum; (3) borrowing of elements from actual folk dialect to aid in the interests of (2); (4) implementation of (2) and (3) in the avowed spirit of ennobling rural life. *The Shepherd's Week* is a sincere effort on the part of its author to fulfill all these conditions, yet Gay himself voices some doubt about the extent of his achievement. He considered himself at the vanguard of a literary movement, and, given his position, he felt he could only break with tradition just so far without also breaking the lines of communication with his readership. This seems to be at the heart of his message when he writes: "It may so hap, in meet time that some lover of Simplicity shall arise, who shall have the Hardiness to render these mine Eclogues into such more modern Dialect as shall be then understood."[7] That "meet time" would come less than forty years after *The Shepherd's Week*. By the mid-century mark, the *Zeitgeist* of rustic pastoral had arrived, accompanied by such lyrics as James Thomson's *The Seasons* (1748) and Thomas Gray's *Elegy Written in a Country Churchyard* (1750), already discussed in Chapter 2. The musical offerings would follow shortly thereafter.

Oliver Goldsmith's *Deserted Village*, written at the same time as the *Elegy*, and in the same vein, is perhaps more "sentimental":[8]

Sweet Auburn, loveliest village of the plain,
Where health and plenty cheared the labouring swain.

How blest is he who crowns in shades like these,
A youth of labour with an age of ease.

Here, the term "sentimental" is used not as it was applied to Virgil earlier, but in its more uncomplimentary acceptance, where it refers to a distortion of everyday reality through "prettification." The problems of sentimentality will be taken up in another place. But apparently, the sentimental aspects of the poem were already a point of contention in Goldsmith's time, judging by George Crabbe's biting denunciation:[9]

> Yes, thus the Muses sing of happy Swains
> Because the Muses never knew their pains.
>
> O'ercome by labour and bow'd down by time
> Feel you the barren flattery of a rhyme?

Jacob Bronowski, who quotes these lines in *The Ascent of Man*, sides with Crabbe, and says that Goldsmith's "lost paradise" is a "fable," the country being a place where "the labourer lived not in the sun, but in poverty and darkness."[10] Crabbe and Bronowski are no doubt generally right in their facts, but they have missed the essential point about *The Deserted Village*. Goldsmith was writing a pastoral, not a polemic; his aim was not to point the finger at the well-to-do and prod them into action. If he had any practical aim at all, it was to reinforce in the minds of his readers a notion of a society whose existence was day by day gaining further entry into their collective consciousness. If Goldsmith's rendering of the notion was exaggerated—if the poet had cast his laborers in too beautiful a light—it had the proper psychological effect; for the country folk thereby took on a significance which, according to the poet, they should have, and, given the right conditions, they would have. *The Deserted Village* may be sentimental, but it is also idealistic, and in a very real way, it helps to spread its own ideals.

By Goldsmith's time the ideals in question had long since become part of the *Zeitgeist*, having been initiated and then vigorously supported through a succession of philosophical programs known collectively as the Enlightenment. The generality and timeliness of Enlightenment ideas could not fail to involve the leading intellectuals of the 18th century. No person of conscience (and that included many rulers) could ignore either the reasonableness of Enlightenment principles or the urgency of the social realities they addressed. It is also true that, among other things, such reasonableness had some material part in the cataclysm of the French Revolution, though it would be wrong to conclude from this that the passionate rallying cry of the Revolution was fully anticipated in Enlightenment thought. Liberty, certainly: it was the basis on which the Enlightenment had been founded, the freedom of opportunity due every man, irrespective of class, to realize himself and make a better life. Even more than that, the idea of a man breaking away from lowly circumstances and moving dramatically up in the world was readily imagined and encouraged. But equality and fraternity were something else again; they signalled as a logical conclusion the *eradication of class*, a notion that simply could not form part of the orderly process envisioned in Enlightenment theory. Maynard Solomon has written:[11]

The Enlightenment abjured superstition and dogma and supplanted theological formulations which negated the possibilities of earthly salvation with a harmonious and optimistic view of man's freedom to develop his potentialities within a framework of natural law and political reconstruction.

"Political reconstruction," however, must be understood in its proper perspective, that is, according to both its aims and its limitations. That it implied wide-ranging social reforms, many of which were put into effect by the more "enlightened" leaders of the day, there is no doubt. But that such reconstruction meant a significant overhauling of the social and political structure is another matter entirely: the lot of those who suffered had to be improved, but the assumption was that the improvements would take place within the prevailing social framework and that the social framework would prevail.

If these socio-political concerns seem to have little to do with musical imagery, their relevance to the *ethos* of rustic pastoral should not be underestimated. In point of fact, the reliance of rustic pastoral on the distinction between classes was absolute. Practically speaking, of course, the vanishing of a peasant class would have meant the dissolution of the European economy, if not the unraveling of the total society. But on a somewhat less apocalyptic note, with the disappearance of the peasantry would have also disappeared the central myth of the honest laborer and the spiritual superiority of country life: rustic pastoral would have lost its reason for being. Although rustic pastoral may not be the only mode of the 18th century to transmit Enlightenment content in artistic form, it is very likely the purest. And unlike the philosophical tracts of the Enlightenment, which deal, at least theoretically, with their contents in a spirit of dispassion and detachment, rustic pastoral, as artistic expression, deals with *pathos* on its own terms, which is to say that there is a built-in tendency in the genre to sweetness and sentimentality.[12]

The fact could not have escaped Haydn's notice that he was the living fulfillment of the Enlightenment dream—a man risen from the peasantry to become one of Europe's most illustrious figures. There is some poetic justice, then, in the fact that he should have become the leading exponent of rustic eloquence in his time. The folk element in his work has long been recognized, but the independence with which he cultivated a folk idiom and the effect this idiom had on his entire style have perhaps only lately been appreciated.[13] As the most efficient way of approaching this question, we will examine Haydn's last completed piece, *The Seasons*, since, in its encyclopedic impulse to summarize a lifetime of creative activity, it reveals the most personal features of his work. Using texts from James Thomson's poem, *The Seasons*, Haydn's oratorio has as much to do with the depiction of country life as with the yearly cycle in whose image human action and feeling have always been so graphically symbolized. Indeed, since human existence is represented here through the life of the country folk, Thomson universalizes that life by bringing it into an interaction with the eternal theme of the seasons. As with any pastoral expression, the possibilities for creating vivid imagery are a great attraction to the artist, and Haydn exerts himself to the fullest. Such scenes as the passage from winter to spring, the ascent of the sun, the storm, the hunt, and the wine fest are a tremendous challenge to Haydn's coloristic imagination; and Zelter, in a contemporary appreciation of the piece (1804) calls particular attention to the poetic and dramatic use of the orchestral resources, adding that such a sonorous achievement would not have been possible without the advances of instrumental techniques made in the previous twenty-five years.

But it is the folk idiom that is of particular interest here, and there are many striking examples of it. The most obvious is probably the vineyard scene with its succession of (1) march accompanied by peasant shouts, (2) rough-hewn German dance in ⁶⁄₈ time accompanied by a drone bass, and (3) climactic chorus, energetic and earthy. But the opening numbers quickly set the tone: the idyllic, softly undulating chorus of the country people, "Come lovely spring" in G major and Allegretto time (No. 2) and Simon's aria, "At dawn the eager plowman" (No. 4), which ingeniously integrates the famous theme from the Surprise symphony with a rhythm that could be only an inadvertent forecast (but no less significant for that) of Schubert's *Die Forelle* and "Ich hör ein Bächlein rauschen" from *Die Schöne Müllerin* (Example 9.1). Another forewarning of Schubert is given late in the work by the haunting spinning song, in ⁶⁄₈ D minor; here, the old siciliana has been left behind and we have entered the plainer, more direct expressive world of *Gretchen am Spinnrade.*

Example 9.1: Haydn, *Schon eilet froh* (*At dawn the eager ploughman*)

Perhaps the most impressive embodiment of plain speech makes its appearance in the Spring section, in the development which leads from the Bittgesang (Song of prayer) to the climactic fugue at the end of the episode. The climax itself is festal pomp at its most emblazoned pitch—clearly beyond the theoretical bounds of pastoral decorum—but preceding it is another tone, the one coming from the worshipping congregation, carrying the attitude of humble piety. The device by which Haydn captures this tone is a slow ³/₄ hymn in the major mode; with its broad, unadorned melody, its close, covered texture, middle-to-low range tessitura, and lack of color, it re-creates the old Christian pattern of humilitas to sublimitas. In itself this music may not bear any accurate resemblance to a true hymn of the Austrian folk; and it need not, for it is intended to capture only the essence of demotic thought, which is the discovery of greatness in lowliness. The hymn as a genre is an expression of a community of worshippers; and the body of singers that the Greeks called "chorus" comes by its communal associations rightly, given its origins in ritual.

As with Arcadian pastoral, the influence of rustic pastoral can be decisively felt in certain instrumental categories of the period. One striking case is the change from the andante serenade-type to an adagio-type that overtakes Haydn's slow movements in the 1760s, a change that is usually described as the composer's attempt to "deepen" his expressive powers. This would be true for Haydn only in the sense that what he could express more "personally" he would express more "deeply." But it would be erroneous to conclude from this that adagios are by nature "deeper" than andante serenades: J.C. Bach and Mozart seem to have no trouble in producing serenades of deep feeling. Generally, the movement from serenade to adagio has to do not with a search for more depth but with an inclination toward demotic expression—a movement away from elegance and toward plain speech, or to put it even more precisely, a transposition of *penseroso* feeling from Arcadian to rustic pastoral. The existence of a rustic variant of *penseroso* goes a long way toward explaining why Beethoven's slow movements in which the adagio-type predominates strike us as being "deeply reflective" in character. Beethoven expresses himself infrequently in the serenade idiom, and examples are confined almost exclusively to his early years. There is the second movement of the piano sonata, Op. 31, No. 1 (a piece that bears almost too much comparison with Mozart), the theme of the slow movement of the Quintet, Op. 16 (an acknowledged imitation of Mozart), and not much more. In his more accustomed mood, Beethoven gravitates toward a stately but simple hymn-type in ³/₄ time (sometimes in common time), usually marked Adagio, and an Andante cantabile-type in ²/₄ or ³/₈. The label "cantabile" should not lead us to think that we are in the presence of a serenade, since the low tessitura and covered sonority do not agree with the airiness and transparency we expect from the typical serenade. Here again, the song-like aspects still have a stronger bond with the sober discipline of the hymn than the soaring flight of the serenade.

The hymn-type (in ³/₄ or ⁴/₄ time) is frequently represented in Mozart's later work (second movements of K. 465 and K. 570), and one can imagine it stimulated by his interest in the Masonic movement. Indeed, the concept of pious community and brotherly love, expressed with particular conviction in the text of Mozart's *Lasst uns mit geschlungen Händen*, is the precise meeting point of Masonry and rustic pastoral. It must be acknowledged that this hymn-type invites close comparison with the Baroque sarabande, a dance whose stateliness, as we know, bears an unequivocally hieratic stamp. Nevertheless, in simpler evocations of sarabandes such as are found in Handel's late period—"Ombra mai fu" from *Serse*, for example—there are signs of an evolution in the direction of the rustic hymn. (This demotic kind of sarabande experiences a reincarnation in such late expressions as the slow movement from Beethoven's *Archduke Trio* and the Schubert Impromptu, Op. 142, No. 2.) Still another form of sober, slow movement is found in Mozart—a type descended from the siciliana because of its basic ⁶/₈ impulse and moderato tempo, but which has strong affinities with the hymn because of a restricted melodic compass, close homophonic texture, and fairly low tessitura. The slow movement from the last quartet, K. 590, is a particularly good case in point, and if this assessment of a cross between siciliana and hymn is correct, then it bears witness to a process in which an Arcadian type subtly evolves into a rustic one.

As a final case to be discussed here, we mention a kind of instrumental music that Robbins Landon, with specific reference to Haydn, has called *più tosto allegretto*. In $2/4$ time, and with a melodic line that Robbins Landon describes as "pert, almost prim,"[14] it radiates an unassuming, amiable cheerfulness that makes it perhaps the purest expression we have of the comic vision in the context of the demotic archetype. With this kind of music, we have in fact returned to the idyllic tone already encountered in Simon's aria from *The Seasons*. And the virtual equivalence of the vocal and instrumental imagery leads us to realize that here is a kind of musical expression unknown to Arcadian pastoral. Depending on one's point of view, there are two ways to explain why this is so: either we can say that this music is not sophisticated and elegant enough to conform to the requisites of Arcadian decorum, or we can say that the imagery of Arcadian pastoral is too sophisticated to capture the underlying significance of what is being expressed here. To take the latter position enables us to define this significance and to reaffirm the honest laborer (or, as he is known in Simon's aria, the "eager ploughman") as the central figure of rustic pastoral. The basic qualities attaching to this laborer—an attitude of cheerfulness manifesting itself in clear-eyed and relaxed behavior—are embodied in the music of this *più tosto allegretto*. Arcadian pastoral does not generate such an image, because the practitioners of Arcadian pastoral, like Plato, saw relaxation only as a form of languor. Rustic pastoral music, on the contrary, answers both Plato and Arcadian pastoral by producing an image which is *soberly* relaxed—that is, relaxed and temperate at the same time. *Allegretto* may well be the most accurate term we can find to designate the character of this image, but in the sense of connoting a fundamental kind of human behavior, not a mere tempo marking.

To approach an understanding of this larger connotation requires taking another glance at Milton's *L'allegro ed il penseroso*. *Allegro*, as everyone knows, is also a tempo marking in music, but Milton used it in its more human acceptance to characterize a kind of personality that is cheerful and buoyant, full of "mirth" and "jest and youthful jollity."[15] Indeed, more than merely cheerful, the *Allegro* personality is a reveller—carefree, dedicated to a life of pure pleasure, terrified of being sad ("Hence loathed Melancholy" is the opening line). To Milton, *L'allegro*, for all his fun and frolic, finally represents a superficial conception of the world, one unequipped to deal with suffering in any form. *Il Penseroso*, on the other hand, is presented as a character who knows how to absorb suffering and turn it into fruitful reflection, which is the deepest kind of pleasure. The ultimate message of Milton's poem is that pensive melancholy is the serious—the "divine"—way to live in the world. A hundred years after Milton, his single-minded view of "jollity" would be provided a viable alternative. *L'allegretto* can be as jolly and cheerful as *L'allegro*, but not out of a compulsion for lighthearted pleasure. The cheerfulness comes from a sense of doing an honest day's work and living according to a code of homely, simple virtues. To lead such a life is to be relaxed and at peace with oneself, to be able to meet adversity and see with a clear and sober eye what values really count. *L'allegretto* is a balanced version of *L'allegro*, a less excited, more measured form of it—cheerfulness with a serious backbone. In 1632, Milton could not have imagined this human type, however great the poet's affection for the English countryside and its inhabitants; the European mind needed more time and the experience of many intervening social and political events before it would be able to see the honest laborer in sharp focus. When finally the *ethos* of rustic pastoral took definitive shape in mid-18th-century English poetry, musicians were quick to find the musical imagery to match. And with a keen intuition for its meaning in terms of human character, they applied the new tempo marking *Allegretto* to the music that epitomized their cheerful peasant.

In its own way, rustic pastoral is every bit as much of an idealization as Arcadian pastoral, perhaps more so, insofar as Arcadian pastoral makes no pretense at representing the "real world" of the everyday countryside. Given what the life of the laborer must have actually been in the heyday of rustic pastoral, one can understand the charges of sentimentality brought against the genre. Pure unadulterated enjoyment of the countryside was the privilege of those who visited it, not those who lived and worked there. A significant part, one imagines (though not the totality), of the rustic pastoral *ethos* was in reality a projection onto rural life of feelings that derived from the relaxed and happy experiences of urban dwellers in a rural setting. As if to obviate any suspicion of sentimentality, this literal point of view is precisely the one adopted by Beethoven in the Pastoral symphony. Having thus taken the stance of the urban observer, Beethoven is free to depict the peasants and the surroundings not as they literally are but as they appear to be when filtered through the observer's tender feelings. This seems to be the real significance of his caveat, "Nicht Malerei aber Ausdruck der Empfindung" (not painting but expression of feelings).

Easily the most remarkable aspect of this work is the utilization of the symphonic form—a type proper to *heroic* expression in terms of scale and sonorous weight—without any sacrificing of the pastoral tone. Though not truly intimate, the symphony nevertheless succeeds in avoiding grandeur, and in its careful selection of subjects—the country walk, the scene by the brook, the peasants' dance, the hymn of thanksgiving—it stays well within pastoral limits. Even the agita-tion of the fourth-movement storm is not out of character, for as it has often been observed, Beethoven is simply following in the tradition of Vivaldi and Haydn, in whose pastoral music the storm appears as a violent interlude before peace is restored. Solomon writes of this moment: "In the fourth movement, 'Fate' intrudes as the thunderous voice of the God of wrath, but withdraws without a serious struggle, leaving his children their moment of innocent rejoicing."[16] Considering the primary role of "Fate" in the symphony preceding the Pastoral, we understand its place here as indeed an interlude, an episodic disturbance whose passing will only enhance the ensuing calm. Thus, the last word goes to the hymn of thanksgiving reaffirming feelings of piety and community. The Pastoral symphony is a summation of all the conventions of rustic pastoral; and not insignificantly, the final movement is marked *Allegretto*.

Although the diverse folk and national movements of the 19th century osten-sibly trace their parentage back to rustic pastoral, the *ethos* of the parent pattern ceases to have much of its original social relevance in the new age. Love of the land and of the people who work it continues to serve as a common bond, yet what the urban observer selects out of the rural setting for special attention—what he finds in rural life that promises to be particularly edifying in terms of his own life—changes to just the extent that Europe moves from an essentially Classical perception of the world to a Romantic one. The first stirrings of change are felt as far back as the 1760s, with the British publications of Percy's *Reliques of Ancient English Poetry* and MacPherson's so-called translations of the poems of Ossian.[17] Since these developments are effectively concurrent with those of the "mainstream" rustic pastoral movement we have been discussing, it is under-standable how the two could be mistaken for one, but it is important to keep them separate, not only because of their divergences in outlook, but mainly because they have very different artistic consequences.

At first glance, the chief difference between them seems to center on a simple reversal of perspective: classic rustic pastoral takes what it needs from folk culture in order to substantiate its own specific distortions, while the folk movement immerses itself in folk culture in order to unveil that culture's literal realities, its innermost secrets. Both of these descriptions are distortions in their own right, incomplete with respect to the aims of both developments and particularly prejudicial against the aims of classic rustic pastoral. By this view, it is all too easy to see only the sentimental side of rustic pastoral—its function in providing urban society with a concrete outlet for experiencing and expressing tender emotion—whereas there is the ethical side as well, the side by which the urban class can apply the lesson of the country laborer to its own mode of existence. This ethical aspect has already been touched upon, but it can be made more explicit here. In effect, the lesson in question may be paraphrased as a succinct directive to the members of urban society: follow the example of the country laborer; do honest work, take pleasure in that fact, and you will be happy. The tenor of this message is unimpeachable, dedicated as it is to a simple homely virtue; and the promise of the message is optimistic without being unrealistic or unduly sentimental. Nevertheless, as a content primarily conceived to be transmitted through works of art, it imposes one severe limitation on the poetic and musical genres to which it is attached: the chief protagonist of classic rustic pastoral having been defined in terms of a specific emotion, he is thus rendered incapable of expressing (and feeling?) the total range of emotions normally experienced by human beings; because the country laborer must by definition be "cheerful," the emotions that fall on the tragic side of experience are closed off to rustic pastoral. The kinds of tragic expression routinely found in Arcadian pastoral—the elegiac and a muted form of tragic *pathos*—are missing in the rustic repertoire, and any image of anger or violence, such as the storm in the Pastoral symphony, can be explained away as incidental or even picturesque.

The folk movement surmounts this limitation by performing an important variation on the rustic image. Though there is no conscious intention involved, the pioneers of the folk movement successfully create a human type the basis of whose identity is free of any reference to *pathos*. Their implicit injunction to urban society becomes: Follow the example of the country laborer, and you will discover the purest, the deepest, the best part of yourself. This message will have resonances in every corner of the folk and national tradition all the way to Bartok. Leon Plantinga writes that certain thinkers in the original folk movement[18]

saw simplicity, naïveté and spontaneity as the most desirable attributes in works of art and literature. Thus the sensibility of the unspoiled peasant, the "noble savage," and the child were held up as models for the artist by Jean-Jacques Rousseau and his contemporaries in England.

Plantinga is surely right in emphasizing the artistic objectives of the folk movement, for an artistic enterprise is what it literally and essentially was. But the conception of an unspoiled peasant sensibility went beyond mere admiration and imitation of the artifacts of the folk; it extended to the notion that the folk song was the authentic instrument of human feeling, because it had escaped being weighed down by all the forms and thought patterns of centuries of court and urban life. Dahlhaus effectively says this when he writes that "the romantic evocation of folk ways and folk art was intended as the expression of a deeper layer of human life and experience which had been overlaid by civilization."[19] Though ultimately as much of an idealization as rustic pastoral's vision of the "eager ploughman," the picture of the peasant drawn by the folk movement (or *Volkstümlichkeit*, as it would shortly come to be known in the German-speaking world) was of a human type not consigned to be the embodiment of honesty and good cheer but rather, subject to all the changes of fortune that could be visited upon humankind and capable of feeling them with an unaccustomed intensity. Such was the depth and utter simplicity of his feeling that he would express it with a kind of eloquence never heard before in the "civilized" world.

For us today the paradigm of such eloquence is the Schubert song. To consider only the two cycles, *Die Schöne Müllerin* (1823) and *Winterreise* (1827), is to appreciate how Schubert found within the compass of *Volkstümlichkeit*, if not his total expressive range, at least the unique power of his musical personality. That power, of course, is responsible for the status of these songs as masterpieces. But there are also cultural reasons why the stories attached to the music—stories of protagonists who suffer misfortunes against which they have no recourse and of which therefore they are the ultimate victim—should strike the modern Western sensibility as extremely moving. Prior to the mid-18th century, observers would not have uniformly responded to the *pathos* of the situations represented; the ethical type embodied in these "heroes" would have been deemed both lacking in significance and unworthy of deep sympathy. Thanks to rustic pastoral, this kind of figure begins to take on the dignity necessary for elevating demotic heroes above the ironic plane, in other words for persuading us that they are inferior to the ordinary person neither in moral fortitude nor in power of action. Once rustic pastoral has won for such a protagonist some degree of admiration and interest, more than just his proverbial cheerfulness may be explored; the roundedness and psychological complexity that were previously granted only to the high-born warrior or the Arcadian shepherd are now conferred on the honest laborer. It is Schubert's particular genius to understand what musical features make up the eloquence of the demotic hero: a plain, almost severe, though lyric, melodic line; a modest, understated demeanor (accomplished in the case of "Wirtshaus" (No. 21 of *Winterreise*) through the device of the pious hymn); a touch of tender sweetness, usually conveyed through major-mode harmony. In contrast to Baroque composers, 19th-century composers learned how to express tragic feeling in the major mode, thus sharply juxtaposing images of the bitter and the sweet. In Germont's aria from Act II of Verdi's *Traviata*, as well as the "Trepak" from Mussorgsky's *Songs and Dances of Death*, each composer intersperses a situation of personal conflict, or fear, or grief with images of what might have been had fate been less cruel. Against the general context of suffering, such images of sweetness can achieve an intense, almost unbearable degree of tragic *pathos*, for they mean for us to hear the voice of a sufferer who, but for a few momentary lapses, succeeds in concealing his grief. In "Wirtshaus," the hero sings his own noble elegy, only twice faltering on the words "nur weiter" when he realizes that however weary he might be, he must wander on.

Although both of Schubert's cycles are concerned with the theme of disappointed love, they take up the theme at different stages of development. *Die Schöne Müllerin* records the whole trajectory of the love experience, from the hero's initial exuberance to his disappointments and on to his ultimate suicide. In the final song, "Der Baches Wiegenlied," in which the brook simultaneously claims the hero's body and sings him sweetly to sleep, Schubert shows that music designed for the cradle is also fitting for the grave. With *Winterreise* all hopes of a happy outcome have been dashed before the story begins. The opening song, "Gute Nacht," sets the tone of muted bleakness heard frequently throughout the cycle: Songs 1, 7, 10, 12, and 20 are related in terms of tempo (moderate to slow), meter (²/₄), mode (minor) and accompaniment figures built out of ceaseless eighth-note motion. Unlike the new species of "noble" understated elegy in the major mode represented by "Wirtshaus," "Gute Nacht," with its drooping melodic lines and minor mode, is in the old plaintive elegiac tradition. "Gute Nacht" maintains an elegiac tone throughout, while in "Auf dem Flusse" (No. 7) and "Einsamkeit," the declamatory outbursts toward the ends of both songs are two of the rare moments in the cycle in which tragic passion breaks past the pastoral confines of the cycle as a whole. "Der Wegweiser" (No. 20), on the other hand, finds no need to raise its voice in order to create the darkest effect of all these "leitmotif" songs: here, the eighth-note motion of the accompaniment has taken over the vocal line as well and has reduced the melodic profile practically to speech-like monotone. The vocal line speaks the raw, unadorned emotion of recitative, except for the fact that this recitative is held tightly within the eighth-note straitjacket which represents the hero's tromping over the frozen land. "Der Leiermann," the final word of the cycle, is a song apart. *Die Schöne Müllerin* ends in sweet death, but here the hero meets up instead with his mirror image—the blind organ-grinder who keeps on mindlessly turning the handle of his hurdy-gurdy in spite of the fact that everyone passes him by without thinking of dropping the meanest coin into his cup. The static and fragmented misery of the music is the voice of the innocent victim reduced to inarticulate and random babbling. There is no redemption here, no dignity, and the pastoral world has been left far behind. And yet, it is precisely in terms of the *ethos* of rustic pastoral that this terrifying picture of alienation in the big city makes sense, for the nightmare presented to us is the tragic underbelly of pastoral, the beautiful idyll gone wrong. The key symbols point to this dismantling of the rustic *ethos*—the blind beggar who was originally from the country himself, and the hurdy-gurdy, a country instrument which, once displaced to the city, loses its value and becomes an object of scorn. The *Winterreise* is by way of being a cautionary tale, a warning that if one chooses to put one's entire faith in the lovely pastoral illusion, one risks losing everything. As if heeding this warning, Schubert in a musical sense embraces all faiths, not confining himself to *Volkstümlichkeit*, but applying his gifts to the epic/heroic mode of symphonies, the ritual ceremony of masses, the gallant worldliness of ballroom dances. But *Volkstümlichkeit* remains the ultimate reference point for his style.

In the later 19th century, *Volkstümlichkeit* enters a new phase, one in which the folk music of a country becomes the expression of its "national soul." In one sense, this represents a narrowing of the *Volkstümlich* idea, ethical superiority now based on national identity instead of rustic purity (a criterion which, besides being genuinely inward, cuts across national lines); in another sense, the later phase represents a broadening, the new music being embraced, theoretically at least, by an entire nation and thus cutting across class lines. To what extent this latter conception responds to historical reality, to what extent it is mere illusion, is debated at length by Dahlhaus in an essay on musical nationalism:[20]

In the uses to which the expression "the people" is put, referring variously to the lower strata of the population and to the nation as a whole, the concept of the lower classes mingles with the idea of nationality. This is a source of confusion, insofar as nineteenth-century nationalism was not at all an expression of self-awareness on the part of the lower classes but a bourgeois phenomenon, while for the nobility dynastic loyalties counted more than national ones.

For Dahlhaus, then, nationalism is a bourgeois myth, a point he makes even more forcefully at a later stage of his essay:[21]

... the "spirit of the people" that was thought to speak in the music of the "national schools" was heard only by the educated, not by the "people" themselves. The artistic character of this music was separated from the folk music it invoked by a social gulf which amounted sometimes to a ravine.

The main intent of this statement is to show that the class division underlying earlier phases of rustic pastoral was still at work in nationalistic art. But the statement has the secondary effect of proving the power of a myth; strong belief is possessed of its own reality. If, in the present case, only the educated segment of a nation was in a position to feel that a European art-music infused with the elements of the nation's folk music captured the "national spirit," that was enough for the magic to take effect, for the members of that segment of society to be genuinely moved and inspired by the experience of listening to a successful product of musical nationalism. The nationalist composers themselves certainly had no intention of passing themselves off as folk musicians (though some of them may have harbored the illusion that were the folk to be exposed to the nationalist music, they might spontaneously embrace it as their own). But neither did they see why their work could not represent a nation in its entirety, irrespective of the divide separating nationalist music and genuine folk music. In their minds class distinction did not preclude nationhood as a valid notion; nor, indeed, is there any reason that it should have, given the metaphysical orientation of nationalism, its obsession with "spirit" and "soul."

The terms in which the basic premises of nationalist art are normally set forth give the impression that art was to serve the nationalist cause, but the proposition seems to work equally well in the opposite direction. That the composer was primarily motivated by the thought of what the fervor of nationalism could do for his music is more than likely; for inasmuch as ethnicity and national identity were highly emotional issues, a music that dipped into the wellsprings of ethnic art stood to gain considerably in emotional power. Dahlhaus presents what appears to be a parallel assessment of the case when he speaks of the "popular appeal" of nationalist music, though in the long run his view carries some very different implications. In effect, he conceives nationalist music to be a neat solution to the problem facing later 19th-century composition, namely how to write a music that will succeed in being both avant-garde and popular at the same time:[22]

[The] ideal of popularity was obviously in direct opposition to the search for constant novelty enforced by the doctrine of originality; something for which the listener is unprepared, and which requires a certain amount of application to understand, is not simultaneously capable of being appreciated and welcomed by a wider public—or so it would seem. But musical nationalism offered a way of escape from the dilemma, and this is what gave it the power to intervene in the aesthetic situation. Music which was prompted to harmonic experiment by procedures or material originating in folk music was on the one hand technically progressive, thus meeting the requirement of novelty; on the other hand, its appeal to national sentiment—or, for foreigners, its picturesque charm—could make it immediately popular.

Eminently intriguing and plausible as this idea may be, the fact remains that Dahlhaus puts the issue on a more pragmatic—one might say, less idealistic—basis than the composers themselves might have liked their artistic motives to be represented. Leaving aside the merits of his suggestion that the same nationalist music might affect the native listener differently from the foreigner, we cannot overlook the fact that by placing national sentiment and picturesque charm on something of an aesthetic par, Dahlhaus effectively reduces our chances of pinpointing the philosophical core of nationalist art, of defining its chief expressive aim. Above all else, nationalist musicians wanted their music to be deeply affecting; and while affective power and wide popularity are not incompatible realities, they rarely share equal place in the minds of serious artists. "Picturesque charm" is something else yet again: traditionally connected to the domain of "exotic music," it connotes an aesthetic emotion that operates on the plane of fantasy and wish fulfillment. The purpose of exotic music was to transport the listener to faraway places, to provide a pleasurable adventure tinged with equal doses of danger and *volupté*. Imitations of near-Eastern and Spanish music became the stock-in-trade of 19th-century exotic expression precisely because the source materials were so remote from the listener's day-to-day experience: the seductive colors could alternately whet and gratify the senses without making further demands.

Conceptually, then, exotic expression falls into the category of escape art, along with the music of carnival entertainments and medieval revels. Though far more delicate and formally subtle as a rule than their simple ancestors, works of exotic music in the 19th century share essentially the same basic expressive aim, which is to offer artistic experiences of "harmless delight." Not so nationalist art, whose *pathos* is of a very different kind. Nationalist artists styled themselves as "realists," as a means of putting the public on notice that the art in question dealt in everyday reality—was meant, in short, to stir deep waters and to leave the listener permanently marked. In this vital respect, nationalism emerges as a genuine variant of rustic pastoral, its expressive sights focused squarely on the theme of the "people" whose destiny, just as Dahlhaus has remarked, comes to be indistinguishable from that of the "lower classes" (i.e., the folk). What was ascribed in an earlier form of pastoral to a single rustic hero now applies to the ethnic group as a whole. The ethical purity of the late 18th-century and early 19th-century peasant is transferred to an entire nation, and the artwork is expected to record the collective joys and sufferings of the people in what might best be called a spirit of "communal *pathos*."

Images of nationalist art, then, typically take the form of a group of piano pieces or a dance suite, such as Grieg's ten sets of *Lyric Pieces* or Dvorak's *Slavonic Dances*. The listener may well hear "picturesque charm" in the sweet, sentimental mood of Grieg's "In My Homeland" (Op. 43, No. 3) but it should be remembered, if we think back to Haydn's *Seasons*, that sentimentality originates in rustic pastoral thinking, not in exoticism. For some listeners Grieg may have succeeded in creating surface effects of delicious local color, or, at the very most, a muted yearning for a life that exists only in dreams. But the response he intends to strike is avowedly more emotional than sensual; eventually he means his quiet songs and piano pieces to be gently touching rather than delicately seductive.

Pastoral is the "natural" province of gentleness, and so there is no question that in large-scale orchestral works, nationalist music has superseded its pastoral bounds and gone over to the heroic camp. Even then, the essential pastoral connection is not broken. For one thing, heroic symphonies invariably contain gentler moments, the subsidiary themes of first movements providing classic examples. But even if such moments did not exist, the rustic pastoral roots of nationalist art would not have been obscured, for the key to nationalist expression is its reliance not on folk material directly but on re-creating in its own musical image the "sound" of the folk. Capturing that sound has been a basic strategy of rustic pastoral music since its inception, which is to say that nationalist composers respectfully follow a time-honored pattern.

Rustic pastoral continued to flourish in the first part of the 20th century, mainly as an updated form of 19th-century nationalism. Vaughn Williams and Sibelius became the leading exponents in the first two decades of the century, Milhaud and Copland in the following generation. The significance of Bartok's nationalism is so all-embracing for the development of his music that it transcends the bounds of both nationalism and rustic pastoral and becomes something quite different from either; his case will be discussed as an aspect of modernist "Primitivism" in Chapter 15. If we concentrate on Copland here, it is because certain unique factors in the American experience yield implications that are not suggested in the original rustic pastoral pattern: the American social structure permitted nationalist and rustic pastoral interests to converge in a way that seemed closer to the historical truth than what was possible in 19th-century Europe.

Of course, for such a convergence to appear genuine, American artists had to perform a considerable feat of historical amnesia: they had to forget that the traditional European division between privileged class and peasant had been replaced in America by something far more extreme, namely the division between free men and slaves. Black Americans are right to regard the ideals of liberty and equality upon which the nation was founded as a mockery vis-à-vis their own situation; but such was the facelessness of black society until very recently that the rest of America could readily and quite sincerely believe that the myth of "liberty and justice for all" had been essentially realized in everyday American life. In view of the potency of the myth, certain rural types—the pioneer, the cowboy, even in a curious way, the outlaw—emerged from historical reality to take on mythic importance, to embody, in other words, values deemed particularly indicative of an "American spirit," qualities such as enterprise, adventurousness, determination, and unpretentiousness of manner. It is in reference to these specific qualities that we see how the interests of nationalism and rustic pastoral are closely joined in American art and how an artist like Copland finds in "local" music like cowboy tunes and Shaker songs the voice of the nation as a whole.

Copland himself has written that "a hymn tune represents a certain order of feeling: simplicity, plainness, sincerity, directness";[23] but he adds that the composers of his generation who were interested in integrating folk material into their works were "after bigger game" than the mere quotation of that material:[24]

We wanted to find a music that would speak of universal things in a vernacular of American speech rhythms. We wanted to write music on a level that left popular music far behind—music with a largeness of utterance representative of the country that Whitman had envisaged.

In short, a cowboy song or country tune, however indicative of the American spirit it might be, was still a seedling expression; it would take music of greater scope to give voice to the vision the new generation of American composers had in mind.

Copland then goes on to say that, unbeknownst to him and his contemporaries, such a music had already been written, namely that of Charles Ives. Copland is quick to distinguish between the Romantic and American impulses in Ives's work, choosing to "stress not so much the mystical and transcendental side of his nature—the side that makes him most nearly akin to men like Thoreau and Emerson—but rather the element in his musical speech that accounts for his acceptance of the vernacular as an integral part of that speech."[25] Yet, as well taken as Copland's distinction is, there still remains the interpretation of the two principles in question in an actual work of Ives, hence the question as to the degree to which they influence each other when they come into contact. The fact is that, with respect to the large-scale instrumental works for which Ives is best remembered, the "American vernacular" becomes a function—serves in the interests—of the transcendental vision; the grandeur of the net result is such that the "American spirit" breathing through these pieces is of an epic order—has, in other words, little to do with rustic pastoral.

If we are looking for a music that combines the American vernacular with the moderate proportions of the pastoral mode, it is in Copland's own scores for the ballets *Billy the Kid, Rodeo,* and *Appalachian Spring* that we will find the quintessential examples. These pieces may fall short of Whitmanesque "largeness of utterance," if that is what Copland was really aspiring to, but in terms of fulfilling the archetypal requirements of rustic pastoral—gentleness, freshness, and dignity through the eloquence of plain speech—they stand unrivaled in the American canon. It must be noted that the Neoclassic character of Copland's personal utterance helps very much in the matter, the clear, crisp outlines of Neoclassic expression reinforcing the crispness already celebrated as a virtue of the American vernacular. Indeed, at times the sonorities are of such a crystalline clarity and delicacy and the formal arrangements so carefully poised that one feels that the music may well have left the demotic world of rustic pastoral for the more rarefied climes of hieratic Arcadia.

Notes

1. John Bull's variations on *Walsingham* appear as the first piece in the *Fitzwilliam Virginal Book*. William Byrd's set on the same tune is found in *My Lady Nevell's Booke*.
2. John Gay, *The Shepherd's Week in Six Pastorals*, p. [A4v].
3. *Ibid.*, p. A4.
4. Lines 65–68 from Milton's poem; see Chapter 8, n. 18.
5. See Wilfrid Mellers, *François Couperin and the French Classical Tradition*, p. 61.
6. See Gay, p. [A4].
7. *Ibid.*, p. [A5].
8. Goldsmith's poem, like Gray's, is included in the anthology *Adventures in English Literature*, Rewey Belle Inglis et al., ed., pp. 296–301.
9. Quoted in Jacob Bronowski, *The Ascent of Man*, p. 260.
10. *Ibid.*, p. 260.
11. Maynard Solomon, *Beethoven*, p. 142.
12. It might be added that "sentimentality" must have had long-standing appeal, to judge only by the fact that rustic pastoral far outlived the 18th century and its original Enlightenment connections.
13. The five-volume biography of Haydn, H.C. Robbins Landon, *Haydn: Chronicle and Works*, is chiefly responsible for this enhanced appreciation. See in particular Vol. I, pp. 35–36; Vol. III, pp. 377–404; Vol. V, pp. 93–120.
14. *Ibid.*, p. 249.
15. From lines 13 and 26 of Milton's poem (see Chapter 8, n. 18).
16. Solomon, p. 206.
17. See Robbins Landon, *Haydn*, Vol. II, pp. 266–271.
18. Leon Plantinga, *Romantic Music*, p. 107.
19. Carl Dahlhaus, *Between Romanticism and Modernism*, p. 93.
20. *Ibid.*, p. 92.
21. *Ibid.*, p. 99.
22. *Ibid.*, p. 99.
23. Aaron Copland, *Music and Imagination*, p. 110.
24. *Ibid.*, p. 111.
25. *Ibid.*, p. 111.

10 The Epic/Heroic Mode

Music of the epic/heroic mode proceeds from two points of origin: ceremonial pomp and military combat. These two sources define two distinct views of the same human type, the kind of man Aristotle called "better than ourselves."[1] Aristotle's value system—his *ethos*—is based on considerations of power of action and toughness of spirit; by "better" we should not understand what would be considered virtuous according to Judeo-Christian standards. Music of ceremonial pomp, which has a longer written history than military music and is therefore more easily traced, represents the hero in his aspect as authority figure—as near-divinity—while military music concentrates on qualities of decisive action and discipline. In view of its older vintage, we will take up ceremonial music first, though the impact of military music on modern Western culture may eventually prove to be the more significant, due to the place of military imagery in the development of our central large-scale instrumental forms, the concerto and the symphony.

As a means of reinforcing the solidarity of institutions and the personal glory of their leaders, the function of ceremony is well understood. Martines gives some vivid accounts of the "orgiastic splendor" that accompanied public occasions—court marriages, religious processions, state visits, carnivals and the like—in Renaissance Italy. Assessing the significance of these events, he writes:[2]

Luxurious ostentation at the courts was a display of power. Without such an exhibition, there was somehow no sufficient claim or title to the possession of power. Therefore the need to show. At the same time, to show was to act out a self-conception: I am prince and I can show it. The more I show it, the more I am what I claim to be. It was a dialectic of ambition and being.

The experience of Renaissance Italy bears out what has already been claimed in this study for hieratic thinking in general; medieval pageantry, whether attached to church or court, partakes of this mentality as well. While music is an integral part of all medieval and Renaissance ceremony, there are some very specific reasons why such ceremonial music may not convey the grandeur and monumentality we associate with later epic-heroic statement. Several of these reasons have been touched upon earlier, but we can elaborate on them here. For one thing, much of the music in question is of an incidental character, meant to form part of a larger whole. The immemorial flourishes of trumpets and drums accompanying the progresses of ruling figures are reported in accounts of specific occasions, but they themselves do not form part of the written record. The momentary significance of this music comes out in the following description of practices in late 15th- and early 16th-century Italy:[3]

Public occasions meant the sound of trumpets, cannon, drums, pipes and the air trembling with bells. Duke Ercole produced eighty trumpeters for Lucrezia Borgia's arrival in Ferrara [January 1502]. At Milan the major public festivities began with the duke's arrival, the rolling of drums and the sound of trumpets and pipes.

Such sounds of pomp were just one element in the ceremonial spectacle, along with the magnificent costumes, coaches, banners, and cavalcades of horses. In themselves, they had no compositional autonomy, the ceremony as a whole being the composition. As isolated motifs, they could give the sign of heroism, but without being integrated into a musical form capable of transmitting a feeling of sustained energy, they did not genuinely embody the heroic vision.

What we are looking for, then, is a kind of self-contained music which, apart from its original ceremonial context, does not merely symbolize grandeur through its imagery but *is* grand by its very weight, scope, and density. The earliest music to qualify on this basis may be the organa in three and four parts of Perotin, though the question of performing forces looms large here: these pieces will make a properly monumental effect, given a sizeable body of singers. When we come to the isorhythmic motet of the 14th and 15th centuries, however, the nature of the performance is less critical, for we know that the kind of piece in question was designed to be sung on great occasions and that the complexity of its internal structure was meant to be received as something grand and imposing. The lengthy description of the musical events taking place at the consecration of the Duomo in Florence in 1436 strongly suggests that Dufay's elaborate isorhythmic motet, *Nuper rosarum flores*, was performed with singers and instruments (trumpets, lutes, flutes) massed together on its separate parts, thus causing a "reverberation" so "joyous and sweet" that "mental stupor seemed as if to regather strength from the wonderful sounds."[4]

Perhaps the chief obstacle in assessing the heroic character of much medieval and Renaissance music is the uncertainty about its actual effect in performance. If voices and instruments joined forces to perform the major musical works written for the dedication of the Florentine cathedral, was this normal procedure or an exceptional solution in recognition of the exceptional nature of the occasion? The traditional image of a Renaissance sacred polyphony floating ethereally around the worshippers' heads in the hushed spirit of Gregorian chant has been largely dispelled by recent scholarship. Though certainly much Renaissance polyphony continues to conform comfortably to that image, a more heterogeneous view of Renaissance sound seems closer to the facts, one in which a mixture of voices and instruments was as likely as a pure *a cappella* realization.[5] However, for lack of specific information regarding assignments of instruments to actual pieces, our modern sensibility, which has been conditioned to respond to timbre and sonority in very precise ways, is left somewhat unsatisfied. The Holy Roman Emperor Maximilian I surely had an impressive retinue of musicians in his employ, but for all the groupings of his instrumental forces into consorts—the pipes and drums, the lutes and viols, the shawms, trombones and krumhorns, the organs, the choir—we cannot be sure whether it was the custom to bring these consorts together in the manner of the modern orchestra or to keep them strictly apart, or whether each consort was conventionally associated with specific kinds of music.[6] Not until the sacred concertos of Giovanni Gabrieli at the end of the 16th century do we find the kinds of precise instrumental designations that have been the norm ever since; significantly, these "sumptuous polychoral motets and grandiose imitative instrumental canzonas"[7] are usually viewed by scholars as being more indicative of Baroque theatricality than Renaissance gravity.

Nevertheless, signs of musical pomp are not altogether missing in the later 16th century. The *cori spezzati* of mid-century Venice—long recognized as the precursor of Gabrieli's later polychoral style—constitute one example, as do the serious multi-voiced motets (usually a 5 or a 6) that make up much of the sacred repertoire of Clemens non Papa, Willaert, and Lassus. In this kind of motet, the opening section, with its staggered homophony, long note values, and widely spaced consonant chords (almost invariably laid out in root position) set the monumental tone. Here, as in the earlier isorhythmic motet (perhaps even more so), the heroic gesture is so clearly delineated through the internal musical relationships that considerations of vocal and instrumental coloring seem extraneous to the central question. Two kinds of instrumental music—the fantasia and the pavane—are recognized in their own time for their specific gravity of character. Though not set out with the same opulence of sound of the motet-type just mentioned, the typical fantasia, with its long-held note values and intricate interweaving of voices, connoted spaciousness and grandeur. The pavane, for its part, was in certain cases so stately and solemn that the dance could appropriately serve as a funeral march.

It is probably only in a relative sense that Renaissance musical "pomp" appears not to live up to its name. Compared against the development in sacred music that followed on the heels of Renaissance polyphony, the stately motets and instrumental pieces of the late 16th century may strike us as less grand than they were intended to be. No music of the West has ever been more single-mindedly devoted to a vision of splendid ceremony than the repertoire known as the "colossal Baroque"—those grand concertato products of the Venetian and German followers of the Gabrielis which elaborated Christian worship in the early 17th century. Monumentality is more than grandeur, it is *static* grandeur, the image of something so immense that it is for all intents and purposes immovable, fixed in place. The impression of static monumentality that issues from many of the *Psalmen Davids* of Schütz (to take the most illustrious examples) is the result of more than vocal and instrumental sonorities ingeniously and variously combined; it is the product of long columns of sound laid out side by side in root position, together with steady dialoguing between the individual voices and a frequency of cadencing that has not been encounterd before or since in Western style. "Hieratic" in the more familiar, and also narrower, sense than the term has been used in this study, these pieces conform very little to the dynamic principle on which modern Western culture has generally proceeded, a fact which may in part explain why they did not have an extended history.[8] But, while they lasted, they succeeded in making a convincing synthesis of two traditionally irreconcilable ideas: the fixity of the eternal and the vibrancy of the worldly and the temporal.

The later 17th century produced a musical image which, if not the equal of grand concertato in hieratic splendor, may have outranked it in pompous intent; this was the French overture. Designed to catch the king's outward bearing as he proceeded godlike before the multitudes, the French overture epitomizes the almost exaggerated majesty that Louis XIV and his court brought to the execution of all public matters. Yet, robed in the formal decorum of this image is an element of *pathos* not detected in the earlier concertato: the rhythmic impulse of a heavy march captures the supernally composed stride of the king and his retinue, but the dotted rhythms add a note of vehemence—the fist of authority insistently pounding out its will to be obeyed. That this reference to a fist is not a flight of fancy can be appreciated if we imagine the dotted rhythms to have had their musical beginnings in the stylized pounding of kettledrums. Given the studied magnificence of the French overture, one would not expect it to have outlived its own time, but it does have a descendant in the slow introduction with which Haydn, and less frequently Mozart, liked to open their mature symphonies. The transition in these Classical symphonies from slow introduction to fast sonata-allegro movement calls to mind the fact that the French overture, too, moves from its majestic march opening to an allegro, often fugal, in the second part. Not content to depict the leader only as supreme authority figure, the French overture means to represent him as military hero as well; in so doing, it embraces in quick succession the two primary expressive types that form the epic/heroic mode in Baroque music—ceremonial pomp, on the one hand, *concitato*, on the other.

Concitato

With *concitato* we come to the central *ethos* guiding Baroque musical expression. Although the term originates with Monteverdi and certain techniques he applied in the *Combattimento di Tancredi e Clorinda* of 1624, the significance of *concitato* for the Baroque period is something of far wider scope than the specific passage given below (Example 10.1). According to Monteverdi, the "affection" to which *concitato* corresponds is anger, the kind of emotion a brave man feels, or should feel, when involved in military combat. The composer of *stile concitato*, Monteverdi says, will come most readily by the expressive materials he is looking for if he imitates the utterances and accents of a man imbued with feelings of "noble rage" while on the field of battle.[9] Excited military music, then, is the paradigm of *stile concitato*, though any excited music of a "serious" kind—that is, of a kind that does not ally itself with revelry—effectively qualifies as *concitato* expression. Indeed, some lack of perception has already been imputed to Monteverdi himself for not having recognized the prototypical signs of *concitato* in the more excited moments of the dramatic madrigal, many of which, needless to say, came directly from his own pen. But if such signs are manifest in music before the *Combattimento*, they are certainly so in music after it. For, as was already said above, *stile concitato* is an expressive pattern of general application to the entire period; as such, it is alive in any rage aria of an *opera seria*, any vivace first movement of a concerto grosso (and many third movements as well) and in fact, in any image in which the crisp, sharply defined anapestic rhythm is predominant. The term "noble rage" is borrowed directly from Alessandro Striggio, who assigns to the personage of La Musica in the prologue of *L'Orfeo* the words:

Et hor di nobil' ira	And now with noble rage
et hor d'amore,	and now with love,
Poss' infiammar	I can inflame
le più gelate menti.	the most frozen hearts.

Characteristically, Monteverdi writes just the type of excited declamation for this line that he will later call *concitato*. In the context of this prologue—which is nothing less than a manifesto of the new aesthetic—*concitato* would seem to be a basic technique for stirring up the emotions, for firing up the iciest hearts; it would be a prime expressive means by which the principle of *pathos* is realized. If this is so, then the precise nature of Baroque *pathos* comes into a new focus. In order to understand this last point, we must carefully examine the expression "noble rage" itself. The word "noble," in short, requires as much attention as the word "rage," for we can accept that rage connotes something like anger or passion or even strong feeling. But this is not any ordinary passion; this is a "noble passion," a passion felt by that sort of man who bears himself *nobly*— whose status ultimately requires that he be self-possessed and in control. And who is that sort of man? He is the hero who strides across the stage of the *opera seria*—the figure in whom the ruling class sees its mirror image and finds the embodiment of its ideals. At the center of the Baroque vision of the heroic is the hero's most precious possession: his *gloire*, which is a power, to be sure, but a power attained—and sustained—through an interaction of passion and dignity. Passion is a positive force, a creative energy leading to effective action provided it

Example 10.1: Monteverdi, *Orfeo*, Prologue

Io la mu - si - ca son ch'ai dol - ci ac - cen - ti so far tran - quil - lo o - gni tur - ba - to co - re et hor di no - bil' i - ra et hor d'a - mo - re pos - s'in - fiam - mar le più ge - la - te men - ti.

is properly tempered and controlled. If left to itself it can get out of hand, become anarchic and destructive.

The idea of emotion out of control echoes the old Greek fear of a Dionysian impulse unqualified and unrestrained. Nevertheless, there is an important distinction to be made between ancient and modern views, for Western thinking about affective experience has undergone a radical change since ancient times. The view that human emotions are individual property—are something distinctly "ours" and nobody else's—is modern and secular in orientation. In archaic thought it is far more natural to think of oneself as being possessed by emotions than being in possession of them. Such emotions are not only not one's own, they are external to the person, and being external, they become personifications in their own right. Each emotion, each separate affect, is attributed to a specifically designated power, whether a god, or perhaps something less clearly defined, like a *daimon*. Richard Hathorn writes: "It would not be too much to say that the gods could enter, and did enter, into human bodies and souls at their own sweet will."[10]

Modern man conceives of his "condition" as something apart from what he plans for himself—as something that happens to him either through fate or by accident—but he does not include his emotions in that picture. The vision of the emotions as alien things coming into the body from the outside could be painful and alarming to the Greeks. Affective experience was so often represented as difficult and unsettling that the *pathe*—the affections themselves—would in time come to take on the connotation of suffering. E.R. Dodds has this to say on the subject:[11]

The Greek had always felt the experience of passion as something mysterious and frightening, the experience of a force that was in him, possessing him, rather than possessed by him. The very word *pathos* testifies to that: like its Latin equivalent *passio*, it means something that "happens to" a man, something of which he is the passive victim.

In this negative reaction to emotion, there is a strong Apollonian tendency: the dislike of human lack of control signifies a decided will to control. To what extent these sentiments were generally felt in Athens of the Golden Age is difficult to say: Euripides, of course, represents the Dionysian "frenzy" in the *Bacchae* as something barbaric and destructive;[12] yet, Aristotle can later report that the same frenzy can be harmless, in fact, even have a therapeutic effect.[13] However, it is important to remember that Aristotle does not have any particular regard for people who need this kind of therapy. They are not his sort of people, which is to say that they are not of the educated class, not born to lead and to shoulder important responsibilities. Here again, we encounter Aristotle's fundamentally hieratic mentality; and indeed, in such a mentality we find the roots of a mistrust, if not of a distinct fear, of Dionysus and all that he stands for. Dodds speaks to this point when he characterizes the Dionysian experience as follows:[14]

Dionysus offered freedom: "Forget the difference, and you will find the identity" ... He was essentially a god of joy ... And his joys were accessible to all, including even slaves, as well as those freemen who were shut out from the old gentile cults. Apollo moved only in the best society, from the days when he was Hector's patron to the days when he canonised aristocratic athletes; but Dionysus was at all periods *demotikos*, a god of the people.

Viewing the Apollonian/Dionysian dichotomy from the perspective of social *ethos* yields an important insight: it reveals not only the close kinship between hieratic and Apollonian tendencies, but it also confirms the great store the upper class sets by appearances. When Dodds mentions the "Greek" fear of passion, we know at least to include the Greek aristocracy in that generalization. In aristocratic terms, passions might well invade the human system, in the form of gods and *daimones*, but it was the responsibility of persons of distinction to resist, to fend off the attack. Even if one were racked with inner torment, it was still a matter of honor to give the outward semblance of calm.

Here we can draw an immediate parallel with the modern European experience and courtly decorum. But the divergence of ancient and modern views must also be recognized. In the modern world, as affective experience is no longer considered something foreign but rather something "human"—originating "inside" us—passion presents itself as more controllable, thus less threatening than it seems to have been to the more Apollonian-minded in ancient times. Passion is not merely something that happens to us, but a force that we can actively harness, a generative power that sets things in motion and inspires feats of heroism. A "heroic effort" is one that transcends the normally human, one that distinguishes itself in action we call "extraordinary." Such an effort requires passion; without passion there can be no aspiration to greatness, to *gloire*. But this passion, as was said above, must be accompanied by discipline and control. The passion works when it is focused and channeled, directed toward the proper end. The mark of the true hero is strength of purpose and clarity of vision; he is master of his destiny because he knows where he is going.

This conception of the heroic was certainly not new to European thought before the 17th century: we find it already overwhelmingly expressed in the hurtling figures of Michelangelo's and Titian's paintings and in the bristling language of Shakespearean tragedy, to mention only the most notable Renaissance examples. Why, then, did it take music so long to come by *concitato* expression? Monteverdi touches upon the answer when he observes, with only a little exaggeration, that up until his own time only the "molle" and the "temperato" modes were known to music. The fact is that until late in the 16th century music had been under the spell of churchly humility and gravity and courtly sweetness. With the unleashing of vehemence in the dramatic madrigal, however, the way was paved for the advent of heroic *concitato*. At the same time, neither the dramatic madrigal nor the recitative provided genuine heroic examples in their own right, for they represented the *pathos* of tragic suffering, not the *ethos* of heroism. In appropriating Plato's device of the battlefield (however much he might have inadvertently misconstrued this device to fit his own ends) Monteverdi endowed anger with an ethical value. What is new in the *Combattimento* is not the expression of anger as such, for vehemence had already been heard in the dramatic madrigal and the recitative, but the emergence in music of a distinct human type, the noble warrior.[15]

Through its association with the battlefield, anger is given concrete direction—a "creative" outlet—and thus becomes worthy of emulation by those aspiring to leadership.[16] Significantly, the most novel passages of the *Combattimento* are not the declamations assigned to the vocal part—though the rapid-fire, "Pyrrhic" rhythms of "et lo sdegno, lo sdegno" are extremely striking—but the instrumental figures designed to represent the thrusts and parries of the combatants at full throttle. In the course of four measures, Monteverdi has created for the future of European instrumental music two of its most enduring clichés: (1) the downward-thrusting cadential resolution of the Baroque concerto and (2) the repetitive V–I cadencing of the Classical symphony (Example 10.2). Monteverdi's efforts endow these impulses with the requisite heroic weight; for the requisite scale to be achieved, music will have to await the development of high Baroque *concitato* style, with its regularity of pulsation, expansion and clarity of forms, richness of texture, and above all, the directedness which comes from the dynamism of the new tonal structure. It is particularly in the larger forms—in the opening movements of concerti grossi or in the monumental organ fugues of Bach—that the *ethos* of the military hero makes itself most unequivocally felt. In the qualities of relentlessness and sustained growth imparted by these pieces—a power held in check and thus giving the promise of hidden reserves—the hieratic vision of passion, not merely subjected to control but made manifest and grandly effective through such control, is completely realized.

The use of the word "monumental" to characterize Bach's organ fugues leads us to realize that in his grandest conceptions the two branches of the epic-heroic mode, concitato and ceremonial pomp, are combined. This is especially felt in the big celebrational D-major pieces with trumpets and kettledrums—the Gloria, Cum sancto spirito, and Et resurrexit of the Mass in B minor, the opening and closing choruses of Cantata No. 11, the opening of the Christmas Oratorio—where principal thematic material, countersubjects, trumpet flourishes and drumbeats are all swooped up in the embrace of a harmonic macro-rhythm rolling inexorably forward. The same heroic techniques serve equally well for grand tragic statement, represented in the opening choruses of such works as Cantatas No. 21, 105, and 198, and the two Passions. In the first ritornello of the St. John Passion the layering of plangently sustained oboes over agitated sixteenth-note string figures over the repeated eighth-note pedal point of the bass line, all operating within the framework of a single and complete harmonic excursion of the key of G minor, shows to what degree Bach has succeeded in integrating the elements of pomp and concitato. By Bach's time this kind of heroic treatment of the Christian ritual had been in force for at least a century. Those with more ascetic leanings, like Thomas Merton, would prefer the slender sublimity of chant to such grandeur. But the overriding feeling among the majority listening to Bach's music today continues to be that the weightiness and splendor of his large-scale works imbue the sacred symbols with a kind of breadth and energy that can come only through the application of heroic means. And from a more general standpoint, one can say that in Bach's heroic style music finally found an equivalent to the gestures that literature and painting had much earlier given the Western world—the first by virtue of its ancient epic poems, the second through the religious and historical frescoes of the Italian Renaissance.

Mature *stile concitato*, then, relies for its *scale* on the qualities of steadiness and continuous growth that we associate with Baroque concertos and fugues. Even so, this scale needs the collaboration of still another feature—the conception of the single affection discussed earlier in connection with the aria—in order to encourage continuity and minimize effects of contrast and interruption. The ostensible forces of contrast in the Baroque concerto grosso—the alternations of *ripieno* and

Example 10.2: Monteverdi, *Combattimento*

concertino, and the introduction of a subordinate theme—are manifestly superseded by rhythmic drive and single-mindedness of expressive purpose. The first movement of the Brandenburg Concerto No. 5 is lyricism in its most monumental form, but it is lyricism, nevertheless.[17] The genres of the high Baroque have, to be sure, pulled away from Renaissance pictoralism; later imagery is endowed with the momentum of a genuine dynamic action. That action, however, consists of forward movement, not change; it is lyric in essence, not dramatic.

In this sense, the *concitato* of the *Combattimento*, clearly more restricted in scope than the later examples, is nevertheless more dramatic, dedicated as it is to volatility and openness of form. This in itself suggests that the conception of *pathos* has undergone an evolution from its origins in the 16th-century madrigal and early monody to its later Baroque condition. And this evolution seems to have taken place in direct proportion to the changing image of *stile concitato*. In terms of the bipartite meaning of "noble rage," there seems to be in the course of the Baroque period something of a change in emphasis toward the "noble" and away from the "rage." *Pathos* given its full voice is vehemence, but high Baroque pathos is hieratic vehemence, a behavior in which Dionysian surrender to Eros and the Apollonian will to resist are involved in a continual interplay of qualification and reassertion. We might say that this interplay defines the expressive center of later Baroque music. In true hieratic thought, passion, however highly charged, is never "raw" but clothed in formality. In the early 17th century, the freedom of recitative signaled the total emancipation of *pathos*, a situation in which human emotions could be vehemently expressed in the total absence of a qualifying *ethos*. But as the Baroque period unfolds and a musical image of the noble warrior emerges, heroic expression in music definitively reclaims the hieratic identity that was always attached to Arcadian pastoral.

Gorgeous Tragedy

In the wake of this discussion, we are led to ask whether *pathos* of a more violent kind—a kind that would break past the bounds of normal Baroque aesthetics—has any chance of expressing itself in later Baroque style. There does in fact exist a type of music in the opera of the period that is designed to deal with the moments in which human emotion overflows with undue spontaneity and volatility, namely, the *recitativo accompagnato*. Most examples of *recitativo accompagnato*, however, are so conventionally artificial that they do not give the requisite illusion of spontaneity, much less the effect of genuine emotion, that one would hope to find in such expression. Nevertheless, the best examples of *recitativo accompagnato* constitute the area where we must look if we are going to find an expression that breaks through the normal hieratic constraints prevailing in the period. In his biography of Couperin, Wilfrid Mellers speaks of Racine's capacity to have achieved moments in his plays in which the "veil of Maya" is rent asunder, and the truth is revealed in all its unprotected horror:[18]

In Racine, as in Molière, the stress is centered on the threat to organized society occasioned by the unruly impulses of the individual. But whereas Molière emphasizes the folly involved in submission to the passions, so that his work is both serious and funny, Racine emphasizes the evil. The intensity of passion in his characters, especially Phèdre, sometimes breaks down the conventional norm; but it is only because of the existence of the norm that the effect of the passion is overwhelming. The sudden glimpses of an un-suspected world in the dark reaches of the mind which the imagery and movement reveal to us, are the more terrible because they appear against the background of "les bornes de l'austère pudeur."

Few who are familiar with the moment in which Phèdre suddenly switches from "vous" to "tu" in her second-act interview with Hippolyte will deny the devastating impact of this event. Mellers is right to talk of the "evil" of unruly passion. Phèdre's tragedy is in direct proportion to her inability to control her dark love for Hippolyte. Indeed, the key to the tragedy of the tragic hero seems to be just that excess of passion which takes hold of him and does not let go its grip until the tragic action has run its course. In all the famous tragic cases of literature—Oedipus, Antigone, Lear, Macbeth, Hamlet, Othello—it is their passion which leads them or drives them or works through them, but which, in any case, is so all-powerful that it seems to have a life of its own.[19] Frye speaks of the way in which tragic heroism bursts the bounds of normal experience and suggests the infinite.[20] And he characterizes Octavius in *Antony and Cleopatra* as a smaller man than Antony, just to the extent that he is more prudent and well-ordered. Antony is the Dionysian hero, giving himself over to passion recklessly, exuberantly, without qualification. Here is a framework in which we see the Apollonian clearly linked with the comic, and the Dionysian with the tragic. For Octavius, like the earlier Odysseus, is a man who will succeed and come out on top, just because he knows how to apply the controls and maneuver his way through. His success comes from his knowledge of how to live within limits; and such limits define him as a finite, Apollonian hero. But the Apollonian hero conforms precisely to the heroic ideal of the Baroque period, to the conception of a passion which, because it does not overreach itself, leads to a triumphant end. This is essentially a comic vision of life: the Baroque vision is fundamentally dedicated to the celebration of the comic hero. After the initial period of the Camerata, where one feels that Aeschylus' dictum of knowledge through suffering is taken seriously[21], the prevailing hieratic mentality places passion and heroism in an essentially finite and comic context.

The artistic imagery will in great part bear out the dominant *ethos* of the age. But there are notable exceptions—moments in which passion bursts out beyond the normal bounds of decorum—and Racine's *Phèdre* is a case in point. Remark-ably, music has been provided with a worthy parallel to Racine's tragedy—the *Hippolyte et Aricie* of Rameau. Rameau's opera, written in 1733, fifty-six years after Racine's play which inspired it, does not have the concentration or tight-ness of construction of the original; nor could it have, given the requirement for *divertissement* in the *tragédie lyrique*. The title of the opera also suggests that the interest has been shifted away from Racine's doomed heroine and toward the young lovers. But the greatest moment of the opera—the one in which suffering is released in all its tragic fury—is reserved for Phèdre. At the end of Act IV, just after Hippolyte has met his violent death (represented spectacularly before the

Example 10.3: Rameau, *Hippolyte et Aricie,* Act IV

Ph

Quels ter- ri - bles é - clats! Fuy -

ons! Où me ca -

cher? Je sens trem - bler la

ter - re. Les En - fers

s'ou - - vrent sous mes pas.

the audience in a manner that was forbidden to French classical tragedy), Phèdre enters inquiring about the commotion (Example 10.3). When she learns the news, the true nature of her suffering is revealed for the first time in the piece, and we are treated to a whirlwind succession of affects which has few, if any, equals in the period. In the overlapping dialogues between Phèdre and the chorus, the swift and unexpected changes between recitative and metered music, the *accompagnato* figures and totally unique orchestral sonorities, and the opulence of the ninth chords that usher Phèdre off the stage toward her death, we have a case in which the artistic intent is to sweep everything and everyone into histrionic gorgeousness and breathless pace. In a sense, the final majestic chords enable Phèdre to retain something of her *gloire*, but the turbulence of the scene as a whole has a lasting effect. This moment from *Hippolyte et Aricie* is far more than *recitativo accompagnato*; it is a dramatic *scena* which, for vehemence at once fiery and massive, must await the mid-19th century to be heard again on the lyric stage. To be sure, the sounds of hieratic Baroque style are still recognizable in this music: Rameau has not made some mad and inexplicable departure from the idiom. But the aesthetic conception anticipates a later age; the curtain of Baroque decorum has given way to the furious assaults of a future tragic spirit, and this condition alone has a startling and overwhelming effect.

The New Festal Pomp

Heroic music in the latter part of the 18th century may be classified under the rubric "new festal pomp." This suggests either that the two branches of heroic expression of the previous era are fused in a single musical image or that one of the branches has ceased to have any bearing on the new style. In fact, neither of these alternatives is quite the case, the redistribution of functions being less symmetrical than represented in this scenario. The new festal pomp has its own distinct character both in terms of musical imagery and archetypal content, which is to say that it differs in all essential respects from the old ceremonial pomp and the *stile concitato*. Yet, one point of common ground is shared with each of its heroic predecessors: like the French overture, festal pomp has its musical origins in a ceremonial march, and like mature *concitato*, its imagery forms the basis of the opening movement of the chief instrumental form of the period. As this instrumental music was the concerto grosso for the high Baroque, so for the later 18th century the genre in question is the symphony; indeed, the gestures of new festal pomp comprise what is commonly referred to as "symphonism."

Taking these connections as a point of departure, we may begin to craft out a definition of the *ethos* of the new musical heroism. Juxtaposition of the French overture and the new military march immediately points up the difference in character between the two types, embodied in the rhythmic impulse. As against the overture's majestic stride, the march of festal pomp means to be buoyant, brisk, light-footed. This is music designed to accompany a leader in public ceremony and to present him in the best possible light, but the notion of what constitutes the best possible light has considerably changed since the days of Louis XIV. While the former ceremonial mode was to hold the onlooker in awestruck thrall, the attempt now is to make a more intimate, gracious appeal. Authority is still to be represented and admired—the stance of firm military discipline in the ceremony assures that; but it needs also to be loved, hence the more amiable public face, the greater charm and lightness of movement. Behind this change of demeanor lurks an important concession to the trend of the times, an effort to redefine one's position in the wake of strong headwinds blowing changes beyond one's control; for it is not as if the monarchies and the princely courts would care to embrace the social ideals of the Enlightenment with unalloyed enthusiasm, but they saw the wisdom in making certain gestures in its direction. Concession is indeed the key word: this was the age of *galant* feeling—an age in which comfort and pleasantness became ideals in their own right, a time when it seemed eminently more pleasant and reasonable to bend to the inevitable than to fight change with implacable resistance.[22] Unfortunately for much of Europe's ruling class, the bending would be too little, too late, while for others, giving up absolutism and divine right was the means of consolidating the considerable power and privilege that remained.

Although the march of festal pomp is a quick music, it has its origins in public ceremony, and is thus properly compared, at least in terms of function, against the French overture, not against *concitato*. *Concitato*, by contrast, begins life as a dramatic representation of a fictional hero in the immediacy of battle. If, on the other hand, we compare festal pomp and *concitato* on the basis of the warrior-hero, the picture of the amiable leader described above should be reinforced; for the military aspect of the march is enough to lend to this leader the characteristics of a warrior—a warrior, nevertheless, who, far from being shown in the heat of battle, is either preparing to go to war, or more likely, returning from the wars ready to greet the milling throngs with all the gracious, good cheer of a man accustomed to basking in the glory of public adoration. In its relationship to the warrior-hero, then, the march of festal pomp is a piece to welcome home a triumphant general and his army; he and his troops are on parade, spanking clean, aglitter with medals.

The amiable leader and the warrior triumphant fuse together in this musical image of discipline and of buoyant good cheer—an image whose slenderness with respect to *concitato* is partly explained by the fact that it is a ceremonial, not a battle, music. In purely rhythmic terms, this slenderness expresses itself in a characteristically brisk quarter-note pulse vis-à-vis the heavier, chugging eighth-note pulse of Baroque *concitato*. Indeed, the new lighter pulse is so characteristic of the time that it is no exaggeration to call the following march rhythm the talisman motive of late 18th-century style: ♩ ♫ ♩ ♩ . The rhythm is ubiquitous, without any preference for genre, figuring in arias, choruses, symphonies, and concertos alike. We are not surprised to find it in such pieces as the march from Act III of *The Marriage of Figaro* or Figaro's aria "Non più andrai," in which Cherubino

Example 10.4: Johann Stamitz, Sinfonia, Op. V, No. 2

is given a proper send-off to the front; but it is equally at home in extended movements of instrumental music and it forms the basic thematic substance of a number of the most famous symphonies of the time, among them Nos. 34, 35, and 41 of Mozart.

In itself a musical idea of great charm and verve, one can understand its special appeal for a public devoted to the comic vision. But the musical idea on its own does not have the capacity to generate an extended symphonic movement: in order for such an amplification to take place, the motivic elements of festal pomp must be integrated into a larger dynamic structure than is provided by a mere march. The credit for the development of that structure falls in great part to the efforts of the Mannheim school. With its famous crescendos, tremolos, drum rolls, and Roman candle effects, together with its achievement of controlling harmonic rhythm on a grand scale, Mannheim symphonism removes the "talisman" rhythm from its original ceremonial setting and creates around it a "universal" expression of triumphant heroism (Example 10.4). If the hero represented in the later 18th-century symphony is slighter in stature than his *concitato* counterpart, it is for the reasons already given: scaling down the hero is a question of choice, the result of a deliberate attempt to create a public persona who is every inch the noble leader but who is at the same time less exalted, less remote, more charming and lovable than his ancestors. And just as the large-scale design of the concerto grosso, dominated as it is by the conception of the single affection, serves to bring out the dogged, unrelenting character of *concitato* heroism, so the equivalent design of the opening movement of the later symphony—the sonata-allegro form—reinforces the new heroic *ethos*. To understand this last point more clearly, we must consider that the sonata-allegro conception is dedicated to recording *changes* of behavior and that such changes of behavior occurring within the public and jubilant climate of festal pomp suggest a certain nonchalance with respect to the significance of the passions.[23] The hero of *stile concitato* is fundamentally driven by his passions, despite the fact that he knows the need of harnessing them for the purpose of achieving certain ends. The hero of festal pomp, on the other hand, believes that the ends he has in mind can be largely achieved through a graceful and personable manner. Passion comes to mean proportionately less to him, how he appears in the eyes of others proportionately more: the *ethos* of social (as opposed to personal) identity takes pride of place.

Sturm und Drang

C.P.E. Bach, deploring the waning fortunes of the contrapuntal style, says in his last years: "I believe with many intelligent men that the present love for the comic accounts for this more than anything else."[24] The triumph of festal pomp appears to be twofold, first in the sense that triumph is the very content of festal pomp, second in the sense that the source of that content, the comic vision, is, just as C.P.E. Bach suggests, the dominant spirit of the age. That having been said, we cannot ignore an opposing spirit that broke onto the German literary scene around 1770 and died out as quickly as it had flared up: *Sturm und Drang* may hold a marginal place in the total network of late 18th-century artistic tendencies, but its presence in the musical imagery of high classic style adds an undeniable expressive potency and its consequences for future musical developments cannot be overstated. Allied at one and the same time with the tragic vision and the large-scale gesture of the new symphonism, the music of *Sturm und Drang* would seem to be nothing other than the reverse face of festal pomp, in short, the music of tragic or solemn pomp. But solemn pomp invokes distinct images of the funeral march, and this is not at all the character of *Sturm und Drang*. Quick and feverish, *Sturm und Drang* music has in fact nothing to do with pomp, being dedicated to a vision of individual passion unattached to ceremony and thus expressing what would soon come to be routinely known as *agitato*.

To what extent *agitato* expression is divested of public connotation, and thus of any notion of social decorum, may be appreciated if we consider briefly the principles underlying the *Sturm und Drang* literary movement. Robbins Landon describes the movement as bringing together three independent impulses into a single focus: (1) a reaction to the social and philosophical tenets of the Enlightenment; (2) a verbal imagery inspired by the climate and landscape of Northern Europe; and (3) a cult of genius which holds that the artist must speak out, "unimpeded by the dictates of morals or scholarship."[25] This last principle outlines with particular clarity the proto-Romantic character of *Sturm und Drang*:

traditional aesthetic concerns about the effect of the work of art are exchanged for emphasis on the process of creation, the person of the artist, and the work of art *per se*. The specifically poetical component of this idea lies in the artist's image of himself as a "creature of nature": he must be a free spirit, as free and unrestricted as the winter storms, wild ocean cliffs, and scudding clouds of Ossian's poems. The metaphorical identification between man and nature is a connection between inner and outer life, and, for a moment this sounds simply like a variant of the typical conceit of a rage aria which compares the storm in one's breast to the storm on the sea. But this is not a conceit; it is a general condition, a total program of artistic behavior by which the poet ceases to be the faithful courtier and spokesman for his society and declares his isolation and disaffection. If such an artist has little use for the Enlightenment, however noble and compassionate its basic outlook, it is doubtless because Enlightenment horizons are too reasonable, too limited by social imperatives. The *Sturm und Drang* poet seeks out the unreasonable—something beyond the civilized social norm, some new and fresh poetic device like the *Volkslied* which he can name "the true expression of feeling and of the entire soul."[26] *Sturm und Drang* literature had its moment, but its wild and woolly features would prove out of place in the *Zeitgeist* of high Classicism: it remained an episode, an additional expressive ingredient, not the main attraction. In time, however, a form of *Sturm und Drang* would come to occupy center stage: the early movement may have been short-lived (within very few years the chief exponents had abandoned it), but its fundamental beliefs would have effects reaching into the Romantic century and beyond.

If *Sturm und Drang* was a brief literary affair, it is not even certain that a movement as such ever existed for music. The term is currently used to refer to a few symphonies of rather extraordinary character written by Haydn c. 1770, and very little else. Moreover, there is no indication that Haydn was aware of the literary activity, nor is he quite the person to equate with the artist envisioned in the new manifesto. Still, the emotional climate of these symphonies is thought to be sufficient cause for the *Sturm und Drang* epithet, and the epithet has stuck.[27] Another category deserving of the name is the instrumental music written for storm scenes in dramatic stage works, such as we find in both Gluck's and Piccini's settings of *Iphigenia in Tauris*.[28] Curiously, the music of these two examples is not particularly distinguishable from the festal pomp imagery of the Mannheim symphonies: drum rolls, tremolos, brief chord-outlining motives proliferate, all set in the festal key of D major. Where Haydn strikingly departs from the festal sound is in his use of minor keys: E minor, F♯ minor, F minor. To what extent the shift from major to minor, unaided by any other musical element, was intended to signal a dramatic change from the comic to the tragic can be shown by taking the Stamitz excerpt above and converting it into the minor mode. In fact, more than a dramatic change is at work here; it is rather a transformation to the diametrically opposed affection, the triumph of festal pomp turned into the chaos of wild fury. The reasons for such a transformation are several. First, there is the increased homophony of later 18th-century style: with the passing tones, auxiliary tones, and suspensions greatly reduced, the primary colorings of tonic, dominant, and subdominant chords are stronger, the major-minor qualities starker and more sharply differentiated. This is especially true of the new symphonism, in which melodic building is more purely triadic than ever before and a single chord, particularly the tonic chord, will be extended for measures on end. But finally, and most significantly, there is the overwhelming presence in the style period of major-mode pieces, and what that means in symbolic terms: by necessity, the minor mode becomes an abnormality, a kind of tragic subversion of the prevailing comic superstructure. The wildness of *agitato* relative to the older *concitato* (which is equally at home in major and minor) is surely due to the exceptional connotation of minor for late 18th-century thinking, though a faster tempo and the volatile nature of the symphonic action are also material factors.

In the final analysis, *Sturm und Drang* expression belongs first and foremost to the tragic, not the heroic, mode. Measured against the noble rage of the *concitato* warrior, the *agitato* feelings of the *Sturm und Drang* poet appear to be without ostensible direction, out of control. It is paradoxical that an age so dedicated to diversion and good cheer should finally produce such an acute form of the tragic vision. But it takes very little to see the logic of this paradox, for the rebelliousness of the *Sturm und Drang* poet is pointed squarely at the *ethos* of festal pomp itself, an *ethos* confined and rendered small (at least in the eyes of the *Sturm und Drang* poets) by an excessive optimism and an overdependence on pleasant circumstances and the good will of others. In *agitato*, the late 18th century finds a new affective function for musical imagery: reversing the basic thrust of elegy and muted tragic *pathos* toward pity, *agitato* concentrates on fear to the near exclusion of pity. *Pathos*, then, is the ruling principle of *Sturm und Drang* art, the *Sturm und Drang* hero being governed essentially by his angry and rebellious emotions. But in the end his revolt against festal pomp carries its own heroic *ethos*, for it implicitly defines a willingness to embrace danger and plunge into extreme circumstances. Given to excess in its own right, *Sturm und Drang* expression can be made to blend with other expressive modes of the late 18th century to form the balanced language of high Classicism. But even unto itself, its alliance with the grand gestures of the new symphonism ultimately justifies its association with the epic/heroic mode.

Heroic Drama

Beethoven's heroic credentials would be secure were it only for the intentions and achievements of his third symphony. Solomon, however, thinks of the third symphony as a starting point, an explosion that unleashed a host of heroic works running clear through Beethoven's so-called "Middle Period" from 1803 to 1810; indeed, Solomon calls these years the Heroic Period.[29] The grandeur of the Eroica symphony itself—the expanded formal designs, the expanded time-scale, the expanded orchestral palette—could be viewed as the festal pomp of the 18th century carried to its ultimate limits. But there is more—a dimension so characteristic of Beethoven's manner that it is often called simply "Beethovenian striving." Solomon writes the following:[30]

Beethoven took music beyond what we may describe as the pleasure principle of Viennese Classicism; he permitted aggressive and disintegrative forces to enter musical form: he placed the tragic experience at the core of his heroic style. He now introduced elements into instrumental music that had previously been neglected or unwelcome. A unique characteristic of the Eroica symphony—and of its heroic successors—is the incorporation into musical form of death, destructiveness, anxiety, and aggression, as terrors to be transcended within the work of art itself. And it will be this intrusion of hostile energy, raising the possibility of loss, that will also make affirmations worthwhile.

Solomon is right to identify "overcoming" or breakthrough (he calls it transcendence) as the key to Beethoven's brand of heroism and to recognize tragic experience as the necessary ingredient by which "overcoming" will be deeply felt. By "tragic experience," however, is meant something more than the inclusion in the Eroica symphony of a colossal enactment of solemn pomp (indeed the most extended and elaborate funeral march ever written). This is not to deny the tragic—and heroic—impact of the second movement of the Eroica symphony, but its tragic significance is immediately recognizable in the conventional image of a funeral march. Moreover, funeral marches are ceremonial by definition: they commemorate tragic events that have already taken place, they do not depict such events in the making. Great as this movement is, its identity as a funeral march actually obscures rather than reveals the places in which Beethoven's true originality in treating tragic experience will be found.

These places, as a number of critics have pointed out in the past, are the very continuities of Beethoven's large-scale instrumental conceptions—the underlying contentiousness between musical ideas, the stressfulness of the internal action as it seeks out points of repose. Solomon puts it perhaps too poetically when he talks about "the incorporation into musical form of death, destructiveness, anxiety, and aggression";[31] what he means in more prosaic terms is that Beethoven saw the contrast inherent in sonata-allegro form as the ground for conflict and discord; for Beethoven, a harmonious and satisfying resolution could not be won before much debate had transpired in the musical discourse. The struggle to bring about resolution is thus both tragic, because difficult and stressful, and heroic, because beyond the ordinarily human. Solomon points to the famous C♯ at the beginning of the Eroica symphony, and notes how it destabilizes the tonic chord and sends the movement on an arduous journey to recover its stability:[32]

The dissonant C♯ ... in measure 7 acts as a fulcrum compelling a departure from the common chord, thus creating a dynamic disequilibrium that provides the driving impulse of the movement, an impetus that continues almost unbroken until the restatement of the tonic chord in the final cadence. The result is music which appears to be self-creating, which must strive for its existence, which pursues a goal with unflagging energy and resoluteness—rather than music whose essence is already largely present in its opening thematic statement.

The notion of Beethovenian striving has, of course, become a cliché, but only because it has been too often restricted to the specific picture of the common man struggling to win his social identity. If we extend the idea of human effort to apply to all levels of experience—thought and feeling as well as social action—we begin to understand with what tenacity and variety Beethoven treats this idea. Moreover, we are interested to pursue the significance of the idea not merely on its own terms but also to see how it relates to certain archetypal contents. In a very real way, Beethoven's music re-creates the pattern of *humilitas* to *sublimitas* envisioned by early Christianity, now worked out in the context of individual aspiration in place of mythic truth. The movement from *humilitas* to *sublimitas* betrays, as has been said earlier, a demotic impulse, if for no other reason than that the demotic is the only one of the modes to embody the feeling of beginning low and aiming upward. Archetypally speaking, the characteristic pattern of uncertainty, struggle, and breakthrough expressed in Beethoven's discourse would mark (1) the intersection of two cardinal points: the Dionysian and the demotic, and (2) the dynamic metamorphosis of the tragic into the comic.

In the Eroica symphony this pattern is dramatized within the context of a single movement, but not from one movement to the next: Beethoven's hero is presented in the form of four loosely connected episodes or tableaux, not through a continuous narrative in four acts. It is in the fifth symphony that the conscious attempt is made to link the four movements in a unified drama. E.T.A. Hoffmann seems more than dimly aware of this when he writes, in a statement that remains more definitive for Romanticism than for Beethoven:[33]

Beethoven's music sets in motion the lever of fear, of awe, of horror, of suffering and wakens just that infinite longing which is the essence of romanticism ... Can there be any work of Beethoven's that confirms all this to a higher degree than his indescribably profound, magnificent symphony in C minor? How this wonderful composition in a climax that climbs on and on, leads the listener imperiously forward into the spirit world of the infinite!

Having experienced the several succeeding stages of music after Beethoven which are commonly called Romantic, we find it difficult to think of Beethoven as the quintessence of Romanticism that Hoffmann saw in him. Certainly Hoffmann's conception of "longing" has little, if any, of the erotic coloring it acquired in later, ultra-Romantic associations. Not so certain are the connotations of the words "fear," "awe," "horror," and "suffering": they seem intended to convey less of the tragic dimension we attach to those words in everyday parlance and more of what we think of—and what Hoffmann has in fact pictured—as our emotion before the incommensurable and superhuman. The tragic tone surely enters into Beethoven's imagery, in the sense that struggle and serious effort involve their measure of pain. But the object of that effort is ultimately reached. All

Beethoven symphonies resolve gloriously, in a spirit of joyous affirmation. And if Hoffmann is less inclined to note that point, it is no doubt because Romantic infiniteness occupies center place in his thoughts. But it is by virtue of that point that Beethoven's essential adherence to the late 18th-century comic vision can be seen to hold good: fulfillment may be long in coming, but it does come, and not tentatively, but totally and decisively.

The imagery of the fifth symphony shows Beethoven staying strictly within the limits of the late 18th-century conventions to create his new drama: the first movement is pure *Sturm und Drang*; the fourth movement, but for a brief recollection of the third movement, is pure festal pomp. Where Beethoven's originality comes in is to have created the effect of a progression between them; the C minor *agitato* of the former gives way to the militant C major triumph of the latter. In between these outer antipodes, we find a second movement serving as a respite from the preceding storm—a pastoral interlude in which the urgent military flourishes, the calls to heroic action, are never far away and at times disturbingly close—and a third movement, ironically labeled "scherzo," in view of the fact that the piece is a triple-time funeral march, all the more gloomy for being subdued almost throughout and therefore sharing none of the rock-like duple-time solidity and military splendor of the Eroica funeral march. But the subdued gloom is deliberate, because it is by means of keeping this piece open at the end and leading it directly into the festal pomp of the fourth movement that Beethoven creates the experience of coming out of a dark tunnel into blazing, glorious light. As if to state the difficulty of the breakthrough, Beethoven has the fourth movement lapse back into the gloom of the tunnel one further time before reemerging once and for all. In this turning of the corner from the third to the fourth movement, we have, of course, the most concentrated moment in the symphony by which the transformation from the tragic to the comic is expressed. But there is the distinct impression, perhaps only retrospectively felt, that the seeds of this transformation have been sown from the opening movement and that every part of the symphony is involved in it. Beethoven has thereby managed to fashion a narrative plan for pure instrumental music that means to approach the unity of literary drama, and he will work according to this plan for the remainder of his creative life. Indeed, the design he has made is so powerful an idea that large-scale instrumental music for the entire extent of the 19th century, irrespective of genre and of alternative meanings that might arise in individual cases, will uniformly respond to its influence.

In view of the simplicity—one might say obviousness—of the concept of going from the agitation of *Sturm und Drang* to the triumph of festal pomp, and in view, also, of the fact that these materials were already fully developed in the late 18th century, one might ask why Haydn and Mozart did not see their dramatic potential—the possibility of connecting them through the linear progression eventually realized by Beethoven. In fact, there are certain tentative forecasts of Beethoven's idea. Something of a tragic-to-comic transformation is perhaps felt in the progression from slow introduction to sonata-allegro form that we find at the opening of a late 18th-century symphony, but such a transformation is not necessarily made with the specific images of *Sturm und Drang* and festal pomp; besides, this action could only be considered embryonic vis-à-vis Beethoven's all-embracing conception. Embryonic events, however, are precisely the sources of full-blown events, and another source for Beethoven's narrative structure is doubtless the opening of Haydn's *Creation*, in which Beethoven's teacher musically depicts the light and order of the world emerging from dark chaos. But here, the action is motivated by a specific extramusical circumstance; it does not address the original question regarding Haydn's and Mozart's attitudes toward their instrumental music.

If we examine such late 18th-century works as Haydn's Farewell symphony in F♯ minor, Mozart's C minor serenade (K. 388), D minor concerto (K. 466), and G minor quintet (K. 516), we will note the same progression in all of them from *Sturm und Drang* opening to major-mode ending. The parallel with the pattern of the fifth symphony is obvious, and yet there is a sharp difference as well: the major-mode endings of the earlier examples do not express festal pomp; they are lighter, more playful, they are in a distinctly *buffa* style. This state of affairs yields a number of implications. First, late 18th-century instrumental works do not close heroically; on the other hand, they have the tendency to *open* heroically, the first movements in festal pomp style far outnumbering those using any other expressive type. *Sturm und Drang* first movements are so rare as to constitute an abnormality, as earlier said. These facts, of course, have been well-known for a long time. What is not so well understood is what this means in terms of the late 18th-century view of heroism. We must not forget the precise nature of the heroism that festal pomp represents: essentially ceremonial and decorative, it is the image of a leader who means to look disciplined and wear a pleasant face at the same time. This is not at all the weighty hero of Beethoven's third and fifth symphonies, who has gone through serious trials in order to arrive at a plane of being considerably above the one on which he started. Haydn's and Mozart's great instrumental works are passionate and profound, but they are simply not heroic either in the *concitato* or Beethovenian sense. Their festal pomp movements make a bow to military brilliance and spiritedness, but they show by their finales that they prefer, in the comic tradition of their age, to leave the listener on a lighthearted note.[34] By placing the festal pomp movement at the end of his work, Beethoven not only lent a heroic character to the work as a whole but also gave to festal pomp itself more weight than it was originally conceived to have. This he could do, because he had learned how to invest his internal musical action with the effects of great struggle and vicissitude. Heroic drama is Beethoven's original conception; and Beethoven's hero is a new human type for music, because he is the first we can follow in the process of becoming.

The aesthetic watershed that Romanticism signifies for the history of Western music suggests strongly that an essentially different approach to the subject of musical content is in order when it comes to studying the music of the period after 1825. That approach is put into effect in Chapters 13–16. Meanwhile, we can observe that much of the old imagery, especially the old heroic imagery, continues to function, with meanings virtually unchanged (albeit with expected updatings in style) in a variety of 19th-century contexts. Though this state of things may at first seem surprising, given the novelty of the Romantic vision, it becomes less so when we consider that heroic themes of glory, military prowess and magnificent ceremony neatly fall in with Romanticism's central vision of transcendence, and can thus readily serve Romantic artists in imaging and elaborating their own world view. In any event, the image-types of *concitato*, solemn pomp, festal pomp, and *Sturm und Drang* all find application in Romantic music, and examples abound in the best-known pieces of the time.

Before enumerating some of these, we should note once again that the pattern of heroic drama set by the Beethoven symphony maintains itself throughout the 19th century for large-scale instrumental works in general. The pattern can be greatly magnified (Bruckner and Mahler symphonies) or significantly altered with respect to its internal episodes (Liszt's symphonic poems), but the overall plan of striving to breakthrough is inalterable, the quest for and achievement of individual fulfillment being a permanent fixture of Romantic thinking. The destiny of the individual, we will come to see, is one of Romanticism's chief preoccupations, and so not unexpectedly, the pre-Romantic imagery least affected by the new aesthetic would be that kind which is the most social in character. Direct counterparts of 18th-century dances and marches of festal pomp—polonaises, marches militaires, and valses brillantes—represent 19th-century privileged society putting on its most glittering and affable outward face. Particularly light-hearted examples of this festal type are usually referred to as "salon music." More serious, though no less ceremonial in character, is the music of solemn pomp, which contributes so significantly to the grandeur of grand opera; *Tannhäuser* (the pilgrim's chorus and the Wartburg scene), *Götterdämmerung* (Siegfried's funeral music), *Parsifal* (Good Friday music), and *Aida* (the triumphal scene) furnish our most memorable examples.

The Good Friday spell and the long stretches of brass-choir music in Bruckner symphonies (the spiritual kin of 17th-century German "Turmmusik") illustrate the thin line dividing religious and secular solemnity in 19th-century style. In the Coronation Scene from *Boris Godunov* both the music and the visual spectacle serve to remind us that separation of church and state is a relatively new idea in the West, and that even in societies far more evolved toward the secular than 17th-century Russia, the most significant ceremonies of state rarely take place without their token invocations and benedictions. *Boris* is most notable, however, for containing long stretches of music specifically designed to be sung by the Russian people, whom Mussorgsky represented as the true composite hero of his opera. This demotic form of heroism, applied characteristically to a community rather than to an individual (and significantly to a community that has suffered hardship and oppression), comes to occupy center stage in the third quarter of the 19th century, when it is realized, as already mentioned in the last chapter, that music can serve as a powerful tool in arousing nationalistic fervor. If our immediate tendency is to associate the nationalist movement in 19th-century music with Eastern Europe, where political independence has long been a matter of urgency, we should not forget a music with popular origins which, for political or other reasons, seeps into earlier Italian opera and spreads its demotic charm; the Anvil Chorus from *Trovatore*, the marches from *Macbeth*, and the even earlier marches accompanying the Roman troops in *Norma* attest to a heroism rising up from below. In this regard, the Toreador song from *Carmen* may be the single most famous case of a down-to-earth "martial" music designed to characterize a hero who is one of us, who comes from the people. On a more specifically nationalistic note, the orchestral works of Sibelius and Ives represent the effort to give music of a markedly national character epic dimensions. Here, the grandeur can at times become so cosmic that, without studying the individual case at close range, it would not be possible to tell where demotic heroism leaves off and Romantic transcendence begins.

The numerous battle pieces and portions of pieces devoted to battle music in the 19th century show that the conceptions of *concitato* and *Sturm und Drang* are still very much alive throughout the period. Although the orchestral literature furnishes the most striking cases—the opening of Berlioz's *Romeo and Juliet*, the entire development section of Tchaikovsky's fantasy overture on the same subject, long passages of Mahler's *Resurrection* symphony and Strauss's *Ein Heldenleben*—battle music appears in nonorchestral scores, also; for instance, the final movement of Chopin's B minor sonata, or the first, third, and fourth movements of the Brahms F minor piano quintet. A *concitato* image-type that seems to be the particular invention of the 19th century is a quick $6/8$ rhythm that may be called the "cavalry motif." It is not that earlier music is lacking in quick $6/8$ imagery, but whereas the older types proceed in the lighthearted categories of the hunt or medieval revelry, the aggressiveness and drive of the new convention lend it an unmistakable *concitato* cast. The development of this new pattern is most likely due to the Romantic taste for imaging the hero as a medieval knight-errant. Mid-19th-century German instrumental music is particularly rich in this type, the coda of the first movement of the Schumann piano concerto, the opening movement of the Mendelssohn Scottish symphony, Wagner's *Ride of the Valkyrie*, and the finale of the Brahms piano quintet constituting a mere handful of the dozens of works that could be cited. In the Scottish symphony, we see how the same $6/8$ thematic material shifts in expression from its original, relatively disciplined, *concitato* character to something more agitated, more akin to the wayward, out-of-control quality associated with *Sturm und Drang*; indeed, this shifting effect is typical of large-scale dramatic movements that feature a cavalry motif as their principal idea.

With the exception of the second movement, the F minor piano quintet of Brahms uses battle motifs so persistently that a battle "program" could easily be worked out for the entire piece. The finale of Brahms's third symphony, also in

F minor, is also a battle piece, but here the struggle, rather than being worked out (as in the finale of the piano quintet) in terms of the actions comprising the struggle, turns in the last moments to a flickering, sunset reminiscence of the main theme of the opening movement.[35] Einstein dubs the symphony "pseudo-heroic," by which he presumably means something akin to what we have earlier described as heroic elegy. The proverbial "autumnal quality" of Brahms's style will be discussed as an aspect of Romanticism in Chapter 14; here, in the context of the epic/heroic mode, the same quality has the effect of surrounding heroism with an elegiac glow, as if recording not the rise or fall of a hero but the passing of heroism itself. At the turn of the century the mantle of heroic elegy passes from Brahms to Richard Strauss, who wears it with characteristic luxuriance. The apotheoses of *Death and Transfiguration* and *Ein Heldenleben* feature themes which, though elegiac in essence—that is, smooth, rounded melodies which could have made their point quietly and on a small scale—are magnified into statements of full-bodied, opulently colored grandeur.

If heroic images in 20th-century music are in short supply (at least relative to their representation in 19th-century music), the reason must be at least twofold; not only are 20th-century images couched in unconventional "languages," but also traditional notions of heroism—indeed, traditional notions altogether—are being called systematically into question. This is especially true of the avant-garde music that arrived on the scene around 1910, where the radically new imagery emerges in direct response to the need to express radically new contents. With the advent of Neoclassicism after World War I, its modernism tempered by significant appropriations from the 18th century and even remoter past, heroic conventions had a chance to reassert themselves. Large orchestral pieces were the most logical source of these conventions, but any large-scale work of this period can be expected to contain its measure of "Beethovenian striving." Hindemith is perhaps the most consistently "monumental" Neoclassic composer (long stretches of *Mathis der Maler* and the Konzertmusik for brass and strings), Shostakovich the most consistently militaristic. As with passages in the Mendelssohn Scottish symphony, the development section of the Shostakovich fifth symphony provides a particularly good example in which battle music flows readily back and forth between *concitato* and *Sturm und Drang* phases.

The importance of ceremony as a stimulus for Stravinsky's image-making will be specifically dealt with in Chapter 15. For the moment, it can be said that the dramatic element of *Oedipus Rex* is structured so as to call attention to the ritualistic, choric underpinnings of ancient Attic tragedy, while the music which begins and ends this work appeals so strongly to the Neoclassic taste for spare and solemn pomp that it will sound in one variant form or another in countless contemporary scores from Milhaud's *Maximilien* to Piston's Symphony No. 3 to Poulenc's *Dialogues des Carmélites*.[36] In the long run, and mainly through the intermediary of Neoclassicism, traditional categories of heroic imagery, with one notable exception, make a respectable showing in serious 20th-century music, the exception being the music of festal pomp. The fact that festal pomp images are virtually absent from the pages of contemporary music speaks volumes not only for the selective eye of Neoclassicism, its romance with Classical humanism notwithstanding, but even more for the controlling force of modernist thinking, which is clearly in back of the selection process. The simple truth of the matter is that the central content of festal pomp—the pleasantly brilliant and unclouded face of privilege which festal pomp wears—is something in which serious artists, under the sway of modernism, have long since ceased to believe.

Notes

1. Aristotle's discussion of this ethical point appears close to the beginning of the *Poetics*. See S.H. Butcher, trans. and ed., *Aristotle's Theory of Poetry and Fine Art*, p. 11 and p. 17.

2. Lauro Martines, *Power and Imagination: City-States in Renaissance Italy*, p. 233.

3. *Ibid.*, p. 234.

4. The full account is given in English in Piero Weiss and Richard Taruskin, ed., *Music in the Western World: A History of Documents*, pp. 81–82.

5. Howard M. Brown, *Music in the Renaissance*, p. 119, writes: "The '*a cappella* ideal' (a term that used to be associated with sixteenth-century music) has... little or no historical validity, even though it does draw attention to the homogeneous texture of much of this music, a texture that sounds well, it must be admitted, whether played by groups of like instruments—consorts of flutes, recorders, or viols, for example—or sung by consorts of unaccompanied voices."

6. Of course, we know at least some of the precise musical functions fulfilled by pipers and drummers, for instance; but whether the music they customarily played corresponds to anything that has come down to us in the prints and manuscripts, we are much less certain.

7. Brown's characterization in *Music in the Renaissance*, p. 370.

8. In Schütz's case the short-lived nature of his large-scale sacred symphonies and concertos is perhaps better explained by practical circumstances: the depletion of his musical forces in Dresden through the encroachments of the Thirty Years' War.

9. Monteverdi's preface to his eighth book of madrigals is provided in English in Oliver Strunk, ed., *Source Readings in Music History*, pp. 413–415.

10. Richmond Y. Hathorn, *Tragedy, Myth & Mystery*, p. 136.

11. E.R. Dodds, *The Greeks and the Irrational*, p. 185.

12. See *ibid.*, pp. 270–278. See also Hathorn, pp. 113–142.

13. See Chapter 3, *supra*, pp. 15–17.

14. Dodds, p. 76.

15. In the battle music of the 16th century, peripatetic and full of effervescence as it is, such a human type does not emerge. In the *Combattimento*, the action scenes are interspersed with the harrowing recitative of the narrator, taking on great tragic weight in the process. Janequin's *La Guerre* and Byrd's *The Battle* are picturesque by comparison.

16. The fact that we today might see nothing "creative" about war should not blind us to the significance of military glory for modern hieratic Europe. The following lines of Tasso from the *Combattimento* show that the ghosts of Homer's heroes still hover over Renaissance epic poetry: Thou, night! whose envious veil with dark disguise / Conceal'd the warrior's acts from human eyes, / Permit me from thy gloom to snatch their fame / And give to future times each mighty name: / So shall they shine, from age to age display'd / For glories won beneath thy sable shade!

17. The secondary, contrasting motive of the Brandenburg Concerto No. 5, announced by the concertino flute in m. 9, is a genuine pastoral figure, but it is made out of the initial heroic material and is eventually reintegrated into the primary heroic action. I like to think that this absorption of the pastoral into the heroic is a paradigm for high Baroque musical thinking in general.

18. Wilfrid Mellers, *François Couperin and the French Classical Tradition*, pp. 38–39. "Les bornes de l'austère pudeur" refers to a line from Act III, Sc. 1 of *Phèdre*.

19. This excess of passion, more than the proverbial *hubris*, may well be the true flaw of the tragic hero.

20. Northrop Frye, *Fools of Time*, p. 5.

21. The relevant passage in Aeschylus is from the *Agamemnon*, Opening Chorus, Strophe 3.

22. In this and the following chapters, there will be certain mentions of the *galant* spirit where necessary; a more throughgoing discussion of *galant* as the reigning spirit of the age and of its significance for musical developments will be given in Chapter 12.

23. Further discussions of the ways in which later 18th-century music deals with changes in behavior are in Chapters 11 and 12.

24. Quoted in Charles Rosen, *The Classical Style*, p. 96.

25. H.C. Robbins Landon, *Haydn: Chronicle and Works*, Vol. II, p. 268.

26. This is in fact Herder's description of the *Volkslied* when he first championed it in 1778. The link between Herder's cause and Schubert's *Volkstümlichkeit* marks one enduring offshoot of the *Sturm und Drang* impulse.

27. There is no question that these symphonies deserve to be singled out and recognized as something different from what Haydn had been writing up to that time; and it is also true that the concept conveyed by the words *Sturm und Drang* is not inappropriate to the highly charged atmosphere of these works. But if affective character, and not connection to the literary movement, is the real criterion for use of the term, the term *agitato* might be preferable, in view of the fact that it suggests connections with activities on both chronological sides of the works we are discussing. Not only does the concept of *agitato* encourage a comparison with *concitato* but it also looks forward to works as far into the future as the Beethoven fifth symphony and the Chopin "Funeral March" sonata.

28. Excerpts from these operas are quoted and discussed in Leonard G. Ratner, *Classic Music: Expression, Form and Style*, pp. 369–384.

29. Maynard Solomon, *Beethoven*. Part III (pp. 111–216) is called "The Heroic Period."

30. *Ibid.*, p. 194.

31. *Ibid.*, p. 194.

32. *Ibid.*, p. 196.

33. Quoted in Strunk, *Source Readings*, pp. 777–778.

34. Mozart's Jupiter symphony is an exception. Since this symphony is also his last, it may presage a direction he would have followed more regularly had he lived longer.

35. The outcome of this reversion is thus neither the tragedy of the quintet nor the triumph of Brahms's first symphony ("Beethoven's tenth"), but rather a mood of quiet acceptance.

36. Stravinsky's *Symphony in Three Movements* bears a curious parallel to the "noble rage" of mature *concitato* in the sense that the symphony, long recognized as echoing in more overt terms than any other of Stravinsky's Neoclassic works the jagged, pulsating rhythms of the *Rite of Spring*, integrates and contains these impulses within the framework of a traditional symphonic design. Unbridled Dionysian "rage" is kept in check, so to speak, by forces emanating directly from "noble" civilized Europe.

11 *The Satiric Mode*

Frye's conception of the satiric as a cross between the ironic and the comic is a good theoretical starting point, but a broader definition is eventually necessary if the chief variants of satiric expression are to be accounted for. The satiric mode is formed essentially out of the human types found in the high comedy of Aristophanes, which imitates the actions, according to Aristotle, of men "worse than ourselves."[1] That such men should be deemed worthy of interest in the first place is due in part to a human tendency to mockery and to a deep-seated need for humor, in addition to which there is the ethical value to be gained in examining basically "unethical" types. The tendency to mockery reflects that fault-finding faculty which is the seat of the ironic perspective and by virtue of which the world appears riddled with imperfections. Given the potential destructiveness of ironic feeling, humor emerges as the saving grace of satiric art, a safety valve that permits unhealthy thoughts to find their way to the catharsis of laughter. Humor thus comes to have its own ethical force, even (or perhaps especially) in the absence of instructiveness; and this will seem particularly true of music, where a genuine instructive element is thought possible only with the collaboration of words.

Because of the extremely disparate character of the expressive types belonging to the satiric mode, it will be useful, before making a review of these types according to style period, to attempt to break down satiric musical imagery into certain general classes. Paralleling the division of the pastoral mode into the Arcadian and the rustic, the satiric mode can been seen, too, as dividing along hieratic and demotic lines, the resulting categories being (1) wit, the humor of superior commentary and (2) the broad form of humor known as burlesque. At the center of wit is the mocking of foibles, dramatized in the form of actions of questionable character. Here, the artistic strategy is to assume a position at some distance removed from (invariably *above*) the actions being examined and to affect a tone, if not of moral elevation, at least of elegant dispassion. Burlesque, on the other hand, which appears to have started out life as the mocking of authority, locates itself *below* the object under scrutiny in an effort to bring the object "down to size."

In early Christian Europe, burlesque grew naturally out of its connections with Carnival, topsy-turvy days, the Feast of Fools—those moments of the year set aside for the mocking of authority by no other than the authorities themselves. In time burlesque would broaden its range to include the imitation of "low types," with the purpose of adding to Carnival revelry the clumsy gestures of peasants or the fast-talking prattle of characters from the demi-monde. By contrast, witty imagery is constrained to maintaining an elegant surface at all times. We might, in fact, go so far as to say that the degree to which a given example of satiric music appears weighted toward wit or toward burlesque will depend on the cruder or more delicate handling of musical materials (finely woven counterpoint vs. coarse-grained textures, light, airborne rhythms vs. heavy accentuation) as well as the use of conventions for the force of their archetypal associations (dance-types, local mannerisms, the deliberate borrowing or avoidance of rustic and urban low-life patterns). Something of all these criteria will be illustrated in the course of this chapter, though anything approaching comprehensiveness is clearly out of the question.

Wit and burlesque may be the chief categories of the satiric mode, but the richness, if not the basic identity, of satiric expression relies probably more on elements which would better go by the name of "strategies" than "categories." In Chapter 2 it was said that at the root of the satiric mentality is a sense of discrepancy and incongruity; if that is true, then strategies involving combination and juxtaposition of images would be likely candidates for creating discrepant and incongruous effects. One obvious case in point is a parodistic use of musical reference such as we find in the banquet scene of *Don Giovanni* or the "Tortoises" episode from *Carnival of the Animals* or the several *Tristan* drolleries of Chabrier and Debussy. This kind of quotation is as limited as it is obvious. A more thoroughgoing example of juxtaposition is provided by the scherzo movement from Haydn's Op. 33, No. 2 quartet, in which an elegant courtly minuet is played off against the frank flatfootedness of a peasant dance. More thoroughgoing still is the mixture of images that provides a basic stratum of continuity for late 18th-century sonata-allegro movements. If it is true that not all the images in question are "satiric" in character, there is still much to suggest that the driving force behind such continuity is the satiric impulse itself. A case will be made for this point several pages ahead.

Of course, a basic context of revelry and high spirits is expected of satiric expression in general. If the imagery is too consistently dark, the context will become ambiguous or even slip from the satiric into the mode of tragic irony. Such seems to be the case of much modernist music in the satiric vein, where the ironic archetype has gained the upper hand over the comic, and the humor has taken on a harsh and cruel edge. Quite the opposite is observed in the above-mentioned Haydn example. There, we are left wondering which of the two styles, the peasant or the courtly, is actually being mocked, for the irony is so tenderly applied that one comes away from the experience with the impression that each of the originals has been parodied and then reaffirmed for its own virtues. The net effect is almost to proclaim the power of romance over satire. We might call this a "loving" kind of satire, one that reminds us that teasing in everyday life is often a sign of closeness and affection.

It remains to mention the category of ribaldry, of which the oldest extant musical examples are the bawdy songs identified by Goldin as the songs of the *leis de con* (the kind of song Guillaume IX of Poitiers sought to replace, or at least to complement, with the song of courtly love). If this category figures in vocal genres to the exclusion of instrumental music, that must be because ribald humor needs to be expressed primarily by verbal or visual means. Music can participate in ribald expression by giving appropriate support to a text, but it has no way of being ribald on its own. This may be the only case in which music is at an expressive disadvantage relative to the other arts. In all other categories of satiric expression, musicians have consistently shown their art to be eminently capable of producing a variety of images, both subtle and trenchant.

The element of mockery in the medieval *pastorela* (or *pastourelle*) has already been addressed in Chapter 5; here, it can be added that the genre, on the basis of the text alone, falls squarely in the category of ribaldry. The proverbial story of the *pastourelle* tells of a knight who, for lack of anything better to do, sets out in search of a bit of diversion at the expense of a little country lass with whom he hopes to have a pleasant but momentary dalliance. As was noted in Chapter 5, this is the very antithesis of the classic pastoral spirit, which idealizes human action by representing it as pure and innocent, "unspoiled by irony."[2] Stevens is aware of an ironic element in the *pastourelle* when he writes: "It is important to realize how disingenuous the literary style is; Robin and Marion may be innocent, but the poet certainly is not."[3] But the poet's ironic outlook is not restricted to style; it includes the action as well, for the country shepherdess (sometimes called Marion) is hardly so innocent that she does not know what the knight wants of her and hardly so bereft of stratagems of her own that she does not know how to fend off his advances and rather gracefully send him on his way. In ending happily, this enterprise upholds two major aspects of traditional satiric expression: it has no evil consequences, yet it is conducted on a level that one must recognize as being distinctly less than high-minded.

How does—or more precisely, to what extent can—the music of the *pastourelle* express this story? What kind of medieval music is most appropriate in underscoring the satiric energy of the *pastourelle* text? When we think of the thematic kinship between the *pastourelle* and the old *leis de con* and of what Goldin says of the older type—"The festival spirit breathes where it will, seeking encounters without consequences. That is why these songs are merry"[4]—our minds run immediately to the dance-song and the world of revels. Nevertheless, Stevens points out that *pastourelle* music is something of a cross between narrative song and dance-song, inclining toward the former when there is no sign of a refrain. In cases where the refrain is present, the melody is often "written out in a clear measured notation,"[5] showing its unequivocal origins in dance. Then again, the pre-refrain music is notated nonmensurally, which raises questions as to how that portion of the *pastourelle* should be performed. Stevens asks:[6]

Should we assume [from this] that the association of narrative with *refrain* in the *pastourelle* means that some narratives at least were sung in a metrical, even in a 'measured' style? At this stage it would be foolish to close our minds to this possibility, even though it is diametrically opposed to what a modern might regard as a 'natural' way of singing narrative—that is, with the flexibility experienced in the recitation tones of Gregorian chant, such as psalmody.

Yet, even granting the fact that rhythmic flexibility is an element common to secular narrative and psalmody, one can scarcely imagine a performer bringing the same accents and tones of voice to both. Contrary to the irregular phrase lengths of the psalms, the pastourelle texts are broken up into short, strongly rhymed lines of equal duration: such lines may well have been performed in unmetered fashion, but as their internal structuring is almost identical to that of dance-song texts, they lend themselves easily to a "measured" style.

As with all the secular music of the Middle Ages, much of the effect of a piece can be learned only through a performance; and about the original modes of performance of medieval music we know virtually nothing. But if story telling *à haute voix* involves a good measure of dramatization (and what self-respecting amateur storyteller has ever read a bedtime tale to children without dramatizing the events and impersonating the characters?), it is only common sense that a medieval professional singer would, through the appropriate inflections of voice, make some effort to convey the buoyant and mocking spirit of the *pastourelle*. Admittedly, the melodies themselves are a little "flat"—not as developed in terms of phrase contour as those of the typical dance-song and not as well differentiated with respect to open and closed endings. Still, the "music" of the poetic structures serves as an important aid to the performer if and when it comes to finding just the right balance in the vocal delivery between vigorous high spirits and offhandedness.[7]

Of course, the custom among medieval singers may have been to resist any kind of dramatization—to assume a neutral tone and let the ribaldry simply speak through the situation depicted in the text. We have so little information on medieval performance practice that it is virtually impossible to form a coherent picture; yet, Guillaume of Poitier's injunction to his *joglar*, Daurostre, to "sing sweetly and not bray" is the beginning of a suggestion that medieval singers knew how to be actors. At any rate, there is no reason to rule out the possibility that singer-performers acted out their narratives, especially in those places where the characters in the stories are allowed to speak for themselves.

The patter-song, made familiar to the English-speaking world primarily through Gilbert and Sullivan operetta, is among the most clearly delineated

forms of satiric musical expression. Its chief ingredient is a rapid vocal utterance
with no hint of *concitato* energy. It is easy to imagine this kind of delivery to
be a staple of the ancient Greek and Roman comedies, attached in particular to
those comic types who had no social power and whose tirades, therefore, came
across as so much ineffectual frustration instead of genuine anger. While it is
not an object of this study to trace the history of the patter-song, one of the
earliest examples must be a 3-voice motet by Guillaume de Machaut which uses
Pourquoy me bat mes maris (a well-known 13th-century dance song) as its cantus
firmus. The triplum-descant of this motet requires the same labial nimbleness as
the "Nightmare" song from *Iolanthe* or Figaro's aria from *The Barber of Seville*.
Since ancient comedies could not have served as Machaut's model, one wonders
where he got the idea. It is true that the triplum of late 13th-century and early
14th-century motets had the habit of moving at a far faster rate than either of
the other two voices, but no satiric intent is usually adduced from this fact;
indeed, one tends to hear only a sophisticated elegance in these rapidly moving
tripla. However, the line separating a sophisticated rapid-fire delivery that is
smoothly charming from a kind that provokes outright laughter may not be so
wide after all, and actual performances could have easily crossed that line, thus
suggesting to an observer as perspicacious as Machaut the potential for musical
mockery contained in excited speech. Two important points emerge from this
example. The first is that however much the text of the piece may be useful in
confirming the satiric intent, the humor is clearly in the music. The second is that
this late medieval motet signals an unambiguous change in the balance between
ethos and *pathos*. Behavior, here, is represented as spontaneous expression of
personal feeling, not the target of ethical prescription. And Machaut's work is not
another lighthearted monophonic dance-song, but a motet of some polyphonic
complexity: one is struck to find such musical distinction lavished on a subject
matter of so little ethical account.

This last fact may explain why *Pourquoy me bat mes maris* seems to be an
isolated case and why we must wait until the second quarter of the 16th century
to find a true *corpus* of polyphonic patter-songs. When they did arrive, they
did so in force: the leading Parisian composers of the day, such as Janequin,
Certon, and Passereau threw themselves into the writing of narrative chansons
(*chansons rustiques*, as they were classified by Attaignant and other publishers),
"many of them humorous and some as wittily indecent as Clément Marot's tale
of an amorous priest, *Frère Thibault*, whose plans are foiled when his young
lady friend gets stuck halfway through the latticework while attempting to enter
his bed chamber."[8] This sustained interest in the ribald and rudely comic may
well be attributable to a general relaxation of older traditions at a court greatly
affected by the new humanist values and dominated by the restless, freewheeling
François 1er. Brown writes of the musico-literary climate:[9]

Like the formal schemes, the subject matter and diction of the poems chosen by Parisian
composers also reflect a new freedom and a release from the strictness of late medieval tra-

ditions. The subject matter was more varied; it encompassed fulfilled as well as unrequited love, and comic as well as serious aspects of the amorous predicament. Many poems mix popular with courtly elements. Clément Marot, the leading chanson poet of the time, even edited anthologies of the song texts that were presumably those most frequently heard in the streets of Paris. And the poetic diction, less strained and artificial than in fifteenth-century chansons, took on a more relaxed, natural, sincere, and individual tone.

The opening of Passereau's *Il est bel et bon* is typical of the emphasis placed on *"parlando* style declamation," with which these Parisian composers had learned to "exploit imitation as the language of wit rather than of Netherlandish seriousness"[10] (Example 11.1). Indeed, it is precisely this "witty counterpoint" that places the patter-song of the period squarely in the first and central category of the satiric mode defined above. Belying the label "chanson rustique," the patter-chanson shows no evidence of rustic manners: it is a music that belongs entirely to the city and the court. And in the spirit of witty satire, it speaks with two separate voices, the one characteristically commenting on the other. In the first voice, we hear the rapid fire of undignified naughtiness, the thumbing of the nose at loftiness. But in the second voice, we find the elegance and harmony of superior workmanship, the reassurance that everything is quite under control. The secret of wit is that it be *knowing*, that it show its awareness of its peccadilloes. If it only commits the peccadilloes, it has pretty much failed in its task. It is testimony to the genius of Janequin, Certon, and Passereau that they succeeded so often in creating the commenting voice of wit, for that is not an easy thing to do in music. In treating the "undistinguished" with such distinction, the patter-chanson foreshadows the best of the *opere buffe* of the 18th century.

The *canzone villanesca,* or *villanesca alla napoletana,* which also had its vogue in the second quarter of the 16th century, is usually taken to be the Italian counterpart of the French patter-chanson. There is, however, an essential difference: the polyphony of the patter-chanson belongs exclusively to the realm of "art" (i.e., "court") music, while the canzone villanesca, albeit a polyphonic genre, imitates the regional folk songs of the unwritten tradition with the deliberate aim of incorporating into its polyphonic fabric their most striking features. Einstein says, referring to the time of the frottolists, that "Good society, patricians and nobles laughed at the melodies and texts sung by peasants, artisans, and sailors."[11] One assumes that the laughter was more good-hearted than scornful, for musical performances of these songs can be described as "bellissimi," and in one account we read: "for the entertainment there appeared five who sang certain peasant songs in the Paduan dialect which were marvelous to listen to."[12] The appeal of this music, as of the canzone villanesca which was its conscious imitation, doubtless lay in the invigorating freshness and sharpness of accentuation that provided a welcome complement to the fluency of the madrigal.

Complementary status, however, does not necessarily lead to equal partnership; the madrigal remained queen of secular polyphony because it was highborn. In the case of the *canzone villanesca,* both subject matter and musical treatment

Example 11.1: Passereau, *Il est bel et bon*

relegated it to a lower rank in the hierarchy of musical forms. It hardly mattered that the style of the *villanesca* was a question of conscious choice, that the parallel fifths and choppy melodic lines were the work of men who in other situations could write the smoothest counterpoint. Unlike the patter-chanson, which kept its urbane voice, the *villanesca* had taken on certain aspects of the rustic manner and thus belonged to the world of burlesque. A broader form of satire than wit, burlesque theoretically got the bigger laughs, but in so doing it had to settle for being a lesser species. If these value judgments bear a distinctly hieratic stamp, they have been long-lasting: to this day, wit occupies a higher place in our critical thinking than burlesque.

Of the eventual destiny of the *canzone villanesca* Einstein writes:[13]

The three-voiced *canzone villanesca* maintains itself until near the end of the century, keeping intact its characteristic features: its coarseness, its response to every regional suggestion from below, its tendency to parody. At the same time there slowly develops a leaning toward the madrigal ... The *canzone villanesca* discards its rustic dress; it remains a canzone, it remains song-like; but it becomes respectable, it becomes a canzonetta.

Perhaps more than the result of "leaning toward the madrigal," the evolution of the *villanesca* may be described as an absorption into the great pastoral vogue that overtook both Italian music and literature in the last decades of the 16th century; for becoming "respectable" in this context points strongly to the civilizing spirit of the pastoral at work. But if this is so, what, if anything, does the gentle canzonetta retain of a satiric character? Should it be classified as belonging to the satiric or the pastoral mode? When we turn to the canzonetta's Elizabethan equivalents, what we see in examining, for example, the opening measures of Weelkes's *Four Arms, Two Necks, One Wreathing* is a delicate harmoniousness typical of the best three-voice fa-la-la madrigals of the period, a music which appears to have no aim other than to express simple, tender love (Example 11.2). Later verses of the text actually suggest a less high-minded love, but even if the verses were of the sincerest, most high-minded sort, as in fact they often are, the fa-la-la refrains themselves would come along to sound a disingenuous note. In the very utterance "fa, la, la," they toss off tender sentiment, subtly warning us to beware of attaching too much importance to our deeper emotions. In short, the fa-la-la refrain plays the *coquette*—a satiric type well-known to Renaissance literati as having trouble deciding whether to give in to or resist feelings of tenderness. Politely as this ambiguity of feeling may be expressed, the ambiguity itself signals the presence of irony, and this is why these charming canzonettas eventually take their place alongside more obvious artifacts of satiric expression. As the emotion of authentic pastoral is totally innocent of irony, any touch of ironic feeling in a given work should incline the work toward the satiric mode: this may well serve as a rule of thumb for identifying the kind of expression in which general sweetness gives off mixed signals.[14]

Example 11.2: Weelkes, *Four arms, two necks, one wreathing*

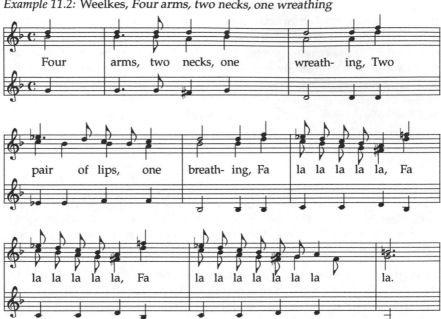

Theatrical Types

Although opinions differ as to which work should claim the title, "first comic opera" (*Che soffri spiri*? *Orontea*?), there is no question that the taste for including satiric episodes in operas that would not essentially be classified as comedies grew rapidly in 17th-century Italy. The most frequently cited mid-century example is *L'incoronazione di Poppea* (1642), Monteverdi's last stage work. Much is sacrificed when the comic scenes of *Poppea* are cut in modern productions (indeed, the opera loses an essential equilibrium, it being Monteverdi's scheme to cover the whole range of human behavior). Of these scenes, the most striking is Act II, Sc. 5, the love-dalliance between Ottavia's page, Valletto, and her lady-in-waiting, Damigella. For Valletto, in particular, Monteverdi writes a music whose melodic character is entirely new to his style. Made out of short patterns arranged sequentially, small pitch intervals, and a curious quarter-note rhythm broken occasionally by eighth notes, the melody is deliberately rudimentary, as if meaning to pass for a true "country song." There is a hint of the same quarter-note rhythm in an earlier scene with Valletto, in which he complains to Ottavia about Seneca's windy philosophizing (Act I, Sc. 6). But there the comic touches, however effective (and they are extremely funny), are made almost wholly in a vocal way (a parody of the vocal concitato found in the *Combattimento*), whereas in the opening of Act II, Sc. 5, the melody is cast in strict duple meter, suggesting an origin in dance.[15] Inevitably, satiric music was to be as much affected by the Baroque tendency toward dance-based imagery as pastoral and heroic music. Quick duple-meter, with its points and angles, would prove particularly apt for satiric expression, though quick triple meter also had its uses, to be sure. But all other things being equal, the durational inequality of accent and nonaccent in triple time will always give it an airborne feeling relative to duple time: pieces in $^3/_8$, for instance, must work against that feeling in order to achieve rude choppiness, a quality that $^2/_4$ pieces readily come by.

Perhaps for that very reason, the lion's share of the satiric passages in Cavalli's *La Calisto* (1651) are in duple time; indeed, one rhythmic pattern that appears periodically throughout the opera seems lifted directly from Monteverdi's bouncy continuo madrigal of 1620, *Chiome d'oro*. In spite of Diana's lofty arias in Act II and Calisto's ethereal apotheosis at the end, one is tempted to dub this work a "comic opera," not only because of the sheer bulk of the satiric episodes but even more because of the way they are used to make 'ethical' points. Jove and Calisto, ostensibly the leading pair of lovers, have the least memorable music; by contrast, Diana and Endymion as the second pair and Linfea and Satirino as the third are brought to vivid life by theirs. The unifying theme of the opera—the force of erotic desire—engulfs them all, the inner conflicts of Diana, the goddess of chastity, embodying, logically enough, the theme in its most intense, moving, and anguished aspects. Linfea, a "nymph" who, as a follower of Diana has remained chaste well past her prime, has the same inner conflicts, but hers, according to dramatic convention, must be subjected to ridicule, while Diana's are exalted. The music dutifully underlines this treatment. It is Linfea's fate to be dragged off, not totally against her will, by Satirino and the rest of the troupe of satyrs. This is all carried out with such good humor that feelings of resentment on the part of the spectators are inappropriate, even allowing for the fact that Linfea's plight commands our sympathy. Meanwhile, the arrows of satire are so freely distributed that some hit unlikely targets, including Diana herself. The fact that the goddess can be made to look silly on occasion has the effect of reducing the distance between the second and third pairs of lovers: the goings-on of Linfea and Satirino on the satiric level are seen to be more than mere diversion, they become a commentary on the interviews between Diana and Endymion on the pastoral-heroic level. The music itself rarely "breaks rank," but quick dramatic shifts from one level to another, with consequent juxtapositions of music from the different levels, bring home vividly the message that distinctions of social station and behavior can get fairly scrambled in face of the great "leveller," erotic passion. The satiric strategy, in short, has its immediate impact here in the release of laughter, but it also has an ethical aftermath—one so long-lived that it can be found still motivating the actions of the great *opere buffe* of the late 18th century. Indeed, the skill with which Cavalli mixes material from the pastoral, heroic, and satiric modes without any loss of coherence is not only remindful of Mozart but worthy of him.

However, we should be careful not to interpret this mid-17th-century *dramma giocoso* too much from the late 18th-century point of view. If, to our modern way of thinking, the satiric element of *La Calisto* is of such a force as to be responsible for creating the central world within which the action moves as well as for its psychological sophistication, most probably few members of the 17th-century community saw it that way. Satiric expression continued to be at the bottom rung of the aesthetic ladder, heroic expression occupied the top rung, and pastoral expression was somewhere in between. Commenting on Purcell's contribution to the comic plays of his day, Curtis Price writes the following:[16]

The music for comedies does not fall into neat categories. Purcell's metier was the tragic extravaganza and the semi-opera; with a few exceptions he was usually allotted seemingly insignificant lyrics in the lighter plays, while the majority of the important songs for the actor-singers were set by other composers ... This is not to say that Purcell was uninterested in musical comedy ... Rather, his work on the operas and serious dramas, which carried greater prestige, left proportionally less time for the lighter forms.

The "greater prestige" of heroic music stemmed, presumably, from a general perception of its power to be "greatly moving," while pastoral music was perceived to be elegantly charming and touching, and satiric music, merely diverting. The 17th-century public, however, liked to be diverted; and so, perhaps in spite of their highest aspirations, the best artists were enlisted to satisfy public taste.

Nor did they perform their tasks indifferently, judging from the results. The output in the satiric sphere from Purcell in England and Lully in France is ultimately considerable, both as to quantity and quality. In developing his powers as a writer of comic music, Lully had the advantage of being born Italian and of having to compose for the mainstay of French court entertainment, the *ballet de cour*. Principally a pastoral genre, the *ballet de cour* had its measure of burlesque episodes, for which appropriate dance music (*airs* as well as instrumental dances) was required. Inevitably, the intense association between dance and theater would heighten the connotations already acquired by individual dance types in the context of court ceremony and social dancing. Differentiations of character became more sharply delineated, the conventional symbolisms more deeply ingrained in the European sensibility, until context could be forsaken altogether with no concomitant loss of understanding. In the innumerable orchestral and keyboard suites of the period, one dance follows another, the different *ethe* being registered by the experienced listener and, as it were, subconsciously classified. Stately dances such as the slow march and sarabande fall into the heroic category (as discussed in Chapter 10), minuets, siciliane, and passepieds are most congenial to pastoral, and the fast-paced types—bourrées, rigaudons, gigues—cluster around the satiric.

Occasionally, a dance balances ambiguously between two categories (though the very mention of ambiguity suggests a tendency toward satire). Such is the case of the gavotte, which straddles the line between the satiric and the pastoral. By a long-standing tradition the gavotte is said to be naturally linked to the pastoral. Yet, the quick alternations of smoothness and angularity in the mature court gavotte point to something beyond the limits of pastoral—

something more complex and less reassuring than, say, the rounded evenness of a minuet, whose gestures seem so quintessentially Arcadian. According to Arbeau (1588), the gavotte he knew was a dance of courtship, crowned with a kiss.[17] If the gavotte had lost this function by Lully's time, it seemed to retain its underlying flirtatiousness, beckoning with one gesture, warning off with the other. The ambivalent signals it sent out laid it open to a variety of treatments, so much so that in the Bach repertoire alone we find the fiery Gavotte of the English Suite No. 3, the mincing Gavotte of the Orchestral Suite No. 2, the triumphant Gavotte of the Orchestral Suite No. 3.[18] The dance seems almost to have become emblematic of a national character, dramatizing the way the French would like to think of themselves—elegant, seductive, witty, elusive, contradictory.

Rameau showed a particular fondness for it, using it more than any other dance in the *divertissements* of his operas. Lully may have favored it less but he could take pride in knowing that the gavotte, along with the other dances "of character," had come into its maturity in his own time, and mainly due to his efforts. Collectively, these French court dances traveled beyond their original borders and became an "international" language, indeed, the most important code that European music had at its disposal for delineating human character and conduct. Satiric expression was particularly enhanced by this development, for certain dance-types seemed to align themselves neatly with certain satiric categories, the playful bourrée with innocent revelry, the rigaudon and the more rugged kinds of gigue with burlesque. As for the ambiguous gavotte, there is no question that it ultimately belonged to the satiric, not the pastoral world: pointed delicacy, air of superiority, and elusiveness were aspects of its makeup that placed it among the subtlest forms of satire and qualified it unequivocally for the category of wit.

Lully's collaborations with Molière between 1662 and 1671 resulted in a series of *comédies-ballets* that remains a high-water mark in the history of comic art.[19] But as James B. Anthony tells us, "After *Thésée* [1675] Lully's comic muse was silenced, the victim of an inflexible attitude that allowed no mixture of comic and tragic genres such as existed in Venetian and Roman opera."[20] In all deference to Anthony's implication that the sharp cleavage between comedy and tragedy was not a particularly happy decision for the future of French opera, it should be pointed out that the possibility of writing comic music was not closed to Lully; he could, after all, have continued to compose *comédies-ballets*. That he shunned them in favor of *tragédies-lyriques* from 1672 until his death in 1687 says in effect that he considered the tragic genre to pose the greater artistic challenge and in consequence to carry the greater prestige.[21]

No such separation of styles hampered English music drama of the same period. The rollicking sailors' air and chorus at the beginning of Act III of Purcell's *Dido and Aeneas* and the sly Envy trio in Act II of the *Indian Queen* ("What flatt'ring noise is this at which my snakes all hiss?") roam freely, as it were, among the serious events that surround them. In the case of the sailors' chorus, the placement of the piece not only affords musical variety but also throws the ensuing tragic denouement into stark relief. Curtis Price notes the vein of cynicism underlying the sailor's verse which begins "Take a boozy short leave of your nymphs on the shore"—"a crude quayside version of Aeneas' heroic crocodile tears to be shed later during the confrontation with Dido."[22] Locating the chromatically descending tetrachord that filters through the middle portions of the piece, Price rightly calls it "a distinctly unsubtle foreshadowing of the ground in Dido's lament."[23] Unsubtle it may be, but it does have the singular virtue of pointing up the commenting power of satiric expression—the fundamental impulse of irony to call into question the grandeur of heroic feeling and bring it, albeit temporarily, down to size. To bring out the commenting factor musically, Purcell casts the sailors' chorus in the form of a strongly accented, robustly textured jig, heavy with masculine cadences. Buried in the context of this crudely rollicking dance, the chromatically descending tetrachord, a conventional symbol of lamenting, indeed gets transformed into crocodile tears. This example is important, if only to point up the fact that discrepancy and incongruity, traditionally considered the province of satiric literature, can be handled by music as well.

Whether the interaction of the satiric with the heroic is a good or bad idea finally comes down to a question of taste—of taste on a national scale. If the preference is for a heroic grandeur free of any compromising impurity, then the solution is to impose a set of rules that will effectively isolate the heroic and protect it from the risk of being compromised; such was the solution devised for French stage music around 1675 and for Italian opera about a quarter of a century later. If, on the other hand, the prevailing taste runs toward the ironic, a world of pure heroism will appear artificial and signify a loss of psychological complexity. For all of late 17th-century England's purported celebration of the heroic as the primary mode, the example of Purcell's dramatic work seems to say that heroic expression benefits in richness and meaning when it is brought into contact with the other modes.

In the 18th century, satiric expression came into its own, dominating not only all musical activity but artistic activity in general. This development was not particularly foreseen as the century opened. The reform of Italian opera c. 1700 had been undertaken with no other view than to weed out the satiric elements from serious dramatic music and leave the heroic and pastoral elements undisturbed.[24] We are told that the appearance of the *opera buffa* and the intermezzo, which "coincided roughly with this ... reform ... suggests that these forms arose as a reaction against the exclusion of comedy from the musical theatre."[25] If this is true, perhaps some credit is due the reform movement itself for having sent satiric music on its way, thereby causing it to develop independently and thus more fully. But we should not be overly grateful to the reformers of *opera seria*, for they certainly did not have the interests of *opera buffa* at heart. The fact is that as the century wore on, *opera buffa* made headway because significant changes in attitude were taking place with respect to satiric entertainment in general. Initially a success in the popular theater, *opera buffa* by the mid-century mark had gained adherents in all sectors of society and was coming to be accepted as a serious art form. Indeed, what distinguishes later 18th-century comic theater from its predecessors is precisely its perceived status as something to be admired as well as enjoyed. The ethical value of satiric expression, understood in an intuitive way in earlier times, now took on a more conceptual, more self-conscious cast: treatises on comedy abounded, literary critics were discovering as if for the first time the instructional and therapeutic benefits of humor.[26]

Opera buffa plots were much affected by contemporary ideas of the role of comedy in theatre. Italian theorists made no distinction between the social function of comic opera and that of any other kind of comic drama. All comedy, according to the current theory, should morally instruct the audience through the art of caricature. The sorts of human foible thought most suitable for caricature included vanity, miserliness, stupidity, cowardliness, and affectation; against these, Antonio Planelli wrote (*Dell'opera in musica*, 1772), 'laughter is the most powerful and effective antidote'.

The wider cultural ramifications of Planelli's thought (by 1772, a well-digested, though still vital, idea) will be discussed in the next chapter; for the moment it is enough to acknowledge the heightened fortunes of satiric art in the 18th century and to try to assess the impact of those fortunes on the musical practice of the day, instrumental as well as theatrical. Beginning with the theatrical, we note what is universally agreed to be the single most important development for mid-18th-century opera, the invention of the ensemble-finale. As the special preserve of *opera buffa*—indeed, as the feature most responsible for bringing a new dramatic force to music for the stage—the ensemble-finale has been much applauded and studied. Yet, for all the ink spilled on the subject, a truly integrated account of the expressive significance of the finale, in terms of both its specific operatic functions and its purported connections to instrumental procedures, has yet to be made. While no such picture will be attempted here, what can at least be done is to distinguish between aspects of the picture which have gained wide acceptance and those about which significant questions remain. To begin with the points generally agreed upon: easily the most important of these pertains to the opportunity the ensemble-finale of the *opera buffa* offered composers to write "action music," that is, a musical equivalent of the actions represented on stage.[27]

The tendency toward greater unity of plot and music in finales was especially promising for future developments. To begin with, ensembles like the *arie finali* in *opera seria*, of a purely reflective content and with no relation to plot, were often thought enough. But from the 1740s onwards composers were more and more concerned to evoke, at the end of the act, the action itself in music; and to place the dramatic situation within a musical frame that would be appropriate and at the same time provide a musically satisfactory form of close to the action. Thus it was that the complex structure of the finale came into being. Its existence set composers new and difficult problems which in the second half of the century they tried to solve by the most various means.

Although the following passage refers specifically to Mozart's work, we can reasonably assume that Mozart's achievement is what would have been generally expected of *buffa* finales:[28]

> The importance of the Mozart finales within the opera as a whole cannot be placed too high: they gather together the disparate threads of both the drama and the musical form and give them a continuity that the opera had never before known.

Both passages above emphasize the constructive implications of the ensemble-finale, its role in creating a sense of wholeness. If the tendency to describe the 18th-century composer's experience strictly in terms of problem-solving smacks too much of a 20th-century point of view, there is no denying the unifying potential of the ensemble-finale (not to mention the unified outcome when skillfully handled). Indeed, the specific anatomy of this outcome is inseparable from the nature of the "musical action" itself—an interplay of heterogeneous musical images in which the succession of events proceeds as much by contrast and surprise as by gradual unfolding. Effects of growth, decline, and definitive change have never before been recorded with such variety and on such a large scale.

The historical importance, then, of the ensemble-finale in terms of its strategies and effects is certainly not in question, nor have recent accounts of these in the musicological literature been anything less than consistent. But consistency and balance are not synonymous things: what the same accounts quite as consistently overlook (possibly because of an over-attentiveness to formal issues) is the basic rationale of the finale, its underlying expressive aims; or if these aims do get mentioned in connection with the *dramatic* apparatus of the opera, rarely is anything said as to how they are captured in the *musical action*. This is a curious state of affairs, especially since 18th-century practitioners of *opera buffa*, when writing of their craft, rarely mention anything else. Here is Lorenzo da Ponte on the subject:[29]

> Everybody sings, and every form of singing must be available—the *adagio*, the *allegro*, the *andante*, the intimate, the harmonious, and then—noise, noise, noise; for the *finale* must always close in an uproar: which in musical jargon is called the *chiusa* or *stretta*.

Peter Kivy, who quotes this statement in his study, *Osmin's Rage*, draws out of it certain conclusions that merit comment. He begins by telling us that da Ponte mistook "the conventions governing the operatic finale" for a "dogma of the theater" when in fact (according to Kivy) they constitute nothing more nor less than "a dogma of pure instrumental music."[30] Kivy proceeds to show how the inclusion of "solos, duets, terzets, sextets," etc., in the ensemble-finale embodies a "principle of permutations and combinations," the same principle that underlies the working out of, say, a "*sinfonia concertante* for violin, cello, oboe, bassoon, and orchestra" where a major objective of the composer would be to give each of the solo instruments a fair share of solo passages and to combine the different instrumental timbres in a variety of mixtures. What Kivy calls "the additive principle"[31]

is an even more primitive and ubiquitous musical parameter. To take the most obvious cases, the fugue, canzona, ricercare, and various informal imitative forms start with one voice and end with them all. And it is a fairly well-recognized principle, at least in practice, that a composition usually ends with everyone playing. It may not start that way; but all forces come together at the close, to make a satisfying musical climax ... The additive principle is, needless to say, what eventuates in the finale, in "noise, noise, noise"; as Da Ponte correctly observes, "the *finale* must always close in an uproar ..." When an ensemble does not, as in the case of the quartet in *Idomeneo*, that is for dramatic purposes; and the violation of the convention underscores it. ("Alone I go to wander" [Exit Idamante]).

Pertinent as this common-sense argument may be to numbers of cases, one wonders whether it sufficiently explains the present case; for what is missing in the argument is the least notion that an expressive imperative *specific and proper* to *opera buffa*, namely the spirit of burlesque, might share some responsibility for the "uproar" of the finale. An incomplete explanation is often a misleading one, as is the case with regard to Kivy's final remark quoted above. Whatever conventions *Idomeneo* is subject to, they are not those of *opera buffa*, since *Idomeneo* is an *opera seria*. Idamante's exit represents no violation of a convention, the convention Kivy mentions being inapplicable to *Idomeneo*. The opera certainly has its measure of ensembles and "noisy" music—for example, the quartet Kivy refers to, the interlude of the storm in Act I, the immense choral invocation to the gods in Act III—but what it most assuredly does not have is a musical *uproar* of the kind that da Ponte specifically had in mind when he used the Italian word "strepitoso." If such an uproar had occurred in *Idomeneo*, Mozart would indeed have been guilty of violating a convention, earning in the bargain the disapproval of spectators who would have justifiably felt that he had either misjudged his genre or tried to mislead them into believing they were witnessing an *opera buffa*.

 Da Ponte's "noise, noise, noise," then, corresponds to the bustling, frenetic, tempest-in-a-teapot atmosphere of the 18th-century comic theater: the *buffa* finale is quite simply the satiric archetype expressed in its quintessentially 18th-century form. It is through the musical *action* of the finale, of course, that this atmosphere will be most forcefully conveyed. The "additive principle" can assist in the process: indeed, it is well-known that the opera-finale grew directly out of the strategy long familiar to the *commedia dell'arte* of populating the stage with more and more *personaggi* in order to produce the proper climax of frenzy and confusion. But the individual parts that "add up" to such a climax in *musical* terms must be of a particular character: they must come from the storehouse of musical gestures traditionally associated with satiric expression—little repeated scurrying figures, fast-paced vocal patter, rapid tempi, the rhythmic inflections proper to the lighthearted dance-types. That the significance of this last point, however self-evident, must not be taken for granted is brought out clearly by the important historical fact that the strategy of the ensemble-finale, which had originated with *opera buffa*, eventually made its way into the *opera seria*. *Idomeneo* is a case in point, *La Clemenza di Tito* is another.

Tito, written in Mozart's last year, 1791, is a prime example of an old Metastasian libretto being converted into a "real opera" (as the composer himself put it), in other words, being altered to include the very ensembles and instrumental "action music" which artist and audience alike had come to regard as indispensable dramatic fare. But though *Tito*'s ensembles may be structurally akin to those of an *opera buffa*, they are gesturally from a different world. The scurrying figures, rapid-fire parlando, and light peasant dances that dot the landscape of *The Marriage of Figaro* would simply be "out of keeping with the dignified proceedings" of *La Clemenza di Tito*.[32] In the end, *opera seria* could adopt the formal strategies of *opera buffa*, but not its behavior; if it were to avoid extinction, *opera seria* had to preserve its own *ethos*.

To acknowledge the lines of division that continued to separate the two main genres of opera up to the end of the 18th century (and well into the next), is in a certain sense to disavow a notion dear to high-minded artists of the classical stamp—the idea that their style was capable of reconciling, within the context of a simple artwork, every expressive type with every other type. This idea may prove to be truer, or at least more easily demonstrable, of instrumental music than of stage music. At any rate, the classical synthesis—Goethe's "harmony of opposites"—will be explored in earnest in the next chapter. For the remainder of this discussion, two related questions are in order: (1) to what extent might the forms and procedures presented above anticipate such a synthesis? and (2) what is the place of the satiric impulse in the entire process? To begin to approach these questions, we may do well to invoke the theme of "musical action" introduced several pages back. Not a few writers consider this theme to be the central impulse of later 18th-century style, viewing it as applying equally to instrumental and operatic forms. Charles Rosen writes: "The sense of form in the [opera] finales is very similar to that in the symphonies and chamber music; the dramatic exigencies of eighteenth-century comedy and musical style have no difficulty walking in step."[33] In another place he says: "Dramatic sentiment [in opera] was replaced by dramatic action. This requirement of action applies equally well to nonoperatic music."[34]

Kivy, in the following statement, carries Rosen's thought one step further:[35]

[T]he ensemble-finale is indeed something like sonata form. In a rigid and pedantic sense this may not be true. But in any understanding of "sonata form" that is really faithful to the enormous variety and flexibility of what Haydn, Mozart, and Beethoven actually wrote, Mozart's ensembles are bona fide examples of it.

The idea of there being some firm common ground between operatic and instrumental procedures is more than plausible, though we must be careful not to overstate the case. As a first matter of caution, we need to be more specific about the very term "musical action": what is its precise anatomy? We spoke earlier of something called "action music," that is, a kind of flexible musical continuity capable of recording quickly changing action on an operatic stage. The portions of an opera that best illustrate such a continuity are none other than the ensembles. For all intents and purposes, then, "action music" and "ensemble" are synonymous terms; or, perhaps more precisely, action music is the kind of music of which ensembles are composed, the ensemble being an entire musico-dramatic form. Initially, the ensemble was the exclusive province of *opera buffa*, but when the practice spread to *opera seria*, the individual gestures of the accompanying action music had to be differentiated according to the *buffa* or *seria* character of the dramatic situation.

"Musical action," however, though often synonymous with "action music," connotes something broader, something belonging as much to the domain of pure instrumental music as to opera. It would seem that the gestures making up the musical action of, say, the opening movement of an 18th-century sonata or symphony would not be bound by the considerations of character that regulated the choices of operatic imagery: music without a text was presumably free to follow any number of expressive routes. In actual fact, expressive conventions were as much in force for instrumental music as for opera, the tone of festal pomp, for instance, predominating (as already noted in Chapter 10) in the overwhelming majority of first movements of symphonies, with *Sturm und Drang* taking over this role on rare occasions. Similarly, second movements tended toward *penseroso* feeling, finales were the scene of buffa gaiety and peripeteia. And yet, within the confines of a prevailing mood, there was room for variety and contrast: festal pomp movements consisted typically of gestures of heroic, pastoral, and satiric character mixing freely within the space of a few measures. In the following excerpt from Mozart's violin sonata, K. 376, the opening three military strokes immediately give way to a smooth cantabile figure, which twelve measures later grows rapidly into something resembling the opening military strokes (Example 11.3). All of this is superseded in m. 19 by a wispy buffa motive and a chattering dialogue between piano and violin. It seems more the shifting interplay among the elements rather than the elements themselves that endow each work with an individual profile. This fluent coordination of heterogeneous gestures—this unity within variety—is doubtless the late 18th century's great legacy to composition in the West. Mozart may be the most masterful exponent of the practice, but the practice belongs to the age as a whole.

That much is not open to question: on the other hand, the reasons for such a state of affairs may well be more debatable than we have traditionally been led to believe. One of the few ostensibly unproblematic areas in the study of music history has always been the theory of the *affections*—the notion that early 18th-century composition expressed the affections as discrete entities, while it was the tendency of later 18th-century practice to represent them in terms of an emotional continuum. There is much testimony from composers and theorists of the time to buttress this notion: Quantz writes in 1752 that "the player should change—so to speak—in every measure to a different affection, and should be

Example 11.3: Mozart, Violin sonata in F, K. 376

(Example 11.3, continued.)

able to appear alternately sad, joyous, serious, etc., such moods being of great importance in music."[36] Sulzer, writing in 1771, is even more specific: "Every emotion involves a sequence of images ... somewhat akin to motion; the very phrase 'motion of the affections' already indicates as much ... Music is ideally suited to the portrayal of all such movements."[37]

Here, musical action is pictured as the expression of affections which, once treated in a succession of separate and discrete musical units, are now brought together in a kaleidoscopic succession within the same unit. Kivy reinforces this traditional view by drawing sharp parallels between musical practice and philosophical inquiry. After reviewing the by-now familiar notion that Descartes' theory of the passions had its musical reflection in the later Baroque habit of treating the affections one by one, Kivy proceeds to discuss the associationist theories of the somewhat obscure mid-18th century philosopher, David Harley, representing Harley's ideas as indicative of the kind of thinking about mental states and feelings that led to the new dramatic procedures of later 18th-century composition. Kivy's attempt to find links between music and the general thought of the times is appealing, if only for its archetypal bias. But beyond the approach are the specific propositions themselves, which are persuasive as well as appealing, in that they provide philosophical support for observations hitherto only proclaimed as true.

Without wishing, therefore, to take anything away from Kivy's argument, we must nevertheless recognize that his view of musical action (like those of the 18th-century authorities he invokes) relies strictly on affective criteria, whereas the same musical action has been represented just above on the basis of ethical criteria—that is, as an interplay of heroic, pastoral, and satiric gestures. The advantages of the ethical approach will not be defended here (they have in any case been suggested in several previous places) beyond saying that behavior is a more concrete, and palpable—and thus more easily identified—conceptual material than feeling. Besides, behavior does not conceptually oppose feeling, but rather suggests and encompasses it by virtue of being its manifestation (even in the negative sense of suppressing feeling, as happens more often than we might think). Also, much of the evidence presented in these last chapters leads us to believe that as a principle, *ethos* is far more responsible for the development of stable and conventional meanings attached to musical imagery than is *pathos*. For all the humanist talk about the *affections*, many of our most familiar conventions seem to have taken shape out of ethical, not affective, considerations; this is certainly true of the reform movement of Italian opera at the beginning of the 18th century, to cite only the most recently mentioned example.

But over and above this accumulated evidence, there is good reason to believe that, more than any other single factor, the growing taste for the satiric in the 18th century should be credited with the emergence of "musical action" as the new language of the age. In reference to the Mozart excerpt given above, the smooth cantabile melody, the choppy little scurrying gestures, and the military flourishes flow in and out of each other, as already noted, with the ease and grace of elements that give no suggestion of coming from separate worlds. This surely has something to do with the nature of the military flourish itself, a gesture of the new festal pomp language which has already been described as signaling a smaller kind of heroism than either Baroque pomp or *concitato*. In short, the gap between heroic and satiric behavior seems to have been reduced. And this effect in its own right must finally be the work of the satiric spirit, for the image of the amiable authority figure who is the hero of the new festal pomp is of someone who readily sees the humor in the comings and goings about him. He shares actively in the satiric mentality, not to the extent of being confused with the types that actually inhabit the satiric world but in the sense that certain traces of their character can be found in his own. By the same token, traces of buffa imagery are not absent from Mannheim symphonism, which was earlier described as the gesture of festal pomp endowed with the sustaining power of a large-scale dynamic design. Indeed, if the opening movement of a Mannheim symphony can be heard as a sustained "march of festal pomp," it can also be heard as a greatly amplified buffa action, for weight of texture and accent are the chief features distinguishing buffa from festal pomp gestures, while only rhythmic vitality marks the common ground. In the final analysis, it is the peripatetic character of their respective musical continuities that attests to the satiric spirit strongly at work. Weight and scale account for the heroic component in what we think of as typical late 18th-century "symphonism," but the dramatic nature of its action—the propensity for mercurial change—points directly to the satiric.

Does this mean that "action music" led chronologically to "musical action"? Rather than pinpoint any causal connection between them (especially since the allegro movements of Italian keyboard sonatas of the 1730s already show them- selves to be worthy exponents of the new musical lightness), it would probably be wiser to say that the prevailing satiric impulse was being felt in the instrumental and operatic arenas simultaneously. To return briefly to the case of opera, we can see one further way in which the satiric principle made lasting inroads. Earlier it was mentioned that the formal strategies of the buffa finale (though not its general behavior) were eventually carried over to the *opera seria*; what was not mentioned at the time was the fact that *seria* elements had already been incorporated into the *opera buffa* with even more vigor and completeness than would ever be made in the reverse direction.[38]

The more *opera buffa* spread and the greater the demand for texts, the more the librettists were forced to extend the narrow limits of their material and to widen their scope. The need was met, from the middle of the century onwards, in two ways. First and above all, the plays of Carlo Goldoni introduced fresh, serious characters (*parti serie*) ... Secondly, the libretti of the Neapolitan Francesco Cerlone opened up the realm of the marvellous, the fabulous, or the exotic ... As harmless and coarse comedies of the old sort and parodies of *opera seria* persisted alongside such new libretti in the second half of the eighteenth century *opera buffa* came to avail itself of a variety of material (with possibilities for dramatic conflict) and types of character with which *opera seria* could not hope to compete.

Although this development appears to speak for the continued strength of heroic and pastoral feeling, it can be read in quite another way. It is true that by virtue of the presence of the *parti serie* alone, the overall personality of *opera buffa* had noticeably changed. But the elements that had constituted its original vitality were still there: the burlesque antics, the rapid *parlando* recitative, the uproar of the climaxes (endowed with increased force through the expansion of the ensemble-finales). All in all, the initial satiric spark continued to set the proceedings afire. Without betraying its original posture, the *opera buffa* had gained breadth: the more serious moments were the means by which to give legitimacy to satiric expression, to bring it up to the level of the pastoral and the heroic—even at times, to push it beyond that level, in the sense of portraying the richness and variability of the human condition. As the theater of operations in which characters from the heroic, pastoral, and satiric worlds could freely intermingle, the mixture embodied in mature *opera buffa* attests to the inclusiveness to which satiric art aspired in the 18th century. And if this is true, then the contribution of satiric expression to the ultimate synthesis of high

Classicism has already been partially accounted for.

As Romanticism superseded Classicism, the fortunes of the satiric proportionately waned. This was less true of conservative Italy, where the 18th-century
buffa pattern continued to serve for the comic operas of Rossini and Donizetti.
Indeed, in respect to the operetta, both formal patterns and general character
remain essentially unchanged throughout the century. But by 19th-century standards, of course, the operetta was a lighter genre, of lesser consequence. It stands
to reason that Romanticism, committed as it was to the sublime, would have little
time for the ridiculous. Nevertheless, over and above the so-called "lighter"
categories, several outlets for satiric expression still present themselves in the
Romantic period, though the "social" contexts in question have notably changed
vis-à-vis their 18th-century counterparts. This change of context is clearly seen in
the example of the scherzo, which, having started off life as a witty admixture of
peasant clumsiness and courtly banter, becomes "elfinlike" in its Mendelssohn-
ian incarnation and "demonic" in a whole range of subsequent 19th-century
versions. Transporting the scherzo to the world of magic and fairy tale is a logical
consequence of Romantic thinking for two basic reasons: in the first place, such
a world is particularly adept at dramatizing the cherished Romantic themes of
strangeness and the powers of the human imagination; secondly, the hallmarks
of satiric music—rapid tempi, light and dry textures, sharp pointed accents (often falling on offbeats to heighten effects of comic surprise)—are as indicative
of the behavior of fairies and sprites as they are of the actions taking place on
an *opera buffa* stage. Creatures of the magical world bear certain resemblances
to traditional satiric types, whom, we will recall, Aristotle described as "worse
than ourselves"; though possessed of certain powers beyond human scope, they
have nothing of either the subtle intelligence or the complex inner life of humans,
a fact which, taken on its own, would grant them only subhuman status. On
the other hand, they are alien beings with mysterious powers and uncertain alle-
giances; and these endowments clearly do not leave them open to the treatment
normally accorded peasants and churls. In the Queen Mab scherzo from Berlioz's
Romeo and Juliet, a reassuring elfin revel in the main section is filled with the
sounds of an unsettling, alien world in the trio. In the "Menuet des Follets"
from the same composer's *Damnation of Faust,* the will-o'-the-wisps cavort about
like so many hyperactive children, disappearing and popping up again at the
most unpredictable times. But the poppings-about of the music are also intended
to remind us that these minions of Mephistopheles can be dangerously as well
as amusingly unpredictable forces over which we have no control and whose
benevolence toward humans is not very likely.[39]
    With the Romantic penchant for turning fear into adventure, 19th-century
musicians no doubt viewed the objects of the magical world as more fascinating
than threatening. But there was also more curious amusement than easy laughter
to be found in the satiric treatment of these objects. Even so, satiric patterns with
traditional connotations continue to figure, if infrequently, in Romantic music,

and, once again, Berlioz is the source of some of the best examples. In the *Damnation of Faust*, the entire scene in Auerbach's cellar is an extended study in low-mindedness. We are treated to the rowdy opening chorus of the drinkers, the Brander's song of the rat, the cynical Amen fugue commemorating the rat's unhappy demise, and Mephistopheles' song of the flea, not to mention an earlier recitative passage in which Mephisto wryly comments on the virtues of the Amen fugue, "so lovely that one would have thought oneself in church." The humor is by turns broad and witty, with an underlying cruelty not found in *opera buffa*. Biting irony is even more in the open in the witches' sabbath movement of the *Symphonie Fantastique*; here, the *idée fixe* theme, sweetly melancholy in its first appearance at the opening of the symphony, has turned grotesque through the rhythmic and instrumental transformations to which it has been subjected. As Berlioz's program reads:[40]

At last the *melody* arrives. Hitherto it had appeared only in graceful form, but now it has become a vulgar tune, trivial and mean; it is the loved one coming to the sabbath to attend the funeral procession of her victim. She is now only a prostitute, fit to take part in such an orgy.

Liszt, following Berlioz's lead, performs a similar metamorphosis on the opening theme of his *Faust Symphony*.

Berlioz's natural wit, so abundantly revealed in his *Memoirs*, happily made its way into his music. Besides the examples already noted, there is the unrestrained revelry of numbers of instrumental works, with their orchestral glitter and unique rhythmic quirkiness: the *Roman Carnival, Benevenuto Cellini*, and *Beatrice and Benedict* overtures are only the three best-known among many others. If Berlioz is the most striking exemplar of satiric expression in the first half of the 19th century, there are other figures who should not be overlooked. Those who have belittled Schumann's music for its total lack of irony have simply missed an abiding satiric strain in the style, especially in the early character pieces for piano. *Carnaval*, Op. 9, boasts the most explicit references, with its parade of *commedia dell'arte* characters, Pierrot, Coquette, Pantalon, and Columbine. A carnival atmosphere dominates *Papillons*, Op. 2, as well, which, like Op. 9, opens and closes with parade pieces. "Mit Humor" and "Mit guten Humor" are frequent visitors among the tempo markings in the *Davidsbündlertänze* and *Phantasiestücke*; in "Grillen," No. 4 of the *Phantasiestücke*, as in the "Lettres dansantes" and the "Valse Allemande" from *Carnaval*, rhythms and sforzando accents pop about as erratically as Berlioz's "Follets." Schumann's proverbial sentimentality is momentarily offset here by rhythmic point and textural dryness, though the dominant impression created by the warm harmonies and uncomplicated melodies is one of tenderheartedness. The satiric element in Schumann's style thus takes on a quality that easily enables the irony to go unnoticed: he does not fail to depict erratic behavior, but he sees it as whimsically charming instead of ridiculous. His characters are to him like so many wayward children, to be indulged and eventually exonerated for their faults. Ultimately, these creatures are the creations of an imagination that sees the world as essentially free of fault; such a romantic imagination thus performs an inadvertent irony of its own, rendering irony impotent by turning conventional faults and foibles into acceptable traits of character.

From this, one readily understands why Schumann was attracted to the theme of children, who, in their combination of rascally impulsiveness and sweet innocence straddle the line between the satiric and pastoral worlds. Mussorgsky's song cycle, *The Nursery*, and "Children in the Tuileries" from *Pictures at an Exhibition* reflect a similar interest in children, while several other character sketches from *Pictures* show that domestic themes in general (the age-old theme of women haggling in the marketplace at Limoges, or baby chicks being hatched from their shells) fall into the same category of benign satire.[41]   At the same time, the rough edges of Mussorgsky's style—his deliberate "unprettiness"—lend themselves to less playful treatment of satiric subjects. In "The Gnome" and "Baba Yaga's Hut," he explores the grotesque, which is a yearning on the part of the satiric to break past its comic origins and suggest tragic feeling. An interesting corollary to these cases occurs at the end of *Boris Godunov*, where the Fool, the archetypal image of revelry and high jinks, appears invested with prophetic powers, the result of great personal suffering. This linking of the Fool type with tragic experience has a long and continuing history, as King Lear's Fool, Watteau's Gilles, Hugo's Triboulet (Verdi's Rigoletto), and the sad saltimbanques of Daumier and Picasso all attest: Stravinsky's Petrouchka furnishes an early 20th-century musical example. As Mussorgsky's Fool keeps tripping over the same fragments of his broken melody, as if powerless to break loose from its grip, his whining is remindful of the static impotence expressed in Couperin's "Les Viéleux et les Gueux" and Schubert's "Der Leiermann." All three are sharp portrayals of society's ultimate victims, all three are testimony to the possibility of investing the inarticulate with unlikely eloquence. Mussorgsky's most complex piece of psychology in the satiric vein may well be "Samuel Goldenberg and Schmuyle," the sketch of two Polish Jews in *Pictures at an Exhibition*. Both figures are at one and the same time mocked (the first for his pretensions to dignity, the second for his total unawareness of dignified behavior) and pitied, this last in view of the Jew's immemorial tragic stance as scapegoat and outcast.

As the 19th century merges into the 20th, the growing taste for the grotesque gives satiric imagery a new cruel edge. Interrupting a typically Romantic lyric passage with vulgar "street" music becomes a favorite technique, a means of representing the intrusion of the grotesque into sublime experience and, by extension, of symbolizing the fragility of the Romantic dream. The third movement of Mahler's first symphony is a much cited example. But the juxtaposition of images of the grotesque and the sublime gets extremely varied treatment throughout Mahler's work, so much so that the mature Mahler sound seems permanently affected by use of the device: in the first movement of the ninth symphony not only do the idyllic moments slip unexpectedly into grotesque transformations of their former selves but even these very moments, dominated by the strings, are characteristically toughened with an ironic lining of clarinets and trumpets.

As Mahler's direct spiritual descendant, Berg carries Mahler's vision to further limits, with concomitant changes in emphasis: the fragility of the Romantic dream approaches near-hopelessness. Berg's two operas are riddled with images of a world gone out of control—the strident pianola music in Act III of *Wozzeck*, for instance, or the garish prologue of *Lulu*, in which a circus master presents the protagonists as so many caged beasts (Lulu is dressed, significantly, in a Pierrot costume). In *Lulu*, the tradition of unalloyed high spirits and good cheer initiated in the topsy-turvy revels of the Middle Ages is given a harshly ironic twist; the opera's topsy-turvy action warns us that high spirits gone unchecked are destined to end in violence. The same stance is characteristic of Shostakovich, in whose 15th symphony the carnival-like opening (the connection with *Petrouchka* is striking) turns darkly ominous on several occasions thereafter. In Schoenberg's *Pierrot Lunaire* the integration of carnival elements and nightmare is so complete that what seems threatening one moment looks ridiculous the next. Giraud's poems, of course, set the stage for the tragicomic convulsions of the music, placing as they do the conventional characters of the *commedia dell'arte* into contexts of deadly violence, to which by tradition such characters were unaccustomed—"a cruel red fleshy tongue," the sun cutting its wrists, a head with a hole bored into it.[42] One's defense against exotic horrors of this sort is not to take them altogether seriously, with the result that even the horror seems mocked in the poems and the equivocation between the comic grotesque and the tragic macabre is never resolved. The music, meanwhile, with its multiple hoots, swoops, and cascading cries, records a state of effervescent delirium—the state of a primal psyche, too long bottled up, finding its voice for the first time.[43]

Not all 20th-century uses of traditional satiric imagery are meant to produce such disturbing transformations. Composers who borrow from the music hall (Les Six were especially noted for this) aim essentially at playfulness and diversion, though there is an ethical dimension as well. Here, the "reverse ethics" involve an offstage but clearly identifiable target, namely respectable society. The connotations of low-life bawdiness associated with the music hall are used both to "épater les bourgeois" and to thumb the nose at middle-class smugness. But as with the *opera buffa*, which, among other things, was often a thinly disguised opportunity to ridicule the upper class, the objects of the ridicule are to take it in good stead and treat it as "harmless entertainment." Thus, Poulenc and Prokofieff, whose satiric styles are particularly connected with the music hall, have reputations for being "humorous" composers, whereas amusement is outweighed by fear in the sinister carnivals of Berg and Shostakovich.[44]

Although the music of "low urban manners" constitutes a fresh resource for 20th-century satire, the traditional appeal of country-bumpkin humor is not dead. Poking fun at clumsy rustic manners is the basis of Bartok's comic music (as might be expected, given the inspiration Hungarian peasant culture represented for all of Bartok's work). The early piano piece called *Burlesque* and the second movement of the sixth string quartet are straightforward examples of Bartok's satiric side; in both, the humor is broad and good-hearted. Stravinsky adopts this tone, as well, in portions of *Les Noces* and *Mavra*, but it ceases to have any place in his music after the Russian period. Indeed, in establishing 18th-century images of cool abstraction and delicate grace as the main models for his Neoclassic phase, Stravinsky patently shows himself, among other things, to be trying for highly urbane displays of wit. Game-playing is usually thought of as a conscious avoidance of seriousness, but in his works of the 1920s Stravinsky proves just how serious his musical games can be. Especially in those moments in the Concerto for piano and winds and *Capriccio*, where hitherto incompatible or unrelated impulses—Bachian anapests, *buffa* flourishes, snatches of ragtime and jazz—are made to combine effortlessly and turn into their opposites, punning commentary reaches a new level of complexity. The effects of these essays in musical parody are of great charm for a select audience that is aware of the references. And awareness seems to be the key consideration, for the references are intended not merely to be absorbed intuitively, but rather to be registered intellectually.

If this kind of wit sounds a new note for satiric expression in music—one that hitherto seemed to belong only to literature—it also has its limitations, and just to the extent that music on its own can never aspire to the precision and explicitness of cross-reference that is possible in literature. A more traditional view of wit in the Stravinsky *oeuvre*, though of far wider scope, is given by *L'histoire du soldat*. Here, several older satiric patterns—the cautionary tale, the world of magic, rustic manners, the motive of carnival revelry—are brought together to form a new and unique atmosphere, one that eventually cannot be separated from the extremely sophisticated music that plays in and around the dramatic action. Beginning with almost exclusively popular materials, Stravinsky endows them with a density that the originals could never have been expected to yield; a little fiddle tune and a trivial waltz melody are transformed into self-contained objects of exquisite poise; a tango is raised to a plane of abstraction of a kind found in the line drawings of Picasso, Matisse, and Modigliani. Ultimately, the measure of the piece's wit is its musical elegance, earning *L'histoire* an honored place alongside the best of its patter-chanson and opera buffa predecessors.

However important satiric expression may be for Stravinsky's work taken as a whole, even to the point of dominating the proceedings in individual works, it is never utilized to the exclusion of other expressive genres (no more than it is in Poulenc, Prokofieff, or Shostakovich). There is one composer, however, in whose output the satiric mode takes over almost completely, and that is Satie. As has been observed, Satie seems to have won his unique place in music history at some cost: diverse and vigorous as satiric expression can be, an obsession with the satiric tends to bring out the expressive limitations, not to speak of the "ethical" dangers, of the mode. Even in what might pass in his work for poignancy (extended passages from *Trois morceaux en forme de poire* come to mind), the stark diffidence of the style is enough to render the effect ambiguous, as if the composer, recoiling before a too frank avowal of feeling, must counteract the possibility with mock-naïveté and self-effacement. Some have explained this deadpan posture (apparently as true of Satie's personality as of his art) as a rather titanic effort to protect a vulnerable psyche as well as compensate for a less than major talent. This may or may not be the case; but beyond that, might not such a posture also signal a loss of faith in traditional ideals, or even more, a loss of faith in holding to any ideals whatsoever?

Whether or not these questions actually apply to Satie, we are aware of the several absurdist groups which follow him and rather proudly trace their roots back to him. Absurdist artworks have their own irreverent charms—certainly, the "happenings" of the 1960s, stimulated in great part by the philosophy of John Cage, are remembered fondly by many for having brought a breath of fresh, if ephemeral, air to an often stifling music scene. But irreverence unchecked is nihilism, and "absurdist" artists have yet to demonstrate that the world is not basically meaningless. Cage, who acknowledges his links to Dada, nevertheless insists that his absurdist techniques are motivated by a non-nihilistic vision. He would wish only that the composer relinquish control over his composition, that he cease exerting his own will: "ways must be discovered that allow noises and tones to be just noises and tones, not exponents subservient to [the composer's] imagination."[45] One can easily sympathize with the notion of not overly imposing one's will, but Cage seems to have confused will and imagination. The idea, proposed very seriously by Cage, that our imagination should be engaged in finding ways to curb our imagination—that is, to curb our natural human impulse to make things, and make them as good as we know how—is an irony that strikes the majority of artists as something that had best be taken lightly, even though—or precisely because—the irony has very little humor in it.[46]

Extreme propositions of this kind lead us to wonder how much the satiric attitude is at the root of no-holds-barred experimentation in 20th-century art. In the past, satiric expression would present itself as the corrective to pastoral wish fulfillment and heroic pretensions to glory, but in our own ironic age, what is there to check possible satiric excesses? This may prove to be a less troublesome question, once it is examined against 20th-century aesthetic premises. At any rate, we will have to search for some answers to this question in the final chapters of this book.

Notes

1. Aristotle's brief references to comedy in the *Poetics* come in the opening portion. See S.H. Butcher, trans. and ed., *Aristotle's Theory of Poetry and Fine Art*, p. 17 and p. 21.
2. This is intended as an application of a thought of Northrop Frye's, who writes in *Anatomy of Criticism*, p. 36: "The elegiac presents a heroism unspoiled by irony."
3. John Stevens, *Words and Music in the Middle Ages: Song, Narrative, Dance and Drama, 1050–1350*, p. 472.
4. Frederick Goldin, ed., *Lyrics of the Troubadours and Trouvères*, p. 7.

5. Stevens, p. 233.

6. *Ibid.*, p. 233.

7. See Stevens's discussion of Adam de la Halle's *Le jeu de Robin et Marion* in *ibid.*, pp. 175–178. This dramatized "pastourelle-cum-bergerie," as Stevens calls it, contains nine songs, all of them *dance-songs* (that is, not narrative types).

8. Howard M. Brown, *Music in the Renaissance*, p. 214.

9. *Ibid.*, p. 213.

10. *Ibid.*, p. 214.

11. Alfred Einstein, *The Italian Madrigal*, Vol. I, p. 340.

12. *Ibid.*, p. 345.

13. *Ibid.*, p. 383.

14. This point will be further explored when we come to the *style galant* in the following chapter. I should add that while situations portrayed in pastoral works may well have an ironic element in them, the emotions of the protagonists do not. To what extent we think of a work as bending toward the ironic (satiric mode) or toward the romantic (pastoral mode) will very much affect the performance of it. In a fa-la-la madrigal, smooth and pointed phrasing will play off against each other, the smooth and pointed presumably not differentiated sharply, but enough to reflect the ambiguities of feeling involved.

15. Valletto's irritation in Act I, Sc. 6 bears comparison with Nerone's second appearance in the opera (Act I, Sc. 9), where the emperor sings true Monteverdian concitato.

16. Curtis A. Price, *Henry Purcell and the London Stage*, p. 147.

17. Thoinot Arbeau, *Orchesography*, p. 175.

18. The variety was such that 18th-century theoreticians felt it necessary to distinguish between a *gavotte tendre* and a *gavotte vive*. See Wye Jamison Allanbrook, *Rhythmic Gesture in Mozart*, p. 50.

19. Happily, *Le Bourgeois Gentilhomme* (1670), replete with Lully's music, can still be enjoyed on a regular basis at the Comédie Française in Paris, the institution Molière founded in 1668.

20. See entry "Lully, Jean-Baptiste" in *The New Grove Dictionary of Music and Musicians*, Stanley Sadie, ed., Vol. XI, p. 321.

21. Another, more practical, reason for Lully's abandonment of the *comédie-ballet* must have been the sudden death of Molière in 1672, leaving Lully at a loss for a collaborator of even remotely equal genius.

22. Price, p. 254.

23. *Ibid.*, p. 254.

24. The practice in musicology of referring to this reform as the strict separation of "tragic and comic genres" was continued a few pages back more out of convenience than inadvertence: I found it useful to quote a certain author's statement and then to elaborate on his thoughts in kind. However, this was done somewhat against my better judgment, since I feel strongly that our critical language, in respect to this issue of the Italian operatic reform, would be improved if we dropped the terms "tragic" and "comic" and substituted in their stead "pastoral", "heroic", and "satiric". While no real objection can be raised against the use of "tragic" as an equivalent for "serious," the connotations of suffering evoked by the word "tragic" are somewhat misleading where *opera seria* is concerned. To be sure, *opera seria* plots contain their measure of

sorrow and anguish, but as they always end happily, suffering is only a provisional experience. But finally, the argument against "tragic" and "comic" lies elsewhere; it lies in the fact that the basic expressive premise of *opera seria* does not proceed from *pathos*—from the sufferings and emotions of the protagonists—but from *ethos*—from the kinds of individuals they are or even more precisely, their modes of behavior and self-expression. As discussed in Chapter 8, the protagonists of *opera seria* sing music appropriate primarily to noble warriors and women of power, and secondarily to Arcadian nymphs and shepherds. In other words, the traits of *opera seria* protagonists are a composite of those archetypally assigned to the inhabitants of the heroic and pastoral worlds. This being so, it seems more precise to say that the creation of an *opera seria* distinct from an *opera buffa* is the result of a strict separation made between heroic-pastoral expression on the one hand and satiric expression on the other.

25. See entry "Opera: Italy—18th-century," in *New Grove*, Vol. XIII, p. 559.

26. *Ibid.*, pp. 558–559.

27. Anna Amalie Abert, "Italian Opera," in *The New Oxford History of Music*, Egon Wellesz and Frederic Sternfeld, ed., Vol. VII, p. 56.

28. Charles Rosen, *The Classical Style*, p. 303.

29. Quoted in Peter Kivy, *Osmin's Rage*, p. 235. In the original Italian, "noise, noise, noise" reads "Lo strepitoso, l'arcistrepitoso, lo strepitosissimo" (Lorenzo da Ponte, *Le Memorie di un Avventuriero*, p. 78.) These remarks are touched off in the memoirs by da Ponte's recollecting the first time he was assigned the task of writing a libretto on a buffa subject (*Ricco d'un giorno*, *Rich for a day*), to be set to music by Salieri. The project was begun but it never saw the light of day. He describes the *finale* as "una spezie di commediola."

30. *Ibid.*, p. 235.

31. *Ibid.*, pp. 235–236.

32. "Out of keeping with the dignified proceedings" is a deliberate paraphrase of Aristotle's thought in the *Poetics*, which reads: "Tragedy should represent on stage kings and other personages of high rank, in keeping with the dignity, elevation, and significance of the proceedings." I invoke Aristotle's statement here to call attention to the longevity of an archetype, as well as to point out how hieratic and neoclassic the attitude of 18th-century *opera seria* was. Also see Abert, "Italian Opera," pp. 165–166, for her assessment of the distinctions between *seria* and *buffa* conventions relative to *La Clemenza di Tito*.

33. Rosen, p. 304.

34. *Ibid.*, p. 43.

35. Kivy, p. 220.

36. Quoted in Paul Henry Lang, *Music in Western Civilization*, p. 586.

37. Quoted in Kivy, p. 225.

38. Abert, "Italian Opera," p. 48.

39. In a more classically satiric sense, the poppings-about, set as they are in the framework of a slow, old-style minuet, are intended to represent characters singularly unequipped to deal with the smooth, decorous, and self-controlled movements of their dance.

40. Quoted in Berlioz, *Fantastic Symphony*, p. 9.

41. Bizet's *Jeux d'Enfants*, Saint Saens's *Carnival of the Animals*, Debussy's *Children's Corner*, and to a lesser extent Fauré's *Dolly Suite* are the French contribution to this category of expression.

42. *Commedia dell'arte* characters were accustomed to some level of violence—farcical slaps, hitting each other over the head—but not deadly violence.

43. The Freudian connotations of Expressionist art, recognized by many of the Expressionists themselves (not to mention by all commentators on Expressionism), will be discussed in its proper place in Chapter 15.

44. Milhaud tells us that at their Saturday evening get-togethers in the years 1918–20, the members of Les Six would regularly visit the music halls and circuses of the Montmartre area and end up back at Milhaud's house to play their latest compositions. "Some of them, such as Auric's *Adieu, New York*, Poulenc's *Cocardes*, and my *Boeuf sur le toit* were continually being played. We even used to insist on Poulenc's playing *Cocardes* every Saturday evening, as he did most readily." Quoted in Piero Weiss and Richard Taruskin, ed., *Music in the Western World: A History of Documents*, p. 471.

45. Quoted in Weiss/Taruskin, p. 323.

46. This discussion was written before John Cage died on August 12, 1992.

12 *The Many Faces of Classicism*

If the term "classicism" invariably evokes thoughts of balance and proportion, what, precisely, is being balanced? How numerous and heterogenous can the elements be that go into making up the well-proportioned whole? The diversity of answers to this last question must account in great part for the welter of movements and ideologies either dubbed or given to stylizing themselves "classical" over the course of Western history. Although the ultimate aim of this chapter is to examine the anatomy of the specific brand of classicism that inhabits later 18th-century music, it will be useful to begin by considering certain notions that have caused the five preceding chapters to be gathered under the rubric "Classical Humanism." Certainly, in the early days of Renaissance humanism, the all-consuming effort to re-create the artifacts of classical antiquity in modern garb was stirred by no greater concern than that of uncovering the ancient secrets of harmony and proportion. When Michelangelo complains of Flemish painting, "Though the eye is agreeably impressed, these pictures have neither art nor reason; neither symmetry nor proportion; neither choice of values nor grandeur,"[1] he is speaking on behalf of formal unity, the implicit presence of which in Italian painting confirms its superiority.

The polyphonic music of Michelangelo's contemporaries shows a like concern for unity. It is understandable, of course, that the extreme limpidity of Josquin's *Ave Maria* has much to do with the symbolic force of its subject; the striving for formal perfection in that motet seems motivated by a need to do justice to Mary's perfection. But that Josquin should seek to render that perfection as a formal interplay of parts—in terms of fastidious planning—is eventually significant in the "classical," not the Christian/symbolic sense. The modern sensibility receives a significant jolt of gratification from a work like the *Ave Maria*. Formal beauty contains, so to speak, its own justification, its orders being so palpable, so demonstrably the cause of the achievement. In its call to imitate nature, Renaissance art theory indirectly reinforces this sense of formal beauty, the implication being that by taking the best parts of nature, artists will arrive at fashioning models of clarity and proportion which nature on her own could not quite carry off. Such theory, however (a thought-product, it should be added, with a distinctly Apollonian thrust to it), can dictate to practice only up to a point. Toward the end of the 16th century ideas of a more Dionysian cast set in: composers of tragic madrigals, consumed by a passion for imitating the chaos of "inner human nature," find themselves willing to sacrifice a large measure of balance for something less aesthetically gratifying but emotionally more compelling. The same spiritual motivations guide the exponents of early opera in their shaping of the new, open, restless recitative. In neither the tragic madrigal nor the recitative is formal organization necessarily abandoned, but neither is it the first order of business. Notions of moving the audience, as opposed to pleasing it, carry the day; the feeling prevails that a heightened expressive power is to be found in extremes—in *dis*proportion.

But in time comes another swing of the pendulum toward the Apollonian side. The latter half of the 17th century—the period musicologists like to call the "phase of codification" in the Baroque era—sees the emergence of modern tonality and the definitive crystallizing of a number of concise tonal designs—the da capo and binary forms—and their large-scale manifestations—the concerto grosso, the trio sonata, the modulating fugue. Indeed, the devising of formal schemata continues unabated throughout the 18th century, so much so that the repertoire of what we consider today to be the conventional formal schemes is effectively completed by the year 1800. All of this is to say that however much the expressive aims of composers may have differed over the 150-year span from 1650 to 1800 and from one locality to another, a feeling for giving musical ideas their full measure of development—for providing them with a well-conceived and self-contained formal environment in which they could play themselves out—is for all intents and purposes universal and consistently pursued.

This renewal of interest in formal orderings and the simultaneous emergence of musical types which have strong social—in certain cases, ceremonial—origins, namely the French court dances and the vocal literature fashioned out of dance material, are not coincidental happenings; at least, they do not appear coincidental to those who believe that music's expressive power derives in large part from its habit of imitating patterns of human self-expression. By such a belief, the analogy between a well-balanced work of art and a well-balanced human personality makes implicit sense, because both phenomena spring from the same mentality, the same classical disposition toward balance. Moreover, the social identity of the individual is implicitly understood throughout the era of Classical humanism as a key factor in shaping the balanced personality. An individual in isolation can be defined strictly in terms of his emotions, but real balance comes when what an individual feels is complemented by who he is; and who he is corresponds in the eyes of the ruling class (in the eyes of those, in short, whose mentality rules over the entire period under discussion) to the place he holds in society.

Thus, what may be called a modern "classical" view of the human personality is ultimately based on some kind of *ethos/pathos* relationship—a relationship involving the mutual interpenetration of private feelings and socially authorized behavior. But in its own turn, this all-embracing classical view breaks down into a number of variants, each of which determines the precise configuration a given *ethos/pathos* relationship will take—the precise manner in which the ethical and pathetic elements will combine. The "classical" heroic vision of the personality that predominates toward the end of the 17th century predicates passion as the seminal force leading to effective action, but a passion, all the same, which must be channeled by considerations of propriety and decorum to bring about certain desired ends. The well-balanced personality of late 18th-century classicism, on the other hand, sets less store by passion than his earlier *concitato* counterpart; motivations are more inward, less dictated by end results. Our task here is to identify the characteristics of this more philosophical, less warrior-like hero, and in particular to discover what cultural forces were at work over the century to lead to the installation of this later classical variant as the heroic ideal.

Style Galant

Somewhat indirectly, these issues have been touched upon earlier—in discussions involving the Enlightenment, rustic pastoral, and opera buffa. But a piece of the puzzle has all the time been missing—one so significant that the picture of the puzzle cannot really be seen until the piece is supplied. This is the conception of *galanterie*, a catchword for courtly manners that sprang up in the last years of the 17th century at the court of Louis XIV and quickly spread to the far reaches of Western court culture. By the turn of the century, "galant" had acquired all the cachet that "Romantic" would take on a century later. Galanterie is a complex notion, and compounding the complexity, in musical terms, is the fact that the term "galant" is applied to music of quite divergent styles written at different stages of the 18th century. To make matters manageable, historians generally tend to break down "galant music"—the *style galant*—into three phases, the first coinciding with the development of "rococo" expression c. 1715 and best embodied in the intimate pieces of the French harpsichord repertoire; the second taking characteristic shape in the Italian keyboard style, c. 1740; and the third represented by the smooth cantabile melodic style of Neapolitan opera, c. 1760. Einstein, in his biography of Mozart, is probably thinking of this last phase when he sets up a "galant-learned" dichotomy for characterizing a number of Mozart's works (though the dichotomy itself suggests a broader sense in which the term could be understood).

To make sense of the *style galant* requires first knowing how "galanterie" originated as a spirit, a general way of life. If to us today galanterie appears to stand for a collection of hypercivilized formalities whose usefulness has long since been served, we should remember that in its own day such behavior carried the makings of an ideal, which came in the form of a human type. The "galant homme" was a man who, besides being thoroughly versed in the social graces, showed marks of higher virtue as well: probity, self-discipline, and a kind of detachment necessary for dealing with complex situations and difficult people. At the court of Versailles, the first personal quality in order of importance was *gloire*; *gloire* was the indispensable mark of *noblesse*, the quality on which depended the very identity of the noble personage attached to the court. The portrait of the warrior/leader—commanding, master of his own destiny—is the most prized image the nobility holds of itself during Louis XIV's reign, and it has resonances, already seen, in all the art forms of the period: it is the dominating narrative of the *opera seria* in Italy and of the *tragédie-lyrique* in France. *Galanterie*, by contrast, is not heroic in essence; its vision is smaller, more domestic. But to read La Bruyère is to discover what combinations of political skill, forbearance, and personal charm it took to keep from ending up on the shoals of a courtly intrigue.[2] *Galanterie* may be second in importance at the court of Versailles to *gloire*, but as a concept that stood for a particular set of human qualities, it was the specific invention of the court—an invention, one might add, so timely and well-conceived that it was being practiced within less than a generation in all the other courts of Europe.

The "galant homme" is the warrior/leader's alter ego, his gentler side, the incarnation he must assume when he comes home from the wars. If it was the aim of every nobleman to be as successful in court as on the battlefield, he must employ means more charming and seductive than warlike; he must borrow some of the delicacy and grace of the Arcadian shepherd. The rise of the galant impulse itself goes some way in explaining the waning of the old pastoral in the 18th century, and with it the decline in popularity of its chief genres, the cantata and the masque.[3] The smooth transition from Arcadian to galant has already been implicitly noted in Watteau's series of paintings known as the *Fêtes galantes* and in the line joining Watteau to Couperin. The connection between the languor of Scarlatti's *siciliane* and the cool eroticism of the later *style galant*, though less familiar to us, is also not difficult to see. Ultimately, however, galant separates itself from Arcadian pastoral, in that the world envisioned by pastoral is purely idyllic, while the element of wit in galant expression signals a generous infusion of irony. There is a weakening of idealism in galant mentality, or to put it more positively, a strengthening of realism. The galant world is not fictional Arcadia, it is the historic court; though physically beautiful, it is neither innocent nor perfect, and one deals with it as best one can, with a mixture of skepticism and good cheer.

Unquestionably, it is the strongly pragmatic tone of *galanterie* that separates it from its earlier counterparts—from the medieval doctrine of courtly love and the program of Renaissance courtliness elaborately spelled out by Castiglione in *Il Cortigiano*. By earlier standards, the *galant homme* celebrated in the new social code would undoubtedly have been found wanting—too eager to please, too little one's own person, too conscious of social values, too inattentive to individual ones. But there was one virtue of the *galant homme* unknown to the human types of the earlier programs, a virtue which *galanterie* had rediscovered, if not actually invented, and which gave it its singular novelty—that was the capacity to take the world a little bit lightly, with a grain of salt. "Keep gay and lively," Bussy-Rabutin advises Mme de Sévigné, "and never take things too solemnly; then you will live another thirty years."[4] Traditionally, the satiric attitude is compared unfavorably to the heroic and pastoral attitudes because of its purported lack of idealism. But the genius of satiric feeling is precisely its lightheartedness, and now, here was the galant spirit raising lightheartedness beyond its traditional associations with revelry and escape to a level of significance where it was to be recognized and sanctioned—indeed institutionalized—as a viable and useful way of dealing with the world.[5] Lightheartedness was being invested with ethical weight.

Such worldliness, while genuinely looked upon with favor at the time, could easily be indicted in individual cases for promoting superficiality and affectation, not to mention hypocrisy. One reads of charges of "fausse galanterie" leveled at members of Louis XIV's court, presumably on the grounds of showing more style than substance, of practicing the letter of a code without its spirit. It would be a mistake, however, to take *galanterie* at face value, to see it as merely an elaborate program of social behavior; for what is particularly fascinating about this program is the intensely complex dynamic it sets up with the inner life. To practice galant manners may have meant repressing an enormous part of one's true emotion, but that hardly meant doing away with emotion altogether. On the contrary, *galanterie* in a very real sense made emotion more fascinating and mysterious, because it was more difficult to probe, thus more of a challenge to the prober. Those who expected to succeed in a galant setting had to work to read what others were feeling deep down; it was a matter of becoming adept at interpreting gestures specifically designed to cover up emotion. Galanterie, in short, proposed an interaction between *ethos* and *pathos* of an extreme psychological subtlety; and this is as true of "galant" as an artistic principle as it is of the galant social code. To appreciate this more fully, we may use the heroic attitude of the era as a point of comparison. The well-balanced hero of Baroque classicism, though directing passion in such a way as to bring events to a triumphant end (in conformity with the comic vision), exalts passion and embraces it as a positive force, so much so that the breadth and intensity of the passion envisioned makes it proper for the expression of tragic as well as comic experience. Galant expression, by contrast, has no connection with the tragic; it tempers passion by wit, which is to say that, far from embracing it wholeheartedly, galant makes an accommodation with passion, all the while persuaded that the emotions are fundamentally not to be trusted, that they are indeed unruly.[6] To wear your emotions on your sleeve is to leave yourself vulnerable to the outside world, while to live too much by or in the emotions is to become vulnerable to yourself—to become prey to your moodiness and lose all hope of maintaining detachment and self-control. Manner thus takes on a new value: more than merely functioning as a sign of social worthiness and cultivation, it becomes the means of protecting oneself both from outside difficulties and one's own passion. Although these motivations may strike us as self-centered to a degree, they can also be interpreted as a kind of thoughtfulness and delicacy of feeling, in the sense of sparing others the embarrassment of unseemly emotional displays. However one may assess today the relative merits of the galant system for developing personal and social virtue, there is no question that the emphasis on manners was contrived to enhance the pleasantness of the environment. In the final analysis, the galant spirit is the most comprehensive embodiment of comic "play" yet witnessed in Western culture, circumventing evil by means of diversion and delicate eroticism, instead of confronting it (like tragedy) head-on.

It is undoubtedly this satiric attitude toward evil—this determination to ignore evil or wave it off with a well-placed witticism—that has caused historians of music to see galant art as having severe expressive limitations. The fact that at the mid-18th-century mark the traditional aesthetic of *pathos* continues to hold firm—that the main business of music is still conceived to be the revelation of the inner life—does pose a dilemma for galant art, if indeed the galant spirit is dedicated to suppression of that inner life. According to historians, the galant solution to the dilemma is characteristic and logical, turning passion into sentiment and restricting its expressive range to the more delicate affections—tenderness, plaintiveness, languor, and gentle wit. Historians can find, in fact, substantial corroboration on this point in the commentaries of the period, regardless of whether the judgment about galant music tends toward the favorable or the critical.

Very possibly the first musical application of the term "galant" appears in Mattheson's *Das Neueröffnete Orchestre* of 1713, in which the author writes that "galanterie" is as necessary an element of good composition as melody and harmony, acquired only through good taste and judgment.[7] Here *galant* has connotations of finesse and discernment—the kind of discernment we expect to find in a man of good breeding and education—in the *galant homme*. These are qualities Mattheson obviously admires. Later views of musical "galanterie" can be less enthusiastic. Buttstedt, in 1717, laments the replacement of "correct knowledge" with "mere Galanterie";[8] Quantz admits that although little galant pieces may well flatter the ear, their great uniformity renders them eventually wearisome.[9] And Kirnberger, writing in 1775, says:[10]

It is a very serious error when the composer allows himself to be seduced by the applause that unpracticed and inexperienced listeners give to the pleasant so-called *galant* pieces, and thereby introduces small, chopped-up dainty music into serious works and even into church music.

Evidently, as the century wore on, and with the gradual passing out-of-fashion of the galant ethic, things associated with the ethic began to lose their appeal. This is hardly to say that the above-mentioned mid-18th-century observers are altogether, or even basically, mistaken: we are all aware of the pretty, inconsequential, platitudinous little pieces they are talking about; there were thousands upon thousands of them written at the time and served up interminably to a public which, we would hope, grew quickly indifferent to them. The question is not whether such pieces existed in great numbers but whether the term "galant" is being too narrowly interpreted in being applied solely to a certain kind of piece; for what seems to be missing in these observations is an appreciation of the multifaceted personality and the psychological awareness envisioned in the original conception of the *galant homme*. We should remember that the galant spirit has clear links to all three of the archetypal modes—the heroic, the pastoral, the satiric—that it is a perspective of many parts. Who is the amiable leader of the new festal pomp—the replacement of the *concitato* warrior of Baroque classicism—if not a new type of hero shaped by the galant perspective? What is the insatiable mid-century appetite for *buffa* opera if not a product of the *galant homme*'s lightheartedness, of his new-found forbearance for creatures of the satiric world?

In the previous chapter, the *buffa finale*, as a type, and a specific movement from a Mozart violin sonata were cited as examples in which wispy buffa motives, military flourishes, and smooth cantabile melodies freely intermingle in an extended field of musical action. Now it can be said more fully that this integration of satiric, heroic, and pastoral gestures gives every impression of being guided by a *central and unifying galant impulse*. To put it very precisely: the peripatetic nature of the action—its impulsiveness, its changeableness—is directly traceable to the satiric mode; but the buoyant spirit that presides over the entire action is the galant spirit itself. Indeed, it is not too much to say that the overwhelming majority of instrumental pieces written in the later 18th century bear the same general galant character. But here, *galant* is clearly intended to mean not the overdelicate, hothouse bouquets named by Quantz, Kirnberger, et al., but rather a vital kind of music involving heroic, pastoral, and satiric gestures alike. Galant is the force binding these gestures together because it is through the galant spirit of accommodation, in the first place, that the divisions between heroic, pastoral, and satiric worlds have come to be considerably narrowed over the course of the 18th century. These worlds continue to maintain their separate identities, but common interests and perspectives have led to a newly perceived interdependence. And so, as actions once confined to a single world now come to move fluidly in and out of those of its neighbors, so too the action of a typical later 18th-century piano or violin sonata can be understood as nothing more nor less than the musical embodiment of that fluidity.

Finally, the galant influence on certain far-reaching changes of style cannot be overlooked. This discussion began with an enumeration of three phases of *style galant* identified by music historians. Except for the lighter pieces of the first phase, it is debatable whether rococo music as a whole qualifies as a galant category. Although it stands in opposition to grandeur and pomp, it has not necessarily abandoned intensity and even tragedy, as so many of the Couperin examples make clear. There is in this intensity a forecast of the hypersensibility to be encountered in the later *Empfindsamer* style of Northern Germany. The two later phases of style galant are at least related in their inclination to affect a generally urbane and unassuming air. In this respect, historians who have attempted to connect the Empfindsamer movement with galant practice seem to be ignoring the basic spiritual discrepancy between them. The two later phases are also related with respect to matters of texture, which show an ever-increasing devotion to the treble register and to the neutralizing of inner voices. In and among all the regional differences of style alive in European music of the time, certain fundamental changes in the way of handling musical materials are taking place: the old tension between soprano and bass is exchanged for melodic primacy and harmonic support; the vigorously articulated basso continuo is given up for iterated quavers and Alberti accompaniments; the melody itself, now invested with expressive responsibilities beyond anything seen since the days of the single melodic line, is fitted out with patterns and motifs quite distinct from its Baroque antecedents. Could it be that these changes, which contemporary musicology views as having profound consequences for the subsequent course of events, could have been accomplished strictly in the names of delicacy and pleasing grace?

Opposing Trends

By virtue of the definition given above, "galant music" is not merely a style, or even a tripartite complex of styles, but rather a music generated by the "galant spirit"—a spirit informed in its own turn by a genuine, if somewhat controversial, conception of human character. Such a music is expressively broad enough to cover the peripatetic actions of opera buffa as well as the heroic gestures of Mannheim festal pomp, not to mention the pretty, polite cantabile style that usually goes by the name "galant." As has already been noted, much of the instrumental repertoire of the later 18th century can be readily described as an action in which various galant elements rise up, interpenetrate, sustain themselves, and recede in an extended glimpse of the comic vision. But in this last characterization—"extended glimpse of the comic vision"—resides the key to both the range and the limitations of galant music, for if the galant feeling holds central place in the musical expression of the age, the presence of other tendencies, some strongly opposed to the prevailing aesthetic, cannot be ignored. In a word, the chief limitation of galant feeling is its unswerving commitment to the comic vision, its incapacity to deal with tragic experience.

In the 1750s and 60s, there may be few who are much concerned with this incapacity, though C.P.E. Bach, who has already been cited as bewailing the excessive love of the comic in his own time, is surely one. Indeed, the outlook expressed in much of the music of the North German School is strikingly antigalant: the small-scale intensity, the declamatory emphasis of details, an unusual interest for the time in the minor mode—all reflect the artistic philosophy of *Empfindsamkeit*. The frequent characterization of eccentric for C.P.E. Bach's manner must in part be due to its separateness from the mainstream, although it unquestionably has to do with a problem of compositional coherence, also. *Empfindsamkeit* separates itself from galant because of its attachment to the inner life, and it aligns itself with its somewhat younger contemporary, *Sturm und Drang*, for the same reason. The line dividing the two is indeed very thin, except for the tendency of *Empfindsamkeit* toward intimate expression and that of *Sturm und Drang* toward the large-scale tragic gesture.[11]

Empfindsamkeit may well have been the muted beginnings of a reaction against galant, of which *Sturm und Drang* was a later and more aggressive form. But even granting all this, neither *Empfindsamkeit* nor *Sturm und Drang*, taken on their own, have anything but sporadic histories in the 18th century. Eventually, *Sturm und Drang* found a more congenial outlet, albeit in somewhat transformed guise, through Romanticism. But later 18th-century music had another destiny in store for *Empfindsamkeit* and *Sturm und Drang*—as expressive factors representing the tragic side of high Classicism. In short, the definitive answer to the exclusive good cheer (and thus purported superficiality) of the galant attitude is not given by the rebellious elements of *Empfindsamkeit* and *Sturm und Drang*, but rather by a milder and yet more comprehensive form of expression—a new kind of classicism which succeeds in incorporating tragic moments into a musical action ultimately dominated by galant feeling. Occasionally, the emphasis is changed, the tragic elements dominating the comic, but the avowed aim of this classicism, as with any other kind, is to achieve a balance, an effect of harmony and wholeness.

The Anatomy of Late 18th-Century Classicism

Traditionally, the achievement of balance in high Classicism is described by music historians in purely formal terms. There is good reason, however, to see the balance of comic and tragic imagery from a specifically ethical standpoint, as will be argued below. It is, of course, possible to read much of the commentary on high Classical art as if it had only formal implications, even when more is intended. A case in point is provided by the following statement by the intellectual historian, Alan Menhennet, in which it is clear from context that the author assumes ethical principles behind formal procedures: "For the more intellectually inclined Classical thinkers (like Schiller and Kant), the pattern is one of opposed categories, which need to be clarified and then reconciled, or at least balanced."[12]

In any event, whether understood in a formal or ethical sense, the pattern of "opposed categories" that Menhennet refers to is clearly what separates the 18th-century view of balance from earlier classical conceptions. In the 16th century, the artist is thought to take the "best parts" of nature and integrate them into a "harmony." The late 18th-century formulation is somewhat more complex: Goethe speaks of the "balance of the unidentical, the contrast of the similar and the harmony of the dissimilar."[13] In this picture of antitheses overcome and reconciled, the antithetical parts would preserve something of their antithetical nature, lending in the process an element of dramatic tension to the harmonious whole. The "unity articulated into variety" characteristic of Mozart's mature works would seem to be primarily a question of continuity—a question of the composer's mastery in regulating what Rosen calls the "rhythmic levels of coherence."[14] Along with the more traditional elements of the impeccable Mozartean surface—a sense of vertical spacing and doubling equal to anything the late 16th-century madrigal could provide in textural ingenuity and a control of the melodic arch worthy of Palestrina—we have a hierarchizing of rhythmic and tonal shapes such that the smallest detail is functional in terms of the ultimate superstructure.

This last factor is the special delight of the contemporary analyst, who sees in it the fundamental condition of musical integrity, if not of artistic greatness. The importance of this dimension as a mark of formal beauty is certainly very considerable, so much so that it can lead us to believe that 18th-century classicism distinguishes itself through an almost exclusive concern for clarity, order, and proportion. Winckelmann, however, speaks of "noble simplicity and quiet grandeur,"[15] which is something beyond formal beauty. And it is more than reasonable to believe that the classical artist saw in his forms the symbols of a human inner harmony and stability. As late as 1829, Goethe will write: "The least of men can be complete [i.e., balanced, in harmony] if he moves within the limits of his abilities and capacities; but even fine talents are darkened, suspended, and destroyed if that absolutely essential quality of proportion is lacking."[16]

The correlation between balance in the work of art and balance of the human personality was not lost on the late 18th-century thinker; nor were the affections considered any less responsible for such a correlation than they had been earlier. However, the musical view of the affections had undergone a change: no longer were they interpreted as a collection of single and discrete states of mind, but as a continuum of affective matter, where moods shift suddenly or intermingle smoothly, and feelings generate their own dynamic life. To regulate this interplay, a fairly large-scale structure was needed: nothing serves better to confirm the formalizing tendency of late 18th-century thought than the process that would eventually be called sonata-allegro form. But is the sonata-allegro process to be understood as having only a *formal* function? Is it merely the *means* to create a unity out of a multiplicity of ideas?

What we must remember is that the creation of that unity is *itself* an idea: it is no less than the central vision of high Classicism, identical with Goethe's conception of balance referred to above. Sonata-allegro form is not simply a formal device, but a symbol—an embodiment of the high Classical vision. Perhaps the most concrete way to grasp this proposition is to imagine it in a historical context—to think of the heterogeneous gestures that sonata-allegro form draws together as nothing other than the variously opposing tendencies of the era—galant, buffa, Empfindsamkeit, Mannheim festal pomp, Sturm und Drang, etc.—and to see high Classicism standing at the end of the era ready to reconcile the oppositions.

As the structure capable of unifying these historical realities within the confines of a single movement of a given piece of music, mature sonata-allegro form would then have demonstrated in a very specific way how late 18th-century classicism (as against other kinds of classicism) carries out its vision of absorbing and synthesizing opposites. But, in fact, this action was already tentatively suggested when we spoke several pages back of the mercurial interplay "between a wispy buffa motive, a hammer blow, and a lyrical effusion." Looking at the opening movement of Mozart's piano concerto, K. 467, we can now see how this interplay is expanded to include all the basic elements of the era. The buffa motive of the opening (foreshadowing Leporello's first aria from *Don Giovanni*) is no sooner stated than it is amplified by means of an orchestral tutti replete with Mannheim tremolos and placed in combination with the broad, heroic countersubject of mm. 12–20. Later, when the piano has entered, a sudden Sturm und Drang outcry in G minor gives over to a moment of pathetic pleading directly out of the Empfindsamer tradition (mm. 109 ff.). Finally, after a flurry of passage work most closely associated with the mid-century Italian keyboard style, we hear the galant/cantabile charm of the second main theme (m. 128) (Examples 12.1a–d).

Example 12.1a: Mozart, Piano concerto No. 21, K. 467, opening

Example 12.1b: Mozart concerto, mm. 11–15

Example 12.1c: Mozart concerto, m. 107–114

Example 12.1d: Mozart concerto, mm. 126–131

A New Seriousness

As the instrument by which the entire musical history of an era can be encapsulated in the succession of events of a single piece, the sonata-allegro form is a *composite* image. But late 18th-century music may also yield an image which expresses the high Classical ideal in even more distilled form. In order to identify that image, we must begin by briefly reconsidering the attributes of Baroque "classicism." Baroque aesthetics places the affections at the very center of musical expression and these affections have heroic weight. The later Baroque conception of "passion controlled" is still motivated by the desire to *enhance* passion, not reduce it. At the same time, the "controlling" operation itself is the essence of what is "classical" in Baroque art—the particular stability achieved when inner feeling is qualified by outward behavior.

Late 18th-century thought predicates proportion, not heroism, as the basic quality of affective experience, and affective experience itself is offered a wider interpretation than previously. No longer are the affections seen to occupy the central (if not exclusive) position in such experience: rather they share equal place with the other phases of human consciousness. Replacing the older dualism of *inner* feeling and *outward* behavior, late 18th-century Classicism envisions a balance which is totally interior, the mixture of the elements of consciousness in such proportion as is necessary and proper to create an inner harmony. On this point, Menhennet has written:[17]

The Classicists revere the reason, but in its form as 'Vernunft', that is, as a harmonious whole, formed by an equal partnership between the understanding, the heart, and the will imbued with right moral principles. The 'Aufklärer' had tended to use the word 'Vernunft' in a way which was more or less synonymous with 'Verstand', i.e., the faculty which knows theoretically and intellectually and which, at the non-philosophical level, is 'gesunder Menschenverstand,' sound common sense. The Classicists did not deny the validity of this faculty, but were not content to remain within its confines. They defined reason more widely to mean something very like the conscious centre-point of man's innate, if often only potential Humanity, the prerogative which marked him off as 'free' by contrast to other creatures who were totally circumscribed by nature ...

Essentially, the Classicist has extended reason to merge with intelligence and imagination and finally with "feeling." This explains why Classical art of the late 18th century does not deal directly with emotions as such—i.e., those entities which are still in this period referred to (though less and less) as the "affections"— but with feeling pure and simple, which is a continuum of consciousness and of which the affections, as previously constituted, form only a part. This explains, too, why the large-scale instrumental music of the period seems more dedicated to flow than to affect, as if flow were the true heart of inner feeling, not any given moment of affective intensity.

Late 18th-century Classicism, then, expands on the philosophy of the *Aufklärung* (the Enlightenment) by joining reason with feeling and by thinking of them as creating together a higher plane of intelligence—a kind of wisdom. This is quite a far cry from galant aspiration, which seeks to temper feeling with the cushioning effects of what amounts at times to little more than pure manner. Yet, the musical phenomenon of high Classicism is comprehensible only when seen in the context of galant style. Late 18th-century musical imagery shows unmistakable signs of its galant roots by virtue of a strong attachment to melody, a multitude of galant formulas and figures, and a general preference for elegance over weight. But if this imagery is to have real weight, artists must find the means to transcend the limits of the galant viewpoint; they need not deny galant expression, they must learn only how to incorporate it into a larger vision.

The composite actions of mature sonata-allegro form represent, as we have seen, a significant step in this direction; there is in this effort a sense of complicating and toughening the fabric by placing a number of ethical alternatives against and in interaction with the galant imagery. But the balance described above as being the central vision of late 18th-century Classicism seems, by its very *interiority*, to run counter to the galant ethic, which prizes outward behavior over the inner life. In his study, *Transformations in Late Eighteenth Century Art*, Robert Rosenblum calls attention to a parallel antithesis in the painting of the period:[18]

The moralizing plane of Greuze's painting rejects not only the amorality of Boucher's interpretation of erotic goals but also the amorality of his style. For Greuze has pruned Boucher's garden of what eighteenth century critics referred to as "chicory" in order to reinstate a new and sobering monumentality. Powdered, pastel tints yield to lean and somber hues; impulsive, errant contours are clarified and disciplined; diminutive, pampered dolls capable only of pleasure take on full-scale, even heroic, human proportions; a sinuous, meandering composition gives way to geometric stability.

One has the impression from this description that galant has been not so much supplemented as totally supplanted. The "moralizing" current Rosenblum speaks of seems closely related to Gluck's innovations in *Orfeo ed Euridice* and *Alceste*. Indeed, Rosenblum shows himself to be aware of such a relation when he writes: "Like Gluck's operatic reforms of the 1760s, Greuze's purging of the florid artifice of Rococo style permitted a new legibility and seriousness of dramatic narrative."[19] Greuze's influence for the future of painting may have been stronger than that of Gluck for the destinies of music: one finds little in the music of the 1780s that resonates the severe monumentality we find in David's paintings of the same decade—the *Death of Socrates*, for instance, or the epoch-making *Oath of the Horatii*. It is not that Gluck leaves no mark whatsoever: his most permanent contribution is no doubt felt in the reduction of ornament and a growing taste for naturalness and clarity in the melodic line. But melody is not totally deprived of delicate ornament, at least not to the extent Gluck would have liked; no more than are the activities of the hedonistic *opera seria* greatly curbed, continuing as they do throughout the century and well into the next. Nor does the eventual achievement of large-scale design in instrumental music have much to do with Gluck's heroic conceptions: the hierarchical power of the mature sonata-allegro movement surely reconciles antitheses and opposites into a harmony, but the antitheses themselves are still evident and their individual effects still felt. What Gluck seems to be envisioning is something akin to what the literary Classicists have in mind when they speak of the fusing of reason and feeling into a sober and compassionate wisdom—Goethe's "quality of proportion" in the inner life and Schiller's "morally attuned soul."[20]

Is there an example of late 18th-century music which distills into one single image-type this Classical idea? If such an image exists, it is perhaps most eloquently embodied in "Dove sono," the Countess' aria from the third act of *Figaro* (Example 12.2). Here, at the beginning of the aria proper, with its extraordinary *dépouillement*, yet plasticity of line and textural and harmonic simplicity, Mozart shows us what it is to face misfortune soberly and with restraint. There is almost an element of stoicism in the Countess' emotion, remindful of the honest dignity of Gray's unsung peasant. But the crystalline quality of the aria separates it from any association with rusticity; at the same time, it refrains from the aristocratic flow and bittersweet delicacy of *penseroso*. In the end, "Dove sono" is neither quite hieratic nor demotic, brushing alongside both but also transcending both. That it transcends *galant* as well is clear from the fact that it expresses an essentially different relation to the world: galant makes as if misfortune did not exist, and with the subterfuge of "play" turns misfortune into the tempest-in-a-teapot intrigues of *opera buffa* or into plaintive but seductive little billings and cooings. The classicism of "Dove sono," on the other hand, reveals a difficult world which resembles the everyday world we live in and whose difficulties must be met with all the inner strength one can muster.

Example 12.2: Mozart, "Dove sono"

In spite of the little that was made above of Gluck's influence in later 18th-century music, the shadow of that composer hanging over "Dove sono" cannot be denied. For Mozart's aria is a clear echo of Gluck's famous lament "Che farò senza Euridice," also in C major, also in moderate tempo and delivered in a most sustained and unadorned cantabile style (Example 12.3). The extreme restraint of the piece led Hanslick to make it the key example in his attack on the emotive theory of music, claiming that it made no difference whether Orpheus' music was sung to the words "J'ai perdu mon Eurydice" (the French version of "Che farò") or "J'ai trouvé mon Eurydice."[21] It is doubtful that Gluck would have understood

Hanslick's reasoning. He may have understood somewhat better Zuckerkandl's more subtle approach, which is to conclude from the example of Gluck's aria that music is neutral with respect to the expression of "grief" or "joy" but not with respect to the expression of psychic life in general. As Zuckerkandl goes on to explain, the difference between "J'ai perdu" and "J'ai trouvé" is negligible; but change "mon Eurydice" to "mon parapluie," and the discrepancy between musical elevation and textual triviality is immediately apparent.[22] Gluck may have agreed with this last point, but he would have also insisted that the music is finally intended to express grief—the grief, however, of a man who must reach into the depths of his being and summon up the moral fortitude to bear his grief with uncommon dignity. The quality of the response of Gluck's Orpheus is hardly recognizable in terms of the conception of spontaneous and intense emotion that governs Monteverdi's setting of the same tragic events.[23] But it is not tragedy that has been diminished, or even softened; it is the sense of how one meets tragedy that has changed.

Example 12.3: Gluck, "Che farò senza Euridice" ("J'ai perdu mon Euridice)"

The late 18th-century view of dignity may be in the long run psychologically more profound than its Baroque counterpart, and socially more egalitarian. In the Baroque view one expresses oneself with dignity because such expression is worthy of a hero-leader. In late 18th-century Classicism, dignified expression has become the reflection, limpid and direct, of a balance that is entirely inward and that each individual must create for himself. That such an inner harmony can be achieved by every human being is in great part the product of Enlightenment thinking, with its implicit faith in the ultimate perfectibility of mankind. We have already seen evidence of that faith in the emergence of the honest laborer of rustic pastoral—a human ideal who earns his dignity precisely by virtue of an honest day's work and also through an acceptance of life's hardships. The musical embodiment of this demotic dignity is the simple communal hymn. What binds this demotic hymn on the one hand to the more hieratic "Che farò senza Euridice" on the other is the sober restraint common to them both. In these sober images, late 18th-century music has found a modern equivalent for Plato's Dorian mode, a music Plato describes, we remember, as being designed to capture the expression of a temperate man in the face of adverse circumstances. Gluck's aria, we feel, is a music of which Plato would have thoroughly approved.

The distance separating Gluck's subdued Orpheus from Monteverdi's demonstrative hero brings to mind once again Monteverdi's misreading of Plato, wherein the great Baroque innovator believes himself to be patterning his *concitato* warrior after Plato's ideal type. Of course, the inner life of the Baroque warrior is anything but temperate; it is fraught with high feeling, even anger, and that anger is meant to express itself openly and vehemently. The only tempering force comes from the warrior's sense of himself as an authority figure: in order to keep vehemence from running out of control—in order to maintain some balance of personality—a modicum of dignified behavior, befitting rank and authority, must always be brought to bear. With the "morally attuned soul" of the late 18th century, on the other hand, the tempering function has already done its work *prior* to any manifestation—any expression—of inner life: the inner life is, by definition "tempered." This should not lead us to think, however, that the high Classical ideal is identical in all respects to Plato's ethical type; for Plato envisions the gaining of temperateness through the quelling of emotion, whereas the Classicist equates temperateness with a harmonious blending of reason *and* feeling. Typically more mild-mannered than mature Baroque expression, the 18th-century music must nevertheless give the impression of being warm, of having heart. In that respect, "Che farò senza Euridice" may be almost too cool a representation of Classical restraint; Hanslick may well have hit on just the right piece to illustrate his principle of expressive neutrality. But in the case of "Dove sono" there is no question: in the opening of this aria, the high Classical ideal of a sober dignity concealing (but in the sense of ultimately revealing) genuine emotion has been brought fully to life.

With almost exaggerated symmetry, this chapter ends as it began—with music written in the key of C and conceived in a spirit of exceptional elevation and purity. Surely, the equilibrium and formal perfection of Josquin's *Ave Maria* make it as deserving of the term "classical" as Mozart's "Dove sono," and for much the same reasons. The persistence of "noble simplicity and quiet grandeur" since the time of the Parthenon and its pronounced emergence at recurring intervals in Western history show the idea to be a genuine archetype of Western thought. The Apollonian restraint of this art can lead one to imagine that such an art is dedicated to the sole pursuit of formal beauty; but the coolness corresponds to a probity which contains—especially when we consider the examples immediately at hand—a great tenderness. Midway between Josquin and Mozart is a music that expresses human emotion more openly; yet, even in their enthusiasm for strong affective experience, Baroque artists work for clarity and balance. The need for some kind of control and discipline seems almost instinctive with the hieratic mentality. But now, at the end of the 18th century, with the passing of a world dominated by hieratic thought, a profoundly serious challenge to the ideals of clarity and balance would get under way.

Notes

1.   Quoted in Johan Huizinga, *The Waning of the Middle Ages*, p. 265.

2.   Jean de la Bruyère, *Les Caractères*, pp. 202–224. See in particular the section "De la cour."

3.   Of course, the other and perhaps more compelling reason was the rise of *rustic* pastoral. In any event, the 18th century was seeing important changes in the overall configuration.

4.   Quoted in Wilfrid Mellers, *François Couperin and the French Classical Tradition*, p. 32.

5.   The same conclusions have been arrived at by way of a somewhat different route in the discussion of *opera buffa* in Chapter 11. It will be seen, as the present discussion continues, that I think of *buffa* in its more mature mid- to late 18th-century form as a distinct offshoot of an all-embracing *galant* spirit.

6.   This reference to "unruliness" is intended to remind the reader that the Baroque heroic attitude, though fundamentally trusting in the passions, nevertheless, saw some passion as excessive, thus unruly and destructive and leading to tragic ends.

7.   See Beekman Cannon, *Johann Mattheson, Spectator in Music*, pp. 115–116.

8.   Quoted in *ibid.*, p. 136. Since Buttstett's work, *Ut, Mi, Sol, Re, Fa, La* (1717) is an avowed rebuttal of virtually all of Mattheson's ideas as laid out in *Das Neueröffnete Orchestre*, he may have attacked *Galanterie* simply because Mattheson was in favor of it.

9.   Johann Joachim Quantz, *On Playing the Flute*, pp. 317–318.

10.   Quoted in William S. Newman, *The Sonata in the Classic Era*, p. 44.

11.   The main discussion on *Sturm und Drang* has already appeared in connection with the epic/heroic mode in Chapter 10.

12.   Alan Menhennet, *Order and Freedom: German Literature and Society, 1720–1805*, p. 194.

13.   Quoted in *ibid.*, p. 184.

14.   Charles Rosen, *The Classical Style*, p. 89.

15.   The original German: "edle Einfalt und stille Grösse."

16.   Quoted in Menhennet, p. 184.

17.   *Ibid.*, pp. 187–188.

18.   Robert Rosenblum, *Transformations in Late Eighteenth Century Art*, p. 52.

19.   *Ibid.*, pp. 52–53.

20. Schiller's entire statement (quoted in Friedrich Blume, *Classic and Romantic Music*, p. 10) reads: "In the beautiful stability of a musical composition is reflected the still more stable beauty of a morally attuned soul." The strong ethical thrust of this idea speaks for itself.

21. Eduard Hanslick, *The Beautiful in Music*, pp. 31–34.

22. Victor Zuckerkandl, *Man the Musician*, pp. 150–154.

23. I must qualify my remark, "the same tragic events." It should be noted that in the story of Orpheus and Euridice, the hero loses his wife not once, but twice. The Monteverdi lament referred to above (and in several other places in this book) appears in the second act of the opera, at the moment when Orpheus learns that Euridice has been fatally poisoned by a snake. This great monody includes not only Orpheus' expressions of grief but also his resolution to go down into the Underworld to plead for Euridice's return. Orpheus' second loss of Euridice occurs when, having been successful in his plea, he is leading Euridice back to the world of the living and makes the fatal mistake of turning around to see that she is still following. It is at this point of the action, when Orpheus has lost Euridice for good, that Gluck has his hero sing the aria, "Che farò senza Euridice." So, while it is true that the two settings in question are not in response to literally the same tragic event, they both involve the same people and the same kind of loss; in short, the situations are tragically equivalent in every way.

PART IV

Transcendental Humanism

... and Beyond: Logos

13   *Romanticism*
and Melodrama

The remarkable thing about Romanticism is that it is a fundamental content of its age without being a religion, science, philosophy, social code, or system of moral values. It is first and foremost an aesthetic idea, though one that endows art with powers beyond any prior conception; for Romanticism also proposes a vision of ultimate significance and in so doing names Art as the means of realizing that vision. It has been shown often enough that the seminal ideas of Romanticism are not original with the movement: they can be found in Vico, Jakob Böhme, St. Teresa, Renaissance alchemy, Ficino, Giordano Bruno, even Bernard de Clairvaux, and perhaps most strikingly in Gottfried von Strasburg's version of the *Tristan* legend.[1] Hugh Honour writes:[2]

Admiration for the wilder natural phenomena—mountains, waterfalls, storms at sea—has been detected in the eighteenth century and earlier: similarly the fascination of esoteric religious and superstitious beliefs in ghosts, vampires, werewolves, nightmares and so on. Interest in, and even the imitation of, medieval literature and architecture extends far back from the nineteenth century, back to the Middle Ages, in fact. Exoticism, especially the lure of the mysterious East, which appealed so strongly to several painters and writers of the early nineteenth century, is now seen to have been, like so many other "Romantic" tendencies, a recurrent element in Western culture ever since Antiquity.

What is unique about Romanticism is that for the first time in the Western experience these themes and ideas enter into the mainstream of European thought. No longer are they the underground outpourings of an occasional mystic or heretic, or an alternative mode of thought to the socially authorized belief of a given locale, but the core of a new and widespread spirituality. The causes for such a change must be left to the cultural historian to deal with, but there is no question that the subject of individual fulfillment is at the very center of it. Like religion, Romanticism aims at transcendence—not, however, through the instruments of myth and ritual, but by virtue of modalities that each individual must work out for himself. The path of individuality envisioned by Romanticism is something very close to what Peter Brooks has described in a related context: "a way of perceiving and imaging the spiritual in a world where there is no longer any clear idea of the sacred ... no clear system of sacred myth, no unity of belief, no accepted metaphorical chain leading from the phenomenal to the spiritual, only a fragmented society and fragments of myths."[3] Here, "fragmented society" must be understood basically in a religious sense; for surely, the 18th century had been busy in many sectors reconstructing *society* in the secular sense, creating the social programs by which all men would find the freedom to realize themselves in a manner suited to their own individual tastes and needs. But by and large mid-18th-century philosophy had not interpreted individual fulfillment in spiritual terms. Romanticism presents itself as a kind of delayed reaction to the Enlightenment by dealing with a dimension of human significance left vacant by Enlightenment thought: it proposes, in effect, what human beings do about the area beyond the immediate here-and-now when organized religion has begun to lose its universal hold. Certain adherents of Romanticism may remain avowed Christians, but Romanticism itself asserts its independence of Christianity. It does so not openly, but implicitly, predicating a beyond devoid of Christian myth. In Romanticism we have the most intense and complete expression of the Dionysian principle modern Western thought has yet encountered.

The vision of mysterious infinite power, nonhuman, unpersonified, and ineffable, is transmitted in countless statements over the course of the 19th century, though never more incisively than in E.T.A. Hoffmann's characterization of Beethoven's music: "Beethoven's music wakens just that infinite longing which is the essence of romanticism."[4] As humans can know the infinite world by sensing or feeling it out, the only sure means of coming into contact with mysterious power is art. Precisely because the infinite has often failed to be revealed in divinely sanctioned doctrine, it is something that the individual must discover for himself, something that he comes to know only through the immediacy of sensuous experience. This reaffirms the Baroque aesthetic of heightened sensuousness, only with wider implication: the content now being not human emotion but a reality which transcends the human, the sentient subject must have the freedom to feel totally and unqualifiedly, to live at the very edge of feeling. As this freedom is achieved through art, only artists and those who sense that art is dedicated to revealing ultimate truths can participate in transcendent experiences. "Art was a divine language to be understood only by the few, Wackenroder and Tieck declared. Runge called it a secret *Familiengespräch*, incomprehensible outside the family circle."[5]

As a self-appointed member of this circle, the artist is confronted with a dual, and somewhat paradoxical, image of himself. On the one hand, he is the rebel against bourgeois values, a voluntary exile from society at large; on the other hand, he is instrumental in creating a new society, a constituency with decidedly elitist leanings. But the new elite is founded on very different prin-

ciples from the old aristocracy. Whether artists band together for protection
against the Philistines, or for the sake of sharing insights and inspirations, the
loosely organized societies they form legislate essentially only one law, namely
the sovereignty of the individual imagination. As the imagination is the nerve
center of the artistic sensibility, so the content of the new art centers about the
artist: he becomes the hero of the piece. By contrast, the leader-hero celebrated in
Baroque art is first and foremost a warrior and only secondarily a singer-shepherd.
This tenacious image will perpetuate itself in the symphonism of the later 18th
century, while the hero of high Classicism—Goethe's "balanced man"—has more
the character of a philosopher than an artist.

Common to all these earlier images is a strong social element; it is not too
much to say that the function of the hero idealized in each of these images is
incomprehensible apart from a social context. The Romantic hero, on the other
hand, means to be taken strictly on his own terms; the artist's need to "rise
above society" constitutes no small part of Romantic transcendence—his will to
eliminate the middle term in what Pope in the early 18th century had classified
as man's three-way relationship with the existential world—with himself, with
society, with the "cosmos"—and be free to pursue steadfastly and directly his
communion with the beyond. To live on a plane above society and its strictures is
to be a free soul. This is something essentially different from Schiller's "morally
attuned soul," where the notion prevails of a mechanism in fairly constant need
of delicate regulation and care. The Romantic soul is Herder's "dark abyss,"[6] an
essence wild and obscure like the cosmos itself.

The identification of microcosm with macrocosm gives nature a new meaning. Traditionally the innocent and ordered world of pastoral art, nature gets
reinterpreted as the leading symbol of the vast and uncontained. Philip Otto
Runge writes:[7]

Where the sky above me teems with innumerable stars, the wind blows through the
vastness of the space, the wave breaks in the immense night ... then my soul rejoices
and soars in the immeasurable space around me, there is no high or low, no time, no
beginning and no end.

In the mesmerizing pictures of Runge's compatriot, Caspar David Friedrich,
we have the enduring feeling of a spectral and unknown realm—a landscape that
looks like nature but which is actually nature divested of any sound, movement,
or time. Simultaneously in England, Turner's *Snow Storm: Hannibal and his
Army Crossing the Alps* gives us what Hugh Honour has described as an "overwhelming feeling for the senseless violence of nature ... with diminutive figures
perilously poised on the verge of a vortex which seems to suck them back into the
primal chaos."[8] Wild nature is the true home of the Romantic soul, as Rellstab's
Aufenthalt, among countless other German poems of the time, attests:[9]

Rauschender strom,	Wild roaring wood,
brausender Wald,	stream white with foam,
starrender Fels	high on the crags
mein Aufenthalt.	I make my home.

Wie sich die Welle	As rolling wave
an Welle reiht,	follows wave to the shore,
fliessen die Thränen	tears flow in torrents
mir ewig erneut.	renewed evermore.
Hoch in den Kronen	Untamed the treetops
wogend sich's regt	surge wild around,
so unaufhörlich	and so my heart beats
mein Herze schlägt.	with endless pound.
Und wie des Felsen	Like hidden ore
uraltes Erz,	in the rocks below,
ewig derselbe	so thru the ages
bleibet mein Schmerz.	ever my woe.

This imagery, to be sure, can be traced back to the *Sturm und Drang* movement, and even more remotely to Edmund Burke's seminal essay on the sublime and the beautiful (1756). The relation Burke draws between the terrifying and the sublime is one of those insights so startling and revolutionary that only a handful of people can absorb, or even dare to understand, their implications when they first appear.[10] Today, with customary hindsight we see both Burke's conception and the *Sturm und Drang* movement as harbingers of Romanticism; and Blume is certainly right to qualify these events, along with others happening in the later 18th century, as being "romantic" in inspiration.[11] But they are not part of Romanticism, if only because Romanticism, in order to exist as such, must have already become the *Zeitgeist*. In the time of Burke and *Sturm und Drang*, the romantically oriented elements were still many years removed from crystallizing into a "prevailing aesthetic," a "temper of the times." What must crystallize first (as indeed the facts make clear) was Classicism itself. Rather than look upon the late 18th century, like Blume, as a random mixture of Classic and Romantic tendencies, we may see instead a pattern of dominant and recessive features. *Sturm und Drang* is a disruptive element that got absorbed into the roomy, great-spirited, and stabilizing environment of high Classical style, the effect of its own force neutralized by the greater power of Classicism. But the seed of disruption had been planted and would produce hardy offspring at a later time. Classicism is the regulation and synthesis of a heterogeneity of expressive signs, while Romanticism singles out one sign in particular and magnifies it to grandiose proportions. In the process, however, the character of *Sturm und Drang* gets qualitatively changed. In terms of Burke's fundamental equation between the terrifying and the sublime, there is a noticeable shift in emphasis from the terror to the sublime. As will be demonstrated later in this chapter, Romanticism expands the tragic vision of *Sturm und Drang* into something essentially Dionysian.

Music, the Quintessential Romantic Art

If Romanticism's great innovation is to have proposed Art as a means of getting to ultimate significance, then music is the art most affected by this development. By its very indefiniteness music becomes the modality supremely equipped to embody the Romantic vision of transcendence. To pinpoint the origin of this idea is probably not possible. Herder begins to sound like Hoffmann and Schopenhauer when he speaks of a genuine content in music, but one that remains essentially mysterious because it is untranslatable in words:[12]

Music rouses a series of intimate feelings, true but not clear, not even perceptual, only most obscure. You, young man, were in its dark auditorium; it lamented, sighed, stormed, exulted; you felt all that, you vibrated with every string. But about what did it—and you with it—lament, sigh, exult, storm? Not a shadow of anything perceptible.

Contemporaneous with Herder is Kant's more sober assessment. For Kant, music has less worth than the other arts because it appeals primarily to the senses and has no way of touching the intellect. Music, he writes, "speaks by means of mere sensations without concepts, and so does not, like poetry, leave anything over for reflection; it yet moves the mind in a greater variety of ways and more intensely, although only transitorily."[13] Within very little time of this statement, however, contemporaries of Kant are coming more and more to see in the very transitoriness of music its great value: its superiority can be proclaimed on the same grounds that Kant argued against it, namely, that in order to express its content it bypasses conceptual thought and relies on sensation.

In predicating the most sensuous of the arts as the one most capable of dealing with the totally metaphysical, Romanticism seems to be guilty of a contradiction. Blume calls attention to this problem when he writes: "Here the Romantic composer finds himself in the ever-present dilemma between the inspiration flowing into his creative work as pure 'content' and the 'form' he needs for shaping it into a work of art."[14] In the medieval view of things, this does present itself as a contradiction: music is too sensuous a material to be considered an adequate language in its own right for symbolizing the divine; it can participate in the symbolizing process, but only in a secondary capacity. But in the Romantic view, where to really know something is to experience it totally, unqualifiedly, in all its sensuous immediacy, music—and especially instrumental music, free as it is of all limiting description and representation—becomes the true way to ultimate knowing. To experience a great piece of music is to experience transcendence itself; just as Hoffmann says, Beethoven's music leads artistic sensibilities "into the depths of the spirit-world," to an "awareness of the Infinite." We may say of Romantic music that it imitates the sensation the individual undergoes in reaching for the immaterial world, and in so doing, it means literally to become that sensation.

The question persists, however, whether the main thrust of Romanticism is toward knowledge of the unknown or toward rapturous feeling. Even the early German Romantics are vague—perhaps deliberately so—as to the essential direction of their gaze: is it fixed on the self and individual fulfillment, or does it look out primarily toward an incommensurable and mysterious beyond? The intermingling of "my soul" and "immeasurable space" described by Philip Otto Runge comes close to Schopenhauer's realization that the distinction between the psychological and the ontological—between the microcosm and the macrocosm, or "inner" and "outer" being—is negligible, by reason of the infiniteness of both. Runge's experience is the raw material of mysticism, the sensation of terror and joy which Burke was the first to articulate in conceptual terms and which, subsequently, Cassirer would call the "momentary god" and Rudolf Otto the "wholly other." Perhaps in view of Schopenhauer's insight the effort to distinguish between the self and the Self is specious and unnecessary. And yet, in the "momentary god" experience two separate effects are clearly discernible. On the one hand, there is the flash of comprehension itself—the conviction on the part of the sentient subject of having come into contact with some immense presence, some absolute power. On the other hand, there is the emotional charge that accompanies the conviction, the exhilaration that results from having grasped something ultimate and sublime. When Runge exclaims, "my soul rejoices and soars in the immeasurable space around me," there is, to be sure, the sense of a reality far greater than Runge himself, but there is also the reality of his own *private* transport, of an exaltation that is his and his alone.

To what extent Romantic art encourages the psychological over the ontological can be determined only by examining a particular artist's style or an individual artwork, but there is little doubt as to the existence of a dualism running through Romantic thought. We can begin to explore this dualism in terms of two fundamental (and fundamentally opposed) categories, which we call here *melodrama* and *Innigkeit*. In time it should be seen how these two expressive types—archetypal contents with a considerable history behind them—had to await the advent of Romanticism in order to come truly into their own.

Melodrama, a Vision of Extremes

Of all the terms current in criticism today, none suffers from a worse reputation than melodrama. This unfortunate development (unfortunate because legitimate artistic categories being the rare commodities they are, we can ill afford to lose one to a value judgment) is the result of a number of factors which, taken together, amount essentially to a self-fulfilling prophecy. Falling out of favor with serious artists at the beginning of the 20th century and henceforth relegated to wandering the valleys of popular entertainment, melodrama thrives today only in the form of pulp fiction and TV soap opera where, understandably, it would hardly be suspected of ever having contained a particle of substance. Yet, even quite early in the 19th century voices critical of melodrama had already been raised. The following commentary on Sir Walter Scott dates from 1828: "It is the doom of such men to compound melo-dramas, and the prize of their high calling to produce excitement without thought ... on the whole [Scott] has ministered

immensely to the diseased craving for mere amusement."[15] Frye treats melodrama as a serious genre but does not much advance its cause when he calls it a
"less authentic version of tragedy ... where we feel impelled to applaud the hero
and hiss the villain."[16] In another place Frye speaks of a "kind of melodrama
which may be defined as comedy without humor."[17] It is true that melodrama
seems to be related to tragedy in terms of process (intense conflict) and to comedy
in terms of outcome (hero's triumph), but such comparisons are not calculated to
bring out its unique features, much less its best points. In the final analysis, the
essence of melodrama is to be found neither in a process nor in an outcome but
in certain internal expressive signs—in the highly charged, hypervivid emotional
climate we have come to call, almost by reflex, "melodramatic." Melodrama is
committed to representing extreme states of mind on the basis of assumptions
almost diametrically opposed to those of tragedy. The central vision of tragedy is
suffering, while that of melodrama is excitement. Tragedy looks upon conflict as
essentially painful and teaches us to endure—to grow more human—by facing
up to misfortunes it is no use to try to wish away. Melodrama accepts conflict
unconditionally, indeed goes further than that by pointing to a deep impulse in
our psychological makeup that attaches a positive value to conflict, as if conflict
were the only means by which life could take on excitement and meaning and we
ourselves become an object of surpassing interest.

If this sounds suspiciously like fantasy and neurosis, the 20th-century science of psychology has at least taught us that fantasy and neurosis are undeniable
presences in human nature; and if art purports to deal with human nature in its
totality, then a genre which concentrates on these psychological elements has
legitimate artistic claims. Yet, serious art has always been assumed to produce
some *edifying* effect; and it is in the context of this assumption that we may begin
to explain the proverbial misgivings about melodrama. For fantasy and neurosis,
at least before the advent of Freudian science, could not have been considered
edifying—i.e., socially acceptable—emotions. They may have been thought to
shed light on human motivation, but only on what would have passed for its
more ephemeral and trivial, if not baser aspects: by the standards of tragedy, they
could have no ethical value. In short, the most, it seems, that one could make of
an art that concentrated on emotions with no social connotation—without "re-
deeming social value"—would be to conclude that it was dedicated to "harmless
entertainment"—to "mere amusement." In terms of melodrama's only ethical
connection, namely its attempt to confirm "the audience's stock moral responses
... by applauding the hero ... and punishing the villain,"[18] the justification for
taking melodrama seriously is even further diminished. Compared to the deep
and hard-won purgations of tragedy, the black-and-white situations and the neat
moral solutions of melodrama look like so much instant gratification. And so,
whether assessed on the basis of its superficial moral treatment or as a vicari-
ous form—a kind of sublimation—of "real" excitement, melodrama is difficult to
accept as serious art.

Still, one must ask whether the true nature of melodrama is missed when it is measured against the standards just discussed. That melodrama is less high-minded than the genres presented earlier in this book is fairly safe to say; that it is lacking in deep significance is another question entirely. It seems more reasonable to believe that the full potential of melodrama's significance cannot be realized until certain ethical restrictions are removed, until Romanticism steps in to proclaim a new relationship between social mores and individual moral responsibility. In order to understand this point better, we must realize that long before melodrama's emergence as a recognized genre, the melodramatic impulse is alive in places where it remains nevertheless hidden from any conscious identification on the part of the practitioners—in Hellenistic sculpture, for instance, or Baroque painting and music. We have only to remember the writhings of the ancient *Laocoon*, the head of Rubens' *Dido in Suicide* tossed backward, her eyes glazed over and rolled upward, or the multitude of outstretched arms in one epic Baroque canvas after another to realize that the gestures of melodrama span the better part of the history of the visual arts in the West. As for music, the examples of recitative style and the French overture are sufficient testimony to the pervasiveness of the melodramatic convention in Baroque style, while the plots of *opera seria* are laced with just those tragicomic mechanisms Frye has associated with later literary melodrama: sharply drawn antagonisms and the happy outcome. In addition, and perhaps most importantly, there are the physical movements employed by the singers of the *opera seria* to accompany their singing and to animate the total dramatic effect—stylized, larger-than-life gestures hardly distinguishable, we can be fairly sure, from those found in contemporaneous paintings. Indeed, these gestures are in all probability the factor most responsible for the eventual dissemination of the word *melodrama* outside music and into every walk of life.

Yet, in all these cases, there is a quality of emotion that separates them from genuine Romantic melodrama. In Chapter 10, we discussed at length the Baroque interest in excited emotion, which comes out plainly in Monteverdi's efforts on behalf of *concitato*. But we also observed that *concitato*, or "noble rage," involved a vision of strong passion qualified by the heroic ideal. Because our assumptions have been greatly shaped by the experience of Romanticism, we are inclined to equate Baroque and Romantic versions of passion by defining them both from the Romantic point of view. But we must bear in mind that in all hieratic thought lies the inevitable balance between individual and social identity, between how a man feels and how he should act. Romanticism predicates the notion of feeling *unqualified*, and thus dispenses with the limits to feeling and behavior imposed by traditional ethical views. In encouraging *stile concitato*, Baroque *pathos* shows more than a passing sympathy for melodramatic excitement; but only with Romanticism does melodrama have the chance to emerge as a primary content in European expression—in short, to take its place as the quintessential Romantic mode.

We may begin to understand why the high voltage of melodrama is the very essence of its content. Peter Brooks speaks of Balzac's chief motivation in his novels as being the "drive to push *through* manners to deeper sources of being."[19] These deeper sources, according to the melodramatic vision, are nothing other than primitive human desire—Eros, as we have called it earlier in this book— which asserts itself no matter how much we deny it and demands that we live and feel life totally and unconditionally. The practice of literary melodrama for representing supposedly normal, everyday people acting in ways far more violent and emotional than they would act in everyday life is often bemoaned by critics as gross exaggeration, but it simply corresponds to what melodrama sees as the central reality of the world, namely, the overwhelming human will to power and self-expression. With Baroque *pathos*, passion is segmented into discrete affections, and overweening passion is represented as leading to tragedy. If in melodrama the passions appear differentiated to an extreme degree, it is only because they refer back to the essential energy without which the passions would never have been known, namely, Eros: to the melodramatic mind, it is necessary to live at the brink of desire—to *feel* to the very limits of one's being—because giving full vent to desire is the only way to total freedom of action and expression. Frye mentions the inclination of the audience to hiss the villain in melodrama; this is true to the extent that the audience's response is conditioned by the reasonable ethical laws imposed by society. But the experience of melodrama can be complicated by another, more irrational response, namely, our secret attraction to the villain, by which he becomes less an object of fear than of fascination, the personification of everything that is free, of our individual will given full throttle, of naked desire with all social interdictions lifted. Especially when the villain is a beautiful woman, the seductiveness latent in melodramatic action rises to the surface and the texture becomes frankly "erotic." Once again, it should be noted that the degree to which these contents are expressed in the 19th century is made possible only by virtue of the new Romantic ethic: it is only the emphasis Romanticism places on individual—as against social—prerogatives that enables the fundamental impulse of melodrama to take full flight.

Melodrama and Music

That an object can be simultaneously fearsome and seductive is no doubt the great discovery of Romanticism. Nowhere is this reality displayed with more sense of its mystery than in Romantic music, particularly in the styles of several composers flourishing between 1830 and 1880. The melodramatic in music is perhaps given its simplest embodiment in the bel canto operas of Donizetti such as *Lucia di Lammermoor* and *Maria Stuarda*. The excitements of bel canto opera depend obviously, and almost totally, on the power of a human voice to spin out a floating cantilena and perform the death-defying leaps of coloratura pyrotechnics. As Gary Schmidgall observes:[20]

For no period in the history of opera is the phrase "on wings of song" more apt. The image both warns and promises. It warns that if we wish to soar with bel canto singers we shall have to do so unhindered by ponderous ideas or complex human themes; it promises a kind of untrammeled exhilaration or, as Shelley put it, "unbodied joy" in the simple ecstasy of sound ... The heart of bel canto lies in this almost orgasmic pleasure ... in the powerful airborne melody climaxing somewhere above the staff.

The melodramatic tenor of these operas can of course be aided by their connection to stories taken from Schiller and Scott, but there is no question that the true melodrama of bel canto stems from the sensations delivered by the "catapulting vocalism."[21] In the operas from Verdi's middle period, on the other hand, the fusion of dramatic action and music is more complete. Especially in *Rigoletto*, where event follows event with a swiftness that leaves the audience fairly gasping for breath, the music is intended to match the plot in recording the hypervivid reactions of creatures grappling with their sudden changes of fate. Here, the voice remains sovereign—not for the purpose of calling attention to itself, however, but in order to use its effects to push below manners and explore the regions of pure, raw passion.[22] In this respect, *Rigoletto* is a classic example of melodrama (its tragic ending notwithstanding), for all the hieratic overtones and elevated heroism of the old *opera seria* have disappeared and emotion has been stripped down to bedrock.

Nevertheless, it is in the sphere of instrumental music, or in musical works where the instrumental factor predominates, that the melodramatic impulse gets its most sustained and complex realizations, and has at the same time the greatest opportunity to further Romantic ideals. Romanticism, we already know, prizes music for being the most visceral of the arts, but as melodrama is particularly dedicated to sensational response and immediate excitement, the music of the "melodramatic" composers—of whom Chopin, Liszt, Wagner, and Tchaikovsky are the leading exponents—surpasses anything written earlier with respect to range and ingenuity of tonal coloring and brilliance and splendor of sound. Taken in this light, the B♭ minor scherzo of Chopin, often criticized for a certain obviousness and superficiality of feeling, and though certainly lacking in the complexity and richness of discourse of the Funeral March sonata or the fourth ballade, becomes an acceptable and representative piece of melodrama. Played as a tragic monument, the scherzo is blown out of proportion into something both pretentious and dull. Played for variety of color and striking effect, it regains some of its original demonic charm. The opening of the piece, in particular, with its sharp juxtapositions of high and low, forte and piano, full and incomplete sonorities shows to what extent 19th-century music can embody the vision Brooks has described for literary melodrama as a clashing of the "forces of light and darkness."[23] The scherzo in C♯ minor is an even more sustained treatment of the same subject matter, in view of the specifically Christian references of its imagery: a devil's dance for the first theme, a religious hymn for the second.[24] Since these are the only two musical ideas in the scherzo, it is easy to read the entire work as a protracted struggle between good and evil, a struggle that becomes wildly violent in the last stages of the piece and ends (somewhat uncharacteristically for melodramas) with the triumph of the forces of evil.

If the scherzo in C♯ minor is a beautifully crafted example in musical terms of an enduring melodramatic archetype, the first movement of the Funeral March sonata carries melodrama one step further by supplying it with a specifically Romantic content (Example 13.1). In the exposition of this movement, we have a curious parallel in musical continuity to the opening of the Beethoven fifth symphony (curious because Chopin was, by his own admission, no great admirer of Beethoven). Yet, in the succession of basic events—the stentorian announcement at the opening, followed by the agitato section, the abrupt and economic change to major, and the quiet lyric moment that follows, we have a close resemblance between the two pieces. The *Sturm und Drang* influence is particularly strong in both agitato sections (the Chopin section displaying a bit more "melodramatic" color than the Beethoven). But here the resemblance ends: for while the closing section of the fifth symphony returns to the opening ideas and elaborates a character of orthodox heroism, the agitato C minor now changed into a confident E♭ major, the closing section of the Chopin sonata develops its quiet theme into a climactic effusion which is redolent with the new spirit. This new spirit is expressed in the form of a full-blooded lyricism, one that resembles neither the steady, relentless momentum of the Baroque concerto grosso nor the alert and radiant fluency of the Mozart sonata-allegro: it is rather a wave of sound, heaving, rolling, surging, billowing, carrying us forward and upward to the final peak of excitement, to a region beyond normal limits.

"Beyond normal limits" signifies transcendence, the avowed goal of Romantic art. But more than the goal itself is the means of getting there: what Romantic melodrama, in all its billowy fullness and sumptuous color, appears to be celebrating is the power of sensuality itself. In a remarkable reversal of traditional Western thinking, Eros is represented as the very path to transcendence. Wagner, of all the Romantic composers, not only carried out this insight artistically but was the one most capable of articulating it intellectually. The final phase of this discussion on melodrama, therefore, will concentrate on what he said about transcendence and how he determined to realize it through his music. We will begin with the last moments of *Tristan*, in which the sensation of being at once physically and emotionally overwhelmed is not only conveyed in the rising tumult of the music, but also explicitly spelled out in Isolde's words:

In dem wogenden Schwall,	In their billowy well,
in dem tönenden Schall,	in their resonant spell,
in des welt Athems wehendem All-	with the world's lifebreath,
-ertrinken	breathing o'er all,
versinken,	Sink down in
unbewusst,	and drown in
höchste Lust.	dreamless rest,
	highest, best.

In romantic writings on art, the frequent references to "transport" not only bear the connotation of rapture and intense emotion but actually suggest the

Example 13.1: Chopin, Sonata No. 2 in B♭ minor, Op. 35

idea of being removed from one place to another. At the end of *Tristan* Wagner envisions such a transport in the form of Isolde's soul soaring upward and uniting with Tristan's, the two finally merging with the world-soul; pain and suffering are thus overcome by mystical rapture. The *Liebestod* records the rapture in process: the music becomes the sensuous metaphor by which Isolde's soul undergoes its transport and is carried from wave to wave of thrillingly vibrant sound. But eventually Wagner means his music to serve on another plane of reality, namely in the interests of *our own* transcendence; for if we follow Isolde's example and give ourselves totally over to the music, as we experience it, we will come to understand how ecstatic feeling is everything, the way to ultimate knowing.

Serenity is finally achieved in the last measures of *Tristan*, but it is a long time in coming. The greater part of the opera is taken up with tumultuous heavings and eddyings representing the restless and tormented yearnings of the lovers. There is, nevertheless, an image in the melodramatist's repertoire which comes in the form of an intense hush stealing over the listener and wrapping him in a resonant mantle of sound. In psychological terms, this image imitates the Dionysian experience of surrendering to a tranquil or depressed state of mind (an action, we will remember, that results in languor, the polar opposite of violent excitement. We remember, too, that from the Platonic, and thus, traditionally "ethical," standpoint, both languor and violence are equally unacceptable modes of behavior because, unlike Apollonian temperateness, they represent a surrender to Eros). The languor is especially well captured in certain nocturnes of Chopin, where the sonorities are at once coloristically dark and texturally soft and velvety. At the opening of the 14th nocturne in F♯ minor, one feels a hint of excitement running through the sonorous torpor of the accompaniment figures— a subtly growing restlessness in the melodic line.[25] By the end of the piece, this undercurrent of excitement has risen frankly to the surface, culminating in the piercing scream of the single F♯ of m. 113 and then tumbling down by means of the recitative line which follows. Finally, in the temperamental no-holds-barred cadence of mm. 126-127, there is realized the condition that Romantic melodrama envisions as the ultimate goal, the experience of total release. The melodramatic essence of this nocturne is in its having swung from one behavioral extreme to the other—from torpor to fever pitch—without settling into, or even passing through, temperateness along the way.

Ecstasis: The Aesthetic Emotion of Total Release

One significant effect of the kind of fluctuation just described is that of sudden change, the impression of an event coming as if from nowhere. In that respect melodrama can be said to imitate the mystical sensation referred to already several times in this book as the "momentary god." In ancient Greece, Dionysian ritual re-created this original mystical experience by inducing trance (or, to use Nietzsche's word, "intoxication"). The end objective of this practice—union with the god—could be effected only through an *ec-stasis*, literally, a "being out of one's (normal) state." Wagner, with characteristic self-awareness (though somewhat rarer humor) writes: "I am an ecstatic by nature: I am never so much myself as when I am beside myself."[26] In drawing a connection between the ancient Greek rites and the melodramatic attitude, we realize that to live "at the brink of emotion" is to surrender to one's emotion totally and unqualifiedly. Ultra-Romantic rapture, like the ancient ecstasis (though realized through art instead of ritual), is the feeling of total release, acquired through leaving the everyday self, with all its built-in censors and controls, behind.

Ecstasis can now take its place alongside the aesthetic emotions discussed earlier: catharsis and affect (purgation and arousal). While catharsis and affect connote, respectively, detachment from and identification with an object, ecstasis signifies absorption into something which is less defined than an object, something better understood as an energy or a power. If melodrama is the kind of expression that aims to re-create in artistic form the momentary-god experience, then ecstasis is the aesthetic emotion by which terror is converted into the sublime. Catharsis and affect are intimately connected to tragedy, for reasons discussed earlier. In the experience of ecstasis, the signs of tragedy can still be detected (conventional tragic images are quite apparent in the nocturnes of Chopin, as they are in Wagner's operas), but their essential meanings have been changed: the painful darkness of tragedy has been transformed into—or at least superseded by—the thrilling darkness of infinite mysterious power. The lesson of melodrama is that desire overcomes fear by turning it into dangerous charm. In that sense, melodrama stands with the most romantic—i.e., least ironic—of the archetypal contents in art.

The composers dedicated to ecstasis create their effects as discussed above—through opulent and melting sonorities, chromatic iridescence, the sustained archings of *ewige Melodie*, in short, by means of all the paraphernalia we commonly equate with mid-19th-century ultra-Romantic style. To consider for a moment an earlier style: we can accept Hoffmann's view of Beethoven as a Romantic in the sense that Beethoven's music aims at (and achieves) transcendent feeling. But Beethoven's illuminations are too much the product of struggle and breakthrough to have any connection with ecstasis. If the essence of Beethovenian expression is the process of human effort, then the dramatic twists and turns, holdings back and thrustings ahead, of that process do not provide the continuing current of lyrical sound by which the experiencing subject will be "carried away." Especially in a piece such as the first movement of Op. 59, No. 1, where interruptions and digressions are inserted almost in imitation of rational discourse, one has the distinct impression that Beethoven does not intend the listener to operate primarily on that level of consciousness which will lead to ecstasis. In order to take in the ideas of this Rasoumovsky quartet, a more active mental state is necessary, a measure of detachment which implies an emotional response analogous to catharsis.

Melodramatic art, on the other hand, must work by striking effect and vivid sensation, in keeping with its central vision of the world as sensual excitement. And we now see that a significant aspect of Romantic rapture—perhaps the most significant—is the direct product of melodramatic treatment. As important, however, as melodrama is to the Romantic cause, it constitutes only one part of Romanticism (and not its best part, if we are to believe the majority of the critics). There is no question that melodrama's aesthetic ambitions fall short of Romanticism's ideals, and that is principally because melodrama is itself not a conventionally idealistic art. Focused on the notion of individual desire and the aesthetic gratification of that notion through ecstasis, it is not designed to elicit much general admiration, at least not on traditionally ethical grounds. But the best realizations of melodramatic music suggest something beyond melodrama's original aims. At least one composer—Wagner—was intensely preoccupied with the possibility of turning ecstasis into ultimate revelation, and he was supremely confident that his music had accomplished the task.

Eros and Thanatos

In order to clarify Wagner's intentions, we once again invoke the opposition Eros/Thanatos first introduced in Chapter 2. There Thanatos was described as a "desire to know," a fundamental impulse to wonder about the world. Eros, by contrast, was defined as a "desire to be," the human craving that comes from having a body and an individual selfhood.

In 19th-century writings the expressions boundless desire and infinite longing are used so persistently and interchangeably that any distinction that might have obtained between them in the early days of Romanticism must have quickly disappeared. If, in any case, we create such a distinction here by connecting "boundless desire" with Eros and "infinite longing" with Thanatos we have improved our chances to understand certain statements which Wagner made on the subjects of *Faust* and *Tristan* and which ultimately serve to shed light on his fundamental vision of the power of music. In a letter to Mathilde Wesendonck of 1858, he writes:[27]

Faust's despair of the world at the beginning [of Goethe's poem] is either based on knowledge of the world ... or alternatively—and this is more likely—Faust is just an academic with a wild imagination and has had no deep experience of the real world. But then it would surely be better if he really did learn what there is to learn—and that at the first—so suitable—opportunity, Gretchen's love. But goodness, how happy the author is once he has got him out of his deep spiritual involvement with this love, so that one bright morning he has forgotten the whole affair without a trace. So for me this Faust simply represents a lost opportunity; and this opportunity was no less than the only hope of salvation and redemption.

Later in the same letter he adds:[28]

What a load of nonsense I am writing. Is it the pleasure of talking to myself or the happiness of talking to you? Yes, to you. But if I look into your eyes I cannot speak another word, for then all is naught that I could say. Look, then everything is so incontestably true to me, then I am so sure of myself, when this wonderful seraphic eye rests upon me and I can lose myself in its gaze. Then there are no object and no subject; everything is then one and indivisible, deep immeasurable harmony.

This is simultaneously a letter *of* love and *about* love; in declaring his feelings to Mathilde, Wagner is also seeing himself as a Faust who will not make Faust's (and Goethe's) mistake. Love, for Wagner, is the ultimate—and fundamental—thing to understand about the world. We might paraphrase Keats and say, on behalf of Wagner: "Love is truth, and truth love, and that's all ye need to know." And in *Tristan* Wagner means to commemorate that truth:[29]

My greatest masterpiece of the art of the most subtle, most gradual transition is certainly the big scene of the second act of *Tristan und Isolde*. This scene begins with pulsating life at its most passionate—and ends in the most mystical, innermost longing for death.

This transition from one state to the other is usually taken to mean that Tristan and Isolde's love can become eternal when it exists solely in spirit. But on another plane Wagner is telling us that their love, because it is a *true love*—because the lovers' souls have been previously knitted together—is of the spirit as well as of the flesh, and therefore already contains the essence of the eternal. Act II of the opera shows us that it is *through* their sensuality that Tristan and Isolde come to an awareness of the transcendental mystery: in their ecstasis they achieve revelation.

So, too, the composer, through the very seductiveness of his music, provides the means by which the listener at one and the same time experiences ecstatic release and gains knowledge of mysterious power. In fulfilling the boundless desire of Eros, we simultaneously satisfy that "infinite longing to know" which has all along been the Romantic ideal; while following our melodramatic impulse to gratify the individual will, we have ended by discovering the universal "Will." In Wagner's view the opposition between Eros and Thanatos is removed through ecstasis because, although the nature of aesthetic rapture is totally sensual and *personal* (like the experience of true love itself), it is paradoxically achieved only through a giving over of one's person—a giving up of the self—to the seductive power of art. You get everything back only when nothing of yourself is left. In this ecstatic action great melodramatic music realizes the central Romantic prophecy of art as transcendence, and the symbiotic relation between melodrama and Romanticism takes on a new dimension.

Notes

1. See Hugh Honour, *Romanticism*, pp. 11–20.
2. *Ibid.*, p. 12.
3. Peter Brooks, "The Melodramatic Imagination," in *Romanticism*, David Thorburn and Geoffrey Hartman, ed., p. 216.
4. Quoted in Oliver Strunk, ed., *Source Readings in Music History*, p. 777.
5. Honour, p. 253.
6. See Friedrich Blume, *Classic and Romantic Music*, p. 13.
7. Quoted in Honour, p. 73.
8. *Ibid.*, p. 34.
9. Schubert set this poem in his last year, 1828. The song forms part of the collection known as the *Schwanengesang*.
10. A thorough discussion of Burke's idea appears in Michel Le Bris, *Romantics and Romanticism*, Chapter VI ("Transformations of the Sublime"), pp. 107–121. A number of magnificent full-page color plates adorn this volume, including reproductions of Turner's *Hannibal Crossing the Alps* and of several of the seminal paintings of Caspar David Friedrich.
11. See Blume, pp. 99–103. Blume's opinion on this point, like practically everything else he says, proceeds from his central premise that, unlike the situation for the Medieval,

> Renaissance, Baroque, and modern eras, no separate Classic and Romantic eras exist; instead, there is a single Classic-Romantic entity: "There is no 'Classic' style period in the history of music, only a Classic-Romantic one, within which those forms that are 'classically' determined can at most be characterized as phases." (p. 9).

12. Quoted in Blume, p. 13.
13. Quoted in Honour, p. 120.
14. Blume, p. 113.
15. Quoted in Gary Schmidgall, *Literature as Opera*, p. 134.
16. Northrop Frye, *Fools of Time*, p. 79.
17. Northrop Frye, *Anatomy of Criticism*, p. 40.
18. Frye, *Fools of Time*, p. 116.
19. Brooks p. 200.
20. Schmidgall, p. 113.
21. *Ibid.*, p. 113.
22. Reference to manner here invokes the notion of galanterie and helps us to understand how, in everyday situations, the galant and melodramatic mentalities represent polar opposites in dealing with those situations. When we are in a galant frame of mind, our inclination is to defuse the difficulties of a situation by making light of them—by seeing them as unimportant annoyances at most, by finding humor in them at best. To the mind under the influence of melodrama, the same situation looks totally different. Regarding this last point, see my article, "Claude Debussy, Melodramatist," in *Music and Context*, Anne Dhu Shapiro, ed., p. 147.
23. See Brooks p. 204.
24. This example, of course, leads us to realize that Christianity is the source of the melodrama which has had the greatest impact on the modern Western imagination, the struggle between God and Satan.
25. Could this effect correspond to the "guns behind flowers" feeling that Schumann detected in Chopin's music?
26. Quoted in Paul Henry Lang, ed., *The Symphony, 1800–1900*, p. xxix.
27. Herbert Barth et al., ed., *Wagner: A Documentary Study*, p. 187.
28. *Ibid.*, p. 187.
29. *Ibid.*, p. 189.

14 *Innigkeit,*
the Romantic Alternative

That a German word should be chosen to designate the mid-19th-century complement to Romantic melodrama is due to the fact that the type of expression for which the word seems most appropriate is not only particularly representative of German music of the mid-19th century (perhaps most clearly recognized in certain works of Schumann) but also related to a number of older, specifically German, manifestations—the philosophy of Hoffmann, Schlegel, et al., the contemplative music of Beethoven, and the more intimate kind of chorale prelude found characteristically in Bach's *Orgelbüchlein.* The closest equivalent term to *Innigkeit* in English is, perhaps, "introspection," which signifies a "peering through" an object to its metaphysical essence. Innigkeit may therefore be said to be more spiritually oriented than melodrama, representing the more "elevated" side of the Romantic vision.[1] The musical products of both Innigkeit and melodrama are calculated to lead to the transcendence promised by Romanticism, but they do so by opposite routes, melodrama allying itself essentially with Eros, Innigkeit with Thanatos. Innigkeit does not deny the inherent sensuality of human nature but to the extent that it does not place the sensual element in primary position, its "imagery" is expectedly less pungent, less sumptuous, less highly colored, less given to striking contrast, than that of melodrama.

What is it to arrive at transcendence by way of Thanatos? If "Innigkeiter" as well as melodramatists are true Romantics, then the distinguishing feature between them must be the way they interpret the transcendent experience, the aspects of the experience they choose to emphasize; that, in its turn, must depend on how they relate to the world generally, what aspects of the world are of ultimate importance to them. For the melodramatist, that significance is rooted in sensory things: the melodramatist finds the world spilling over with signs of the life force—movement, color, turmoil, human passions and conflicts, physical being in all its abundance and variety are what greatly move him. All of life, its terrors as well as its pleasures, is a spectacle, breathtaking and alluring. In response to the impact that the living immediacy of the world has had on him, the melodramatic artist seeks to fashion a work of art that faithfully celebrates that impact: melodramatic images must in themselves be pungent and alluring, they must have the power to intoxicate, to overtake our senses, to enfold us in their powerful embrace.

No less moved and excited by the plenitude of life than the melodramatists, the adherents of Innigkeit nevertheless extract a different truth from their emotion. For the melodramatic artist, it is the life force itself that strikes him as the chief reality; for the adherent of Innigkeit, it is his own deep understanding. He recognizes the basic fact that this understanding would have no reality at all without there existing in the first place a human capacity for being deeply moved. The philosopher of Innigkeit thus concentrates his efforts on identifying the seat of this capacity as the "deepest recesses of our individual soul." If we seem to be falling into the familiar trap that hazy Romantic language typically lays open for its victims, we will simply have to work our way out. As a first step, we must remind ourselves that the deep emotion envisioned by Innigkeit is of a different order than that of melodrama, and thus differently expressed. The essence of melodramatic emotion being sensual excitement, melodramatic expression behaves accordingly. The emotion of Innigkeit is something less sensually immediate, it is rather something filtered and processed in a deep inner recess of our being, a super-*penseroso*, so to speak. Having been so processed, it becomes less what we commonly call emotion and more what we think of as a power of perception, a way—the profoundest way—of understanding the world. But perhaps it would be more faithful to the ideology of Innigkeit to reverse this formulation and to say that such an understanding of the world is the most profound because it is the most deeply metaphysical, bypassing in the final analysis both the rational and the sensual.

The spirituality of melodrama, then, seems to rely on discrete and periodic manifestations, in contrast to which Innigkeit would be a characteristically sustained spiritual condition, a general disposition of the soul. The specific nature of Innigkeit transcendence might well be defined in a negative way, that is, as an experience deprived of the thrill of sensation—without the "momentary god." Or said more positively, each of us need not have undergone a momentary-god experience in order to feel that Innigkeit is a basic part of our makeup, in order to be sure of our capacity to sense the world deeply. But if this is so, identifying Innigkeit music becomes a particularly problematic thing, for what form does a piece of music take which seeks to re-create an emotion as interiorized as the kind envisioned by the Innigkeit philosophy? What does musical imagery sound like that is meant to capture someone in the act of peering intently into the world? The problem is not unlike the one confronting demotic expression in those various stages of Western history dominated by hieratic thinking: in face of the manifestly splendid and exquisite products of hieratic artistry, how have demotic artists managed to get themselves understood? How have they conveyed the inherent significance and dignity of their wares in spite of relatively humble appearances? Like hieratic expression, melodramatic gestures are there for everyone to hear and see; not so those of Innigkeit, which must make themselves felt in less overtly sensory ways. And yet, "nonmelodramatic" 19th-century music is hardly proof positive of the presence of Innigkeit. To be sure, we have some clues as to the quality of image we are looking for: certain prototypes of contemplative emotion in musical imagery—the floating cantilena of Gregorian chant, the meditational character of the preludes of Bach's *Orgelbüchlein*, Beethoven's "penseroso" slow movements—have conditioned us to equate quiet hush with spirituality (in addition to which the opposition between spirituality and sensuality is an archetype deeply implanted in our cultural consciousness). But contemplation is no more the extent of Innigkeit content than *penseroso* is the only mood in Beethoven's expressive arsenal.

The viewpoint advanced below is that Innigkeit images are among the most diverse in Western musical literature. Far from being restricted to the familiar guises of spirituality presented earlier in this book, Innigkeit images can roar as well as whisper, they can charge aggressively ahead or flow gently on. They can come in the form of symphonies or songs; they can encompass all the heroic, pastoral, and satiric paraphernalia that music of the classical humanist era has left as its legacy to the 19th century. What the following discussion intends to show is that the major composers in question—Schubert, Schumann, Brahms, and Bruckner—represent, each in his own way, a significant aspect of the Innigkeit vision, despite marked divergences of style and procedure. With melodrama the gestural overtness is such that one can imagine characteristic qualities in advance of encountering any specific work. With Innigkeit art this is not possible, because the essence of Innigkeit expression is not behavior, but pure feeling. One's only recourse is to confront the individual work and attempt to extract from the host of diverse and opposing images one finds there a prevailing aura that corresponds in some significant way to the Innigkeit "emotion" described above. Such a method proceeds on the conviction that out of the multiple observations will emerge a set of phases or patterns, each of which will serve to confirm Innigkeit's fundamental *ethos*.

Voice of Mitleid: Schumann

Schumann's work may be said to represent the most accessible phase of Innigkeit, in view of the intimately human element that permeates his early piano pieces and songs—themes of domesticity, youthful love, fanciful daydreaming. Of all the Romantics, Schumann in particular leads us to discover what is wondrous in the ordinary and familiar little corners of everyday life, thereby continuing a tradition already developed in genre painting and rustic pastoral poetry, though with an emphasis more on the private than the social implications of the archetype. To find the wonder and significance in ordinary things presupposes some initial spark of sympathy for them. Jack Stein has spoken of Schumann's evocations as being "always tinged with sentimental innocence,"[2] a characterization which is clearly not intended to disparage the composer but presumably to point out how Schumann, in the spirit of the original romantic impulse, means to express what it is to feel one's heart going out to other things and other beings. Schopenhauer makes a great deal of this experience in his prize essay, "On the Foundation of Morality":[3]

The sort of act that I am here discussing is not something that I have merely dreamed up or conjured out of thin air, but a reality—in fact, a not unusual reality: it is, namely, the everyday phenomenon of *Mitleid*, compassion, which is to say: immediate participation released from all other considerations, first, in the pain of another, and then, in the alleviation or termination of that pain, which alone is the true ground of all autonomous righteousness and of all true human love.

Schopenhauer's conception is not essentially different from Christian *agape* or Enlightenment brotherhood or Theocritan communal sharing (though it certainly has a more mystical "Eastern" flavor than these earlier versions of compassion, due to the fact that he sees in the capacity of one soul to connect to another the basis of "singleness of Being," that is, the existence of the One Soul from which all individual souls derive and to which they return).[4] The love envisioned by Schopenhauer is, in any case, clearly different from the self-centered, erotic kind embodied in melodramatic art. Here, the center of the love feeling is tenderness; and tenderness is what radiates forth most prominently from such scores of Schumann's as the *Frauenliebe und Leben* and the second movement of the Trio in F major (Example 14.1). Tenderness, of course, is hardly unknown to earlier styles, but its effect is usually mitigated by other influences. In Zerlina's aria, "Bati, bati," Mozart tempers tenderness with expected Classical restraint and some gentle irony. In the climactic adagio from the fourth movement of the Eroica symphony, the expression is unrestrained, but it is also motivated by a long and complex development leading up to it. Moreover, Beethoven's tenderness is delivered on a grand scale, as if addressed to all creation at once, and it is surrounded by a variety of contrasting ideas that enrich and complicate the central feeling.

Schumann's tenderness focuses, rather, on the intimate and the particular; but even more important, it is so single-minded that it effectively obliterates other inclinations and perspectives. This is, indeed, the heart of sentimentality—the tendency of the sentient subject to get wrapped up in the beauty of his own tender emotion in such a way that the complications of everyday reality get reduced to sweetness and light. The danger of oversimplification in sentimental expression—the inclination to view the world through the romantic prism without the countervailing presence of ironic awareness—is what 20th-century criticism has held against much 19th-century art—is, in fact, what has earned for sentimentality the same bad name as that which stalks melodrama. Yet, what appears to be an obvious weakness becomes in Schumann's work a strength. This

Example 14.1: Schumann, Piano trio in F, Op. 80

is due in certain cases (for instance, Nos. 2, 4, and 5 of the *Dichterliebe* or certain pieces of the *Kinderscenen*) to an extremely delicate, almost aphoristic treatment of the sentimental feeling, as if the emotion were so intensely personal and fragile that it could only be rendered in hesitating whispers and semistatements. In other cases the limitations of the sentimental perspective are offset by the rhythmic verve of "guten Humor" ("Grillen") or by an intensely sustained (usually falling) melodic line, supported by a sequence of steadily pulsating, full-bodied chords, the outpouring of a heart brimming over with limitless sympathy (again, the slow movement of the F major trio). In short, Schumann's art at its best persuades us of what is truly noble in sentimental feeling, namely, its power to reach that infinite dimension contained in Schopenhauer's conception of *Mitleid*.

Current criticism has the habit of applying the characterization "sentimental" to a class of work which is idyllic or nostalgic, but not sentimental in the sense just described. It is understandable how intimate reveries such as the *Liebesträume* of Liszt or the Andante Spianato and Nocturne in E♭ of Chopin can be confused with Schumannesque sentimentality, but the two types must be distinguished. In the Chopin and Liszt examples, the central emotion is not tenderness but gentle seduction, something closely akin to the languor of Scarlatti's *siciliane*. The "guns-behind-flowers" quality which Schumann observed in Chopin's music—an erotic energy alive under the lovely mask—is something in which Schumann's style is almost utterly lacking. Chopin is not incapable of expressing tenderness, as he shows in the second theme of the B minor sonata or the opening themes of the B major and E major Nocturnes. But the surface glamour of his music attests to an underlying movement toward melodrama, which is the losing of the self in one's own sensual exhilaration, and away from sentimentality, which is the losing of the self in one's own tender emotion. Sensual excitement usually leads our minds to the seductive and alluring stimuli that bring the excitement on, whereas the welling-up of tenderness makes us think of the source from which the emotion issued and which we have come to identify as something inherently human—as "belonging to us" and thus, as being "in us." This must be why melodramatic images convey an overwhelming sense of outward action, while with Innigkeit expression, even images of action seem ultimately embedded in a chrysalis of contemplation.

Voice of Innocence: Schubert

Earlier it was said that with the oncoming of Romanticism, the artist himself becomes the hero of the piece, the chief protagonist among the cultural types of the West to play out the human drama of the 19th century. This is totally consistent with Romanticism's elevation of art to the status of spiritual experience. Nevertheless, the artist does not always appear as himself; as a man of many parts he can assume a number of guises. He is first and foremost a sensitive and poetic figure, but he must also possess physical and moral courage (a conception that effectively reverses the Baroque self-image of warrior first, shepherd second). Romantic stage works may cast the hero in such diverse roles as the simple huntsman, the fairy-tale prince, the gypsy troubadour, the knight of the Holy Grail; what comes through from each of these personalities is refinement of sensibility, a certain aura of the supernatural, a spiritual purity. We commonly say of the older epic hero that he is "larger-than-life," of the Romantic hero that he walks "a little off the ground." It is not for nothing that the Romantics look less to the ancient epic poems for inspiration than to medieval legend and the quest romances of the 12th and 13th centuries.

Schumann's characteristic hero is less magical than the operatic personalities just mentioned, more one of us; indeed, in the *Dichterliebe* (better translated "The Poet in Love" than "The Poet's Loves"), the artist retains his original identity. One imagines an adolescent of somewhat hypersensitive nature, well-meaning and goodhearted but vulnerable, unpracticed in the art of love and destined for disappointment. He has much in common with the heroes of Schubert's song cycles, though Schubert's protagonists seem remote by comparison with Schumann's, in part because of the rural surroundings which we urban dwellers find unfamiliar. But the core of the remoteness is eventually not in the rural setting: it is in Schubert's music, in a style that represents an important phase of Innigkeit expression.

To understand the nature of this dimension, we must first remind ourselves what the countryside signified for Schubert and his *Volkstümlich* contemporaries. A society that lived in close contact with nature was by definition unspoiled, immune to the corrupting influences of the court and the city. Members of such a society expressed themselves openly and sincerely, free of courtly and urban pre-tension. Imitating the folk ways therefore seemed a sure and practical means by which to capture this openness for one's own music. But the unaffected character of Schubert's melody goes beyond the demotic conception of a heroism rooted in humble purity: in the simple poise of the melodic line and the extraordinary freshness of the sonorities, one hears the voice not merely of what the English poets liked to refer to as the "country swain" but of someone who is *in*, though not really *of*, this world.[5]

It is easy to understand why the subject matter of *Die Schöne Müllerin* and *Winterreise* appealed to Schubert, for the situations described in the poetry represent protagonists quite incapable of dealing with daily life on its own terms. The "heroes" of these cycles (if such they can be called, since they are really victims) are so unworldly as to be otherworldly. If Müller's poems suggest this otherworldliness, Schubert's style expresses the true essence of it, and in a way that goes beyond the quality that Marcel Schneider has described for the music as a "longing for Heaven." "Heaven" seems too limiting a term in the present case, evoking only images of paradise and perfection, and none of the destructive forces that play throughout Schubert's work. Nothing in the total range of human feeling is outside of Schubert's power: have effervescence (*Abschied, Fischerweiser*) and desolation ("Wegweiser," "Wirtshaus") ever been conveyed more vividly, more directly? But in the ultimate analysis, it is not the human passions themselves, but the directness with which the passion is expressed, that points to the specific type of Innigkeit we are trying to identify. The Schubertian hero speaks with intense clarity precisely because that is the way he inherently sees the world. The effect is of someone who, having been set down briefly among us and thus less accustomed to the world than we are, sees it more lucidly. Wordsworth, in *Intimations of Immortality*, speaks of children having this power, because they have come more recently than adults from immortal realms.[6] Schubert's style retains the lucid tone of Wordsworth's children while concerning itself with adult emotions. In his human incarnation, the Schubertian hero feels in the ordinary human way, while at the same time he is able to rub off the film that envelops everyday reality for the rest of us, and to cut through to a primordial essence. This idea may be best understood if we turn momentarily to an example of Schubert's instrumental music, where the complicating factor of an explicit situation has been eliminated. In the Moment Musical, Op. 94, No. 2, there is no actual protagonist to be identified; we cannot observe a behavior, and yet we hear a longing, an exhilaration, a despair (Example 14.2). Above all, we hear a voice, a sound of pure limpid lyricism. This sound embodies the specific kind of Innigkeit we have been trying to define—a spirituality that comes on unbidden because it is so totally native and instinctive; not acquired through practice, not induced by some exceptional experience, it thus manifests itself effortlessly and spontaneously; it flows forth. Schumann's brand of Innigkeit seems more accessible to us because it is so eminently the product of a consciousness we live with from day to day, namely the human heart. Still, Schubert's style reminds us of those flashes of illumination that occur to us every now and then, when the "immortal element" in our consciousness is upon us. And conversely, listening to Schubert's music enables us to experience those flashes in more sustained chunks of time.

Example 14.2: Schubert, Moment Musical, Op. 94, No. 2

Voice of Faith: Bruckner

Bruckner's spirituality seems tangibly Christian in view of his proverbial faith and the fact that his symphonies, no less than his church works, were, by his own assertion, glorifications of "my dear God."[7] The imagery of the symphonies, too—from the string tremolo openings to the massively choired apotheoses, is easily interpreted in conventional religious terms. Nevertheless, the Bruckner symphony is not liturgical: it follows a conception of its own time, which is the narrative design of the Beethoven symphony and what that design connotes of a process leading to transcendence. If Bruckner's work has any links to the medieval past, it may be seen in the way his symphony-type re-creates in musical terms the spiritual quest which forms the basis of the 12th- and 13th-century grail stories. Implicitly stated in the one type as in the other is the important Christian message that faith is well in hand as long as it is being reexamined and renewed; the road of faith is in constant need of being traveled.

Authors of grail romances had the habit of representing their quests, however spiritual and Christian their ultimate didactic value, as action-packed adventures, a sequence of episodes full of color and swift movement. Bruckner ignores this strategy almost entirely. Repressing virtually every sign of what had been understood and practiced as "musical action" since the later 18th century, he writes first and last movements at slow speeds, organizes material in block-like sections, offers little, if anything, in the way of transition. Except for the scherzo, the Bruckner symphony is static and monumental, the very opposite of action. But this clearly serves to strengthen an impression of the quest experience as something essentially internal and psychological: from Bruckner's example we gain insight into a unique musical treatment of the Innigkeit vision, for the effect is not of motion forward—of a protagonist in active pursuit of a goal—but of events passing before and around him. And these "events," so-called, may be nothing more than the outward projections of inward states of mind—the protagonist's thoughts and feelings felt so powerfully within him that he experiences them as if "occurring" to him from without. At the opening of the ninth symphony we hear the gathering of mysterious, inchoate forces (tremolo strings, muted and fragmented horn calls). These sounds draw closer and take on more definite shape with the announcement by the horns in unison of the first recognizable melodic idea. As the horns split into rich harmonies and a sighing motive moves urgently upward, we have a sense of approaching illumination, of the onset of the first instance in the piece of blinding, overpowering awareness. This moment comes in the form of an octave-leaping theme proclaimed fortissimo by the entire orchestra and followed by a titanic full cadence in the home key. The immense power having been felt at close range, it begins almost immediately to dissipate (pizzicato strings in overlapping downward motions), and it will be quite some time into the first movement before a similar amount of energy accumulates. A strictly Christian interpretation would view these waxings and wanings as the drawing near and slipping away of godlike feeling; the final apotheosis of the movement would then be a solid establishment (or reestablishment) of union with the divine. But whether taken in an ontological, Christian or a psychological, Romantic sense, the Bruckner symphony conveys an experience of manifestly transcendent character; it is meant to be the imaging of an individual in search of oneness.

Since the symphonies of Mahler are conceived with the same end point in mind as Bruckner's, it is of interest to consider briefly how vastly different are the means they employ for getting to the end point. Mahler's continuities involve such emotional extremes—are so action-packed, so volatile, so full of tumult—that he seems clearly to belong with the "melodramatists." The essential difference between the Mahlerian and Brucknerian quests may be viewed as revolving symbolically around the problem of belief: Bruckner portrays the search of one who is already a believer; Mahler portrays the search for belief itself, hence the crises, the reversals, the underlying anguish of the journey. The anguish is directly related to the quester's sensuality, which, in keeping with traditional ethics, is contrasted unfavorably with spirituality and is thus the blocking force to transcendence. Whereas Wagner in *Tristan* proclaims the sensual and the spiritual to be mutually reinforcing principles, Mahler sees them as naturally antagonistic. One might say of the Mahlerian hero that his quest is the desperate search for Innigkeit made by an inveterate "melodramatist." The transcendent end point of the Mahler symphony thus marks the triumph of spirituality over sensuality, though because the effort to reach the end point has been fraught with conflict, and because, also, of the melodramatic protagonist's basic nature, much sensuality has been expressed along the way. Curiously, both symphonic types— the Mahlerian as well as the Brucknerian—support a spiritual vision rooted in Christian ethics. Brucknerian transcendence serves as a straightforward and unclouded reaffirmation of Christian redemption. Mahler's expression of breakthrough is a displacement of the Christian archetype of man's Fall and ultimate salvation: in one work after another, Mahler places images connoting triviality, decadence, and grotesquerie in a musical world of cosmic scope, in an effort to show how modern, sensual man, in spite of significant lapses in moral strength, struggles to hold on to an exalted vision of reality. This conception is already prefigured in Liszt, whose style (indeed, whose very career) seems to embody the capacity of the new European of the 19th century, mired down in banality and given to excess as he can be, nevertheless to scale the heights from time to time and reach for the sublime.

Voice of Experience: Brahms

Examples such as Liszt's no doubt served to confirm Brahms in the conviction that grandiosity had replaced grandeur in mid-19th-century art. In order to preserve true grandeur of feeling, it was necessary to re-invent the older heroic imagery. Brahms's commitment to the past has encouraged a fairly widespread idea that he was interested merely in pouring old wine into new bottles. His detractors have criticized him for being out of step with his own time: a classicist in Romantic clothing, a master of extraordinary technical command with little in the way of genuine inspiration and vision. It seems clear enough that Brahms was not particularly comfortable with much of the "visionary" aspect of Romanticism—notions of transcendental experience and ecstasis, for instance—but that is no reason to believe that he fashioned a style from negative considerations—out of rejection of the prevailing aesthetic of the day.[8] If 18th-century equivalents are readily found for his musical images, it is only in isolation—that is, taken one by one—that such images might appear "conventional." When images and gestures are powerfully combined in the context of a large-scale work, it is more than likely that they will yield some new significance, some as yet undiscovered insight. What repeatedly emerges from Brahms's work—from the Brahms style as a whole—is the "discovery," so to speak, of a new species of Innigkeit; moreover, Brahms's example is particularly instructive, because it serves to reveal Innigkeit as something totally distinct from transcendent sensation, which is an action or the state of mind resulting from an action, while the essence of Innigkeit is contemplation.

The violin concerto effectively shows how the species of Innigkeit we are speaking of is embodied in the Brahmsian musical fabric. Rarely have so many diverse images and gestures been compressed in so short a time frame (Examples 14.3a, b, and c). In quick order, we go from the pastoral peace of the opening to the urgent call of authority in m. 16, to the blazing glory of mm. 27 ff. No sooner has pastoral gentleness been restored (mm. 41) but it begins to be threatened by an uneasy mood in the low strings (mm. 69 ff.), which leads directly to the sound of alarm of m. 78. In addition to this rapid succession of events, there is something else: rarely has Brahms felt inclined to use such expressive extremes as he does in this work. Extreme gestures imply the presence of melodrama, and indeed, with the first entry of the solo violin, we are treated to an extraordinary moment of melodramatic violence, a truly demonic scream (mm. 90 ff.). The following thirty-odd measures are spent trying to dispel this outburst, and this is fully accomplished with the return of the opening theme, now outfitted with such a dulcet, floating support of cellos and horns that one has the impression that pastoral peace has been transformed into the ultimate serenity of paradise. Within a few measures, Brahms has brought us from one extreme to the other, from one form of the sublime to its polar opposite, from the terrifying to the heavenly. Uncharacteristically for him, Brahms is dealing here with "sudden ultimates"; he seems to have involved himself in the very "momentary-god" experience he is reputed to like to sidestep. But then we must ask how much of the entire movement is actually spent with these "ultimates." The fact is that the solo violin makes its "forces of darkness" entry in m. 90 and never appears in that guise again, while the heavenly music, though less momentary than the demonic scream, does not represent the general climate of the piece, either. With genuine melodramatic music, by contrast, we expect the demonic and heavenly images to predominate: Brahms evidently prefers not to live in a land of expressive extremes. Given, therefore, the exceptional nature of extremes in Brahms's work, one is prompted to ask why they figure at all. The answer must be that they are included because the action of a large-scale work is, in Brahms's way of thinking, *inclusive*: he means to portray a world in which every kind of action and feeling can find a place. At the same time, not all the actions and feelings presented need necessarily be shared by the "Brahmsian hero," the sentient subject whose voice is transmitted through Brahms's style. To hear that voice properly is to be able to extract a "primary tone" from Brahms's imagery and to have a firm sense of how the composer goes about relating his images and integrating them into a unified whole.

Example 14.3a: Brahms, Violin concerto, Op. 77, mm. 78–84

Example 14.3b: Brahms concerto, mm. 90–94

Example 14.3c: Brahms concerto, mm. 132–142

Brahms's music is characteristically unmelodramatic, not only for the reasons given above, but more so for the fact that it does not *move* melodramatically— it does not undergo radical changes, it does not work by shock or surprise. At the beginning of the violin concerto, the sequencing of events is rapid, as earlier stated, but it is also smooth and logical. Even the demonic scream, striking as it is, involves a chain of preparations, the uneasy strings of mm. 69 ff. anticipating the sound of alarm of m. 78, which in its turn gives ample warning of the oncoming violence. As mentioned earlier, this violence dissipates gradually over the course of the following thirty measures, and this is only one of a number of "imperceptible" transformations encountered during the movement, another particularly telling instance being the subtle blooming of the languorous, full-bodied secondary theme (m. 206) out of the delicate figurations of the solo part immediately preceding.

A continuity as elastic and logically motivated as this one recalls the fluency of Mozart (notwithstanding the differences in gesture and sonority). Could Brahms be a Classicist in Romantic clothing, after all? Although comparison with the great Classic composers is no mean tribute, it also does not bring us closer to discovering what is uniquely Brahmsian in Brahms. If his music truly represents the Innigkeit vision, then its uniqueness must somehow proceed from the specific kind of Innigkeit it expresses. What can our observations of the violin concerto tell us about this content? In one sense, a work of art within whose confines a multitude of images have been molded into a unity imitates nothing more nor less than our capacity to feel the diversity of things as an integrated whole. That could be said of any coherent entity which is composed of heterogeneous parts; it says nothing in particular of Brahms's work. True, this perception involves a level of consciousness deeper than the purely rational, but it also involves the participation of the senses; Innigkeit consciousness, by contrast, though it may have its beginnings in the rational and the sensual, is apparently conceived to transcend them both.

Yet the functioning of Innigkeit consciousness varies according to what one imagines the primary "seat" of consciousness to be. We have seen concrete evidence of this by way of the music of the three composers recently discussed. From Schumann's standpoint, the primary seat of consciousness is the human heart; with Bruckner it is religious faith; with Schubert a preternatural power which, according to Wordsworth, is strongest at birth and diminishes as we continue to live in the world. Bruckner's symphonies appeal to our sense of the traditionally sacred: we understand the world best at those moments when we feel closest to God. Schumann's music expresses in sustained form what it is to grasp the real essence of things when we love them unconditionally, when we open our hearts fully to them. Schubert's imagery captures that part of us that remains young, that part by means of which we continue to see the world with the direct penetrating gaze of childhood.

This last-mentioned conception, most clearly transmitted through Schubert's work, now helps us to pinpoint the notable features of Brahmsian Innigkeit. If, as Wordsworth says, most of the mysterious "gift" with which we are born is lost in the process of growing up—in the process of becoming "worldly"—we are led to wonder whether there is any compensation for this loss. Is this kind of Innigkeit replaced by any other kind? It is, indeed; and the replacement, so familiar and ordinary that it could be easily overlooked, is quite simply the deep sense of the world that we gain precisely in the process of growing up, in the process of undergoing, step by little step, the world's frustrations and exhilarations. This is what Brahms's music quintessentially expresses: the deep understanding of the world acquired through experience. We infer this content in his music—just as we do for any other composer—through his style, through his habitual way of working musically, his choices of musical images, the manner in which he combines images, his characteristic sound. In the first movement of the violin concerto, the images run the gamut of world experience such as it was conventionally understood in the mid-19th century: the demonic and the heavenly, together with less extreme states such as Arcadian quiet, concitato restlessness, pastoral languor, and festal grandeur, are all present. The net effect, however, of this range of imagery—the result, in short, of Brahms's combinations and choices of emphasis—reflects the distinct point of view of the Brahmsian hero, a type who has known both the highs and lows of life and opts for something in between. Just as the Schubertian hero speaks with the crystalline voice of innocence, so the Brahmsian hero speaks with the resonant but tempered voice of experience: the archetypal condition of having journeyed through the world, no matter how many the moments of pleasure and triumph, is to have felt the world's tempering effects. A characteristic sound for Brahms—heavy texture, low tessitura, descending motifs—is often called "autumnal," indication that the journey is well into its third quarter.

The business of attaching the label "Classical" to Brahms is both limiting and uninformative, but it does have the virtue of opening our minds to the fact that late 18th-century Classicism prepared the way for the Innigkeit conception of the inner life. Up until the later 18th century, the inner life was essentially composed of a number of discrete parts: there was the mind, governed by the rational principle; there was the heart, the seat of the "affetti umani"; and there was the immortal soul, preserved intact by conduct deemed proper according to Christian ethical standards. When, however, Schiller speaks of the "morally attuned soul," we feel that a new formulation has been born. This kind of soul is one overseen by certain individual prerogatives, the inner life of the new Classical man becoming a carefully constructed balance of the intellect and the heart: only a fluent interaction between these two seats of consciousness produces true intelligence. This Classical conception endows the inner life with a complexity it has not known before, though it must be recognized that in the spirit of Classical reasonableness, only a balance has been struck: the new entity (the morally attuned soul) is visibly made out of the old parts. With the Innigkeit conception, and talk of feeling out the world "in the deepest recesses of one's being," one has the impression of an extended and indivisible consciousness: the formulation has become mystical and Romantic. But as is the case in confronting so many Romantic formulations, one's explanatory powers are found to be wanting: it seems virtually impossible to describe, theoretically at least, either the functions or the emanations of this inner life. It is not even clear whether the term "perception" is more appropriate than "emotion" or "spirituality" to describe the quality of consciousness in question. Perhaps the quality embraces all three concepts in one, in which case it may best be called "deep understanding" and left at that.

Nevertheless, the Brahmsian phase of Innigkeit may show the way to a more concrete formulation than the Romantics themselves might have troubled to make; for it stands to reason that an understanding that proceeds from having broadly experienced the world would involve the same faculties as come into play in everyday life, namely the reason, the human emotions, and the senses. If this is so, then the resulting entity could be construed as an amalgam of the three faculties just named, though they would be blended—one might say, fused—in such a way that their individual identities would no longer be recognizable. Still, the inclusion of an element responsive to sensory stimuli signals a conception of the inner life more richly layered than the Classical conception. There is also the implication that Classical "intelligence" is an awareness limited to things of this world, functioning especially well in social contexts, while the inner life envisioned by Innigkeit philosophy is capable of penetrating to greater mysteries.

One cautionary note is in order: in our eagerness to devise a precise configuration for this most all-embracing of conceptions, we may well have been guilty of an overdetermination. The vagueness of "deepest recesses of one's being" resonates with the very limitlessness of the idea, an effect that gets reduced when the formulation takes on any hint of materiality. The configuration just devised may well only apply to a view of the inner life represented best in Brahms's music, in which case it would more properly be described as a "seat of consciousness" equivalent to those identified earlier in connection with the styles of Schubert, Schumann, and Bruckner. Even in this more restricted form, the formulation has a decided usefulness. Finally, it should be repeated that Brahmsian Innigkeit shows the possibility of feeling "infinitely" about the world without there being a concomitant "momentary-god" experience, that is, a sense of sudden rapture. (Schumannian and Schubertian forms of Innigkeit, on the other hand, involve a measure of rapture—of momentary thrill—if only because the "insights" of the human heart and of childlike innocence come on spontaneously and immediately.) The separateness of rapturous (i.e., ecstatic) experiences from those of Innigkeit enables us indirectly to restate and thereby clarify the fundamental distinction between Innigkeit and melodrama. This distinction is more a question of process than of vision. Melodrama begins with the general condition of excitement, an excitement which can be made so intense under certain influences that it turns into the experiencing of overwhelming, ultimate significance; Innigkeit, by contrast, begins with the understanding of the ultimate significance of something, from which can (but need not) emanate a feeling of rapture. The connecting link of "ultimate significance" between the two processes confirms the place of melodrama and Innigkeit as the chief—and complementary—modalities of Romanticism.

That Romanticism offers art as a *logos*—a way of true knowing—is its radical and lasting contribution to Western culture. At one and the same time, art is elevated to a new level of meaning, and the meaning of *logos* itself is considerably broadened. Above all, the commitment to art is a deeply personal thing, an adventure made in solitude but rich in rewards for the solitary traveler. From the standpoint of traditional ethics, of course, this quest for ultimate significance independent of the conventional, socially authorized routes is something of a scandal. Even more scandalous is Wagner's proposition of arriving at *logos* by way of Eros. The priority that Romanticism gives to the individual principle over the social principle is destined eventually to result in a significant splintering of values, the effects of which we continue to live with today. Yet, in itself Romanticism remains a coherent ethic because it keeps faith with certain fundamental ideas, not the least of which are those just enumerated; it holds to its belief in ultimate revelation, in the power of feeling to bring about that revelation, in true love, in the boundlessness of the artistic imagination. In the final analysis, Romanticism's great strength is belief itself—or, perhaps more precisely, the kind of belief which grows out of an impulse to "romanticize" the world. We cannot forget that the Romantic attachment to what is alien and darkly mysterious points to seductiveness, not pain. We should remember that both Eros and Thanatos are forms of desire, not fear.

The business of turning fear into a promise of pleasure, whether that promise comes in the form of (1) an adventure, as with exotic and magical art, (2) a fulfillment of strong private passion, as with melodrama, (3) a fulfillment of childlike intimations of a spirit world, or of feelings of compassion or religious faith, as with Innigkeit, or (4) an actual contact with the sublime, as with the most metaphysical aspirations of the Romantic movement—this ingenuity on the part of Romanticism is at the heart of its genius. Yet, there are those who would say, with some justification, that the ingenuity itself signals a fatal weakness; they would call attention to Romanticism's persistent dependence on wish fulfillment, its willfulness in ignoring the unpleasant realities of everyday life, its need to escape the limitations imposed by any social system—limitations which might signify certain minor restrictions to one's freedom of action, true, but without which individuals could not reasonably be expected to function, let alone survive. Even a critic as sympathetic to 19th-century art as Northrop Frye will write: "Romanticism has a reputation for taking a facile or rose-colored view of things, and even great works of Romanticism sometimes show us a mental quest achieved without having passed through any real difficulties or dangers on the way."[9] It is true that Romanticism is often faulted, and perhaps rightly so, for having projected an object of desire that is not won through the normal human order of striving and hard work. However, we would do well to remember that these objections are mainly the reflections of the present century about the century before. To these objections the Romantic artist would most probably answer: "I am not unaware of the difficulties of everyday life; on the contrary, it is precisely with these in mind that I seek to provide through my art the means to transcend everyday reality and thereby hold out one of the few hopes of true redemption." It is very much an open question—and probably always will be—as to which perspective, the Romantic or the one prevailing today, offers a more satisfactory way of looking at and dealing with the world.

Notes

1. "Elevated" is placed in quotation marks, because here again we have a case of a traditional "ethical" prejudice, a question of the immaterial being prized above the material.

2. Quoted in Joseph Kerman, "How We Got into Analysis and How to Get Out," in *Critical Inquiry*, Vol. II, No. 2 (1980), p. 329.

3. Quoted in Joseph Campbell, *Creative Mythology*, Vol. IV of *The Masks of God*, p. 72.

4. Schopenhauer was much influenced by Eastern philosophy, as he himself attests. Of the Hindu Upanishads, he wrote: "[They have] been the consolation of my life, and will be of my death."

5. The archetypal example of this sort for modern Western culture is the brief presence of Jesus on earth.

6. Lines 85 through 128 of *Intimations of Immortality* read: Behold the child among his newborn blisses, / A six years' darling of a pygmy size! / ...Thou, whose exterior semblance doth belie / Thy soul's immensity; / Thou best philosopher, who yet dost keep / Thy heritage, thou eye among the blind / ...Thou little child, yet glorious in the might / Of heaven-born freedom on thy being's height; / Why with such earnest pains dost thou provoke / The years to bring the inevitable yoke, / Thus blindly with thy blessedness at strife? / Full soon thy soul shall have her earthly freight, / And custom lie upon thee with a weight, / Heavy as frost, and deep almost as life!

7. See Derek Watson, *Bruckner* in *The Master Musician Series*, p. 133.

8. Dvorak was once supposed to have turned to Brahms and said, "Oh Master, you have such a great soul but you believe in nothing!"

9. Northrop Frye, *A Study of English Romanticism*, p. 38.

15   *Age of Irony:*
Modernist Music

Histories of painting usually mark the "Modern Era" from the time of David and Goya, and the "modernist tendency" from the time of Manet and the Impressionists. Here, too, Impressionism will be represented as the first definitive step away from Romanticism and toward the building of a new sensibility. It is paradoxical that this essentially mild-mannered art should be the harbinger of such radical change: Impressionism seems to be a movement whose intentions are outweighed by its ramifications. Yet, part of the paradox is due to the incompleteness with which the Impressionist painters understood their own aims. On the face of it they intended only to please a public already greatly experienced in the business of looking at pictures; in reality, they were asking this same public to do something it could not immediately do, namely to adjust to a different way of organizing line and color on a two-dimensional surface. We today have no trouble in seeing Impressionism as coming directly out of the plein-air tradition of the Barbizon school and constituting another distinguished chapter in the story of pastoral expression. To most serious connoisseurs of the 1870s these flimsy, unprofessional, and undignified looking canvases, which were being perpetrated as high art, simply represented the lowering of standards.

In this example we see the beginnings of an all-too-familiar pattern—the breakdown in communication between artist and audience: increasingly a public otherwise prone to enjoying art and considering it an essential element of living finds itself embroiled in mystifying, if not altogether repellent situations. Who is to blame for this state of affairs—the artist for speaking a radical new tongue or the public for not being able to follow? The difficulty of deciding, in any given instance, which side is at fault only heightens the tension. Modernist art becomes by definition problematic; it enters as if permanently into a condition of crisis, and the condition itself grows to be a part of the artwork's essential content. Whether the core of the modernist problem is more a question of content than of form is not immediately clear. The vehemence with which both the musical and pictorial languages were radicalized around 1910 would indicate the latter. What we hear first and foremost in a piece like *Erwartung*, even when placed alongside an immediate predecessor like *Salome*, is its stark difference, its seeming abandonment of every traditional aspect of form. Strauss is a logical consequence of Wagner. Not so Schoenberg in his atonal mode; to claim otherwise from our present vantage point is to use the illegitimate privilege of hindsight. Schoenberg's music contains the *sine qua non* of modernism, the irresistible urge to strike a blow for the future, no matter how deep one's veneration for the past.[1]

To judge by this tentative characterization, however, one might conclude that the essence of modernism is nothing but a healthy spirit of adventure—the quality inherent in any moment or movement in history that has ever styled itself "modern." On that basis, the *Ars Nova* of Philippe de Vitry would qualify as a "modernist" event, as would the activities of the Florentine Camerata or Wagner's *Art Work of the Future*. No one would deny the great thrust forward that each of these cases represents in terms of the development of musical resources, but none of them, in the final analysis, makes a particularly instructive parallel for the events taking place around 1910. Nor do we learn much more by considering the notion that Romanticism, a potent force in music for a good hundred years, had finally outlived its usefulness, and that the new artist, in order to find himself—to claim his proper identity—must break with what he had known and set out on a new course. The idea of finding liberation through rebellion is as old as Zeus overthrowing Cronos and does not much serve in explaining the case at hand. If we wish to identify the specific ingredients of 20th-century modernism, we must simply look more closely at the specific historical and cultural circumstances that attended the opening of the 20th century. That is not done with a few strokes, but one thing can be proposed in advance of a fuller discussion: the artists setting out on their own "modernist" course did so with less help from the past than at any other time in Western history. Or to put it somewhat differently, the way things had been done pointed less clearly to the future than in any other period.

If there is any truth to this last idea, then perhaps 20th-century art—or more precisely, "modernist" art—is a beast of a very different color and should be considered as separate from all previous artistic endeavor. Perhaps the art historians are wrong to have joined 19th- and 20th-century developments in painting and sculpture under the rubric "modern." Perhaps Friedrich Blume's conception of a "Classic-Romantic" unity makes more sense than it is sometimes given. Formally speaking, Blume is right: Romantic music takes over all the vocal and instrumental genres that Classic music brought to fruition and, above all, maintains the tonal structure which works to ensure the coherence of these genres. "Modernist" music gives up the traditional tonal structure and is thus bent on inventing diverse and hitherto unknown modes of coherence. Conceptually speaking, however—in terms of the place art and the artist had come to occupy in the cultural scheme of things—Romanticism and modernism share entirely common ground. What they share is the prevailing view of art itself, which in the eyes of its practitioners remains nothing less than the surest way of getting to the ultimate meaning of things. Moreover, the picture of the artist and his mission as being removed from the sphere of routine affairs is by the end of the 19th century deeply entrenched in the popular as well as the artistic imagination.

In one very real sense much of the crisis of modernism may be traced back to this legacy of Romanticism, for if the Romantic vision of art as the supreme *logos* had not continued to hold firm, the modernist artist would have been able to carry his burden more lightly. As it stood, there emerged a new and acute self-consciousness, born of the discrepancy between the vision of art as ultimate revelation and the uncertainty as to what there remained to reveal. This self-consciousness in art had not had to await the opening years of the 20th century to come of age; it had already become a dominant factor in the Symbolists' perception of their historical position. The dilemma of Symbolist artists was double-edged: on the one hand, they were confronted with the question of what there was left for them to say if Wagner had indeed said it all; on the other hand, ambivalence and disaffection stretched even to Wagner himself, for there was the growing suspicion that his message might have been overextended and less important than it sounded.

Here, in the Symbolist example, we find later 19th-century art in the firm grip of an ironic mood, one which does not necessarily connote despair about the artistic future but suggests nevertheless a withholding of belief in any conventionally prescribed value. The irony of the Symbolist stance gives modernism a concrete identity. Art, its status as spiritual quest still solidly intact, is now stripped of romantic aura; the quest has turned into flight and predicament. At the beginning of the 19th century, the Romantic artist could declare his aims with the exuberance of one who knew they would be fulfilled; at the end of the 19th century, the new artist sets his aims high but with little hope of seeing them reached. And yet, in spite of this important difference in outlook, Romanticism and modernism form a curious alliance, locked together in their belief in art itself, in its significance as society's only true promise. It is no small testimony to the modernist's commitment to art that the quest will be pursued even in the face of small rewards—even if it means extracting from the morass of previously accumulated truths a mere scintilla of truth, even if the artistic results should prove fragmentary, unresolved, and meager by comparison with the sumptuous imagery of yesteryear. As for the new imagery itself, it will be gathered from the most diverse and unexpected sources. On examining the material presented in the following pages, we should have confirmed for us the fact that content—something envisioned, whether sharply or vaguely—precedes form. The drastic changes imposed on the musical language in the name of "modernism" in the first years of this century are ultimately a question of content, for art being a language of images, a need for fresh content engenders the search for new imagery.

Impressionism/Symbolism

In Chapter 8, where Impressionism was discussed as a late variant of the Arcadian archetype, it was said that the significance of Impressionism extends beyond the pastoral idyll to dimensions "more pertinent to modernist concerns." These dimensions will now be considered. Essentially, it is a question of responding to Impressionist images with a broadened awareness of what is meant by the "fleeting moment." From the idyllic point of view the "fleeting moment" is an experience of quiet beauty to be recorded and given permanence in a work of art. In a modernist frame of mind, however, we interpret the same Impressionist moment as more ephemeral than beautiful; such a moment is construed as the vanishing of loveliness. Symbolism builds on this connotation by viewing ephemerality in terms of meaning rather than in terms of experience: the fleeting moment becomes a symbol of human incapacity, a projection of our own failure to grasp the reality of the world in anything longer than a flash, a momentary intuition. What is left around these occasional glimmers of understanding is obscurity. In Monet's *Impression: View of Le Havre*, with its multiple differentiations of gray light and confusion of figure and ground, this fundamental Symbolist idea is given what may be called an Impressionist rendering, a conscious attempt to represent light, the archetypal symbol of clarity, as something hazy and ambiguous.[2] Shadowiness is no longer meant to be seen as the opposite of light but its *alter ego*; the former opposites interpenetrate to the point where it becomes impossible to tell where one leaves off and the other begins.

Debussy's *oeuvre* provides numerous musical parallels to this effect, with perhaps more potential impact than Monet's painting, in the sense that music is capable of recording the interpenetration of the shadowy and the luminous as motion, as transformation in process. *Pagodes*, the first of the set of three piano pieces entitled *Estampes*, is a particularly striking example. Although the atmosphere of the piece is largely built out of images borrowed from the East—the ever-changing pentatonic combinations, the explicit reference to the pagodas of Buddhism—the underlying vision is Symbolist inspired. Twice during the work, which is otherwise concerned with the soft, hazy murmur and blanket of static harmony that constitute the hallmarks of Impressionist texture, there emerges a succession of sharply delineated sounds—strict homorhythm, melody outlined in four octaves, *forte* dynamic. Clarity, brief and spasmodic, has arisen out of the enveloping cloudiness: as an image of our capacity to hold on to reality only in flashes, the pagodas momentarily appear in all their stark splendor, only to recede once again into the shadows. In *Voiles*, from the first book of Preludes, five luminous measures of pentatonicism break out from the surrounding whole-tone blur, their incandescence consumed almost before they had the chance to burn bright.

The effect conveyed in these examples is one of paroxysm—a spurt of physical, or mental, energy that can no longer be contained "below the surface." Debussy applies this effect repeatedly in his work and appears to have learned it from the example of Mallarmé's faun, who is alternately visited during his summer reverie by sudden illuminations and lapses of memory (if not total blanks).[3] Here, Impressionism and Symbolism are closely joined in their view of the artwork as a way—truly, the only way—of counteracting existential impermanence and our inability to hold on to the true meaning of things. This is a particularly life-and-death issue with Mallarmé, who never ceases to waver in his ambivalence about the ultimate significance of existence: is the universe totally sublime or utterly meaningless? Whichever it is, the poem continues to be our only salvation, the only hope of combating the void.

As captivated as Debussy is throughout his career by the brilliance, suggestiveness, and integrity of Mallarmé's art, his encounter with the work of another Symbolist poet, Maeterlinck, will prove more fateful in terms of the formation of his mature style. If Mallarmé's poetry is filled with the tension of the poet's urge to overcome the resistance of ultimate meaning, Maeterlinck's way of dealing with the mystery is softer, more resigned. In *Pelléas et Mélisande*, it is as if the human compulsion to know—or rather, to have answers—as dramatized in the character of Golaud, constitutes the chief evil in the world. In mock-naïve language whose negations and failures to say would seem to point to man's inability to find concrete answers, Maeterlinck suggests that Mélisande, of all the personages in the play, is most in tune with the universe precisely because she does not seek answers, because she refrains from asserting her will, refrains from active pursuits of any kind. In her very passivity, she embodies, by Western standards, a novel and even strange way of dealing with the world, one which leads us forward to a fresh insight as to what "the failure to say" could mean. Richard Langham-Smith shows how Maeterlinck's insight was shaped by a Pre-Raphaelite conception of an idealized woman—an "ange-femme"—through whose example silence signals not a lack of understanding but a profound knowing.[4]

Curiously, the Impressionists and Symbolists may have been headed toward this conclusion all along. From the beginning, they had resisted the full-blown expressiveness of Romanticism, no longer capable of believing in the Romantic dream. "Prends l'éloquence et tords-lui le cou," wrote Verlaine in his *Art poétique* of 1884 in a thinly veiled attack on Wagnerian grandiloquence. That Impressionists and Symbolists alike had taken to expressing themselves more moderately and tentatively than the Romantics was not only because they were less confident about understanding the immensity of it all, but, in a more positive sense, because deep down they felt that understatement was somehow closer to the truth. Now, here were the Pre-Raphaelites and Maeterlinck to confirm and extend this intuition. In Maeterlinck's drama, silence is not merely embodied in the person of Mélisande, it is a force that pervades the entire atmosphere, a mysterious underlying power that comes to feel like the source of everything. When he turns to setting Maeterlinck's drama as an opera, Debussy, to match this stillness, invents a music that approaches literal silence—a silence broken only, but then paroxystically, by Golaud's violence, as when Yniold is held up to the window and Mélisande is dragged along by her hair. As a consequence of these outbursts, the stretches of quiet music in the opera become full of disquiet, anticipation of impending disaster. Debussy returns to this mood in later pieces: *Nuages*, for instance, is dedicated entirely to a premonition of disaster which never comes, but turns into a festival instead. In a more general sense, however, Debussy's stillness does not necessarily signify disaster; it is, in fact, attached to neither a tragic nor a comic mood, since it is meant to represent something above mood, something prior to human experience. Indeed, it is meant to embody the source out of which experience is born, the unknown power lurking beneath the surface of "mere appearances."

This having been said, the paroxystic effect described earlier as an energy breaking through the surface is subject to reinterpretation. The shadowy areas surrounding the paroxysm itself were represented above as what surpasses our understanding, what remains veiled and closed off to us. This connotation continues to hold good, but with a difference, for now we are enabled to identify more clearly than before these veiled and mysterious areas: they become nothing more nor less than what lies underneath the surface, the "eternal ground of being," the primal source of world action and energy. So all-encompassing is this primal source that it will indeed surpass our understanding if we take active, intellectual—"Western"—steps to penetrate its mystery; we arrive at "knowing" it, like Mélisande, only through acknowledgment and affirmation. In extended portions of *Pelléas* and *La Mer*, Debussy brings us into knowledge of this source of being by re-creating it for us musically. *Sirènes* is the clearest example of all, for here the elements in question are combined in a discourse which is simplicity itself: the bubbling and rocking of the musical surface at the opening of the piece contains an energy which only for a brief moment at mm. 80–83 breaks through the surface in a compressed paroxysm of opulence and power and then dissolves into its bubbling and rocking once again.

The paroxysm of *Sirènes* is the one brief but totally unambiguous sign of what has been contained beneath the surface all along, namely, the life force itself—Eros, the desire to be. And with the mention of Eros, we come to realize that Debussy in *Sirènes*, and by extension in his mature large-scale works in general, has quite simply reversed the process of transcendence with which the musical masterpieces of Romantic melodrama have made us familiar. We must recognize, of course, that Debussy has not invented his bubbling, eddying music of near-silence out of nothing: such music has many antecedents, not the least of which are the images of the serene/sublime with which numerous ultra-Romantic works conclude. That they should so conclude is significant. The music of *Tristan*, in all its churnings and upward spirallings, is the dynamic action of Eros as it longs for ultimate merging with the mystery, for total oneness. Attainment of the longed-for state is thus appropriately accompanied by the sounds of harmonious quiet and rest. Debussy, on the other hand, characteristically begins with these sounds; for him, the mystery—the undifferentiated whole, the static principle—is not the endpoint but the *given*. *Sirènes* definitively changes the emphasis of the earlier melodramatic relationship between Eros and the mystery, Eros appearing only long enough to confirm the primacy of the "ground of being."

It is not, of course, that the Romantics did not recognize this primacy themselves—the animating, creative force, the "motion and spirit … that rolls through all things."[5] They chose, however, to dramatize its essence in terms of a quest, in terms of a spiritual experience of a distinctly human character, and to record, in all its excitement and dramatic conflict, the process by which the human being moves toward transcendence. Debussy records something more impersonal, something more in the nature of first principles—the dynamic born out of the static.[6] As such, he provides an alternative world view to Romanticism or perhaps a different emphasis of the same world view.[7] But even if only the latter case should prove to be true, the result is imagery—indeed, a total musical experience—of a strikingly different order. And the differences do not stop with individual images; they extend to questions of structure of the musical language itself. For if Debussy's music means, in the first instance, to reduce the sharp oppositions characteristic of Romantic drama, and even more, to embody nothing less than the ground of being (the static principle), the fundamental changes in tonal thinking that his later style represents follow directly from these expressive aims. Clouding and fragmentation of individual shapes, among other kinds of discontinuity in the musical discourse, already signal a certain degree of amorphousness, though the musical form, if it is to remain such, cannot be literally amorphous. In Debussy, amorphousness is ultimately withstood by structures which embrace a general forward movement and fulfill expectations of resolution. That means that tonality in its most fundamental sense has not been abandoned; but what remains is a far more static version of tonality, one that has had to leave the dynamic, common-practice version behind.

Primitivism

The influx of non-Western ideas into Europe, especially into France, had become something of a trend in the later 19th century, though we should be careful not to see in such a trend a uniform disaffection with Western values. Above all, there is no reason to credit a connection between 19th-century exotic art and modernism. Exoticism is a branch of Romanticism, an aspect of the wish fulfillment dream that harbors no aspirations to transcendence or to probing the deepest recesses of one's being; it means only to carry out the dream to the point of creating images of faraway places and pleasurably dangerous adventure. This is not to condescend to the general category of exotic art, which has produced its quantity of seductive masterpieces—songs of Gounod, Bizet, Delibes, *Scheherazade* of Rimsky-Korsakov, *In the Steppes of Central Asia* of Borodin, to mention the most familiar. French composers of the pre-Impressionist generation are known to have been particularly adept at integrating middle-Eastern and Spanish elements into their individual styles, and the French taste for exoticism is strong enough to have continued well into the 20th century, finding important outlets in

Debussy and Ravel. All this does not change the fact that exoticism is essentially an art of escape and maintains an exclusively Western point of view. It borrows alien imagery in the same spirit of delight and sympathy that the typical Western traveler takes in the sights of Meknes and Marrakech, Bali and Boroboudor— without making any real connection with the indwelling spirit of the culture or imagining that the way of life there could have anything to do with his own. But perhaps exoticism is a necessary phase of contact with the alien culture before anything of consequence can rub off. In that sense, and without sharing anything of the later modernist view, exotic art could be considered a preparatory step for what happened in France close to the end of the century.

So far our discussion has centered on modernist art that draws from non-Western sources of "high culture." What distinguishes the movement known as Primitivism is that it is strongly attached to the artifacts and functions of "traditional" or archaic societies—societies which, relative to those of the West or of India, China, and Japan, have, so to speak, not, or only partially evolved. The initial impetus in Primitivist art is felt in painting—first, with Gauguin in the 1890s ("Barbarism," he said, "is for me a rejuvenation"),[8] and then a decade later with the Fauves, together with a mounting interest shown by a number of artists living in France for the African and Melanesian works exhibited at the Musée Ethnographique de Paris. Yet, while the high colors and flat surfaces of Gauguin and the Fauves constitute a clear departure from Impressionism, the decorative effect of their work may bring it short of "barbarism." In Gauguin, in particular, the aura of stasis and mystery that surrounds his Tahitian pictures types them as yet one more phase of Symbolism. It is only with Picasso's *Les Demoiselles d'Avignon* (1907) that the content of Primitivism gets delivered with full force. Six years later Stravinsky's *The Rite of Spring* will supply *Les Demoiselles* with a precise musical parallel.

What distinguishes the Picasso and Stravinsky works is the ability they have of bringing elemental power out into the open. In Debussy's work, primal energy comes in the form of near-silence; it is essentially suggested, contained mainly beneath the surface. In *The Rite of Spring*, the power is overt, blatant, there is no escaping it. There is no escaping the fact, either, that the last vestige of Romantic rapture has disappeared. Has the sweet harmoniousness of Romantic sonority no longer a place in Primitivist works because the premise of the serene/sublime has ceased to have any hold over the imaginations of these artists? Debussy carried on an ambivalent relation with Wagner all his life and never entirely freed himself from the "ghost of old Klingsor."[9] Stravinsky, on the other hand, is the young composer who fell asleep at Bayreuth, impervious from the start to Klingsor's charms.[10]

In *The Rite of Spring* Stravinsky relies on the anecdotal stimulus of a pagan ritual to focus his musical ideas. But both the "pagan" and "ritual" elements have ramifications beyond the work itself. The series of actions which make up the plot of the ballet, in which the life of the Chosen One is exchanged for the rebirth of Spring, dramatizes the oldest conception of human history—the myth of the eternal return. At the center of this myth is the basic observation that "life lives on life" in an inevitable cycle of destruction and creation: the eternal law has it that something must be lost from the world in order that something be gained. For the so-called higher religions, this is not an eternal law, but simply a law of nature, one that is transcended when man envisions a more permanent end—a state beyond nature—and works toward achieving that end. The chief aim of the higher religions has always been to show how man can avoid temporal pain and transcend the ills of the world. But primitive religion accepts nature as an eternal realm and takes its law as the definitive truth, which it is man's sole function to maintain and carry out. As Campbell has written:[11]

There never was a time when time was not. Nor will there be a time when this kaleidoscopic play of eternity in time will have ceased. There is therefore nothing to be gained, either for the universe or for man, through individual originality and effort. Those who have identified themselves with the mortal body and its affections will necessarily find that all is painful, since everything—for them—must end. But for those who have found the still point of eternity, around which all—including themselves—revolves, everything is acceptable as it is ... The first duty of the individual, consequently, is simply to play his given role—as do the sun and moon, the various animal and plant species, the water, the rocks, and the stars—without resistance, without fault; and then, if possible, so to order his mind as to identify its consciousness with the inhabiting principle of the whole.

What is so striking about primitive thought, because so remote from our own, is the impersonal nature of its conception of evil: evil is simply a given of the world, a necessary alternative to good, and was not invented for the purpose of causing suffering, especially human suffering. It is not visited on man capriciously or unjustly, since it can always be explained as the result of human error or misunderstanding which it is then the responsibility of the community to correct. Primitive myth has little if any time for pity and lamentation, for it gets directly to the business of translating suffering into appropriate action—action which will deal with the error that brought out the evil in the first place. By such a view, human intervention can have an effect on the balance between good and evil, though never eliminate evil altogether. Above all, primitive religion clearly recognizes the harshness of the human condition but not as something that happens directly to *me*; thus, it does not concentrate on the emotional response to that condition, preferring instead to anticipate evil rather than react to it, in an effort to mitigate it.

The human emotional response to harsh fate, as expressed in epics and tragedies since the time of the Greeks, constitutes the basis of the tragic vision in the West. Indeed, the precise texture of this vision, with its focus on pity and fear—but especially pity—is so deeply entrenched in the Western mind that it takes a very conscious mental effort—or perhaps the shock of a work like *The Rite of Spring*—for us to realize that the emotions portrayed in Western tragic art are not inherent or universal, but shaped by the culture.[12] *The Rite of Spring* does not work along the traditional tragic/comic lines; nor does its brand of modernism involve irony, either, for irony is the product of a personal relation to the world, while *The Rite of Spring* functions on a plane that bypasses the personal. Stravinsky's ballet hardly advocates reversing a 3000-year-old mental trend and embracing the primitive perspective, but it does suggest that contemporary society stands to learn something from that perspective, insofar as primitive philosophy regards the human condition with a clear-eyed, unself-pitying emotion with which the modern European mentality has almost totally lost contact. The dispassionate element in primitive emotion comes from the fact that, unlike modern secular thinking, which places human desire—Eros—at the very center of the universe—and in so doing, identifies that desire (to paraphrase Campbell) "with the mortal body and its affections"—primitive myth sees the human element as just one of many orders involved in the eternal flux of good and evil.

It is *pathos*, then, which is absent from the emotional world of *The Rite of Spring*. *Pathos*, as expressed in traditional humanist art, is designed to move the spectator to identify strongly with the object or situation represented. Identification presupposes the arousal of sympathy, which turns to pity when the representation is vehement and tragic. But *The Rite of Spring* does not elicit pity, for its action is situated above tragedy in the Western sense, it does not lie in the field of personal suffering. In the second act of Monteverdi's *Orfeo*, the hero makes a heroic resolve: to risk everything—to make the supreme sacrifice—by descending into the underworld and pleading for the return of Euridice. But before he decides upon this action, he surrenders to lament, he weeps openly and bitterly for his loss. As the action is framed in *The Rite of Spring*, there is no room for lament; the proceedings move directly to the stage of the sacrificial preparations, they focus immediately on the momentous and the superhuman. Solemnity and monumentality, not lamentation, are the expressive order of the day, though it is more than understandable how the pounding rhythms of the famous "Rite chord" that accompanies the first rise of the curtain would not have been recognized in 1913 as solemn by an audience to whom solemnity in music meant something akin to the measured, larger-than-life strides of the French overture. Of course, the relentless energy of long passages of Stravinsky's score do ultimately invest the music with a larger-than-life quality; it is rather the violence and convulsiveness of the musical gestures which fail to conform to traditional notions of "monumental composure" and which thus require a considerable process of familiarization on the part of the listener before he will be able to hear in these gestures what Stravinsky would have him hear, namely the sound of solemn decorum.

The harsh and brutal character of this new decorum responds directly to that "pitiless" vision of reality which Stravinsky saw as constituting the center of belief and experience in archaic societies. From the general modernist standpoint, then, primitivism becomes an important vehicle for weaning the contemporary art lover away from his "sentimental" expectations with respect to art. If primitivism represents an extreme means of achieving this end, *The Rite of Spring* is quite certainly an extreme case within the framework of Primitivism. The later works of Stravinsky's first period are generally acknowledged to be a retreat from the position he established in *The Rite*. *Les Noces* has the relentless rhythmic propulsion and sharp accents of the earlier work, but the level of dissonance has been significantly lowered, perhaps because burlesque has largely replaced solemnity as the dominant mood. As for *L'histoire du soldat*, its small scale, both in terms of forces and format, together with the introduction of elements from a variety of traditions, reduces the primitivist impact while highlighting the effect of irony. Though it is true that the ironic attitude is by definition antisentimentalist, it is also true that irony maintains a relation with sentiment in the very act of calling it into question. Primitivism, on the other hand, at least the kind of primitivism envisioned by Stravinsky, has no relation to sentiment whatsoever.[13]

The Primitivist Voice: Bartok

Although *The Rite of Spring* is a striking example of Primitivism, and for that reason alone (not to mention its historical notoriety) is a useful means of introducing the Primitivist ethic, it is, as already noted, an extreme example. Being so, it poses the danger of diverting us from recognizing other, less radical alternatives as qualifying for Primitivist status. *The Rite* may be a less than ideal standard against which to measure Primitivist influences in early 20th-century art, if only because of the specificity of the ballet's scenario. Bartok deserves, no less than Stravinsky, the labels "modernist" and "primitivist," even though no specific reference to archaic society is to be found throughout his work. What will be found instead, and constantly, are the references to the peasant culture of his native Hungary, a kind of culture which, falling midway between the archaic and the courtly/urban types, can be properly called "semi-evolved." Bartok's case, as opposed to the scenario of *The Rite of Spring*, reminds us that Stravinsky's primitivist style builds on a similar "semi-evolved" source, Russian peasant music. We are also reminded that Stravinsky turned from being a primitivist quite early in his career, while Bartok never broke with his peasant connections. Stravinsky's motivations for taking the course he did may be due to a fear that Russian peasant music had lent his style too definite a personality; he is known to have once assessed Bartok's identification with Hungarian peasant melody—in spite of the general admiration he possessed for Bartok's work—as excessively dependent. Ultimately, both composers' decisions are understandable in view of the nature of the relationships that developed early on between them and their folk material—the one selective, the other comprehensive. Bartok's attitude toward peasant music is both more traditionalist and enduring than Stravinsky's by virtue of its function in shaping a total world view. Stravinsky's reluctance to embrace any single world view is symptomatic of a cosmopolitan and detached kind of modernism.

An important lesson to be learned from Bartok's music is that *pathos, pace* Stravinsky, can have a place in primitivist expression, after all. It may be more to the point, in fact, to invoke the name of Mussorgsky than that of Stravinsky when defining the precise nature of Bartok's primitivism. Mussorgsky is usually typed a "nationalist"—in keeping with his period and with one of its dominant philosophies. But he is more than that, if what is meant by nationalism is, in the first instance, an *ethos* which seeks to raise the people of a certain ethnic type to heroic status, and in the second instance, a *pathos* which seeks to record the joys and sorrows of that same people. In both instances, the common ground is ethnicity, the focus on a group defined by its locale and local history. Mussorgsky moves beyond the local to the "universal," for, although the basis of his style is Russian, even aggressively so, the music is finally the expression of a communal *pathos* whose main order of business is that of recording not the joys and sorrows of a stated nationality, but rather those of the entire class of social subordinates. This class, which clearly cuts across national lines, just as clearly points to the strong demotic core of Mussorgskyan expression.

In this matter of communal *pathos*, Bartok figures as Mussorgsky's direct descendant. Human interest in the peasantry and their everyday life, intimations of the peasants' collective destiny, affirmation of their intrinsic worth, but with the distinct aim of drawing them unadorned, warts and all—these ideas the two composers share in common. Where Bartok's conception diverges from Mussorgsky's is in its primitivist emphasis. For Mussorgsky, the central aesthetic aim is still oriented toward expression of the full range of human emotion, while at the same time the Christian ethic of "humilitas to sublimitas" continues to be a central theme, though in somewhat reworked form. The ugliness and freshness Tchaikovsky noted in Mussorgsky's style is intimately connected to Mussorgsky's belief that the sublime lies in the lowly—even in the grotesque—and that the truth of that thought will be revealed to us only through our compassion.[14] With Bartok, sublimity is exchanged for a far older concept: his picture of reality, while including human emotion, places it not at the center of things but rather into a relation with something more comprehensive. What Bartok envisions is not the cosmos in the traditional Christian sense—that is, the physical universe plus an immaterial beyond—but something more akin to primitive thought: a cosmic feeling captured in the earth itself. In an episode from Agatha Fassett's revealing biography of Bartok's last years, the three principals of the book—Bartok, his wife Ditta, and the author—are strolling in a Vermont woods on a warm summer's day when they suddenly come into a clearing.[15]

"The herd is not at home," [Bartok] remarked with distinct regret. "But they were here yesterday." He pointed to the big dark droppings in the short grass. "Dung," he said, using the strongest of Hungarian words, the one I had never expected to hear spoken aloud, let alone articulated with so obvious a relish in its substantial rhythm. I tried to look unconcerned, but Bartok detected my embarrassment. "It didn't occur to me that you might be offended, although I should have known."

"What a pity," he continued with sympathy, "not to be able to feel the strength and purity of real words, words that stand for the very thing they are expressing. How vulgar substitute words are, by suggesting that they cover something ugly or evil. These words were accepted naturally by people who lived in close connection with the earth ..."

He sang then a little song full of those startling words, pronouncing them as clearly and roundly, with such uncompromising force, that it seemed miraculous how rightly they blended into the melody ... the joyful rhythm, so accurately repeated as one verse followed another, rising and falling as naturally as one's own breath.

Bartok's country song is clearly not identical with the "sweet bukolikos" of Theocritus which initiated the pastoral tradition. In a classic reversal of the definition of ugliness, Bartok attempts to show that what is truly ugly is the false veneer with which "civilization" has covered over the rude strength and beauty of the creations of country people. Bartok's interest in the peasants is not in their joys and sufferings *per se* (as it is with Mussorgsky), but in their values, in the unencumbered clarity with which they view the world. And there is no question that for Bartok this clarity derives directly from their "close connection with the earth": the earth is intensely alive, and thus contains life's secrets.

In another passage from Fassett's book we read the following:[16]

[Bartok] sat down again, and leaning forward, dug his hands into the pine needles at his feet. "Must be knee deep—the accumulation of centuries, I suppose." As he spoke his voice was resonant even at its quietest. "I don't imagine that you two women would care much to have your floors covered with this kind of carpet, but you can be sure that it took more time and more work to make than even the most precious of hand-woven rugs. Sun, rain, frost and snow and wind beating down incessantly on these trees above us, as the seasons rapidly turned, the leaves and needles falling, dying, making room ... for the numberless new ones that were born in their places—these elemental things—and don't forget the bugs and birds and worms, too, helping the process along in their own ways, for they all have taken part in the creation of this pungent-smelling carpet composed of equal amounts of life and death."

As we listened to him there in the summer night this first time, his words unfolded before me a mysterious abundant existence until then unknown to me. And by the end of the summer this recurrent theme of his had become so familiar that I myself began to hear those hidden sounds, that hidden movement beneath all surfaces, dead or alive.

These hidden sounds and motions are doubtless what Bartok's music makes heard and felt in the soft murmurings of his "nocturne" movements (String Quartet No. 5, movements 2 and 4) and in the harsher, more frenzied buzzings of certain scherzi. But Bartok's essays in nature painting, however much they confirm his love for peasant life and thus assure him a solid place in the hallowed tradition of rustic pastoral, do not define his *style*, any more than does his persistent use of Hungarian peasant melody and dance-types. Or rather, all these serve to *describe* the style, but they do not explain its real content; indeed, they have the effect of leading our minds away from the fact that for all of Bartok's liberal borrowings of the source material, his style is a thoroughgoing transformation of it. We need only look at one of his folk song settings to see where the folk-song ends and Bartok begins. The sustained energy of the last movement of the fifth quartet, to take only one example, takes much from the vigor of Hungarian dance music, but it is not synonymous with that vigor; the specific energy, variety of means, and complexity of that piece are Bartok's doing.

The cardinal point to keep in mind here is that we are in the presence of an authentic artifact of 20th-century European high culture, not an imitation of a product "rooted in the national soil." Though this point is obvious once it is said, it can be easily obscured by the enthusiasm and seriousness with which Bartok has embraced the source material, along with its basic world view. It is in this last respect, in particular, that the primitivist of the Bartokian stamp goes beyond his spiritual forbears, for while rustic pastoral aims to capture the peasant's personality and *Volkstümlichkeit* the entire range of his emotions, the primitivist is not content with anything less than taking over the peasant's very way of looking at the world. That Bartok has done exactly this is absolutely clear from the passages quoted above: the fervor with which he holds forth before his women companions about the earth's hidden wonders leaves no doubt that the image of nature and its cycle of creation and destruction has come to be for him one of life's deepest and most inspiring truths.

We would expect that this conception would figure as an important content in his style, but it is not the total extent of the content: the music expresses more. In order to understand why this is so, we must ask ourselves once again just who the primitivist is; we must know precisely where he stands with regard to the objects he admires. All primitivists are joined in their belief that the viewpoint of rustic society is healthier than that of sophisticated European society and that Europeans would do well to learn its eternal lessons. But when all is said and done, the primitivist is not a member of rustic society. He may succeed in getting deep into the peasant mind, even to the point of adopting the essence of the peasant world view and making it his own. But this world view cannot constitute the extent of the primitivist's mentality, if only because he continues to carry, willy-nilly, his urban dweller's cultural baggage, with all that connotes of social sophistication, inner conflicts, emotional repression, overeducation in false and outworn values, ambiguous and uncertain thoughts about the world and its future.

Bartok, of course, is aware of the distance separating his culture from that of the peasants: he knows his place. But this awareness only adds to the irony of the situation, for he realizes that the central *ethos* of primitivist art, which is that of replacing contemporary European values with the healthy viewpoint of an archaic or semi-evolved society, will always be subject to limitations, the limitations being directly related to the inability, not to mention the unwillingness, of the contemporary European to deny his own culture, to unlearn what has already been learned. Bartok is himself one of these contemporary Europeans, as his modernism unequivocally attests. Exactly how all of these ideas get translated into his musical imagery, however, is not so unequivocal. Are the harshnesses of Bartok's style directly explained by what the contemporary ironist sees as the dissonances and imperfections of contemporary urban life? Or do they merely reflect the "beautiful rudenesses" of peasant life? Or are they due to the ironies inherent in trying to reconcile the two divergent cultures in question?

One thing is certain: the breadth and complexity of Bartok's large-scale designs are in no way the work of Hungarian peasant music, they belong strictly to the Western tradition. That these complexities, over and above those encountered in traditional Western music, are the result of a failure (more likely a refusal) to work out matters according to the traditional modes would appear to conform to that ironic element in modernist thought which believes in the possibility of only partial solutions. But the irony of a partial solution need hardly be a bitter irony; there is a redemptive side as well, and the redemption is that, in the face of everything that militated against finding it, a solution, however partial it may be relative to the total sublimities of the Romantic past, has been found, and realized. And Bartok's solution must be no small redemption if we listen to the numerous voices that have been raised in recent times to proclaim him the most "universal" of 20th-century composers, the one to have fashioned the most satisfying synthesis. Indeed, he has managed to combine the music of two divergent cultures to an extraordinary degree, and his primitivist optic has been wide enough to include communal *pathos* as well.

If we were to take Bartok at his word, we would have to conclude that his musical *ethos*, in an ideal world, would have been to make his contemporary language speak as simply and clearly as folk melody and dance. Perhaps he has accomplished this in some of his folk-song settings. But his large-scale works bear witness to a reality rather than to an ideal, namely that of the contemporary composer's inescapable destiny (inescapable because it is the result of a cultural legacy) to speak in the complex terms of his own time and place, to express an ambiguous and even anguished vision of the 20th-century urban West. Because Bartok's style, from very early on, is inextricably linked to Hungarian peasant music, it is difficult to know whether to characterize his synthesis as a modernist transformation of the source material or as an integration of the source material into a modernist language. The latter characterization may finally be closer to the truth, in which case his achievement could be termed a "modified *ethos*" and summarized as follows: to the extent that the power of Hungarian peasant music courses through Bartok's style, modernist expression has succeeded in creating a "primitivist hero" who speaks with exhilaration and emotional directness: and on this primitivist hero rests the hope that sophisticated European society may yet be invested with renewed health.

Viennese Expressionism

The paradox of Expressionist music is that of all modernist modes of expression, it presents the most extreme transformations of the Western musical language without ostensibly borrowing anything from outside.[17] Expressionism has long been described as the logical conclusion of Romanticism—Romanticism in its final decadence, the underlying neurosis of German Romantic culture brought out into the open. Opponents of this view have argued that to take Expressionism to be merely, or even essentially, the final stages of Romanticism is to miss its unique content. Both views contain a certain measure of truth. On the one hand, it is difficult not to hear the echoes of Romantic melodrama in the hyperactivity of Expressionist imagery—in the peripatetic discourse of swoopings and swoonings, piercing screams and cascading sighs (not to mention the brooding murk of the textures, heavy with melodramatic atmosphere). At the same time, by dwelling on the Romantic connections of this discourse in terms of its gestures, we risk overlooking its radicalism in more formal terms—that aspect of Expressionist expressiveness which Romanticism could never have anticipated. Is Expressionism merely the reverse side of the Romantic coin, the Romantic dream of sublimity turned into strident nightmare, as has often been suggested? Such an opposition seems strident in its own right, an oversimplification of the case. An opposition, however, which is a genuine kind of relationship does have the virtue of clearly pointing to common ground between the two opposing terms. Since there is reason to believe that common ground is shared by the two conceptions in question, one approach to the problem of identifying the contents of Expressionism is to begin with the premises of Romanticism and to see to what extent Expressionism may be construed as a displacement of its predecessor.[18]

Let us, therefore, briefly review these premises. Romanticism is a vision of a spiritual transformation the end result of which is a feeling of oneness. Its *logos*, like that of mysticism, is totally personal, of a kind that must be experienced rather than known in the rational sense. Those who pursue such a *logos* will do so through the modalities of true love, communion with nature, and the experiencing of great art. Such modalities having been removed from the inhibiting and trivializing influences of society, the individual is free to find his real self and life's essential values.

In its disenchantment with this vision, modernism has tended to represent Romanticism as a dream of pure wish fulfillment, an illusion, a philosophy of escape. This assessment, as unfair as it is simplistic, has the ring of truth about it in one respect at least, which is that Romanticism provides no program for practical living. The Romantics themselves (or at least the more perceptive among them) would not argue this point; on the contrary, they would argue more subtly that the program they provide for leaving society and the practical world behind is for the sake of spiritual replenishment. The moments spent in the world of freedom (and one should claim as many of these moments for oneself as one can) strengthen us—they are our reward for the obligations, annoyances, reversals, and stark tragedies we must face in the world of necessity (the world to which common wisdom assigns the names "real" and "everyday"). Unfortunately, the precepts of Romanticism have often been mistakenly applied to practical living (sometimes even by Romantics who should have known better) and always with pernicious results. One such result—a side effect of Romantic thought that still seems to be with us—is the cult of artistic genius which has it that the artist, because of his exceptional gifts, is somehow above the social law—untouched by the rules of conduct that bind ordinary mortals. According to this kind of thinking, Wagner is justified in behaving like Wotan and Tristan and bullying his way past whole clusters of betrayed colleagues, benefactors, and intimates. At best, Romanticism is useless in dealing directly with the practical affairs of this world; its *ethos* is rather to better mankind by showing the way to the world of freedom and urging each of us to spend as much time there as possible.

Such an aspiration could presumably be called Utopian, but then Romanticism would hardly be the first philosophy to be guilty of Utopianism. The Enlightenment before it had displayed "an unquestioning faith in the reformation of the world." Voltaire could write in the middle of the 18th century (and Beethoven could still believe it at the beginning of the 19th century): *"Some day all will be well*, is our hope; *all is well today*, is illusion."[19] For the new modernists at the end of the 19th century, such a hope had itself become an illusion: the *mythos* of the perfectibility of mankind was fast being relegated to permanent obsolescence. When the Aufklärer and the Romantics looked out onto the world, they saw the same social evils that the modernists would see a hundred years later—hypocrisy, prejudice, greed, oppression and humiliation of the underclass, inability to harbor noble thoughts and feelings and express them sincerely. The Enlightenment solution was to look forward to the day when these social evils would have been eliminated and to work unceasingly for their elimination. The Romantic solution was to walk away from society and to create an environment of wild nature, true love, and poetry closed off from such evils. The modernists looked upon the Romantic solution as containing a glaring error: into this pure environment of theirs, the Romantics had introduced one inevitable impurity, namely themselves; for as a child of "civilized Europe," of his corrupted society, how could the Romantic artist imagine that somehow, he, unlike the ordinary citizen, unlike the Philistines, had escaped carrying the societal corruption in the innermost recesses of his being? The modernist artist was under no such illusion; he knew he was tainted like everyone else, and the best he could do was to fashion an art that reflected that incontrovertible fact.

For the modernist, then, Romantic art expresses inner life only at its best and most beautiful moments, not inner life in its entirety. Even when representing the most anguished and tragic situations, Romanticism contrives to cast them in a beautiful and exciting glow. In the modernist view Romantic tragic expression is not true tragedy, it is only tragic romance; it is an incomplete form of tragedy because it contains no part of tragic irony: or perhaps, more precisely, because what would have been experienced as tragic irony in ordinary life has been converted by the romanticizing spirit into the sublime. Try as one might to represent the Romantic position as an *ethos* designed to improve the world, albeit indirectly, by filling it with ravishing and inspiring images and in the process elevating those who come into contact with these images, the modernists will have none of it. The *ethos* of modernism is that the world becomes better when we face up to its—and our—imperfections, even if imperfection should extend to the artwork itself. In the final analysis, a partial solution with a total content is to be valued higher than a total solution with a partial content. In modernist terms, a partial content is clearly one that is too beautiful to contain the whole truth.

To the extent that Primitivism shares these views about Western culture and the place of art in the culture, it is a genuine modernist conception. But it also holds out the promise of notably improving Western culture by bringing in infusions of new life, beauty, and health from a culture with a better world view. Does Expressionism make any similar offer? The Primitivist artist finds fresh inspiration in the artifacts of archaic and semi-evolved societies; he uses these artifacts as direct models, even to the point of integrating them or parts of them into his own work. Where does the Expressionist look for similar inspiration? In the sighs, shrieks, and murky sonorities that make up much of the action of Schoenberg's and Berg's orchestra pieces, we hear the unequivocal voice of hysteria, we seem to have stumbled into a place of pure tragic irony, a place beyond redemption. "Beyond redemption" signifies the total absence of *ethos*, the impossibility of making things better. One has justifiable misgivings about an artistic vision that shows nothing more than the reality of imperfection. Since it is unimaginable that artists of the maturity and sensibility of Schoenberg and Berg could have fashioned an art with no ethical purpose, we must look further for an answer.

In fact, the art dedicated principally to tragic irony (extremely uncommon, if evident at all, in music prior to the 20th century) has traditionally fallen into two types: the cautionary tale and the kind of action represented by the darkest of the Greek and Elizabethan tragic dramas. First appearances to the contrary, the effects envisioned by both types are positive and hopeful—to be felt, if not immediately as such by the spectator, at least eventually. The cautionary tale effectively tells the spectator that if he behaves properly, unlike the characters of the tale, he will avoid having all the ills of the world topple down upon him. Expressionist art does not seem to be of this type, however, if only because it proceeds on the premise that we have already passed the stage where the cautionary tale can do any good: the ills of the world are already in our midst, "civilized" Europe is in a state of disrepair, we ourselves are seriously infected. Expressionist art presumably works more along the lines of Greek tragedy, which contrived, through the representation of fearsome and pitiful actions, to bring the spectator face to face with himself and thereby (at least according to Aristotle's theory of catharsis) achieve a purification. This age-old idea of the therapeutic effects of artistic experience (derived, almost certainly, from observations of ritual practices of therapy) comes to enjoy new life in the guise of Expressionist aesthetics. Expressionism is revealed to have an *ethos*, after all, which is: if we seriously wish to rid ourselves of our ills, we must begin by acknowledging their existence; and, what more effective way of doing that than coming face to face with an Expressionist artwork with all its harsh nightmarish action laid before us?

Mention of "therapy," of course, brings to mind Freudian science and the fact that it and Expressionism were coming to the fore at the same time. Before examining that parallelism, however, we should first explore a comparable parallelism between Primitivism and Expressionism, for it stands to reveal something essential, indeed unique, about the Expressionist viewpoint. What both share in their common disaffection with European society Primitivism seeks to rectify on a purely *societal* basis: a one-to-one exchange will be made between the values and artifacts of Western culture and those of a healthier culture outside the Western orbit. The standpoint of Expressionism—or at least that aspect of Expressionism expressed in the music—is more *personal* and the logic of its rationale more involved. As the Expressionists assess the ills of "civilized" Europe, these ills come in personal as well as social forms, and there is a clear cause/effect relation between the two kinds. Expressionism has much to say about the human inner life, which it views from a distinctly modernist standpoint. In the idealized Romantic view, the inner life is the deepest recess of our being, the mechanism which, properly stimulated, leads us to transcendent experiences and by which we understand life's deepest meanings. To the Romantic, although society is corrupt, the inner life of the artist and those who feel like artists remains pure. The Expressionist no longer harbors this illusion: the gifts of the artist do not afford him any special immunity as regards the state of his inner life; he is as much of a "civilized European" as the next person. Now the key factor linking the personal to the social in Expressionist thinking comes clear: it is "civilization" itself which is responsible for the ill health of the European's inner life (of his *psyche*, as it will henceforth be identified by Freudian theory). There was once a time in a bygone age when the Western psyche must have been healthy, when the individual was truly in touch with the deepest recesses of his being (as the Romantics liked to believe was true in their own time but were mistaken in believing so). In Freudian language, "deepest recesses of one's being" gets translated into "primal core of the psyche"; and it is precisely this primal core with which the individual loses touch in the process of being inducted into the mysteries of European high culture.

Encrusted within layers of social artifice, the primal core becomes inaccessible to the only one to whom it is of any use; and while this primal part of the psyche recedes further and further behind walls of cultivation and ultra-respectability, the psyche as a whole loses the function of its natural instincts: it ceases to feel spontaneously, to be able to distinguish between the essential and unessential. But this is not the worst, for the fact is that the primal core, as fiercely kept down as it is, fights for life; it cries out for its freedom, it struggles to break loose of its bonds. What has resulted from this, according to Expressionist thinking, is a communal neurosis afflicting an entire segment of the population, namely the educated, hypercivilized class of Europe. This situation points to serious emotional disability: a conflicted inner life, the individual set against himself, the human psyche a constant battleground between the forces of nature and the strictures of culture. Freud's aim is to get back to the primal self by way of a new scientific method of purification. Expressionism means to follow a method that Western art has used intermittently from the time of Attic tragedy: the business of holding up to the spectator the mirror of his own ills, so that he might recognize them as his own and thus take the first step toward effecting a purge.[20] In order to prepare the hypercivilized European for coming to terms with his predicament, the Expressionist artist devises actions which bear the essence of that predicament. So inward are the actions of Expressionist music that we can imagine hearing the primal self battling to break out of the emotional prison in which it has been held by a lifetime of respectability. In certain cases we are witness to the actions of female hysterics of the type who were Freud's first patients. At the very least, we hear the imitation of neurotic behavior.

Of all the musical products of early Expressionism, Schoenberg's *Erwartung* (1909) is the most explicitly Freudian. Subtitled "monodrama," but also referred to by the composer as "Angsttraum," this work of some twenty-five minutes' length portrays a woman in the deep throes of what today would be called an "anxiety attack." Very agitated already at the opening of the work, for having waited three days for her lover to show up, she becomes increasingly disoriented as she goes searching for him in the woods outside her house, and then collapses in complete hysteria when she trips over his body running with fresh blood. The typically Freudian aspects of the scenario are reflected in the number of mysteries left unsolved. It is never revealed how the man died, though there is the distinct possibility that the woman herself has killed him out of jealousy and is now returning to the scene of the crime in a state of shock.[21] Even more Freudian is the surreal, dream-like atmosphere surrounding the woman's actions and reactions; in the final analysis it is not at all clear whether what we have witnessed has really happened or is merely a product of the woman's hyperactive imagination. The treatment of the events seems a conscious attempt to reinforce Freudian notions of the vivid and distressing character of dreams and of their power, despite—but finally, precisely because of—the tendency of dreams to move away from the logical sequencing of waking experience in unlocking the doors to our inner selves.

Robert Craft has written the following on the Freudian overtones of *Erwartung*:[22]

The soliloquy is composed entirely of short phrases or anacoluthons; few grammatically complete sentences can be found in the whole text. The broken manner of speech suggests a patient on an analyst's couch remembering in discontinuous bits and snatches ... [This strategy] is the essential clue, I think, to an understanding of both the musical complex and the dramatic form.

The broken speech that Craft identifies as a key to the music of *Erwartung* extends to the Expressionist style as a whole, the chief ingredients of which George Perle has named as being (1) absence of key, (2) consistently dissonant harmony, (3) rhythmic asymmetry, (4) textural complexity, and (5) melodic angularity.[23] The combined interaction of these elements produces effects so daunting to the average listener that it is doubtful whether he has ever recognized in this music what the Expressionists intended him to recognize, namely the mirror image of his own psychological predicament. Over and above the general difficulties of the Expressionist style, *Erwartung* is particularly inaccessible because not only is there no letup from beginning to end, but even more, because no image, with the exception of the extraordinarily striking measures of motoric rhythm that join Scenes 3 and 4, is clearly differentiable from any other image.[24] Craft attributes one of *Erwartung*'s difficulties to a total absence of repetition. But the real difficulty in this regard stems from the paradox that while there is no repetition in a literal sense, there is much that is repetitive in terms of effect. Indeed, one may say that the continuous fabric of *Erwartung* is composed of countless variations of a single parabolic gesture.

Schoenberg's method of interweaving many strands of melody in a dissonant harmonic context proves the main impediment to the listener's ability to follow. But this composite prosody is complex, one feels, precisely because it is designed to correspond to the way in which the Expressionist artist imagines information to be processed by the psyche. The procedures of tonality bear direct analogies to the orders and phrase structures of rational discourse. In Schoenberg's atonal polyphony, images overlap, break off, pile up, and engage in non sequiturs in much the same way that we experience images in dreams: what we sense in Schoenberg's continuities is the action of an unconscious mind at full throttle. No element may be more indicative of this action than the vocal part in *Pierrot Lunaire*; by means of the hoots, swoops, and cascading cries of the Sprechstimme, the psyche, uninhibited and uncensored, finds a voice. Perhaps not since the time of the Florentine Camerata has the question of declamation as giving a vivid and faithful account of inner life been considered so seriously and acted upon so literally.

The central implication of the above discussion has been that Expressionism is responsible for taking no more than the initial step in the psyche's rehabilitation. Yet, Berg's two operas appear to carry the healing process of the psyche further along the way. On the face of it, both works look like cautionary tales about the dark consequences of obsessive behavior. The chief protagonist of each of the operas is best understood as a function of obsession, Wozzeck the victim of his inner demon, Lulu the obsessive object, the siren who both promises pleasure and leads to destruction, her own included. Berg finds the imagery to match the tragic-ironic tone: in *Wozzeck* the murky textures and lethargic, yet periodically convulsive, rhythms, along with the strident pianola music of Act III; in *Lulu* the garishness of the opening, the *Verwandlungsmusik* between Sc. 1 and 2 of Act I, the dialogues of Act II, Sc. 2. Nevertheless, neither opera stops with tragic irony, each being drawn into the realm of traditional tragedy through the softening power of elegy. In *Wozzeck* tragic *pathos* finds its most concentrated expression in the orchestral interlude following Wozzeck's death, a wordless lament by which we, the spectators (the surrogate chorus), testify to Wozzeck's worthiness of being pitied and thereby elevate both him and ourselves. Tragic *pathos* in *Lulu*, more diffusely spread through the opera by means of a recurrent love theme of ravishing iridescence, is an admixture of elegy and seduction redolent with ultra-Romantic associations—indeed, redolent with reminiscences of the Siegfried-Brünnhilde love music from the *Ring*. Comparison with Wagner, however, serves to point up a distinction between Wagnerian and Bergian conceptions: the tragedy in Wagner is followed by pure *ecstasis*, whereas in *Lulu*, ecstasis can never fully break loose of Expressionist irony. Reciprocally, however, ecstasis must be recognized as having had its part in softening the unrepentant edge of early Expressionism—in showing us that even the fearsome images of the psyche can be subject to the pitying impulses of the heart.

Although the soft—one might say, languorous—element in Berg's style may establish links with traditional expressions of *pathos* more readily than do Schoenberg's harsher and more active images, the fact remains that Expressionism, in all its manifestations without exception, takes *pathos* to be its chief motivating principle. In this respect, it distinguishes itself from Impressionism, Symbolism, and Primitivism, indeed, from every other major form of early modernist art. We need no explanations from experts in the field to realize that the characters represented in Expressionist stage works exist primarily through their emotions. If those characters behave strangely and irrationally—if the world they inhabit looks like a grotesque and lurid distortion of the everyday world—this is in the interests of showing us contemporary Europe underneath the smooth veneer; now we see Western culture as it truly is, with the masks of civility removed. But Western culture is ultimately interpreted by Expressionism in distinctly personal, not communal, terms. That is why the mad worlds created by Expressionist artists resemble nothing so much as bad dreams—the spontaneous and thus most deeply felt effusions of a disturbed inner life. Similarly, the wildly angular melodic gestures of the music connote nonrational behavior—raw emotion unqualified by any sign of self-control, the cry of a primal self too long suppressed—while the overlappings and fragmented utterances of Expressionist musical discourses correspond to the nonlogical and nonchronological narratives of dreams.

On several levels, then—in the traditional mode of the "human affections" as well as the more modernist mode informed by Freudian theory—Expressionism reasserts its prime allegiance to *pathos*. Even more, *pathos* is at the bottom of a specific Expressionist *logos*, insofar as the Expressionist artwork means not merely to express emotions but rather to embody the very mechanisms of emotion, to act out its functional anatomy. Yet, in the deeper sense in which Romanticism first envisioned the artwork as a *logos*, Expressionism assumes a characteristically modernist attitude. We implicitly and palpably feel the effects of this attitude in the difficulty of the Expressionist musical language—for many still today a difficulty amounting to impenetrability. Unquestionably, the chief cause of the difficulty is the atonality—the dissonant chromaticism which has severed all ties with the concept of tonal hierarchy and thus dispossessed its own tonal configurations of the capacity to generate a sense of beginnings, middles, and ends. Though this loss of formal structuring through tonal means does not rule out possibilities of compensating by other means, it severely limits the possibilities. In addition to contributing to the kind of musical discourse already discussed above, this strategy is consistent with the modernist idea of finding it difficult to extract ordered patterns of meaning from existential experience and in particular, to bring problems to a satisfactory point of resolution.

This failure to resolve becomes almost *de rigeur* in Expressionist works. The end of *Wozzeck* is doubtless the classic case, but the end of *Erwartung* may be even more instructive, in the way it brings words and music together to deliver a familiar but essential modernist truth. Toward the end of the piece, the woman, bending over her dead lover, alternately berates and speaks tenderly to him; for a few brief moments, Schoenberg provides her with lines that will enable her to sing from the "pitying impulses of the heart." At the very end, she suddenly imagines seeing him (or, if the "Angsttraum" is a literal and not metaphorical dream and she has only imagined him murdered, she may actually be seeing him walking through the door), and she says: "Ah, bist du da, ich suchte ..." (Oh, there you are, I was searching ...). We imagine the object of her search to have been her lover; but we cannot be entirely sure: it may have been some*thing* as well as some*one*. At this point the woodwinds tumble upward in a gesture of repeated spirals and then quickly trail off—a bold way to end because it is not a way to end by the standards of 1909. "Ich suchte ...," in combination with this musical gesture, forms an extraordinarily concise metaphor about the difficulty of grasping meaning. More specifically, the metaphor is an answer—or, at least, a challenge—to Romanticism's supreme confidence in the artwork as a quest which yields up at the end a magnificent resolution, a total fulfillment. The Expressionist artwork leaves the quest open-ended, which is to say that the significance of the quest is not in its fulfillment but in the questing. We must be careful at this point, however, not to blur a crucial distinction. The skepticism of the Expressionist artist regarding his own understanding does not apply to art directly but to the resistance of meaning itself. The world, according to the modernist, doles out its revelations very sparingly; the experience of grasping meaning is onerous and painful, and so the artist has no recourse but to pass that experience on to the spectator/listener by re-creating its essential qualities. However, like all modernist artists, the Expressionist believes that to the extent deep meaning can be captured, the artwork is the tried-and-true means, the saving grace.

Formalist Music

By formalist art is meant a kind of art-product that meets the basic conditions set forth in the aesthetic position known as formalism. The governing principle of formalism, mentioned briefly in the opening pages of this book, warrants re-stating. In essence, it is the idea that the old conception of a content as existing independently of artistic form is an illusion, content being an inalienable aspect of form, not something revealed through it. This idea has two serious ramifications, the first affecting the way the artist goes about making his artwork, the second having to do with the kinds of responses stimulated by the artwork in the viewer/listener. Musical formalism can trace its roots back at least to Hanslick's theories in the middle of the 19th century, though 20th-century "formalist music," as such, may be guided more by the example of Cézanne in painting than by any actual musical development. Cézanne's development, in its turn, is anticipated by a distinctly intellectual phase of Impressionism in which light becomes less a symbol (of either pastoral innocence or ambiguity) and more an object of analytical interest in its own right. In his innumerable studies of haystacks and in the famous series of Rouen Cathedral, Monet asks the viewer to make a conscious response to the effects of light—to observe, in other words, along with the painter, the infinite changes that light can produce. Conversely, the application of paint on these canvases—the very daubs, the relationships of complementary colors, the gradations from light to dark—calls attention to itself: the painting is the vehicle by which we come to understand the essence of nature, that essence being embodied in light and color. The formalist strategy, here, in which the artist deliberately distances the spectator from the artwork by explaining his subject in the process of revealing it, is carried even further in the work of Cézanne. Cézanne's backhanded compliment about Monet, "He is only an eye, but what an eye!" fairly much summarizes his feeling that light and color are (to borrow from Nietzsche) the "mere appearance" of nature, the evidence of its variety and changeability; what he is searching for is something truly permanent—nature's "eternal laws." He finds these in the spatial order of nature, in fundamental shapes underlying that order—"the cylinder, the sphere, the cone."[25] It is characteristic of his analytical standpoint that these shapes are not given directly by nature but have been "abstracted" from it by geometry. Characteristic, also, is the fact that light and color for him have no intrinsic value, but rather function in the service of rhythm and volume.

It is not enough, however, to make Cézanne's art the paradigm of modernist formalism without at the same time calling attention to the particular kind of formalism it represents; Monet, too, has formalist leanings, as already noted. Light and color, however, are less quantifiable aspects of form than cylinders, spheres, and cones. It is the rational emphasis in Cézanne's painting, then, which provides the essential key to his formalism and by extension to the fundamental attitude of formalist art criticism from the time of Roger Fry and Clive Bell.[26] This is hardly the first time in the history of art and art appreciation that the rational properties of form are accorded greater honor than its nonrational properties. All "classical" ages have tended toward this emphasis—the same emphasis that we hear in Socrates' advice to encourage a "sober and harmonious love of the orderly" or in Aquinas's observation that "aesthetic pleasure has to do with the intellect, even if it does so through the mediation of the senses."[27] But 20th-century formalism carries the proposition farther, for it reaffirms Romanticism's vision of art as an ultimate *logos*, an idea that would have occurred neither to

Socrates nor to Aquinas. And yet, formalist critics propose the acquisition of this *logos* by a route diametrically opposed to the one taken by the Romantics: the art lover is promised a sublime experience—an "exaltation"—in contemplating an artwork, but only if he is willing to approach the work in the belief that it is a world unto itself, a world of rational structures and proportions having nothing to do with the existential world around it.

In the presence of a Cézanne painting, then, one feels that Fry and Bell were unerringly right in finding in Cézanne's example the justification of their aesthetic position. For all his devotion to nature, Cézanne effectively reverses the age-old primacy of nature over art, by abstracting from nature its essential forms rather than imitating its existential completeness. His painting confirms with unaccustomed force the unity of the "world" of the work of art as opposed to the multiplicity of the world of everyday; in the best of Cézanne's pictures, every part uniquely intersects with every other part, as if held in place by the power for which Plato and those following him could only find the name "principle of form." The same effect is given by virtually any one of the mature sonnets of Mallarmé, where the poet has created a field of extreme compression, an intricate system of multiple idea-and-sound relationships that one feels would simply fall apart or explode if one detail were misplaced.

Musical works written in conformity with the aesthetic principles just identified can be said to account for the greater part of the output of "advanced music" in the period 1920–1950. The so-called Neoclassical literature presupposes construction, not expression, as the chief concern of the composer, while at the same time having in view a considerable enhancement of the perceptual powers of the listener; indeed, nothing less than a major revamping of the listener's aesthetic expectations is envisioned. The question looms large, however, as to whether these aims have been realized in the works themselves—whether, in other words, the literature of formalist music supplies equivalents to Cézanne and Mallarmé either in terms of formal achievement or of transformation of the language.[28] Much of the equivocal character of Neoclassical music vis-à-vis these last two criteria seems due to certain fateful choices made by the leading composers of the time—especially by Stravinsky, whose influence was already strong enough by 1920 to bring an entire generation along with him. It is ironic that the modernist aesthetic to be most preoccupied with form should turn out to effect in the long run the least radical transformation of the musical language. The irony, to be sure, is somewhat understandable in view of the state of modernist music just after World War I, the mission of Neoclassicism being to a great extent consolidation—the task of providing for modernist music the opportunity to take account of itself and give some system and order to its innovations: if the language of music had indeed been restructured, then its structure should conform to certain "rational laws." Still, Stravinsky's Neoclassical structures do not evolve out of the more radical forms alive in his "Russian" pieces, but rather fall back on procedures closely wed to those of traditional tonality. Little correlation, in short, obtains between Stravinsky's Russian and Neoclassical languages; the latter emerges not as a consolidation of the former, merely as an alternative.[29]

As for the question of formal achievement, the Neoclassical strategy has a certain material effect in that area as well; for one may wonder whether the purported single-mindedness with which the formalist composer pursues his goal of shaping a form with no identifiable content is not compromised when the imagery he fashions is so closely derived from styles whose conventional contents are so readily recognized. Contrary to cubism, for instance, for which no earlier tradition of Western art can be found, Neoclassicism makes continual and deliberate references to earlier styles, evoking inescapable associations in the process. Since the styles in question are overwhelmingly of 18th-century origin, the associations are preeminently *concitato* and *galant*. Hindemith leans toward the former, Stravinsky toward the latter. Indeed, Stravinsky's pieces of the 1920s may well be called "neo-galant" in their emphasis of urbane wit and conscious avoidance of "deep emotion."

That Stravinsky's reworking of galant gestures reflects sympathy for galant values is undeniable; delicate grace, self-composure, and emotional distance make up the habitual content of Stravinsky's pieces of the 1920s. And yet, with the very reworking of the galant elements comes a qualitative difference, an impulse to get past content by interpreting it as an aspect of form. In Chapter 11 mention was made of Stravinsky's seriousness with regard to the business of playing "musical games." These games can have considerable satiric charm, but in the end it is a kind of charm where little trace is left of galant coquettishness and plaintiveness. The qualitative difference of Stravinsky's reworking of the original galant imagery lies in the fact that while both place the emphasis on behavior, galant aims primarily at social manner, Stravinsky at perception. Whereas, from the galant viewpoint, behavior is always defined in its relation to emotion (either as an expression of refined or subdued feeling or as a means of actually covering up strong passions), for Stravinsky behavior becomes a manifestation of awareness—the business of taking in a complex of events and seeing them in proper relation. This is an *ethos* of sorts, insofar as it envisions providing an experience by which to improve a human capacity. Unlike Plato, there is no intention of improving human character, but that, in itself, is what gives the conception its specifically formalist distortion—what removes it from the sphere of existential human concern and locates it squarely in a world unto itself. Eric Salzman has written the following on this point:[30]

Just as cubism is a poetic statement about objects and forms, about the nature of vision and the way we perceive and know forms, ... so is Stravinsky's music a poetic statement about musical objects and aural forms, about our experience of musical art and the artistic transformation of musical materials, always measured in that special domain of music experience, time.

Evidence of the degree to which Stravinsky realizes his formalist aims would seem to be found more in certain choice passages than (as in the case of Cézanne, Mallarmé, and the cubists) in whole works. The primary aesthetic intention being to avoid at all costs the business of engulfing the listener in the sonorous excitements deemed indispensable by the ultra-Romantics for bringing on the spiritual sensation, formalist music tries for the unexciting; it yields imagery designed to be interesting rather than exciting—imagery calculated to give the listener the Apollonian distance necessary to focus, while in the very act of experiencing a piece of music, on aspects of proportion and relation. The Concerto en ré for strings by Stravinsky supplies two excellent cases in point. In mm. 54–76 from the first movement, there is no immediately recognizable melody, no harmonic moment that strikes one as even mildly memorable: differentiation of shapes is held to a minimum, as if to prevent them from being *striking*, from making any direct appeal to the senses. What we have in place of the familiar sensory stimuli and formal designs is a continuity of infinitely graded variations of a single motif—a narrative of melodic and rhythmic snippets pieced together in such a way as to leave no doubt about the aesthetic intent. That intent is to bring the listener to a new level of awareness about certain ideals of form, notably the importance of pacing and the dynamism of change within the confines of sameness.

Even a higher level of awareness seems demanded by a second example from the Concerto en ré (first movement, mm. 146–173). Modulatory passages of this kind in Stravinsky's work display such an extraordinarily subtle treatment of the tonal material that the result can impress the listener as being totally ordinary rather than extraordinary, of no consequence whatsoever. Only after repeated hearings do such passages begin to take shape for the listener: blandness—even blankness—becomes absorbing detail, aridity turns into arid beauty. The aesthetic pleasure of this kind of experience is only partially intellectual; it comes also from knowing that one has stretched something other, and perhaps more, than one's intellect—that is, not so much one's ability to reason as one's perceptual powers.[31] Formalist music can thus represent a rare combination of *ethos* and *logos*, in the sense that it seeks to improve a specific level of human consciousness. To the extent, then, that Stravinsky produced passages of the kind just discussed, it may be said that he achieved the same level of formal integrity for music as did Cézanne and Mallarmé for painting and poetry, and by virtue of the same aesthetic criteria. At first, these criteria seem extremely elitist and exclusionary, demanding as they do aptitudes which nature gives out very rarely and which, therefore, are usually developed through training. But on second thought, the formalist vision probably means to be Utopian rather than elitist; that is, it presents the formalist work of art as a training ground in itself, as a means of changing traditional aesthetic expectations and of teaching art lovers how to appreciate new and higher orders of organization. In view of the wide acceptance and even reverence gained by certain types of formalist art, such a Utopian vision, it seems, has not been based on false hopes.

It should not be thought that formalist music after World War I was restricted to the Neoclassicists; it extended as well to those who had represented Expressionism before the war. More than one critic has called attention to two kinds of Neoclassical speech in the period 1920–1950—one, an extended diatonicism spoken by Stravinsky, Hindemith, et al.; the other an autonomous chromaticism represented by Schoenberg and his followers. Doubtless, the most striking sign of a formalist (if not Neoclassicizing) presence in Expressionist music after 1920 is the birth of twelve-tone theory. Indeed, Schoenberg's motivation behind the dodecaphonic development—that of providing a system, a structural justification, so to speak, for the earlier Expressionist style—addresses the problem of consolidation much more directly than Stravinsky's Neoclassical tonal solutions. Yet, for all that, and in spite of his adoption of traditional formal schemes (most notable, perhaps, in the Suite, Op. 25, but evident in all his instrumental works of this period), Schoenberg does not emerge a genuine formalist, if only because the linchpin of formalism, which is to inculcate as formalist an attitude in the art lover as is already implanted in the artist, is not uppermost in his mind. In the ultimate analysis, Schoenberg sees the importance of construction not as an end in itself but as a means for expressing the content, for conveying powerfully what there is to be said. Berg is clearly of the same mind when he writes of the formal devices in *Wozzeck* that, as crucial as they are to the coherence of each of the fifteen scenes of the opera, their presence should in no way be registered consciously by the listener.

In its aesthetic priorities, Expressionism seems undeniably to place content over form; and yet, this contention comes into serious question when we confront the music of Webern. Already Adorno had written in 1931 with some prescience:[32]

Webern pursues to its furthest extreme the subjectivism which Schoenberg first released in ironic play in *Pierrot*. He is the only one to propound musical expressionism in its strictest sense, carrying it to such a point that it reverts of its own weight to a new objectivity.

The opaqueness of this statement, which derives from Adorno's failure to explain why Webern's "subjectivism" ought to be equated with "a new objectivity," is nevertheless offset by the intuition that somehow extreme opposites will meet at a common point. How can this be shown to be true in Webern's case? The beginnings of an answer to this question may be found in his early Expressionist works, where already the qualities of compression and silence distinctly separate him from Schoenberg and Berg. Their tragic irony expresses itself as horror, degradation, and grotesquerie—objects of fear squarely located in the world of everyday human experience. Even when these objects are subjected to "surreal" treatment, we are never in doubt as to their real significance, namely as projections of deep-seated psychological disturbances. With Webern, the compressions and silences signal something different from the psychological—an ontological dread, a kind of fear which begins with the human, to be sure, but which projects outward toward something not of human making, beyond our ken.[33] The third of the six orchestra pieces, Op. 10, is the most acute case in point, but this tendency to symbolize the unknown in terms of negation—in terms of elimination of everything unessential and impure—is characteristic of all his work in this period.

The transition to the increased reductionism of the twelve-tone period is therefore entirely logical (a reductionism, by the way, which stands in direct opposition to the rhetorical expansion encouraged by the new twelve-tone means in Schoenberg's work). In Webern's twelve-tone music, the attempt to rid the rhetoric of any conventional gesture, together with the persistent use of canon, produces an effect of extreme formal density. In this regard, Webern's art is particularly remindful of Mallarmé's sonnet distillations in which content is transformed into poetic "essence." With Webern, however, content can hardly be conceived as something distinct from form, for along with the denial of the conventional rhetoric, the conventional content associations also disappear. A notable exception in this last respect is the vestige of tragic *pathos* still alive in the archetypal chromatic sigh of Webernian declamation—echo of passages such as the opening of the third act of *Parsifal* and the soprano aria from Bach's Cantata No. 21. As with these pieces, chromaticism figures as a sensual factor in Webern's style, adding a certain restrained richness, contributing significantly to the luster and polish of the music's surface. The texture is not without some dissonant asperities; but the real asperity—the "sternness"—of this music is in its aphoristic character, in its tendency toward compression and negation. Here, the Eastern conception of emptiness, epitomized in the Zen sculpture garden, is not far off. In Webern's experience, as in Mallarmé's, artistic discipline is tantamount to monastic *askesis*, with the difference that neither musician nor poet means to deny sensuality entirely. With Webern, man exists as much sensually as metaphysically, and the duality is never overcome. At one moment the artwork is a distillation—an essence—at another moment, a perfectly crafted jewel.

But with the mention of the "perfectly crafted jewel" we have hit at the very heart of Webern's relation to sense material, which is nothing more nor less than raising such material—like Cézanne, like Stravinsky—to the level of pure form. Webern's mature style enables us to see that pure form was where he was heading all along, even from the time of the early Expressionist works. Reference to a human need to leave the messiness—the tragic irony—of the existential world behind for something better has been made on several occasions in this book, and various ways to fulfill that need have been cited. In Webern's case a solution was found by creating a second world—an art world—free of any sign of imperfection and waste—free, too, of any symbolic connection (or so far as that was possible) to the "first" world. Here is the formalist impulse operating at full tilt. That this impulse may be stronger in Webern than it is even in Stravinsky seems borne out by the facts—especially by the harmonic language Webern chose to use, which, based on no earlier tonal tradition, casts no Neoclassical backward glances and carries no content associations that threaten to run interference with formalist single-mindedness. Stravinsky apparently realized this as well, for whom should he take as his model for the final stage of his career but Anton von Webern? Nor would Stravinsky stand alone, as it turned out, given the fact that a whole generation of serialists would harken to the astringent voice of this so solitary and unlikely figure. We began this discussion on formalism taking Cézanne as the standard against which subsequent formalist attitudes and achievements should be measured. Since Webern's example meets the three essential criteria on which the standard was based—(1) creation of an art world free of outside references; (2) establishment of a language with important consequences for the future; (3) education of the listener with respect to the intellectual dimension of aesthetic pleasure—we must conclude that formalist music of the first half of the 20th century finds its most complete fulfillment in his works.

Notes

1. Schoenberg's sincere respect for the past is nowhere in doubt. Afraid that his modernism might appear a rejection of the past, he had to justify it as a direct outgrowth.

2. Monet's painting of Le Havre was first exhibited in 1874, and its title apparently suggested to a critic present at the exhibition the name "Impressionism." One of the most frequently reproduced Impressionist paintings, it is now used as the cover illustration for the Dover publication of Debussy's piano music. Its most recent history is less illustrious: it was stolen, along with eight other works, from the Musée Marmottan (Paris) in September, 1985, and has yet to be recovered.

3. In *Afternoon of a Faun* (definitive version, 1876), Mallarmé, rather than using the fading-in-and-out technique typical of Impressionism, resorts to the more radical strategy of self-interruption. For this reason alone, Mallarmé's poem may well deserve the label "first modernist artwork": Debussy's *Jeux* (1913) is a thoroughgoing musical application of self-interruption, though moments in earlier pieces (*La Mer, Iberia*), show the strategy already tentatively at work. In my article, "*Prelude to the Afternoon Faun* and *Jeux*: Debussy's Summer Rites," in *19th-Century Music*, Vol. III (1980), pp. 225–238, I try to show how *Jeux* (1913) bears closer comparison than the Prelude to Mallarmé's procedures.

4. Richard Langham-Smith, "Debussy and the Pre-Raphaelites," in *19th-Century Music*, Vol. V (1981), pp. 95–109.

5. From Wordsworth's *Lines Written a Few Miles above Tintern Abbey* (1798).

6. In terms of these principles the Romantic vision could be defined as the dynamic aspiring to the static.

7. Debussy could also be said to have provided a positive answer to the more intellectually oriented, and thus anguished, phase of Symbolism represented by Mallarmé. And he carries out Maeterlinck's imperative with perhaps greater effect than the poet was able to create, for the simple reason that music is more readily prepared than words to embody "primal stuff." Because words are such an evolved and articulate human artifact, Maeterlinck must use language extraordinarily delicately and suggestively in order to convey a sense of the ground of being behind the actions of his characters. Music can function much more directly in pursuit of the same goal.

8. Fernand Hazan et al., ed., *Dictionary of Modern Painting*, p. 112.

9. See Edward Lockspeiser, *Debussy, His Life and Mind*, Vol. I, p. 191.

10. *Ibid.*, p. 94.

11. Joseph Campbell, *Oriental Mythology*, Vol. II of *The Masks of God*, pp. 3–4.

12. I have avoided the use of the word "archetypal" here, for fear of its being taken in the "inherent" Jungian sense. As used in this book (and in Frye) "archetype" means a basic pattern of thought of the culture, not a product of the universal "collective unconscious." I'm not necessarily denying by this the existence of a "collective unconscious," I simply have no opinion on the matter.

13. Over and above the "pitiless" vision of reality expressed in *The Rite of Spring*, there is the element of the ritual itself, a strategy that works toward reinforcing the effect of formality and thereby further removing the action from the sphere of the personal. The importance of ritual in Stravinsky's development cannot be overestimated. Perhaps the most enduring influence in this respect is the ritualistic source of Stravinsky's rhythm—Russian folk incantation and dance. In addition, there are the religous works proper, ranging across the whole career: the *Symphony of Psalms*, the *Mass*, the *Canticum Sacrum*, the *Requiem Cantiles*. In each of these, the treatment bespeaks an emphasis away from personal meditation and toward communal participation. Thoroughly communal in orientation is *Les Noces*; in *Petrouchka* the carnival "background" finishes by swallowing up the personal drama, deliberately reducing the effect of *pathos*; and although there is no explicit program attached to the *Symphonies for Wind Instruments*, the grave impassive character of this piece resonates with ritual associations. This preoccupation with ritual indicates a tendency of a certain branch of modernism to reverse that original impulse in Greek art to bring forth drama out of ritual, to see emerge, in short, the humanistic from the mythic. Stravinsky's formalizations move toward diminishing the humanistic impact of a work in favor of its presence as icon and exemplum.

14. This is also a major idea in Dostoevsky. This connection between the grotesque and the sublime is, to my mind, the chief ingredient of what Mussorgsky liked to call his "realism," though he may well have called it an anti-romantic Romanticism. Mahler's work contains important examples of the type (see Chapter 11).

15. Agatha Fassett, *The Naked Face of Genius*, pp. 158–159.

16. *Ibid.*, pp. 105–106.

17. By contrast, the effects of primitivism in German Expressionist painting—in Kirchner and Nolde particularly—are very pronounced. Perhaps there is a primitivist element in Schoenberg's style as well, though presumably it would be much less overt than what one meets in Stravinsky and Bartok. If such an influence does exist in Expressionist music, I don't hear it, and therefore can't identify it, but I would be happy to have it pointed out to me.

18. I am greatly indebted to John and Dorothy Crawford, authors of a forthcoming study on Expressionism, for a series of intense discussions we had on the subject in December, 1987. Their ideas helped immeasurably in getting my thoughts crystallized, though they are of course in no way responsible for whatever distortions I might have made of their own thinking.

19. Quoted in Maynard Solomon, *Beethoven*, p. 142.

20. It leads one to think that before Freud, art, especially tragic art, might have performed an important service as psychotherapy. We should remember that Aristotle's idea of artistic catharsis was most likely derived from the experiences of Corybantic (or some such) therapy (see Chapter 3 *supra*).

21. In *Erwartung*, there is the "other woman with the white arms" who lives on the other side of the woods. One can see how this love triangle corresponds to the relation-

ship Freud observed early on between his typical female patient and her parents—competition with the mother for love of the father. The Oedipus complex is the same situation with the sexes reversed.

22. Record booklet from the Columbia recording of the complete works of Arnold Schoenberg (M2S679), volume I, p. [5].

23. *Ibid.*, p. [4].

24. It strikes me that this exceptional moment is distinctly Freudian, tantamount to a Freudian slip. It has no business being in the piece because it doesn't belong or relate to anything else; but of course, it deserves to be there after all, because, like a Freudian slip, it *must* have significance, having been produced by the subconsious.

25. Hazan, *Dictionary of Modern Painting*, p. 24.

26. This becomes very clear by comparing Fry's and Bell's theories with those of an art critic of one generation earlier, namely Walter Pater. Pater's formalism is what would be called "Aestheticism" in the third quarter of the 19th century, involving a deep appreciation of detail—delight in motifs and arabesques, nuances of shadings and color, iridescence—rather than a preoccupation with hierarchical design.

27. See Umberto Eco, *The Aesthetics of Thomas Aquinas*, pp. 57–58.

28. It is somewhat ironic that the two exemplars of modernist formalism in painting and poetry should chronologically belong to the 19th century. Cézanne barely made it into the 20th century, dying in 1906. Mallarmé died in 1898.

29. This statement is rather an oversimplification, I admit. Pieter van den Toorn's work on Stravinsky's tonality has done much to change our impressions of Stravinsky's middle period, representing it as both more adventurous and more coherent than has been traditionally thought.

30. Eric Salzman, *Twentieth-Century Music: An Introduction*, p. 49.

31. This seems to bear out exactly Aquinas's definition of aesthetic pleasure (see n. 27 above) as an intellectual experience touched off by the senses.

32. Quoted in Hans Moldenhauer, *Anton von Webern, A Chronicle of His Life and Work*, p. 49.

33. Frye has identified three kinds of fear: (1) *horror*, or fear at close range; (2) *terror*, or fear at a distance; (3) *dread*, or fear without an object, i.e., fear of the unknown. In Chapter 8, Frye's definition of *penseroso* was given as a *dread* that is turned to pleasure through romance. More particularly, *penseroso* is a quality connected to the pastoral tradition; and if this is so, we can say of the quality of dread in Webern that it belongs to the world of tragic irony because no aspect of pastoral is present to soften or "romanticize" the effect.

16   *Formalist Alterations of the Archetypes*

Commentaries on music written since 1945 tend to gather around two concerns: (1) the techniques used to bring a piece into being and (2) the aesthetic premises on which the piece is based (together with those which it calls into question). The latter concern may appear to bear more directly on the present study than the former, but neither truly comes to terms with the problem of the musical image as such. This is hardly surprising, given the problem archetypal criticism has in finding content in images purportedly stripped of conventional associations. Indeed, the problem only grows worse if we persist in thinking of artistic content as a separable quantity, originating outside the artwork—if, in short, we refuse to take seriously the possibility that the content of a given work might be, just as the formalists proclaim, merely an aspect of its form. On the other hand, if we give up struggling against the formalist proposition and embrace it wholeheartedly— with the understanding that this is done specifically for the sake of dealing with the body of music now under discussion—the problem instantly disappears. And the reason must lie in the aesthetic beliefs guiding the new music, in the fact that the new avant-garde is driven by what might appropriately be called a "super-formalism," a conception of music that carries formalist aspirations beyond anything imagined in the previous half century.

What Eric Salzman has written in connection with Stravinsky's aesthetic— that it is "art about art, or more to the point, about the experience of art ... the entire range of musical experience"[1] applies with even more force to the avant-garde activities of the early 1950s in Paris and Darmstadt as well as to the group dominated by Milton Babbitt in the United States during the same period. The operative word here is "language": though we must take care to shake ourselves loose of the old connotations of "mode of expression" that can still cling to that word. Expressionism and Primitivism were movements guided by a specific view of reality or set of values for which it was necessary to find the proper expressive "language," in other words, to invent the means with which to embody the world view in question, to capture the inspiriting ideas. But in the avant-garde music now under discussion, language *is* the inspiriting idea: it has ceased to be a means and has become an end in itself. General histories of music usually deal with this avant-garde period in terms of techniques by which the composer has striven to assemble his work, leaving the unsuspecting reader to believe that these techniques—the means—must be in the service of something that the entire work is meant to express. In point of fact, if anything is expressed, it is the means themselves; they are what the work is about, they are what holds the key to the composer's "world view," this world view being situated not outside the artwork but in the squarely self-contained world the formalist calls art.

This is hardly to say that the secrets of formalist avant-garde music will be revealed by a simple enumeration of the means used to put a representative piece of music together. On the contrary, means and effects remain two distinct properties of the piece of music, with the means presumably responsible for the effects. As with any other kind of art, it is assumed that only through the effects of the music will its contents be known. Where the almost insurmountable obstacle arises for the listener faced with the new music—especially faced with the music fashioned according to the procedures of total serialism—is in the huge disparity between the character of the means and the character of the effects. If the new kind of serial work is organized on the basis of Schoenberg's original conception of the tone row, only now applied to the parameters of duration, intensity, and timbre in addition to that of pitch—if, in other words, the piece of music is brought into being by means of a system of interlocking structures more rigorously ordered than anything seen heretofore in Western music—why is it that the products of such order give off such seeming effects of disorder? To take a comparable example from the traditional literature: given a brief explanation of how Ockeghem organized the four canonic voices in the *Missa Prolationum*, a reasonably educated listener will readily hear a correlation between Ockeghem's craft and the musical outcome. Without necessarily being able to follow the organization in all its intricacy, he will nevertheless have an overall impression of relatedness, a sense of parts interacting to form ordered patterns. To be told, on the other hand, that the five instruments of Stockhausen's *Zeitmasse* are simultaneously engaged in playing their parts at different rates of speed, some of them metronomically fixed, some of them free, is no insurance that even a highly trained listener will recognize—i.e., *perceive*—such an interaction, either immediately or eventually. If we are to believe that the practitioners of total serialism were acting in good faith—with a positive purpose in mind and not out of some perverse interest in making victims of their audiences—there is only one, quite obvious conclusion to draw from this example, namely that these composers were out to explore the limits of human perception itself, at the very least to stretch those limits beyond what had been demanded by earlier music, and perhaps most important of all, to inquire into the number of forms that human perception could take when confronted with intensely complex configurations. In light of these motivations, the strategy of total serialism becomes manifestly clear: it is simply a very systematic way to produce a density of musical information, to arrive at a language that will either push perceptions to the breaking point or elicit from the listener a variety of responses which are different from each other in kind rather than merely in degree.

That total serialism was adopted largely for these ends is reinforced by the composers' own observations, especially those of Boulez. Before looking into some of these, however, we must clarify one point having to do with the relative ease or difficulty involved in making sense of formal patterns. When a language appears difficult to us, we often confuse the reasons for its difficulty; we tend to blur the lines dividing two aspects of the language which should nevertheless be kept strictly apart—its newness and its complexity. That this distinction has particular significance for the music in question is brought out by the fact that while the language in which this music speaks is no longer new, there is every chance that it will always be considered complex. Newness, in any case, has always proved something of a false idol, partly because of its inherent impermanency, partly because the ideals on which it is based are largely illusory. In the present case, the "new" language grew old, perhaps more quickly than one might have anticipated, because so many dreary, second-rate works were composed in its name. Where the pioneers of the language envisioned setting off in a direction that not only meant a definitive break with the past but was specifically aimed at determining the future course of events, we see from our present vantage point that this last aim has largely gone unfulfilled. The avant-garde language (or collection of dialects) is no longer spoken by the great majority of composers active today and the passing of its heyday seems regretted by very few. While it should continue to share a modest place alongside other contemporary languages and structures, its promise as the dominant cohesive force in the future evolution of Western composition has not come to pass: to that extent, the newness that the early practitioners of total serialism saw in their language turned out to be an illusion.

And yet, in one major respect, there has been something enduring to come out of this language, something that is enduring precisely because it need not remain proper to total serialism but is general enough to be integrated into other languages as well. What this something is can perhaps be best identified in reference to a plea Stockhausen once made for rethinking the craft of musical composition down to its last detail. "It was as if my whole musical education had proved totally useless,"[2] he said, a remark in which one plainly hears the urge to bypass all of musical "civilization" and return to a kind of original Golden Age—an environment where music will have a second chance, where musicians, like a new race of primitives who have something to say but no codified language with which to give it voice, will invent a language from ground zero. However pure a conception the project of disencumbering oneself of the baggage of the past may be, there is some question as to its practicality, if only because (and contrary to the situation of the original Golden Age) there is already a language in place. Thus, even to those who are eager to see a new language born, this new language will appear as more of a dismantling than a mere bypassing of the old one. To eradicate a language, one would have to eradicate memory itself. It is more realistic to expect that listeners, in assimilating a new language, will have to relate it to the one they already know. Applying this principle to the case at hand, the new music would appear, at least for an initial period, as the breaking up of the continuities of the old syntax, as if the new race of musical primitives were learning to sing by means of structures that departed appreciably in shape and function from the central structure of traditional syntax, namely the *phrase*.

This process is already significantly under way with Webern's points and fragments (thus not strictly "new"), but the syntactical departure that his innovation represents is kept in check by the rhythmic and motivic consistency of any given work, movement, or extended section. With his successors, the breaking up of the old syntax is carried much further, resulting in unforeseen syntactic juxtapositions and continuities so unpredictable as to create persistent effects of discontinuity. Tape music of the 1950s provides especially striking examples— Stockhausen's *Gesang der Jünglinge* or Berio's *Omaggio a Joyce*, for instance, in which normal utterances are initially pulverized into shards of their former selves and then gradually reconstituted to create extended unarticulated drones. But the presence of accent impulses, motivic fragments, and drones—of structures designed to sidestep the interior "completeness" of the traditional phrase shape—is as general for performed instrumental and vocal music as it is for sound material transformed by electronic means. Most important of all, this syntax is a permanent legacy of a kind of speech in which virtually all composers of the present generation become fluent and whose inflections can be heard in works which might otherwise show little sympathy for avant-garde aesthetic expression. In this one long-range effect, the "newness" of the language seems to have found a valid claim.

Complexity, however, is another matter, a function of the handling of a language, not of its historical evolution. By the traditional standards of complexity, the *Grosse Fuge* of Beethoven preserves its identity as a complex work, as much even for the performing groups who know the work inside out as for the listeners who are coming to it for the first time. To what extent, if any, must those traditional standards be altered in light of the experiences of total serialism? Of all the composers of the post-Webern generation—and there is hardly an exception among them who cannot argue his position with considerable skill—Boulez is perhaps the one to provide the most comprehensive, if not always the clearest, answer to this question. At first glance, his view of complexity would seem to conform to the traditional view, connected as it is to a special feeling for large-scale continuities. He is devoted to Debussy's *Jeux* "because it was the first time, I think, that he kept for such a long stretch to a completely continuous form and this is what I believe to be important."[3] With respect to Berg's chamber concerto, he says: "What thrilled me as I went along was the complexity of his mind: the number of internal correspondences, the intricacy of his musical construction, the esoteric character of many of the references, the density of texture, that whole universe in perpetual motion revolving constantly around itself."[4]

Boulez refers to the effect of his early pieces as an "organized delirium,"[5] and there is no question that the contradiction contained in these words holds much meaning for him. In distinguishing between the influence of "overall control" in *Le Marteau sans maître* and the "room for what I call 'local indiscipline',"[6] the composer points to the way in which his contradiction can be realized. In terms of what the listener experiences, the action of "organized delirium" converts directly into a "contrast between really total perception and overall perception where details are lost":[7]

In a passage that is obvious, simple, and clear, you assimilate a hundred percent of what is said because all the articulations can be easily distinguished—the direction of the music, its general form, and so on. On the other hand, in an extremely complex passage, the superimpositions are sometimes so dense that they cancel each other out, and ultimately give only an overall impression.

The question looms large as to the identity of the "you" Boulez is referring to in this passage: who is the person assimilating a hundred percent of the "obvious, simple, and clear" information—is he an ordinary listener or one with particular qualifications for dealing with difficult musical situations? Assuming that Boulez has the latter type of listener in mind, for otherwise the comment would not have much point, we are faced with still another question: how complex does a passage have to be in order to have crossed the borderline between the totally assimilable and only the partially so? Boulez neither attempts a definition nor cites examples of this distinction, though we can imagine that the juxtaposition of the first two movements of *Le Marteau sans maître* (the rhythmically unstable followed by the rhythmically regular) would serve as a good illustration. Whether or not the above ever really has a satisfactory answer, it does at least bring us closer to what Boulez means by "complexity," namely that quality which inheres in something not totally assimilable by the rational level of consciousness; complexity for Boulez would thus be the point of union—as well as the point of distinction—between the rational and the nonrational. Célestin Deliège has caught the substance of this when, addressing Boulez directly, he makes the following observation:[8]

A great deal of your reasoning propounds something that seems permanent in your case: the dialectical character of your thought and attitudes, which causes you to move between rational and irrational poles. You have mentioned 'hysteria according to Artaud'; you have given vent to irrational desires, and also spoken of 'delirium', though stressing at the same time that 'it must be organized'. In your search for a new 'poetics' you feel the need to have a considerable technical apparatus in the background; your development constantly takes you from one pole to the other.

Boulez's response to this is:[9] "I have the sort of temperament that tries to invent rules so as to have the pleasure of destroying them later: it is a dialectical evolution between freedom of invention and the need for discipline in invention."

On the face of it, Boulez's remark seems to reaffirm the conventional notion of the creative process in art, by which the material from the rational and nonrational levels of consciousness meet on the image-making, or aesthetic, level proper. What separates Boulez from the traditional view is the emphasis on *dialectic*, the interaction between levels without the resultant synthesis. Whereas in traditional art we are left with a sense of aesthetic fusion of the rational and nonrational strands of information, in Boulez's music there is a deliberate effort to keep the fusion from happening; hence the complexity, which leads the listener to recognize the separateness of the entities, and the necessity of the receiving mind to run "from one pole to the other."

Another factor contributing to the emphasis of dialectic over synthesis is the absence of a clear symbolic function. In traditional music the presence of the archetypal associations provides a certain unifying coherence, even in the face of intensely complex continuities (the *Grosse Fuge* is a good illustration). But the symbolizing-associative process, which is the connection the mind makes between sensory and metaphysical content, is something that Boulez's poetics and procedures discourage. The following statement fairly much summarizes his formalist position: "This key-word, structure, leads us to a conclusion … drawn from Rougier, which can equally well be applied to music: 'What we can know of the world is its structure, not its essence.' "[10]

Further along in the same discussion, Boulez says, "Form and content are of the same nature, subject to the same analytical jurisdiction."[11] Since "essence," or the metaphysical, plays effectively no part in the Boulezian aesthetic scheme, it is inappropriate—or at least somewhat beside the point—to analyze his own works in symbolic terms. Traditional image making has been defined in this book as a *lateral* transfer of information between two "substances" of a different order (or more precisely, between "substance and nonsubstance"). Boulez sees his music as activating a nonrational level of the consciousness, but only in terms of its perceptual, not its symbolizing, capacity; indeed, this restriction is imposed for the express purpose of concentrating attention on the number and kinds of *vertical* transfers of information capable of being made between the rational and nonrational levels of consciousness. Since the metaphysical is an important mechanism by which we resolve contrasts and tensions into a synthesis, the absence of the metaphysical in the Boulezian canon of ideas goes a long way toward explaining why much of the meaning of a work by Boulez depends on the need for keeping contrasts and tensions alive, and thus strongly felt.

Boulez may be the most articulate spokesman for these aspirations, but the general effect of instability—the condition of "dissonance" on every level of the musical action—constitutes the common ground of all those engaging in total serialism. Schoenberg had shown how tonal instability could be *systematized* by devising his conception of the total chromatic; if analogous systems could be found for the other musical parameters, then what Boulez often refers to as "the principle of constant variation, or nonrepetition"[12] would have been given its most complete expression. Of course, as far as Boulez was concerned,

Schoenberg had misunderstood his own serial conceptions by allying them with architectonic structures from traditional tonality: "These architectures annihilate the possibilities of organization inherent in the new language. The two worlds are incompatible ..."[13] The remarkable achievements of Schoenberg's early Expressionist period—the three pieces for piano, Op. 11 and *Pierrot Lunaire*, with their "violence and frenzy, their considerable density of texture," and their "manifest attempt to construct contrapuntally"[14]—had been betrayed in Schoenberg's later misapplication of his own twelve-tone method. Schoenberg, according to Boulez, had, at one and the same time, brought the dodecaphonic system into being and undermined it by working it out in terms of large-scale designs that were diametrically opposed to the spirit of openness and ceaseless action which serialism stood for. Boulez's reference to "the possibilities of organization" in the above statement helps us to understand more precisely what he means by "organized delirium": in terms of the realities of the works governed by the methods of total serialism, "organized delirium" becomes nothing other than the condition of "constant variation and renewal"—the effect of "delirium," in short, arrived at by the most deliberate, rational, and acutely *organized* means possible.[15]

The image of a delirium consciously organized seems altogether appropriate for artists who had come to be deeply preoccupied, one might say, obsessed, with the idea of human consciousness and all its ramifications—its capacities, the variety of its functions, its essential restlessness. When Boulez speaks admiringly of the "violence" and "frenzy" of *Pierrot Lunaire*, we can be reasonably certain that he is not thinking of those effects in the same *pathos*-laden sense in which Schoenberg created them. Frenzy for the Expressionists was the peripeteia of a disturbed psyche, the emotions in disarray; Boulez's frenzy is the quality of a peripatetic mind, the consciousness as *perpetuum mobile*.[16] What is consistently conveyed, both implicitly and explicitly, in the remarks of the serialist composers is their ultimate belief in the expanding capacities of the human consciousness and in music itself for testing these capacities out. The *ethos* of the new music is thus essentially the same as was made by an earlier brand of formalism, only with more insistence—the challenge the new music makes to our perceptions, its call to stretching them to a point beyond anything we hitherto imagined possible. Boulez has called serial thought a "universe in perpetual expansion" and in that characterization we understand serial music to be the direct mirror image of that other universe called the human consciousness.

In one important respect, the aesthetic of the new generation represents a significant departure from the earlier formalism. For all their devotion to Webern, the new serialists do not share his aspirations with regard to the finished work. It is true that he works with the structures of the total chromatic—he uses the language of tonal instability—and yet, he does so in the somewhat paradoxical interest of creating an object of extreme consistency, a network of ultimately harmonious parts. Harmony is clearly not uppermost in the minds of the new serialists; indeed all indications point to the contrary—to the harmonious effect being studiously avoided. This seems especially true of Stockhausen's large orchestral pieces—*Gruppen* and *Carré*, for example—where the composer, led on by his diverse and outsized forces to perform some startling exploits of the sonic imagination, gives little if any thought to making the sonic effects part of a coherent design. The result is a grab-bag of unpredictable and seemingly unmotivated juxtapositions: passages of exquisite instrumental delicacy jarred out of their complacency by honks, squeaks, and other indelicate noises, compositional non sequiturs, extended anticlimaxes, gestural babblings. But given Stockhausen's immense skill in handling musical detail, it would be extremely ill-advised to cite ineptitude or inattention on other fronts: indeed, the discontinuities and seeming incoherences of *Gruppen* and *Carré* seem quite precisely calculated, a deliberate attempt by the composer to break the listener of the habit of assimilating musical information in strictly linear ways. Stockhausen's radical conception of form as elaborated in his theory of the "moment" is summarized below:[17]

Each individually characterized passage in a work is regarded as an experiential unit, a 'moment' which can potentially engage the listener's full attention and can do so in exactly the same measure as its neighbours. No single 'moment' claims priority, even as a beginning or ending; hence the nature of such a work is essentially 'unending' (and, indeed, 'unbeginning'). Significantly, each 'moment' is, in Stockhausen's view, equally dispensable, rather than equally indispensable, to the listener: his unending forms are the outcome not only of his pursuit of equality among all constituents of a work, but also of his leanings toward indeterminacy, which he accurately enough attributes to the durations and intensities of his listeners' attentiveness. The listener's unpredictable ecstatic involvement with the 'now' of one 'moment' can be bought only at the risk of his equally unpredictable withdrawal from some other.

It is arguable whether the listener's attentiveness is as unpredictable as Stockhausen claims. The traditional view of composition, of course, is that the listener's attention will be held by the persuasion of continuity of a work, provided that that continuity is persuasive enough. In order to make it so, the composer must manipulate time in such a way as to keep the listener engaged in the forward movement of the musical current. Stockhausen's denial of the necessity of forward movement, by which he effectively contravenes the principle of beginning, middle, and end held inviolate since the time of Aristotle, does not find much favor with those who, like Elliott Carter, maintain a deep concern for "the problem of time-continuity and of producing feelings of tension and release and therefore of musical motion in the listener."[18] Although Carter intends his musical events to interact in ways that would take them far beyond the stage of mere "linear succession," he is nevertheless committed to the idea of an organically integrated artwork, in which the individual events "owe their musical effect almost entirely to their specific 'placing' in the musical time-continuity."[19] In short, without sacrificing the organicity and forward thrust of traditional composition, Carter is at the same time trying for the multilayered actions characteristic of serial music; to that extent, he shares Boulez's and Stockhausen's fascination with the protean character of human perception. To realize this somewhat bifocal aim, he resorts to a number of strategies, of which David Schiff has cited stratification, mosaic texture, and neutralization as the three most important. Stratification, doubt-less the technique most closely associated with Carter's mature style, involves a striking interplay of musical events, for which the word "interplay" is almost a misnomer, given the single-mindedness with which each musical element pur-sues its individual course, as if oblivious of the others. Schiff presents an example from early on in the first string quartet, in which[20]

each instrument plays at a different metronomic speed, with highly contrasted colours, intervals, and expressive gestures. Unlike a Bach fugue, where the harmonic resultant of the lines is not only clear, but is the controlling structure, here the differentiation of character is the clearest structural guide, and the overall harmony seems unimportant, especially because the different speeds of each line prevent the sounding of simultaneous chords. Bach's counterpoint merges separate voices into a unified chorale. Carter's counterpoint lets voices move individually, like people on a city street.

The analogy to "people" here is significant, for Carter is far more willing than the serialists to view his musical elements in human terms—as "characters." He describes the instruments of his second string quartet as being "type-cast," each having "its own special expressive attitude and its own repertory of musical speeds and intervals. In a certain sense each instrument is like a character in an opera made up primarily of 'quartets'."[21] He speaks of the ballroom scene from *Don Giovanni* and the final act of *Aida* as providing models, however stylistically remote, for developing his own specific techniques.[22] Nevertheless, for all the theatrical references, we must keep in mind Carter's primary ded-ication to his idea of musical continuity; to remind ourselves of the formalist emphasis of his vision is to realize that his instrumental character assignments have only secondary importance. The techniques of stratification, mosaic, and neutralization are alternated in a complex interplay to produce in the listener a sense not so much of the individual personalities of either the instruments or the musical ideas given to them as of the kinds of relationships that result from the interplay itself—relationships which the composer has identified as assum-ing essentially "three forms of responsiveness: discipleship, companionship, and confrontation."[23]

Schiff describes a moment from the Adagio of the first quartet in which viola and cello, on the one hand, and the two violins on the other begin to exchange material and to take on the other pair's "mood." Confrontation seems to give way to cooperation, writes Schiff, and in this last action, we see a very concrete ex-ample of how Carter means to realize his initial ambition of moving from states of relative tension to states of relative release and thus produce in the listener "feelings ... of musical motion."[24] From this example, we come to understand quite precisely that the highly differentiated "characters" of the musical mate-rials and their instrumental assignments have been devised not for their own sake but in order to permit the listener to follow closely—to perceive with some certainty—the transformations that proceed from the characters' interactions. Carter has perhaps said it most simply when he writes: "The total effect at any given moment is the primary consideration, the contribution of each instrument secondary."[25] That the character elements are a secondary factor is, of course, no reason to ignore them: they are a definite presence in Carter's music—an essential content—thus an important indicator of how the imagery is to be read. If we think back to Boulez's aesthetic, we are reminded of his almost exclusive focus on the perceptual, the essential reduction of the content to concerns, albeit subtle and diversified, about the human consciousness. Carter's notions of "character" show a concern for invoking the total human personality—Eros in interaction with Thanatos, impulses of the "desire to be" working to fulfill the "desire to know." This inclination to maintain some link with traditional notions of content goes hand in hand with Carter's persistence in upholding traditional principles of form. His "epiphanies" are clearly not as resolved as Beethoven's, nor may they even mean to be as complete as Bartok's, but much of the feeling of momentousness in his large-scale works places them in the Beethovenian tradition and proceeds from the mainstream principle of "urgent continuity." Where he differs from his predecessors is in the ultimately formalist—and antisymbolist—emphasis of his expressive point of view. In experiencing the music of Beethoven or of Bartok, we hear the voices and feel the steps of the chief protagonists embodied directly in their imagery—the "Beethovenian hero" in the case of the former, the "primitivist hero" in the case of the latter. In Carter's images, we hear the voices and feel the steps of a number of secondary characters, but not those of a "Carterian hero"; Carter permits himself to *represent* in a secondary sense, but not in a primary sense, for, in the final analysis, it is the essence of formalist content to be conveyed to the viewer/listener *as form*, not as representation.

Carter's solutions with respect to large-scale composition have worked well for him, but his complaint that the Darmstadt composers "have not shown the proper seriousness about the problems of time-continuity" but have "dealt rather with unusualness of aural effect, thus reducing music to mere physical sound"[26] undervalues both their aims and their achievement. For one thing, the rhetorical impact of numbers of gestures in Stockhausen's music—the sense of contrast and change they produce—is enough to assure us that the composer has a keen concern for musical time, however little that concern may conform to the traditional one. But even if this were not true, Stockhausen's treatment of "mere physical sound" is of such an order as to make us recognize that the formalist imperative of stretching the listener's perceptions has been genuinely carried out in terms of a world of new densities, textural and timbral combinations, and sonic juxtapositions that have been revealed to composer and listener alike by virtue of his aural originality. In one respect, however, Carter's point does carry some weight. Stockhausen's moments, however aurally and rhetorically effective they may be in their splendid disconnectedness, suggest neither the possibility of being sustained nor a way in which they might metamorphose into a neighboring moment. Since the absence of these two fundamental effects of traditional composition constitutes a severe formal limitation, one legitimately wonders whether new notions of continuity arise to replace the old. With characteristic ingenuity, Boulez anticipates this question with his conceptions of "interlocking cycles," as worked out in *Le Marteau*, and of mobile units, as designated for the third piano sonata, the intention being not to displace continuity with discontinuity but to propose several continuities at once, thereby offering the possibility of seeing the work from several vantage points "while leaving its basic meaning unaltered." Although it is not precisely clear what a formalist has in mind when he speaks of a "basic meaning," nor how a listener should go about following serial continuities at once, it is more than possible to imagine that with good will and practice, we can learn to find connectedness between things that once seemed disconnected. At any rate, as points of arrival and climaxes are of less significance to nonlinear conceptions of time, Stockhausen's and Boulez's works of this type would seem to deal less in "epiphanies" than in "illuminations," thus supplying one more way by which to image modernism's proverbial struggle with resistant meaning.

The radical nature of Stockhausen's concept of musical time is perhaps superseded only by John Cage's extreme attitudes toward music as a whole. If Stockhausen has redefined form, Cage has redefined art by claiming that form is not necessary to art. Form invokes the notion of aesthetic intention, and Cage has distinctly said, "My purpose is to eliminate purpose."[27] The idea of the composer giving up artistic control for a place alongside the listener, from which both set forth in a spirit of innocent discovery—"let's find out together what happens"—has the immediate appeal of openness about it. As we begin with no expectations—no preconceived notions—we should also not be disappointed if the end of a musical adventure yields little in the way of a revelation. This is a somewhat veiled way of saying that what there is to reveal depends primarily on the observer and his ability to concentrate. To Boulez's rather impatient remark, "It is quite beyond me to sit through a million uninteresting events in the expectation that I might eventually hear one that is interesting,"[28] Cage would respond that the listener gets back what he puts in. The degree to which the listener is now made responsible for actively completing the artwork signifies a radical change in the roles traditionally played by composer and audience: if during a performance of *4'33"* (Cage's famous essay in silence, in which a performer sits before a piano for exactly four minutes and thirty-three seconds without making contact with the keyboard), the listener finds his mind wandering and ends up with a diffuse instead of focused impression of the experience, this does not signify a defeat for the piece of music; on the contrary, it suggests that the listener did not take advantage of the opportunity the piece of music offered.

By proposing a fluid intermingling between art and the everyday world, Cage has as his chief aim, quite like the formalists, to push to new limits the listener's perceptions, yet by means directly antithetical to the formalist vision of a self-contained world of art. The effects of this difference are felt not so much in the area of the perceptions themselves as in the attitude behind the perceptions. Cage asks that we approach "his" work in a totally accepting frame of mind, in a mood of maximum tolerance; the approach to the formalist artwork is critical, selective, evaluative. The essence of the Cageian experience is that whereas perceptual activity is maintained at a high level, judgment has no place—a situation which strikes traditional thinking as a paradox. But the issue of abandoning judgment in the experiencing of an artwork is finally an ethical issue, and Cage's position makes us realize that the question cannot be decided on purely objective grounds. The *ethos* of formalism is that our perceptual powers will be enhanced when the musical materials are of such a kind as to permit us to make fine distinctions and to unravel complex situations. The *ethos* of Cage's philosophy is that our musical perceptions are improved when we open ourselves to sound phenomena of all kinds and are struck by their diversity and specificity.

In the final analysis, however, the most radical aspect of Cage's aesthetic does not concern the relation of artwork to listener but the relation of artwork to composer. Cage wants to dispossess the creative artist of his purported dictatorial control but in so doing he has also effectively relieved him of his artistic responsibilities.[29] In the Cageian view of things not only is the artist dislodged from the position of visionary accorded him since the early days of Romanticism but he also loses his proverbial status as craftsman, as maker of images. It is not that images altogether disappear in Cage's musical experience; it is simply that they are found rather than invented, loosely or randomly assembled rather than carefully matched to form a complex of coherent shapes and functions. In this transformed picture of the composer's activities lies the single most troubling moment of Cage's aesthetic; art ceases to be a genuine *logos*, because although Cage continues to believe in the art experience as producing a kind of knowledge, the "artwork" no longer comes into being as the result of a conscious and deliberate questing after, and processing of, images. The mythos of the artist grappling with his material, working to get the resistant stuff to conform to the idealized vision in his head, is now replaced by the picture of a figure wandering through an unfamiliar wood, happening here and there upon this amiable creature or that curious object, all the while listening intently to the crackling of the leaves and needles beneath his tufted steps. Like Galilei earlier, who asked his European contemporaries to give up all the delights of polyphony, Cage is asking the present age to sacrifice something with which it will not part willingly, namely its belief that composers, being endowed with special gifts, are alone in their capacity to bestow on society certain revelations which society will not have in any other form. Cage may argue that these revelations are no less diffuse and ephemeral than the ones offered through his method of releasing the controls, that the hope of getting richly layered meanings from intensely crafted forms is mere illusion; but certain illusions die hard.

Formalism and Cage's aesthetics may represent the extreme poles of thought with respect to musical craft, but they are essentially agreed in their view of the nonrepresentational, nonassociative character of musical meaning. Still, this has not prevented referential contents from getting attached to primarily formalist works—an inevitable situation where texts are involved, as is generally the case in the later works of Stockhausen and Berio. Indeed, the relative importance of the referential content in the output of these two composers has noticeably gained strength as they have increasingly removed themselves from their earlier commitment to total serialism. Of course, no more than a brief program or an evocative title is needed to create an association, nor does it take long for an association to turn into a convention. In certain early works of Xenakis (*Metastasis, Pithoprakta*) the treatment of the strings can hardly be separated from a mood of fear and alarm because of the similar sounds in Penderecki's more famous (though later) *Threnody for the Victims of Hiroshima*. Paradoxically, where conventional associations are largely missing, the listener's associative inclination will almost inevitably go to work to fill in the void. In the early days of *musique concrète*, the public heard eggs frying and water gurgling through pipes instead of anything resembling musical continuity, though with familiarity these contents have generally come to be supplanted by less trivial ones. Still, tape music tends to evoke a sense of the nonhuman and the "unearthly" (if not the "otherworldly") and this, hardly at all because the sounds are produced by a machine but because the sounds are not those of instruments with any clear connection to traditional vocal music. The use of acoustic instruments and voices in a way that does not correspond to traditional vocal treatment will result in a similarly nonhuman effect. Much the same sense of cosmic space, for example, is suggested by the instrumental-choral combination of Stockhausen's *Carré* or Ligeti's *Atmosphères* as by Xenakis' electronically produced *Orient-Occident III*, by virtue of the slow-moving, monumental masses of sound common to them all.

With all these allusions (and often overt references) to extramusical contents, two questions persist: (1) what is the relative importance of such contents in a given work? and (2) for what expressive purpose have they been included? With regard to the first question, something of an answer has already been provided in the distinction made a few pages back between primary and secondary contents. As for the second question, the ever-present danger in explicating the meanings of contemporary musical imagery is to read them in ways more appropriate to traditional music. Here, the very comments of the composer are sometimes open to interpretation and thus cause for misunderstanding. For example, Stockhausen tells us that the first sketches of *Carré* "were made in the air during a six week long tour in America, where I daily flew great distances, experiencing above the clouds the slowest times of change and the widest spaces."[30] The poetic tinge of the final part of this statement can lead us to believe that *Carré* is meant to evoke, in some latter-day Romantic sense, the "mysterious reaches of the universe"; whereas, what the composer is really after is to transmit to the listener by way of *Carré* the intensified awareness of slowly moving time he himself experienced when flying in a plane. The content has perceptual, not mystical connotations: *Carré* is ultimately intended to challenge our ability to follow the slowest continuity yet perceived in a musical work up to that time. On the other hand, when we come to later works of Stockhausen, the likelihood of a mystical interpretation gains considerably, as has been noted by G.W. Hopkins, who writes of the text-scores of *Aus den sieben Tagen* and *Für kommende Zeiten* (1969–70): "Sympathetically treated, the music can yield a meditative, even yogic quality, highly characteristic of the composer's work after *Stimmung*."[31] The ritual element in a number of the later works, together with the religious overtones in Stockhausen's prose writings, leave little doubt that the music means to appeal to a nonrational level of consciousness akin to the deepest recesses of the inmost self envisioned by the Romantics. And yet, the rational/perceptual basis of Stockhausen's efforts throughout the 1950s and most of the 1960s remains an indelible point of reference. As Hopkins writes:[32]

[I]f one bears in mind the important influence of Indian religion in Stockhausen's thinking, it could be argued that the music is one of the century's supreme examples of religious expression. In his essays Stockhausen has constantly related his music to abstract conceptual propositions of a philosophical and religious nature and conversely, his music has frequently been a concrete, or symbolic representation of such propositions. But the philosophy of Stockhausen's music remains an unscaled peak; no scholar or critic has yet gained the perspective from which a comprehensive exegesis would be feasible, and consequently, discussion of his ideas and his system of reference necessarily remains somewhat piecemeal.

This assessment could equally apply to several contemporaries of Stockhausen who, like him, see the existential universe (*musica mundana*) and the universe which is the human consciousness (*musica humana*) as reflections of each other in their unresolved complexity and who therefore have no choice but to fashion a *musica instrumentalis* that embodies an ambiguous and unresolved content. Often the ambiguity prompts a composer to characterize his work with such oracular simplicity as to reinforce the ambiguity, as when Xenakis (who, being Greek, might have more right to be oracular than most), after describing the materials and processes that went into the making of *Orient-Occident III*—a cello being drawn over various substances, signals from the ionosphere electronically transformed—refers to the final climax of the piece as "an apotheosis of the new man."[33] The ethical implications of this reference are enticing, and we would like to know what the qualities of this new (and better?) man might be. Are these the qualities of someone who, in a purely formalist sense, has extended his appreciation of sound phenomena to the point of embracing the materials of *Orient-Occident* as genuine music and of hearing the succession of its sound events as a highly organized and continuous whole? Or does Xenakis mean to include more spiritual aspects of the human personality—the kind of man who is prepared to live with both the wonders and horrors of the new technology, or, as the title suggests, who sees an eventual synthesis between Eastern and Western ways of thinking? None of these interpretations can be ruled out, and the composer might well tell us that all of them are valid whether they originally occurred to him or not.

Although evocative titles or the explicit commentaries of a composer are the most efficient means of encouraging a listener's interest in the referential contents of a musical work, another category—that of musical quotation—has been pursued with surprising energy by a number of the most notable and ambitious exponents of the new music, among them Berio, Stockhausen, and Peter Maxwell Davies. Musical borrowing, of course, is a time-honored practice, as old as polyphony itself; but the very character of musical quotation has changed qualitatively as the opportunities for borrowing have increased exponentially in recent times. It is not merely that the musicological activities of the past several decades have made available whole categories of music that once seemed permanently lost to Western culture; it is also a question of attitude—a feeling on the part of the sophisticated intellectual musician that he must command his entire past. And in some cases, even the Western past is not enough; musical material from alien folk and popular cultures is also mined and integrated into new contexts by extremely diverse and resourceful means. Stockhausen has spoken of creating a "music of the whole world," and he has sought to realize this aim with his customary ingenuity. Berio's *oeuvre* also provides a number of examples of an extraordinary combinatorial imagination at work, the central movement alone of the *Sinfonia* (1968–69) incorporating quotations from Debussy, Strauss, Wagner and others, all "judiciously stitched" into the scherzo from Mahler's second symphony.[34] The extent to which the original materials are transformed and made to mix or disappear in the new melting pot varies from case to case, and only inspection on an individual basis would reveal where a work falls along the axis framed by the two polar techniques that Griffiths calls "collage" and "integration."[35] Similarly, the associative meanings of the old materials could only be determined by intensive study of their relations and combinations in any given work, though sharply satirical treatment of the materials (as happens routinely in Davies' earlier uses of chant and medieval polyphony) are not easily missed. However, whether done primarily in the interests of satire or in a more benign "ecumenical" spirit, the recent techniques of musical quotation ultimately show their modernist leanings, insofar as the quotations are left to coexist and collide rather than converge into a total unity. There has been a recent tendency to compare Stockhausen, because of the scale and scope of his later undertakings, to Wagner, but the comparison seems misplaced, if only because Wagner's encyclopedic aspirations are realized by means of a world in which every dramatic event is clearly motivated and every musical thread is woven into a single fabric; Stockhausen's "music of the whole world," by contrast, is a collection of heterogeneous actions that show little sign of giving up their restless multiplicity.

In most recent times, the dominance of the formalist aesthetic has gradually given way to a freewheeling eclecticism represented by the loosely related three-pronged alliance of total serialism, electronic music, and indeterminacy, which points in no clear direction. The changes have come about for both philosophical and practical reasons—partly in reaction to what numbers of artists took to be a relentless "scientism" on the part of the postwar avant-garde, partly as the result of efforts to win back an audience that was lost mainly because of that scientism. These problems had to some extent already been sensed by the avant-garde composers themselves and certain steps taken to deal with them. But steps independent of the avant-garde were also under way. Perhaps more out of a need to find some order in the new developments than to address comprehensively the complexities of the situation, critics have come up with the concepts "Neo-Romanticism" and "Minimalism" to cover the patchwork of viewpoints and procedures that the new developments represent. The "Neo-Romantic" label, in particular, seems much overworked, a catch-all term designed to embrace everything from nostalgic yearnings for quiet, *cantabile* lyricism to lavish reincarnations of late 19th-century Austro-Hungarian exuberance, replete with the robust gestures and glittering sonorities of the originals, though simultaneously sprinkled with telltale signs of the contemporary idiom.

Perhaps the only force to unite all branches of "Neo-Romanticism" would be the impulse to utilize and rework traditional structures—the harmonic progressions of functional tonality as well as the phraseological syntax of common-practice melody. Minimalism, too, has reclaimed harmonic progression as its fundamental tonal language, though in limited ways and without the periodic structure characteristic of traditional Western syntax. Philip Glass himself has noted the bow to Western tradition that the introduction of harmonic progression signalled for his music at the time he composed *Einstein on the Beach* (1975–76), the music written prior to that time ("rigorous and highly reductive") being "more radical in its departure from the received tradition of Western music than what I have written since."[36] Yet, his impression that this infusion of harmonic movement "marked a sharp break with the very rhythmically charged, but harmonically static, music I had written before"[37] is overstated, for it is hardly conceivable that the descending tetrachord ground bass, used throughout the seven scenes of an opera of several hours' length, as it is in *Satyagraha*, can produce anything but a harmonically static effect. But this seems only right, since tonal stasis—at least relative to the dynamic procedures of the common-practice period—is at the very heart of minimalist expression; or more precisely, the variability of durations and the irregularity of patterns and accents played against harmonic predictability are what constitute the expressive tension in Glass's style. Indeed, if this tension is the *sine qua non* of the minimalist effect, as it seems to be, one might say that a composer closely associated with minimalism ceases to be so, when, like John Adams in *Harmonielehre* (1987), he writes a piece of music in the frankly dynamic mode of traditional Western tonality.[38]

The minimalist preoccupation with the treatment of tone and rhythm bespeaks a decided formalist orientation, though the actual effects may eventually suggest more. Steve Reich's early essays with repetitive processes moving in and out of phase with each other make neat perceptual points, but the variants he introduces into the process of his later music complicate the perceptual situation; they point to the activation of at least two distinct levels of human perception.

On the one hand, the listener is invited to respond to the delicate shifts in patterning created by the intermittent alternation of a single tone in a harmonic complex, resulting in periodic refreshments of the harmonic palette; on the other hand, given the fact that these alterations are "minimal" relative to the entire duration of a work, it is only a matter of time before the drone-like effects of harmonic stasis and steady pulsation take over and the consciousness of the listener switches from rational awareness to something approaching trance. While the effect varies according to the attention span of the listener—both Reich and Glass have spoken at length about the importance of the listener in completing the artwork and contributing to its meaning[39]—the tendency to descend, over time, into a state of nonrational consciousness is virtually irresistible. As those sympathetic to Glass's theater pieces have repeatedly witnessed, the hypnotic character of the experience is what they take away as its lasting and therapeutic effect, the feeling of being wrapped in a shroud of sound.[40] Mention of nonrational consciousness gives rise, as in the case of Stockhausen's meditative rituals, to comparison with ultra-Romantic music, and again, the differences must be pointed out. Large-scale Romantic music is alive with momentous events, a field of dramatic contrasts, multifarious gestures, and "climaxes that climb on and on."[41] Large-scale minimalist music is not devoid of event, nor need it dispense with changes of sonority and dynamics nor with effects of sustained energy that proceed, in large part, from tensions of nonsynchronizing patterns. The sustained energy is not, however, the kind that builds to climaxes—that climbs on and on— but rather that achieves a steady state; the rhythm of minimalism is motoric, its gesture mechanistic; the inescapable fate of minimalist music, for all its diversity of pattern, is to suggest no diversity of gesture.

The minimalist preference for steady propulsion over gesture is at once the unique feature of its language and in the eyes of its critics its chief limitation (self-imposed though that limitation may be). But where the subject of musical language is concerned, minimalism is hardly alone in being cited for its faults; the language of every musical movement of the postwar period has been found wanting in some significant respect. With indeterminacy, the complaint has been directed against its having abandoned the search for a language altogether and with that, the belief, held sacred since the early days of Romanticism, that art music offers the myth of a profound and dependable, though in all likelihood, incomplete, knowing. With Neo-Romanticism, the complaint is scarcely less serious, this time lodged against the tendency to regress or at best to try to resuscitate an outmoded language. Minimalism, by contrast, has produced a genuine language, but one, it is alleged, so reduced in variety of event and information that it leaves the perceptual resources of a reasonably sophisticated listener largely untapped. Total serialism is charged with having moved in the diametrically opposite direction, becoming in the process a monstrous *super-logos* guilty of pushing perceptual powers beyond the point they should be made to go.

Is there any hope of finding a language which would allay the criticism and serve the future of Western music, as classical tonality and its structures served the past? In the closing comments of his excellent history of avant-garde music since 1945, Paul Griffiths writes:[42]

If a new common language is to be found whether at IRCAM or elsewhere, it seems likely that it will not be able to ignore the recent past, and that it will therefore have to be a synthesis of the most diverse means and methods. Perhaps it is more probable that the present condition will persist, and that new directions in music will forever fork more than they intertwine.

A common language presumably speaks for a sizeable community. But in this case, a community of approximately what size and shape? One that reunites the aspirations of "high" and popular art, that represents both the East and the West? There is no doubting one point: a common language will not materialize until there arises a genuine desire for such a thing, until artists themselves embrace the idea in such numbers that it becomes the prevailing aesthetic (or more generally still, an important *mythos* of the culture). Since the advent of Romanticism, the creative emphasis in Western art has been on individuality and difference; should that emphasis change, a common language would not only be a distinct possibility, it might come about more quickly than recent musical history would permit us to imagine.

Notes

1. Eric Salzman, *Twentieth-Century Music: An Introduction*, p. 49.
2. Quoted in "Stockhausen, Karlheinz," *The New Grove Dictionary of Music and Musicians*, Stanley Sadie, ed., Vol. XVIII, p. 155.
3. Pierre Boulez, *Conversations with Célestin Deliège*, p. 18.
4. *Ibid.*, p. 24.
5. *Ibid.*, p. 64.
6. *Ibid.*, p. 66.
7. *Ibid.*, pp. 51–52.
8. *Ibid.*, p. 64.
9. *Ibid.*, pp. 64–65.
10. Pierre Boulez, *Boulez on Music Today*, p. 32.
11. *Ibid.*, p. 32.
12. Quoted in Piero Weiss and Richard Taruskin, ed., *Music in the Western World*, p. 507. See also Paul Griffiths, *Modern Music: The Avant Garde since 1945*, p. 26.
13. Quoted in Weiss/Taruskin, p. 508.
14. See *ibid.*, p. 508, and Griffiths, p. 22.
15. For Babbitt's disagreements with Boulez and Stockhausen on their applications of serial methods, see Griffiths, pp. 38 and pp. 93–94.
16. Certain gross aspects of Expressionist imagery figure in Boulez's style—the enormous vocal range, the wide leaps, the active and supple counterpoint; but the Expressionist *Angst*, captured in what Boulez himself once uncharitably called "the clichés of

the most ostentatious and obsolete romanticism... those constant anticipations, with expressive leaning on the key note... those false appoggiaturas... those formulas of arpeggios..." is missing.

17. "Stockhausen, Karlheinz," *New Grove*, Vol. XVIII, p. 152.
18. See Weiss/Taruskin, p. 528.
19. *Ibid.*, pp. 527–528.
20. David Schiff, *The Music of Elliott Carter*, p. 57.
21. Record notes from the Nonesuch recording of Carter's first and second string quartets, No. H-71249.
22. Schiff, p. 55.
23. Carter, record notes (see n. 21 *supra*).
24. Schiff, p. 57.
25. Carter, record notes (see n. 21 *supra*).
26. Weiss/Taruskin, p. 528.
27. Roger Kamien, *Music, An Appreciation*, p. 492.
28. Boulez, *Conversations*, p. 84.
29. See Griffiths' extended discussion on this point, pp. 66–70 and pp. 124–126.
30. Record notes from the DGG Avant garde recording of *Gruppen* and *Carré*, No. 137 002.
31. "Stockhausen, Karlheinz," *New Grove*, Vol. XVIII, p. 154.
32. *Ibid.*, p. 155.
33. Record notes from the Nonesuch recording of a number of electronic works of Xenakis, No. H-71246.
34. Griffiths, p. 208.
35. *Ibid.*, pp. 200–219.
36. Philip Glass, *Music by Philip Glass*, p. 62.
37. *Ibid.*, p. 62.
38. Indeed, *Harmonielehre* easily lends itself to being dubbed "Neo-Romantic."
39. See Griffiths, p. 179, and Glass, p. 35.
40. This is a paraphrase of a comment made by a journalist that Glass himself thought astute enough to quote: "Leighton Kerner (music critic of the *Village Voice*) remarked that the key of A minor envelops the opera [*Akhnaten*] like a shroud, a description I find both poetic and accurate." (Glass, p. 174).
41. The reference is to E.T.A. Hoffmann's seminal description of Beethoven's fifth symphony, quoted in Chapter 10 of this book.
42. Griffiths, p. 298. The reference to IRCAM is to the Institut de Recherche et de Coordination Acoustique/Musique located at the Centre Beaubourg, Paris.

Epilogue

17 *Analysis and Culture*

Despite its bow to chronology, the survey presented in Parts II, III and IV of this book is not a history of music in the usual sense, providing no adequate coverage of genres, techniques, or formal schemes. Nor is it a history of aesthetics, since, despite numerous references to aesthetic theories, it does not deal with these in any systematic way. Rather, it is a history of ideas which happen to express themselves in the form of music. In this understanding of the word, "idea" is not a concept, but a *conception*—something which has the potential for being a concept but which could just as readily take the shape of a poem or a painting or a ritual or a musical image. By including the musical image in this picture, I am proposing that musicology participate in the history of ideas in the same unquestioning way that literary criticism and the fine arts have been doing for lo these many years. Western music being an artifact of Western culture, it must make up something of the patterns of thought of that culture, in the nature of any symbolistic mode. Music criticism, therefore, has a right, if not a responsibility, to explicate the musical symbols.

This presupposes that we understand art as expressing its contents through a modality other than the discursive symbol. Art operates by means of the image, which is to say that its primary target is not the rational mind but the aesthetic field of our consciousness, that "field" being the interaction of what Nietzsche identified as the Dionysian, intuitional level of our consciousness and the Apollonian, image-making level. The aesthetic field of consciousness is often referred to as our "sensibility," the capacity in us to respond to the sensuousness of an image and convert the sensuous material into an "essence"—into something virtually metaphysical, existing outside of time and space. The sensibility, in other words, is our way of grasping the artistic experience as a whole, of reducing it to "a single *quality*," as John Dewey writes, "that pervades the entire experience in spite of the variation of its constituent parts."[1] Frye has referred to this unifying quality as the "underlying tonality,"[2] and Edward Cone calls it the "context."[3] We realize that sensibility is the passive complement, so to speak, of the imagination, the latter working as it does to convert an intuition into an image. Archetypal criticism thus promotes the sensibility as the chief agent for reading artistic imagery. But for formalists—and for critics of other persuasions as well—the sensibility presents itself as a categorically unreliable tool. For what rigor is there in relying on a mechanism that operates below the level of rational consciousness and whose thought-product is in the nature of an overall impression?

It is at this point that archetypal criticism advances its central principle— the principle that serves as a unifying framework for the concepts of image, content, and sensibility—namely, the archetype. By virtue of the archetype, it is possible to show that the sensibility need not be some subjective mental apparatus dealing loosely and haphazardly with artistic imagery, but can be a finely tuned instrument conditioned in its own right by the commonly held values of a culture. In short, archetypal criticism finds it as natural to call the sensibility a "cultural product" as the artistic phenomena to which it responds. The sensibility itself may not operate on the rational level of consciousness, but the conventions which have gone into shaping it can be rationally classified and described.

Frye has written that poetry is "a body of forms and categories to which every new poem attaches itself somewhere,"[4] and this is as complete a statement of purpose as archetypal criticism needs in order to go about its business. The challenge to the critic is to fashion artistic categories which will correspond to widely held views of reality. In Chapter 1, it was noted that the conception of the archetype can be applied to an image as well as to a pattern of thought. In its connection with the former the archetype was characterized as the "conventional aspect of the image" or as "the name we give to a collective corpus of images which closely resemble each other." We gradually discovered, however, that working from the point of view of the archetypal image had its limitations. We could perhaps identify hunting or military archetypes as having a relative stability throughout music history, but how many more image types of this sort would be forthcoming? Just as literary symbols such as "the rose," "the sea," and "the garden" do not figure in Frye's critical framework, so it was soon clear that musical images, no matter how "archetypal" in appearance, could not directly serve in the construction of the model worked out in Chapter 2. To be sure, certain strong image-associations have emerged in the course of this study: the major and minor modes with the comic and tragic visions, respectively; declamatory expression with strong *pathos*, lyrical expression with elegy; "harmonious sweetness" with romance, "contentiousness" and "asperity" with irony. But any one of these associations is only semidefinitive in character, being subject to continual qualification in a given image by the presence of other associations which have as much claim in creating the ultimate "tonality" of the image as the initial association. Reading an image for its content, in short, involves a number of interlocking frames of reference. With that in mind, it becomes increasingly clear that the only sure way of building a systematic structure of associations is to begin from the standpoint of the archetypal content and proceed toward the conventional image.

This procedure results in the identification of a number of expressive types which symbolize views of reality that are of fairly "universal" significance. Our tendency to glorify and exalt gets crystallized in heroic expression, while our inclination to belittle is best projected through satire; it is in pastoral that our will toward peace and serenity is most completely worked out; in melodrama we get a definitive sense of the world as excitement and mystery. The principle of archetypal content enables us to cross the boundaries not only between style periods but also between the various arts themselves, leading us to find common elements running through seemingly unrelated areas. Thus, "nihilistic play" would seem to be the "tone" linking such disparate images as Aristophanic satire, the troubador *leis de con*, the trouvère *pastourelle*, the *canti carnascialeschi*, the French patter-chanson, comic scenes from Cavalli operas, opera buffa finales, Dada, and happenings à la John Cage.

At the same time, we can study the evolution of an archetypal content as it comes into contact with the attitudes of a given society and gets reinterpreted—and enriched—in the process. The original thrust of pastoral, for example, is deeply antiheroic, envisioning a world far from the tumult of great deeds and warlike glory. This central idyllic tone pastoral never loses; but over the ages new tones and new meanings are interpolated. Thus, Arcadian pastoral in modern Europe becomes the archetypal vehicle for embodying the ideals of cultivated beauty and behavior. The Baroque version of Arcadian pastoral performs a variation on the Renaissance version, adding languor to tenderness. Impressionism incorporates all these elements, but effectively transforms them by enlisting their connotations in the service of a qualitatively different vision, namely, ephemerality. Rustic pastoral is the reaction against Arcadian pastoral: it preserves the idyllic archetype but it says that the idyll is not to be found in cultivated beauty and behavior, but in a serenity of spirit which is an inner beauty. Bartok takes rustic pastoral one step further by indicting the socially accepted canons of beauty of "civilized"—may we say "Arcadianized"?—modern Europe, as leading to preciosity and veneer, in other words, to "vulgarity" and ugliness. The result of this reversal is that we will miss the new idyllic tone in Bartok's music if we look too closely for the old Arcadian convention.

Heroic, pastoral, and melodramatic archetypes do not constitute the most comprehensive categories of the archetypal system; that status is reserved for the five dichotomies introduced in Part I. The dichotomies are the most comprehensive categories because they are the most elemental—the structures which help us to unravel the mixtures and compounds of which individual images, and even archetypes such as the heroic and pastoral, are made up. The dichotomies bring us into contact with the most fundamental visions of reality. With regard to Western culture they encompass the ideas with which the various segments of the culture have tried and continue to try to meet the fundamental problems of living in the world. These ideas and their variants form the primary conceptual framework of the book—primary in the sense of corresponding to the content of the culture as a whole. But a secondary conceptual structure is introduced in Part II, which, though not superseding the dichotomies in importance, determines the course of the rest of the book. Organized around a triad of concepts called here "ethos," "pathos," and "logos," this structure proceeds from the notion of a changing aesthetic relative to the capacities of Western music in dealing with the archetypal contents. In other words, it is one thing to study content as a function of *Zeitgeist*, the beliefs, ideals, values, etc., of a given community; it is another to determine the place accorded to music itself in the community's value system. Is music thought primarily to be in the business of (1) shaping human character (*ethos*) or (2) exploring human emotion (*pathos*) or (3) leading to ultimate truth (*logos*)? The book makes a case for a general progression from (1) to (3) over the course of Western musical history, though the presence of one tendency should not be understood to exclude the others.

The above questions have been subjected to elaborate discussion throughout Parts II, III, and IV, but it may serve some purpose here to quickly review the main points. We begin with the musical aesthetic dominated by *ethos*, according to which musical imagery is designed to embody—and in turn foster—a certain comportment. Comportment is of the "ethical" type when it is deemed appropriate to a way of life whose virtues are held in high regard by a considerable body of adherents. Ancient Dorian hymns, Gregorian chants (especially of the syllabic variety), and songs of courtly love are "ethical" kinds of music because they embody codes of human behavior sanctioned—indeed, prescribed—by institutions with wide and persistent appeal (the Socratic school of moral philosophy, the early Christian Church, the courts of medieval Provence). According to such an aesthetic (one may quite as readily call it an "ethic"), behavior reflects character; and in the cases just cited, since the codes of behavior are by definition virtuous, the music in question reflects "good character."

When the musical philosophy is guided by the principle of *pathos*, it is believed that music records human beings acting according to the way they feel: behavior is thought of as a sign not of character but of emotion. In themselves, emotions carry no ethical value; they are neither good nor bad, merely pleasurable or painful. Thus, at the end of the 16th century, we find composers insisting on the expression of stormy and violent feelings because such feelings are a fact of human nature; to deny music any part of its responsibility in covering the full range of the inner life would be to deny truth itself. This kind of thinking is most purely expressed in the dark madrigals of Wert, Gesualdo, and Monteverdi and in the monodies of early Italian opera. However, it is not long before an ethical concern has been introduced—or more accurately, reintroduced—into the picture. Tempestuous feelings are qualified as "noble," the property of warriors and authority figures. Tragedy in music becomes grandly heroic, and the ancient hieratic division between high and low styles is reaffirmed. But, in fact, the division itself was never absent from Classical humanistic thinking; it is rather that in the 17th and 18th centuries, the notion of separate heroic, pastoral, and satiric characters asserts itself in musical terms with particular clarity, and thus engenders a fund of images the basis of whose expressive life is an interaction of ethical and affective factors.

The fact that aestheticians of the period rarely explain musical content in anything but affective terms (or in terms that they, at least, take to have affective force) does not argue against the presence of strong ethical connotations. One of the main premises of this book, buttressed and supported in particular by the discussions devoted to the three "modes" in Chapters 8–11, has been that ethical considerations dwell implicitly in the imagery in spite of the fact that they have not been acknowledged explicitly in the critical literature. If I have insisted on this point, it is not only because musical imagery appears considerably enriched when recognized as containing an ethical as well as an affective component, but even more, perhaps, because the critic's vocabulary becomes increasingly flexible *and objective* as he deals with the ethical implications of affective behavior. In the 17th and 18th centuries, it was customary to say that a certain musical image expressed a certain emotion. What archetypal criticism prefers to say is that a musical image from the period in question confronts us not with an emotion directly, but with a behavior from which we infer an emotion. Moreover, this behavior is a function not merely of how a person acts under the sway of a certain emotion but how a certain kind of person acts in general. The aesthetic assumption here is that a musical image expresses *something*, but a major part of what we designate as the content of the image has to do with the *manner* in which that something is expressed. If that seems to complicate matters, it also clarifies them, for the manner of expression enables us to know who is doing the expressing. And the kind of person identified in turn signals a reliable and objective meaning, because the meaning is shared and conventional; it has cultural backing, it corresponds to the various ways members of a given society prefer (and in some cases, prefer not) to see themselves. Or we might reverse this proposition by saying that musical imagery is one further means by which the preferences of a given society find expression—"take concrete form."

The above formulation works very well, I think, for the period of Classical humanism, much less so for the period following. The reasons are several. In the first place, an aesthetic governed by the principle of *logos* implies a quite radical alteration in the relation between the artwork and its receiver. In contradistinction to the traditional conception of that relation, in which the listener finds directly through the musical imagery the emotions, actions, and character-types he believes he knows from the everyday world, the new conception proposes an artwork which is intended to be the projection of "deep inner life," with all that connotes of an amalgam of emotions, sensations, and higher spiritual longings. The artwork at one and the same time expresses the content of that inner life and becomes the experience whereby the inner life of the individual listener can be significantly fulfilled. This new relation between artwork and listener brings in its wake important changes in the way post-18th-century musical imagery is (or should be) read.

It is not that heroic, pastoral, and satiric themes cease to have a place in the new imagery and to carry much of their old meaning; it is rather that they cease to carry the same weight of meaning. Initially conceived by societies to image their most cherished ideals, the traditional heroic, pastoral, and satiric character-types are individuals whose identities come into focus within (indeed, only within) a social context. The hero of Romanticism, by contrast, is an individual who operates independently of, if not against, society (this in spite of the proverbial need of Romantic artists and art lovers to form their own society). Heroic, pastoral, and satiric masks may well be—and are frequently—donned by the Romantic hero, but their proper meanings will be understood only as they are filtered through the primary contents of Romanticism. In short, these masks come to represent secondary contents, adjuncts to the central ideas of the new aesthetic, the means by which the new ideas—themes of transcendence, sensual exhilaration, and deep inwardness, themes consistent with the vision of art as a *logos*, as a pathway to an ultimate kind of truth—get translated into concrete form.

We might say that the central archetypes of the period of Classical humanism continue to figure prominently in the period of "transcendental humanism" so long as they reinforce the main issues of the later period. Heroic images are important to Romantic music because of the tendency to glorify which is common to them both; but it is important to remember that in the new context, the old heroic archetype no longer directly represents itself, it serves in the interests of another archetype to which the evolution of ideas has forced it to give way. Thus, heroic elegy is a recurrent pattern in Brahms's work, so much so that it might be said that Brahms's music expresses the pattern more completely and memorably than any other music. But heroic elegy does not form the basis of Brahms's style; it does not apply to the style as a whole. That function is reserved for the quality described in Chapter 14 as the "Innigkeit of the Brahmsian hero," whose specific inwardness comes from a long and continued familiarity with life's occasional triumphs and more frequent disappointments. In its turn, Brahmsian Innigkeit does much to explain the prominence of heroic elegy in Brahms's work, the conventional images of heroic elegy materially aiding in expressing the central feeling of the "voice of experience," the feeling we call "autumnal." Similarly, the "Schubertian hero," though resembling in many particulars the *Volkstümlich* version of the rustic pastoral hero, is finally something else, something essentially mystical and without social identity. The special "visionary" gift attaching to this protagonist is the kind of Innigkeit that defines Schubert's style in general— running like a current, so to speak, throughout the style—whereas the images of *Volkstümlichkeit*, prevalent as they are in Schubert's work, also give way to other contrasting images. As for a more recent example, galant images play a significant part in Stravinsky's Neoclassical music, because they help create the climate in which to carry out the core aim of Stravinsky's formalist position, namely, awareness of complex orders and fine distinctions.

Just as the vision of music as a *logos* influences the way we read 19th- and

20th-century musical images, so it has been the determining factor in the point of view adopted in Part IV of this book. The already philosophical tone of the earlier pages becomes even more emphatic in the discussions on the 19th and 20th century, in no small part because the correspondence between image and *primary* content in this period ceases to be a direct one-to-one relation. It is, of course, necessary, no matter what the period in question, to establish the cultural context for the period's imagery—necessary, that is, if we are interested, to begin with, in reading an image for what has been defined in these pages as its content: the gestures of an image will not—cannot—point unequivocally to a content all on their own. But with 19th- and 20th-century music, the necessity for establishing a context—for knowing the precise aesthetic motivations behind the imagery—is particularly acute. To understand better why this is so, we may think back once again to the kinds of "hero"—the human types—that have been identified in the course of this study. Running our minds over the list, we notice that all the types emerging before 1800 have been defined by their *behavior*, all those after 1800 by their *consciousness*. Consciousness and *logos* being the complementary principles of a single process, this is as it should be; but the problem looms large of how to *image* consciousness—how to represent consciousness in terms of vocal and rhythmic gesture—whereas the concreteness of behavior suggests *mimesis*, or the business of making correspondences between human gesture and musical gesture, as if immediately and self-evidently.

The disjunction between the materiality of behavior and the immateriality of consciousness in turn causes something of a disjunction in the progress of this book: Parts II and III have as their main thrust to show the emergence of images whose gestures, however stylized and subject to convention, are taken to represent patterns of behavior observed in everyday life. If this had been the main thrust of Part IV, the resulting image-conventions would have indicated only secondary contents—the older heroic, pastoral, and satiric archetypes done up in Romantic and modernist dress. (Indeed, these are precisely the kinds of content presented in the final portions of Chapters 8–11).

In order to be certain about getting to the primary contents of 19th- and 20th-century music, we have had to focus on quality of mind—on a conception that we may call "seats of consciousness"—as the means of distinguishing between the human types emerging in this period. Thus, the heroes of Romanticism are identified in terms of a deep consciousness operating far below the rational level: the melodramatic hero is a function of surpassing exhilaration which has its origins in the natural connection to life and life's primal energy; the Innigkeit hero is a function of his unusual capacity to understand the world, a capacity whose diverse sources may well go beyond the four—selfless love, Christian faith, visionary innocence, and worldly experience—enumerated in Chapter 14. The chief characteristic of the Expressionist hero is a troubled unconsciousness, which, raised to the formal level of art, becomes a means to self-revelation and exorcism of inner demons. The identity of the Primitivist hero is revealed chiefly through his cultural perspective, which he seeks to improve by taking on a fresh world view. Located far closer to the rational domain than those just described are the "seats of consciousness" envisioned in formalist art. The heroes associated with Stravinskyan and Webernian formalism express the will to escape the disorder of the existential world by entering into worlds whose complexity is ultimately seen as constituting a perfect order. The hero of total determinism, by contrast, is defined by his very tolerance for disorder, by the stimulation he receives from the experience of having his consciousness buffeted back and forth between the rational and nonrational poles.

Such character-types, based as they are on an immaterial principle, do not indicate the gestures of their corresponding musical images with anything of the concreteness of the old "behavioral" conventions, but they do form a solid cultural context for and around the images: they serve to reassure us that conventional connotations attach to 19th- and 20th-century styles quite as much as they do to earlier ones. They also serve to point up the sharp differences in connotation between later and earlier images, the fact that the growing tendency to nontraditional expression reflects a growing disaffection with the European cultural tradition. Above all, they organize the history of 19th- and 20th-century music in two significant ways. First, the notion is confirmed that the Romantic and modernist periods are unified by virtue of their belief in art as supreme significance. Second, we see that the same two periods are distinctly separated in terms of ultimate ethical consequences. Romanticism, with characteristic optimism, views art as the sure path to oneness, to total integration of the personality. With its ironic turn of mind, modernism has given up hope of oneness, it settles for the fragmented and the incomplete. But it should be realized that this modernist attitude applies to the human condition as a whole, not to art in particular. Art is limited only because the human capacity to understand is limited; for the modernist as for the Romantic, art has enormous value, despite its limitations.

To conceive of a group of human types as being "in back of" characteristic vocal and rhythmic gestures of Western music has been the concrete means by which to show not only that music has the symbolizing capacity of its sister arts but also how and to what extent the popular idea of music expressing human emotion and behavior has a cultural basis and a long history. A more abstract or philosophical way of stating the matter would be to say that musical images came to be invested with certain contents in accordance with the desire (perhaps, need) of a community to have its fondest beliefs expressed musically. This, in brief, is the book's substance—what it set out to do in a conceptual sense. In the page or two remaining, I would like to return to a couple of practical considerations touched upon in the opening chapter. In particular, I would like to call attention to something the book did not set out to do—something which could not have been done, given the specific parameters of this study, but for which a cornerstone has at least been laid.

Before turning to this issue, one other practical matter should first be mentioned: I see as an immediate outlet for the ideas of this book their incorporation into Introduction to Music and Music Appreciation courses. Traditionally, these courses have been conducted as history surveys, and, in their turn, history surveys have provided little more than a dutiful accounting of the rises and falls of techniques, genres, and styles. In such an accounting, one style period changes inexorably into another, as if changes in style were everyday occurrences in the life of music—occurrences obeying some unspoken law of musical nature, without reference to a world outside. What needs to be added to this approach is a sense of music as an expressive language; for that is the sense in which students coming to music appreciation courses think of music, and they want confirmation that changes of style correspond materially to ways in which people over the ages have felt about their own music—how it has spoken to them, how it has functioned in their lives. The present book is designed to provide some guidance in this respect.

But it is actually in another respect—in the area of analysis—that I envision certain long-term possibilities for this study. That I should make analysis the final consideration here may strike some readers as curious, given the fact that it has figured virtually nowhere in the discussion. Indeed, this book being a "theory" pure and simple, there was no place for practical analysis, either of the structural or archetypal kind. It is true that twice in the course of Part I—in particular, in the summary to Chapter 2—I have briefly proposed what form an archetypal analysis might take. I also make clear in the same summary that I have no intention of acting on my proposal. As I explicitly state there, all musical examples in the book are introduced as illustrations of conventional types; they are never meant to stand on their own. My point about the first movement from the Mozart concerto, K. 467, is not about *it*, but about a conventional relation that develops in the late 18th century between sonata-allegro form and high Classicism. The concerto movement in question is merely the one example that has to stand for literally hundreds of Mozart and Haydn sonata-allegro movements, any one of which could have served as illustration because all contain the same buffa, festal pomp, *Sturm und Drang*, and cantabile elements. Of course, each work contains these elements in different strengths and concentrations. From the first measures of the D minor concerto, K. 466, we can tell that the *Sturm und Drang* pattern is going to predominate, as opposed to its almost parenthetical role in K. 467; but, given the theoretical posture of this book, I have had to stop short of going into such differences.

The analytical method I have in mind, however, does not end with "archetypal analysis": it presupposes the archetypal findings to be brought into an interaction with certain techniques of structural analysis, notably those belonging to the area of rhythmic theory. To be somewhat more precise about the procedure: before an individual work is studied on its own, its function as a member of an entire tradition of individual works—its place in a general cultural context—must be ascertained; only then can its own context—its "primary tonality"—be extracted and molded from the total body of contents the culture provides. Once this operation is completed, the methods of syntactic analysis can be brought to bear, for the context thus established is now understood to be the background against which the interior interactions and continuities of a given work take place. In archetypal thinking the individual gestures do not so much build up a context as articulate it. This two-phased process, then, is more than a syntactic analysis: it is a *formal* analysis, insofar as the form of a work is defined by two distinct principles, the one that shapes the work, the other that contains it.[5]

What music criticism is searching for, above all (and I believe I am speaking for everyone involved in the new movement without exception), is a coherent method for dealing with an individual piece of music—a method utilizing the tools of analysis as traditionally practiced, but in a culturally more informed way than analysis has traditionally allowed. With a view to that end, critics have already come up with a variety of methods, none of them fully coherent, some of them providing equal parts of brilliance, fancy, and precious little to build on. Perhaps one day we will see a consensus of approach, perhaps not. Where there is clearly no lack of consensus already today is in the desire to convince the professional analysts that musical meaning can be something more than syntactic organization. I understand the analyst's preoccupation with objective findings, because I share that preoccupation. And that is precisely why I believe every effort should be made to put the nonsyntactic aspects of music on an objective footing. I have almost forgotten that the present study began, quite a few years ago, as a method of structural analysis. I am periodically reminded of this fact when I come across a sheaf of discarded pages with Schenker-like graphs and schematic designs. What hampered progress in that project and eventually led to its abandonment was the inadequacy, so far as I could see, of any of the existing formulations of the form/content relationship. It became more and more apparent to me that before it was possible to deal with the continuities of a given work—the interactions of its parts—it was necessary to know it as a whole. I am enough of an analyst to believe that studying the inner workings of a piece in an effort to understand how it makes its effects and comes by its power is still the most absorbing process of all. But I would maintain that to carry out this process in proper order, setting the context is the indispensable first step.

Notes

1. John Dewey, *Art as Experience*, p. 37.
2. Northrop Frye, *Anatomy of Criticism*, p. 50.
3. Edward T. Cone, *The Composer's Voice*, pp. 162–165.
4. Northrop Frye, *Fables of Identity*, p. 44.
5. This bifocal conception of form comes from Frye; see *Anatomy*, p. 83.

Bibliography

Abert, Anna Amalie, "The Operas of Mozart," *The New Oxford History of Music*, ed. Egon Wellesz and Frederic Sternfeld. London: Oxford University Press, 1973.

Adams, Henry, *Mont-Saint-Michel and Chartres*. New York: G.P. Putnam, 1980.

Adorno, Theodor W., *Prisms*, trans. Samuel and Shierry Weber. Letchworth, U.K.: Garden City Press, 1967.

Allanbrook, Wye Jamison, *Rhythmic Gesture in Mozart*. Chicago: University of Chicago Press, 1983.

Alpers, Paul, *The Singer of the Eclogues: A Study of Virgilian Pastoral*. Berkeley: University of California Press, 1979.

Arbeau, Thoinot, *Orchesography*, trans. Mary Stewart Evans. New York: Dover Publications, 1984.

Aristotle, *The Poetics*, trans. W. Hamilton Fyfe. Cambridge, Mass.: Harvard University Press, 1927.

Auerbach, Erich, *Mimesis*, trans. Willard P. Trask. Princeton: Princeton University Press, 1953.

Austin, William, *Music in the 20th Century*. New York: W.W. Norton, 1966.

Bach, C.P.E., *Essay on the True Art of Playing Keyboard Instruments*, trans. William J. Mitchell. New York: W.W. Norton, 1949.

Bach, Johann Christian, *Temistocle*, ed. Edward O.D. Downes and H.C. Robbins Landon. Vienna: Universal, 1965.

Barker, Andrew, ed., *Greek Musical Writings*. Cambridge, U.K.: Cambridge University Press, 1984.

Barth, Herbert et al., ed., *Wagner: A Documentary Study*. New York: Oxford University Press, 1975.

Barthes, Roland, *Image, Music, Text*, trans. Stephen Heath. New York: Farrar, Strauss, and Giroux, 1977.

———, *Mythologies*. Paris: Editions du Seuil, 1957.

Barzun, Jacques, *Berlioz and His Century*. Chicago: University of Chicago Press, 1956.

————, *Classic, Romantic, and Modern*. Chicago: University of Chicago Press, 1943.

————, *Pleasures of Music*. Chicago: University of Chicago Press, 1977.

Beardsley, Monroe C. and Schueller, Herbert M., ed., *Aesthetic Inquiry*. Belmont, Calif.: Dickenson Publishing Co., 1967.

Bell, Clive, *Since Cézanne*. Freeport, N.Y.: Books for Libraries Press, 1969.

Berman, Laurence, "*Prelude to the Afternoon Faun* and *Jeux*: Debussy's Summer Rites," *19th-Century Music*, Vol. III (1980).

————, *Words and Music: The Scholar's View*. Cambridge, Mass.: Harvard University Department of Music, 1972.

Berman, Marshall, *All That Is Solid Melts Into Air*. New York: Simon and Schuster, 1982.

Bernstein, Lawrence F., "The 'Parisian Chanson': Problems of Style and Terminology," *Journal of the American Musicological Society*, Vol. XXXI, No. 2 (1978), pp. 193–240.

Beye, Charles Rowan, *Ancient Greek Literature and Society*. Garden City, N.Y.: Doubleday & Co., 1975.

Black, Michael, *Poetic Drama as Mirror of the Will*. New York: Harper & Row, 1977.

Blume, Friedrich, *Classic and Romantic Music*, trans. M.D. Herter Norton. New York: W.W. Norton, 1970.

————, *Renaissance and Baroque Music*, trans. M.D. Herter Norton. New York: W.W. Norton, 1967.

Boman, Thorleif, *Hebrew Thought Compared with Greek*. New York: W.W. Norton, 1970.

Boulez, Pierre, *Boulez on Music Today*, trans. Susan Bradshaw and Richard Rodney Bennett. London: Faber and Faber, 1971.

————, *Conversations with Célestin Deliège*. London: Eulenburg, 1976.

Bower, Calvin, "Natural and Artificial Music: The Origins and Development of an Aesthetic Concept," *Musica Disciplina*, Vol. 25 (1971).

Bronowski, Jacob, *The Ascent of Man*. Boston: Little, Brown, 1973.

Brown, Howard M., *Music in the Renaissance*. Englewood Cliffs, N.J.: Prentice-Hall, 1976.

Bruyère, Jean de la, *Les Caractères*. Paris: Garnier-Flammarion, 1965.

Buchanan, Scott, ed., *The Portable Plato*. New York: Viking Press, 1948.

Buelow, George J., "Music, Rhetoric, and the Concept of Affections," *Notes*, Vol. XXX (1973).

Burckhardt, Jacob, *The Civilization of the Renaissance in Italy*. New York: Harper and Row, 1975. 2 vols.

Burgess, Anthony, *This Man & Music*. New York: Avon Books, 1982.

Butcher, S.H., trans. and ed., *Aristotle's Theory of Poetry and Fine Art*. New York: Dover Publications, 1894.

Butler, Ruth, *Western Sculpture: Definitions of Man*. Boston: New York Graphic Society, 1975.

Cairns, Huntington, ed., *The Limits of Art*. Princeton: Princeton University Press, 1970. 3 vols.

Campbell, Joseph, *The Masks of God*. Harmondsworth, U.K.: Penguin Books, 1976. 4 vols.

Cannon, Beekman, *Johann Mattheson, Spectator in Music*. New Haven, Conn.: Yale University Press, 1947.

Cassirer, Ernst, *Language and Myth*, trans. Susanne K. Langer. New York: Dover Publications, 1953.

Chatwin, Bruce, *In Patagonia*. New York: 1977.

Cohn, Robert Greer, *Toward the Poems of Mallarmé*. Berkeley: University of California Press, 1980.

Coker, Wilson, *Music & Meaning*. New York: Free Press, 1972.

Cone, Edward T., ed., *Berlioz, Fantastic Symphony*. New York: W.W. Norton, 1971.

————, *The Composer's Voice*. Berkeley: University of California Press, 1974.

————, *Musical Form and Musical Performance*. New York: W.W. Norton, 1968.

Conrad, Peter, *Romantic Opera and Literary Form*. Berkeley: University of California Press, 1977.

Conze, Edward, *Buddhism, Its Essence and Development*. New York: Harper and Row, 1951.

Cook, Albert and Dolin, Edwin, ed., *An Anthology of Greek Tragedy*. Indianapolis/New York: Bobbs-Merrill, 1972.

Cook, Olive et al., ed., *The Praeger Picture Encyclopedia of Art*. New York: Praeger Books, 1958.

Cooper, Grosvenor and Meyer, Leonard B., *The Rhythmic Structure of Music*. Chicago: University of Chicago Press, 1960.

Copland, Aaron, *Music and Imagination*. Cambridge, Mass.: Harvard University Press, 1959.

Croix, Horst de la and Tansey, Richard G., rev., *Gardner's Art Through the Ages*. New York: Harcourt, Brace, & World, 1970.

Dahlhaus, Carl, *Between Romanticism and Modernism*, trans. Mary Whittall. Berkeley: University of California Press, 1980.

————, *Richard Wagner's Music Dramas*, trans. Mary Whittal. Cambridge, U.K.: Cambridge University Press, 1979.

Davison, Archibald T. and Apel, Willi, ed., *Historical Anthology of Music*. Cambridge, Mass.: Harvard University Press, 1946, 1950. 2 vols.

Dewey, John, *Art as Experience*. New York: Paragon Books, 1979.

Dodds, E.R., *The Greeks and the Irrational*. Berkeley: University of California Press, 1951.

Eco, Umberto, *The Aesthetics of Thomas Aquinas*, trans. Hugh Bredin. Cambridge, Mass.: Harvard University Press, 1988.

————, *The Name of the Rose*, trans. William Weaver. London: Picador, 1984.

Edmonds, J.M., trans., *The Greek Bucolic Poets* in Loeb Classical Library. Cambridge, Mass.: Harvard University Press, 1912.

Ehrmann, Jacques, ed., *Structuralism*. Garden City, N.Y.: Doubleday & Co., 1970.

Einstein, Alfred, *The Italian Madrigal*, trans. Alexander H. Krappe, Roger H. Sessions, and Oliver Strunk. Princeton: Princeton University Press, 1949. 3 vols.

Eliade, Mircea, *The Myth of the Eternal Return*. Princeton: Princeton University Press, 1954.

————, *Myth and Reality*, trans. Willard R. Trask. New York: Harper & Row, 1963.

————, *The Sacred & the Profane*, trans. Willard R. Trask. New York: Harcourt, Brace, & World, 1959.

Ellis, Willis D., ed., *A Source Book of Gestalt Psychology*. London: Rutledge & Kegan Paul, 1969.

Epperson, Gordon, *The Musical Symbol*. Ames, Iowa: Iowa State University Press, 1967.

Fassett, Agatha, *The Naked Face of Genius*. Boston: Houghton-Mifflin, 1958.

Frazer, Sir James George, *The Golden Bough*. New York: MacMillan, 1922.

Friedlander, Walter, *David to Delacroix*, trans. Robert Goldwater. Cambridge, Mass.: Harvard University Press, 1952.

Frisch, Walter, *Brahms and the Principle of Developing Variation*. Berkeley: University of California Press, 1984.

Fry, Roger, *Vision and Design*. Cleveland, Ohio: World Publishing Co., 1963.

Frye, Northrop, *Anatomy of Criticism*. Princeton: Princeton University Press, 1957.

———, *The Educated Imagination*. Bloomington: Indiana University Press, 1964.

———, *Fables of Identity*. New York: Harcourt, Brace, & World, 1965.

———, *Fools of Time*. Toronto: University of Toronto Press, 1967.

———, *A Study of English Romanticism*. Chicago: University of Chicago Press, 1968.

———, *The Well-Tempered Critic*. Bloomington: Indiana University Press, 1963.

Gardiner, Patrick, *Schopenhauer*. Harmondsworth, U.K.: Penguin Books, 1967.

Gay, John, *The Shepherd's Week in Six Pastorals*. London: Scolar Press Limited, 1969. Facsimile.

Gilman, Richard, *Decadence*. New York: Farrar, Strauss, and Giroux, 1975.

Girdlestone, Cuthbert, *Jean-Philippe Rameau: His Life and Work*. New York: Dover Publications, 1969.

Glass, Philip, *Music by Philip Glass*. New York: Harper & Row, 1987.

Goldin, Frederick, ed., *Lyrics of the Troubadours and Trouvères*. Garden City, N.Y.: Anchor/Doubleday, 1973.

Gordon, Cyrus H., *The Common Background of Greek and Hebrew Civilization*. New York: W.W. Norton, 1965.

Grant, Donald J. and Palisca, Claude V., *A History of Western Music*. New York: W.W. Norton, 1988.

Graves, Robert, *The Greek Myths*. Harmondsworth, U.K.: Penguin Books, 1955.

Graves, Robert and Patai, Raphael, *Hebrew Myths: The Book of Genesis*. New York: McGraw-Hill, 1963.

Griffiths, Paul, *Modern Music: The Avant Garde since 1945*. New York: George Braziller, 1981.

Haar, James, *Essays on Italian Poetry and Music in the Renaissance, 1350–1600*. Berkeley: University of California Press, 1986.

Hanslick, Eduard, *The Beautiful in Music*, trans. Gustav Cohen. Indianapolis/New York: Bobbs-Merrill, 1957.

Harrison, Jane Ellen, *Themis*. New York: University Books, 1962.

Hartman, Geoffrey H., *Criticism in the Wilderness*. New Haven: Yale University Press, 1980.

Hathorn, Richmond Y., *Tragedy, Myth & Mystery*. Bloomington: Indiana University Press, 1962.

Havelock, Eric A., *Preface to Plato*. Cambridge, Mass.: Harvard University Press, 1963.

Hawkes, Terence, *Structuralism and Semiotics*. Berkeley: University of California Press, 1977.

Hazan, Fernand et al., ed., *Dictionary of Modern Painting*. New York: Paris Book Center, Inc., no date.

Herodotus, *The Histories*, trans. Aubrey de Sélincourt. Harmondsworth, U.K.: Penguin Books, 1954.

Hesiod, *Theogony*, trans. Norman O. Brown. Indianapolis/New York: Bobbs-Merrill, 1953.

Highwater, Jamake, *The Primal Mind*. New York: New American Library, 1981.

Hildesheimer, Wolfgang, *Mozart*, trans. Marion Faber. New York: Random House, 1983.

Hillman, James, *Re-Visioning Psychology*. New York: Harper & Row, 1975.

Hofmann, Werner, *The Earthly Paradise*. New York: George Braziller, 1961.

Hofstadter, Douglas and Dennett, Daniel C., *The Mind's I*. Toronto: Bantam Books, 1981.

Holroyde, Peggy, *The Music of India*. New York: Praeger Publishers, 1972.

Honour, Hugh, *Romanticism*. New York: Harper & Row, 1979.

Hoppin, Richard H., *Medieval Music*. New York: W.W. Norton, 1978.

Houston, John Porter and Tobin, Mona, trans., *French Symbolist Poetry*. Bloomington: Indiana University Press, 1980.

Huizinga, Johan, *The Waning of the Middle Ages*. Garden City, N.Y.: Doubleday & Co., 1954.

Huray, Peter Le and Day, James, ed., *Music and Aesthetics in the Eighteenth and Early-Nineteenth Centuries*. Cambridge, U.K.: Cambridge University Press, 1981.

Inglis, Rewey Belle et al., ed., *Adventures in English Literature*. New York: Harcourt, Brace, & Co., 1948.

James, William, *The Varieties of Religious Experience*. New York: New American Library, 1958.

Jonsson, Ritva and Treitler, Leo, "Medieval Music and Language: A Reconsideration of the Relationship," *Studies in the History of Music:* Volume I. New York: Broude Brothers, 1985.

Jung, Carl G., *Man and His Symbols*. Garden City, N.Y.: Doubleday & Co., 1964.

Kamien, Roger, *Music, An Appreciation*. New York: McGraw-Hill, 1984.

Kapleau, Philip, ed., *The Three Pillars of Zen*. New York: Harper & Row, 1966.

Kaufmann, Walter, *Tragedy and Philosophy*. Princeton: Princeton University Press, 1968.

Kerman, Joseph, "How We Got into Analysis and How to Get Out," *Critical Inquiry*, Vol. II, No. 2 (1980).

Kirk, G.S., *The Nature of Greek Myths*. Harmondsworth, U.K.: Penguin Books, 1974.

Kivy, Peter, *The Corded Shell*. Princeton: Princeton University Press, 1980.

——, *Osmin's Rage*. Princeton: Princeton University Press, 1988.

——, *Sound and Semblance*. Princeton: Princeton University Press, 1984.

Kott, Jan, *The Eating of the Gods*. New York: Random House, 1974.

Kramer, Lawrence, *Music as Cultural Practice, 1800–1900*. Berkeley: University of California Press, 1990.

Landon, H.C. Robbins, *Haydn: Chronicle and Works*. Bloomington: Indiana University Press, 1976–80. 5 vols.

Lang, Paul Henry, *Handel*. New York: W.W. Norton, 1966.

——, *Music in Western Civilization*. New York: W.W. Norton, 1941.

——, *The Symphony, 1800–1900*. New York: W.W. Norton, 1969.

Langer, Susanne K., *Philosophy in a New Key*. Cambridge, Mass.: Harvard University Press, 1957.

Langham-Smith, Richard, "Debussy and the Pre-Raphaelites," *19th-Century Music*, Vol. V (1981).

Lattimore, Richmond, trans. and ed., *The Iliad of Homer*. Chicago: University of Chicago Press, 1951.

——, *The Odyssey of Homer*. New York: Harper & Row, 1965.

Lawall, Gilbert, *Theocritus' Coan Pastorals*. Washington, D.C.: Center for Hellenic Studies, 1967.

Le Bris, Michel, *Romantics and Romanticism*. New York: Skira / Rizzoli, 1981.

Leppmann, Wolfgang, *Winckelmann*. New York: Alfred A. Knopf, 1970.

Lévi-Strauss, Claude, *The Raw and the Cooked*. New York: Harper and Row, 1976.

Lipking, Lawrence, *The Ordering of the Arts in Eighteenth-Century England*. Princeton: Princeton University Press, 1970.

Lockspeiser, Edward, *Debussy, His Life and Mind*. London: Cambridge University Press, 1962 & 1965. 2 vols.

Lockwood, Lewis, ed., *Palestrina, Pope Marcellus Mass*. New York: W.W. Norton, 1975.

Lowinsky, Edward, "Secret Chromatic Art Re-examined," *Perspectives in Musicology*, ed. Barry S. Brook, Edward O.D. Downes, and Sherman Van Solkema. New York: W.W. Norton, 1972.

MacClintock, Carol, trans. and ed., *Readings in the History of Music in Performance*. Bloomington: Indiana University Press, 1979.

Macksey, Richard and Donato, Eugenio, ed., *The Structuralist Controversy*. Baltimore: Johns Hopkins Press, 1970.

Mallarmé, Stéphane, *Poems*, trans. C.F. MacIntyre. Berkeley: University of California Press, 1971.

Martines, Lauro, *Power and Imagination: City-States in Renaissance Italy*. New York: Knopf, 1979.

Matarasso, P.M., trans., *The Quest for the Holy Grail*. Harmondsworth, U.K.: Penguin Books, 1969.

Mellers, Wilfrid, *François Couperin and the French Classical Tradition*. New York: Dover Publications, 1968.

Menhennet, Alan, *Order and Freedom: German Literature and Society, 1720–1805*. New York: Basic Books, 1973.

Merton, Thomas, *The Seven Storey Mountain*. Garden City, N.Y.: Doubleday & Co., 1970.

Meyer, Leonard B., *Explaining Music*. Berkeley: University of California Press, 1973.

———, *Emotion and Meaning in Music*. Chicago: University of Chicago Press, 1956.

———, *Music, the Arts, and Ideas*. Chicago: University of Chicago Press, 1967.

———, *Style and Music: Theory, History and Ideology*. Philadelphia: University of Pennsylvania Press, 1989.

Mitchell, Donald, *The Language of Modern Music*. New York: St. Martin's Press, 1963.

Moldenhauer, Hans, *Anton von Webern, A Chronicle of His Life and Work*. New York: Alfred A. Knopf, 1979.

Monsman, Gerald Cornelis, *Pater's Portraits*. Baltimore: Johns Hopkins Press, 1967.

More, Thomas, *Utopia*, trans. Paul Turner. Harmondsworth, U.K.: Penguin Books, 1961.

Morley, Thomas, *A Plain and Easy Introduction to Practical Music*, ed. Alec Harmon. New York: W.W. Norton, 1952.

Murphy, James J., *Rhetoric in the Middle Ages*. Berkeley: University of California Press, 1974.

Myers, Henry Alonzo, *Tragedy, A View of Life*. Ithaca: Cornell University Press, 1956.

Nattiez, Jean-Jacques, *Music and Discourse: Toward a Semiology of Music*, trans. Carolyn Abbate. Princeton: Princeton University Press, 1990.

Neubauer, John, *The Emancipation of Music from Language*. New Haven: Yale University Press, 1986.

Newman, William S., *The Sonata in the Classic Era*. Chapel Hill: University of North Carolina Press, 1963.

Nietzsche, Friedrich, *The Birth of Tragedy*, trans. and ed. Walter Kaufmann. New York: Random House, 1967.

O'Flaherty, Wendy Doniger, ed., *Hindu Myths*. Harmondsworth, U.K.: Penguin Books, 1975.

Palisca, Claude V., ed., *Hucbald, Guido and John on Music: Three Medieval Treatises*. New Haven, Conn.: Yale University Press, 1978.

———, *Humanism in Italian Renaissance Musical Thought*. New Haven: Yale University Press, 1985.

Panofsky, Erwin, *Idea, A Concept in Art Theory*, trans. Joseph J.S. Peake. New York: Harper & Row, 1968.

———, *Meaning in the Visual Arts*. Garden City: Doubleday & Co., 1955.

Pater, Walter, *The Renaissance, the 1893 Text*, ed. Donald L. Hill. Berkeley: University of California Press, 1980.

Paz, Octavio, *Alternating Current*, trans. Helen R. Lane. New York: Viking Press, 1973.

———, *The Bow and the Lyre*, trans. Ruth L.C. Sims. New York: McGraw-Hill, 1973.

Philipson, Morris, ed., *Aesthetics Today*. Cleveland, Ohio: World Publishing Co., 1961.

Pirrotta, Nino, *Music and Culture in Italy from the Middle Ages to the Baroque*. Cambridge, Mass.: Harvard University Press, 1984.

Plantinga, Leon, *Romantic Music*. New York: W.W. Norton, 1984.

Plato, *Timaeus and Critias*, trans. Desmond Lee. Harmondsworth, U.K.: Penguin Books, 1971.

Pope, Alexander, *Collected Poems*, ed. Ernest Rhys. London: J.M. Dent & Sons, Ltd., 1924.

Prall, D.W., *Aesthetic Judgment*. New York: Thomas P. Crowell, 1929.

Price, Curtis A., *Henry Purcell and the London Stage*. Cambridge, U.K.: Cambridge University Press, 1984.

Prior, Moody E., *The Language of Tragedy*. Bloomington: Indiana University Press, 1966.

Quantz, Johann Joachim, *On Playing the Flute*, trans. Edward E. Reilly. New York: Free Press, 1966.

Radcliff-Unstead, Douglass, *The Birth of Modern Comedy in Renaissance Italy*. Chicago: University of Chicago Press, 1969.

Ratner, Leonard G., *Classic Music: Expression, Form and Style*. New York: Schirmer Books, 1980.

Raynor, Henry, *A Social History of Music*. New York: Taplinger Publishing Co., 1978.

Reese, Gustave, *Music in the Middle Ages*. New York: W.W. Norton, 1940.

———, *Music in the Renaissance*. New York: W.W. Norton, 1954.

Reimer, Bennett, *A Philosophy of Music Education*. Englewood Cliffs, N.J.: Prentice-Hall, 1970.

Rosen, Charles, *The Classical Style*. New York: W.W. Norton, 1971.

Rosenblum, Robert, *Transformations in Late Eighteenth Century Art*. Princeton: Princeton University Press, 1967.

Rougement, Denis de, *Love in the Western World*, trans. Montgomery Belgion. New York: Fawcett, 1969.

Ruwet, Nicolas, *Langage, musique, poésie*. Paris: Editions du Seuil, 1972.

Sachs, Curt, *The Rise of Music in the Ancient World*. New York: W.W. Norton, 1943.

Sadie, Stanley, ed., *The New Grove Dictionary of Music and Musicians*. London: Macmillan Publishers Ltd., 1980. 20 vols.

Salzman, Eric, *Twentieth-Century Music: An Introduction*. Englewood Cliffs, N.J.: Prentice-Hall, 1967.

Santayana, George, *The Sense of Beauty*. New York: Dover Publications, 1955.

Saussure, Ferdinand de, "Course in General Linguistics," *The Structuralists from Marx to Lévi-Strauss*, ed. Richard and Fernande De George. Garden City, N.Y.: Doubleday & Co., 1972.

Schiff, David, *The Music of Elliott Carter*. London: Eulenburg, 1983.

Schmidgall, Gary, *Literature as Opera*. Oxford: Oxford University Press, 1977.

Schneider, Marcel, *Schubert*. New York: Grove Press, 1959.

Scholes, Robert and Kellogg, Robert, *The Nature of Narrative*. New York, Oxford: Oxford University Press, 1966.

Scholes, Robert, *Structuralism in Literature*. New Haven: Yale University Press, 1974.

Schonberg, Harold, *The Great Pianists*. New York: Simon and Schuster, 1963.

Schopenhauer, Arthur, *The World as Will and Idea*, trans. R.B. Haldane and J. Kemp. Garden City, N.Y.: Doubleday & Co., 1961.

Schrade, Leo, *Monteverdi, Creator of Modern Music*. New York: W.W. Norton, 1949.

————, *Tragedy in the Art of Music*. Cambridge, Mass.: Harvard University Press, 1964.

Schweitzer, Albert, *J.S. Bach*, trans. Ernest Newman (1911). New York: Dover Publications, 1966.

Searle, John, *Minds, Brains, and Science*. Cambridge, Mass.: Harvard University Press, 1967.

Seay, Albert, *Music in the Medieval World*. Berkeley: University of California Press, 1973.

Sessions, Roger, *The Musical Experience of Composer, Performer, Listener*. Princeton: Princeton University Press, 1950.

Seward, Desmond, *Prince of the Renaissance: The Golden Life of François I*. New York: MacMillan, 1973.

Shapiro, Anne Dhu, ed., *Music and Context*. Cambridge, Mass.: Harvard University Department of Music, 1985.

Solomon, Maynard, *Beethoven*. New York: Schirmer Books, 1973.

Spalding, Frances, *Roger Fry: Art and Life*. Berkeley: University of California Press, 1980.

Steblin, Rita, *A History of Key Characteristics in the Eighteenth and Early Nineteenth Centuries*. Ann Arbor: University of Michigan Press, 1983.

Stevens, John, *Words and Music in the Middle Ages: Song, Narrative, Dance and Drama, 1050–1350*. Cambridge, U.K.: Cambridge University Press, 1986.

Strassburg, Gottfried von, *Tristan*, trans. A.T. Hatto. Harmondsworth, U.K.: Penguin Books, 1960.

Stravinsky, Igor, *An Autobiography*. New York: W.W. Norton, 1962.

Stravinsky, Igor and Craft, Robert, *Conversations with Igor Stravinsky*. Berkeley: University of California Press, 1980.

Stravinsky, Igor, *Poetics of Music*, trans. Arthur Knodel and Ingolf Dahl. Cambridge, Mass.: Harvard University Press, 1947.

Strunk, Oliver, ed., *Source Readings in Music History*. New York: W.W. Norton, 1950.

Thorburn, David and Hartman, Geoffrey, *Romanticism.* Ithaca: Cornell University Press, 1973.

Toynbee, Arnold J., *Greek Historical Thought.* New York: Mentor Books, 1952.

———, *A Study of History.* New York: Weathervane Books (Oxford University Press), 1972.

Tuve, Rosemond, *Elizabethan and Metaphysical Imagery.* Chicago: University of Chicago Press, 1947.

Underhill, Ruth Murray, *Singing for Power.* Berkeley: University of California Press, 1938.

Wagner, David L., ed., *The Seven Liberal Arts in the Middle Ages.* Bloomington: Indiana University Press, 1983.

Watson, Derek, *Bruckner.* London: Dent, 1975.

Weaver, William and Chusid, Martin, ed., *The Verdi Companion.* New York: W.W. Norton, 1979.

Weiss, Piero and Taruskin, Richard, ed., *Music in the Western World: A History of Documents.* New York: W.W. Norton, 1984.

Weston, Jessie L., *From Ritual to Romance.* Garden City, N.Y.: Doubleday & Co., 1957.

Wimsatt, William K. and Brooks, Cleanth, *Literary Criticism: A Short History.* Chicago: University of Chicago Press, 1957. 2 vols.

Winn, James Anderson, *Unsuspected Eloquence.* New Haven: Yale University Press, 1981.

Yates, Peter, *Twentieth Century Music.* New York: Minerva Press, 1968.

Zuckerkandl, Victor, *Man the Musician*, trans. Norbert Guterman. Princeton: Princeton University Press, 1973.

———, *The Sense of Music.* Princeton: Princeton University Press, 1959.

———, *Sound and Symbol.* Princeton: Princeton University Press, 1956.

Subject Index

Composers who appear in the text only in connection with a musical example do not appear in this index. See the music index for entries.

action
  musical   242–247
adagio-type   185
affect   112, 368
  and tonality   123–126
affections   14, 243–246, 266, 269
agitato   213–215, 218, 224
alleluia   83
American music   194–196
analysis
  archetypal   *See* archetypal criticism
  structural   372–373
Antony and Cleopatra   208
Apollo   52
Apollonian/Dionysian dichotomy   53
Arbeau, Thoinot   151
Arcadian shepherd   260
archetypal criticism   2–18, 76, 344,
  365–366, 372–373
  elements of   19–58, *see also*
    dichotomies
  model of   3–5

archetype   8–14, 19, 22
  definition of   9, 342, 365–366
  demotic   186
  hieratic   25
aria   146–154, *see also* opera
  and dance types   150–152
  in pastoral   172
aristocratic mentality   44–45
Aristotle   6, 43–45, 63–66, 69–74, 169,
  203, 255
artist   279–280, 300, 355
atonality   333
Aubry and Beck   96
Auerbach, Erich   45–46, 81
Augustine   79–81, 84–87, 112–113
avant-garde music   344–361, *see*
  also Minimalism; Neoclassicism;
  Neo-Romanticism; Serialism
  continuity in   351–354
  means and effects   345–346
  stratification in   352

Bach, J.S.   82, 205
balance   266–274

Bartok, Bela 322–326, 353
battle music 221–222
beauty 46–48
  formal 257, 266
Beethoven, Ludwig van 215–220, 298, 353
Boethius 89
Boulez, Pierre 348–350, 354, 361
Brahms, Johannes 304–310, 369
brightness 22–24
Bruckner, Anton 302–304
Burke, Edmund 281
burlesque 226–227, 233

caccia 158–159
Cage, John 253, 354–355
canzone villanesca 231
Carter, Elliott 351–354
catharsis 69–74, 137, 290–291
  definition of 69
ceremonial music 197–200
  in Renaissance Italy 197–199
Cézanne, Paul 335–336
chanson 131–135, 158
  chanson de complainte 132–134
  chanson de cour 132–135, 154
  chanson rustique 230
  patter-chanson 231
chant 76, 80, 82–89, 112–116
  performance practice 114–116
character 6, 65, 68–69, *see also ethos*
  types 68, 167, 247
Chopin, Frédéric 300
chorus
  tragic 72–73
Classicism 257–274, 281, 308
  high 265–274
Claudin de Sermisy 133–135
collective unconscious 342
colossal Baroque 199
concerto grosso 205
concitato 139–142, 200–207, 211–215, 221, 285
consciousness 302, 309, 360, 370–371
content 2–3, 5–8, 15–18, 370
  in courtly love song 92
  and form 314, 334, 339–341
convention 15, 24–25, 34, 243

Copland, Aaron 194–196
Corybantes 71–72
courtly love 91–107, 131–134, 167
  code of 92–94

dance songs 104–107
dance, courtly 150–152, 236–237
darkness 22–24
Debussy, Claude 315–318
decorum 153
  liturgical 126–127
  of rusticity 181
deities 38–40, 43–44, *see also* Apollo; Dionysus
delirium 348, 350
Descartes, René 147–148
desire 21, 26, 286, 317–318
dialectic 349
dichotomies 19–58, 88, 366
  Apollonian/Dionysian 51–56, 73, 203, 258
  comic/tragic 20–26, 125
  Eros/Thanatos 21–22, 55, 292–293
  ethos/pathos 130–131
  hieratic/demotic 42–51, 179
  major/minor 24, 123–126, 129
  mythic/humanistic 36–42
  romantic/ironic 26–27
  tragic/comic 254–255
dignity 272–273
Dionysian impulse 71
Dionysian ritual 52
Dionysian spirit 74
Dionysus 39, 52–53, 203
drama, heroic 215–223

ecstasis 52–53, 290–291
  Christian 87
elegiac statement 168
elegy 31–32, 50–51
  heroic 369
  in pastoral 162–166, 168, 174, 191
emotion 69, 126–127, 367, *see also* passions; *pathos*
Empfindsamkeit 264–265
English music drama 237
Enlightenment 182–183, 213, 269, 328
ensemble-finale 239–242

ephemerality 315
epic/heroic mode 197–223
eros *See* desire
Essay on Man 7, 18
ethos 6, 43, 62, 153, 367
    of Christian liturgy 76–89
    of courtly love 99, 106–107
    of Expressionism 329–331
    in Greek thought 62–69
    of modernism 328
    of primitivism 325–326
    of Romanticism 328
Euripides 39
exotic music 193
exoticism 193–194, 318–319
Expressionism 326–334, 342
    elements of musical style 331

favola in musica 165–166
festal pomp 210–213, 218–220, 223, 246
folk idiom 184
folk movements 188–189
folk music 180, 184–186, 192, 324–326
    hymn type 184–186, 195
folk tunes 180
formalism 334–341, 344–361, 371
    in art 335–336
French court dances 237
French overture 200, 210
Freudian theory 21, 329–331
Frye, Northrop 8–10, 14, 28, 56, 58, 365

Gaffurio 122
galant 259–265, 294, 337
    galant homme 260–262
Galilei, Vincenzo 142–146, 149
gavotte 236
Gay, John 49–50, 180–181
genre painting 48–49
Ghirardello da Firenze 158
Glarean, Heinrich 120–123, 137–138
Glass, Philip 359–360
gloire 260
gods 43
Goldin, Frederick 93–95
Goldsmith, Oliver 181
Gray, Thomas 50
grotesque 250–251, 342
Guarini 160–162

Guido d'Arezzo 111–113
Guillaume IX 93–95

harmonic principles 120–126
Haydn, Joseph 183–185, 214
hero 67–68, 369–371
    Apollonian/Dionysian 208
    Beethovenian 219, 353
    Brahmsian 308, 369
    demotic 190
    Expressionist 370
    of festal pomp 246
    hero-leader 166–167
    Innigkeit 370
    madrigalian 137
    melodramatic 370
    Primitivist 370
    Romantic 280, 301, 369
    Schubertian 302, 369
heroism 83, 201–204, 219
    demotic 220
    in music 210–213, 222–223
    tragic 208
Homer 38, 40–41, 57
humanism 111, 116–120, 369
    role of antiquity 118–119
humility 81–82
humor 32
hymn 185
hymn tune 195

image 12–14, 365
    definition of 7
    musical 368–371
    tragic 22–24
impiety 38–40
Impressionism 315–318
    in art 312, 341
    spiritual impulse of 175–177
improvvisatori 119
Innigkeit 295–310, 369
instrumental dance-types 150
instrumental serenade 172
irony 32–36, 227–228, 233, 314, 322
    and humor 32
    and satire 34–35
    tragic 35–36, 328–329, 340

Johannes of Afflighem   112–115
Josquin des Prés   117, 119–127, 132, 257
joy
  Christian   87
  in courtly love song   95
jubilus   83–87

Kaufmann, Walter   20
Kivy, Peter   16–17, 240–246

languor   169, 290
leis de con   94–95, 228
liberal arts   78
logos   21, 36–38, 53–56, 367–370
  art as   309–310, 314, 355
  of Christianity   76–77, 88
  Dionysian   53–56, 71–72, 74
  Expressionist   333
  formalist   336
love song   91–103
  courtly   93–101
Lully, Jean-Baptiste   236–237

Machaut, Guillaume de   124, 230
madrigal   135–146, 233
  declamatory   143–145
  dramatic   204
  pastoral   167–169
  rhetoric in   136–139
  tragic   258
  use of instruments in   139
Maeterlinck, Maurice   316–317
Mahler, Gustav   304
Mallarmé, Stéphane   176–177, 316, 341
march
  funeral   216, 218
  military   210–212
Marenzio, Luca   160–162, 169
meaning   15–16, 315–316
melisma   83, 86–88
melodrama   294–295, 305–306, 309
  in music   286–290
  sensuality in   288–290, 300
  villain in   286
Merton, Thomas   82
Milton, John   180, 186–187
Minimalism   359–360
Mitleid   297–300

modernism   312–341, 369–371
modes, musical   62–63
  of the Church   112–116, 120–126
Molière   34
momentary god   10, 283, 290, 296
Monet, Claude   335
Moniot d'Arras   157–158
Monteverdi, Claudio   102–103, 146, 149,
  162–166, 201–202, 204, 234
moralism   270
More, Thomas   110–111
motet   230
Mozart, Wolfgang Amadeus   240–243
musique concrète   356
Mussorgsky, Modest   323
myth   9–11, 14, 36–42
  Christian   40–42
  Greek   38–40
  primitive   320–321

narrative songs   104
nationalism   221
  and modernism   323
  in rustic pastoral   191–196
natural music   77
Nature   22–24, 46–47
  in primitive myth   319
  in Romanticism   280
Neo-Romanticism   359–360
Neoclassicism   336–339
Nietzsche, Friedrich   51–52, 54–56
noble rage   201–202, 207, 225, 285

Oedipus Rex   *See* tragedy, Greek
opera   146–152, 165–167, 172–173,
  234–242, 286–287
  bel canto   286
  comic   234–236
  opera buffa   238–242, 247–248, 251, 263
  opera seria   247, 254
operetta   248

paroxysm   315–317
Passereau, Pierre   231
passions   147–148, 154, 203–204, 208,
  261–262, 285–286, *see also* emotion;
  pathos
  expression of   136, 138, 150

pastoral 28–32, 46, 157–177, 179–196, 236–237, 366, *see also* Theocritus; Virgil
  Arcadian 46, 159–177, 179, 187, 260, 366
  Barbizon 175
  rustic 49–51, 179–196, 366
  sensuousness in 167–170
  social/political aspects of 182–183
pastourelle 159, 228–229
pathos 64–66, 110–127, 321–323, 367
  in Baroque music 207
  in Greek philosophy 69–74
  in madrigals 135–136
  in modern music 332–334
patter-song 229–233
  polyphonic 230–233
peasant culture 322–326, *see also* Primitivism
penseroso 170–175, 178, 185, 343
phrase, musical
  beginnings of 99–101
Plato 6, 9, 62–70, 74, 112, 169, 273
polyphony
  medieval 88–89
  Renaissance 117, 119–127, 199
Pre-Raphaelites 316–317
Primitivism 318–326, 329, 342
  in art 319
  concept of evil in 320
psalmody 79–80, 85
psyche
  individual 332–333
  Western 330

quotation, musical 358

Racine, Jean 207–210
recitative 142–146, 155
  recitativo accompagnato 207–210
Regino of Prüm 76
Reich, Steve 359–360
Rembrandt van Rijn 23–24
resolution 334
rhetoric 80–82, 112–118, 136–139
ribaldry 228
ritual 342
  Christian 41–42
  Dionysian 290
rococo 263

Romanticism 217, 219, 248, 278–293, 300, 309–310, 313–314, 326–330
  ultra-Romantic style 291
  wish fulfillment 310, 318–319, 327–328
Runge, Philip Otto 280, 283

Satie, Erik 252–253
satire 34, 226–253, *see also* irony
  in modern music 250–253
  in theatrical types 234–253
scherzo 248
Schoenberg, Arnold 313, 339, 349
Schubert, Franz 300–302, 369
Schumann, Robert 249, 297–300
sensuousness 168
sentimentality 181, 298, 321–322
serenade 172–175
serialism, total 345–348
  language of 346–347
seriousness 101–103
sermo humilis 81
solemnity 25, 321
sonata-allegro form 213, 216, 266–268, 372
soul 63, *see also* character
spirituality 302–304
Stevens, John 85–87, 91–92, 95–99, 111–116
Stockhausen, Karlheinz 346, 350–354, 356–357
  theory of the "moment" 351
Stravinsky, Igor 15, 222, 225, 252, 319–322, 336–338, 340
Sturm und Drang 213–215, 218–219, 224, 265, 281
  literary movement 213–214
style 11–13
  definition of 12
sublime 83
sublimity 83–88, 281, 323
symbolism 349
  art movement 314–318
  of harmonic types 124–126
symphonism
  Mannheim school 210–215, 246–247
syntactic analysis 6

Tasso, Torquato   140–142
tenderness   *See Mitleid*
text-music relationship   95, *see also*
   psalmody; rhetoric
   in chansons   131–142
   in medieval music   91, 99, 111–115
   in recitative   142–145
Theocritus   28–30
tonality
   of art   56–58
tract   85–88
tragedy   20–26, 31–32, 137, 255, *see also*
   elegy
   constituents of   72
   gorgeous   207–210
   Greek   20, 43–45, 51–52, 57, 69–74,
      329
   in melodrama   284–286, 291
   in pastoral   174–175, 191
transcendence   278–280, 282–283,
   288–293, 295–296, 304, 309, 317–318
troubadours   93–98, 134
twelve-tone music   339–340, 350

types, human   152–154

understanding   296, 307–309
universals   2, 6–7, 9
Utopianism   328

villain   286
Virgil   28, 30–32
Volkstümlichkeit   189–191, 369, *see also*
   folk movements; nationalism

warrior-hero   167
Watteau, Antoine   170, 178
Webern, Anton von   339–341, 350
Wert, Giaches de   140–142
wit   226–227, 231
word-painting   160
Wordsworth, William   302, 307, 311,
   341

Xenakis, Iannis   356–357

Zarlino   122–123
Zeitgeist   11–12

Music Index

Page numbers in roman indicate textual references; italics indicate musical examples.

Adam de la Halle
  D'amourous coeur 97
Alleluia for Easter 83, *84*
Anonymous
  A l'entrada del temps clar 107
  Spring song *105*

Bach, J.C.
  "Fosca nube" *173*
  Temistocle 172
Bach, J.S.
  English suite #3 (gavotte) 24
  Fugue 8, *WTC* I *102*
  Mass in B minor 83
  Sarabande *25*
  St. John Passion 205
Bartok
  Nine Little Piano Pieces, #1 *102*
Beethoven
  Appassionata sonata 5
  Eroica symphony 215–217
  Pastoral symphony 187
  Piano sonata, Op. 31, No. 1 185
  Quartet, Op. 59, No. 1
    ("Rasoumovsky") 291
  Quintet, Op. 16 185

Symphony #5 217–218
Berg
  Lulu 251, 332
  Wozzeck 251, 332
Berio
  Sinfonia 358
Berlioz
  Damnation of Faust 249
  Symphonie Fantastique 249
Bizet, Georges
  Carmen 56
Boulez
  Le Marteau sans maître 348
Brahms
  Symphony #3 221
  Violin concerto *306,* 305–308
  Violin sonata, Op. 100 *102*
Bruckner
  Symphony #9 303

Cage
  4'33'' 354
Carter
  String quartets #1, 2 352
Cavalli
  La Calisto 235

Chopin
  B♭ minor scherzo 287, *289*
  C♯ minor scherzo 287–288
  Funeral March sonata 288
  Nocturne in F♯ minor (#14) 290
Claudin de Sermisy
  J'attends secours *135*
  Tant que vivray *133*
Couperin
  "L'âme en peine" *171*, 171–172

Debussy
  Pelléas et Mélisande 316–317
  Prelude to the Afternoon of a Faun
    176–177
  Sirènes 317–318
Deus, deus meus 85–87
Dowland
  Lacrimae Antiquae Pavan 25
Dufay
  Nuper rosarum flores 198
  Pour l'amour de ma doulce amye
    158

Ghirardello
  Tosto che l'alba 158–159
Gluck
  "Che farò senza Euridice" *272*,
    271–273

Handel
  Acis and Galatea 32, *33*
  Giulio Cesare 166–167
  L'allegro ed il penseroso 180
  Semele *102*
Haydn
  Schon eilet froh *184*
  Seasons, The 183, 186

Josquin
  Absalon, fili mi 120, *121*, 123–124,
    126–127
  Ave Maria 257
  Déploration (Nymphes des bois)
    123–125
  Douleur me bat 123–124, 132
  Plaine de deuil 132

Machaut
  Lai *102*
  Pourquoy me bat mes maris 230
  Rose, lis, printemps, verdure 124
Mahler
  Symphonies #1, 9 250
Marenzio
  Ah, dolente partita 162, *164*
  Scaldava il sol *161*
Mendelssohn
  Scottish symphony 221
Moniot d'Arras
  Ce fut en mai 157–158
Monteverdi
  Ah, dolente partita 162–164, *165*
  Combattimento di Tancredi e
    Clorinda 200, 204, *206*, 223
  L'incoronazione di Poppea 146, 149,
    234
  L'Orfeo *103*, 165–166, 200–201, *202*
Mozart
  "Dove sono" 270, *271*, 273
  Idomeneo 241
  La Clemenza di Tito 242
  Piano concerto, K. 467 173, 267, *267*,
    268, 372
  Quartet, K. 590 186
  Serenade, K. 375 173
  Violin sonata, K. 376 243, *244*
Mussorgsky
  Boris Godunov 220, 250
  Pictures at an Exhibition 250

Ockeghem
  Missa Prolationum 345

Passereau
  Il est bel et bon 232
Purcell
  Dido and Aeneas 237–238

Rameau
  Hippolyte et Aricie 208, *209*
Rore
  Hor ch'el ciel 137, *138*

Scarlatti
  Sono amante *168*

Schoenberg
  Erwartung   331, 334, 342
  Pierrot Lunaire   251
Schubert
  Die Schöne Müllerin   301
  Moment Musical, Op. 94, No. 2   *302*
  Winterreise   301
Schumann
  Dichterliebe   301
  Piano trio in F major   *299*
Stamitz
  Sinfonia, Op. V, No. 2   *212*
Stockhausen
  Carré   350, 356–357
  Gruppen   350
  Zeitmasse   345
Stravinsky
  Concerto en ré   338
  L'histoire du soldat   252
  The Rite of Spring   319–322, 342

Ventadorn
  Be m'an perdut   98
  Can vei la lauzeta (Courtly love song)
    100
Verdelot
  Madonna, il tuo bel viso   136
Verdi
  Il Trovatore   104
  Rigoletto   287
Vivaldi
  Four Seasons   172

Wagner
  Tristan und Isolde   288–290, 292–293
Weelkes
  Four arms, two necks, one wreathing
    234
Wert
  Ah, dolente partita   163
  Giunto a la tomba   140, 141

About the Author

LAURENCE BERMAN is a pianist, and Associate Professor of Music at the University of Massachusetts at Boston, where he gives courses in the history and theory of music. His areas of academic specialization include turn-of-the-century French music as well as music aesthetics and criticism, and he has published articles on composers, most frequently Debussy, in reference books, journals, and essay collections.